The Elaethium

Andrew Rydberg

iUniverse

THE ELAETHIUM

Copyright © 2022 Andrew Rydberg.

All rights reserved. No part of this book may be used or reproduced by any means, graphic, electronic, or mechanical, including photocopying, recording, taping or by any information storage retrieval system without the written permission of the author except in the case of brief quotations embodied in critical articles and reviews.

This is a work of fiction. All of the characters, names, incidents, places, organizations, and dialogue in this novel are either the products of the author's imagination or are used fictitiously.

iUniverse books may be ordered through booksellers or by contacting:

iUniverse
1663 Liberty Drive
Bloomington, IN 47403
www.iuniverse.com
844-349-9409

Because of the dynamic nature of the Internet, any web addresses or links contained in this book may have changed since publication and may no longer be valid. The views expressed in this work are solely those of the author and do not necessarily reflect the views of the publisher, and the publisher hereby disclaims any responsibility for them.

Any people depicted in stock imagery provided by Getty Images are models, and such images are being used for illustrative purposes only.-
Certain stock imagery © Getty Images.

ISBN: 978-1-6632-3464-3 (sc)
ISBN: 978-1-6632-3465-0 (e)

Library of Congress Control Number: 2022904524

Print information available on the last page.

iUniverse rev. date: 06/08/2022

Chapter 1
Sunset

Sixth Era. 124. Febris 3.

It was just the two of them ascending the frozen reach—an old man with a near-empty rucksack leading his eight-year-old granddaughter. As the wind kicked the powdery snow into his face, the old man took off his woolen cap and placed it on the girl's head. His bald pate was briefly exposed to the wind until he pulled up the hood of his leather cloak. While no longer debilitating, the wind and snow swirled persistently around them. Trees and rocky terrain on the mountain reduced the raging gales from the tundra below into a gentle but chilling breeze. They had left their coastal home country, Armini, all those months ago, and it had offered nothing like the brutal cold of Svarengel.

"Grandfather?" the little girl asked quietly. "Grandfather Celus, I'm tired."

The old man paused to look at her. Her eyes fluttered and were barely open. "And you think I'm not? We're in the final stretch, Elaethia, and I'd like to get somewhere safe by nightfall."

Celus looked at the sun and realized it would be setting soon. The days were much shorter now. Celus had grown to hate the sun here. Back home, the celestial being would grant warmth and life. But up here it was nothing but a beacon of false hope. No matter how brightly it shone, he would shiver furiously. The old man felt sure he would never get the chill out of his bones. Anywhere else in the world, this would be the final month of winter. But apparently Svarengel winters lasted anywhere from six to eight months.

But the mountain's weather wasn't the only concern. An elderly man and a young girl would be easy prey for wolves, snowbears, or sabercats that had made their homes within the many caves. There were undoubtedly monsters residing here as well. They would make quick work of humans like him. Not even demihumans, with their light fur, could survive this cold for long. He continued up the mountain until the girl staggered and fell to her knees behind him.

The old man turned around. Elaethia had been silent the entire time, and that was concerning. The brat hardly ever shut up. He hoisted her up from under her arms and brushed the snow off her coat. He felt her neck to make sure that her father's gold-and-sapphire pendant was still secure. He did *not* want to go hunting for it again. Celus looked into the little girl's face. Her cheeks were bright red, and her eyes were dry and droopy.

"Damnit, Marcus," Celus muttered to himself as he pulled the girl along. "Why would you leave me alone with this daughter of yours? You just had to dump her on me and then send me on this fool's errand."

He looked back at his granddaughter. "Come on, Elaethia; be strong for your father. You and I both are doing this for him."

"I can't. My feet won't move another step," she mumbled.

Celus noticed the violent tremble in her legs. He couldn't tell whether it was from fear, exhaustion, chill, or any combination of the three. Either way, he knew they wouldn't make it at this rate. He pushed past his own fatigue to hoist her onto his back and continue the trek.

Elaethia spoke after a while. "Why didn't any of the villagers want to talk about the dragon? Is he really that scary?"

"My only concern is getting to him as soon as possible. I've lost count of how many places we've tried to get help from. This is our last hope."

"Will the dragon kill Emperor Rychus?" Elaethia asked.

"In the best-case scenario, he grants you his power and you become a dragon hero. What's probably going to happen is we'll both get eaten."

Her fingers squeezed his shoulders. "I-I don't want us to get eaten. Are you sure no one else will help?"

"We've come too far to turn back," Celus snapped. "Bargaining with this damn dragon is your only hope."

"You'll be with me the whole way, won't you, Grandfather?"

"Only as long as I need to be," he muttered. "You know your role. Don't let your father's sacrifice be in vain."

She nodded gently and pressed her cheek to the back of his head. "I won't let you or Father down. I'll train as hard as I can."

"You'd better," Celus said. "I didn't do all of this for you just for you to give up."

Elaethia felt for the gold-and-sapphire necklace around her neck. "I'll do it. I'll be a dragon hero if that's what it takes."

The sun continued its course along the clear sky, beginning to disappear behind the jagged peaks. Celus looked back at the route they had taken and sighed. The two of them had made a decent amount of progress. This was the only good luck they'd had today. The locals were not able to give any specifics of their endpoint, but it seemed that nothing and nobody wanted to go anywhere near the crest of the snowy mountains.

But there was undoubtedly a reason for that. A sense of unease grew inside of him. He paused—and instantly regretted doing so. All the fatigue from his ascent suddenly caught up with him. He was too old for this kind of exertion. The young girl, still clinging to his shoulders, groaned as the sudden stop woke her.

"Have we made it?" she asked.

"Shh! Be still!" Celus held up his hand and looked around with wild eyes. It had dawned on him why he felt a sense of unease. He surveyed their surroundings again, silently and thoroughly. It was quiet. Dead quiet. Time seemed to halt entirely.

A sudden roar to his left made his heart leap into his throat. An enormous snowbear burst from a dense snow-covered thicket. The creature rose to its full height. Four meters of muscle and fur glared down at them with unmistakable intent. Its giant mouth opened to bare its teeth and pink maw. The old man snapped back to his senses. Celus broke out in a run, clutching the child on his back. From the corner of his eye, he saw the giant shape of the beast crash through the brush to pursue them. Celus stopped to set the girl down for a moment and scrambled to ready a torch. He wanted to save it for when it became dark, but the situation demanded he use it now.

The ground shook as the snowbear thundered toward them. Celus's shaking hands struck his flint and steel over the pitch-covered torch. The sound of heavy breathing and crunching snow grew louder behind him. The torch ignited with a flash of heat and orange flame. A shadow fell over them. Hot, rancid breath rolled down his spine as he seized the lit torch.

Elaethia screamed. He lunged forward with his granddaughter as a paw the size of his chest swiped just over his head. Adrenaline surged through his old and freezing veins. Celus and Elaethia scrambled up the incline, desperate to find something, *anything*, to help them escape from the beast.

What caught his eye would have left him breathless had he not been near panic. Enormous crystalline formations protruded from the snowy landscape. Nearly a dozen of the tall constructs stood in front of them. Their murky light-blue color was nothing like he had ever seen before.

A heavy, furry mass slammed into him from behind. Celus found himself pinned to the ground as Elaethia was sent tumbling away from him. His face was thrown into the powdery snow as his breath was crushed from his lungs. A sharp pain erupted from his arm as he felt the beast take hold of his elbow in its mouth.

"Grandfather!" Elaethia screamed.

Celus tried to cry out to tell her to run but could only manage a strained groan. The groan turned into a growl and then a cry as his arm was pierced and stretched away from his body. With a tear and a snap, the viselike grip on his elbow was replaced with searing agony. Celus's vision began to turn dark until a bright orange light illuminated the corner of his vision. The crushing weight on his body lifted with the sound of the bear roaring in pain. The old man slowly looked up to see Elaethia waving the torch back and forth in front of the beast as it backed away.

"Grandfather! Please! Please get up!" she cried.

Celus weakly tried to push off the ground and fell. He couldn't feel his left arm. He pushed again with his knees and struggled to get to his feet. Blood pulsed in spurts down Celus's side. He clutched the bleeding space on his torso where his arm used to be. He felt nothing—not the cold, not the blood, not even the stump that used to be his left arm. His eyes turned empty, yet determined. As the bear began to pursue them again, they staggered to the line of crystals.

Just as the beast was about to run them down, it lurched to a halt, its eyes fixed on the landscape ahead of them. The snowbear turned its gaze to Elaethia and her bleeding grandfather. It growled in frustration, let out another bone-shaking roar, and then turned and lumbered back to where it came from. Celus turned to see what had saved them, only to see an area in the distance where the ground opened into the enormous mouth of a cave.

"Grandfather, it's gone. It left." Elaethia said.

Celus didn't meet her gaze; nor did he respond.

"Grandfather, what do we do? Where do we go, please, say something!"

He stayed silent as he began to sway. He looked at the cave. Whatever was inside was enough to drive away an angry bear from easy prey. The sun had disappeared beneath the horizon. Their torch was rapidly becoming their only source of light. The thought of whatever monster might lie within made his legs buckle. But they had to take shelter before darkness fell completely. Both took deep breaths and stepped into the darkness.

The ground beneath them descended sharply, and the icy floor robbed them of their footing. Celus slid on his back down the steep incline, coming to a rough halt at the bottom. Elaethia wasn't so fortunate. She struck her head at the bottom of the slide and rolled limply across the cold floor. From the flickering light of the torch, Celus saw she wasn't bleeding but was only unconscious from the impact. He tried once again to rise to his feet but found his body unresponsive. His adrenaline had run out. The only other thing he could see within the cave was a large pile of discarded weapons, armor, and skeletons.

A deep scraping noise broke the silence. He turned his head further into the cave, trying to comprehend what was in front of him

From the dwindling light, he saw a massive form begin to move; the shape was larger than his house back in Armini. Deep azure scales glistened along the enormous body, leading up to a serpentine neck as thick as the snowbear's torso. Attached to it was a head as wide as a wagon and twice as long. The creature's blue reptilian eyes were encased in deep blue markings that grew outward and downward to its jawline to come to a point.

Celus exhaled heavily. The legends were true. He smiled gravely, knowing he had fulfilled his promise. Perhaps now his son could rest in peace. Celus looked once more to the still form of Elaethia, which lay on the ground next to the flickering torch. Elaethia, now the only surviving member of the Soliano family, had reached her destination. She was in the clutches of the last dragon.

The dragon tilted his head. For the first time in a thousand years, he was taken aback. He had heard nothing of brehdars for over a century, let alone seen one. Yet two of them, humans apparently, had walked directly into his cave. He had deliberately taken steps to avoid contact with other intelligent beings. He had no qualms with brehdars, so long as they left him alone. He turned his gaze to the assorted pile of brehdar equipment and corpses near the bottom of the incline. The brehdars from his time always wanted one of two things: his power or his life. This pair, however, did not seem capable of violence.

He turned his gaze once again to the humans that had walked, or rather fallen, into his home. The bigger one was already dead, and the little one would probably join him if she didn't wake soon and warm herself. Humans were sturdy creatures. Of all species of brehdar, they were certainly the most adaptive. That being said, the mountain conditions were less than habitable for one as small as her.

The dragon sighed, deciding to take action. He reached over with one claw, lifted the little one off the ground, and grabbed the fur-and-leather cloak off the deceased man with his other. He lay the coat on the floor and placed her on top of it. He decided the little one should be clothed enough to keep warm from the frigid air, and the wind couldn't penetrate into the cave. Time would tell whether that would be enough. He tilted his head. There was no logical reason for him to take this action. Perhaps his millennia of solitude had softened him, or maybe it was the fact she might be able to tell him of the outside world.

Once again he pondered the reason why they had come to him. Looking at the dead man, he decided they were seeking refuge from beasts or monsters. They couldn't have known he was here; meaning it was shelter they were seeking. This was troubling. That would mean the predators on the mountain had grown less cautious of him. Perhaps he would have to make an appearance to reinstate his dominance. He furrowed his brow. He didn't like leaving his cave. There was always some sort of commotion every time he did, and prey on the mountain evaded him with ease.

The scent of blood from the older one's corpse had enveloped the enclosure. The dragon pondered on the last time he ate. It had been several years, and it wasn't often that food came to him. He moved a clawed hand to remove the rucksack attached to the man and proceeded to dispose of the old human.

The dragon recalled why he didn't like to eat brehdars. They were bony creatures that always wore clothing or armor that got stuck between his teeth. The taste wasn't very appetizing either.

This one was particularly bony, and the lack of blood further diluted the taste. Realizing that what he had just accomplished would most likely traumatize the little one, he began to lap at the ground to remove any trace of the dead man. He found it disappointing. The old human could hardly be considered a snack. He shuddered, belched, and decided he would seal the entrance after the little one had left.

He was old, even by dragon standards, and wanted to live out the last of his years in peace. He was not powerful compared to some of his kin that devoted their lives to combat. Supposedly he was a wise dragon, but he never paid much mind to such claims. More so, he saw himself as one of the few that chose to stop and think, as opposed to making rash decisions based on honor or rage. He would often shake his head at his brothers and sisters that acted blindly. Their impulsive behaviors were the very reason he was now alone in this world. Brief waves of loneliness and mild regret washed over him. He decided to return to his slumber so they would not dwell in his thoughts.

He was awoken the next morning by a sudden crash followed by a shrill scream. He opened his eyes and slowly lifted his head to where the sounds came from. His eyes widened and then hardened as he beheld the source of the outburst. The little one was awake, and seemed to have fallen into his pile of assorted brehdar equipment. She kicked away from the rolling skull of a dwarf, crashing and scrambling over the weapons and armor as she did. Once free from the pile, her breath hitched, and she shakily looked up to meet Frossgar's gaze.

Another scream resonated in the open cavern. The girl fell on her behind and kicked back, seemingly desperate to escape from him. The dragon watched with curiosity as the tiny human scrambled back toward him, grabbed a shield that had slid between them, and dashed back to the wall to do a surprisingly good job of hiding completely behind it. Only her hair and rear were still exposed. He paused for a moment and tilted his head.

"What are you doing, little one?" asked the deep but patronizing voice. He heard no response from the shaking circle of wood and steel. "Come now, I have no intention of hurting you. However, it is rude to enter someone's home and sift through their belongings."

The shield shifted slightly. A set of shaky fingers gripped the top of the shield. Then the top of her head appeared, followed by large, watery blue eyes. Her messy black hair dangled in her face down to her reddened cheeks.

"Well?" the dragon asked. "Perhaps customs have changed since my time, but an elder has addressed you. Is it not respectful to give me a response?"

She looked down behind the shield and mumbled something softly.

He grunted. "The courtesy of manners must have become highly lax these last several hundred years. Try again, this time with a clear voice and while looking me in the eye."

Her face appeared again, her fearful gaze glued firmly to his. "Y-yes sir! I-I'm sorry for bothering you, sir. P-please don't hurt me!" she shrieked.

The dragon winced. "When I say clearly, I mean firmly, child. I can hear your speaking voice just fine."

"I'm sorry, sir; I won't make you angry again," she said

"Somehow I doubt you will manage that. Brehdars are quite good at being nuisances. Now return that shield to me. I intend to speak with you, and you are making it difficult by cowering behind it like a cornered animal."

She held out the shield, her arms quaking as if it felt too heavy to hold straight.

He only stared at her. "Do you expect me to come to you? Bring it here."

Elaethia stood up and shuffled toward him, the shield held closely to her chest. She shyly held it out once more, flinching as his claw moved to take it from her.

"You must let go before I can take it, little one," he said gently.

Elaethia quickly dropped her hands behind her back, and he returned the shield to the scattered pile of armor.

"That is better. First and foremost, we should learn each other's names. Since you have come to me, it is proper that you introduce yourself first."

"Elaethia. Elaethia Soliano," came the small reply.

"Now, Elaethia Soliano, explain why you have come unannounced, uninvited, into my home."

The little girl shifted "Um, a-are you that dragon the legends talk about?"

The dragon tilted his head. "You have heard of me? So you have sought me out. Very few brehdars have tried since the end of the dragon wars. I cannot imagine you are here to kill me."

Her eyes bugged. "No! No, Mr. Dragon, sir! I … we … came here for your help!"

He raised an eyebrow. He knew she was talking about the older human, but he decided to feign ignorance. "We? But you are here alone, little one."

"No, Mr. Dragon, sir! My grandfather Celus! He's hurt! A bear attacked us, and he lost his arm … and … I don't know where he is." She looked down, her tears pattering to the ground.

A pang of sympathy suddenly struck the old dragon's heart. "I understand your kind mourns the death of a companion. I am sorry for your loss."

"He's not dead!" she shouted. "He can't be! He fell with me! Maybe he went back outside or is hiding! You have to help me! He's all I have left; I have to save him!"

He recoiled at the sudden demand. Then his eyes hardened. "Listen to me, little one. If he was as wounded as you say, he could not have survived the night. If the beast that pursued you did not kill him, then the mountain weather surely would have."

Elaethia stopped and stared at him, her eyes wide and distraught. Then she began to cry. His eyes softened and his jaw began to lax. Unsure of what else to do, he handed her a cloak to dry her tears. However, instead of taking hold of it, she grabbed fiercely onto his finger and bawled into it. The great dragon froze. He remained in a semiparalysed state until the small human's sobs seemed to end. She finally let go and slumped to her knees, using the cloak to clean the tears and snot from her face.

The dragon cleared his throat. "You mentioned you were looking for me. What was it you were hoping to achieve?"

Elaethia sniffled and hugged the cloak. "We heard stories of people becoming heroes with the help of dragons. They get really strong and can use magic. My home has been ruled by the same horrible emperor for over a hundred years. He … he killed my mother and father and the rest of my family because they stood up to him. Now they're all gone, so we ran away. We wanted to find someone to teach me how to fight, but nobody would. But then we heard about you. We came all this way to find you so you could help me kill Emperor Rychus. Mr. Dragon, sir, I need you to—"

The dragon groaned and shifted his body. "Referring to me as 'Mr. Dragon' has become quite bothersome. You may call me Frossgar."

"F … Frossgar?" Elaethia repeated. "Wh-what about your last name?"

Frossgar tilted his head. "I do not understand the question. I hold only one name. All dragons do. What use is another?"

"I … I don't know either," Elaethia said. She sniffed once again. Suddenly she shot to her feet, clenched her fists, and looked up with eyes filled with a newly-kindled fire. "So … so please, Mr. Frossgar! Train me to be a dragon hero!"

Sixth Era. 139. Mertim 15.

She strode alone through the city of Breeze. In one hand she held a flyer advertising the regional guild. In the other she held her visored helmet. Sheathed on her back was a massive twin battleaxe with a spearhead at the tip. Underneath the long handle was a rucksack containing her travel belongings. Its single strap passed between the two protruding breastplates. Beneath that was a one-handed crossbow strapped to her tailbone. Her equipment made little noise as she moved along. Her axe and armor were a blue so deep that they were almost black.

Her black hair cascaded down between her shoulder blades with a single braid in the center. Her most prominent features, however, were her eyes. Blue-green and almost reptilian, they were complemented by the deep blue markings that encased them. Looking closely, one would notice that the skin under these markings was not flesh, but scales.

Her aim was to reach the guildhall before it got dark, and dusk was little more than an hour away. She stopped at the city square and looked around. The large clock in the center proved her correct. Elaethia had entered populated cities before, but this was the largest she had been to in many years. Hundreds of eyes remained fixed on her, but she paid no attention. She was used to being stared at. They could gawk all night, so long as they didn't pester her with small talk or inquiries. That became bothersome after a while, especially since it was always the same questions.

"What is your business?" they would ask.

"My business is my own," she would reply.

"Where are you going?"

"I am going to the city of Breeze."

"Do you have hostile intent?"

"Not as of yet."

"Why are you wearing all that armor?"

"It is easier than carrying it."

And so on.

Even as she walked down the streets, guards would nervously approach her and question why she was in full armor with such an unreasonably large battleaxe. After expressing her irritation with this to an older-looking guard, he suggested she carry her helmet instead of wearing it. She didn't understand how that would help. Yet much to her surprise, all the soldiers and guards left her alone—besides eyeing her from a safe distance.

Elaethia didn't dislike talking with others, as it could benefit her with information. But unlike them, she hardly found pleasure in idle chat. Few people were worth exercising conversation with. Every interaction felt like a task.

It dawned on her that she might be lost. An exasperated sigh escaped her lips. She would have to ask for directions. Glancing at some of the nearby citizens, she tried to identify someone to ask. However, as she met their gazes, they quickly turned away. Her focus shifted to an open-air restaurant. She made her way to the small building and stood in line behind a loud elf in his early twenties with a bow slung behind his back. He appeared very displeased with the girl behind the counter.

"You call this food?" the blond archer shouted. "You've cooked it brown all the way through! How the hell am I supposed to eat this hunk of leather?"

"Sir, you asked for a well-done rabbit haunch," the teenage girl stammered as she shrunk away from the customer.

"Imbecile!" he shrieked and threw the wooden plate to the street. "I meant the best one you had! Cooked to perfection! Your finest score! What you served me isn't even fit for a dog!"

"I-I'm sorry sir; if you would like, we can retake—"

"No!" The elf slammed his fist on the counter, causing the girl to shrink further away. "I want my money back *and* a free meal! We adventurers risk our lives to keep you sniveling citizens safe, taking the quests you're too weak to handle! How about you show some gratitude!"

The warrior sighed. This was taking too long. "Pardon me," she announced.

The elf wheeled around to confront her, his left index finger pointing straight to her nose. "You can wait you're damned tur—"

He stopped himself. The elf stepped twice to the right as his hand slowly dropped to his side. His eyes widened as he noticed the thick armor and enormous weapon slung across the stranger's back. She was half a head taller and more muscled than he was. The warrior ignored him and turned her attention to the shaking girl behind the counter.

"I apologize for interrupting, but I am pressed for time."

The archer turned away sharply. "Oh i-it's not a problem at all, I was j-just leaving!" With his nose in the air, he quickly walked away before she could respond.

"It would appear I have driven away one of your customers," the armored woman stated. "However, your transaction did not seem to be going very well."

The serving girl's brow furrowed. She shook her head and clapped her cheeks, and she then put a hand to her chest and exhaled in relief. "Oh no, i-it's fine. Thank you very much! Honestly, if you hadn't stepped in, I don't know what I would have done."

"Given the direction of the ordeal, I assume you would have broken into tears and agreed to his demands."

The serving girl blinked and cleared her throat after a few seconds. "Right. Um, well, thank you again. Is there anything I can get you? I'll give you a discount for chasing away that rude adventurer."

"Yes there is," she replied, holding up the flyer. "Could you tell me how to get to the guild? This pamphlet is incorrect."

The girl took it from her and frowned. "This is our guild all right, but it isn't in this location. How old is this flyer? Where did you get it?"

"From a farming market north of here, one week's ride by wagon."

The girl scratched her head. "All right, I guess. Well, go down that way and take the third left on Birch Street. After a few hundred meters you should see a large three-story building with two chimneys and glass windows. Banners with the guild's insignia will be flying over it. You can't miss it."

"Thank you." The warrior turned and began to walk in the indicated direction.

"Um … F-feel free to stop by anytime you're hungry!"

The woman nodded.

"H-Hey!" the girl called once. "What's your name?"

Elaethia halted. She pondered for a moment and realized this was the first person to ask her name out of personal interest. And the girl did not seem to be afraid of her anymore. She decided she liked her.

"Elaethia," came the light reply.

The girl beamed and waved energetically in farewell. "I'm Cathrine! Good luck!"

Elaethia reached the guildhall soon after. As described, it was a very large building. Two chimneys, more like smokestacks, produced dark smoke that smelled of wood fire. She took a deep breath, and could sense it was magical in origin. Warped windows made it so she couldn't see clearly through them, but she could make out tens, if not dozens, of silhouettes sitting and milling about. Erupting laughs and shouts from within indicated this was a rather boisterous place. But that seemed reasonable, as this was one of the most prestigious adventurer guilds in the country.

Several enormous banners bearing the guild's insignia were draped all around the exterior, showing a silhouette of a long, tusked mammal with flat feet and a curved back. Two spears pierced it in a cross. She could tell it was meant to be a behemoth. But since the monstrosities were the size of hills, as well as the second largest creature after leviathans, she found the rendition highly disproportionate. As the sun barely dipped past the rooftops, she inhaled deeply and stepped inside.

Elaethia halted in her tracks. There must have been a hundred men and women on the first floor, all species of brehdars among the celebrating masses. Waiters and serving girls darted around with trays of food and mugs of alcohol while the adventurers drank, ate, and laughed heartily. She inhaled again and braced herself for the stench that accompanied multiple fighters in one room. Surprisingly, it was tame. Soap, smoke, and alcohol wafted from the bar and kitchen; the smell of finished wood rose from the desks and tables. She hadn't expected this place to be so clean.

A pair of heavy-looking warriors near the sidewall suddenly butted heads. The drunken demiwolf and human began to throw fists at each other while the onlookers roared their approval. The combatants grappled and hurled insults with each blow, until the human grabbed a chair and lifted it above his head to clobber the demiwolf. Before he could bring it down, he was interrupted by an air spell. The sudden and precise burst of wind struck him in the torso and sent him crashing into the table behind him. Everyone turned their heads to see a slick female demicat with her staff leveled at her target. After a moment of silence, she suddenly burst out in laughter. The demiwolf and other onlookers joined her and traded high-fives.

"Can I help you?" A friendly male voice asked from her right. A waiter with a tray full of dirty plates had stopped to address her.

"Where is the front desk?" she asked.

The middle-aged dwarf pointed further to her right. "The receptionists are over there in those teller booths. Do you need anyth—" He was cut short, as she already began walking to the gated desk.

Elaethia approached the rightmost one. A small, brass bell hung from the side with a sign above it that read: "Ring For Assistance." She rang it.

"Be right there!" a woman's voice called from further back. Its owner made her appearance a few seconds later.

She was a pretty elf, about Elaethia's age, with white hair stopping at her neck. A pair of rimmed spectacles rested on her freckled nose. She wore a blouse with ruffles protruding from her *very* pronounced breast; the guild insignia was displayed on the left shoulder.

"I'm sorry, but we aren't posting any more requests tonight," she said. "You can take a form to fill out and submit it tomorrow morning, however."

"I am not here to post a request," came the mildly confused response.

The receptionist looked up and examined Elaethia. "Are you from another guild? I'm sorry, I don't see an insignia on your person. If you have a complaint or a challenge, I can issue you the proper forms, and you can submit them right now. Under 'receptionist on duty' you can put my name—Maya."

"I am here to apply. I understand that guilds may provide funding while giving opportunities to hone one's skills."

Maya blinked. "Um, we're not accepting any more members. We haven't for almost three years. Whatever propaganda or information you heard should have told you."

Elaethia presented the flyer to the receptionist.

Maya took it and adjusted her spectacles. "I see … This flyer is over ten years old, advertising the original location in the center of town. Where did you find this?"

Elaethia ignored the question. "So I cannot apply here?"

"Have you been rejected by other regions' guilds?"

"No. This is the first one I have applied to."

Maya inhaled slowly and furrowed her brow, clenching the old flyer. She looked at Elaethia, down at the paper, and then back at Elaethia. She exhaled and closed her eyes.

"I would really hate for you to come all this way just to be turned down. But our guild's policy is rather strict. Tell you what: I can bring it up with the guild master, but don't expect a miracle. The old man rarely makes special—"

"The hell are ya talkin' about, Maya?" a loud, slurred voice demanded from behind them.

Elaethia turned to see the same human warrior from the brawl before. Cheeks red from intoxication, he leaned on a greatsword as his glazed eyes focused intensely into hers.

Maya put her hands up nervously. "Now, Peter, this is nothing to get yourself worked up about."

Peter sneered. "Nah-nah-nah, we don't need another newbie wanderin' in here, takin' all our quests. Get lost, milk drinker; nobody wants you in our guild!"

"You are referring to me, are you not?" Elaethia replied coldly. "I assume that was some sort of insult?"

The drunk warrior smirked and spat at her feet. The entire hall focused on the pair as a chorus of low jeers filled the giant room. The swordsman puffed out his chest and laughed. "Oh yeah? Whaddya gonna do about it? Can you even move in that equipment? I bet your daddy bought it for you, didn't he? Nah, that looks way too expensive for a greenhorn like you. You musta stolen it from him. He oughta be disappointed in you."

Elaethia's eyes steeled as she unbuckled her rucksack and unsheathed her battleaxe, leveling it on her shoulder.

"Do not speak disrespectfully of this armor and axe. They are Frossgar and Jörgen's final gifts."

The swordsman howled in laughter. "This stupid tramp wants to fight! Perfect. My blood's still boiling from my unfinished fight with Liam. I'm gonna take that one out on you as well!"

"Please, no using weapons inside!" Maya cried, hiding behind her counter and covering her eyes.

Peter charged her, his sword raised above his head in an obvious tell at an overhead strike. Elaethia hefted up the handle of her battleaxe to intercept the blow. The large greatsword collided with the handle of the axe, stopped entirely by her block.

"How—?"

It was the only word that could escape his lips before the butt end of the battleaxe handle slammed into his brow. He doubled backward and managed to stay on his feet. But as his right foot touched the ground, Elaethia swung around from her left, hooking his ankle where the axe head connected with the shaft, and yanked him off his feet. In the same motion, she whipped the great blade over her head, and down to the ground next to his head. Frost spread from where it hovered not a centimeter above the stone floor.

Gasps came from the astonished onlookers, and murmuring followed.

"Did you see that?"

"Have you ever seen a battleaxe move so quickly?"

"Forget that; she stopped it right before it hit the ground!"

"At that speed?"

"What kinda human *is* she?"

Peter trembled, still lying on his back. Blood leaked from his swollen forehead and trickled down his face to the floor.

"W-who the hell are you?" he stammered.

"Apologize" was the only response.

Peter nodded furiously. "All right, all right! I'm sorry, I take it back, okay? J-just let me up."

Elaethia grunted and lifted her axe, resting it on her shoulders. Cheers and howls erupted throughout the guildhall. This reaction made no sense to her, but it mattered not so long as she could continue her conversation at the reception desk. Unfortunately, that was not an option. Elaethia found herself swarmed by the crowd and their deafening roars of approval. On the verge of snapping once more, her fist clenched around her weapon's handle. Before she could take any action, a gruff, booming voice overpowered the noisy spectators, resonating throughout the entire building.

"All right, all of you *shut up*!"

Everything went dead quiet. All eyes looked up to a balcony on the second floor. Elaethia followed their gaze, which rested on an enormous demihuman. He was a demibear, judging from the rounded ears atop his head, coarse fur on his forearms and chest, and lack of a visible tail. He appeared to be in his midfifties, with greying hair and a thick, well-kept beard. He crossed his giant arms and swept the floor below with a disapproving gaze. His eyes rested on Elaethia and Peter, both of whom were at the center of the mob. This man was obviously the guild master.

"You two, my office, now!" he barked.

"Yes, Master," Peter grumbled as he rose to his feet.

Elaethia sheathed her weapon, grabbed her ruck, and followed him in silence.

"Now for the rest of you!" the guild master continued. "I've got enough problems with you lot giving me mountains of paperwork by causing mischief out in town. I don't need everyone hollering in here so the whole damned city can hear you! Keep it down before I close the bar for the night!"

"Yes sir," came the sheepish chorus.

The guild master sighed and rubbed his eyes with his fingers. "By the Sun and Moon, you rascals give me a headache. Maya! I want you up here too."

"Understood, Master! On my way." The elf grabbed some papers and disappeared into the back room.

Elaethia and Peter followed the guild master down the hall to the last room. He opened the door and lumbered inside. The first thing Elaethia saw was a long couch. In front of it was a mahogany desk with a stein, a pitcher of mead, and a fountain pen standing neatly on top of it. A comfortable high-back armchair stood behind it.

The demibear pointed to the couch. "Sit."

They promptly obeyed. The demibear dropped into his own seat, shaking the room slightly. He rested his head into his folded hands. Silence briefly filled the spacious, elegant room, until it was broken by the sound of the door shutting. Maya stepped in with the small stack of paper.

"Peter Stone," the guild master began. "I know I've said I condone friendly brawling in my guildhall. It keeps comradery and competition present while making sure you rascals don't get fat and lazy. I also know I said no using weapons or magic in those brawls. So either you blatantly disobeyed me or you were trying to kill this woman."

"No sir!" Peter said quickly. "It was just a quick test of mettle. There was no ill intent at all."

Elaethia responded immediately. "You deliberately swung your weapon at me with a harmful intent. I had no choice but to retaliate."

"No, no, because you purposefully missed when you swung at me, right? There was no way that was an accident; that means it was a show of force, see?"

She shook her head. "A drunken fool is no opponent. There would be little to gain in killing you."

"Drunken foo …? Now wait a damn minute, I'm the strongest warrior in the guild! I apologized to you, but you oughta show me some respect in return!"

The guild master slammed a meaty fist onto the desk, bouncing the pitcher upward. Elaethia turned back to him to see that his eyes were ablaze in anger. The two warriors fell silent.

"That high and mighty attitude has put us in hot water several times, Stone," he growled. "I would've banned most other members at this rate. I'm not about to kick out my number-one warrior, and you've caught on to that. You need to be brought down a few notches, and we're gonna start by putting you on dish duty until the end of the month."

Peter seemed to choke. "Dish duty! Master Dameon, I'm not gonna do something so embarrassing. That's a punishment for the apprentices!"

"Then quit acting like a spoiled brat!" the demibear thundered back. "Or maybe you'd prefer I have Maya here get a discharge sheet from downstairs?"

Peter clamped his mouth shut and looked down. His face turned a deep red.

Dameon looked at the strange woman. "As for you, let me start by introducing myself. The name's Dameon Greatjaw. And if you haven't figured it out by now, this is my guild. As its master, I have final say on everything that happens in this hall and what I choose to do with those who cause a ruckus in it. Now. Who are you?"

"Elaethia."

"That's it? You don't have a last name? A reason for being here? You weren't here just to poke around, were you?"

"Elaethia Frossgar, sir. I came here with intent to apply."

Dameon looked intently at her. "Frossgar? What kind of name is that? It sounds like one of those ancient dragons."

"It is. I am his champion."

The room froze. A grandfather clock in the corner ticked a few times. The sounds of the hall downstairs murmured through the door. Suddenly the guild master burst out laughing with a hearty belly laugh that shook his whole person. He wiped his eyes and regarded her with a lighter tone.

"My word, girl, I didn't take you for someone with a sense of humor." His face quickly fell as Elaethia's expression didn't falter. "By the Moon … you're serious?"

She nodded. Silence filled the room as the guild master looked harshly into her reptile-like eyes.

"You've got me completely at a loss, girl," Dameon said after a while. "Nobody's seen a dragon hero in hundreds of years, so I have no clue what they look like. On the other hand, I've also never seen anyone put Peter on his ass like that. Even when he's drunk. You look like a regular human, despite your eyes and … are those scales around them? You're also wearing plated armor and carrying a battleaxe that few men could even lift. Hell, *I* wouldn't take that thing into battle. What material is that made of anyway?"

"They are made of Frossgar's bones and scales," she said.

"Y-you mean to tell me that's *dragonite* equipment?" the demibear sputtered.

Elaethia nodded solemnly.

Dameon slumped back in his chair and ran his hands through his thick hair. "I still can't bring myself to believe it. There has to be some way to prove all of this."

"Master, if I may," Maya interjected. "Part of the legend surrounding dragon heroes is their ability to use their respective magic without a conduit. She froze a portion of the floor in her fight with Peter. If she is a dragon hero, it seems like it was a frost dragon."

"Well done, Maya," Dameon praised. He suddenly planted the pitcher of alcohol in front of him. "But I can hardly account for that, as I wasn't there myself. So, Elaethia! If you can freeze this mead without any conduits or touching it, I'll take your claim seriously."

Elaethia didn't know what a conduit was, but she had been given a task to aid her standing. She was going to comply. She walked to the desk and extended her hand above the pitcher, putting her power into it. Instantly the liquid inside began to harden in a crystalline pattern. Frost gathered all around the outside of the container. After a couple of seconds, she put a finger on it and tilted it off the desk. The wooden pitcher made a solid thud as it hit the floor and began to roll.

The room was in shock. Maya's mouth was agape. Dameon's eyes were wide in disbelief. Even Peter, who had sulked in silence, was fixated on the rolling jar of frozen mead.

Elaethia faced the guild master once more. "I heard from your receptionist that you were no longer taking applicants. Is that still in effect?"

The giant demibear looked directly at her and began to chuckle. The chuckle turned into a laugh, and the laugh turned into a hearty roar of amusement.

"We put that policy in place because I had those rascals pouring out of my ears! We were completely overfilled. But Sun be damned if I turn away the first dragon hero to appear in centuries after she went and sought out *my* guild. Maya, go dig out some application requests. I'm going to fire up the tag brander."

The elf held up the papers in her hand. "Already got them, sir. I had a hunch you might take this one."

"*That's* my girl; you know your old man well!"

The demibear laughed again as he stood and clapped her on the back. Maya stumbled forward a few steps from the impact. She caught herself and reached a hand up to fix her glasses, beaming as she handed him the stack of paper.

"She is your child?" Elaethia asked.

Dameon spread his arms as he rounded the desk toward her. "All members of this guild are my children, girl. Once that form is filled out and I make your tag, you will be too!"

Maya sat Elaethia down and began to fill out the paperwork, while Peter's jaw seemed to stretch to the ground. Dameon watched from overhead and wrote down certain information on a separate piece of paper. After a minute or so, he took it over to a press in the corner and began entering the information on magic-projected characters. Maya filled out the same information on identical forms.

"We have to make several copies," she explained. "One is for your own records, one for the guild itself, one for Linderry's National Guild Department, and one for the city of Breeze. This way your registration is officially recognized."

All that seemed unnecessary to Elaethia, but it was required, so she nodded in agreement. The sound of the press dropping behind them indicated her tag was complete. Master Dameon walked over carrying a small, flat piece of metal with wire going through the top.

"This is your guild tag," he announced proudly. "Make sure you have it on you at all times, as it allows you to travel freely throughout the country. I'll also have our seamstresses make you an insignia. Wear it whenever you're out on a quest to let everyone know not to bother you."

Elaethia's eyes brightened.

Maya read her expression. "But if you wear it all the time everywhere you go, people will notice. Then they'll ignore it and try to come up to you anyway."

The warrior's face fell slightly. She took the tag from the guild master and examined it. It read, "Elaethia Frossgar. Female. Aged twenty-three. Dragon Hero Human. Warrior. Breeze Guild.

Hair, black. Eyes, blue. Skin, pale. Unarmored weight, 270lbs. Height, 72 inches." She found it an adequate description. She stood and placed it around her neck with the gold-and-sapphire pendant that she never took off.

The guild master faced her in full and extended a hand as a smile formed on his lips. "Welcome to Breeze, rascal."

She extended her hand to meet his. "Thank you very much. I will work hard in your guild."

Master Dameon grinned as he herded her and Peter out of his office. "Yes, I don't doubt that you will. Now both of you get outta here. I have paperwork to submit. Peter, show the new girl around. Get her well acquainted. When you're done, you can start on those dishes."

"Yes, Master," he replied grudgingly.

Maya and Dameon turned and walked back to the office. The two warriors stood side by side in silence at the top of the stairs. Peter stared at his feet. His fists were clenched, and sweat beaded on his brow.

"We can look past the recent events," Elaethia said. "Please show me around if you would."

He spat through his teeth, "Figure it out yourself."

"I do not know where to begin."

"Stupid bitch," he muttered.

A blur of deep blue shot from the dragon warrior's shoulder. Her blow sent him clattering down the stairs into the bar below, where his head wedged itself in a barstool. The guild went quiet and stared up at the dragon hero. She held a fist poised in front of her. Her blue-green eyes burned down at the blond man. Dameon's bellowing laughter resounded from behind her. The guild master leaned over the balcony as he addressed his bewildered members once more.

"All right, you rascals, today you have a new sister!" He pointed at her with his opening announcement. "This here is Elaethia. I'll let her introduce herself as she sees fit. But just be warned: you'd better play nice with her unless you want to end up like Mr. Stone down there!"

All of the onlookers turned their heads to watch as members of Peter's party dislodged his head from the barstool and carried him into the basement.

Master Dameon continued. "She may be soft on the eyes, but I'd bet this whole guildhall she could put any one of you in the dirt. Now start cleaning up! Taps are shut off! I've got even more administrative duties piling up, and I don't need you lot distracting me."

"Yes, Master," the masses responded.

Dameon grunted and disappeared into his office. The adventurers all turned to where Elaethia had once been, ready to ask even more questions, only to see that she had already disappeared out the front door into the night.

Chapter 2
Child and Dragon

Sixth Era. 124. Febris 3.

Frossgar mulled over the reasons for agreeing to the child's request. He had lost count of how many brehdars had come to him with the same goal. The need for dragon heroes had long passed, and the dragon wars were nothing more than ancient history. It was almost impossible that there would be any other dragon heroes still alive today. If he did choose her as his champion, it would be an easy life. But he would no longer be able to live as he was. That is why he rejected so many.

So why was this young human different? It wasn't that she struck him as promising in any way—the opposite, in fact. She was small, weak, naive, and timid. For quite some time, he had considered doing something with his existence besides sitting in a cave and waiting for the world to end. But was Elaethia really the one worth changing tides for? His mind rejected the notion in an instant, but his heart spoke otherwise. He furrowed his brow and considered the possibility. No. That would not be possible for several reasons.

First and foremost, she was by no means an acceptable host. Elaethia's tiny body would not withstand the conjoinment. They would both perish in a horrible fashion if they were to attempt it now. Secondly, her will was strong, but her mind was weak. It didn't matter how strong she was physically if her mind crumbled when paired with his. Finally, he wasn't entirely sure how to even do it.

Reclusiveness had its disadvantages. He racked his brain for memories of any explanation of the process. He had only ever associated with a few of his cousins, and he wasn't sure whether they knew either. Taking all this into consideration, was he really willing to do this? He would lose his grip on this world and entrust everything he was to the human that had come to him last night.

He lifted his head to see where Elaethia had gone. Frossgar scanned the cavern to see her at the pile of discarded equipment. The small human was sifting through it and grabbing everything she could fit her hands around. The shadow cast from a makeshift campfire lit from the torch made her seem like a goblin atop a treasure horde.

"Did I not explain to you that it is rude to play with someone's belongings in his own home?" he scolded.

She whipped around. His chosen hero, the appointed caretaker of his mind, power, and soul had donned a rusted horned helmet twice the size of her own head and was attempting to hide a six-foot spear behind her back.

"I wasn't playing, sir," replied the girl. "I was just looking."

"I see. Then I suppose that helmet and spear happened to appear on your person by magic."

"No sir." Her face flushed as she returned the equipment to the pile of mismatched items. Elaethia stepped down and shuffled over to him, eyes down and hands behind her back.

"While old, some of those weapons are still sharp. Should you cut yourself, I would not be able to render you aid."

"But I'm so bored, Mr. Frossgar! There's nothing to do in this cave."

He tilted his head. "It has only been a day, little one. How could you possibly be bored?"

"A whole day is forever! I just want to have some fun, and you won't play with me. You don't even know any games!"

Frossgar pondered her statement. There was a hint of truth in her words. A brehdar's perception of time was significantly faster than his own.

"I am old, little one. I do not 'play.' You should be more concerned about your next meal as opposed to your entertainment."

"But I already ate most of the food we brought with us."

"Then I suggest you go out and hunt."

The small girl stared at him. "Hunt? But I don't know how to."

"That will be problematic then. Nevertheless, you seem too small to wield a weapon. It seems I will have to do it for you until you are strong enough. But there are alternatives to meat. This mountain used to be home to a tribe of druids. If memory serves me correctly, they were able to create certain flora that can withstand the harsh climate."

Elaethia's eyes lit up. "All right, Mr. Frossgar, I'm off. I'll show you how strong I am and bring back a whole bunch!"

She ran over to her pile of furs to grab the empty rucksack and thick, hooded coat. Elaethia threw them over her body and then began scampering up the incline to the mouth of the cave. It wasn't half a minute before she slid back down and sheepishly walked to the dragon.

"I … don't know what any look like," she said.

"You should have thought of that before you departed. If you intend to be *my* champion, you must learn to think and reason." He searched his mind for a way to describe the plants, until he realized that he, too, was ignorant of the vegetation in question. "I could not give you an accurate description, as I have not made an effort to see them in hundreds of years. But I am confident I would recognize them if I saw them."

Elaethia's eyes brightened. "Come with me, then! You can show me!"

Frossgar was about to refuse, but he stopped. He looked into the innocent eyes of the girl that was now bouncing with excitement. The dragon could produce no excuse other than his desire not to move. Frossgar sighed, enveloping the girl in a gentle cloud of freezing vapor.

"I suppose I should show myself and reestablish my presence. The local fauna have certainly grown confident around my territory."

Elaethia brushed the frost out of her hair and jumped into the air with a fist pump. *"Yes!* C'mon, Mr. Frossgar! Let's go right now!"

The ancient dragon groaned as he rose to all fours and moved up the incline. His clawed feet thumped deeply with each step, breaking through the ice as he pulled himself up. Elaethia eagerly clambered up after him, using the indentations from his claws as handholds and footholds. She inhaled sharply as she emerged.

The great dragon stretched out his neck and tail, and spread his enormous wings to their fullest. His dark scales faded into a lighter blue near the edges. His leathery wings were an even brighter shade. Long, black spikes ran down his spine from his head all the way to his tail. His underbelly was sky blue, the armor-like scales turning into a smoother, less shingled pattern. He folded his wings and shook from front to back. Frossgar looked back at Elaethia, his white beard waving gently in the breeze.

"Are you coming?" he asked. She nodded in response and trudged through the deep snow to catch up with his front end. It took nearly a minute.

He tilted his head. "Is that as fast as you can move, little one?"

Elaethia looked up at him and stuck out her bottom lip. "I was the fastest girl in my class back home. It's not my fault you're so long."

"This may take a while," Frossgar noted.

The small girl fiddled with her fingers. "Um … Maybe I could ride you?"

"Ride … me …?" his response was incredulous.

"I wasn't thinking about you like a horse! You said this may take a while, and I don't want to make you stay out longer than you wanted."

He regarded her explanation. Never had he heard of dragons allowing brehdars to ride them. He doubted even the benevolent moon or air dragons would allow it. However, she made a valid point, and she was going to be his champion anyway. If he had to take one step for every ten of hers, it would be dark before they could accomplish their mission.

"Very well. Climb on my back, near the base of my neck. Place yourself between my spines." He sank down onto his haunches. The snow crunched beneath his form as Elaethia clambered up his rough blue scales.

After a few minutes, he called back to her again. "You may ask for assistance if you are having difficulty."

"I'm already up here, sir. I have been for a minute now."

Frossgar hadn't felt her climb up or settle onto his back. She was even lighter than he had thought.

"I see," he replied plainly. "Let us be on our way. Be sure to call to me should you fall. I would not notice otherwise."

He stood and had just started to move when he heard a delighted shriek erupt from behind him. He felt a peculiar emotion bubble in his chest from the jubilant giggles of the human girl on his back. Frossgar paused for a brief moment to try to comprehend the odd feeling. He grunted, shook his head, and continued to walk past the icy blue structures outside his cave.

"How could you see all those, Mr. Frossgar?" Elaethia inquired as they began their return. "Your eyes are so far from the ground!"

"Dragons are aerial hunters, little one. Our vision must be keen to spot prey below," he replied.

"Don't your eyes get worse as you get old? My grandmother had awful eyesight, and you're *much* older than her!"

The dragon exhaled deeply from his nose. "We are different from short-lived brehdars. Magic courses through our bodies. We do not get sick; nor do our senses degrade over time."

Elaethia rested her head against the spine in front of her. "It must be nice being a dragon. How old are you, Mr. Frossgar?"

"I have stopped counting, but I know I have spent around thirty-four hundred years on this earth."

Elaethia shot up. "That's a really long time! What was it like back then?"

"That is a very broad time frame."

"Did you have a lot of friends?"

"I never had need for 'friends,' but there were a couple whose company I found reasonable."

"I bet you've been around longer than most cities!"

"I have seen the rise and fall of many an empire."

Elaethia's eyes widened. "So that means you have seen a lot of wars, too?"

"Yes. Though I never involved myself in any of them, including the dragon wars."

"Did you ever kill people?"

"You ask a lot of questions, little one," the dragon chided.

"Well I don't know very much," she mumbled.

"Have I not explained to you that it is improper to mumble?"

Elaethia corrected her tone. "Yes sir, you have."

"Why are brehdars so quick to subjugate themselves?" he asked no one in particular.

A grin appeared on the girl's face. "See, now *you're* the one asking questions."

"That was nothing compared to the barrage you beset upon me," he retorted.

The little girl laughed as she hugged his spine. He again felt that new emotion in his chest.

"You seem to have recovered from the death of your grandfather. Do you not mourn him, as your actions from the other day would suggest?"

Elaethia was quiet for a moment. "Grandfather Celus wasn't around very much. He hated Mother. Always said she was a 'harlot,' whatever that means, and only after my father for his money. But I don't believe it. Mother loved me and Father, and she always cared for him when he came home hurt or tired. Grandmother usually told me to stay away from Grandfather, since I reminded him of Mother. She said I had Father's hair and skin but Mother's eyes and face. Father always wore this necklace, saying that when he looked at it, it was like he was looking at me and Mother—the gold being her skin, and the sapphire being my eyes. He liked to say he imagined my mother as the gold, holding me, as the sapphire. Then he said he would hold it to his heart so that it was like we were all together, even when he was away."

"So did you feel distrust or fear toward your grandfather?"

Elaethia pursed her bottom lip. "I guess I was afraid of Grandfather. He would throw things at me if I got near him, or call me mean things. Sometimes I think he would have done worse if Father hadn't told him to leave me alone. I was sad when you told me he was dead, because I thought he was all I had left. But I still have Father's pendant. As long as I have it, my mother and father are always with me. I don't dislike Grandfather anymore, because I know he didn't really hate me. If he did, he wouldn't have gotten me here. I'm not glad he's gone, but I won't really miss him. Besides, you're much nicer than he was, Mr. Frossgar!"

"I never knew your grandfather, so I can neither agree nor disagree," he said, unsure how to take the compliment.

"Well, I knew both of you," The girl countered "And I say you're better."

"You have spent merely a day with me, little one. I do not believe that is enough of a basis to make such a claim."

Elaethia hugged him more fiercely. "Maybe not, but you seem nice! Mother always said I was good at judging people. And you've been way friendlier this one day than Grandfather was my whole life!"

"Do not compare me to the rest of the brehdars that you knew back home. The difference between us is far too vast."

"But you're still a person!" she insisted. "I don't think it matters if you have scales or skin, two legs or four, or are one meter or one hundred meters. If you have a mind and feelings, I think that makes you just like everyone else."

"Is that what all brehdars believe, or simply your own opinion?"

The little girl leaned against his spine. "Well, it's how I think. I'm pretty sure most people think so, too. While we were traveling up here, we met people from every race. All of them were different in their own way, but nobody was ever treated differently. Grandfather wouldn't let me talk to anyone, but I could tell just by hearing and watching."

Frossgar turned back to look at her and tilted his head. "Even the demihumans? They freely exist together with the other brehdars?"

"Yeah!" Elaethia exclaimed, "I know they were used for slaves or soldiers a long time ago. But our schools say they've been just like regular people for hundreds of years now."

"Hmm," he noted, turning his head forward again. "That is good to hear, I suppose."

"Where did demihumans come from, anyway? I know they haven't been around as long as humans, dwarves, or elves."

"They were created by an anatomy sorcerer that specialized in body matter transferal. He believed he could produce his own army by conjoining humans and animals into new species— creatures intelligent enough to follow orders and fight, but dull enough to be mass-controlled and lack a will of their own. As you can tell, he experimented with sabercats, wolves, and bears. At one point they became as intelligent as regular humans. The sorcerer had no intention of allowing a sentient species as his final product and attempted to kill them off. But he forgot that they could think and reason. The demihumans quickly learned of his plans and turned on him.

"Now free of their bondage, the three new species of brehdar scattered into the world. Unfortunately the world was not prepared for their arrival. Their presence was considered an abomination at the time. Neither children of the Sun and Moon nor naturally occurring, they were shunned from civilization. The last I had heard about demihumans was that they were sold as slaves or used in conscripted soldiering."

"Well, those days are over, Mr. Frossgar," Elaethia announced. "There weren't as many demihumans in Armini as there are here or in Linderry, but they're just like normal people. Father would have loved to see how they're treated up here."

"You speak highly of your father, Marcus I believe. What of your mother?"

"Mother's name was Naomi. My family never told me much about her past. Grandmother said Father rescued her from a bad place and told me I would understand when I was older. I know Grandfather always called her that 'harlot' name, and that had something to do with where she came from. But that doesn't matter to me. She loved me and Father very much and always took care of us."

"Is that so? Unfortunately I do not recognize that word either. 'Harlot' must be a new term that I have not encountered."

"Mother loved to tell me the story of how Father met her. She was supposed to be a slave for Emperor Rychus, but Father rescued her. He pretended that he wanted her as a slave for himself as a reward for being loyal. He tricked Rychus and saved my mother!"

"You mentioned this 'Rychus' before. Who is he?" Frossgar asked.

"He's evil," she said. "He's ruled Armini for over a hundred years. Even though he's so old, he still looks young. Father said his strength and magic are unbeatable, and that's why he sent Grandfather and me away. Anytime people stand up to him, he kills them. My father tried to stop him, but he couldn't. That's when we all ran away. Only Grandfather and I escaped."

"What makes this man so evil?"

"I don't understand it very well, but Mother said that if you don't work directly under him, you have no freedom. He makes the people pay a lot of money to him, and he doesn't protect them. He tells his soldiers to do whatever they want if the citizens don't obey the rules. But the people can't even have weapons to protect themselves. If he finds out you can use magic, he takes you. People aren't allowed to leave, and if they do, he sends spies to hunt them down. After Grandfather and I escaped, we found out that Armini is the only country to use slaves."

"Is that so?"

Frossgar felt anger well up within him. Rychus reminded him of the tyrant kings from back during the dragon war who ruled with an iron fist over their subjects. Men like him were responsible for the dragon wars. Men like him sent the world into chaos. Men like him were the reason he was alone now, and it burned him that such men still existed. He despised anyone who used their power to harm others. More so, he hated it when they would come to positions of absolute power. If Elaethia spoke the truth, then this Rychus was corrupted beyond redemption. If he stayed in power, he would undoubtedly act to spread it and send the world into chaos again.

"And you wish to destroy Rychus, do you not?" he asked.

"Yes sir!" Elaethia stated firmly.

"You hold a commendable cause, little one. Men like him must not exist."

"So you're really going to help me all the way?" Elaethia exclaimed. "You're going to show me magic and make me strong?"

"If that is what it takes." He turned once more to face her, his reptilian eyes burning with a purpose he had never felt before. "If Rychus remains in this position, he will undoubtedly cause a shift in tides in the world for the worse. I will not sit idly by while that happens. Not again. I will grant you my soul and power, and you, Elaethia, will be my champion."

The girl suddenly squealed in delight and ran up his neck to jump onto his giant face, which she hugged fiercely. "I love you, Mr. Frossgar! I'm going to work as hard as I can!"

The great dragon was shocked by the burst of endearment. But that strange new emotion that had bubbled in him before suddenly burst forth like a spring. A warmth flowed through the ancient frost dragon's heart as an indescribable attachment for the tiny human clinging lovingly to his face flowered to life.

"Come now," he chided, almost laughing. "I cannot walk properly with you on my face."

"Thank you, sir. Thank you so much." The little girl looked up, a wide smile on her face and tears in her eyes.

"You are quite welcome, little one." His once gruff and patronizing voice now gave way to something gentler. "Now return to where you were; we are nearing home."

Sixth Era. 139. Mertim 16.

Elaethia strode back into the guildhall early the next morning. It was quieter than the night before, as most of the members were still asleep or back in their own homes. Some staff members nodded a greeting to her as they catered to an exhausted party of three. She presumed this party had just returned from a quest. There were also several passed-out adventurers that had drunk too much the night before, as well as a cloaked man that tended to the string on his recurve bow. She made a mental note to continue making her appearances early in the morning. She approached the reception desk to ring the rightmost bell.

"Coming!" Maya called from the back room, and she appeared soon afterward. "Oh, Elaethia! Where'd you disappear off to last night? Everyone was looking forward to meeting you."

"It would have felt more like an interrogation than a meeting," the warrior said. "I dislike such crowded atmospheres. I will make my acquaintance with the other members as time sees fit."

"That's hardly the problem, really. You left before we could give you an orientation. Where did you even sleep last night?"

"In the forests outside the city."

Maya's jaw seemed to hit the desk. "You spent the night *outside?* What about predators, or monsters, or ... or bandits?"

"Creatures smell the dragon on me and keep their distance, and I am perfectly capable of concealing myself from brehdars at night. They would not be able to penetrate my armor should they find me regardless."

Maya put a shaking hand to her hair. "You slept in your armor ... Elaethia, that is so uncouth."

The warrior tilted her head. "Were my actions problematic?"

"Yes! Well, no, but. Augh!" the receptionist groaned and put her head in her hands. "Listen, we have rooms for our members here. If you had stuck around last night, you could have rented one, and you wouldn't have had to sleep outside."

"Sleeping in the wilderness has never bothered me. Besides, is it not normal for adventurers to do so?"

"Okay, but that's while they're on quests! You're here in civilization; you don't have to do those kinds of things!"

"I appreciate your concern for me, but you do not need to worry. I cannot catch sickness like other brehdars do. I am not so sensitive about where I choose to sleep, and I would prefer to avoid being surrounded by so many people."

"Elaethia"—Maya reached out and softly took her armored hand—"that's tacky. You're with the guild now, meaning you represent us with everything you do. Being as strong and outstanding as you are, you're sure to become one of our most famous adventurers. We can't have a star member sleeping outside like a vagabond. Do us the honor, and carry yourself with a bit more dignity."

Elaethia tried to read her expression. She didn't completely understand what Maya was saying, but the term 'dignity' meant something to her as well.

"All right," she said after a moment. "I understand maintaining the guild's reputation is important. If my actions tarnish it, then I will work to adjust them. How much is a room here?"

"Thank you. I have a feeling you're going to have a lot of conversations like this down the road." Maya sighed and slumped onto the counter to bury her head in her arms. After a second, she popped back up with a cheerful smile. "Rent is six gold a month, or sixty gold for a year. Now, let's finish your orientation."

Elaethia tilted her head. "Orientation?"

"Geran!" Maya called out into the guildhall.

The man who was working on his bow stood up and walked over. He wore a short, plain leather tunic with padded gambeson armor. With the exception of his green-hooded cloak with a gray interior, his clothing was a simple brown. On his left hip was a steel longsword, and on his right side a sheathed dagger. A dark brown recurve bow and its respective quiver were slung across his back. His stride and demeanor showed he was very experienced.

"You called?" he asked.

Geran was maybe an inch taller than Elaethia and looked a year or two older. His brown hair was on the shorter side but was long enough to be neatly combed. A trimmed stubble beard enveloped his face, which held brown eyes that were slightly darker than his hair. With his chiseled features, a firm jaw, and toned muscles, he was an attractive man.

Maya turned back to the warrior. "Elaethia, this is Geran Nightshade. Geran, Elaethia Frossgar. Geran's one of our veteran members, and my closest friend. We've both been hanging around here since we were fourteen. He's turned into our best ranger over the years and consequently won't work with others. Despite that, he's actually very friendly!"

"Helluvan introduction, Maya," the ranger sighed.

"It is a pleasure to make your acquaintance, Geran," Elaethia greeted him politely with an extended hand.

"Likewise, Elaethia," he responded warmly, grasping it with a firm shake. "Heard you were the one that thrashed Peter last night. Sorry I wasn't around to see it."

"I apologize if my first impression has been a negative one. Hopefully I can correct any misunderstandings."

"Absolutely not," the ranger laughed. "That was the best possible way you could've introduced yourself to this dysfunctional family of ours. Part of the 'initiation' some of the veteran warriors have is coming together and beating the snot out of the new ones. Something tells me you're going to be the first one they skip that tradition for."

"They would be wise to do so," she said.

Maya stepped in. "Geran, would you be so kind as to show her around? She pulled a disappearing act last night before we could get down to it."

"Sure thing. We'll start here." The ranger patted the wooden surface. "This is the reception desk. It's where you, as an adventurer, come to sign up for and turn in quests. If there's any paperwork or letters for you, someone will come tell you, and this is where you can find them. Now, if you'd follow me."

He turned and walked in with Elaethia in tow. They rounded a corner and faced a cork poster wall that stretched about fifteen meters in length and two meters tall.

"This is our quest wall," he continued. "Every morning, quests from all over the region get posted here. They're separated by difficulty into the five levels, although technically there are six. B for beginner, I for intermediate, A for advanced, V for veteran, and R for raid. Raids are unique because they require multiple groups. An individual adventurer is ranked by the caliber of quest they can consistently complete. Once you or your party chooses a quest, you take it to the reception desk, where they will either stamp it with approval or decline it. You'll get in serious trouble if you take a quest that's been declined. Even if you complete it without being caught, you won't get the reward. And then you'll still get reprimanded."

"What about the sixth level?" she inquired.

"That's G, for 'guild.' Those quests are ultra-rare and are on a level so intense that the whole guild is needed to handle them. There's only ever been one G-level quest as long as I've been here, and that was ten years ago when the guild took down a behemoth. That's also where we got our emblem from."

Elaethia's eyebrows rose. "A behemoth? That is most impressive."

His face dropped. "True, but it wasn't all glory and triumph. A lot of adventurers died trying to kill the thing."

"I see," she replied. "You must have lost some very close people."

"My mentor, Adrian, as well as some of our other best members. I wasn't there to see any of it happen, because I was too young to partake, but there's no nice way to be killed by a behemoth. They never let us youngins see the bodies, because, well …" He trailed off.

"I see. I am sorry for your loss."

"Yeah. Let's move on, huh?"

They walked to their left and came to a door that led into a room resembling a huge pantry. Inside there were three stations, the first being the largest and having a wall of prewrapped packages of food. An old dwarf with a bald head and long black beard sat behind a small desk.

"This is our provisions section," Geran said. "Once you have a quest stamped off by the reception desk, you bring it back here and run through all these stations for your supplies. Mr. Brodric here is in charge of the rations."

"Bringin' in th' new whelp are ye, Nightshade?" Brodric said in a thick Svarengel accent.

"Yessir," Geran said. "She's that dragon hero everyone's been buzzing about. Quickly made her mark as a tough warrior."

"Aye, and a lovely one at that." He turned to address her. "How d'ye plan to keep all th' men around here offa ye?"

"A bruise or broken bone usually dissuades wandering hands," Elaethia said with a straight face.

The dwarf roared with laughter. "That it does, lass, that it does. Where'd ye find this gem of a woman, Nightshade? Th' ones that normally chase after ye are flaky youngins."

"Actually, she came to us," Geran corrected him. He then turned to Elaethia. "Brodric here is our field cook. He's an alchemist who uses his magic to prevent things from spoiling. Once you come here with your sheet, he'll issue you enough meals to last the duration of the quest."

"Not accountin' for taste, mind ye," Brodric said. "I make em' as good as I can, but th' liquids that keep em' fresh dilutes it a bit. Careful not to eat several in a row, either, 'cause they can clog up yer insides."

"I will remember that," the warrior promised. "I have never heard of this type of magic before. I must applaud your ingenuity and dedication to the guild."

The dwarf gave her a long, bewildered look and then looked over at the ranger.

"Now ye take good care of this lady, Geran. She's got a level head on her shoulders, and it'd be a shame if it got lopped off."

"I will, Brodric, although she's very good at taking care of herself."

They continued down the line and passed the wall of rations, stopping at a massive five-meter-tall barrel.

"This is the canteen," Geran announced. "Here is where you can fill up on drinking water. Nobody runs this station though, because we encourage the adventurers to take as much as they can. Hydration is essential in combat."

Elaethia nodded in agreement as they moved over to the final station. Behind the counter was a middle-aged human woman with greying brown hair. She wore a long white coat with black shoes and pants. A pair of goggles sat around her eyes.

"Finally, this is the potion shop," Geran said. "This one is optional, since it costs money, and the guild isn't going to make you buy potions, considering they can be expensive. Michelle back there is our guild's main alchemist, who makes and sells a variety of potions to the adventurers. Her duties also include purifying the canteen and bath water. She's a little … eccentric, and she's very involved in her work. It's best you only talk with her if you're going to buy or request a potion."

Elaethia looked up at the woman, who was fiddling around with sets of glass beakers, tubes, and boilers. The alchemist muttered to herself as she cast spells on the multicolored liquids in front of her.

"Don't worry; she's harmless," the ranger assured her. "Just odd. Let's go over to the bar."

They crossed the main hall over to the opposite side, where the massive serving area was located. Several bartenders and servers were behind it, cleaning dishes and wiping the counters.

"Citizens come in here all the time for food and drink. But we adventurers have the right-of-way. You don't strike me as a drinker, but the food made by our chefs back there gets better by the year. It's a bit pricier than some of the other places you'll find out in town, but it makes sense, as a guild can be expensive to maintain. The menu is posted above the bar up there. Whenever you're ready to order, just wave down any of the servers."

They turned toward the stairs leading to the second level

"Up here are the adventurers' quarters. They aren't exactly luxurious, but they accommodate our needs well enough—although a lot of members prefer getting their own place out in town. If you don't mind the occasional rowdy neighbor or people going to and from quests at night or in the morning, you should be fine. Down the hall at the very end, as you already know, is the guild master's office. Don't ever go in there unless you are asked for or he's needed for something.

"On the opposite end are the baths and facilities. They're always open unless under maintenance, and they are completely free if you choose to live here. The left side is for the women, the right side for the men. And please, for the love of the Moon, cover yourself appropriately when walking to and from the baths. Some of the guys here, and girls for that matter, are a bunch of filthy animals who may try some funny business. Do *not* wash your gear in the baths. We have faucets and racks out back for that. Also out there is a decent training area, mostly for beginner members."

They started to walk back downstairs toward the receptionist's desk.

"Those are all the main places you need to worry about. The third level is storage for all old files, accolades, and awards. If you've got more stuff than your room can handle, you can rent space up there, too. The basement is the infirmary as well as staff and apprentice quarters. Unless you get a room here, you'll spend the majority of your time on the first floor. This concludes my orientation; do you have any questions?"

"Yes," she replied. "I wish to take a quest. Which level do you recommend for me?"

Geran gave her a blank look. "What?"

"You mentioned the quests were separated by difficulty. Which level set should I choose from?"

His expression turned incredulous. "You literally just got here, and the first thing you're doing is asking to go on a quest. Alone."

"Correct," she replied.

Geran's hand flew up and smacked his face. He inhaled sharply, lowered his hand, and rubbed his finger and thumb into his eyes. Exhaling, he looked at her expression, which was now slightly confused.

She spoke again. "Can I not take a quest? I thought I was fully indoctrinated in the guild."

"Well, you can. And you are. But what about living arrangements? Forming a party? Getting settled in? You don't even have a guild insignia yet."

"None of those are necessary. If I recall, you do not have a party yourself. But perhaps living arrangements should be addressed. Maya did mention that as well, and I promised I would correct it."

Geran looked into her determined blue eyes and sighed. "All right, let's go see Maya then. Hopefully she can talk some sense into you."

On their way to the reception desk; Elaethia halted at the quest board and began scanning the requests at the basic level.

"What are you doing?" Geran asked.

"Your B-level quests are quite novice," she stated. "Deliveries, sewer cleaning, jury requests … These are only fit for an inexperienced adventurer."

"Yeah. That's why they're called 'beginner' quests," he responded with heavy sarcasm.

She ignored him and jumped up to the advanced requests. "These are more attuned to my expertise. I have already done several tasks similar to these in my travels."

"Come again?"

She pulled a request off the cork wall and made her way to the desk. "This one seems beneficial and complementary to my skills."

"Where are you going with that?" Geran called after her.

"To give it to Maya so she can stamp it."

Elaethia marched around the corner to the reception desk. Maya was still sitting there and working on some papers. A quick glance told her they had something to do with a completed quest, presumably relating to the party of three from earlier. Elaethia unhesitatingly planted hers on top of it in front of Maya. The elf jumped a little in her seat and looked up.

"Oh!" she exclaimed. "E-Elaethia. Hi."

"I would like to accept this quest, please," Elaethia said.

"Um …" the receptionist murmured, and she looked helplessly at the ranger, who shook his head while slightly raising his hands. "I suppose I could check it out."

She grabbed the flyer and straightened it out. After a second, she dropped one hand and turned the flyer around to face the dragon hero.

"This is an A-level quest, Elaethia," she stated with mild irritation.

"I am aware," the warrior replied. "I would like to acquire a room here, but I do not have the funds to afford it. This quest has a reward large enough to purchase a year's rent."

"This is a quest meant for a party of intermediate or higher adventurers, and you're asking me to approve you for it, alone?"

"Yes."

"Beyond that, this quest is special in how it operates, and there are engagement restrictions on it."

Geran stepped in. "Which one did she pick?"

"The Westreach tower hostage situation," replied the elf.

"What!"

Elaethia spoke again. "I fail to see the reason for this response."

Geran walked up to the counter and faced her. "Elaethia, this is a watchtower that's been occupied by bandits who have several children imprisoned there. Westreach has its own guild, so normally this quest is out of our jurisdiction. But some of those children are citizens of Breeze, so we're authorized to post it."

"Yes, I have read the request," she replied calmly.

"Look. I don't completely doubt your ability to take care of some bandits, but this is a sensitive quest. Anything happens to one of those five kids, and our guild's reputation could be shot!"

"I do not intend for any of them to be harmed. You are welcome to accompany me if you wish," Elaethia retorted.

Geran stopped and closed his mouth. "I make a point to only work alone," he replied under his breath after a moment.

"Have you ever even done anything like this before?" Maya interjected. "This one specifically requests all children to be returned to their homes *alive*. Do you understand what you're applying for?"

Elaethia shot the elf a look cold enough to make her sit back down. "Many times have I gone into a fort or cave to dispose of bandits or sorcerers, and every time they have had prisoners. I will not stand idle while those children are used for entertainment or experimentation. They will not be collateral damage, as they are usually kept together in a solitary location. If you will not allow me to take this as an adventurer, I may very well do it alone out of charity. Now, will you sign me off on this quest?"

Maya stood in silence for a few moments. She swallowed hard and blinked. After a moment, she sighed, looked at the request once more, and stamped it.

Maya and Geran observed Elaethia as she went through the provisions line and out the main doors. They stood together, watching the dragon hero make her way toward the city's front gates.

"Geran—" Maya started.

He held a hand up. "Don't ask. I was gonna do it anyway. You and I both know what happens when you interfere with another party's quest. If I get caught, I don't want the blame falling on you too."

"Thank you … I owe you one."

Geran pulled his hood up and laughed under his breath. "As if we're still keeping count of favors."

Elaethia took instant use of her new guild tag. The warrior presented it to a wagoner who was headed in the same direction. She fully expected him to demand payment, but the old demiwolf actually offered to pay *her* instead. The elderly trader had apparently been recently attacked by roadside bandits and was very excited at the thought of having a large, intimidating warrior with him until the next town. As she climbed in back, she made a silent tally of the pros and cons of the last two days. So far, joining the guild was proving more beneficial than not.

Sixth Era. 139. Mertim 17.

Elaethia stared up the hill at the watchtower. The road was open and wide. Any lookouts would be able to see her approach. The warrior ducked into the thick woods on the side and continued her ascent under the cover of brush and foliage.

There was only a single guard in front of the stone structure. The grungy demicat leaned against the shade of the wall; his iron and fur armor was poorly kept and rusted around the edges. There was no one else outside. Elaethia decided to launch her assault at night, when they would be at their most lax. The hostages would also not likely be present. She quietly set down her gear and sat down to wait.

The bandits rotated their shifts every couple of hours. The oncoming guard started alert and attentive, only to quickly lose interest and stare off into space. A few even fell asleep at their posts. Light started to shine through the windows as the sky darkened. Sounds of laughter and reveling shortly followed. They reminded her of a quieter, more malicious version of a guildhall. The lack of young or fearful voices could be either good or bad news; it meant the five hostages were either in a separate location, already dead, or gone.

It was nearing the time to engage, but Elaethia didn't know what was on the other side of the door. Her use of magic was going to have to be held off until she could confirm the immediate interior was free of innocents. The current watchman suddenly snorted as the last of the light faded from the sky. He hocked, spat on the ground, and opened the door to head inside. Elaethia stood after it closed behind him and carefully walked across the road through the darkness.

After about five meters, she heard the strum of a bow and felt an impact on her shoulder. Unfazed, she stopped and watched as an arrow bounced off of her dragonite plates. The warrior looked up to see that an archer had spotted her from the high tower. Elaethia looked around and realized she was silhouetted by the light from inside. She cursed at herself. She knew to pay attention to how she stood out in her surroundings. Another strum of the bow broke her consideration. The arrow ricocheted off her helmet, tilting her head back slightly. She sighed, pulled out her crossbow, loaded a bolt, and fired at the archer twenty meters above her. She heard nothing over the sound of the bandits inside, but the longbow fell from the tower and clattered on the gravel path.

The sounds of eating and laughing inside subsided.

"The hell was that?" a bandit whispered.

"Luis, check it out," a gruff voice barked.

"Right, right; I'm goin'," a third voice grumbled.

The sound of a stool scraping on cobblestone was followed by nearing footsteps. Elaethia listened intently and braced herself. Moving shadows blocked the light from under the door, indicating that Luis had reached it. Just as the latch was released, Elaethia unleashed a savage kick. The heavy oak door blasted inward, splintering and ripping itself off its hinges. The bandit was thrown back into one of his compatriots and rag-dolled lifelessly off a table and onto the ground.

"Holy Sun and Moon!" the demicat bandit yelped.

A quick evaluation of the room revealed five enemies standing, one on the ground, and one dead near the back. There were no hostages in the room.

Elaethia lunged forward with the battleaxe and cleaved through the front of the demicat, cutting him diagonally in half. She stepped with the momentum to the next man and continued the axe's arc across to sweep it sideways into his left side, where it lodged halfway into his torso. The other three charged at her with their weapons drawn. Elaethia maneuvered her axe with the bandit still on it and leveled it at her attackers. She kicked the dead elf off of it, which knocked the closest enemy over.

The warrior thrust the spearhead into the throat of the next bandit, tore it out, and stepped back to whip the great axe sideways around with a spin. The axe hummed through the air as it sang through the neck of the next assailant, sending his head flying. Still carrying its momentum around, she brought the massive blade down from overhead onto the final bandit on the ground, shattering the cobblestone floor beneath as it crushed through his chest. Elaethia's eyes shot up to meet the gaze of the final man that had initially been knocked over. With a terrified cry, the dwarf scrambled to his feet in an attempt to run up a set of spiral stairs along the wall. He had taken two steps when a stool Elaethia had thrown crashed into his head.

Elaethia stood and took in her surroundings. It would have been a cozy little room had it not been for recent events. Even then she doubted the bandits kept it clean. Some now broken and bloodstained furniture was scattered across the room. Food and eating utensils littered the floor. A fireplace crackled comfortably near the stairs that lead up to the top of the tower.

The sound of bare feet on stone rushed up the stairs from the basement. Another bandit emerged wearing nothing but shirt and trousers, his belt undone. He looked wildly around the room until his horrified eyes rested on the plated warrior in the center. Elaethia inhaled deeply. She emptied her lungs, and a cloud of freezing vapor billowed out toward her target. A stifled scream that was quickly smothered by the sound of cracking ice filled the room. When the mist cleared, it revealed the slain bandit mounted on the wall behind him, impaled by a cluster of sharp crystals.

Elaethia followed the stairs down from where he had come from. She rounded the corner at the bottom and opened a door to reveal five shaking children. A very young girl and slightly older boy were holding each other in the near corner. They trembled with wide eyes that watched her as she walked in. Their matching blond hair and blue eyes suggested they were siblings.

A black-and-white-haired, teenage demiwolf was chained to the opposite wall. He eyed her warily and attempted to hold himself up despite how exhausted he looked. Most notable were the other two. A young teenage girl lay naked in a pile of straw, covered only by a blanket. She was crying and attempting to make herself as small as possible. A slightly younger boy crawled to her from the far wall. Tears streamed from his face and blood poured from his forehead.

"Don't come any closer!" he screamed at Elaethia.

Elaethia stopped and leaned her axe against the wall. She removed her helmet and settled it on the axe's hilt.

"I will not harm you," she assured them. "My name is Elaethia; I am with Breeze's guild. I have come here to bring you home."

The boy paused and then scrambled to the girl beside him.

"I told you someone would come," he sobbed as he clung tightly to her. "I promised you, didn't I?"

Elaethia knelt in front of the chained demiwolf and held his face to her eyes.

"Can you speak? Do you know where the keys to unlock these cuffs are?"

"Wall … Peg … Other side … of door."

She stood and walked out. As he said, the ring of keys dangled next to the entryway. She took them, walked back to the boy, and released him from the shackles. He sighed heavily as he fell, but Elaethia caught him before he could hit the ground. She leaned him against the wall and pulled out her water and a stamina potion. She tilted the skin of water into his mouth and gave him short, controlled sips. After he was swallowing comfortably, Elaethia poured the potion into his mouth as well. Seconds later he gasped and lurched forward.

"Are you all right?" she asked.

He blinked heavily as his chest heaved. "Yeah, yeah. Thanks."

She handed him the healing potion and water. "I will return shortly. Stay here and see to the others. I must make sure there are no other enemies in the tower."

He nodded as he took the vial and waterskin from her.

Elaethia stood and made her way to the door to head upstairs. She retrieved her pack and sheath from outside and set them on the floor by the fire. The warrior then searched the corpses for signs of life or anything of value. She found little more than a fair amount of gold and silver coins. She continued her search up the spiral stairs, which housed only a ladder to a trapdoor. She recalled the archer from before and climbed up.

The archer wasn't dead but was clearly wounded and in pain. The elf's breathing was strained as she leaned against the turret, and she was bleeding heavily. The bolt was lodged in her left leg and had ruptured an artery.

"You … You bitch." The bandit growled.

Elaethia calmly walked over to her and grabbed her by the shirt. The bandit groaned in pain as she was hoisted to her knees.

"Get your damn hands off—" She was cut short as she was thrown over the edge.

The archer plummeted silently before she impacted the gravel below with a crunch and lay still. Elaethia made her way back to the main floor and took whatever food was still good. She returned to the basement once she was content with her progress. All the children sat together when she entered the room. They were huddled closely around the now-dressed girl, who sat with her legs to her chest. Elaethia couldn't see her face through her knees.

"I'm sorry; I'm so sorry!" the young boy sobbed. "I promised your pa I wouldn't let anything happen. I tried, I swear I tried, but … but he just … I couldn't …"

The demiwolf put a hand on his shoulder. "It's okay, Henry. You couldn't stop a grownup like that. You can't put the blame on yourself; there's nothing any of us could have done."

Henry shook his head furiously and was about to respond when he heard Elaethia enter. They looked up at her as she once again set her axe and helmet along the wall. She walked into the center of the room and offered them the food.

"Eat slowly so you do not get sick. Save the water as best you can."

The blond siblings and the demiwolf scrambled over to food. Henry led the girl over behind them. Elaethia pulled up a stool and addressed the black-and-white-haired demiwolf, as he was clearly the oldest.

"What is your name? How did you come to be here?" she asked.

He swallowed. "My name's Michael Finway, ma'am. I've been here as long as those bandits have. Pretty sure they were trying to abduct us for ransom or slave trades, but I dunno for sure. I was out hunting in the woods near my village when they appeared out of nowhere and nabbed me. We all moved in here almost two weeks ago. They used me mostly for cleaning up and washing their gear. A few days later, some of them spotted this blond-haired brother and sister and snatched 'em. Don't know their names; I've never heard them speak. A few days ago, Ana and Henry over there were walking along the road back to Breeze when they got grabbed."

The two looked up at the sound of their names.

"I assume you are also related?" Elaethia asked them.

Henry shook his head. "No ma'am. Ana's my neighbor. Her pa asked me to walk with her while she was visiting family in Westreach. We've done this so many times we didn't think we'd be in any danger."

Henry sat very close to Ana. The girl was silent as she looked down at the untouched piece of bread in her hands with empty eyes. Elaethia knew what had happened to her in this tower. It was a scene she was unfortunately familiar with. This wasn't the first time she had saved a girl like her. It also was unlikely it would be the last. Elaethia never knew what could be said to console girls like her.

"I see," she said simply. "We shall sleep here for the night. Tomorrow I will take you home."

Henry's eyes shot up. "What about the bandits?"

"There are none," she said. "All that were here are dead. I will check to make sure there are no more in the area if that would comfort you."

"But what if more come while we're sleeping?" he persisted.

Elaethia sighed, stood up, and walked to the door. After closing and locking it, she took her stool and planted it in front of the closed entryway.

"Then I will be sure to not fall asleep."

They all woke midmorning, except Elaethia, who had fulfilled her promise and stayed awake throughout the night. The children gathered their remaining belongings and then went upstairs to leave the watchtower. The ice from the night before had melted, and the corpses were still strewn around the area. The children stared in awe and horror at the destruction around them. Elaethia tilted her head, realizing that normal children were uncomfortable around this kind of spectacle. She would have to remember that for next time.

Once outside, they were suddenly greeted by four adventurers, all of which wore the Westreach guild insignia in various places. A tall warrior with two hammers on his back led them, and he walked directly up to Elaethia.

"So *you're* the one that rampaged in there last night," he began. "I don't see an insignia on you; who're you with?"

Elaethia pulled out her tag and the quest flyer. "Breeze. If you are with Westreach's guild, I am sorry, but I have already completed this quest."

Surprisingly, he smiled. "Not a problem, actually. You just did all the hard work for us."

"I beg your pardon?" she said.

He took out a flyer of his own. "See, our description mentioned bandits, so we came prepared. But it seems like you already took care of that."

"My mission had nothing to do with killing the bandits, but simply returning the hostages. My quest is nearly complete, so we will be returning home."

The warrior planted a firm hand on her left shoulder. "Uh, no."

She glared at him. "Is there a problem?"

His expression wavered, but he stood his ground. A female demibear with a spear stepped next to him

"See, that's the thing," she continued. "Our quest also asked to get the kids home. So we'll be taking them off your hands."

The other party members started to surround her. The five children began to tremble and looked up at Elaethia.

"Although," the leader mused, looking at her throat. "I can see some pretty high-quality gold around your neck, there. If you hand that pendant over, we might be okay with letting you take all five of—"

In a flash, Elaethia's left hand flew up to grab the warrior's hand, lifted it off, and twisted it to her side.

"Ow! *Shit*, lady!" He fell to a knee and scrambled around on the gravel to ease the constant pressure. The other party members drew their weapons but halted as she pulled the massive battleaxe from her back with her free hand.

"Tell your party to stand down," she told him.

"Suck a cock!"

His furious expression turned nervous as frost began to spread on his arm where she held him. "Woah, woah, woah! Hold on, we can talk this out."

Elaethia kept her grip as the ice spread faster.

"Don't do anything rash, okay? This doesn't need to turn into an incident."

She remained silent. He tried to pull free with a growl, but it quickly turned into a yelp.

"Okay! Okay! Guys, sheathe 'em! Sheathe 'em'!"

The Westreach party slowly returned their weapons to their holsters. Elaethia released the warrior's arm, who clutched it shakily to his chest. Vapor flowed from his mouth as he breathed heavily.

Elaethia turned to Michael. "You said you and those siblings are from Westreach, is that correct?"

The demiwolf's ears perked up. "Yes ma'am! Well, I'm from a village in the region. I don't know about them."

"Very well. You three will follow these adventurers to Westreach; I will take Ana and Henry back to Breeze. Do you have any objections?"

The question was addressed to the Westreach party. None of them said anything.

"I trust you will not attempt to harass or take advantage of these children as you did with me?" she continued.

The warrior growled. "We wanna get paid, same as you, lady. Even if we *wanted* to do anything to them, our asses would fry."

"I see. Do you trust them with your care, Michael?"

He stepped closer to her, eyes bright and tail wagging. "Yes ma'am, adventurers never hurt people like that! Though I'd rather go with you—you're way cooler!"

"Then it is decided," she said. She directed Ana and Henry in front of her and led them down the hill back home. Michael waved after her as the other group walked in the opposite direction.

The ranger Geran exhaled in relief from his cover in the thick foliage. He had been trailing her the entire time, observing her closely through the mission. She was calm, ruthless, and, most importantly, efficient. She was still sloppy by his standards, but definitely a cut above the other armored meatheads in the guild. Geran watched as they disappeared in the distance. He emerged from the brush, stretched, and rolled his shoulders. The hard part was over. All he had to do now was beat them home.

Chapter 3
Dragon Hero

Sixth Era. 124. Febris 4.

A dragon's concept of time was significantly different from a brehdar's. Frossgar had been alive for over three thousand years and knew patience like no other living being. Yet, somehow, this little human had managed to test it to its fullest. The child's incessant questions alone were enough to test his temper. But those on top of her unbridled curiosity, abysmal patience, and insistent touching drove him near to the brink. Several times he snapped at Elaethia's obnoxious behavior, only for her to respond with watery eyes and stifled hiccups. This pouting was undoubtedly an attempt to incite pity in the old dragon's heart. Frossgar would be lying if he said it didn't work.

Frossgar had sired offspring before, but frost dragons were the least social of the nine species. He never knew his children. But all of that was before the dragon wars and hardly more than a passing memory. It felt odd knowing that he had outlived them. He felt no remorse, as there was no attachment to the sons and daughters he never met. But this human, Elaethia, had sparked a sense of kinship and an urge to protect he had never felt before. It served as an odd pairing with the irritation she would instill.

Between Elaethia's inexperience toward life and Frossgar's ignorance toward nurturing brehdars, raising this child would prove difficult. They would have to learn from trial and error, and their first trial quickly made itself known. The single torch that had accompanied her on the trip had sputtered out, and the makeshift campfire was dead upon their return. The dragon lowered himself into the dark cave and watched as the small child approached the lifeless coals with her hands clamped to her chest.

"It would seem your first priority would be to reignite the flame," Frossgar said. "I doubt you will freeze, but it would be very uncomfortable at night. I also recall that brehdars cannot eat raw flesh as I can. You will need some method to cook your meat. Given that the daylight is fading, I suggest you relight the fire as soon as possible."

"How do I do that?"

Frossgar tilted his head. "You do not know? Did your grandfather light the torch by magic?"

Elaethia shook her head. "No sir, he used a flint and steel."

"That term is unknown to me. Is it a tool?"

"Yes sir. I've never used it before, though."

"Surely you have watched him use it, have you not? Was he so irresponsible as to not teach you?"

Elaethia wrung her hands. "I tried once but I couldn't get it fast enough. He just got impatient and snatched it back."

"Go and retrieve it. We shall see if you can produce fire with it now."

Frossgar watched as Elaethia hopped up and jogged to the rucksack. After rummaging around in it, she pulled out a small, curved, metal bar and a chunk of mineral. Elaethia brought them up and explained them to him.

"This piece of metal is called the striker. You hit it against the flint, and it's supposed to throw out sparks."

Elaethia held out some dried pine needles and twigs, and she placed them in a structure on the ground. She began to hit the flint with the striker, filling the cavern with a sharp clacking sound. After a few minutes, she leaned back and groaned.

"It's so hard," she complained. "I don't wanna do this! Grandfather made it look so simple. Why isn't this easy?"

"Life in and of itself is not easy. We must strive to achieve what we want."

"You're a dragon; can't you just make some fire with magic?"

He tilted his head. "I am a frost dragon, little one. My arsenal of spells is specialized in frost-based magic."

"So you can't make fire?"

"No. I cannot make fire."

"Well that's stupid," the little girl folded her arms and stuck out her bottom lip.

"Pouting is very unbecoming of a hero. You are the only one who can do this. Complaining will bring you no closer to your goal."

She gave the tool a long, hard look. Placing the flint in her left hand and the striker in her right, she struck out with the piece of metal and banged it on her finger.

"Ouch!" She yelped, and she dropped the tools. She then stuck her finger in her mouth.

Frossgar closed his eyes and tried very hard not to scold her again. Once again she picked up the ignition tool, this time keeping her fingers away from the striking surface. She shot the steel forward, making an audible clack as it hit the flint. Nothing happened. She frowned and tried again, harder this time. A small piece of the flint broke off, but with it came a tiny single spark. She froze, eyes wide and mouth agape.

She whipped her head toward the dragon. "Mr. Frossgar, did you see that!"

"I did, little one. Try again."

Elaethia grunted in determination as she once again hit the two together, only to achieve the same result. She scratched her head and furrowed her brow.

"Grandfather once said this worked because of something called 'friction.' Do you know what that is?"

"Yes, although I do not know how to explain it to you. But I now believe I understand how this tool works. Instead of clashing them together, slide the flint against the metal piece as if you are trying to brush something off of it."

Elaethia nodded and braced to try it. She wound up and struck again as instructed. This time, however, she produced a small shower of sparks that fell onto the kindling. She dropped the tool in surprise.

Frossgar tilted his head. "Why are you frightened? You produced sparks, only not big enough. Do it again."

"I wasn't frightened, sir, just surprised! I think I've got it now."

Elaethia grunted with effort as she showered the pile of needles and twigs with sparks. Eventually she was able to produce sparks big enough to light the kindling. Her eyes widened as the small fire grew at her knees.

She leaped up and faced the dragon. "Look, Mr. Frossgar; I did it!"

He gave a single nod. "Indeed you did. Well done, little one."

Elaethia giggled and gave him a giant, toothy smile. Frossgar couldn't tell whether it was the small fire or the endearing actions of the child before him that spread a pleasant warmth through him.

Sixth Era. 127. Jinum 26.

As the years went by, Elaethia began to practice hunting for small prey. She tried replicating some of the traps and snares she had seen from the hunters in the village. It took several months' worth of attempts, but she eventually figured it out with occasional ideas from Frossgar. One day she discovered a rabbit trapped in her snare. The girl nearly tripped over herself in her excited dash back to the cave with the squirming animal tied up in her arms.

"Look, Frossgar! I caught one!" Elaethia announced as she proudly showed her prize.

Frossgar lifted his head. "That is all well and good, but why does it still live? Do you intend to have it as a companion?"

The girl laughed. "No sir, we're gonna eat it!"

The dragon gave her a hard look. "We? You think I am going to share a rabbit with you?"

"Well …" She paused. "I guess I could let you have it."

"That is neither here nor there," he continued. "That is for you. You caught it. You are going to eat it. I am asking why you have not killed it yet."

Elaethia's face fell. She looked at the terrified animal in her arms and then back at Frossgar. "I-I thought that you might do it," she responded quietly.

"You are mumbling again. Have we not fixed that problem?"

"Yes sir! I'll fix it! I was hoping that you would kill it for me, since I caught and brought it back."

Frossgar shifted himself so he was facing her in full. "You want me to kill it. I assume, then, that you also want me to skin it, cook it, and then feed it to you?"

Elaethia shrank back. "No sir, it's just … I don't want to hurt it. I don't like blood."

"You intend to wage war against an emperor with powers and cruelty beyond your comprehension. Do you think that you can go from this time until then without killing?"

"I …"

"If you cannot bring yourself to kill a single animal to sustain yourself, how do you think you will fare in combat against another brehdar? Could you take the life of a person with a mind and soul if you cannot take one of a simple rabbit?"

Tears began to form in her eyes. "Please …"

His tone steeled. "The way you hold back will follow you everywhere you go in life unless you break it now. Your enemies will not restrain themselves because you are hesitant or weak. Instead they will exploit this weakness and strike. It may not even be you that dies. You may have to watch as one you call friend is felled, or worse, because you could not bring yourself to do what needed to be done. Do you understand this?"

Elaethia looked up at him with tears streaming down her cheeks. His expression was stern and unrelenting. He was not going to back down or take pity on her. The girl choked on a sob, shakily took out the sharp knife she used as a tool, placed it to the writhing animal's throat, and pulled. The rabbit shrieked. The sudden noise pulled a cry from Elaethia's throat as well as she fumbled with the bleeding animal. The rabbit squirmed and writhed in Elaethia's arms. She struggled to keep a hold of it, trying as hard as she could to get the knife to the panicking mammal's neck. Through the girl's whimpers and the rabbit's shrieks, the blade met the animal's neck again and tore.

Blood poured from the throat of the dead rabbit. She placed the leaking animal on the ground and dropped the knife, the blade clattering on the stony floor. Blood covered her hands and the front of her coat. Heavy, shaking breaths flowed from her mouth, her small body trembling. Tears began to well up in her eyes as she stared at her red-stained hands and coat.

"The task is not complete, little one," Frossgar pressed with a gentler tone.

Silently nodding, she picked up the knife once more and began to skin the rabbit. As she peeled the flesh and fur off, she skewered pieces of it on a sharpened stick. Elaethia turned to the fire and began to cook the meat over it. She stared blankly into the fire, watching the meat on the end of her skewer hiss and pop in the flames. After a few minutes, she took it off and bit into it.

"*Ah!*" she yelped in pain. "Hot!"

"Of course," Frossgar stated. "You just took it off the fire. Let it sit. It will cool soon enough."

Elaethia nodded sullenly and sat for a few minutes, testing it with her tongue. Seemingly satisfied with the temperature, she bit into it again, chewed, and swallowed. The girl shuddered and grimaced.

"It's yucky …" she whined.

"Perhaps as time flows on you will learn to either endure it or prepare it better," Frossgar explained patiently. "But this is food. It is the fuel that drives the body. And you must make sure yours is a suitable host for me when the time comes."

Elaethia nodded and continued eating until the rabbit was gone. After she had cleaned herself off and disposed of the remains, she sat next to the fire and hugged her knees. The dragon moved himself behind her so she was between his arms.

"I understand this may be hard for you," he began, "but it is crucial. I will never ask you to do something I would not do or have not done myself. Everything I say is necessary. The words I spoke to you were from my own experience. There was a time in my life where I chose not to kill, and this mindset led to the death of an individual I regarded well. For whatever it is worth, I am proud of what you did today. Each lesson is one step closer to you becoming the champion we need."

Elaethia shuffled to the left, leaned against his scaled hand, and wrapped herself in his white beard. "I know. I want to be the best I can be for you. I promised I would work hard for you, and I will."

"I know you will, little one," he replied soothingly. "Tomorrow is another day, and we will continue to work through it together."

Sixth Era. 132. Otoril 17.

The weapons that lay in the cave were old and brittle, but some still held a keen edge or sturdy blade. All the normal bows had rotted away to uselessness, though one crossbow still operated fairly well. Since it was very hard to reload, Elaethia carried only a single shot on her hunts. Besides the smaller hunting knife, her preferred weapon was a sturdy oak spear with a steel head. It was taller than she was, but she could wield it with little issue. Frossgar knew how spears worked, as they were a fairly simple weapon. His instructions were not the best, but apparently they sufficed.

Frossgar could feel nothing but pride for Elaethia. Growing up on the mountain trained and shaped her body in a way that no brehdar could recreate. Tasks such as carrying a doe over two kilometers on her back were simple for her. In tangent, she had become capable of defending her kills from predators ready to steal an easy meal. Frossgar would watch as the teenager would slide down into his cave with a successful hunt every time she left.

"You have grown, little one," Frossgar praised. "Continue as you are, and your body will be an acceptable host within the decade."

"It can wait a little longer, Frossgar," Elaethia replied as she dropped her kill on the floor. "Life on your mountain is not so bad. I make sure to eat and work plenty, as you say. I don't remember any girls my age in Armini being capable of this. To think we were all afraid of a little blood."

"That was you not too long ago, Elaethia," the dragon chuckled. "Time has flowed by strangely. I feel as if I can physically see you growing if I look long enough."

Elaethia laughed as she arranged the cleaned pieces of deer. "And I believe that if I stare at your beard long enough, I can see it inching closer to the ground."

"Come now, I was giving you a compliment," he chortled.

"I know," she said, "but I couldn't resist. Thank you, Frossgar. Would you like some of this venison? I know you've said you haven't eaten in decades."

"You have asked several times over the years, and every time I have declined. Dragons may survive for decades without feeding so long as we remain in a restful state. You must eat as much as you can without taking me into account."

"Surely the smell must drive you mad, though," Elaethia protested.

"I cannot deny its temptation," the dragon admitted with a watering mouth. "But time has taught me discipline—another lesson you are learning as you live with me."

"Then one day I will bring in a whole herd for you. Then both of us can eat without guilt."

Frossgar shook his head. "Prey on the mountain would quickly become scarce should the both of us eat to our heart's content. We must conserve what resources we have and take only what we need, using everything and wasting nothing. That is the way we must live when sharing with nature. But you already know this. I am proud of you, little one."

"Frossgar, I am nearly seventeen now. I am not so little anymore."

"Maybe not by brehdar standards," he agreed. "But you are small and young compared to me. Even when you have surpassed brehdar-kind in power, you will always be my little one."

Elaethia smiled and sighed. "I suppose so. As long as you are with me, there's nothing I won't be able to accomplish. Have you figured out how to conjoin us yet?"

"I have pondered it over the years. It is not a process one can practice, but I am fairly certain I can do it once the time is right."

Elaethia leaped up. "That is wonderful to hear! When will we be ready?"

The dragon thought to himself for a moment. She was definitely not ready yet. They would need a definite point to gauge from. He turned his gaze to the discarded pile of equipment and looked at the heaviest of weapons. The only one still in stable condition was a large single-bladed axe.

"Take that axe from the pile and bring it here," he told her.

Wordlessly she walked over, hefted the heavy weapon, and brought it to him.

"Swing it down on the remainder of your deer carcass, at the thickest part. I want you to strike as hard as you can."

"Of course." She obeyed, awkwardly lifting the long axe above her head. It wasn't too heavy to her, but she seemed to struggle with the length and balance. Once she got into a solid stance, she swung it with all her might. The blade sank a few inches into the deer corpse.

"How was that?" she asked eagerly.

"Hmm." The dragon nodded. "Very well. Once you can take that axe and break through my scales in one swing, I will deem you ready."

Her knees buckled. "Break your scales? Frossgar, I could never do that!"

"This body will cease to exist soon enough, little one. It matters not what happens to it."

"I just can't," she shook her head. "There must be another way."

He slowly reached a claw over to touch her face. With a flick, he pulled out a few strands of hair. She took a small step back while clutching the side of her head and looked at him with confusion.

"Did that hurt?" he asked.

She shook her head. "No, it's nothing. But why did you do that?"

"That is what I am asking you to do to me. Seems trivial now, does it not?"

"I suppose," she agreed. "May I try it now?"

"You may try anytime," he assured her.

Elaethia walked to the flank of the enormous dragon. She again lifted the old axe with a grunt, and brought it down. A harsh clang echoed through the cave. The impact area looked no different from before the hit.

The dragon sighed in disappointment. "You are still holding back. I did not even feel that, little one. Had I not watched, I would not have known you tried. I suggest you carry that axe with you everywhere you go. Get accustomed to it so you may wield it better."

Sixth Era. 137. Febris 11.

Elaethia yelled with effort as she slammed the heavy axe into the trunk of a frozen pine. The weapon sank into the tree and wedged itself partway up the blade. Elaethia grunted and yanked on the handle. It didn't budge. She sighed heavily, her breath turning to mist as it wafted out of her open mouth. She pushed a few frozen locks from her face. The frigid air and wind were so cold they had frozen the sweat that ran through her hair.

Elaethia exhaled slowly to steady her breathing and looked around. She had to venture far from the cave to do this kind of training. Both she and Frossgar had decided the best targets to practice on were trees. But after the first year, she had significantly deforested the area around the cave. At first it took several days for her to fell even one. But after a while, she was cutting them down daily. Now she was at the point where she could practice only in the winter when the trees had hardened.

She rolled her shoulders and grasped the long handle of the axe. With another grunt, she wrenched the weapon free and poised it for another swing. She inhaled, gripped the axe, and roared as she heaved it into the tree again. This time the blade went nearly halfway in. A surge of motivation began to burn in her chest. Elaethia tore the weapon free and instantly swung it back into the tree. Again and again, for an hour that felt like minutes, Elaethia hacked through the tree until it cracked under its own weight and toppled over with a crash.

Elaethia dropped to a knee and propped herself on the axe. Her chest heaved, and her muscles screamed. Her gasps of frigid air made her lungs burn in frozen agony. Her limbs trembled. Sweat poured down her face and froze to her skin. She tried to stand but found her body wouldn't respond. Despite all of this, she found she was smiling. Elaethia felt a laugh build in her throat, but it came out as a cough. After a short fit, she inhaled slowly, heaved herself to her feet, and began the walk back to Frossgar's cave.

"Frossgar," she stated the next day. "I am ready."

"Are you now?" he asked. "As always, I am ready when you are."

Elaethia nodded and walked over to his mid torso. Frossgar watched intently as she inhaled slowly, lifted the axe smoothly, and brought it down with a heavy yell. A deep, resonating clang sounded from the impact. Elaethia gritted her teeth as the axe bounced off and hit the ground at her feet. She had begun to turn away in defeat when she heard Frossgar's soothing voice.

"Little one," he spoke calmly. "Look at where you struck."

She turned and looked intently at the impact point. The scale she had hit was cracked, dented, and beginning to fall off. She whipped her head over to meet his proud gaze as the scale clattered to the ground.

"Congratulations," he applauded. "You are the first brehdar to ever breach my scales."

"Does that mean …" She left it hanging.

"Yes. It is time to make you my champion."

Elaethia gathered her small cache of belongings, packing all the furs and tools they would need for the return down the mountain. She looked around the cave to take in the surroundings one more time before she and Frossgar said good-bye to it. Donning a patched coat of wolf hide and a leather hooded cloak over it, she stood ready for Frossgar to begin their conjoinment.

"Are you ready, little one?" the dragon asked with a fire growing in his heart.

"I am, Frossgar," she replied with equal vigor.

"Today you no longer carry your family's name, Elaethia Soliano. Once the process is complete, you will don my name. You will be Elaethia Frossgar."

The woman clutched at the amulet around her neck, hesitant to leave her beloved family name behind. "As long as I carry my family in this pendant, they will always be with me."

"With us," the dragon corrected. "You will bring me into your family. I will be your newest member. Besides, you would trade that name eventually should you mate. Once the process is complete, you will feel strength and magic you have never felt before. But do not worry; I will be in your mind with you, guiding you along the way."

She inhaled shakily, and Frossgar understood why. All her work and training for the past twelve years was finally coming together. Her life goal of avenging her family and country was about to begin. This was the moment the two of them had built up to together.

"Open yourself to me, Elaethia. I will do the rest. This conjoinment shall change the both of us. I will no longer be a dragon, as you will no longer be a human. I shall take the form of a brehdar, but you will become a dragon in all manners but physical. My mind will meld with yours, and we shall begin your journey together."

The great dragon leveled his head to hers, his marked eyes peering into her own. Elaethia strode forward and embraced his enormous face, resting her head on the bridge of his nose.

"I am already open, Frossgar. I always have been."

"Then I am ready," announced the frost dragon as he stood to his full height and spread his great wings. The cavern was barely large enough to hold his form. "All these years I have raised you to be a dragon hero, but after today I will teach you how to be one. Every spell you have witnessed me use and then some will be at your disposal. But do not worry; I will guide you all the way. Take as many of my scales as you can carry, as well as some of my bones. They can be forged into armor and weaponry, and there is no stronger material than dragonite."

"Very well," she said. "I will collect as much as I can."

"Then let us begin."

The markings around his eyes seemed to glow. His eyes shone with light, and they met her own, which shone in turn. Magic welled out of the great dragon. The very air hummed with the immense power that filled the cavern. A piercing, chilly mist enveloped the two as the surge rushed into the young woman.

Frossgar could see the world through her eyes. He could feel her emotions, her senses, and then her mind. The feeling was indescribable, yet terrible. She was freezing over but burning up at the same time. Her body seemed to tear from the raw strength that was being forced into it. Her mind overloaded to the brink of madness with emotion and memories of the past three thousand years. She screamed. Her body warped with unrelenting power and agony. Elaethia collapsed, clutching her head and wailing in terror as she rolled along the ground.

Frossgar knew what had gone wrong. In their haste and excitement, he had forgotten a crucial component for his host. Her body was nearly perfect, strong and durable to the core. But her mind was still that of a child. Growing up in a cave, alone, apart from others of her kind had closed her world to nothing but the mountainside. Elaethia's mind was far too narrow to withstand his. If he continued to join his with her, she would be driven to insanity, unable to even function. He would sit and wait inside her head until they both died. But it was too late. The process could not be stopped. Frossgar looked down once more at the writhing human he had raised from a child. He refused to allow such a fate to befall her. He would rather cast his own mind into the abyss than let her suffer. He severed the connection between their minds, saying one final good-bye to the human he had raised as his own.

"I love you, little one."

Then he poured the rest of his power and strength into her as everything went dark.

Elaethia's mind ached when she awoke. Her body swelled with a new feeling. Strength and heightened senses that she had never noticed before, and a welling source of energy, bubbled within her. Somehow she knew this new feeling was magic. Sitting up, she rubbed her eyes and opened them. It was dark—very dark. The fire was completely out, and it was night. Normally she would not be able to see at all in such a dim environment, but vision was slowly coming to her. She scratched her head, trying to remember what had just happened.

She was being overwhelmed by something, and then she heard Frossgar's voice. Elaethia remembered his words and smiled. No one had said that to her since her parents were alive. She called out into her mind to talk to him. She was given no response. Concern rose within her chest. She realized her body and power felt vastly stronger, but her mind had not changed as he had described. She tried to call to him again, but this time, too, was in vain. In a panic, she screamed his name.

"Frossgar!" her cry echoed throughout the empty cavern.

She wheeled around as her vision became clearer in the blackness. She would never forget the sight in front of her. The hollow husk of the great dragon lay collapsed on the ground in front of her. The body lay lifeless. All the flesh had completely disappeared, the skull was dry bone, and the jaw lay slack on the ground. The hollow eyes stared straight ahead, boring into her soul. There was no sign or sense of the beloved dragon.

Frossgar was gone.

Elaethia collapsed to the ground and wept. Mournful, gut-wrenching sobs erupted from her as she buried her face in her hands. With tears streaming down her face, she crawled forward to place a hand on the remains of the last dragon. Her forceful sobbing racked and tore at her throat. Elaethia struggled to breathe through her uncontrollable sobs and coughing. There was no reveling or triumph at the birth of the new dragon hero as her wails echoed throughout the cavern late into the night.

Elaethia awoke to light glinting into her face. She inhaled slowly and pulled herself to her knees. She looked around and realized everything was completely encased in frost. The floor, walls, ceiling, and even the campfire were frozen over. A closer look showed the flame itself had frozen. Tongues of solid ice resembling the campfire rose from the pile of frozen wood. She soon realized that the cold no longer made an impact on her. The only things that had not been frozen were her, the giant axe, the pack on her back, and the skeletal form of Frossgar. His deep blue scales glistened with the intruding light.

Elaethia remembered her final promise to him and began to fill her pack with his scales. She dumped out the extra furs she had packed and filled it completely with everything she could to honor the memory of the great dragon. With scales, a few bones, a single three-meter black spine from his back, and the axe, she left the cave that had been her home for so long.

As she emerged, Elaethia was taken aback by the sight around her. The whole area in front of the cavern had a thick coating of ice around it. Trees were bent over, rocks were cracked. Even the unchanging crystalline structures that had always stood guard around the outside were encased. All of them had a thick coat of solid ice warped to their shape. Everything within fifty meters was affected. Even a passing rabbit had been frozen mid-jump and lay entombed in ice. She exhaled heavily. Elaethia started down the mountain, striding with sullen thoughts and unexplainable loneliness. For the first time in her life, she was truly alone.

Once she reached the bottom of the mountain, she would turn south, as it was the only direction she could think to go. Once again, those who had promised to always be with her had left her. She would have to face Emperor Rychus alone.

After a day of walking nonstop, she passed through a coastal village that she barely recognized from the journey up. The locals stared at the disheveled woman who strode intimidatingly through their town. Elaethia stopped at a barrel under a tree that had some fresh water in it and cupped some in her hands to drink. She froze as she saw her reflection.

She looked like hell, but that wasn't what kept her from recognizing her own reflection. Her face was still her own, but it was not her eyes that stared back at her. Frossgar's dragon features had combined with her own. Her once human eyes had a slight reptilian form and a piercing deep blue color. His distinct markings had also appeared on her face. Her once pale skin had turned into smooth scales where the markings traced. It was almost as if it were him looking at her from the barrel. Drops created ripples on the surface, distorting the image. She realized she was crying again. As she silently loomed over the barrel, her ragged breathing began to turn into sobs again.

"Oy!" a gruff Svarengel voice shouted from her right. "If yer done salting up th' rain barrel, I need ye to move so I can fill my skin."

She turned to face the voice. Its owner was a tall human in his sixties. His braided white hair merged into his long, white braided beard. He was muscular, but his arched back showed his strength was giving way to his age. She didn't respond to him.

"Did ye hear me?" he spoke again. "That's my barrel yer cryin' into. I don't mind ye takin' a drink or two, but ye can't stand there all day."

"Leave me be," she said plainly

"Well then move. Yer scarin' the villagers, so unless ye got business here, I suggest ye keep movin' on."

"Please, just …"

"Ye got wool in yer ears, lass? I won't tell ye again. Ye got the looks of a warrior about ye, but Sun as my witness, ye sure aren't acting like one. Hold yer head up and push on. Whoever taught ye to fight wouldn't want to see ye like this. Do them the honor and show some—"

"I said leave me *be!*" Elaethia exploded at the old warrior. She swung the enormous axe with all her might at the tree next to her. The blade snapped off halfway through, but the force alone shattered the rest of the trunk, toppling it over and splintering it. Elaethia dropped to a knee, propping herself up with the broken shaft of the axe.

"Stars above," breathed the old man. "What the hell are ye? Ye aren't one of those demonspawn are ye?"

"Jörgen!" an elderly female voice called from the distance. "What are ye doin' to that poor woman?"

"I haven't done a thing to her, Ingrid!" he called back. "I was just tellin' her she needs to move along before somethin' happens!"

"Can't ye tell yer th' reason somethin' happened? Leave th' poor wretch be!"

"All right, all right, woman. If yer so hellbent on helpin' her, then ye come and deal with it!"

He trudged over to a cottage that Elaethia assumed was his home. An elderly demiwolf the same age as he was passed him and trotted over to her. She wore a plain white-and-tan dress and had long, braided silver hair pinned behind her back. Her wrinkled face was full of concern and kindness.

"Come, dear," she said soothingly. "Let's get ye inside and cleaned up. Don't let my husband get to ye. He was a raider captain most of his life. Sensitive subjects like this are not his strong suit."

"I appreciate your sentiment, but I do not intend to stay here," Elaethia replied emotionlessly.

"Nonsense. You look more haggard than a spriggan. Don't take what he said to heart, but he was right about one thing. Whoever raised ye would want what's best for ye. Just stay one night, and if ye still want to leave in th' mornin', we won't stop ye."

The dragon hero looked up at Ingrid's kind face. She couldn't remember whether anyone had ever looked at her like that. Her chest began to spasm as she threatened to break down again. Elaethia looked down, blinked the tears out of her eyes, and followed Ingrid into her cottage.

Sixth Era. 139. Mertim 16.

Elaethia took Ana and Henry to their homes upon returning to Breeze. It was midmorning, but the families immediately ignored their customers and burst from their houses and shops. They sobbed in relief and wrapped both the children and the warrior in massive, affectionate hugs. Elaethia found this quite uncomfortable. Although she tried to decline, the family of bakers insisted on giving Elaethia an extra reward. They promised any number of special orders, free for the rest of the year. However, she would never take them up on that.

She made her way to the guildhall, passing the small restaurant that Cathrine worked at. Her stomach growled as the aroma of cooking meat filled the air. She had not eaten in two days, as she had given her provisions to the children. Elaethia remembered the pleasant serving girl and decided to stop to order.

"Elaethia!" Cathrine called out. "I'm so glad to see you again! Did you get in?"

"Yes," Elaethia said as she approached the counter. "Thank you again for telling me how to get there. If you would not mind, I would like to purchase some food. I will take whatever special you have today."

"Of course!" Cathrine announced. "My brother brought in some deer from yesterday's hunt. Father will cook you up a nice venison steak. That'll run you two silvers."

Elaethia handed her the coins as Cathrine turned around and called the order through a window before turning back again to face her. "So how have you been settling in? I'm sure you're excited to take your first quest."

"Actually, I just returned from it."

"Wow! That was fast. So where's the rest of your party? Did something happen to them?"

"No, I went alone. It was an A-level quest against some bandits with a hostage situation and jurisdiction constraints. I have not met many of my fellow adventurers yet, but that is fine, because I wanted to go alone to minimize potential casualties."

Cathrine's face went blank, and she blinked twice. "I don't know what any of that means, but it sounds hard! Did everything go all right?"

"It was not particularly difficult. I have done similar things before I was in the guild. The most notable problem was a small confrontation with a party from the Westreach guild."

"Not the bandits?"

"Killing brehdars is a simple task. Negotiating with them proves more troublesome."

"I see. So how'd you get around them?"

"I froze the leader's arm until they backed down."

Cathrine's tone wavered. "You consider that negotiating?"

Elaethia tilted her head. "Is it not?"

"Well, usually when 'negotiating' comes to mind, I think of people calmly talking it out for the best possible outcome."

"I was perfectly calm, and I would say we had the best possible outcome."

"You froze a guy's arm."

"He was being rude and difficult."

Cathrine sighed. "I think we need to work on your negotiating skills."

Elaethia noticed both Geran and Maya as she opened the door to the guild. Geran was sitting at the bar, eating breakfast, and Maya was at her usual seat at the reception desk. The hall was as loud, but not as boisterous, as it usually was during the evening. Geran turned as the door opened. He quickly finished his meal and stood up from the bar when he saw Elaethia enter.

Elaethia approached the reception desk and placed the flyer on the counter. "The quest is complete. All five children have been returned to their homes alive."

Maya looked up at her with a relieved expression as she pulled out a postquest report. "Congratulations, and welcome back. We'll get a full report from the one who filed the request by a verifier. Fill out any line that says "Adventurer," and sign here at the bottom where it says "Party Leader." I will go collect your reward."

Maya stood and walked into the back room as Elaethia filled out the form. She returned shortly with a tray of coins.

"Here you are," Maya announced. "Sixty-eight gold and three silver. Please verify the amount."

Elaethia counted out the coins and nodded her approval. She set aside sixty gold coins and slid the rest into her pouch. "I will use this to purchase a room for one year, please."

"Oh! Very well, I'll have one of our housing managers check on the available rooms." She took the stack of coins and set it to the side. "Just between you and me, I honestly didn't believe you would accomplish that quest as well as you did."

"You doubted me that much?"

"Well, kinda," Maya continued. "I mean, nobody's ever soloed an A-level quest flawlessly before. I knew you were special coming in, but this really seals the deal. I was actually preparing some complaint forms in case the worst happened."

"If it was that much of a concern, you could have asked me to wait. I would have allowed others to accompany me."

"You didn't give me much of a choice."

Elaethia tilted her head. "I did not?"

Maya laughed and started taking the gold to the back room. "No, Elaethia, you did not. By the way, Geran was looking for you. Probably to ask about your quest."

The elf disappeared into the back room. Elaethia turned around to see a familiar ranger standing a few meters in front of her.

"Heard your first quest went well," Geran said. "Something tells me you're about to march right back over to the quest board and grab another."

She shook her head. "Not today. I do have to recover from this one, and Maya is getting a room prepared. I would like to rest a little and get acquainted with the space before I venture out again."

"Were there any problems during your quest worth mentioning?"

Elaethia paused and thought for a moment. "Nothing I have not dealt with before, but apparently my negotiating needs improvement. Then there is the ever-present issue of limited visibility when I have my helmet on, and dealing with enemies that are out of reach. I suppose it would be beneficial to recruit someone who could be my eyes in battle."

Geran was about to open his mouth when a familiar male voice penetrated the conversation. "Oho? Sounds to me like you could use a ranger!"

They turned to see the elven archer that Elaethia encountered at Cathrine's restaurant before. He strutted his way over to them with his long, flowing blond hair bouncing with his elegant stride.

"Allow me to introduce myself," he announced with a bow. "*I* am Sybil Fairwind. Breeze's soon-to-be best archer *and* best ranger."

Geran's eyes narrowed, and his brow furrowed. "What's that supposed to mean?"

The elf scoffed. "Exactly as I said, my dear human. Just because you hold that title now doesn't mean it's guaranteed for long. My keen eyes and steady hand will surely prove myself more capable than your current skills."

"Really?" Geran shot back as the surrounding adventurers tuned in to the growing tension. "I don't remember you even being selected for the annual tournament. And since when have you been so involved in advanced ranger duties?"

Sybil waved the retort aside. "I don't understand why you feel the need to compete here, Geran. It's not like *you* would offer to join her. In fact, I recall you specifically stating your preference to stay solo. The last time you were in a party was over nine years ago. And as for the tournament, we shall see if you can manage this year when I compete with *this!*"

He triumphantly pulled out a sleek, light-colored bow. Elaethia could feel a slight presence of magic on it.

"*This* is my new enchanted bow! Its magical aura relaxes my body and soothes my mind when I hold it, ensuring a stable platform. Oh, it took years to get one, but its lightweight and flawless design will surely put your old, shabby weapon to shame!"

Geran's voice was steady but hot with irritation. "Yeah? Well, she isn't looking for a pompous rich kid with a sparkly toy, so you can sit on it and rotate."

The surrounding adventurers spat out their drinks and covered their mouths, snorting under their breaths. Sybil's face turned red. He forced a laugh and put a finger to his collar to straighten it.

"Perhaps we should ask the lady herself. I'm sure she has a discerning eye for talent! What say you, Elaethia? You have asked for someone with my precise skills, and here I am, coming right to you!"

"I remember you," she said.

His face turned blank. "I'm sorry?"

"You were terrorizing Cathrine the other day," she continued. "I have no intention of having someone as brash and arrogant as you by my side."

The elf's face blanched. "Bu-but you *need* me! Quests at a caliber as high as you want are best done with a ranger watching your back, and you would surely want the best! That's why—"

Geran interrupted him. "That's why *I* am offering to form a party with her."

Everyone in the area went dead quiet. A stool clattered to the ground as a demicat girl shot up from her seat.

"*Whaaaaat?*" she shouted in disbelief. "Geran Nightshade's joining a *party?*"

She leaped over the table, knocking some dishes to the ground, and trotted over to them. She wore a long-sleeved orange tunic with black embroidering on the edges. One orange and one purple thigh-high stocking traveled from her black shin-high boots. Thick but well-kept red-brown hair cascaded down to her mid back. Her catlike ears and tail were the same color. She had fair, clear skin that showed no signs of scars or blemishes. She was very pretty, with a nose on the small side, perky lips, and stunning green feline eyes. Like any other demihuman, the only extra hair she would have would be on her upper legs and forearms. Elaethia suspected she chose to shave it, considering she didn't see any.

Geran sighed as the demicat approached. His attitude shifted from irritation to exasperation, with a hint of amusement. "Do you *have* to make a scene about it, Lilian?"

Lilian stopped in front of him with a bounce and looked up. He was a full head taller than her, even with her feline ears. She started to poke at his chest with her finger, carrying a smug tone. "Of course I do! You've been running solo for longer than I've been here! Now some mysterious woman shows up and you're immediately joining her? What kinda secrets are you hiding, Mr. Nightshade?"

"I'm not hiding anything! She's just a force of nature, and I feel it'd be best if someone kept an eye on her."

"Oooooh?" Lilian gave him a look and then turned to Elaethia. "So? Are you gonna answer the poor guy? Or do you wanna leave him hanging for a bit longer?"

Elaethia nodded. "I would have him by my side in a fight. I have heard nothing but good things about his skill, and his company seems enjoyable."

Lilian squinted and took a step closer to Elaethia. "Hmph. You talk like an old man. Do you hate fun like some of the older adventurers here, too?"

"I see no issue with frivolity when the time permits. Forgive me, I recognize you from my first day, when you broke up a fight between Peter Stone and that demiwolf, but we have not been properly introduced."

"Oh, that fight with Liam? Psh, that was nothing. You're looking at Breeze's third-strongest elemental mage!"

"I see. Well, it is a pleasure to meet you. I am Elaethia Frossgar." She extended a gauntlet to the mage. A mischievous grin formed on Lilian's face but quickly disappeared. She reached out and shook it.

"Gosh, so formal. Well, I'm Lilian Whitepaw, and—huh …?" She glanced down at their clasped hands with a very confused look on her face. She let go and examined her own hand.

"That's strange," Lilian muttered. "Hey, Geran! Shake my hand real quick!"

The ranger extended his hand and grasped hers. "Okay ... though I don't know wh-*hhnnngggggggg!*"

His body seized up and stiffened. His fingers curled, and his back arched as his hair frizzed out. Lilian let go of him and looked at her hand again as the air began to smell of ozone, ignoring Geran as he crumpled to the ground.

"Well, that's odd. I wonder why that didn't work," she muttered, still looking at her hand.

Elaethia stared in confusion at the ranger now lying on the floor. "What happened?"

Lilian placed her hands behind her and rocked back on her heels. The demicat scrunched her eyes shut and flashed a fanged grin. The expression was accompanied with an innocent hum. "Oh, nothing!" she said. "Don't you worry about it. Now, if you'll excuse me, I should get going before—*Ack!* No-no-no-no-*no! Stop! Stop!*"

Geran had shot his hand up to grab her tail. As he stood, he began to pull it up as Lilian's high-pitched rapid-fire objections continued under his reprimand.

"Lilian," he growled. "Wanna explain why you thought it would be a good idea to use *electric touch* on me?"

"*I'm sorryyyyy!*" she wailed. Her ears turned back, and her arms started flailing around. The mage's speech turned whiney and fast, not even pausing for breath. "I-wasn't-gonna-use-it-on-you-at-first-I-swear-it's-just-it-didn't-work-on-Elaethia-so-I-thought-I-did-something-wrong-and*eyaaaaaah!*" She yowled as he yanked her tail higher. She had to stand on her toes to avoid being dangled.

"What? You were going to use it on *Elaethia?*"

"It was just a fun little joke! I-wasn't-gonna-make-it-powerful-enough-to-hurt-owie ow-ow-ow! Leggo-my-tail!"

"Then what the hell do you call what you just did to me?"

"I-thought-the-original-power-was-too-low-to-feel-so-I-tried-it-again-on-you-with-a-little-more-juice! Pleeeeaasse, Geran! I'm-sorry-I-won't-ever-do-it-again-I-promise!"

Lilian stared up at him with watery eyes and a trembling bottom lip. Her hands stopped flailing around and folded in front of her chest. Geran's expression softened. He sighed and released her tail.

"All right. All right, I'll let it slide. This time."

Lilian's attitude did a full turnaround. Her eyes brightened, and her mouth opened into a wide, enormous smile. She leaped onto him, wrapped her arms around his neck, and started nuzzling his chin.

"Awwwww Gerryyyyyy!" she purred. "You're such a big softy!"

"How many times have I told you not to call me that?" the ranger grumbled.

"But it makes you sound so cute!"

"I don't *want* to sound cute!"

Elaethia's head was swimming. "Um, excuse me. I am afraid I do not understand what is going on, Geran, but I can wait for you to finish your discussion with your girlfriend."

Lilian's eyes somehow managed to get brighter as she gasped. "Hear that, Gerry? She called me your girlfriend!"

"We are *not* dating!" the ranger stated firmly as he managed to pry the demicat off of him. "Don't sound so hopeful, either. I know you're into older guys, but just because you're eighteen now doesn't mean I'm scoping you out!"

"Oh?" she egged him. "Then how come you're keeping track of my age like that?"

"Because you wouldn't shut up about it for days after your birthday!"

Lilian gasped with exaggerated amour. "You remembered my *birthday!*"

"It was last week!"

Elaethia began to turn to escape from the situation. "Well, I shall be on my way. Come find me when you are ready, Geran."

"Wait!" Lilian shouted, and she pranced in front of her with hopeful eyes. "I wanna join you too!"

"I-I am sorry?"

"If Nightshade's forming a party with someone, they *have* to be super good. There's no *way* I can pass this up!"

"Now wait a second!" Geran protested.

Lilian ignored him. "Sure, you need a ranger for tracking, spotting people, and picking off faraway enemies. But what if you come across another magician? Or an atronach? Or a group of small, numerous, easy-to-fry enemies? There's no better class to help you there than an elemental mage!"

"Lilian, hold up! What about us?" A teenage boy stood up from the table Lilian had been sitting at earlier. The young duelist's eyes were filled with concern. A male dwarven warrior and elven priestess of similar age watched with him.

"Aww, Dylan," she mewled as she walked over to them. "I like you guys; I really do! But I'm so tired of I- and B-level quests. They're so boring, and I never have to try, while you guys still struggle with them. I want to go out and stop bandits in towers, take down trolls in caverns, or fight orc hordes like the high-level adventurers! I'm so limited when on quests with you. I can't even use half my spells! I've talked about joining another party for a long time now, and you know how fast you have to jump on these opportunities. We knew this day was coming."

Dylan looked down and shuffled with his hands. "No. You're right. We don't want to hold you back anymore."

Lilian rounded the table and hugged her friends. "I had fun with you guys. Honest! That's why I stuck around for so long. I promise I'll visit you when I can, okay? Besides, if she says "no," I'll be right back at your sides."

"All right," the duelist, who looked ready to cry, said with a sniffle.

Lilian stood on her toes to kiss his forehead, and then she turned and waltzed back to Elaethia, eyes bright and tail curled. "So?" she pressed. "Whaddya say? Are you ready to have awesome and destructive arcane arts at your disposal from your lovable local elemental mage?"

Elaethia was still partially dazed. She looked at the cheerful demicat; over to her now former party; back at Lilian; over to Geran, who was equally shocked; and finally back to Lilian.

"I … Do not see why not. You appear friendly, and if your magic abilities are—"

Lilian suddenly pounced onto Elaethia. Now paralyzed with shock, the dragon hero stood as stiff as a board as the demicat clambered over her and emitted loud giggles of glee.

"*Wheeeeeee!*" Lilian shrieked with jubilance. "This is gonna be so fun! Just you and me and Gerry, all goin' on A and V quests, getting fame and fortune, taking on all sorts of enemies and monsters! *Oh*, this is so cool. I promise you won't regret it one bit! Which quest should we go on first? Oh! I'll go check the flyers!"

Lilian leaped off of Elaethia and started for the quest board, but Geran stopped her midstride by the tail. "Hold your horses, fuzz-brain."

"Owieeee! Geraaan let goooo! Ow-ow-ow-ow-ow!"

"I know you're excited to get out of the I ranks, but Elaethia just got back from Westreach and needs to get settled. Why don't you help her move in, since I wouldn't be allowed in her room?"

Lilian stopped trying to pull herself free of his iron grip and crossed her arms. Her ears folded back as she pouted, facing away from him.

"Hmph. Fiiiiine. I'll go see if they have a room ready for you, Elaethia. C'mon upstairs when you have all your stuff." The demicat grumbled and trudged to the stairs as Geran released her tail.

"Quite the handful, isn't she?" Geran asked Elaethia.

"Is she always like that?"

"Yeah. *Oh* yeah. But it grows on you. She's a really sweet girl, as well as a very powerful mage. Everyone says she gets her spell potency from her personality. That and she got an earlier start in magic than most. She's somewhat of a prodigy."

"She is clearly very popular," Elaethia said.

"She's one of the main stars of the guild. Technically so am I, no matter how much I try to avoid it. At this rate, you'll be one, too."

"I do not care for fame or popularity."

"E-lae-thi-aaaa!" Lilian's voice sounded from the second floor. "Hurry up! Your room is ready!"

Geran looked at the waving demicat and then back at Elaethia. "Don't worry. With her in the party, she'll gladly soak up all the attention. I'd get up there before she comes down here and gets you herself."

"I agree." The warrior nodded. After verifying she had all her belongings, she strode across the hall and up the stairs to meet Lilian.

"You're lucky!" the mage announced as Elaethia passed the last step. "You got a room halfway between the stairs and the baths."

"That is one of the more preferable rooms?" Elaethia asked.

"I guess. Folks have their own opinions, but most of us would rather have a room on the *opposite* side of Master Dameon's office. But you probably don't care. The housing manager already put the binding spell on the door handle. All you need to do is put your hand on it to form the bond."

Elaethia tilted her head. "Binding spell? Bond?"

"It's what we use as locks. Normal locks can be picked, and keys can be lost. It's much easier if there's an enchantment on the door that's bound to the owner. Go ahead, see for yourself."

Elaethia placed her hand on the door latch, and a small glow accompanied by a hum came from it. After a second it dissipated, and the latch clicked under her grip.

"There ya go!" Lilian chirped. "Now nobody except you or a manager can open this door!"

Elaethia stepped into her new quarters. It was a plain room. The furniture was a table with an accompanying chair, a bed with sheets and blankets, and a large wooden cabinet. A chest of drawers lay longways underneath the bed. There was also an armor stand next to it. On the table was a single oil lamp that was half full. The far wall had a single glass-paned window with hinged wooden shutters on the inside.

"That cabinet is for all your gear, drawers for your clothes, and that stand is for your armor," Lilian explained. "This is all you're given, but there's nothing stopping you from getting extra furniture or accessories. My room is on the other side, fifth from the left. By the way, sorry for trying to use *electric touch* on you like that, but how come it didn't work?"

"I assume that is one of your elemental spells? My armor is dragonite, and elemental dragon scales already have a resistance to elemental magic. I would not even notice low-level spells."

"Oh. That's cool. Kinda lame, though."

Elaethia tilted her head. "Lame?"

"Well, it means I can't have as much fun with you! Oh well. Anyway, I'm sure Geran explained already, but guys can't go into girls' rooms, and girls can't go into guys'. Master Dameon apparently made that a rule after all the noise complaints. That's a bummer, 'cause I'd really like to drop in and mess with Geran every now and then. Maybe freeze his pillow or put a *lightning rune* under his doormat."

"So you two really are a couple?" Elaethia asked.

"Noooo, I just like to play with him. All guys fluster so easily when I tease them, but he's so nonchalant and cool all the time. It's nice to see him caught off guard every now and then. Although he is rather handsome, isn't he?"

Elaethia had noticed it when they first met but never gave it a second thought until now. "I suppose so. Do you want to be a couple?"

Lilian laughed. "I couldn't tease all the other boys if I were in a relationship! Besides, he doesn't see me like that. I was practically a kitten when I showed up, and he's always regarded me as family. He's been the guild's top ranger even before I first showed up three years ago. Since then he's always been that lone and mysterious man that all the girls fantasize about unraveling. Why? Do *you* like him, Elaethia?"

"I … To be honest, I do not know. I grew up in isolation on a mountain with Frossgar. Then I spent a year with a retired Svarengel sea raider, and I have wandered alone ever since. I have hardly been around any men my age since I was a girl."

Elaethia looked over at Lilian, who gleamed back with a smug expression.

"What?" Elaethia demanded.

"Oh. Nothing," Lilian flashed the same grin from earlier, and she then spun on her heel and walked out of the room. "Come and find me when you're ready to go on a quest!"

Elaethia looked around the room and set her gear down to unpack. It didn't take long, as she didn't have much to begin with. Her ruck and travel gear were all neatly packed into the cabinet. Her deep blue dragonite armor stood mounted on the armor stand. The visored helmet sat on top, and the plated boots rested beneath. Her heavy axe leaned against the cabinet between the two.

After a brief bath, she changed into her only set of clothes: a white shirt slightly open at the chest, and brown leather pants with a black leather belt. She fondled the gold-and-sapphire pendant around her neck and sat on her bed. Elaethia felt no need to light the lamp, since her dragon eyes could see the room clearly through the dark.

This was a new feeling for her. She wasn't scared or uneasy; it was a different sort of emotion. Thinking about it, she decided it was a positive one. It seemed similar to the sense of belonging she'd had with Frossgar and Jörgen, actually. It wasn't as personal, as they were more spread out among the several people she had met over these last few days. Unable to grasp this new feeling, she sighed, lay down, and went to sleep.

Chapter 4
Woman and Warrior

Sixth Era. 137. Febris 12.

Ingrid guided a shaking Elaethia into the wooden cottage. The inside was cozy and surprisingly spacious. White and gray furs covered most of the wooden furniture, which was carved in the western Svarengel fashion. Depictions of dragons, sailboats, beasts, and monsters were engraved on the walls. Jörgen sat down beside a fire, running a whetstone over an engraved battleaxe. Elaethia placed her belongings next to the door as she entered.

The old raider looked up as the two women walked in. "I'm guessin' th' rain barrel is open now. If ye don't mind, I'll go fill th' pot for supper."

He stood so Elaethia could take his seat. The large man exited the house as Ingrid grabbed a blanket for their guest and placed it around Elaethia's shoulders.

"Now. If you'll excuse th' late introduction, my name is Ingrid," the elderly demiwolf said. "What's yer name, dear? What brought ye all the way out here?"

"Elaethia," she replied. "Elaethia Soli- I mean Frossgar. I came from the northern mountain range."

"There isn't anythin' up there but caves and monsters," Ingrid noted. "What have ye been doin'?"

"Living and training. I was raised by Frossgar. I spent most of my life learning from him, but he is gone now. We were supposed to be together, but something happened, and I do not hear his voice."

"So Frossgar was yer master, eh? That name strikes me as odd."

"You would not know him. He chose a life of solitude for thousands of years."

Ingrid's brow furrowed as she thought aloud. "Mountains. Solitude. Thousands of years. Ye aren't talkin' about a dragon or a demon are ye?"

"The last dragon, as far as we knew. I was to be his champion, but something went wrong, and now …" Her voice faltered. "I do not know what to do."

Ingrid didn't know what to believe. She had heard the legends of a dragon still living in the northern mountains since she was a pup. In fact, that was a story told over the generations to scare children out of exploring the mountainside alone. The possibility that this fairy tale was real took her aback. That being said, she knew most legends were rooted in truth. Then she looked back at what this young woman did to that tree outside, and the scale-like markings around her eyes. Maybe it was true.

Ingrid cleared her throat. "Jörgen and I have lived here our whole lives. We've been married for over forty years. In his glory days, he would sail around the Svarengel islands and coast, raidin' other tribes and clans. He was an absolute terror, he was. I would wait for him here and listen to his tales of glory and battle when he returned. Every so often he'd mention the legend of the dragon. It seems it was a tale that every Svarengel knew. For as long as tradition remembers; warriors and adventurers have come from all over th' world to find this dragon, only to come back empty-handed or not at all. But yer tellin' me ye haven't just seen him but were raised by him and made his champion?"

Elaethia nodded.

"Well then," Ingrid continued, "let's just wait for Jörgen to return. I'm sure he would know more about this than I. Until then, make yerself at home. Th' door to th' right will be yer room. It was our girl Erika's until she started raidin' herself."

"She will not mind if I use it?"

Ingrid looked into the fire. "She passed on many years ago. On her fourth raid. She never came back. Jörgen's been kickin' himself all these years because he wasn't with her. Though I am grateful he didn't, as we believe her longboat was sunken by a leviathan."

"Your daughter and husband did not raid together?"

Ingrid's tail drooped to the floor. "Erika insisted she go with a different crew, sayin' she wanted to make her own legacy apart from her father. I can understand not wantin' to live under that shadow. I miss our girl, but I couldn't stamp out her dream like that."

"If you could go back, you would not stop her?"

"That's a difficult question. Ye'll understand one day when ye have children of yer own."

Elaethia tilted her head. "Children of my own?"

The door behind them suddenly opened. Ingrid looked up to see her husband duck as he entered the cottage. He strode past them and hung the pot of water on a hook over the fire.

"Now," Jörgen began. "I don't care about what ye did to that tree. But as long as ye don't do that to anythin' or anyone here, we won't have a problem. Is that understood?"

"Yes sir," Elaethia replied firmly.

The old man grunted as he sat down in a high-back wooden chair. "At least ye seem to have remembered yer manners. Well, Ingrid, what's her story?"

Ingrid's canine ears turned flat. "Ye could ask her yerself, ye meathead. Unless ye forgot yer manners too."

Jörgen sighed and faced Elaethia. "So. I suppose now that ye have regained yer composure, we ought to have some sort of introduction. Th' name's Jörgen Sterkhand. I'm a retired raider captain, livin' out my days with my wife, Ingrid. Th' clan seems bent on makin' me th' next village elder, too, although I'm sure she's already filled ye in on that. Now, what's yer tale?"

Elaethia repeated her story with Jörgen. This time she described Frossgar and her time with him.

The raider rubbed his chin. "So. Frossgar was th' name of that dragon."

Ingrid raised an eyebrow. "Yer choosin' to believe her, Jörgen?"

"And ye don't? I can't say I'm surprised; ye never saw much fightin' yerself. But in all my years, I've never met a brehdar who could knock over a tree in one swing, let alone with a rusty old axe like that. Not to say I know what a dragon hero looks like. Nobody's seen one since those big wars hundreds of years ago. But if there was one, she'd be it."

"Are ye sure? There's a lot of magic in this world. She could have some type we don't know about."

"That's what I thought m'self until I saw what was in her bag over there. If ye still don't believe us, see for yerself."

Ingrid turned to Elaethia. "May I?" she asked with uncertainty.

Elaethia opened her mouth as if she were about to object. Instead she closed it and only nodded silently.

The elderly woman stood and walked over to the rucksack by the door. She pulled the flap back and gasped as she beheld its contents. Inside, packed soundly along each other, were maybe a hundred dark blue scales. They ranged from the size of a coin to the size of a dinner plate. A few were even as large as the seat of a chair.

"By the Moon," she breathed. "Are these …"

"Frossgar's scales and bones," Elaethia said solemnly. "It is all that I could bring of him."

Ingrid walked back to her chair and sat down. "What do ye plan to do with them?"

"Frossgar said they could be used to forge a weapon and armor. My goal is to travel south until I find a smith who can help me."

Jörgen made a face. "Ye think ye can just wander around hopin' to find someone who knows how to make armor out of dragon scales?"

"Is that not something so easily done?"

"Are ye serious?" he asked.

She tilted her head.

"Aye, yer serious. Listen, lass. Dragon heroes haven't existed for centuries. That means dragon armor hasn't either. There probably isn't a living soul that knows how to make it."

"What about the elder's longhouse?" Ingrid thought aloud. "Maybe there's somethin' in there that could send her in the right direction."

Jörgen shrugged. "Could be."

Ingrid glared at him and gave a pointed cough.

Jörgen looked to the floor and shifted in his seat. After a moment he grunted and stood to walk toward the door. "I suppose it's worth checkin.' I've got nothin' better to do for th' rest of th' day."

Ingrid stood as he left. "I'll take yer pack to the room for ye, Elaethia. Just sit there and let me know if the pot boils over."

"That is all right," Elaethia declined as she stood. "I can take it myself."

"Don't be ridiculous. Yer our guest, and we haven't had company in years. I don't mind at all."

The elderly demiwolf reached the bag and took a hold of it. With a pull, she attempted to lift it, only to find it wouldn't budge. She placed a second hand on it and tried again to lift with a grunt. It shifted only a little.

"All right," Ingrid panted. "I suppose I can let ye take it yerself."

Elaethia strode over, slung the bag over her shoulder with one hand, and walked into the room.

"Well that just isn't fair," the old woman mumbled.

Ingrid chopped and seasoned vegetables and pieces of meat to prepare for stew. Occasionally she would glance over her shoulder at the alleged dragon hero. She was greeted with the same scene every time: Elaethia sitting at the table with her hands resting on her knees, her eyes blank and staring at the table. Ingrid sighed and poured some milk into the pot and began to stir it with the rest of the ingredients. This was going to be the touchiest subject she'd ever tackled in her life.

Ingrid walked over to the table once the cooking and other preparations were complete. It had been nearly an hour since Jörgen left, so Ingrid decided to start supper without him. The old woman took a seat at the table across from Elaethia and served the stew into some bowls. Elaethia took a hold of one and was about to drink from it.

"Ye have a spoon, dear," Ingrid chided.

Elaethia looked up from the bowl and then down at the table where the utensil sat. She put the bowl down, grabbed the spoon, and stared at it almost as if she was trying to remember how to use it. She looked again at the bowl and dipped the spoon in slowly. Elaethia brought the steaming food to her face and put it in her mouth. She stayed like that for several seconds. Tears appeared in her eyes as she slowly pulled the spoon from her lips.

"Incredible …" she faltered.

"Well, I don't believe my cooking is *that* amazin'," Ingrid laughed with a gently wagging tail. "But I thank ye anyway. Th' way yer tearin' through that, I'd say ye haven't had a proper meal in years."

Elaethia spoke between spoonfuls. "I have not eaten like this since I was a girl. I've prepared my own meat over an open fire for as long as I can recall. I had forgotten what it was like to sit at a table. I have not gathered to eat like this since … since my family was alive …"

Ingrid felt her heart sink even further. "Ye lost yer dragon *and* yer family, too?"

Elaethia nodded. "I have nothing left in this world. All I have of Frossgar are those scales, and all I have of my family is this necklace."

"It is very beautiful, and I can tell it is expertly made with pure materials. I'm a raider wife, after all. I haven't gone all these years without developin' an eye for quality. I'd say it's worth more than this whole village. Keep it close, dear. It would be very unfortunate if ye lost it."

Elaethia clenched it in her hand. "I always have. It has only left my person once since I escaped Armini."

Ingrid nearly choked on her stew. "Th' southern coastal country? Ye keep revealin' the strangest things. Next yer gonna say ye can fly, too."

Elaethia shook her head. "I cannot fly, but yes I came from Armini. My family was being hunted by Emperor Rychus. It was because of this that my grandfather and I escaped when I was eight. We traveled all through Linderry to find help, but we could find no one to aid us. Eventually we found ourselves in Svarengel and continued north. I believe this was the very village where we heard of the legend of the dragon. Grandfather did not survive, but I found Frossgar and lived with him until a few days ago."

"How old are ye, exactly?"

"I turned twenty two months ago. My birthday is one of the few things I can remember from my childhood."

Ingrid slowly set her bowl on the table. "I see. What was he like? Frossgar, that is."

Elaethia sat back and thought for a moment. "He was firm but kind. He always pushed me to be the best I could, without forcing me to do something I could not. Frossgar was a very wise dragon but chose to live in solitude, away from the world. He knew a lot about a few things but was ignorant of current events. The last he knew of our world was that demihumans had been introduced."

"That was a very long time ago. How old was he?"

"About three thousand four hundred years old. Though he could not say for sure."

"I'm sorry. This has been very hard on you."

Elaethia nodded. "I have lost much in my life. It is a cycle that has been repeated since before I escaped Armini. But you were right. Frossgar would not want me to mourn. He and my father would want me to push on and be strong. I will live to make them proud."

Ingrid found herself in awe at the determination of the woman in front of her—how she could have gone through all that pain and loss, only to have gotten the resolve to push on in the short time since they had met. She had to have the soul of a dragon. Not knowing what else to say, the two finished their meals in silence. Ingrid put the pot back over the dying fire to save some for Jörgen when he returned.

"What is yer plan?" Ingrid asked. "After makin' yer armor, that is. Ye seemed to have a goal in mind when I offered to let ye stay."

"To return to Armini and challenge Emperor Rychus. He has been a tyrant ruling over the country for over a hundred years."

Ingrid cocked an ear. "Ye plan to do this by yerself?"

"Frossgar will always be with me"—she clutched her golden pendant—"as will my family."

"That's very touchin', dear, but I don't think that will be enough to take on an empire."

"Once I have my armor and weapon, I am sure I will be able to manage," she insisted.

Ingrid's eyes landed on Elaethia's gold-and-sapphire necklace again. "That jewelry is somethin' from yer family, ye said? What's it's tale?"

Tears began to well in Elaethia's eyes again. "I would prefer not to talk about that yet. It … I …"

"That's all right, dear," Ingrid soothed, and she placed her wrinkled hands on Elaethia's. "Ye don't need to tell me. Every woman has her secrets, as well as a part of her past that needs time to heal."

Elaethia wiped her nose with the back of her sleeve. "Thank you, Ingrid."

Ingrid smiled as she cleaned up. "But back to the matter at hand. I've never seen a dragon hero in battle before, but they're said to be legendary. Whatever the case, I doubt one woman can wade her way through all that alone."

Before Elaethia could respond, the door opened as Jörgen entered with an old book. "I may have said there were no livin' souls who knew how to craft dragonite. But that doesn't mean there wasn't ever anyone in this clan at one point who didn't."

"What are ye sayin,' Jörgen?" Ingrid asked. "What's the book?"

"In a minute, my dear," he said, and he turned to Elaethia. "The elder's longhouse has a history of all the major events that happened here since this village was built. Seems we had some bits about the dragon wars."

"How does that help Elaethia here?"

"'Cause this village used to be home to a dragon hero durin' th' second war. There are whole books and pictures on how he fought and made his armor."

Elaethia looked up sharply at his words and slid to the edge of her seat.

"Get to th' point, Jörgen!" Ingrid snapped. "What does any of this mean?"

The large human placed the book on the table. "It means we have a step-by-step guide on how to forge those scales and bones into weapons and armor. We need to get studyin'."

"But I do not read very well," Elaethia admitted.

"Then that's where we'll start."

Weeks later, Elaethia and Jörgen stood over a blazing forge. The pack of dragon parts hung on her back. The enormous raider next to her had pliers, tongs, punches, chisels, files, hammers, and even a bellows hanging from his grimy leather apron.

"Th' first thing we need is a new hammer," he explained. "Normal steel can barely dent dragon scales, let alone pound them into plates."

Elaethia looked up at him. "You know how to smith?"

"All true Svarengels learn to smith as they become of age. None of 'em get to experience the glory and privilege of raidin' until they make their own equipment. I'm th' oldest raider here and have tinkered with more gear than any other member of this clan. I know th' ins and outs of this forge like my own axe and armor."

Jörgen reached a pair of tongs into a crucible and pulled out a hot dragon scale. The once deep blue scale was now scorched black and warped. The raider placed a joint bone with molded steel to form a hammer shape in the center of it. He took out a pair of pliers and pulled the hot, malleable scale taut to the mold. As it began to cool, he pounded it into shape with a steel hammer. After many sweltering minutes, he held up his newest creation—a hammer made with dragon scale and bone.

"That is the hammer we shall use?" Elaethia inquired.

Jörgen handed it to her. "This is the hammer that *ye* will use, lass. Ye forge yer own weapon and armor in our tradition, remember?"

"I do not know how to," Elaethia replied.

"I plan to help ye along th' way. I understand livin' in a cave most yer life wouldn't have taught ye thing one about craftsmanship. On top of that, this is the first set of dragonite equipment to be made in hundreds, maybe thousands of years. Of course I'm goin' to be a part of it. Besides, yer th' only one strong enough to do it right."

"I see. Show me where to begin."

Though it took two months for the body armor and gauntlets to be completed, the quality of craftsmanship was indisputable. Longer bones were carved and set to use as the mold, while the scales were forged to conform to it and serve as the armor. The azure scales turned darker and darker as they were heated and compressed, until the entire piece was a deep blue. The sides and back were made with smaller, more versatile scales. The shoulders and chest were covered with large, thick scales layered on top of each other.

But the pieces took up quite a bit of the scales and bone they had, and the helmet took a bit longer than they thought. Instead of the Svarengel open-faced style, Elaethia decided on the visored full helmet she had seen all over Linderry on her journey north. The V-shaped visor was open enough that she could see fairly well in front of her, but her peripherals were obstructed. Elaethia saw no need to decorate the helmet, but Jörgen insisted she include the iconic Svarengel protrusions on the sides.

"We're runnin' out of scales, lass," Jörgen noted. "I think we'd better focus on yer weapons before we get to yer boots."

Elaethia thought for a second. "An axe, to be sure. A large one with a blade on each end. I would also like a sword for closer encounters."

Jörgen looked at the remaining scales. "If we do that, I doubt we'll have enough for yer boots."

"We can make them out of a different material. I do not expect to be hit in the foot often."

Jörgen shook his head. "Yer feet are the contact point between ye and th' ground. If yer going to be swingin' an axe and thunderin' around in heavy armor like this, they'll be shaken to pieces. We've been saving them for last because they're gonna be a delicate process."

"What would you suggest, then?"

"We'll make yer boots and use th' rest on yer weapon. I'd say just stick with th' axe."

After the boots, they forged the remaining scales, as well as the spine that Elaethia had brought, into the massive twin blades. Jörgen carved the spine into a shaft as Elaethia shaped the scales into a large, twin-headed battleaxe. After the long, sweaty process was complete, they took it over to a grindstone for sharpening. Jörgen hefted the giant weapon and rested it heavily on the grindstone. But as he placed his feet on the pedals and began to spin it, he saw that the axe was warping the grindstone, not the other way around.

"What is the matter?" Elaethia asked.

"Yer weapon is tougher than th' grindstone, lass," he grunted. "We can't sharpen it. Not as it is. How many bones do we have left?"

"Only a couple."

Jörgen let out a long breath. "I have an idea, but it won't be easy. Bring 'em out."

With the dragonite hammer, Elaethia pounded the biggest of the bones into coarse grains. As she did, Jörgen strained the grindstone over the forge and heated it to near its melting point.

Once Elaethia was done with her task, she donned her dragonite gloves and pulled the searing grindstone from the flames. As it cooled, Jörgen pressed the dragon-bone grains into its surface, melding the bone with the softened stone all around the surface. Finally they reattached the makeshift dragonite grindstone to its stand.

Jörgen sat down again and held the blades to the grindstone for several minutes. Blue and white sparks leaped from the blade and grindstone and onto the grassy dirt. The white sparks fizzled into nothing, but the blue ones created tiny patches of frost that quickly melted as they landed. Finally Jörgen let off and handed the weapon to her.

"Here ye go, lass." He presented it with a strain. "I gotta say, this is one heavy weapon. I don't know a brehdar alive that could swing this thing properly."

Elaethia took hold and got a feel for it.

The old Svarengel looked on with wide eyes. "Are ye seriously holdin' that comfortably in one hand?"

Elaethia looked up. "You found this extremely heavy?"

"Ye don't?"

"It is certainly the weightiest weapon I have ever held, but I would not say it is heavy.

"Never mind that; give 'er a few swings."

Elaethia took a solid grip on the enormous weapon. She took a step back and swung it back and forth. The blade hummed as it sliced through the air.

"I feel comfortable with this," she announced.

Jörgen said nothing as sweat beaded his reddening brow.

Elaethia tilted her head. "Is something the matter?"

"Well, lookin' past how ye seem to so casually swing that thing around, yer form is giving me a headache."

"My form?"

"Yes, yer form!" he shouted. "Who taught ye to swing like that? What's with that stance? Why're yer arms so close together?"

"Nobody taught me. Frossgar was a dragon and did not know how to use brehdar weapons, except for the spear that I would—"

Jörgen smacked himself in the face. "I can't have ye runnin' amok in th' world in this armor with such shabby technique. Yer gonna stay here until I'm satisfied with yer combat capabilities. C'mere. Plant yer feet shoulder-width apart like I'm doing. Now place yer left foot slightly in front and bend yer knees. No, not that much! There! Yes, like that. That there is a basic stance. Ye get th' most power and stability in yer fights with this."

"It seems rather limited," Elaethia noted.

"Yer holdin' a big weapon and wearin' heavy armor. Mobility isn't an option for ye. Yer a tower of strength, not a light-footed duelist."

"I do not feel restrained," she stated.

"Really? Well, ye see that dyin' tree thirty meters over there? Since ye like to chop them up so much, why don't ye run over and cut it down, quick as ye can."

Elaethia nodded, gripped her axe, ran forward a few steps, and leaped through the air. She came down in front of the tree and slashed the axe completely through it. A blast of icy crystals erupted on the opposite side as the dead tree shattered and crashed to the ground. Jörgen stood in astonishment at both the leap and the magical strike as Elaethia turned to face him through the dust.

"That was a bit simpler than I first imagined," she said. "I have been wondering how to use Frossgar's magic. What do you think?"

"I think," he said, choking on his own voice, "we need to work on yer swingin' next."

Jörgen took her over to a wide open area with his own axe and had her get into the stance again. "Th' thing about battleaxes is they're heavy. So a back-and-forth motion will tire ye out quickly."

"I do not feel any kind of fatigue," she stated.

"Doesn't matter; it's still sloppy. With a battleaxe, it takes more effort to get it up to full speed than most other weapons. It'll take just as much, if not more, to slow it down, only to speed it up again in th' opposite direction."

"What do you suggest I do instead?"

"For a basic starter, ye want to keep th' same momentum from yer initial swing. Instead of stoppin' it, keep it goin' in th' same direction. If ye have to change directions, come around from a different angle. Maintain a constant arc around yer body. Watch me."

The old raider wound up and demonstrated the technique, shifting his body with each swing so the blade moved in a continuous flow. He stopped after a few rotations.

"Make sense?" he asked.

"I believe so, yes."

Elaethia gripped her own axe and attempted the smooth flourish that Jörgen had just performed. Again she put some frost magic into it. A freezing vapor enveloped the dragon hero, and sharp ice spikes flew out directly in front of her. Elaethia stumbled because of the thick armor she was wearing and stopped the flourish.

"There, see?" Jörgen pointed out with ice hanging from his beard and eyebrows. "That's where technique and stance come in. This weapon is meant for berserkers, not heavy warriors. It's not made for long combat, but ye seem to be different. Let me show ye again, this time without th' magic. Ye can practice that on yer own."

"I will, Jörgen. I thank you for your instruction."

The old man grunted in approval. "Just stick with it, lass. Ye will get th' hang of it. Now get into the stance again. Watch me closely. We're goin' to do this step-by-step together, so don't get ahead of me."

Sixth Era. 137. Jalesk 4.

As Ingrid had predicted, Elaethia showed massive improvement as she practiced. Her arcs were more proficient, as were her stance and strikes. While her husband made sure to train her in the proper way, he would also step back and let her develop her own style. Elaethia was definitely a brehdar at one point, but now she was something much more. Ingrid observed the physical strength that the young woman put forth, as well as the mysterious frost magic that surrounded her when she trained. Pride welled in her chest as the villagers looked on at Elaethia in astonishment. All doubt had long left her mind. Elaethia could only be a dragon hero.

Over the months that Elaethia stayed with the Sterkands, she picked skills not just from Jörgen but also from his wife. Elaethia quickly became fascinated with food, and she watched as Ingrid prepared dinner each night. At one point she even began to attempt cooking herself. Elaethia was destined to be great. A formidable warrior. A mighty woman. A beacon of hope, birthed by her will of iron. But a famous chef would never be among these titles. Ingrid decided it would be best if she kept to the cooking.

Elaethia had come very far in ways other than her combat prowess. It was painfully obvious from the beginning that she grew up in a cave with an old, out-of-touch dragon. The dragon hero was truly a pure-hearted woman but was unbelievably socially awkward—so much so that the young women of the village had started to avoid her completely. Ingrid found that she couldn't just sit there as Elaethia struggled to display and understand basic brehdar interaction. Someone would need to help in that regard.

Elaethia would soon learn that Ingrid was just as strict as her husband when it came to instruction. Only instead of strikes and stances, it was pose and posture. The dragon hero never knew when a surprise lesson would be thrust at her, as Ingrid never hesitated to correct Elaethia when her behavior was less than ladylike.

"I always wondered why ye never tried to dissuade th' suitors that always followed ye around," the old woman suddenly asked one night.

"Suitors?" Elaethia asked. "Do you mean the men that would watch me train?"

"Of course I mean them!" Ingrid replied with indignation. "Ye mean to tell me ye don't know what they were doin'?"

"I care not, really. If they got close, Jörgen would chase them away. I hardly dealt with them."

Ingrid put a palm to her forehead, and her ears fell back. "Elaethia, yer a wonderful and powerful woman. But so painfully naive."

"I do not understand."

The old woman sighed and took Elaethia's hands. "Somethin' Jörgen has always said is that he is a man before anythin' else. He may have been a raider captain, and he may be in line for th' next village elder. But he always states that before any of that, he is a man. It is his duty first and foremost to act like one above all else. I believe ye need to look at yerself not as a dragon hero, nor a warrior, but a woman. Remember that first and foremost ye need to be a woman."

Elaethia tilted her head. "How do I go about that?"

"Ye can start by closin' yer legs when ye sit. Ye need to have a more elegant posture about ye."

Elaethia adjusted herself. "I understand. What is the next step?"

Ingrid couldn't help but laugh. "This isn't somethin' ye can learn like a weapon or magic. There is no step-by-step process to bein' a lady. Ye will learn in time, but I will teach ye th' best I can."

"I see. Thank you, Ingrid. What do those 'suitors' want with me?"

"Same thing all suitors want. To make you his bride and continue his generation. Yer strong and have fertile hips and a rather large chest. They'd like to claim and enjoy that."

"Claim and enjoy? How so?"

"Come now, do I have to explain to ye how children are made?"

"I have always wondered."

"Well hasn't this just turned into an odd conversation. Where to start …"

Ingrid described the method of reproduction and the desires of men for quite some time. The old woman was very grateful, although slightly perturbed, that Elaethia showed no shame or embarrassment regarding the explanation. If Ingrid didn't know any better, she would have thought Elaethia already knew and was simply toying with her. The only concern Ingrid found herself having was that the young woman seemingly took detailed mental notes regarding the processes involved in brehdar reproduction.

Sixth Era. 138. Miyan 22.

The time spent with Elaethia in the quiet and secluded village was otherwise uneventful. Her skill was beyond what Jörgen's had been when he was in his prime in no time. The elderly raider was obviously equal parts jealous and proud at her insane ability. The same could not be said about her social skills, however. The damage of her initial introduction to the village, as well as the last fourteen years of her life, had taken their toll on her. Brehdar interaction would be beyond her for a long time. It was quite possible that she would never be considered normal.

As the seasons made a full change, Elaethia and the Sterkhands came to realize one thing. It was time for Elaethia to continue her journey.

"It's been one of th' shortest years I've ever felt," Jörgen stated one morning as they sat down for breakfast one last time. "Ye've made more progress in fourteen months than any of us would have in years."

"I am very grateful for all you have done for me," Elaethia said. "I wish there were an adequate way I could return the favor."

Ingrid shook her head. "Yer company in this home was more than enough. We were delighted to have ye with us."

Jörgen shifted in his seat. "I suppose it's time to say our good-byes then?"

Ingrid nodded. "That's right, dear. Elaethia needs to be headed south."

Jörgen and Ingrid stood together in front of the door as Elaethia donned her armor and pack and rested her great axe on her shoulder.

"Some final gifts for ye," Jörgen announced.

He held out his hands and presented a large sheath, shaped perfectly for Elaethia's battleaxe. He also handed her a coarse blue-and-white stone and a dragonite forge hammer with a wooden handle. He buckled the sheath around Elaethia's torso and guided her axe into it.

"This is made for yer weapon and for travelin'. This is how ye use it."

"I see it is designed to sit so it does not interfere with my pack," Elaethia noted.

"Aye." Jörgen nodded. "It'll be very handy if ye need to pull it out at a moment's notice. That other thing is a whetstone made of dragon bone and scale. Nothin' much out there will dull that axe, but just in case, ye can use that to keep yer blade keen. I also used the last of what we had to give ye a forge hammer of yer own."

"Both you and Frossgar have always taught me to be ready at a moment's notice. I thank you again for everything you have done for me."

"Of course, of course." The big man cleared his throat as his voice faltered. "Now ye should be on yer way. Don't want to lose th' sunlight."

Elaethia looked to the sky. "The morning has just begun. I do not believe the sunlight will be going anywhere anytime soon."

Ingrid stepped in. "Well, it is a ways to th' next village. Ye should get going so ye make it as far as ye can before it gets dark."

"You are correct, Ingrid," Elaethia agreed. "I will be on my way if there is nothing else."

"No dear, that is all." Ingrid stepped up and hugged the armored woman warmly. Elaethia returned the gesture in kind. "Just make sure ye keep yer armor and body clean. A woman shouldn't smell like sweat and blood for long. And remember: ye'll *always* have a place here. You may return any time."

Elaethia nodded and turned to face Jörgen, who seemed to be trembling. Instead of embracing her, however, he held out a hand. She unhesitatingly grasped it in a firm shake.

The elderly raider coughed once. "One thing I think ye should do before headin' down to Armini ... I've heard of groups of adventurers in Linderry that go out together and solve problems in exchange for money. It'd be a good place to hone yer skills and gain some funds before yer war against that emperor."

"I will give it consideration. I do want to get used to combat and my magic."

"Right, right, enough of the fluff and whatnot," Jörgen choked. "Off ye go before ye start growin' moss."

"Of course, Jörgen." Elaethia smiled. "I doubt I will grow moss, but I understand the need to begin my journey. Take care."

Elaethia turned and walked down the road, heading south toward Linderry. Jörgen broke down immediately after Elaethia disappeared from his sight. The raider's body trembled and shuddered as he fought to stay on his feet. Tears welled in his eyes and trickled down his wrinkled face and into his white beard.

Ingrid put her arms around him and comforted him in a soft voice. "We knew this day would come, dear. Ye know she wouldn't be happy if she lived here with us forever."

"I've never met such a fine and headstrong warrior," he choked. "And I was able to train and mold her into what she is."

"She could never replace Erika. It was wonderful to have her, but it just wasn't the same."

"No, no, of course not. But stars above, I hate to say good-bye."

"I know," Ingrid said, soothing him. "But ye made absolutely sure she had all the tools and experience she could possibly have before ye let her go. Ye set her on the right path, and she's not one to stray from it. We have no reason to be worried."

Jörgen nodded, and the two went back inside. He trudged solemnly to their room and closed the door. Ingrid walked over to Erika's room, which Elaethia had used in her stead. It was uncanny how much the strange woman from the mountain resembled and contrasted her late daughter. Erika's short brown hair, her fiery attitude, her short attention span—none of these were things Elaethia had. But they shared their soft eyes, their kind hearts, their strong bodies, their eagerness to learn, and their unwavering loyalty. They would have been best friends, maybe even sisters.

Ingrid felt tears form in her eyes and trickle down her cheek. By the Moon, she hated good-byes even more so than her husband. But now was not the time to mourn. It was all right to be sad, but this wasn't something to dwell on. It was not the end of anything. It was simply the beginning of something new. Elaethia had the whole world in front of her, and she was ready to take it on.

Ingrid let out a small chuckle. She believed it was better to smile because something happened as opposed to cry because it was over. But something about the air in her home felt somber now. But it would pass. The Sterkhand family had been alone before. They could do it again.

In the months leading up to when she joined the guild, Elaethia traveled south. Village by village, town by town, she heard rumors and reports of malicious happenings in the area. She initially decided they would serve as good practice for her skills, until she realized she felt a calling toward these vigilante activities. She continued to perform feat after feat, fueled by the grateful faces of those she saved, the satisfaction of there being one less monster or villain in the world, or the thrill of a new experience. It wasn't long before she became known as the lone armored vigilante whose face no one ever saw.

Elaethia had acquired a good amount of money and decided to investigate a fair in northern Linderry. As she wandered aimlessly through, she noticed a wagoner being harassed by a group of young men. Instinct took in, and she drove them away without a hint of a fight. The old wagoner seemed grateful and went so far as to offer her a ride to the next town. It was once she climbed into the back that she found the old, crumpled flyer for the guild of Breeze.

Sixth Era. 139. Mertim 17.

Elaethia wasn't quite used to her new living arrangements. As Geran had warned, adventurers would stay up later than she did, and groups returning from quests in the morning made a good amount of noise themselves. Though she preferred a quieter environment, she decided she would get used to it.

The warrior changed into her armor and strode outside her room midmorning. It wasn't as lively as it was during the evening, but not as dead as during the sunrise hours. It had been a full day since she moved into her room, and she found she was already bored. It was time to find a quest for her new party. She headed downstairs and walked over to the quest board to scan the A-level requests. The first one caught her eye as being a reasonable task with a good reward. Elaethia took it off the board and walked to the receptionist desk.

Maya greeted the warrior as she approached. "Good morning, Elaethia! How are you enjoying the guild so far?"

"Good morning," she replied. "It is not what I am accustomed to, but I have no doubt I will get used to it."

"I'm happy to hear that! Hopefully you'll meld into our family well enough."

"We shall see."

"Do you own a set of clothes?" the receptionist asked. "I noticed I've only ever seen you in your armor."

"Yes, I have a set. Why do you ask?"

"Normal adventurers only wear their gear when they're questing," the elf explained. "And I realize I'm saying this as you are holding a quest flyer."

"Correct. I intend to take this one."

"Alone again?"

"I assume Geran and Lilian will accompany me."

Maya raised an eyebrow. "Assume? You haven't asked them if they want to go on this one?"

Elaethia tilted her head. "Should I?"

Maya sighed in resignation and closed her eyes. "That would be rather polite, don't you think? Besides, I can't approve a quest unless all party members give consent. Go discuss it with them, and come back when you've all decided you want to go, okay?"

Elaethia nodded. "Very well, thank you."

"Oh! By the way, your insignia was finished last night."

Maya reached under her desk and pulled out a tabard bearing the guild's insignia etched in blue. Elaethia took a hold of it. It was a long cloth designed to go around her waist and hang between her legs, dangling just above her knees.

"Thank you very much," Elaethia said. "I shall return with the rest of my party."

She turned and walked back to the main hall. She scanned the room but saw no sign of the ranger or mage. Then she remembered Lilian's room. Elaethia walked upstairs and across to where the demicat lived. After a few knocks, the door opened to reveal a head of tangled red-brown hair with two cat ears poking through it.

"Whaaaaaat?" the demicat groaned. Her eyes were half-open and mostly covered by the mess of hair.

"Good morning," Elaethia greeted the mage. "I have found a quest I would like to take. Shall we discuss it?"

"Huh?" came the half-awake reply. "It's, like, super early. Why would we be looking for a quest?" Lilian rubbed her face and looked up with a squint. Her eyes popped open at the recognition. "*Oh!* Gosh, hiya, Elaethia! C'mon in! Sorry about the mess."

Lilian opened the door to let the warrior in. The mage closed it behind her and walked ahead into the room. It would have been nearly identical to Elaethia's had it not been for the mess and colorful atmosphere. In utter contrast to the dragon hero's room, Lilian's was full of bright pillows, books, blankets, drapes, rugs, and clothes. It appeared that she had painted her furniture as well. Articles of clothing were strewn across the room. Her sheets and blanket draped to the floor, presumably from when she had rolled out of bed. Lilian stood in the center of the mess and started to pick various clothes and bedding off of the floor. She was barefoot and wore only a purple nightshirt with her furry tail snaking out from underneath it.

"Your living arrangements are … interesting," Elaethia said.

Lilian yawned, revealing her fangs. She walked over the window and opened the shutters to flood the room with sunlight. "Well I'm not used to waking up this early. I don't know how you people do it."

"I could say the same for you. How do you sleep so late after the sun rises? You waste so much daylight."

"Hmph. You really do sound like some of those old geezers," the mage grumbled as she shopped around trying to slip on her socks and boots. "What'd you need, anyway? Why're you all armored up?"

"To discuss a quest. I found one regarding some sabercats running rampant in the western woods. I realize you have not done a quest of this scale before, so I will understand if you are hesitant to join—"

Lilian shot her hand up. "What type and level is it?"

"Kill type, A level. I tried to—"

"I'm in."

"Are you not curious about the details?" Elaethia asked.

"Not really. You can fill me in on the way if you'd like, though. Have you talked to Geran yet?"

"I have not."

"Go and talk boring stuff with him. I gotta finish getting ready."

Lilian stood and pushed Elaethia toward the door. The girl wasn't actually able to make the armored woman move, but Elaethia felt it best to go along with it.

"What all do you need to do? How long will it take? Where shall we meet you?"

"Stop asking so many questions," Lilian proclaimed as Elaethia was fully out of the entryway. "You'll take all the excitement out of it. Now shoo!"

She shut the door, leaving a bewildered Elaethia on the balcony.

"But I do not know where Geran is!" Elaethia called through the closed door. She was given no response.

She blinked a few times and turned to head back downstairs. After a few minutes of asking around, she was able to locate Geran's room. Apparently it was a few doors down from hers, closer to the bathrooms. She knocked on it and waited patiently. After a few seconds, the door opened.

"Mornin'," Geran greeted her.

"Good morning," she replied. "I have found a suitable quest. Shall we discuss it?"

"Yeah, give me a second while I put on some shoes. I'd get Lilian if I were you; I've heard she can take a while."

"I already spoke with her. She was getting ready when I left."

"Good. That should give us maybe an hour to plan."

She peered into his room from the hallway. It was significantly tidier and much less colorful than Lilian's. He had an equal number of books on his shelves, but his clothes were hung in the wardrobe and neatly folded in chests. A large regional map hung directly above his bed. Odd markings had been made all over it in various places. She had no clue what they could mean. On his desk lay a large open book. Her dragon eyes were able to make out some of the wording. Strangely, it was a ledger. She didn't recognize any of the names, but they appeared to be people of interest to the ranger. One line in particular mentioned something about Blackwolf Halfway House. *Curious*, she thought. Geran reemerged, and they walked down together and sat at a small table. Elaethia placed the flyer in front of him. The ranger picked it up and began to read it aloud.

"In the woods about six kilometers northwest of the main city, there have been reports of sabercats frequently attacking anything and everything, both in small groups and alone. Kill as many of the feral sabercats as you can, as they have been restricting trade and travel routes between establishments. The reward will be eight silver per."

He set it down on the table, his face furrowed in thought. "Sabercats? Attacking everything, and in groups?"

"I questioned that as well," Elaethia said. "In my travels I have learned they are solitary creatures and tend to avoid brehdars and well-traveled roads. The fact that they are acting like this disturbs me."

"This is a kill quest, so we won't get any extra reward for it, but I'd like to find out the reason behind this behavior. Keep in mind, I rarely take kill quests, so don't rely on me too much."

"I would like to find the cause as well. If we can locate and neutralize it, we can perhaps prevent similar instances from happening in the future."

"A few adventurers may be rather mad about that, but I agree."

"Why would they be mad?"

"Well, a guild *is* a business," Geran began. "This is an occupation and source of income for us adventurers. Quests are how we earn money, so in a sense, we want there to be a plethora of quests. Of course, that kind of means we live off the suffering of others. By going the extra step beyond killing the sabercats, we eliminate the potential of a follow-up quest, which will lead to another reward. There are a couple members here that would unhesitatingly ignore a problem in the hope it will turn up again in the form of a quest."

Elaethia's eyes hardened. "That is not an admirable trait for someone who claims to help others."

"Yeah, well, nothing we can do about it. It isn't a crime to refuse help to someone outside your quest, and Master Dameon can't discharge someone because of it."

"Why not?"

"Every guild is regulated by an organization in the capital called the National Department of Guilds. NDG for short. The NDG mandated a law to prevent unfounded discharges. This was mainly to prevent incoming guild masters from curbing anyone they didn't want. It also was created to keep guilds from discharging adventurers because of their race, skill, class, or stature. The country doesn't care about who you pick and choose to enter the guild, but kicking someone out who has notable combat expertise, or potentially sensitive information, is not good for national security."

"Why does this department care whom a guild chooses to keep?"

"They don't want to leave dangerous individuals unchecked. Linderry wants to keep an eye on those kinds of people, and they don't want to be looking at excess amounts of discharged individuals. A lot of bandits and whatnot are usually former adventurers. The only way you can be discharged is by committing a felony, or repeated disorderly conduct.

"Anyway, it does a good job of keeping us safe in our jobs, but a small setback is that it keeps morally shifty people in the guild. Peter Stone has almost been discharged a few times for his disorderly conduct, and Sybil Fairwind is on thin ice for his apathetic tendencies. The only thing stopping Peter from getting the boot is his raw talent. A lot of us would love to see Sybil get curbed too, but he's never done anything that could warrant it."

"Is it so bad to be discharged?"

"Well, it practically ruins one's reputation. People find out you got kicked out of the guild, and you're immediately branded as a miscreant."

"I see," she noted. "You say a plethora of quests seems to be a necessity, so I would assume they would be taken very quickly. However, I notice that many quests have posted dates several days old. It seems quests don't disappear as fast as that would imply."

"Obviously you don't even look at B- or I- level quests, but more difficult quests pay good money. A party of three can live comfortably for a few months off a single V-level quest alone. Once they cash in, they're free to just relax until they need money again. As a result, higher-level quests tend to sit for a while before parties take them. The backside to that is that since they are so dangerous, people want them taken care of as soon as possible. So they increase the reward to motivate the adventurers."

"But what of aiding the people?" Elaethia protested.

"This is a high-risk job. Nobody wants to stick their neck out for strangers so often."

"That is unfortunate. Shall we depart once Lilian is ready?"

Geran made a face. "Don't you want to devise a strategy? Form a plan for getting there, scouting it out, attacking, investigating, and returning?"

She tilted her head. "Is that not a strategy in and of itself?"

"No, that's just the basic outline."

"What more detail would we need?"

"Maps, gear, accountability, personnel, provisions, travel method, contingencies, abilities, and assets," Geran listed off as he counted on his fingers. "We should look at everything we have and how we can use it to its fullest potential."

"We have never fought alongside one another," she pointed out. "How would we know?"

"Exactly, so we should all come together and present what we have to offer."

"I … suppose," she faltered.

Geran explained his ranger capabilities for a time. The only pieces of information she found important were his skills with the bow, the sword, tracking, scouting, and intelligence gathering. He talked at some length of how he had used them in previous missions. Elaethia tried to listen politely but found herself tuning out. After a while, the dull atmosphere was broken by the cheerful sound of Lilian's voice.

"Well there you guys are!" she chirped as she leaned over the railing.

The mage trotted over to the staircase and made her way downstairs. She was in her usual getup, except she was now wearing a flowing black cloak with orange embroidery around the trim. She also wore a pointed black hat with identical embroidery circling the wide brim. Holes were cut into the brim so her ears could poke out. In her hand she carried a straight, gnarled wooden staff that was about a meter and a half long. A fist-sized red gemstone was embedded at the top. She had a tan belted pouch fastened to her thigh and waist. She also appeared to be wearing makeup.

"You guys done talking boring stuff yet?" she asked as she reached the table.

"Oh good, you're just in time," Geran announced. "We just finished up discussing my capabilities, although I can do a recap for you. After that, Elaethia can give us a rundown on her contributions. Once she's done, you can take the stage and explain—"

"Okay, so you guys aren't done talking boring stuff. I'm gonna get a drink while you finish up." She turned to walk away but hadn't made it a step before Geran's hand shot out and snagged her cloak. She made a sound akin to a cat choking on a hairball.

"Not so fast. I don't know how your old party ran things, but you're in ours now. This is a completely different league than you're used to, so don't think you can run through it like an B or I quest. Siddown and join the strategy meeting."

Lilian took off her witch hat and dropped into a chair, groaning loudly as she banged her head on the table. She let out another audible groan of contempt, muffled by the wooden surface.

"All right, Elaethia," Geran said. "What can you provide for this mission?"

"Well, I use my armor and axe to push through enemies and cut them down. I have yet to meet one that can halt me. Beyond that, I can use frost dragon magic, although I am still learning the different attacks and spells I have."

Elaethia looked at her two companions. Lilian was still face down on the table, while Geran looked at her with interest.

"You're good. Keep going," he said.

"What more is there to tell? I have covered everything."

He looked at her incredulously. "That's it? There's no way you can expand on that?"

"I do not understand."

"Well you can start by explaining how you can use those skills to create openings, initiate an attack, make a hole in the enemy defense, et cetera. I think we can use you to—"

Lilian suddenly shot up. "Okay! That sounds good enough! Hi, my name's Lilian, I'm an elemental mage. I have a variety of spells under fire, lightning, air, and frost. I'm super powerful, but I can't use spells if I run out of magic. I also can't afford to get hit, 'cause wearing armor makes it almost impossible to channel magic. That's why I need you two to back me up in case I run outta magic or get charged."

"Typical glass ballista," Geran sighed.

Elaethia tilted her head. "How does your magic come back?"

Lilian made a face but answered regardless. "It comes back naturally. Otherwise I could use A potion, *electric drain,* or a get a priest to cast *moonlight* on me."

"Can you explain *electric drain*?" Geran pressed.

The demicat sighed. "It's a lightning spell that sucks my target's magic into me. Doesn't matter if the magic trait is active in the target or not. It's a channeled spell, so it's only active as long as I focus on it. It doesn't hurt … much … so I sometimes use it on friendlies. But I can't use it if I'm totally empty."

"That was great! There's the kind of explanation I'm looking for!" Geran praised. The demicat responded by resting her chin on the table and sticking out her tongue.

"How many spells do you know?" Elaethia asked

"I dunno. A lot?" Lilian muttered.

"Well, you can probably list them off," Geran mused. "We'll get a total, and then a rundown of what they do."

Lilian glared at him with her ears tilted back.

"Okay, maybe some other time then," he sighed.

Lilian whined and leaned back in her chair. "Gaaaah, why are we just sitting here? We can talk on the way there!"

"You don't even know where it is," Geran pointed out.

"Gimme that!" the mage huffed, and she snatched the quest flyer. "It's only, like, an hour and a half away! What's the holdup?"

"And how do you plan on getting there?"

"Walking!"

"No shit! I mean what route?"

"We have a map!" she wailed and slammed her head on the table again, flailing the paper in the air. "We can literally just follow the roads!"

"That's not how maps work! There're no roads in the middle of the woods!"

"Well then, use your tracking skills and ranger us up some sabercats!"

"I can't just … Augh!" He, too, slammed his head onto the table. "This is why I didn't want to be in a party."

Elaethia sat wide-eyed. Her gaze shifted back and forth between the two fed-up party members. "Perhaps we should get it approved and head out. We can continue our discussion on the way there."

They both grunted in agreement as they all stood and headed to the receptionist desk. After Maya stamped it, Geran and Lilian made their way through the provisions line. Elaethia stayed behind to talk with Maya.

"Is Geran always so detail-oriented?" she asked.

Maya laughed. "As far as rangers go, his attention to minutiae is on a completely different level. I can imagine it gets annoying to someone like you or Lilian. Bear with him, though. It'll likely save your lives in the future."

"You seem very confident in that answer. Do you know this for sure?"

The elf nodded. "We came here on the same day, so I've known him for over ten years. He hasn't survived this long on his own by sheer luck. He knows exactly what he can and can't do, as well as where he excels. Everything he does has a purpose and is necessary in his mind. Geran is the best at what he does, and he knows it. That being said, he believes he can always get better. He's seen a lot of death over the years. He understands better than anyone how every second and every detail can matter. That's what pushes him to such lengths every time."

Elaethia nodded and turned to join the others as they emerged from the provisions section. Geran had bought a healing potion, while Lilian got one of her own, as well as a magic potion. They stopped again at the table and made the final preparations and checks on their items.

"Hey, Geeeerry," Lilian hummed, giving him big eyes. "My pouch is a little small for all this stuff. Do you think you could be a dear and put them in your bag too?"

"Nope," he responded instantly. "Shoulda thought about that when you selected your equipment."

"But Dylan always did it for me! Carrying a clunky bag like that would interfere with my presence! You understand that a lady has to maintain her image everywhere she goes, right, Elaethia?"

"I understand maintaining an image is important," Elaethia agreed, thinking back to Ingrid's lessons.

The mage turned smugly to Geran—until Elaethia continued.

"However, in a mission, the most important thing is survival and completion. If you did not prepare yourself accordingly, that is on you."

Lilian looked up at her with a heartbroken expression. "E-lae-thi-aaaaa!" the demicat wailed. She slammed her head into the dragonite chest plate and a hollow bonk resonated from the impact. Lilian slowly shrunk down and clutched her head with her ears back.

"Ow, ow, ow, ow, ow, ow, ow," she whimpered.

Elaethia stared at her in confusion. "Why would you do that?"

Lilian looked up with bleary eyes. "That's not fair! You're supposed to feel bad for me!"

Elaethia tilted her head. "But you did this to yourself."

"So?" the demicat said with a sniffle.

Elaethia held a gauntlet to her while taking off her pack. "Nevertheless, I understand that you do not have the space to carry all of your items, so I shall take some of them for you. Next time be sure to bring a larger bag."

Lilian nodded gratefully and hugged Elaethia's leg while she placed the food and extra water in her own pack.

Finally, they all donned their insignia. Elaethia wrapped the white-and-blue tabard around her waist. Geran fastened a green-and-brown brassard to his left shoulder. Lilian placed a black-and-purple band around the base of her pointy hat. Together, the party of three strode out the door to begin their quest.

Elaethia had always wondered how magic truly worked. All the magicians in Armini had been taken captive by the emperor, and Frossgar had never explained his. Something told her he probably didn't know himself.

"Lilian," Elaethia began as they exited the city walls, "magic has always fascinated me. Now that I have it, I wish to understand it more. What is it, exactly?"

"Magic?" the demicat asked, cocking an ear. "That's a pretty broad topic; could you be more specific?"

"Why can only certain people use it?"

"It's hereditary. Like hair color, eyes, race, et cetera. It's a recessive trait, though. According to some of the Arcane Sages, nearly everyone could use magic during the early dragon wars.

Now only about thirty percent of brehdars have active magic. The Sages believe magic will never disappear naturally but will become more and more rare over time."

"These Arcane Sages—who are they?"

Lilian gave her a sideways look. "Gosh, you really did grow up in a cave didn't you? The Arcane Sages are the highest ranking magicians in Linderry, and they live in this big 'ol tower called the Moon's Pillar in the capital city, Apogee. Like other wizards, they spend their time studying magic and using it to better brehdar-kind. That or just experiment around. *Allegedly* Their power is enough to turn the whole country into a crater if they wanted to. But the bunch of old book-sniffers probably haven't even considered it."

"So they are wizards? What makes their magic different from yours as a mage?"

"Oh there's no difference like that. Magic is magic. Magicians get their titles from how they exercise it. Mages use theirs for combat, and wizards are like scholars or engineers. There's another type called sorcerers, but they aren't formally recognized by the country. Sorcerers are basically malicious wizards who practice in seclusion because they adopted illegal or forbidden magic like necromancy, hypnosis, or one of the types of anatomy magic."

Elaethia thought for a moment. "Frossgar mentioned demihumans came into existence because of an anatomy sorcerer. I understand them a bit better now."

Geran and Lilian both stopped in their tracks.

"What did you say?" Lilian asked, eyes wide.

"Did you just say a *sorcerer* created demihumans?" Geran pressed her.

"That is what Frossgar said, yes. Is this not common knowledge?"

"What? No! Are you serious! You mean to tell me you just *happen* to know exactly how three sentient beings came into existence?"

"Elaethia…" Lilian's voice was rather small. "Could you tell me everything Frossgar said?"

"I was a child when he explained it to me, but apparently at the beginning of the dragon wars, an unnamed sorcerer wanted to build an army of semi-intelligent, strong, terrifying creatures. Demihumans. Eventually he created what we have now, which was fully sentient, lacking basically all of their animal nature. They turned on him and escaped into the world."

Lilian's voice was far away. "We were created by a sorcerer. On accident?"

"I am surprised that you all do not know this. I would assume it would have been documented somewhere."

"No," Geran said. He muttered to himself for a few moments and then nodded. "It makes sense why they'd keep this secret. Can you imagine if people knew there was a way to create a whole other sentient life form? It would be chaos, and unfathomably inhumane experiments would result. I'm willing to bet the Arcane Sages do have a record, but chose to keep it secret for this reason. Both of you, never tell *anyone* this knowledge. Elaethia you haven't shared this with anyone else have you?"

"I have not," she assured him.

"Good. I don't know if what Frossgar told you is true, but the fewer people that know this, the better." He then turned to the demicat "Lilian, I know this is going to be very hard, but you have to keep this information away from your friends and family. This goes to your grave, alright?"

"I know." She nodded, ears drooping.

"Well," The ranger announced. "Now that we have significantly dropped the mood, let's talk a bit more about magic. Elaethia, do you have any other questions?"

She thought for a moment. "I still wish to understand my own. I understand I have frost magic because it was gifted to me. But what about you, Lilian? Were you born an elemental mage?"

The demicat shook her head. "No. We get to choose. Magic starts out neutral in a magician's body, so we can cast any spell we want at first. But once we do, we get locked into that school. Take me, for example. My first spell was *thunderbolt*, so I got locked into elemental magic."

"Their first spell locks them in?" Elaethia asked. "How does one prevent oneself from choosing a school one had no intention of following?"

"Magic isn't like that. You don't just randomly punch someone or jump in the air. To use a spell, you have to know what you're doing and commit to it. You gotta have a conduit to use your magic too. But that's a whole other deal. Don't ask me about that kinda stuff, 'cause I don't really know or care."

"You are not curious as to how it all works?"

The demicat turned up her nose. "Course not! I'm a mage, not a wizard! If I wanted to sit and ponder the meaning of magic, I would be up in that tower with the rest of the book-sniffers. I wanna go out and blast things and get famous, and being an adventurer is the perfect way to do that!"

"You say this very casually. Do you not have concern for your life?" Elaethia asked.

"Well, I mean, a little. But like I said, I just want to blast things, and I can't do that cooped up in a lab or shop. I want to go out into the world. Fame and fortune await as an adventurer, and I have my eyes on going down in history as a legendary mage."

Geran suddenly stopped and pointed off the road. "Hold up; we need to turn north here."

"Do you miss your home?" Elaethia asked the mage as they stepped into the woods.

"Somewhat, but definitely not as bad as you. I still try to visit them every now and then. I grew up in a village southwest of here, in a family of tailors and farmers. I gotta big family, you know. Mama, Papa, an older sister, two younger brothers, a kid sister, and my nana and grandad. All under one roof. I'm the only one who has active magic, though, besides Grandad. I joined the guild three years ago as an apprentice, and I became an adventurer a year after that."

"I imagine your family would be concerned about your choice."

"They're proud of me, but I know they're worried. Mama always said she wanted me to work in a tailor shop making pillows, but she puts on a brave face for me. I know she's afraid I'll get dissolved by a slime, crushed by a troll, taken by goblins, eaten by wolves—take your pick. But my folks see me as a strong girl and know I wouldn't do anything too stupid."

Elaethia tilted her head. "Too stupid?"

"Well, I can't be smart all the time; that'd be boring! Come to think of it, now that you and Geran are here, I can afford to be stupider than usual!"

"I do not believe that is a trait to be proud of."

Lilian fluttered a hand. "Aw, c'mon. Being a little stupid never hurt anyone."

"On the contrary, there have been many occasions where things turned for the worse because someone failed to—"

"Augh, Elaethia! Stooooop! You're such an old lady!"

"I am only twenty-three years old."

"E-lae-thi-aaa!"

"Hey!" Geran snapped in a hushed shout. "Are you guys trying to give away our position?"

"Position?" Lilian asked. "What position?"

"We're trying to track down some sabercats, and you're gonna alert the whole forest where we are!"

The mage folded her arms. "So? We're here to kill them, right? If they come to us, it's that much easier."

"It's a lot better if we can be the ones to initiate the attack."

"That is correct," Elaethia agreed. "However, we are in their territory. It is likely they will find us before we find them."

Lilian groaned. "You two keep goin' on like they're all together in one spot! I thought the quest said they were all over the place in small groups or alone."

"I am one in mind with Lilian. The quest indicated that it was more likely they would attack us."

Lilian frowned. "Yeah, didn't it say they attacked frequently? But frequently according to what? Sabercat attacks were never common to begin with."

Geran reached into his pocket. He pulled out the flyer and flipped it over to the description. "I don't know for sure, all right? All it says is that they're frequently attacking."

"If I recall correctly, it says the sabercats have been restricting travel and trade routes," Elaethia noted. "But I have heard nothing about them interfering with adventurers on quests. How long has this quest been active?"

"Date of request is almost a week ago, but the reports go back for over a month. But you're right. I haven't heard anything about them attacking guild members, and we're in these woods more than anyone else. It's almost like they know not to attack people who are capable of defending themselves."

"Say, does that mean they avoid armed caravans, too?" Lilian asked. "One of the most frequent quests my old party would do were escorts, but I don't think we ever got attacked by sabercats. An angry mama bear or wolves, but that's it for animals.

"That can't be a coincidence," Geran muttered. "And there's no way they all got smart out of nowhere."

"Traveling in groups, avoiding armed brehdars, attacking everything else … Something is definitely awry," Elaethia concluded.

"Then they'll probably avoid us, considering we're armed to the teeth," Geran said.

"Not if we keep investigating. The mastermind would surely make attempts to dissuade us."

"Mastermind?" Lilian asked. "You think someone's behind this?"

"Freeze!" Geran shot out his hand and crouched down. "You two hear that?"

The two women joined Geran in a crouch and tuned their ears to their surroundings. The woods were dead quiet. The ever-present sounds of the forest had ceased. Elaethia understood what that meant. She quickly dropped her pack and put a hand on the handle of her axe.

Lilian looked around. Her ears twitched. "What? I don't hear anything."

"Exactly," Geran muttered. "We're being stalked."

"How can you tell?" Lilian's ears sank but then instantly shot up as she whipped her head to look at the dragon hero. "Elaethia, behind you!"

A sabercat lunged from the bushes behind her. The beast was similar in size to an adult cow, with tan-and-gold fur, powerful legs, and a long tail. Its claws were wicked sharp, as were the pair of foot-long teeth that protruded from its upper jaw.

The warrior's battleaxe sang from its sheath in a wide, underhand arc. The blade came around and embedded itself into the animal's enormous furry belly. She stood and carried the momentum, continuing the arc in a wheel that slammed the beast into the ground. The axe broke through the animal's spine with a crunch. Elaethia wrenched the great blade from the sabercat and held it at the ready. Lilian shrieked as she was splattered with blood.

Geran drew his longsword and rose to a low kneel. "Get ready! They just tried to take out our strongest asset first! These cats know what they're doing!"

"Why are you using your sword? Aren't you better with your bow?" Lilian shouted.

"Look at the size of that thing! My arrows are only gonna piss them off! Stand back-to-back so they can't attack from our rear."

The party complied and looked around, scanning for any sign of movement. A crash from the brush came from Lilian's side. As the beast emerged, she thrust her staff forward, and a loud crack of lightning struck the animal in the head. It tumbled to the ground, its head smoldering from the bolt. Three more instantly charged at Geran. Lilian quickly stepped to his side. She thrust her staff again, except this time a massive torch of fire bellowed out of it. Engulfed in flames, the first two screamed and writhed on the ground. The third's instincts took over, and it turned to flee.

Elaethia hacked at the two on the ground while Geran dropped his sword to draw his bow. The ranger nocked an arrow, drew it back, took a slow breath, and released. The arrow embedded itself into the hamstring of the running sabercat's rear leg. Elaethia suddenly leapt the distance and slammed her axe on the crippled animal. An eruption of several ice spikes impaled it and tore its body apart. Frost spread along the ground outward from the impact, accompanied by a chilly mist.

Geran winced at the sight of the mangled beast. "By the Sun, Elaethia. I don't … I had *no* idea you could do something like that, but was it really necessary?"

Elaethia ripped her axe free and turned. "I was thinking about what Lilian said. It is not often I get to practice my dragon magic. I should take the opportunity whenever I can."

"I mean, I guess. But *damn* that's gruesome. Lilian, are you seeing this?"

"Nope!" The girl looked away from the bloody mess. "I can't see a thing."

Geran ran a hand through his hair and exhaled slowly. "All right, well, let's see where they came from. Hopefully we'll find this 'mastermind' Elaethia was talking about."

Geran picked up and stowed his weapons before moving to where the sabercats had attacked from. The ranger inspected the ground, seemingly following an invisible trail for a few hundred meters.

Eventually Lilian piped up. "What're you doing, Geran? Tracking them?"

"Yeah, I'm following their spoor to see where they originated from."

"Spore? Like the mushroom stuff?"

"Similar word, different meaning. Spoor is anything left over from whatever you're tracking: footprints, impressions, trash, feces, broken branches—anything that could indicate where they've been."

"Sounds kinda hard."

"It is, so if you don't mind …"

"Gosh all right, all right," Lilian sighed, and she turned to Elaethia. "Do you know about this 'spoor' thing?"

"It is a new concept to me as well. However, I believe the best thing to do now is let Geran concentrate. We can learn best by watching him."

"Hmph." The demicat made a face but followed along in silence.

Elaethia intently studied the forest around her as Geran led them through it. She didn't have much else to do, considering how slowly they were moving. Geran wound, twisted, turned, backtracked, and froze so often that she began to wonder whether or not he really knew what he was doing. What stopped her from believing these thoughts was her ability to hear the words he muttered under his breath as he stalked along: "Divots," "gait," "dig," "roll," "fresh." She knew the words he was saying but could not figure out how they were pieced together. Elaethia had been told by many people how experienced he was, so she chose to remain silent and trust him further.

As the hours ticked by, Elaethia became restless. Looking over at Lilian, she saw that the bubbly mage was experiencing the same feelings, only more so. The demicat trudged and meandered around in circles behind them, muttering under her breath about her boredom and how lame rangers were. Elaethia chose to continue her silent watch over the deciduous forest around them. It was no surprise that they had not been attacked since the first encounter. But this meant one of two things: The beasts were either deliberately avoiding them or were setting up for a full assault. Either way, her initial suspicion was confirmed. Someone was behind this.

Geran suddenly stopped in front of a thicket. "This has to be it. There're signs of sabercat activity all over the place."

Elaethia squinted into the thick brush. "There is most likely a large ambush awaiting us within."

"Then we need to flush them out," Geran stated. "Lilian, anything you can do to get the ball rolling?"

"Hm-hmm," the mage hummed confidently. The demicat flapped her cloak and twirled her staff. Her left hand flew up and slowly gripped the brim of her witch hat. She struck a pose with a burning gleam in her eye and took the stage. "'Bout time I got to unleash some heavy-hitting magic! You guys might want to stand back."

Lilian got into a stance as Geran and Elaethia stood a few meters behind her. Lilian inhaled slowly and then thrust her staff forward. Her eyes suddenly flashed. The air in the thicket brightened for a moment before a deafening explosion rocked the forest. The shock from the detonation knocked Geran off his feet, while Elaethia had to take a step back to keep her own footing. The surrounding grove trembled from the blast. Leaves and branches fell from the trees all around them. A smokey orange mushroom cloud billowed up from the now-flaming thicket. Searing heat radiated from the inferno. Sabercats fled in all directions from the blaze, their terrified yowls dissipating into the surrounding woods.

Lilian looked on with enormous satisfaction at her handiwork. She turned back to her stunned party with a thumbs-up. Her once bright green eyes now matched the color of the surrounding forest.

"Welp, that used up almost all my magic. I'll be good to use heavy stuff in maybe fifteen minutes, but I can pop my potion if I have to. Think you guys can take it from here?"

"Idiots!" a shrill, male voice screeched from the thicket. A middle-aged dwarf emerged from the burning grove and flailed a splintered staff around. His tattered robes and hair were smoldering, and there were burns and scars all over his face and arms. The dwarf's voice was riddled with insanity. "Imbeciles! Fools! Stupid, stupid meddlers! You ruined it! You ruined everything!"

"Ruined what?" Geran demanded. "Are you behind these sabercat attacks?"

"Of course! Who else is smart and powerful enough to control these beasts? Certainly not someone so dull and careless as an elemental mage! You *disgrace* of a magician! How can you call yourself a wielder of the arcane arts and do something so moronic! Have you *any* idea how long it took me to perfect the spell? How many clawings and scars I got perfecting this art? Of course not! You're just a *stupid* girl who only cares for destruction!"

Lilian trembled with anger. The demicat's tail had bushed out, and her ears were laid back. Her eyes were ablaze with an intensity equal to the roaring thicket.

Elaethia stepped forward. "What art? What were you doing?"

"Controlling my babies, you dimwit! Were you not listening? This took me *decades*! I had found a way to control animals with my anatomy magic! I could make them do as I pleased! Oh, but it wasn't perfect; it wasn't *quite* perfect. I couldn't make them do anything against their instincts—no, no, no. They wouldn't listen to me then. I was going to take this information to the capital, see? I was going to be an Arcane Sage! But they turned me away! I was too unstable, they said. Inhumane, they said! This magic was forbidden, they said! Forbidden? *Ha!* This should be spread to the world! Can you imagine? If we could control our animals, we wouldn't need to train them! There would be no need to breed or raise them in a certain way! No, no, no, all of that would be unnecessary. But they wouldn't listen, and they threw me away!"

"So why attack civilians? Isn't your beef with the Sages?" Geran asked.

"Practice, practice, practice. I needed to get it right. It needed to be perfect! I couldn't lead an assault on the Moon's Pillar with a half-baked spell and unpredictable animals! No, no, no. And I couldn't have my babies practice on you adventurers; you'd hurt them! I can't attack with injured babies! But you meddled around! You made me turn them on you, and you killed them! I was going to show those fools at the Moon's Pillar! But none of that matters now."

His unhinged gaze turned to Lilian. "You ... You ruined everything. My life's work, my purpose, my dream—gone up in flames! Ruined! If I can't have my revenge on the Sages, I'll have it on you!"

With a wild shriek, he ran toward the mage, his staff raised above his head as spittle flew from his mouth. A maniacal cackle warbled from his lips as he charged the demicat with undeniable intent.

Elaethia hefted her axe but was halted by Geran. The ranger stepped forward and threw Lilian behind him. In the space of a second, he drew his bow, nocked an arrow, aimed, and released in one fluid motion. The shot sailed through the air and into the sorcerer's throat. The old dwarf lurched back and crumpled to the ground. The lunatic choked on his own blood as the life vanished from his eyes.

"Sorry … my … babies …" The sorcerer gurgled as he reached to the blazing thicket. His arm fell, and he said no more. The party stood for a moment to process what had just happened.

"Dull and careless elemental mage?" Lilian suddenly burst out. "Where the *hell* does he get off saying something like that! Does he *really* think we just wave our staffs around, blowing things up? No! Explosions that big take *years* to get right! The first time I got one that size, I passed out from exhaustion on the spot! Does he really think we only care about blowing things up? Well, maybe, but that's beside the point! I just … *Augh!*" Lilian stamped her foot and paced back and forth while muttering under her breath, her tail lashing from side to side.

Geran stepped in. "We can continue our tantrums later. Our next order of business is making sure this fire doesn't spread any further. Lilian, can you get this under control? It's your magic."

"I don't know, Geran!" she snapped. "Can you un-shoot that dumbass sorcerer? It's *your* arrow!"

"Jeez, who put your tail in a knot?"

"Take a wild guess!"

"Excuse me," Elaethia said as she strode past them and stepped unhesitatingly into the raging inferno.

"What the hell, Elaethia! Are you crazy?"

Lilian tried to run forward, but Geran caught her arm. "Hold on; she probably knows what she's doing!"

Lilian wheeled around. "She said her dragonite armor resists minor elemental spells. *Explosion* is *not* a minor spell!"

"She may be naive, but she's not an idiot. She's probably done this before!"

"But …" the mage looked back and forth between the ranger and the fiery thicket.

"Have some faith in your party." Geran's expression did not match his words, but both of them knew there wasn't much either of them could do.

Lilian reached into her pouch and pulled out her potion. "If nothing happens in the next ten seconds, I'm downing this and pouring as much frost magic in there as I can."

Just as she finished the sentence, the heat from the blaze began to subside. After a moment, sharp crackling could be heard from within. In an instant, an enormous eruption of vicious ice spikes exploded from the thicket. The flames gave way to the sudden, overpowering frozen mass. Geran and Lilian's mouths fell open. The vapor of their breath issued in steamy clouds. After a second, muffled sounds of shattering ice began to emanate from the formation. They grew louder and louder until Elaethia burst her way through. Out of breath, she walked over to them and took off her helmet. Sweat flowed profusely down her face, her hair drenched and disheveled.

"That," she panted, "was very unpleasant."

Chapter 5
Samurai

Sixth era. 139. Mertim 17.

Elaethia tried to maintain a watchful eye on the surrounding forest as they returned to the main road. But through her profuse sweating and heavy breathing, she found the task difficult. Her eyes drifted to the ground as she walked, and her head felt heavy. She lifted a gauntlet to push away a lock of sweat-streaked hair that had started to stick to the side of her face and dangle in her eye. This was the first time she had attempted something so drastic. She very much hopped that it would be the last.

"I thought you were supposed to be a juggernaut," Lilian stated as she cocked an ear. "But you look super drained right now."

"I will admit this is the first time I have felt so out of breath since my transformation," Elaethia said. "Walking into that fire was well beyond my comfort level."

Geran looked the warrior up and down. "You all right? You don't have any burns or anything that we need to treat?"

"No, my armor protected me from the flames. It was the heat that was unbearable. If Lilian's spell had affected a reasonably bigger area, I may not have succeeded."

The mage blinked. "You think so? I didn't even go full blowout on that one."

"How much was in it?" Geran asked.

"Most of it. I used a little in the first fight, and I wanted to save a little bit more just in case."

"What would it look like if you had expended all of your magic?" Elaethia asked.

Lilian flashed a mischievous fanged grin. "I can show you sometime if we have a day where nothing's going on. We'd have to find somewhere pretty far away, though. I got yelled at last time 'cause *apparently* clearing an abandoned farm property of bandits by blowing it to hell is 'irresponsible' and 'a public nuisance' or whatever."

Elaethia stopped as she and Lilian suddenly met each other's gaze. "Lilian, your eyes … They are not normal. Are you ill?"

"What, this?" she asked as she pointed at her dim green eyes. "Oh, yeah, I'm fine. This happens when magicians use a lot of magic. Yours are doing it a little too. It's totally normal—and a dead giveaway that a magician you're fighting is runnin' outta juice."

"I see," Elaethia said. "That is valuable information. Can you tell me anything else I should know about magic?"

"Sure. We've got time to kill on the way back."

Elaethia was rather disappointed with the amount of knowledge she obtained in the two-hour return. Her understanding of magic was novice-level at best, and it took half the time for Lilian to figure out where to even begin. All Elaethia could learn was the differences between "casts" (which were instant and versatile spells) and "channels" (which were long-lasting spells that required constant focus). There was a third type of spell called a "transformation." Lilian tried explain that transformations were a cross between "casts" and "channels" but were also completely different. It was at this point that Elaethia started to get a headache and requested a change of topic.

Lilian then directed the conversation towards an advanced practice in magic called specializing. Through a procedure, a magician could dedicate themselves to a single class of magic in their school. Elemental magicians could choose between fire, frost, air, and lightning. Druids could choose between forest, water, and earth magic. Holy magicians had only two options, being sun and moon magic. Once a magician chose a class, they unlocked more advanced spells within it. But as a result they could never use the other classes again. Apparently by becoming a dragon hero, Elaethia was automatically specialized in frost.

Geran halted the party abruptly as they reached the guild. "Hold up! Crap, I can't believe I forgot. Everyone check your gear."

Lilian raised an eyebrow. "Why?"

"Accountability. Make sure you have everything you came here with, as well as anything we may have looted."

"We took nothing from our adversaries," Elaethia said.

"Okay, but do you have everything else? Let's open our bags and make sure we didn't lose anything. Also, Lilian, here's the trash from your provisions." He held out the wrappings of her field meal.

The mage glanced away and started for the door. "Well, I think I ought to take a bath. Gosh, does a girl get sweaty after a quest like that."

"Oh no you don't!" Geran swiped at her to grab her cloak or tail, but she danced out of his reach and darted into the building.

"Don't worry; I'll come collect my share of the reward later!" She called before she slammed the door behind her.

"That girl," Geran muttered. He and Elaethia set their packs on the ground and began to take account of their belongings.

"A reasonable task," Elaethia noted. "But rather unnecessary in this scenario."

Geran grunted as they headed inside. "I beg to differ. But if Lilian loses something and we don't know where to look for it, it sucks to be her. We really should have done this before we started back, but better late than never, right? Let's go turn the quest in and then clean ourselves up. You deserve that bath more than Lilian does."

"Oh! There you two are," Maya said as they entered.

"Have you been looking for us?" Elaethia asked.

"Not me specifically, but someone else. A young man. Foreign, short but well built, very strange facial features and armor. I've never seen a human like him in my life. I take it he didn't find you out there."

Geran narrowed his eyes. "Apparently not. That description sounds a little suspicious. Did he have a weird accent and use strange titles with your names?"

Maya's ears wiggled. "Yeah, how did you know?"

"Now *that* is odd. What's one of them doing here?"

Elaethia tilted her head. "I do not understand. Who is he?"

"Someone from one of the few places I don't have reliable ties with. Maya, where are his escorts? Unless he was one of them?"

"Neither, he was alone," the receptionist said.

"That ain't good. Where did he go?"

Maya shook her head. "I'm not sure. Apparently he came in here frantically looking for Elaethia. I was on break at the time, but Bridgette told me Peter helped him out."

"She let *Stone* help?"

Maya sighed. "That ditz of a dwarf should have known better than to trust Peter. He's over by the bar with his party. Maybe he's feeling generous enough to tell you where that foreigner went."

"I appreciate it, Maya," Geran said. He turned to Elaethia. "It may be a bit before we can clean off, Elaethia. I want to make sure this doesn't get out of hand."

"Understood. Who is this stranger? Is he in trouble?"

"One way or another," the ranger muttered.

Elaethia and Geran approached the portion of the bar that Peter Stone and the rest of his party were sitting at. The muscular blond human held a stein above his head and was guffawing about something with an equally massive demibear. A gray-haired demicat sat quietly on the left with a bottle of pink liquid in his hands. The first of the veteran party to look up was a dwarven priestess who held a glass of what seemed to be juice.

"Good afternoon, Geran," she said.

"How's it going, Blanche?" he greeted. "Is this a good time to talk to Peter?"

The black-haired priestess shrugged. "Depends how badly you want to. He and Micah are both pretty deep in the drink, so they'll either be chatty or feisty."

Elaethia stepped forward. "Then I will be sure to persuade them to speak."

Blanche looked up at the armored woman and quickly averted her gaze back to Geran. "W-well I hope for the best. I've already patched them both up from yesterday's quest, so please don't let Miss Elaethia hurt them."

Peter turned around and sneered. "Ooh, yes, Mr. Geran! Please don't let the big lady hurt us!"

The ranger folded his arms. "No promises."

The air began to chill as Elaethia took another step. "I highly advise you hold your tongue for everything besides the information we wish to acquire."

"Get your panties out of a bunch," the demibear snorted. "Jeez, some people can't take a joke."

Geran held a hand up. "Forget it, Micah. We aren't here on a social call. An Osakyotan came in here looking for Elaethia, and *Peter* here sent him somewhere. We'd like to go collect him."

"Huh?" the human warrior leaned back with bloodshot eyes. "Osa-what now? I don't know what that means. I'm trying to have a contest with Micah here, and you guys are ruining it. Don't try to make me use brain power on your guys' problems."

Geran groaned. "My problem could very quickly turn into *all* of our problems if we don't find him. If that guy is killed or captured, we could be talking about a potential international conflict."

"International conflict," Micah scoffed. "You've always loved making things into bigger problems than they really are, Geran. He'll be back eventually; just go away and let us drink."

"No problem then. Just tell us where you sent him and we'll leave."

Peter flexed and cracked his knuckles. "You're not taking the hint, are you, Nightshade? I don't like being told what to do. And now I *really* don't feel like telling you. Since you've decided to start being unreasonable, it looks like I'm gonna have to teach you some courtesy."

Geran took a step back. "Damn it, Peter, why do you always have to make things so difficult?"

"I think I'm being pretty fair. All I said was I was gonna teach you a lesson. I didn't say anything about seriously hurting you. Keep that mouth running and I'll up those stakes."

"C'mon, you big lunk, I don't have time for this! I'll buy your next round or something; just tell us already."

"The hell'd you just call me? C'mere!" Peter shot a hand out to grab Geran's shirt. The ranger instantly raised his arms to defend himself from the drunken warrior.

Elaethia got there first. Peter obviously expected to get a fistful of Geran's leather tunic. Instead he found his hand clasped with a cold dragonite gauntlet. Elaethia clenched his hand in her own and twisted his arm to the bar. The dragon hero pinned the human to the counter and used her other hand to grab the side of his face and slam it to the wooden surface.

"*Ow!*" Peter shouted. "What the hell?"

"I warned you," she said in a dangerously calm voice. "Answer the question."

Before Peter could respond, the pop of a cork came from behind him. The quiet, gray-haired demicat opened the vial of pink liquid and thrust it into Elaethia's face. The thin liquid quickly turned to mist as it struck her and seeped into her lungs. She felt her muscles turn lax and her eyes droop. She released her grip and took a step back to shake her head. Elaethia blinked and coughed a few times before looking up to see that demicat holding the now-empty bottle level with her face.

"Man," he said in an Eastern Svarengel accent. "Ya really *are* a tough bastard. That was s'pposed to be enough to make a troll sleep fer a week."

"I didn't need your help, Christoph!" Peter growled, massaging his neck.

"If I listen'd to ya every time you said that, ya'd be a constellation by now. I've been workin' on this one fer months, y'know. Ya owe me big time, Stone."

"Yeah, yeah, I get it. I'll buy you whatever ingredients you need."

"Ya can't *buy* these ingredients anywhere near here. Not fer a price ya can afford anyway. We're goin' to have to find them in the wild. This stuff isn't exactly common, either. It'll take at least a month to make up for this, not even includin' the magical alterations I'll have to instill in it."

"Tch," Peter spat. "Alchemists."

Micah sighed and leaned against the bar. "Well, Geran. Now that you've ruined our afternoon, I might as well tell you what you want so you'll leave. We sent that foreigner over to the Lonely Fox. He left about half an hour ago, maybe a little less."

Geran's jaw dropped. "You *what!*"

Peter began to chuckle. "He was such a serious-lookin' fella. We thought he could use something to help him relax."

"Stars above, Peter, that's cruel!"

"You're just a prude, Geran. If you hurry, you might catch him before he's ruined."

"Gaaaah! We have to go, *now!*" Geran grabbed Elaethia by the wrist and started to pull her to the door as Peter and Micah burst out into laughter.

Elaethia's head finally cleared itself from the potion. "What is the matter?"

Geran gritted his teeth. "That foreigner's been sent somewhere pretty unholy. We've got to get to him before something happens."

Her eyes narrowed. "Is his life in danger?"

"It's his dignity we're worried about."

"I see."

"No. No you don't. Just come on!"

The two of them ran down the cobblestone road to the northernmost part of the city. Elaethia followed Geran as he weaved his way through narrow streets and alleys. It was nearing dusk, so the sun was still up, but the surrounding city seemed to darken around them as Geran pushed past citizens and vendors to get to this strange destination.

The ranger suddenly halted in front of a two-story wooden building with no windows. A single sign hung over the front door: "The Lonely Fox." Scantily-clad women leaned over the railing of the front porch, eyeing the ranger as he drew near. A few were taking deep inhalations from long metal pipes. One of them blew out a slow puff of smoke as Geran approached.

"Hey there, handsome," she called out. "I've never seen you around here before. Care to have me show you around?"

"Solid pass. Elaethia, stay out here, please. This isn't a place you'd do well in."

She nodded. "I do not understand. But if you insist, I will keep watch."

"Oh, honey," another woman cooed as she took a step toward him. "Don't want your lady friend to watch? It's all right. I can treat you better than she can anyway."

Geran ran past her up the creaky wooden stairs. "I'm not here for business, just to pick up a friend."

"Hmph, shame," she sighed, and she pushed out her chest. "Let us know if you … change your mind."

"Not likely."

Less than a minute later, he reappeared with a very odd young man. He appeared to be in his late teens or early twenties and was rather short—a few inches shorter than Elaethia. He had stiff, coarse, jet-black hair that was gathered behind his head in a small bun. The sides of his head were shaved in a high fade. The stranger had pale skin and small, dark, slanted eyes. The odd human walked confidently but still held firmly to Geran's arm.

The most noticeable feature, however, was his apparel. She could tell it was armor, but it was nothing like anything she had ever seen before. It was metal, but it was plated in curved layers with padding in between. Several studded sheets lay upon one another, the thickest parts being on his chest, groin, thighs, and shoulders. Underneath it was loose clothing, cut off by tight red leather boots and arm braces. The dark metal armor was held together by red straps that protruded from metal studs. In one hand he held an open-faced helmet with similar long-layered plating that circled the back and sides. In his other he held a sheathed longsword with a small circular hilt and a slightly curved blade.

"Thank you, sir …" he said shakily. "Your friend, Peter-san, told me this location was the place I was looking for. But I think he might have been mistaken."

Geran patted him firmly on the shoulder. "I never said he was my friend. Are you good? They didn't do anything to you, did they?"

"N-no, but they tried to undress me. If you hadn't come, I don't know what would have happened."

"A lot more than you would have bargained for. How much did they charge?"

The black-haired man shook his head. "I don't know. The woman at the counter just took some from my purse. I don't know the amount, but it feels very light now."

Geran turned to one of the girls on the porch. "Hey, how much did your mistress take?"

An elf wearing a translucent gown shrugged. "Dunno. No refunds, though."

"Figures," Geran growled through his teeth.

Elaethia's eyes hardened. "Have these women stolen from this man? Shall I go reacquire his funds?"

"Don't bother." Geran glared at the shady building as he led them back to the guild. "They aren't worth our time."

Geran turned to the strange man as they returned. "All right. We're safe now. Have you recovered enough to tell us your name?"

The stranger's eyes shot open.

"Oh! My apologies." He faced them stiffly and offered a deep bow. "My name is Shiro Inahari! It is an honor to make your acquaintance … uh …"

"Geran."

"Geran-san!"

"Likewise. We've been told you've been looking for us—specifically Elaethia here. What's your business with her?"

Shiro's body seized as he whipped his gaze to the dragon hero. His face lost all color. "Y-you are Elaethia?"

She tilted her head. "Are you well?"

He suddenly threw himself onto his knees and pressed his forehead against the ground at Elaethia's feet. "Forgive me! I had heard your description, but I would never have imagined that you would come to me! I have traveled across this land to find and come before you, in hopes that you will let me journey with you!"

Geran flinched back. "What in the—"

Shiro brought himself to a knee and doubled over in a bow as he pounded his right fist across his chest in salute. "I beg of you! Please allow me to join in your services! Even if I can't fight at your side, I will make use of myself by carrying your belongings and acting as a lowly servant. I humbly offer you my loyalty, Elaethia-sama!"

Everyone in the area had stopped, completely stunned by the sudden action.

"Th-that is not my name" was all Elaethia managed to get out.

Shiro's face turned beet red. "Y-you are not Elaethia?"

"I am, but you said my name differently that second time."

"That's because he's from Osakyota," Geran stated. "You're alone, aren't you? That means you evaded your escorts, they're dead, or you never had any. I'm assuming it's that last option, isn't it?"

"Yes sir!" Shiro shouted, bowing again.

"Well. That answers a lot of questions but brings up even more."

Elaethia tilted her head. "I do not understand."

"I doubt you will for a while. Hey, Shiro, was it?"

"Yes sir!" the prostrating Osakyotan barked.

"By the Moon, stand up. We don't do that here. You're freaking everybody out."

"Right! My most sincere apologies!" Shiro shot up and stood stiffly in front of them again. A noticeable red mark appeared on his forehead from where it had hit the ground.

"You know of this man?" Elaethia asked Geran.

"No, but I've worked with and against people from his country before. They're a ... different bunch. It takes a while to get used to them. But I imagine he's had it even harder coming here."

Shiro looked from Geran to Elaethia and back to Geran, clearly in heavy self-conflict. He slowly looked to the ground after an awkward moment of silence. "It ... has been very difficult, yes," he admitted.

"Then let's go inside and talk," Geran said. "We can't block the entryway forever."

Geran led the nervous Osakyotan and a befuddled Elaethia into the guildhall. Everyone inside stared at the strange group as they opened the door.

"I see you found him," Maya said as they entered.

Geran raised an eyebrow. "Yeah. Did you know that Peter sent him to a brothel?"

The elf's eyes widened. "He *what?* No wonder you two dashed out of here like that. Is he all right?"

"He's fine; he didn't lose anything important. I'd be more worried about Peter if I were you. Blond meathead was practically rolling on the floor when we left. I've got a feeling Elaethia might decide to have words with him later."

Geran led Shiro and Elaethia to their usual table and prompted them to sit. Elaethia took her seat right away, but Shiro remained standing.

Geran sighed. "Jeez, Shiro, relax. All those formalities your people do make me uncomfortable."

"O-of course. Excuse me." He pulled a chair back and sat stiffly in it, placing his hands on top of his thighs. Shiro sat perfectly straight, heels flat on the floor, his back not touching the chair.

The ranger inhaled. "So, Shiro—"

"Yes sir!"

He flinched. "Gaaaah, don't do that!"

Shiro held his hands out tensely. "I'm sorry!"

"He seems nervous," Elaethia noted.

Geran gave her a sideways look. "What was your first clue?"

"His eyes. They do not stay in one place for long."

"I'm genuinely surprised that you noticed that."

"Is that so? Perhaps you can inform me of other traits I should be aware of."

"Yes!" Shiro nodded. "Inform me, too! This seems like valuable information, and I wish to present myself as professionally as possible!"

Geran rubbed his eyes and then exhaled slowly.

"Stars above. I can't believe I have to deal with two of them now. Okay, Shiro, what's your deal coming to us? Yeah, sure, Elaethia is incredible and all, so I'd understand if you wanted to join us to get famous. But there's no way in hell people from your country have heard about her yet. Even then, I can't imagine you sailing over here *just* for that. In fact, last I checked, Osakyota didn't allow its citizens to come to the main continent. Only military men and ambassadors with permission from the emperor. So excuse me if I don't fully believe you."

Shiro planted his hands on the table. "It's true! I mean, I came to Linderry looking for anyone. But the legends and stories I'd heard about Elaethia-sama showed that she was not only a matchless warrior but a righteous one too. I heard of this shortly after leaving the region of Clearharbor. You're correct, though. I didn't come here with the emperor's permission. Nevertheless, I tried to make myself useful to the population, but I'm so utterly lost here. I don't understand anything about this country. I just needed to find someone who could help me clear my name."

"Why did you not stay in Clearharbor?" Elaethia asked.

"I acquainted myself with a bad group of people by mistake. I couldn't stay in one place for long, either. People were doing strange things: making objects and energy appear out of nothing. And there are humans with animal features. It's unnatural! Everywhere I go, it's there!"

"You have never seen magic or demihumans?" Elaethia asked.

"Magic? I've heard stories of it, but I don't know what it is. It's not evil or unholy, is it?"

"Not even close," Geran assured him. "Magic isn't evil; it's a tool—a gift from the Heavens. Magic is evil like a sword is evil; it's all about the person using it. I think I remember an ambassador explaining something to me. They don't have demihumans in Osakyota, and they keep the knowledge of magic a secret. Hmm, Elaethia, it's probably best we keep him away from—"

"Oh, hey, there you guys are!" Lilian's voice sounded behind them.

"Shhhhheeeeit," Geran's eyes widened as the mage bounced over to them in her casual wear.

"Hello, Lilian," Elaethia greeted the mage.

"Hiya!" she chirped. "I was wondering where you guys popped off to. Oh? Who's this?"

The demicat looked curiously at Shiro. The Osakyotan turned red as he noticed her fluffy ears and tail. He shot up to double over in a bow again.

"I-I am, uh, Shiro Inahari! It-It's a meet you to pleasure!"

"Huh? Is there something on the floor?"

Lilian bent over herself to examine the ground she thought he was looking at. Her ears brushed the top of his head as she did. He made an "eep" noise, doubled backward, and knocked his chair over. Shiro scrambled to pick it up and sat down at the table again, as stiff as a board.

Lilian cocked an ear. "You okay?"

Geran introduced the Osakyotan. "Lilian, this is Shiro. Long story short, he uh … wants to join the party."

"Party up with us?" She looked at the Osakyotan. His eyes met hers and then quickly darted away as he turned pink. A devilish grin that reached the demicat's ears spread throughout her face.

"Lilian …" Geran said.

Lilian purred as she took a suggestive step toward Shiro. "Ohhh*hhh*? So *that's* what this cutie wants. Gosh, well how lucky are we to have such a guy come to us."

Shiro jumped out of his seat and extended a hand. "I-I understand a custom here is to, uh, 'shake hands.' Please, um … shake my hand!"

"Aww, you're so sweet," she hummed as she held his hand and brought it up. She gave him a gentle face with big, fluttery eyes. "I'm Lilian Whitepaw. I hope we can become good friends."

Sweat poured down Shiro's face as he started to tremble. "I, um, o-of course, I …"

"If you're not too busy later, I could show you around. I know of a few secluded places where we could—"

Geran reached over and chopped sharply on the top of her head. She mewled and dropped into a crouch, rubbing where she had been struck.

"Ow-ow-ow-ow-ow."

"Lilian, leave the poor guy alone," Geran scolded. "Shiro's having a rough enough time as it is, especially from the local women. Don't make it worse."

Lilian folded her arms and pouted. "Meanie."

"Sorry about her," he said to Shiro with a glare at the demicat. "She likes to play games—sometimes at the expense of others."

She turned away and stuck out her tongue with her ears pointed back.

"Is she … a demihuman?" Shiro asked while his face returned to its natural color.

Geran grunted. "Yep. Demicat. One of the strangest ones you'll ever meet."

"Hey!" Lilian shot up. "Don't do my introduction for me!"

"Someone has to. You can't do it properly yourself."

"Proper? Pfft, that's so lame!"

Shiro piped up and faced her. "Amazing … I've seen demihumans all over Linderry, but I've never been able to talk to one! Well, except for one from this evening, but she was doing most of the talking … and the … feeling …"

Lilian gave him a sideways look. "What does *that* mean? And what's wrong with the demihumans in Osakyota?"

"We don't have them back home. I was very confused when I stepped off the ship in Clearharbor to see humans with animal ears and tails."

"Why didn't you talk with any of the ones there?"

"I suppose I didn't get the chance. That and it wasn't one of my concerns at the time. But now I have an opportunity!"

Geran stepped in. "You do realize that demihumans are just normal brehdars, right?"

"Huh?"

"Yeah, you can literally just talk to her like any other person."

"But. I, um …" Shiro peered over Geran's shoulder to look at Lilian, who was gently batting her eyes. He blushed again and glanced away. Geran turned around to look at the demicat, who had shifted her expression and started to whistle casually. The ranger exhaled with a sigh of exasperation.

"Moon give me patience. All right, we can talk about demihumans and magic later, okay? Shiro, you said you came here without permission. Why? What made you illegally flee Osakyota?"

"To prevent dishonor from befalling my family."

Geran rolled his hand. "Right, right. You guys are obsessed with family honor and all that, but why? How does you coming here accomplish that?"

"Let me start from the beginning." Shiro sat back and inhaled slowly. "I am the eldest son of the Inahari family. My father is the revered general, nationally known as the northern shogun. Because of him, we had wealth and status in Osakyota. Unfortunately that meant a nobleman in the city we lived in hated our family, since the emperor gave my father more respect than him. He became so obsessed with discrediting my family that he forgot about his own. His wife took it with grace, but his only daughter became rebellious and started running with bad crowds. Soon she was being seen with known members of bandit clans. But her father was too occupied to take it seriously.

"With the nobleman not caring about the city, crime began to flourish. Even our own home wasn't safe. One night I awoke to the sound of struggling and screaming from my sister's room. I grabbed my sword and rushed to help her, but I was too slow. I arrived to see the nobleman's daughter standing over my sister with a bloody knife. I remember fighting and trying to save my sister, but it was too late. She was dead …"

Geran leaned forward. "So you killed that daughter in retaliation?"

Shiro nodded. "This feud would destroy both our families' reputations. My killing her was justifiable under normal circumstances, but since she was noble it caused a power contest. I was instantly branded a murderer. Maybe I am. My family knew the safest thing to do was get me out of the country. My father and I fled to the docks, where he was able to sneak me aboard an ambassador's vessel. I was on that ship for three days."

"Gosh, that's rough." Lilian frowned. "Not to be rude or anything, but that's kinduva heavy story to tell us right off the bat. I mean, we hardly know each other."

"I've been told that I trust people too easily … But someone as powerful and famous as Elaethia-sama has to be a good person! And if you're all her friends, then I know I can trust you, too. But you're right. I wanted to prove myself useful to the city of Clearharbor and its communities. But a lot of people took advantage of my desperation and skill, only to cast me aside after they were done with me. But then I heard of a woman in Breeze that was so strong she could take on ten bandits by herself like it was nothing. I instantly set off alone, getting attacked by men, monsters, and beasts the whole way until I got here. From there you know the rest."

Shiro stood and faced the dragon hero. "Elaethia-sama. I know I may never amount to what you are, and may be unworthy to stand by your side, but—" He was interrupted by Geran.

"Hold on a second; this is a lot to take in. I've been around Elaethia enough to know when something is too much for her to process."

Elaethia suddenly stood. "I accept."

"Wai- what?"

She ignored Geran and walked over to Shiro and placed a gauntlet on his shoulder. "I know hardship, loss, and purpose more than anything. Hearing your story reminds me of myself, as well as my own goal. I would never be able to face my father or Frossgar again if I turned away a fate-driven man such as yourself."

"Now hold on!" Geran sputtered. "Elaethia, you can't just allow someone into the party without consulting us first. We don't even know the guy!"

"Do you have objections?" she asked in a dangerous tone. Lilian simply shook her head, while Geran took a step back.

"Well, if he got here on his own with only what we see on him, he's got to be proficient at what he does. He seems like a good guy; it's just so sudden." He paused and then looked at Shiro. "You were able to fight off bandits, monsters, and beasts all the way here and came out unharmed?"

Shiro nodded.

"All right," Geran said, "I suppose. We can always kick him out later if there're any issues."

Shiro regarded him with relief and then looked up at Elaethia. "You're defending me? But you don't even know me."

"I know your story and your heart," she stated firmly. "A man of your dedication and resolve is rare and incredibly valuable. I would be honored to welcome you to the party."

Shiro got down to a knee as he drew his curved longsword to present it to her. "Then I hereby swear myself to your service, Elaethia-sama. I am your sword and servant, and I will gladly lay my life down for you."

Elaethia saw herself as a little girl falling in front of Frossgar with the same resolve. "I understand. More than you know. But I will never ask you to die for me. We fight alongside each other as equals. Do not think of me as your master. None of us is more important than the other."

"Thank you." A single tear streamed from Shiro's eye as he choked on his response. "Thank you so much, Elaethia-sama."

Elaethia too knelt in front of the young man. Shiro's ragged breath told her that he was fighting back tears. For whatever reason, he refused to let them flow. Elaethia didn't understand, but that didn't matter. Shiro was a broken man held together only by his honor and courage.

Lilian quietly turned to Geran. "I almost feel bad for teasing him now."

The ranger raised an eyebrow. "Almost?"

"Well of course I'm gonna keep at it! I haven't gotten a reaction like that since … *ever!* Are all Osakyotans like that?"

"Yes and no. But I think he's just a little bit … more so."

"Hmm," she noted. "By the way, why's he saying her name all funny?"

"It's something they do over there. He'll probably do the same for us."

"What's it mean?" she asked.

"Dunno. You'll have to ask him."

"Why's his armor so different?"

"That's just how they design it."

"How come he does all that bowing stuff?"

Geran threw his hands up. "By the Moon, Lilian, I don't know everything about their culture! Ask him yourself!"

"He seems a little busy."

"I didn't mean right now," he growled.

Once Shiro had regained his composure, he got to his feet and walked up to the two of them with Elaethia behind him.

"Thank you again for allowing me to travel with you. I look forward to fighting together, and I will not let you down. I assure you I will prove both my worth and my heart, Geran-san, Lilian-chan."

"Told ya," Geran said to Lilian.

"Say, what do those mean?" she asked Shiro.

He blinked. "What does what mean?"

"Like the 'san' 'chan' 'sama' thing. Why do you slap those on the ends of our names?"

"That's just how we ... I don't know how to explain it." He looked apologetically at Geran for help.

The ranger shrugged. "The Osakyotans I worked with also called me 'Geran-san.' Pretty sure it's like 'mister' or something close to it. I'm gonna tell you the same thing I told them: don't bother with that; just call me Geran."

"So 'chan' is like 'miss'?" Lilian asked. "Why is Elaethia different?"

"We use 'chan' for children or, um, younger women." Shiro said. He blushed as Lilian smiled at him. "I refer to her as Elaethia-sama because I've sworn myself to her and devoted myself to her will. It's a sign of respect. But if it bothers the both of you like Geran-sa ... I mean Geran ... then I'll do my best to stop."

"It matters not to me," Elaethia stated.

Lilian looked off to the left and waved a hand. "I don't mind, really. But if it makes you feel more comfortable, then feel free to keep using it."

"Okay! Then how about Lili-chan?"

The demicat actually seemed to blush. "Well gosh, I mean, if you want."

Elaethia felt the corners of her mouth turn into a smile. The comfortable yet somewhat awkward air around them had disappeared. She knew not the reason for this, but there was no denying the growing sense of companionship. For the first time in a long time, Elaethia felt as though all that could be right in the world *was* right. Until Geran ground the conversation to a halt.

"All this aside," he said, "we're skipping a crucial step. In order for Shiro to be in our party, he has to be a member of the guild. And I can't say for sure whether Master Dameon will make another exception."

"If I'll make another exception for what?" a gruff voice asked from the side.

Elaethia looked up as the others yelped in surprise and doubled back. Shiro looked forward to see an enormous torso. He looked up further to witness a thick beard. The Osakyotan's neck craned nearly straight up as he locked eyes with the massive demibear that towered over him.

"It-it's a monster!" he shouted, and he drew his sword. Shiro leaped in front of Elaethia, warily holding the blade toward what he obviously perceived as a threat. Geran and Lilian drew in sharp breaths and were about to shout out against the action until Master Dameon put his hands on his hips and guffawed.

"Hah! You've got quite the backbone to draw a blade at me in my own guildhall! I like that. Monster, eh? Haven't been called that in a while."

Geran blew out a sigh of relief. "Thank the heavens ..."

Master Dameon grunted. "Now, I heard there was a foreigner sniffing around here. Thought I'd come down to make sure some bigwig from another country wasn't trying to push my rascals around. Bah, you look harmless. What's your name, kid?"

Shiro returned his sword to its sheath. "I-I-I … You are the master of this guild? My most sincere apologies! I'm Shiro Inahari! It's a pleasure to meet you!"

"An Osakyotan? In *my* guildhall? How'd they let you out of the country?"

Lilian popped a hand in the air. "Ooh! Ooh! He-murdered-the-murderer-that- murdered-his-sister-but-the-murderer-was-a-noble-so-he-ran-away-to-find-someone-to-clear-his-name-and-he-wants-it-to-be-Elaethia!"

Geran rubbed his face. "What …?"

Elaethia nodded. "He is also of honorable blood. His father is called a northern shogun, and aided his escape."

Master Dameon scratched his thick beard. "You accept his offer, girl?"

"Yes sir," Elaethia responded. "I would very much like to have him at our side."

"Hrmph," he grumbled. "Just by lookin' at him I can tell he won't be causing trouble. But will he be an asset to the guild?"

"I am willing to accept all responsibility for problems he may cause," she declared firmly. Dameon met her steely gaze with his own. After a tense moment, he sighed and folded his arms.

"All right, girl, all right. If it were anyone other than you and Nightshade that asked, however, I woulda thrown him out. Now you! Listen up, Shiro!"

"Yes, Master Dameon-sama!"

"Master Dameon-what now? Ah, whatever. I'm allowing you into this guild. For now. We're gonna go up to my office to get you properly integrated, but first things first. Don't think you'll get any sort of special treatment just because you're a foreigner, understand? Let alone some general's brat. I expect you to pull your weight around here and take quests just like everyone else."

"Yes sir! I assure you that I won't be a bother to your guild!"

"Good. Now follow me. *Brittany!* My office! With an application form!"

"On my way!" a middle-aged demicat called from the reception desk.

"More and more paperwork," the demibear grumbled as he lumbered to the stairs with Shiro in tow. Elaethia stood in silence with her other party members as they watched them leave.

Lilian piped up and plucked the quest flyer from Geran's pouch. "Welp! I think I'll go turn this is. I'll come back with the reward!"

Geran called after her. "We know exactly how much that quest was worth and how many we killed. Don't try anything funny!"

"I won't!" she called back.

Geran turned to Elaethia. "You're really bent on keeping Shiro, aren't you?"

"His goal is most admirable."

"Maybe," he mused, rubbing his stubble beard.

"Do you have concerns about his actions or behavior?"

"A little. I don't expect you to understand, but a guy like that definitely has ulterior motives. Shiro seems straightforward, so I doubt it's anything serious. But there's definitely more to him than meets the eye. Besides, Lilian's gonna run away with that nervous demeanor of his, and some people in this guild will try to chew him up and spit him out."

"We will keep a close eye on him. No one will harm him as long as he is with us."

"Yeah, but a guy like that is usually good at getting himself into trouble."

"We shall see," Elaethia stated. They looked up as Lilian bounced back to the table with a sack of coins.

"Okay!" she chirped. "How are we gonna split this? I say forty-forty-twenty."

"Forty-forty-twenty? Who would even be the twenty?" Geran asked.

Lilian gave him a look.

"Oh hell no. In what world would I accept that?"

"Well, you didn't kill any sabercats. Elaethia and I did all the heavy lifting."

"Yeah, and you wouldn't have found any if it hadn't been for me. On top of that, I killed the sorcerer who controlled all of them, so where does that rank?"

"He wasn't part of the description, so he doesn't count."

"Nice try. You're also ignoring my other point."

Lilian gave him an innocent look. "What other point?"

"I tracked them down. You wouldn't have been able to kill them if I hadn't found them for you."

"I'm sure we could have figured it out."

"I'd like to hear how you'd do that."

"That's beside the point. Kills are kills."

"How is that beside the point? I literally explained how you couldn't kill them if it hadn't been for me!"

"Sounds to me like you're whining because you weren't as awesome as Elaethia and me. Just take your share with grace."

"Listen here, you little hairball, I'm not—" He stopped short as he noticed that the two of them had vapor coming out of their mouths and that the temperature had dropped significantly. They slowly turned to meet Elaethia's cold stare.

Lilian shivered. "Even sound good to you?"

"Yeah," Geran said through chattering teeth. "I like even. Even is good."

After some time had passed, Shiro descended the stairs from the guild master's office. The Osakyotan approached the table and proudly showed them all his tag and application form.

"Look, Elaethia-sama!" he held them in front of her. "I'm officially a part of the guild, which means I can be in your party!"

"Indeed." She smiled. "Welcome to it."

Lilian snatched the items. "Lemme see those! Aw, no fair. You're a year older than me. Samurai? What kinda class is that?"

Shiro puffed out his chest and put a hand on the hilt of his sword. "It's the most honorable title a man such as myself can obtain! I've proven myself a capable warrior and have skill recognized by all!"

Elaethia tilted her head. "So you are a warrior."

"No!" he protested firmly. "Much more than that. My abilities and status are distinguished among other fighters and in society, and I have been recognized as an honorable man! Well, I was, anyway … But my skill with the blade is unmatched back home! Father says my discipline is somewhat lacking, but in combat I am a fearsome opponent."

"So like a duelist with heavy armor then," Geran said plainly.

"No, no, no, it's different! Anyone can pick up a sword and fight, but only a few of us have distinguished ourselves in the art and lifestyle! It takes years of training and meditation to achieve! I had to memorize the seven scrolls that entail our code, and fulfill them in everyday life! It's something your culture can't understand."

The ranger put his hands up. "All right, all right, Shiro. We believe you."

"Thank you," the samurai breathed. "I promise I will prove my worth to all of you! You won't regret it!"

The other three only nodded quietly.

Lilian broke the silence. "All righty then! Now that I got my reward, I'm gonna go crash. You should go take your bath, Elaethia. You kinda stink."

"I have noticed I am in dire need, yes. Let us go."

The two women stood to head upstairs.

Geran turned to Shiro once they left. "All right, I know you have a million questions, and I have some of my own. You go first."

"Yes!" he announced. "What does a guild actually do?"

The ranger rubbed his head. "Hooooo boy. We're gonna start *there?* Take a seat; this'll take a while."

Shiro sat down as Geran gave him a thirty-minute rundown of the guild, adventurers, questing, and the party. The samurai nodded furiously at each point.

"I see now. We're here to help the citizens in exchange for money."

"Basically. Don't get it twisted, though. We're neither heroes nor sell-swords. Adventurers are something in between. Every quest that's posted for us is legally submitted. If we accept a job to kill, arrest, rescue, or do anything else to something or someone, we do it. Which ones we do, and how we do them—that is completely up to our discretion and moral standards. That age-old fairytale of "righteous people do not kill because that makes them no different than villains" has no place here. If you are accepting money to do something, you do it to the letter."

"Understood. When do we go out and make our names famous?"

"That comes with time, if at all. Our best bet is the annual tournament. Maybe if we get really good, our party will get named. If we do something absolutely incredible, we'll be nationally recognized as heroes. But the last person to gain that title in this guild was about ten years ago."

"Oh! Who was it? What did he or she do?"

"Merrick Thatcher, druid. He sacrificed himself to kill a behemoth and saved the entire city."

"Sacrificed himself? So he was nationally recognized as a hero …"

"Postmortem," Geran finished.

"I see. Most unfortunate. But because of him, the city lives. He died with honor."

"Yeah, we all owe it to him. What else you got?"

"Nothing at the moment, but I'll be sure to ask if I think of anything," Shiro said.

"Yeah, I'm sure you will. So you plan to stay here at the hall, or out in town?"

Shiro's forehead wrinkled. "What do you mean?"

"I'm asking where you're going to live. You gotta have some place to sleep and keep your gear and money. You own more than what you have on your person, right?"

The two stared at each other. Shiro's face was blank.

"You don't. Do you?"

The samurai's face began to turn red. "I had not considered this until just now."

"By the Moon …" Geran groaned, folding his arms on the table and burying his head in them. "How much money do you have?"

"Um, let's see …" Shiro muttered, and he pulled out a coin purse. "I have fourteen."

"Gold or silver?"

"Coins," Shiro said.

Geran stared at him. The ranger inhaled and then exhaled slowly as he pushed his own reward money toward the new party member.

"We'll talk more later. I'm sure you're even more burned out than I am. Take this and go up to that desk near the door behind us. That's the receptionist desk, as I explained just now. Maya's over there, and she'll help you."

"The pretty elf with the white hair? All right. Are you sure it's okay to give me this? Isn't it your money?"

"It's fine. Just go," Geran replied through clenched teeth.

"I promise I will make it up to you! Thank you again very much for your—"

"Gooooooo!"

"Yes sir! I'll go right now!"

The Osakyotan scooped the reward money into his pouch and ran up to the reception desk. Geran dropped his head in his arms again, inhaled, and shouted with frustration into the table.

Chapter 6
Cohesion

Sixth Era. 139. Mertim 21.

Elaethia lay faceup on her bed. A sudden and unshakable wave of reflection came over her, specifically regarding the guild and party. She certainly didn't regret it, but it was not at all what she expected. Come to think of it, she didn't know what she expected in the first place. In the span of almost a month, she had already completed several quests and gained three companions. Luckily, the company she had chosen had proven themselves admirable, or at least capable. They were a motley crew, but skilled and experienced.

However, it may have been too soon to say that, considering none of them knew how Shiro fared in combat. His survival skills had to be very high, since he had made it all this way to them with minimal belongings and knowledge. Or so he claimed. On the other hand, he lost his composure easily and was unfamiliar with Linderrian customs and standards. Then again, so was she. If all else failed, she knew, Geran would remove him from the party. Elaethia truly hoped it would never come to that.

A knock on the door broke her concentration. She got up to answer it, revealing a cheerful Lilian gazing up at her.

"Mornin'!" the demicat chirped.

"Good morning. Even though it is nearly noon."

"Well then it's still morning, isn't it?"

"I suppose so," Elaethia agreed. "What can I do for you?"

"Nothin.' I'm bored. Thought I'd just drop in and say hi."

Elaethia blinked. "You came to relieve yourself of boredom by speaking to me?"

Lilian laughed. "Yeah, of course! We're in a party and friends after all. Mind if I come in?"

Elaethia opened the door. "Is that so? Well then, if you wish."

"How'd yesterday's quest go?" Lilian asked. "What was it again? A spriggan getting aggressive with a homestead?"

"Correct. I was able to destroy it without any issue."

"Didja use your magic or just chop it up?"

"I stayed to my weapon," Elaethia said. "My magic is still difficult to control. I would rather not experiment when innocents are nearby. Why do you ask?"

The demicat shrugged. "I just like talking about magic with other mages. It's fun to share stories and compare spells."

"Is that so? I will remember that for the future."

Lilian looked around the room and made a face. "Gosh, your room hasn't changed since you moved in, has it?"

"There has not been a need for it. I do not own much."

"Hmph. No wonder you always look so sad. You live in such a bland space. You oughta spruce it up a bit."

Elaethia tilted her head. "I look sad?"

Lilian sat down on the bed and continued to look around. "Well, you're always so focused and serious. Not sure if I've even seen a real smile on you before."

"We live a serious life, do we not?"

"Well, yeah, but that doesn't mean you have to be like that all the time! We chose to live this life, so we can choose our attitude toward it. I say take it easy and have some fun! Let your hair down a little! Work hard, play hard, I say."

"My hair is usually down," the warrior noted while running her fingers through her black tresses.

"Elaethia, that's not what I … It's a figure of speech. It means to relax."

"I see. What would you suggest?"

Lilian cocked an ear. "Are you asking me how to relax?"

"I know how to rest, but I tire of lying around. That is why I take quests about three times a week. Perhaps you could give me some ideas or activities."

"Well I'm not sure why you're asking *me*. I'm dunno what you do in your spare time. I don't think you'd like any of the stuff I do, unless you like shopping, books, practicing spells, and teasing guys."

"I do not particularly enjoy shopping, and reading has never struck me as entertaining. Dragon magic is also quite difficult to practice in closed spaces."

"Nothing to say about the last point, huh? Well, how about we go out in town? Wander around a bit and see if there's anything you'd like to add to the room. It's pretty empty in here."

"Yes, you did mention that," Elaethia said.

She glanced over to the stand that held her armor and axe, and then at the open closet that held only her travel equipment. She remembered Lilian's room and suddenly felt rather lacking with her living conditions. There was beauty in simplicity, but she felt perhaps she should make it feel more like a home. After all, the Sterkhand family had many decorations and whatnot in their cottage. Even Frossgar kept that pile of armor and weapons in his cave. All she had was the stand and empty furniture.

"Very well," she finally said. "There is no reason to continue lying about as I was."

Lilian hummed in satisfaction and hopped up. "Awesome. I know some good places we can check out. We'll have this place brightened up in no time!"

"I do not wish to spend much recreationally."

"No problem! We can just window shop."

"I do not need windows."

"That just means looking around without intending to buy anything. Think of it as scouting ahead."

Finally something made clear sense to Elaethia. Lilian bounced ahead and walked out the door to the balcony as Elaethia put on her rabbit-fur shoes. Elaethia got a few looks from the present guild members, who had never seen her out of her armor. From the corner of her eye, she could tell some were looking a little *too* hard. Staring them down averted their over-interested gazes. As the pair exited the guildhall, Lilian shot a thumbs-up to Geran, who sat at a table with Shiro. The ranger and samurai waved in response.

"Are they not joining us?" Elaethia asked.

"Nah. Shiro's completely lost here, so Geran's gonna sit him down again and get him up to speed the best he can. He's made it my job to … Anyway, you say you don't like teasing guys much, but that top says otherwise."

Elaethia looked at her shirt. "Is there something wrong with it?"

"Well, it's not exactly indecent, but it certainly draws attention to your chest. I never figured you'd wear something that open."

"I find it comfortable and ventilated. It is also easy to put on and take off."

"Figures that'd be your reason," Lilian muttered. "Say, you're always wearing that necklace, too. What is it?"

"It was my father's. It is all that I have left of my family. He gave it to me on the day he died, before he challenged Rychus. It was the last time I saw him."

"Oh. I, uh … I'm sorry … But it's really pretty! Can I hold it?"

Elaethia clenched the necklace and stepped to the side. "You may not."

Lilian's ears fell flat. "Sorry, sorry. I was just curious. I didn't mean anything bad."

Elaethia exhaled and relaxed. "I see. Nevertheless, it will stay on my person."

"That's okay. How about we make our first stop at a tailor and get you some more clothes?"

"I thought we were going to simply browse."

The demicat flashed her signature grin and strutted down the cobblestone streets. "Yeah, well, plans change all the time."

Elaethia followed closely behind as they passed several shops and stands. Lilian halted in front of a glass-paned window with several outfits on display. Elaethia looked up to see a wooden sign bearing a carved spool of thread hanging over the entryway. Lilian grabbed her hand and pulled her in, cheerfully announcing their presence. A brass bell jingled as the door opened.

"Helloooo!" she called into the store.

A demiwolf woman poked her head around a corner. "Welcome! Feel free to look around! Come up to the desk when you're ready."

"Okeydokey! Let's take a look-see," Lilian said, and she paraded herself around the small store.

Elaethia watched the mage hum to herself as she looked everything over. She then turned her own attention to the clothing. The variety of style was anywhere from plain to elegant, but there was nothing either luxurious or simple. This tailor certainly had skill. Elaethia followed behind the girl and took note of everything.

"You seem to be looking at items well beyond our budget," she noted.

"Well, we're here, aren't we? Doesn't hurt just to look," Lilian said as she examined a frilly red dress with ruffles.

"Would you wear something like that?" Elaethia asked.

"This? By the Moon, no, I wouldn't be caught dead in this thing. I guess it's pretty, but it does *not* match my hair—or, more importantly, my figure."

"I see. What would you recommend I purchase?"

"Hm? Oh I wasn't looking at anything for you. I figured you'd pick something boring and leave."

"Perhaps a couple months ago I would have. But since meeting you, I decided to put more effort into my personal appearance. Ingrid would want this as well."

Lilian whipped her head to meet Elaethia's gaze. "Wait. Are you … asking for my help?"

"I would appreciate some assistance and input, yes."

The demicat's face lit up. "Holy crap! Elaethia wants me to help her pick out an outfit!"

"L-Lilian—"

Lilian cheered as she pounced and clambered over the warrior. "Oh-my-goodness-you-have-*no*-idea-how-much-I've-been-wanting-to-do-something-like-this-I'm-so-*excited*-we're-gonna-get-you-something-absolutely-stunning-OH-I-can't-wait-to-see-Geran's-face-this-is-gonna-be-great!"

Elaethia put her hands up as a smile touched her lips. "Please, please calm down. I do not want something that draws much attention. And what does Geran have to do with this?"

Lilian flashed her signature grin and hummed. "Oh, nothing. Now c'mon, c'mon, we don't have all day; Let's try some of this stuff on!"

For nearly an hour, Lilian crammed Elaethia into a dressing room with a variety of clothing. The outfits ranged anywhere from plain jerkins to elegant dresses to official outfits. Lilian even tried to get the strong woman into the frilly red dress from earlier. The dress was taken by Elaethia's hand, only to instantly be flung back out and wrapped around Lilian's face. Eventually Elaethia got overwhelmed with the amount of clothing she found herself getting in and out of. She finally decided on a button-down white shirt underneath a black outer corset. Form-fitting tan pants and laced black boots accompanied them.

Elaethia stepped out and examined herself. "The clothing is comfortable. Even the boots, but they are a little awkward to walk in. Are you sure these are necessary?"

"Absolutely they are! And what are you talking about, those heels aren't even high! They're, like, two inches! Just walk around a bit; you'll get used to it."

"All of this is rather expensive," Elaethia noted.

"Yeah, but you look great!" Lilian insisted.

"I … I suppose you are right." Elaethia stared at her reflection in a wall mirror, wondering how someone like her could look like that.

Lilian nodded intently as she examined Elaethia from every angle. "I know you refused out of personal preference, but I agree a dress wouldn't work on you. You have this weird balance between being beefy and curvy."

"Is that a good thing?" Elaethia asked as they stepped into the street.

"I'd say so. It certainly works for you. Guys can be drawn to that kinda thing, although you really only need to worry about one."

Elaethia tilted her head. "Who would that be?"

Lilian only grinned. "Now let's move onto the next shop!"

"Another store? I thought we were only going to one."

"I never said that, now did I?" Lilian beamed smugly.

The two walked down the street and rounded a corner. A girl with long brown hair and a bag collided into Elaethia. The girl let out a soft "oof" and stumbled back. She fell to the ground, scattering the bag's contents. Elaethia didn't seem to notice until after the girl was already on the ground. Elaethia blinked and looked down extending a hand to help collect the scattered fruits and vegetables.

"I apologize. Are you all right?" she asked.

"Yes, I'm okay. Sorry, I should have been paying attention to—" The girl looked up. "Elaethia?"

"Cathrine?" She recognized the serving girl from the restaurant in the city square.

Lilian poked her head into the conversation. "You know her?"

"I do. She assisted me in getting to the guildhall when I first entered the city."

Cathrine nodded. "Yeah, and she chased away an adventurer that was giving me a hard time."

The demicat turned to Elaethia. "You never told me about that."

"It was not of any consequential value."

"It was to me!" Catherine insisted. "And then you came back! I was actually wondering why you hadn't visited since."

"Elaethia, are you neglecting your friends?" Lilian scolded.

Elaethia's brow wrinkled. "I apologize for not returning, Cathrine. I did say that I would. Life in the guild took more adjustment than I had anticipated."

"Oh! Oh, that's all right!" Cathrine said. "I don't know much about guild life, but I can imagine having trouble dealing with people like that elf ranger."

Lilian's ears perked up. "Elf ranger? Long blond hair, green tunic, bow, pompous asshole?"

"Yes! You know him?"

Lilian wrinkled her nose. "Ugh. That's Sybil. I can't understand how he doesn't realize that nobody likes him. He's been in and out of more parties than anybody else in the whole guild. Nobody can stand him for long."

Cathrine shot to her feet. "I know! He's so arrogant! He didn't even know me and was going on and on about how valuable he was and what the guild would be without him."

"Oh, what did he say to you? I wanna hear the whole story."

Elaethia sighed. "Perhaps we may converse as we walk? Cathrine, if you are not busy, you are welcome to join us."

Her eyes lit up. "Can I? I mean, is it okay? I'm not an adventurer like you guys."

Lilian took her wrist and started to walk. "Oh, that doesn't matter one bit! That means I can tell you all about the stuff I did and you won't get bored! Like that time where I soloed a retrieval from newbie bandits using nothing but *flashbang*. That was so funny! I'm Lilian, by the way; I'm in Elaethia's party."

Cathrine gave an awkward smile. "I understood maybe half the things you just said. I didn't know Elaethia was in a party now, but I'm glad she's got some friends!"

Lilian flashed her grin. "She only keeps the *best* of company. I can tell because of you, too! Isn't that right, Elaethia?"

"I suppose so," the warrior agreed. With a smile, she realized Cathrine was right. Elaethia strode down the cobblestone street, listening and conversing on and off with her friends.

Back at the guildhall, Geran and Shiro had their conversation interrupted by a swarm of male adventurers. The main focus, of course, was the foreigner; who wore a red-and-black kimono with sandals. Most notable of the small swarm were Peter Stone, the demiwolf warrior he once brawled with—who introduced himself as Liam Barron—and Dylan Hartford, from Lilian's former party.

"So," Peter stated, "that sword there is your main weapon? What is that thing, anyway? I can tell it's meant for two hands 'cause it's got a long handle and no pommel, but it's the same length as a normal longsword. Do you use it with one hand, or two like my greatsword?"

Shiro rested a hand on the hilt of the sword. "This is my katana. It can be used in one hand or two. I don't know what a greatsword is, however."

Peter hefted up his giant sword and leaned on it. "Aha, you mean one of these babies? You gotta have some crazy muscles and endurance to use this thing for the long fight. Heavy enough to clobber someone in armor, but sleek enough to cut. Great reach, too."

Liam flipped his hefty spear and rested its bladed head on the ground. "Pfft, you wanna talk reach? You get better reach and placement with a polearm. A heavy shaft also can take care of armored baddies if you hit 'em right."

"You're still on about that? Any lame-brained peasant can use a spear. It takes skill and strength to wield a greatsword."

"C'mon, man! You're so limited and slow. I've got two jabs on you by the time you've even wound up!"

"So you've poked at me once or twice. That's not much compared to getting cut in half like you'd be."

Dylan stepped in. "If we're going with speed and accuracy, there's nothing better than a rapier or saber. I've won several duels with quick slashes and thrusts."

Geran nodded. "Dylan's got a point. Strength only gets you so far. Then again, speed isn't everything. Keep working at it, bud; you won't be intermediate forever."

"Bah! You're just a newbie lover, Nightshade," Peter scoffed. "Goin' easy on them like that is what makes them soft."

"Hey, you gotta bring 'em up somehow," Liam pointed out. "If all you do is talk down to 'em, they'll lose drive."

"You wanna give them drive? The best motivator is to get them in front of some girls! A man's strength doubles when he's got some cuties watching him."

"Speakin' of cuties"—the demiwolf grinned and leaned toward Shiro—"how 'bout that Whitepaw girl, huh? She's certainly something. Bet you didn't have anything like her in Osakyota."

"W-well yes," Shiro stammered. "There are no demihumans back home. She's very unique."

All the guys leaned back and groaned loudly.

Peter thumped a fist on the samurai's shoulder. "Nah, nah, nah, that's not what we wanna hear! Don't you think she's a real looker? You can't tell me you don't get wild imaginations of rescuing her from some sort of dangerous situation? Y'know girls like that can get awful affectionate in those circumstances."

The guys grunted in agreement and looked at him. Geran pulled up his hood and sighed. Nothing short of a miracle would save the poor guy now.

Shiro's face started to turn red. "Well, yes, I suppose she's very pretty."

The crowd growled with approval and banged their fists on the table.

"That's it? That's all you got to say?" Liam pressed. "C'mon, we're all guys here, let's hear what you really think about our little Lilian! We all can agree she's good on the eyes!"

"You guys are so gross!" the elven priestess from Dylan's party scolded from the other end of the bar.

"Don't worry, Dana, we aren't getting too in-depth!" the duelist assured her.

"Yet!" Peter howled.

The mob joined him in laughter as Shiro's face turned almost completely red.

"Where is she, anyway?" Liam noticed. "I'd hate to embarrass our new brother in front of her."

"She's out. With Elaethia," Geran stated.

"That's another thing!" Liam continued. "When are you gonna make a move on that, Geran? You're the only one here who can even talk to her! Hell, Peter got his lights knocked out the last time he tried!"

Everyone guffawed at the remark.

Peter quickly put the attention back on the ranger. "Yeah, Geran, we've all seen you staring! You've got tact and subtlety on just about everything else! Think you got a chance with that ice queen?"

The ranger folded his arms. "There's a lot more to Elaethia than you all know. Sit down and have a conversation with her. You might be surprised."

The group muttered among themselves.

"Course not. You guys are all talk," Geran said.

Shiro suddenly stood up. "Are they talking disrespectfully about Elaethia-sama?"

"Easy, samurai. Not like any of them could hold a candle to her, anyway."

Dylan put a hand up. "Yeah, no need to get worked up, man. We're all just messing around."

Shiro sat back down. "I suppose you're right. Although I have never actually seen her fight."

"She easily cleared a bandit hideout and took down several sabercats by herself," Geran said. "And that's just what I can personally account for. Apparently she's done way more than that before and since she got here. Fought monsters, killed more bandits, took out sorcerers—you name it. If you see it on a kill quest or clear quest, she's done it. Don't think any of these guys can say that about themselves."

"You're one to talk, Nightshade!" Peter pointed at him. "That was your first kill quest in over a year! All those overwatch and scout missions probably left your blades rusty."

"Nice try, Stone. I still completed the bounty on that horse thief. It's a lot harder crossing blades with someone you're not supposed to kill. Also, I'm pretty sure I'm still the only one in the guild who's done every type of espionage quest."

"You rangers and your petty sneakery," Peter groaned. "When are you guys gonna get a *real* man's quest like a kill, a challenge, or a suppression?"

"Not our field of expertise. Why don't we leave the heavy lifting to you and keep the ones that actually require a brain for us?"

Liam pounded a fist on his chest. "Hah! I'd rather stick with *my* class! Glory and fame is the way of a warrior, and that shady lifestyle is far from epic."

"I agree!" Shiro matched the demiwolf's excitement. "There's no greater honor than proving your might on the battlefield!"

"Ha-*hah*! Damn right, foreigner! See, Geran? This guy gets it!" Liam extended a hand to Shiro, who firmly grasped it in a hearty shake.

The samurai looked over to Geran. "No offense to you, of course."

The ranger waved it off. "Doesn't bother me. I know what I do and how people look at it. As long as we're all here to get the dirty work done and get paid, it doesn't matter."

Everyone muttered in agreement. The front doors suddenly opened as Lilian and Elaethia walked back in.

"Geraaaan!" the demicat called. "We need a quest! Pronto!"

Elaethia nodded sheepishly as the room grew unusually quiet. "It appears we have gone over our budget and are in need of funds."

"Meet us at the quest board; we'll be right there," Geran called back.

"Woah, woah, woah, is that Elaethia?" Dylan whispered as he stared at the woman. "I've never seen her out of her armor."

Liam whistled under his breath. "You've been running around with *that*? Nightshade, the hell you doing, man? Look at that *body*! Frosty is packing, bro! If you don't jump on that, someone else might!"

Geran gave him a look as he and Shiro headed to the board. "What, like you?"

"Sun and Moon, no. If the stories I've heard are even half right, I'll keep my distance. We're all rooting for you though!"

The spearman gave him a thumbs-up as the two met up with their party. The women were scanning the A quests as Geran and Shiro strolled up.

"Find anything yet?" Geran asked.

"Not sure," Lilian started. "The best ones I can see are a challenge quest for a gang in the western trade village, a kill quest on a troll, and a clear quest for a goblin-infested cave. There's also a clear quest for a small orc camp in the V section."

Geran made a face. "I don't think we should jump into the veteran-level quests yet. The challenge one should be simple with the four of us. Easily there and back by tonight."

"Yeah, but it doesn't pay as well as the others. I was looking at the troll one, but I feel like Elaethia would be doing everything."

"I am sure you all would be of some sort of assistance to me," the warrior said. "What do you think, Shiro? This would be your first quest, and I believe your input would be important."

Shiro rubbed his chin. "What's this one? A clear for a … Blackwolf fence?"

Lilian's tail flicked. "Blackwolf? They're still in the city?"

"Who are they?"

Geran answered. "A regional crime faction we've been whittling away at. They're criminals, but don't mistake them for just a ragtag crew of bandits. They have hierarchy, organization, and a lot of resources. We're not ready for this one either."

"Then let us take the goblin quest," Elaethia decided. "They are dull creatures that only have strength in numbers. It will be fairly simple as long as we stay together."

Lilian wrinkled her nose. "Goblins are so gross, though. That reward is the second lowest, too."

"Doesn't matter," Geran interjected. "Little buggers like to hoard anything shiny. I guarantee we'll find some junk in there worth selling."

Shiro piped up. "I'd be glad to give you a portion of my share if you are in need, Lili-chan!"

"That's so sweet of you!"

"Yeah right, buddy. You're broke too, remember?" Geran stated. "What's with newbies and blowing all their money? You guys grow up supported by home, then jump in here thinking you're making a fortune. You don't make nearly as much as you think you do, so stop throwing money around every time you get some. This is why you're always broke, Lilian."

The demicat stuck her tongue out.

"Have we decided?" Elaethia pressed.

"Yeah, this one looks good. Lilian, Shiro, any objections?"

"I have none if that's what everyone else wants," Shiro agreed.

Lilian pursed her lips and grumbled. "If any of them get their grubby little fingers on me, I'm blaming all of you."

"Don't worry, Lili-chan. I won't let a single goblin touch you."

"Aww! I *knew* we had a good catch bringing you in!"

Lilian pounced on him and affectionately rubbed her cheek against him. The Osakyotan turned pink and tried in vain to construct a response. He quickly stepped away and escaped up the stairs to his room.

"I-I have to get ready! I'll meet you all downstairs soon!"

"Good plan," Geran agreed. "Lilian, I hope you bought a bigger bag this time."

"Why d'ya think I'm so broke?"

"How would I know? I don't know what you two did out there."

"*Oh!* That reminds me." Lilian stepped behind Elaethia and pushed the woman up to him. "Notice anything different here?"

The ranger regarded Elaethia. "I see you bought some new clothes. I guess that's why you're in need of this quest too?"

Elaethia nodded. "They indeed were rather expensive."

Lilian looked up at him smugly. "Awwwww, c'mon, Gerry! Don't you have something to say about them?"

He coughed and looked at Elaethia again. "Well, it definitely looks good on you. Really highlights your features."

"Doesn't it?" The demicat winked as she wrapped her arms underneath Elaethia's chest and squeezed. Both Geran and Elaethia's cheeks began to flush.

"Lilian!" The ranger lunged forward to grab at her, but she danced out his reach and bounded up the stairs with a maniacal giggle.

"That girl," he growled. He turned around to look at Elaethia and met her eyes. They both grew flustered again and looked away.

"Sorry about that," he said, and he scratched the back of his head.

"It is fine. That caught me by surprise as well." She paused for a few seconds. "Although it makes me glad to hear that you like it."

"Yeah, I, uh … I'm glad that you're glad."

They stood in silence for a few moments until Geran coughed.

"Well, we have plenty of time to prepare, knowing Lilian, but I think I should go get my questing gear ready. I'll meet you down here, and we can make a plan."

Elaethia nodded. "Yes, of course. I will see you then."

Elaethia was the second one down after fifteen minutes. Shiro was just a few minutes ahead of her, and Geran arrived several minutes after. Lilian finally made her appearance thirty minutes after him. As Lilian took her seat at the table, Geran straightened out the quest flyer and read the description.

"A large pack of goblins has holed up in a cave that has been marked on the map. They have grown in size and confidence enough to harass travelers, abduct livestock, raid farms, and break into homes to steal valuables. There are no reports of brehdar kidnappings or deaths as of this posting. The goblin's numbers are too high for the local guard to handle but too small to be recognized as a regional threat. This pack needs to be eradicated before it becomes large enough to pose a substantial threat to the local villages."

Shiro looked at the description. "These little green men are that much of an issue? How come the guard didn't take care of them before they got so numerous?"

Lilian's ear flicked. "They're a bunch of brats. They don't go out like this unless they have large numbers, so nobody would have known about them. They're too dumb to farm or hunt, so they steal from brehdars. When there's enough of them, they start getting bolder. They're attracted to anything shiny, and they multiply like rabbits."

Elaethia nodded. "They are able to reproduce quickly due to high fertility. They are the only creatures that can impregnate any sapien, be it goblin, orc, or brehdar. The offspring are always fully goblin."

"Why do you know more about monsters than you do about people?" Geran asked.

Elaethia only tilted her head in response.

Once they had the quest stamped, they proceeded through the provisions line and headed out the door. Everyone, including Shiro, had donned their insignia. His was a long, thin, white headband with the guild insignia stitched in red. It wrapped around his forehead underneath his helmet, with the two tied-off ends flowing freely behind his head.

Between Lilian and Geran's cloaks, and Elaethia and Shiro's armor, the whole town couldn't help but watch the awesome group: a warrior in blue, a ranger in green, a mage in orange, and a samurai in red. No one would have guessed such an entourage was on a quest to kill goblins. Onlookers talked among themselves as the party made their way to the gate.

"Are they from our guild?"

"That's our crest for sure."

"Who's that young man in red? I've never seen that style of armor in my life."

"Isn't that Lilian? She finally moved up in rank, it seems."

"That ranger's been around for about a decade, but this is the first time I've seen him in a group. What's his name? Garett, Gavin …?"

"Geran, I think."

"Is this the new ace party? I've never seen them before, but they look stronger than Razorback, maybe even Earth Shatter."

Elaethia tilted her head. "Razorback? Earth Shatter? Ace party?"

"Several parties in the guild have been publicly recognized as highly effective," Geran explained. "Once the guild acknowledges it, they assign a name to the party. The ace party is the strongest in a guild. Razorback is Liam Barron's group, and Earth Shatter is Peter Stone's. Earth Shatter's the ace. The third-most-popular party in our guild is an all-female one called Heaven's Light, and a lot of guys go nuts over them. Didn't they try to recruit you at one point, Lilian?"

The demicat shrugged. "Yeah, but I turned them down. There're no guys. Besides, Suzanna's doing fine as their mage. Although she has me to thank for that."

"Did you train her?" Elaethia asked as they exited the town.

"I mean, kinda. We were best friends when we showed up, so I helped her out. Susie just doesn't focus as well as I do."

"Must have the attention span of a goldfish," Geran muttered.

"You're the third-strongest mage, right, Lilian? Who are the other two?" Shiro asked.

"Technically one. The mage in Razorback, Remus Lichen. He's a little self-absorbed, as a lot of elves are, but he's not an ass like Sybil."

"What do you mean 'technically' one? Who's the other?"

"That'd be Mordecai," Geran said. "A specialized fire mage. He runs solo and is hardly ever around. He doesn't technically count since he only appears once or twice a year to take a V quest, and then he disappears again. Actually I think the last one he did was an R level. He doesn't even take part in the annual guild tournament anymore, since it's not even a challenge for him. Last one he attended was a year or two after I arrived."

Shiro's mouth fell open. "He did a whole raid? *Alone?*"

"That guy is *stupid* powerful. I think he's in his early to mid-thirties now. He fights with a dominating presence and is utterly overwhelming with his spells. Even Master Dameon at his peak would have a hell of a time against Mordecai. He's easily the strongest adventurer in the guild, maybe even the country."

Shiro beamed. "I bet Elaethia-sama could take that title if she wanted."

Geran exhaled heavily. "I don't know about that. I've been around him a few times, and his aura is on a different level than hers. Just by standing there, he heats the whole room up."

"I could chill the atmosphere around me if I wished," Elaethia said almost indignantly.

"Yeah, magicians don't just radiate their magic like that," Lilian piped in. "The one time I was around him, I could tell he was doing it on purpose. Probably to flex his power, or maybe to keep people away."

Geran shrugged. "Well then, who knows? He's got about ten years on Elaethia, but she's got dragon magic and a warrior style. Once we figure out your full potential, it'd be a battle for the ages. Huh. That'd be something to see. From a distance, of course."

"How is he not a hero?" Shiro asked.

"Probably because nobody really knows who he is anymore," Geran said. "He's more like a legend or a myth than a hero. If he made an effort to make himself known and popular, he definitely would be. He's got his own agenda, and the guild is more or less a means to an end for him. He cares about it in his own way, but I feel he's ready to drop it any time. At this rate, he'll earn himself a national title."

Shiro perked up. "National title …"

"Don't even think about it. Normal brehdars almost never get them. Throughout history, it's pretty much always been magicians. The only national title I can remember off the top of my head went to another specialized fire mage. Couldn't tell you his real name, as he was only known as the Red Devil. Batshit crazy mage focused his entire studies into only the explosion spell."

"Don't forget about the Westreach Giant!" Lilian added. "He was a monk who could grow almost ten meters."

Geran snapped his fingers. "Oh yeah, there was also the Beast Mother about a century before the Red Devil. Legend says she lived in the Titan's Forest and could turn brehdars into tamed animals."

"So it really is rare for one to gain such a title," Elaethia marveled.

Geran waved a hand. "I'm sure there've been more. But legends tend to get altered beyond recognition."

"Or overshadowed by a new one," Lillian added. "By the way, where are we going?"

The other party members stopped and looked at her.

"Were you not paying attention during the meeting?" Elaethia asked.

Lilian giggled and stuck the tip of her tongue out. "I kinda spaced out."

Geran rubbed his eyes. "By the Moon, Lilian …"

"Whaaaaat? You guys are so boring when you talk like that! I know my job is to blast things, so just leave me at that!"

"You don't even know where we're going!"

"Well, I know I'll start blasting things when we get there!"

Shiro pointed down the road. "Lili-chan, we're going a few kilometers in that direction. There should be a cave off a trail from the main road."

"Ah! Thanks, Shiro!" Lilian said. She beamed at Geran, who sighed and shook his head.

This was Elaethia's first time in this part of Breeze. Most of her travels throughout the region took her across the plains or through the thickets, and perhaps once or twice into the thin forests. The northwestern portion of Breeze was dense woodland, however. The trees grew so thick and tall that she wondered whether it would be possible for her to cut them in half with a single swing. The forest was so dense in parts that sunlight shone only through the small gaps in the leaves and branches of the mighty oaks and maples that towered above.

Eventually they approached their destination. Geran halted the party and motioned for them to get down. "Drop off all the equipment you won't need once we get inside. I'm going to scout ahead."

They complied and set aside their traveling gear. Geran attached a small horn to his belt and began to rub a green-and-brown paste on his face and neck.

"What is that, Geran?" Elaethia inquired.

"Camouflage paint. Helps keep me blended in with the forest. If I'm not back in ten minutes or you hear me blow this horn, come find me."

With that he finished covering his face, pulled up his hood, checked his weapons, and disappeared into the brush.

"What are goblins like?" Shiro asked.

Lilian's tail flicked. "Green, ugly, smelly, and stupid. They're as big as a ten-year-old but can be a real pain when in groups. Last time we tangled with them, Dylan charged off on his own and got overwhelmed, and Dana almost got grabbed. I had to do pretty much everything. Thank the Sun that our warrior, Horst, was able to get her back before they could drag her further in. Since then I've made a personal goal to kill a goblin with every spell I have. So far I've gotten fifteen. Only twenty-five to go."

Shiro inched closer to her. "I didn't know there were so many spells!"

"You bet! There're forty alone for elemental magicians, not including the ones that come with specializing. None of the other schools of magic have that many. Well, except the others are more versatile. But either way, we have the largest arsenal!"

"Woooaaahhh. How do you remember all those?"

"Hmm. I'm just that good." Lilian stood, flapping her cloak and grabbing the brim of her hat. Shiro looked up at her in wonder.

Elaethia tilted her head. "I thought you did not know how many spells you had."

The mage's ears flattened. She stuttered once as her shoulders shrunk. Lilian tapped her index fingers together and looked down. "Well, I uh … After Geran asked that one time, I kinda wanted to know myself. So I sorta went ahead and made myself a list."

"And you did not tell him about it?"

Lilian's eyes moved away from the warrior. "N-no."

"Why not? I am sure he would be pleased to hear about it."

"I … forgot."

"I see." Elaethia's gaze was filled with disappointment. The mage's cheeks turned red as she sat cross-legged and looked at the ground. The party remained in somewhat awkward silence until Geran seemed to materialize next to them.

"All right, you guys want the good news or the bad news?"

Shiro and Lilian yelped in surprise at the ranger's sudden appearance.

"Let us hear the bad news first," Elaethia suggested.

"There're no guards, watches, or any sign of goblin activity outside of the cave. I have no clue what kind of weapons, armor, or numbers we'll see once we get in there. We're going in almost completely blind."

"I don't like the way you're saying that," Shiro said nervously.

"The good news is that means they aren't expecting company. We should be able to take them by surprise. The question is, do we plan on going soft or loud?" He paused to look at the members of his party—namely Lilian and Elaethia. "I don't even know why I asked."

Shiro raised his hand. "What does that mean?"

"Don't worry about it. Here's my plan: I'll go in first, followed by Shiro, then Lilian, and then Elaethia. I'd like to take out as many as we can with some subtlety before you ladies go nuts in there. I'll use my bow for as long as I can, and then Shiro and I can move up with our swords. Lilian, I'd like you to use *torch* to give us a light source. Elaethia, I want you to be our anchor. Watch our backs, and don't let anything get past you."

Lilian shot her hand up. "Hold on! Remind me again why we aren't having the heavy armor go first?"

Elaethia answered. "It could be difficult to swing a weapon as large as mine inside. Caves can be very tight in places. It is wiser to let weapons capable of quick thrusts to go first. Do not worry; I will come to your aid if you are in need."

"I guess, but since I'm not in front, I won't be able to use the majority of my spells. Looks like I'm on lantern duty."

Geran winked at her. "Don't worry. You'll get an even share of the reward."

The party moved quietly through the vegetation. There were no goblins outside as they approached the mouth of the cave. The ranger nocked an arrow, drew back the bowstring, and sharply turned the corner. A curious grunt came from within as he released, followed by muffled gargle and a small thud. Geran nocked another arrow and glided silently inside. The other three followed him as quietly as they could.

Elaethia looked down at the now-dead goblin. An arrow protruded through its mouth as it lay in an ever-growing puddle of blood. It was perhaps a meter tall, with sickly green skin, pointed nose and ears, and beady dark eyes. Crude armor made of leather, metal, wood, and bone covered its chest. It was her first time fighting them in caves. She was glad to have someone as experienced as Geran leading the way.

The ranger halted, laxed the arrow, and put his hand up sharply. Two goblins sat against the wall, speaking back and forth in goblin language. He motioned for Shiro to join him. The samurai came next to him and took a knee, and Geran made a few hand gestures back and forth between him and the goblins. The Osakyotan blinked at him. Geran rubbed his eyes. He pointed at Shiro, and then at the rightmost goblin, and then he ran a thumb across his throat. The samurai mouthed "Oh!" and nodded.

"Go!" Geran instructed in a harsh whisper.

Shiro charged forward as the ranger loosed his arrow into the left goblin. The one on the right stood sharply with a startled yelp. It was quickly silenced as the katana was thrust through its neck. Shiro slowly removed his blade and wiped the blood off on the creature's baggy clothing.

Geran retrieved his arrow and turned to the party. "Stop here for a few minutes to let your eyes adjust to the dark. These things may be dumb and weak, but they've got keener senses than most of us. Lilian, put the light out and get next to Shiro. Let us know if you hear anything coming. Shiro, don't let anything get past you."

The mage and samurai nodded as the flame on the end of Lilian's staff died to nothing. Shiro knelt and faced further into the cave, his sword at the ready. The demicat stacked up behind him and peered deeper into the cave. Elaethia's dragon eyes could see clearly through the darkness, but it was her duty to watch the rear. This would be a good opportunity to test Shiro's capabilities. The party waited in silence for ten minutes until Shiro and Geran could see noticeably better.

"Lili-chan, do you see anything?" Shiro asked.

"Nothin'."

"It goes for a few meters and then turns left," Elaethia said.

Lilian cocked an ear. "Wait, you can see that?"

Geran drew his longsword and stepped forward. "All right. Move up."

They stood as Geran took the front again. Shiro followed closely behind with Lilian, who cast a dim *torch*. Elaethia turned behind them once more and then followed. Rounding the corner, they could see a slight glow coming from within. The sounds of goblins conversing and general ruckus grew louder as the light grew brighter. Geran once again halted the group. He pulled a small mirror from his pouch and peered at it around the corner. He turned back and motioned the party closer.

"There're a bunch of them hanging around in the next room. There don't seem to be any hostages or other passages. I say you three charge in there and take them out with shock and awe."

Lilian gave him a smug look. "Oho? Is that *our* Geran suggesting we go loud?"

"Unless you'd rather keep back and give me and Shiro some light."

"No, no, no, lemme go too!" she extinguished her staff with a twirl.

Geran readied his bow. "I'll stay back here to make sure none of them make a run for it. Lilian, stay near the rear and use low-level spells. Try to target the ones that are off on their own. Shiro, I'm still trying to figure out your style, so move in and do what you do. Just be mindful of the rest of us. And Elaethia …" He paused and stared at her. "I dunno. Go nuts, I guess. Just don't splatter anything against a wall that's taller than your waist."

She hefted her battleaxe. "I would never even consider such a thing, Geran."

"Glad to hear it. Lilian, isn't there a lightning spell that makes a bright light and a loud noise?"

She gave a thumbs-up. "That's *flashbang*. It doesn't hurt, though; it just blinds and deafens everyone around it."

"That's the one. Open up with that, then we'll flow in."

Shiro and Elaethia nodded. Lilian's eyes glinted as she looked up with a fanged grin.

"Let's blast some gobs."

The rest of the party covered their ears and closed their eyes as Lilian thrust her staff at the center of the room. A brilliant flash accompanied by a deafening explosion struck the creatures within. Geran wheeled around the bend, aimed for a moment, and then fired an arrow into the chest of a goblin standing on a makeshift table. The creature gargled as it toppled over onto the ground. Elaethia thundered past, axe wound up at her side, as she cleaved through two of them in a single swing.

A flash of red slid past as Shiro leaped into the fray with his sword above his head. He slashed through the torso of the nearest creature and brought the blade across his body in a sideways cut to sever the head of the next. Lilian stood partly back from the two. The mage sent *thunderbolts*, *icicles*, and *fireballs* into individual goblins that strayed too far from the fighters.

The goblins didn't stand a chance. After one shrieked and attempted to rush to the exit, only to be run through by Geran, the remainder of the nest made a dash into a small opening in the wall. Chopping, slashing, and blasting the whole way, the three made their way to the round hole. Elaethia put on her helmet and bent over to peer inside after the last goblin slid in. Nothing happened for a second, until a short spear thrust out and weakly struck her helmet. Wordlessly, she grabbed the spear and yanked it out with its wielder still holding on to it. The goblin didn't even have time to scream before its face was caved in by a deep blue gauntlet.

"It seems they are trapped," Elaethia said. "There is only one way in and out. I suspect they intend to wait there until we leave."

Lilian frowned. "Well, I don't plan on waiting that long. And I *especially* don't plan on crawling in there after them. Elaethia, can you fit through that gap?"

"Potentially, but my axe will not. Perhaps you can use *torch* to burn them from within."

"Is it airtight in there?"

"I do not know."

"'Cause if it is, the flames will just blow right back out. I don't know why, but I've tried something similar before. I may not be able to smoke them out of there, but I have another spell that might work."

"*Arcing tendrils?*" Shiro asked.

"Nope. I've used that one on goblins before, remember? This one's an air spell I've never even tried. It's called *vacuum*, and I haven't seen a use for it until now."

"What does that do?" Geran called from the entrance.

The Elaethium

"It's supposed to suck all the air out of an area. Mostly used by wizards for experiments or storage. I think we can use that to suffocate them in there."

"All right, give it a shot."

Lilian gripped her staff and stuck the end into the small cavern. A sudden gust of air shot in and almost brought her to her knees. Several yelps of startled goblins warbled from within.

Lilian made a face. "Huh. Well that didn't work. Unless … *Oh!* Wait-wait-wait! I think I remember something. The air will just go back in unless you seal it off. Damn, if only we had a way to do that."

"Can you seal it off with ice?" Geran called down.

"Of course! *Ice wall*! Elaethia, can you channel one for me?"

Elaethia tilted her head. "*Ice wall*? I do not know that spell."

"Course you do; you're specialized in frost magic. You can do all the frost spells I can and then some. Here, watch me," Lilian pointed her staff at the ground. Her eyes began to pulse as a small ice formation began to rise from the stone floor. "There. Try that!"

Elaethia knelt next to the tiny block of ice. She squinted at it, rubbed her chin, and then held her hand out. The air began to chill as her reptile-like eyes pulsed. The same icy formation began to grow rapidly and crudely. Before they knew it, it was over a meter tall.

"Is that satisfactory?" she asked.

"Kinda shabby, but we can work on it. Can you channel another on the entrance?"

"One moment." The warrior stood, approached the hole, and once again built an ice wall to seal off the entrance.

Shiro looked at the frozen structure. "Can you still cast your spell through that, Lili-chan?"

"Watch and learn," the mage announced as she held out her hand. After a moment it began to glow. Shiro held his face closer to it but then recoiled from the immense heat radiating off it.

"Lili-chan! Your hand is melting!"

"Nope! This here is *burning touch*. The *touch* series are the only spells I can use without a conduit. Now shush. Lemme concentrate." She placed her searing hand on a portion of the wall of ice and melted a fist-sized hole into it. She pulled her hand back and shook it until it went back to normal.

"Elaethia, I'm gonna put my staff through this opening," she said. "Once I do, build the wall back around the shaft."

Lilian stuck the gnarled conduit through the melted hole and nodded at Elaethia to seal it off. The dragon hero held out her hand to channel the spell. Once the staff was pinched off, Lilian gave it a few tugs to make sure it was snug. The demicat nodded and put her will into it. A violent splutch sounded through the wall of ice. The three looked at each other in confusion and then shrugged it off.

"How long should we wait?" Shiro asked.

"I dunno, but I'm out of magic now. Geryyyyy! How long can a goblin hold its breath for?"

"How the hell would I know?" the ranger called back.

"I thought you were supposed to be smart or something!"

"Cat, I'm gonna use your tail to—"

"Right, he's got no idea. Elaethia, what do you think?"

The warrior pondered for a moment. "Perhaps thirty minutes. Just to be sure."

"Works for me. I should have a decent amount of magic back by then."

Lilian left the staff where it was and turned over to sit against the stony wall. Shiro and Elaethia took similar resting positions.

About fifteen minutes later, Shiro turned to look at the wall of ice. "They've been very quiet since Lili-chan cast her spell."

Lilian rolled her hand. "Well, yeah. There's no air in there."

"Surely they'd make some sort of commotion. They haven't so much as tried to break it down."

"I agree," Elaethia said. "It is reasonable to believe that they would make some effort in a panic to free themselves. But they have been quiet the entire time."

Shiro rubbed his chin. "Do you think they had an escape passage?"

"It is possible."

Lilian cocked an ear. "So whaddya wanna do?"

"Let us remove the wall. It would not hurt to look."

Shiro nodded. "I agree with Elaethia-sama."

"What are you guys doing?" Geran called from his position.

"We're gonna open it up!" Lilian responded.

"Okay, go for it," he agreed.

The mage rolled back over to the wall, once again using *burning touch* to melt around her staff. A gust of air blasted into the space through the hole. After a second, she suddenly recoiled back and pinched her nose.

"Eugh! That reeks!"

"Stars above, how quickly do goblins decay?" Shiro gagged.

Elaethia exhaled slowly from the stench of rotting flesh and bile, but kept a straight face. "The rest of that wall must disappear before we can investigate. Bear with it until it is done."

Lilian nodded, still covering her nose. She continued to melt the wall down until it was gone and quickly stood up to hurry away from the horrible smell. Elaethia once again donned her helmet and peered inside. What awaited her was something completely unexpected. All of the goblins in the small space, without exception, had fallen over in pools of their own blood. While they were still mostly in one piece, they had clearly been ruptured from the inside out.

"What do you see? What happened in there?" Geran called from behind.

Elaethia stood and took off her helmet. "It appears they have burst."

"Wait, like, exploded?" Lilian asked.

"Not in the literal sense, no, but their eyes have erupted from their sockets and blood is pouring from their orific—"

"Okay, okay, okay, you don't need to explain further; I got it. How did *that* happen?"

"I do not know."

Geran scratched his head. "I've never heard of anything like that before. Maybe it has something to do with the air getting sucked out of the goblins' bodies?"

Elaethia nodded. "They are very weak in structure. If their lungs did not have the integrity to withstand the vacuum, it is believable that they ruptured from within."

Lilian rubbed her head. "By the Moon, guys, stop going so in depth with this. They're just goblins, and they're dead now. We don't need to go all detective on this."

"So the quest is complete then," Shiro stated.

Lilian hopped up. "I'd say so. Let's grab some loot and get outta this stink-hole."

Geran took a look around the shambled, bloody, smelly cave. "Everyone check your stuff. Make sure you have everything you came here with, and get a count for anything extra. Man, I'd hate to be whoever comes out here to verify this one."

"How many goblins were there, anyway?" asked Lilian.

"Quest didn't specify, and we can't exactly count the ones in the panic hole. I'd say maybe twenty?"

"Would it be considerate to leave something for the verifier?" Elaethia asked.

"Nah. We don't know when that's gonna be, and someone else could always stroll in here and take it. Not to mention quest verifiers get their own salary." Geran squinted at the setting sun as the party emerged. "That's always irked me. Those glorified, paper-pushing deskies get almost as much as we do. And just for walking back and forth from the locations and filing reports. And then they can always turn around and dock our pay if they think we didn't do a good enough job."

"I'd say our guild's verifiers are pretty fair," Lilian chimed in. "If they found one or two goblins still alive, they wouldn't deduct anything. They'd probably just have their escorts take care of it. Except that one verifier from a while ago. She'd probably call it negligent, right, Geran?"

"Oh yeah, *that* bitch. I personally never had any issues, since ranger missions rarely require verifiers. But Liam and Peter got screwed over a few times because of her."

"Where is this verifier now?" Elaethia asked.

"Couldn't tell you. Master Dameon curbed her after a year of complaints. She's the reason the guild keeps it anonymous which verifier checks a quest, though. Some of those death threats she got were pretty nasty."

"Let us be thankful those issues are no longer prevalent, as far as we know," Elaethia concluded.

"Yep!" chirped Lilian. "I haven't ever had a reward recalled before either!"

"Don't jinx us, cat," Geran laughed.

She flashed her signature grin at him as they reached the main road. They suddenly halted, as they noticed Shiro had stopped walking behind them. Elaethia realized he had also not spoken since they left the cave.

"Are you well, Shiro?" she asked him.

"I ..." he opened and closed his hands. "I don't understand."

Lilian cocked an ear. "Huh? We're talking about quest completion. If the guild didn't like how we did this quest, they'd confiscate some of the reward."

He shook his head. "No it ... it's not like that. This doesn't make any sense."

"What part?" Geran asked.

"Any of this!" Shiro stated firmly. "I know this is Linderrian culture, but I just can't accept it! This is all wrong; it's not the way it's supposed to be for me at all!"

Geran raised his hands. "Woah, woah, calm down, man. If you want to try a different approach next time, we can. I'm open to ideas."

Tears began to well up in Shiro's eyes. "You just don't get it. I don't deserve this. I shouldn't be allowed to fight with you. I shouldn't be allowed to speak with you. I shouldn't even be paid for my work!"

"Shiro ...?" Lilian hesitated.

The samurai took off his helmet and held it in his shaking hands. "I'm a dishonorable man. I took another person's life out of rage. I passed judgment on my own accord! I deserve all the bad things that have happened to me because I could not control myself! I am here to clear my name, to atone for my sin. I shouldn't be making friends and earning wages!"

Elaethia stepped to him. "What is wrong, Shiro?"

"I'm a terrible person, Elaethia-sama!" he choked. "I murdered someone. I thrust my family into chaos. My grandfather is dead. My sister is murdered. My father is on trial. My mother and brothers are defenseless and alone. The Inahari name has been tainted. All because of me. I left everyone behind to hide my shame, but I can't bear this guilt and loneliness any longer!"

"There was no other way you could have controlled this outcome," Elaethia said.

"I should have restrained myself! If only I could have had the discipline to hold my blade back, none of this would have happened!"

Elaethia held a gauntlet to his shoulder. "You were right to do so, Shiro. If the same fate befell my father, Frossgar, or any of my friends, I would have done the same without hesitation. It is unjust of your country to treat you the way they have."

The samurai wiped a sleeve under his nose. "I know it is. But it's the law, as well as the order of things for my code and family."

"If you know your treatment to be unfair, then why do you inflict such punishments upon yourself?"

"Wh-why? Because I deserve it."

"Who is to say what you do or do not deserve? You are a person, regardless of your flaws. In our eyes you have committed no crimes or wrongdoings."

"But to be allowed to fight at my master's side … I haven't done anything to prove I am honorable enough," Shiro insisted.

"You have done nothing to prove you are dishonorable enough, either," Elaethia assured him. "I am afraid I do not understand what it is that upsets you, but you are by no means a bad man. And of course you should fight at our sides. It makes no sense for you to fight anywhere else. We are stronger united."

Shiro's arms fell limp, his helmet weakly grasped in his hand. "E-Elaethia-sama … I … I don't know what to say."

"Then are you ready to return to the guild? We would all like to go home, and you are one of us. It is only right to return together."

The samurai sniffed once more, smiled gently, and put his helmet back on. "Yes, Elaethia-sama."

Chapter 7
Recovery

Sixth Era. 139. Mertim 22.

The sun had just set when the party opened the doors to the guildhall. The great building was lively and boisterous as usual. Adventurers and a few civilians drank and reveled, while staff and servers darted around to take and fill orders. More tired from the walk than weary from the fight, the party dropped off their gear and turned in the quest. After they agreed to meet at a table downstairs, they went off to bathe and change out of their adventuring gear.

"Here's the plan," Geran started as they all arrived. "Tomorrow around noon, we'll take our loot to an appraiser. The two most common procedures after that are to split the cash equally, or individually based on what we picked up."

Shiro nodded. "If possible, I'd like to watch the appraisal. It will be a good lesson on learning what is and isn't valuable here."

"A wise decision," Elaethia said, and she pushed the coin tray to the center of the table. "I have taken the liberty of splitting the reward. Are we all content with this?"

Shiro and Lilian snatched up their coins, while Geran and Elaethia placed their own in their purses.

Lilian juggled her coins and frowned. "We knew this going in, but that reward was pretty small. We'll have to take another quest soon."

Shiro stood and rested a hand on the hilt of his sword. "I'm always ready to take another! Honor and fame await an adventurer, and fortune favors the bold! Once we pawn our loot, we can set out again tomorrow!"

"Now hold on a second," Geran said as he put a hand on the samurai's shoulder. "You just completed a quest. Now's not the time to think about another. Look around. Other parties have gotten back from their quests too. What do you see them doing?"

Shiro scanned the room. "They're ... celebrating?"

"Bingo. You know what Lilian says: "Work hard, play hard," right? We did a pretty damn good job today, especially for our first time together. I say that calls for celebration."

Lilian pumped a fist. "Awwwww *yeah!* After-quest drinks taste the *best!* Let's grab some seats before they all fill up!"

The demicat snagged Shiro by the elbow and dragged him toward the bar. The Osakyotan turned pink and began to sputter.

"B-but Lili-chan! I'm not old enough to drink!"

"You're nineteen, right? You only gotta be eighteen here, so you're good!"

"But I've never drunk alcohol before!" His voice was quickly drowned out by the sounds of the guild as he was pulled out of earshot.

Geran chuckled. "Wanna grab a round with the rest of us, Elaethia? It would be good for cohesion to celebrate together."

She pondered the invitation. "I myself have never drunk alcohol, and I have no problem with frivolity when the time permits, but …" She paused and looked around.

"Not your kind of atmosphere?"

"That as well. But I have never seen the appeal to these celebrations, nor have I had the heart for it. I cannot find myself willing to celebrate while Rychus still lives. These activities give no preparation or advancement to my goal."

Geran stood. "It couldn't hurt though, could it? There's no way that Svarengel family you stayed with would let you just sit and brood until you go and fight that guy. So neither should we. Besides, you ought to open up a little every now and then. If you don't let yourself enjoy some frivolity here and there, you'll turn sour."

She stood to join him. "If you insist. However, do not expect me to stay as long as the rest of you."

"Right, right. But you said it yourself: We're stronger united."

They joined Shiro and Lilian at the far end of the bar, near the stairs. The pair had just had their drinks presented to them. The demicat swiped up the wooden mug and began gulping down the contents. After a few swigs, she gasped sharply and let out a whoop.

"C'mon, Shiro! Don't leave me to drink alone! Your mead's getting warm!"

Geran raised an eyebrow. "What did you order for him?"

"Same thing I always get! The fruity one!"

The ranger picked up Shiro's mug and smelled its contents. "Yup, that's berry mead. Be careful with this stuff, Shiro. It's not strong, but it goes down easy. It's a good one for newbies, so have a mug or two. Don't try to keep up with Lilian, though. Despite her looks, she's no lightweight. That cat could drink half the youngins here under the table. Something tells me she's got more experience than she admits."

He waved down one of the bartenders and pointed a thumb at Elaethia. "Lemme get another one of those berry meads for the lady here. I'll take a dark ale."

"You're not going to have the same as the rest of us?" Shiro asked.

Geran took a deep swig from his mug when it arrived. "I used to drink that stuff when I started. Most people do. But it's too sweet for me now. I like something a little stiffer. Go ahead, give yours a try."

Shiro nodded and gripped his mug with both hands. He stared into it for a second and then brought it to his lips. He recoiled slightly at the new sensation and then went in for a deeper sip.

"It isn't bad, but not at all what I expected," he said.

Geran chuckled. "Well, since you passed the taste test, lemme tell you a little something about mead. I'm sure you've already noticed; but this ain't tea. You're not supposed to sip it. Go on, take a big gulp."

The samurai nodded again and did as instructed. After a single, large swallow, he slammed the mug down and erupted into a ragged coughing fit. Geran roared in laughter and slapped him on the back.

"Hell yeah, Shiro, get some!"

Shiro looked up at him with a grin and teary eyes. He gave a thumbs-up and took another gulp with a more controlled approach. Once again he broke into a cough, but not as heavily.

The Osakyotan looked up with hunched shoulders and bleary eyes. Through sporadic coughing, he asked, "Can I have some water, please?"

"Sure, buddy," Geran laughed. "Just ask the bartender for one."

Elaethia tilted her head. "This is part of the celebratory process?"

"Well, this is a little special. It's a man's first drink, so we gotta make sure it's done right."

"I see." She watched intently as Shiro finished his mug. Lilian, who was already two drinks in, leaned toward him.

"Well? Whaddya think?" she asked.

Shiro smacked his lips. "It's new and unusual, but I think I can get used to it."

Geran and Lilian laughed and patted his shoulders as Elaethia continued to watch with fascination. Shiro started on his next drink while Lilian enthusiastically cheered him on. Geran turned to see Elaethia's reaction and saw that she hadn't even touched her drink.

"Not to your liking?" he asked.

She followed his gaze and shifted back. "I apologize; I entirely forgot it was there." She picked it up in one hand, smelled it, and took a large swig. She then set it down again without so much as a blink.

Geran's forehead wrinkled. "Are you sure this is your first time?"

"I am sure, yes. I would certainly remember an experience like this."

"Ah. So how is it?"

"It is too early to tell. But I will be sure to let you know my final opinion later."

"Okay, well, I don't expect you to be all that social, so just relax and take it all in. Let me know when you decide you want to head back to your room."

Elaethia smiled. "I will, Geran. Thank you for your concern."

"Well I wouldn't say I was concerned. I guess I shoulda known that nothing gets through your iron will. Even alcohol."

"Is that so?"

Geran rubbed the back of his head. "Yeah. Say, uh, don't take this the wrong way, but I've been pretty curious toward your necklace."

Elaethia's hand came up to grab the golden pendant. "What of it?"

He laughed and put his hands up. "I'm not looking to steal it or anything; I'm just curious as to why you have it. It just surprises me that a woman as simplistic as you would have something so expensive."

"It was my father's," she began. "He gave it to me before he sent my family away while he went to fight. I cannot remember the words he said to me as he put it around my neck, but I can count on one hand how many times it has come off."

"It must really mean something to you."

Elaethia looked down and tightened her grip. "More than you know."

Geran nodded and looked into his mug. "I bet. Anyway, It's nice to know we're making progress on you."

"What do you mean?" she asked.

The ranger leaned against the bar. "When you first got here, you were as unapproachable as an orc with a toothache. Hell, when I was showing you around the place, I was ready for you to start throwing me through walls. But in these last few weeks, that ice-cold aura you have has almost disappeared."

Her tone wavered. "You believe I am losing my frost affinity because of you all?"

Geran laughed. "No, no, no, not like that. I mean your attitude. I think your magic is getting stronger, if anything. Of course, I wouldn't be able to tell. I'd ask Lilian."

He turned to address the mage but stopped himself. Lilian had her arm around Shiro and was waving her other hand in the air. The samurai was blushing furiously but smiling as she told stories about her magical adventures.

"Maybe we can ask her later," Geran chuckled. "I'm glad to see those two are getting along. I was worried Lilian might eat him up."

"Shiro certainly acts odd around her. I am not sure as to why, however."

"You can't tell?"

Elaethia shook her head.

He laughed. "I shouldn't be surprised. You're even worse than he is when it comes to social cues."

"I have been told similar things before," she said. "You seem to understand what is going on between them. What is it?"

"Well, I can't say that it's my place to tell. It's kind of a delicate thing, but it's fun to watch. You might pick up on it one day. It's a special kind of bond we shouldn't get involved in."

"You and I should not involve ourselves in a special bond like theirs?"

He froze for a second and then chuckled uncomfortably. "I meant getting involved in their business. Beyond that, I'd say we should wait a while."

"Indeed. I believe I should understand what you mean before I think further. Information is always necessary before engaging in all things."

"Yeah. Something like that."

Geran looked into his near-empty mug. It dawned on him what she really meant. He felt a little ashamed of himself for getting his hopes up like that. He had sworn off getting involved in romantic affairs a while ago for several reasons. That being said, he found her intriguing, calm, quiet, and powerful. And he frankly felt she was very beautiful too.

Geran shook himself back to reality. He knew those kinds of thoughts were dangerous, especially toward someone within his own party. The very things that drew him to her would be what would undo them. She was too naive, too unaware of the world around her. He was a man of caution, and she was a woman of action. They were nearly polar opposites.

A sudden bump shifted him to the right. He turned to see that Shiro had been pushed off his stool by Lilian. The mage blinked a couple times and scratched her head.

"Whoopsies! Sorry, guys!" She let out a girlish giggle and helped Shiro back onto his stool.

"How many have you two had?" Geran asked.

"I dunno 'bout me, but Shiro's on his third!"

Geran rubbed his eyes. "Shiro, didn't I tell you to have one or two? Wait, don't tell me. Lilian convinced you otherwise."

"Yes!" Shiro exclaimed with a slur. "Lili-chan is wonderful! She's so encouraging!"

Geran sighed with a forced laugh. "All right, buddy, I think we should cut you off for the night. Anyway, you completed your first ever quest today. What did you think of it?"

"It was marvelous!" Shiro said, and he swung his arms out, which sent a few drops flying from his mug. "Elaethia-sama is so strong and awesome! It's like she doesn't even try at all! And Lili-chan is so cool, too, because she knows so many spells! Magic is really awesome and useful. I wanted her to teach me, but she said she can't since Osakyotans don't have magic. *Oh!* And you, Geran! You're so smart and composed. We did so well with your plan, none of us even got hurt!"

The ranger smiled. "Glad you enjoyed it. That was easy as far as quests go for a party of four. Expect greater challenges going forward."

"Wonderful! A true samurai always strives for improvement!"

Lilian pounced over him to put her face right up to Geran's. "Are ya sayin' we'll be takin' a V quest next?"

He recoiled from her alcohol-ridden breath. "Jeez, Lilian, relax. That was hardly an A. We'll build ourselves up."

"Baaaaaaw!" she whined, and she flopped over, which knocked the drink out of Geran's hand and onto his lap.

"Damn it, cat!" he yelled.

"Whoops. Sorry, Gerry. Lemme clean that up for ya." She moved forward again, seemingly unaware she was still draped over Shiro. The two tilted off the stool and into Geran. He barely caught both of them, and he somehow managed to stand them up.

"That's it! Lilian, if you're gonna be a pain in the ass, go do it somewhere else!"

"Aww, Gerry, don't be such a stinker!"

"Then don't be such a brat! Thank the Moon I don't have to worry about Elaethia as much, but you two are turning into a handful. I'm going to get Shiro upstairs, so you can scram until I get that out of the way."

"Mmmmm fiiiiine," she grumbled. Her expression turned devious for a second as she reached toward his face. Her finger crackled dimly with electricity. "Boop!" she sang as she zapped him on the nose.

"*Lilian!*" Geran roared as he held his face.

The mage wheeled around and sprinted off, cackling with girly laughter. He was about to chase after her when he saw Shiro out of the corner of his eye. The samurai had stacked their empty mugs on the counter and had raised his sword above his head.

"Shiro, what are you doing!"

"A true samurai always strives for improvement. I must be able to make flawless strikes, even in my inhibited state."

"Don't break the mugs! What did I tell you about weapons inside?"

"Practice is more important!" Shiro insisted as he poised to strike.

Geran lunged forward and grabbed him. "You never had good common sense to begin with, but this really takes it up a notch!"

"Please, Geran, I don't want to make a scene!" Shiro wailed.

"You were already doing that, you idiot! Stop squirming already. Elaethia, help me out here; he's stronger than he looks!" He looked up to the warrior, who slowly turned to him. Her cheeks had slightly reddened, and her reptilian eyes were droopy. "You're drunk ... How the hell are you drunk? You've only had one drink!"

Her response was slow. "I have decided this beverage is rather good but has a mildly unpleasant aftertaste. I would like another!" she called to the barkeeper.

"No!" Geran shouted. "She's cut off! Elaethia, you're done for the night. This is why I never joined a party. Shiro! Quit fighting me! You talk all about honor and whatnot, and then you start acting like this?"

The samurai stopped. "I ... You're right. I am shaming myself, aren't I?"

"Big time. You done now?"

"Yes sir. I think it's best if I excuse myself for the evening."

Geran placed a hand on the samurai's shoulder. "Yeah, good plan. Let's get you to bed. I'll make sure you make it to your room."

"Yes, thank you, Geran."

They walked over to the stairs and up to his room. Geran looked over the railing to see that Lilian had convinced Liam Barron to give her a piggy-back ride. She giggled madly and shouted "Wheeeeee!" at the top of her lungs while the demiwolf charged around the floor. Geran shook his head at her antics as he guided Shiro to his room.

"Geran-san ..." Shiro mumbled weakly.

The ranger sighed. "I thought I told you just to call me Geran,"

"Geran, you know there's a reason I chose her as my master, right?"

"Who? Elaethia? Because she was the strongest and most righteous warrior in Linderry, right?"

The samurai grunted as he put his hand to the door and pushed it open. "Yes, but that was only my mindset at first."

"What are you on about?"

Shiro's fingers dug into Geran's shoulders as he inhaled deeply. "Please don't tell her this; but she's not the first master I've had here."

Geran raised an eyebrow and rolled the Osakyotan into his bed. "What's that supposed to mean?"

"There were many whom I swore my services to before I found her," he continued as he rested his head on the pillow. "Strong men and women who seemed firm and just. But they were either dishonorable or only used me for a short time before throwing me aside."

"I get it, man; I'm sorry you got screwed over. But I doubt it'd bother Elaethia if she knew you proclaimed your services to others before her."

"Don't you see, Geran-san? That's why Elaethia-sama is the best. None of my former masters talked to me like she does. None of them accepted me like she did. None of them looked past my wrongdoings like she has. Elaethia-sama promised that we would fight and stand as equals. And we did. Did you see us today, Geran-san?"

The ranger chuckled and pulled the blanket over him. "I sure did, buddy. You two did really well together. That was one of the best pairs I've ever seen."

Shiro turned his head to Geran. "Promise?"

"I promise."

A tear formed in Shiro's glazed eyes. "All this time in Linderry, I felt like a sellsword. A samurai with no master: a ronin. But Elaethia-sama fills me with purpose again. I … I don't want her to do away with me. I don't think my soul could take it."

"Don't worry about that, Shiro. I haven't been with her too much longer than you have, y'know. But I know she doesn't have a thought in her mind that involves getting rid of you. None of us do. But you've given her something unique as well. You're honorable, courageous, and dependable. She's never had a person like you to fight by her side."

"I … I'm a person … again …" Shiro mumbled.

Geran only stared at him in silence as Shiro smiled widely. The samurai's eyes began to flutter, and seconds later he was snoring. Geran exhaled heavily and patted him on the chest. He stood and walked to the door, turning back to look at the sleeping man. Geran shook his head and stepped outside.

He made his way back downstairs to collect Elaethia. To his horror, he noticed there was another empty mug next to her. Geran silently locked eyes with the bartender and gave him a glare so sinister it made the elven man drop the mug he was cleaning.

Geran put a hand on Elaethia's shoulder. "Hey, are you there? Can you stand?"

She only looked up at him with bloodshot eyes.

"Hoo boy. Please tell me you can make it to your room."

Her voice was more of a mumble than speech. "I should make it so far without too much difficulty." She rose to her feet and staggered like a newborn deer.

"Nope, nope. You sit here for a second. I'll be right back." He guided her back onto her stool and then walked over to the reception desk.

Maya looked up as he approached. "Hey, Geran. How can I help?"

"Hey there. Elaethia just had her first experience with alcohol, and I could use some help."

Maya groaned and set her pen down. "Oh no. Nothing and no one is broken, I hope? I really didn't want to fill out any more paperwork tonight."

"No, nothing administrative. She's a mellow drunk. I was looking for some help getting her to her room. I need someone I can trust not to try something funny with her."

"I suppose. I'll be right there."

The elf stood and headed into the back room, and she came out a door on the other side of the quest wall. The two walked through and around the other loud and rowdy adventurers over to where Elaethia sat.

Geran put his hand on Elaethia's shoulder. "Maya and I are gonna help you get to bed. Sound good to you?"

Elaethia only nodded in response.

"Wow, she's pretty far gone. How much did you make her drink?" Maya demanded as they each took an arm. Both of them grunted with effort as they strained to help Elaethia out of her seat and up the stairs.

"Just one," Geran said with a strain. "But your bartender there decided to sneak her a second one. She took the first sip so well I thought I didn't have to worry."

"Well, she's going to have a very nasty hangover," Maya wheezed as they reached the warrior's room.

"Yeah, we may have to postpone tomorrow's events."

Geran guided Elaethia's hand to her door handle. The door opened, and he stepped back so Maya could help her get inside. The short elf groaned with effort, stumbling as she lugged the warrior into her room. Geran quickly closed the door behind her as he noticed several adventurers below had taken notice. After a few minutes, Maya reappeared with a red face and a sweating brow.

"She is *not* a light woman," Maya panted, wiping her glasses.

"Was she cooperative?"

"Yes, thankfully. She's in bed. I got her shoes off but left her dressed. That is a *lot* of dense muscle on such a trim woman. Those shoulders and thighs are like *steel*."

"I know, right?"

Maya raised an eyebrow. "Now how would you know, Nightshade?"

"Look, I'm a ranger. I notice things. Call it an occupational hazard."

"I'm going to tell her you said that."

"Oh, please don't."

Maya laughed. "I'm kidding. Would you like help getting your mage to bed, too?"

Geran looked into the guildhall below. The demicat was dancing fervently on top of a table while holding another mug of alcohol. Other adventurers around her were cheering her on while whooping and hollering indistinctively.

"She'll wind down eventually," he decided. "After that, she can be someone else's problem. Thanks again, as usual. You've always been good at helping me with just about anything."

"Not a problem, as usual You've given me plenty of worse scenarios over the last decade. I'll see you around."

Geran woke up a little after nine o'clock. Considering the previous night's debacle, he figured it would be best to see to the other members of his party. Lilian, he knew, probably wouldn't even answer the door, but Shiro and Elaethia needed to be checked on. Deciding the young samurai needed attention first, he grabbed a waterskin and made his way to Shiro's room. He knocked gently and pressed his ear to the door. He heard a thud, followed by a moan. When he didn't hear anything else after a few seconds, Geran knocked again. Rustling and scraping sounds moved slowly toward the door. It suddenly opened to reveal a zombielike Osakyotan cowering in the entryway. Shiro groaned and covered his face as light flooded in.

"Is that the Sun? Why is he at my door?"

"Far from it. It's Geran. Mind if I come in?"

Shiro only grunted in response and shuffled back. Geran stepped in and closed the door as the samurai flopped back onto his mattress.

"My head feels like it's going to pop and implode at the same time," he groaned.

"I suppose there's no point in asking how you feel."

"Truly this is the death of a thousand cuts," Shiro wheezed.

Geran chuckled. "The first hangover is usually the worst, but you're not gonna die. Here. I'm gonna leave this water for you on your nightstand. Make sure you rehydrate yourself. Just take it easy for now; we can go out later if we have to."

"Water? I am truly in your debt." Shiro weakly reached for the waterskin and dribbled some into his mouth.

"I'm sure you'll find some convoluted way to thank me later. I just came here to make sure you were still breathing. Drink slowly, and as much as you can. I'll come check on you again in a few hours if you don't come find me by then."

Shiro swallowed and then turned over to mumble into his pillow. "Thank you very much, Geran-san,"

"It's just Geran," the ranger insisted.

Geran quietly left the room and headed downstairs. He grabbed a clean mug from the bar, filled it with water from the canteen, and went back upstairs to Lilian's room. A gentle knock on her door was followed by complete silence. He tried again with a little more persistence. Again, nothing.

"Lilian? You in there?" he called through the door. "I just wanna make sure you're okay. I've got some water here for yo-"

A heavy impact rattled the door from the other side, while a thud on the floor immediately followed. Geran jolted back, as he realized Lilian had thrown something at him. He decided it was best to leave her alone.

The last stop would be Elaethia, who had been in significantly worse condition than Shiro last night. Judging by the samurai's current state, he didn't even want to think about how she was feeling. The ranger hesitated in front of Elaethia's room. She was probably in no condition to move, let alone get up and answer the door. On the other hand, it was entirely possible her condition had taken a turn for the worse. He turned over the options in his head and finally decided. Someone had to make sure she was okay. He slowly reached his hand up and knocked softly on her door. Geran inhaled deeply, dreading the worst.

The door suddenly opened.

"Oh. Good morning, Geran," Elaethia said.

She stood fully dressed in front of him. She was wearing her fur shoes, and her clothes were straightened and neat. The room was full of light and in an orderly fashion. It looked as if she'd been awake for hours.

"Good … morning …" he faltered.

She tilted her head. "Is something wrong?"

"I … are you … okay?"

"I am well, yes."

"You didn't wake up with a headache or pain anywhere? You don't feel any repercussions from last night?"

She blinked and raised an eyebrow. "No. Why would I?"

"You don't get hangovers … That is so not fair."

"You are acting very strange this morning. Are you sure it is you who should be asking me about my current condition?"

"No, no, I'm just shocked. The other two are completely done for."

"They are feeling unwell, so you came to make sure I was not also?" she asked.

"Yeah, pretty much. I expected you to be worse off, since you were the most intoxicated when I left last night."

"I have never gotten sick or feverish since Frossgar granted me his power. Did I ever mention this to you?"

Geran rubbed the back of his head. "Yeah, you did. I just didn't think that counted for hangovers."

"Will Shiro and Lilian be all right? Should we get them a healing potion?"

"They'll be fine after a couple of hours. Besides, healing potions don't cure this kind of thing."

"I see. Is there something else you need in the meantime? Or something you wish to do? I have grown bored reading the book I borrowed from Lilian."

"Nothing around here that would interest you."

"Perhaps somewhere in the city then? I'm sure you might know of something for us to do while we wait for Shiro and Lilian."

Geran raised an eyebrow. "Are you asking me to take you somewhere?"

"Yes, please. If you do not mind."

"Oh. Yeah, sure. I just wasn't expecting that kind of response."

She tilted her head. "Should I have said something different?"

"Actually, I don't really know what I was expecting," Geran's brow furrowed as they stood in silence for a few seconds. "Well, uh, why don't you meet me downstairs in ten minutes. I'll think of a place that'd be interesting for both of us."

Elaethia nodded. "Very well. I will see you then."

The ranger exhaled heavily as she closed the door. He racked his brain as he made his way across the balcony. What was something around town that Elaethia, of all people, would find entertaining? Geran knew he was a rather uninteresting guy. He'd bored off a handful of girls that had taken an interest in him before, and he did *not* want to have that happen to Elaethia. Restaurants and libraries were probably of no interest to her, which really narrowed their options. Combat and weaponry were really all she talked about. That being said, there *was* an errand he'd been putting off. He felt this might be a good way to kill two birds with one stone.

Elaethia descended the staircase after ten minutes on the minute. She heard footsteps behind her and turned around to see that Geran had also just left his room. The timing was so uncanny that Elaethia realized he must have counted. Then again, so had she. A glint caught her eye, and she saw him holding a silver disc. She focused on it and saw lines and numbers on it in a circular pattern. A pocket watch. She hadn't known he had one. She had always used the clock on the guild's back wall to tell time, but now she felt perhaps she should invest in one. It would make it easier for her to gauge time when on quest.

They walked out the front door together and headed into town. Elaethia glanced at Geran's attire and noticed that his dagger was sheathed at his side. She vaguely remembered that it had odd, toothy indentations along the blade and wondered whether she should have brought her own weapon. She disregarded the thought after a moment.

Geran seemed to notice her stare. "Is something wrong?"

"No. I am merely wondering why you have decided to go out under arms. I realize I would stand out if I did as well, but I do not often see others walking around with weapons while not on quest."

"Oh, I'm just going to get it checked on by my usual blacksmith. I haven't used my swordbreaker in over a year, and I'd like to make sure it's still in good condition."

"You have named your dagger 'swordbreaker'?"

Geran laughed. "That's not the name of this individual weapon, just the type. My primary is a longsword, my secondary is a swordbreaker."

"It seems rather small to be able to break another blade," Elaethia said.

"That's actually not what it's used for. Another name for it is a parrying knife."

He pulled it out and handed it to her. It was a fairly long sidearm, almost half a meter from pommel to point. The grip was designed for comfort and stability, the hilt was wider than that of a normal dagger. Most notable on the weapon was the blade. The top half was sleek and wickedly sharp. The bottom half was entirely unique. Several toothlike gaps ran a few centimeters into the blade, and the tips were pointed in an arrow-like fashion.

"What is the purpose for these indentations?" she asked. "It cannot be a form of serration, for if the teeth embedded themselves into an opponent's body, it would be nearly impossible for a normal brehdar to tear it free."

"It's mainly for defense, designed to trap an enemy's blade" he said. "I can show you how it works sometime, but I don't use it that often, to be honest. Most of the time it's just another piece of equipment to keep track of."

"Then if it limits you so, why do you have it?"

"It's better to have something and not need it than to need it and not have it. It's saved my life on occasion. I'm fairly good with my longsword, but I prefer to keep my distance with the bow. I've got no problem running just my blade against monsters or inexperienced brehdars, but in a duel against an experienced swordsman? I'm hoping Shiro can handle those situations."

Geran continued to rattle on about ideas for various scenarios and how they could best handle them. Most of them involved Elaethia moving in first as Lilian backed her up, while Shiro watched *her* back. Elaethia couldn't help but marvel at his depth and forethought. The ranger certainly put a lot of thought and planning into this group. Perhaps *too* much.

They turned a bend and arrived at their destination. It was an open smithy nearly as large as the main floor of the guildhall. Waves of heat flowed out of the stone structure in buffets of hot air. Dozens of brehdars of all races stood around blazing forges and furnaces. The sound of metal striking metal and grindstones on blades filled the air as the craftsmen sweated and bent over their work. It was almost chaotic. This smithy bore only a mild resemblance to the one in Svarengel.

Geran stepped under an awning. "This shouldn't take long. I'm just getting it checked on to make sure it's good for a fight. You can watch, or take a look around if you want."

Elaethia nodded and headed toward the display area. Having no particular interest in the dagger, she turned her attention to a greatsword that hung from a rack. It seemed fairly well made.

From tip to pommel, it came up to her chest—half a meter shorter than Peter Stone's massive sword. She noticed some carved designs along the blade that formed into the image of a dragon's head at the tip. She found the carvings rather inaccurate as compared to a real dragon.

"Ah, you've got a good eye for weaponry."

Elaethia turned to see one of the blacksmiths approaching her. He was a demicat in his late twenties with short, blond hair and a grimy, shaven face. His tail appeared amputated halfway down.

Elaethia shrugged. "It seems to be a good weapon. It was the design that caught my attention."

"You noticed that. Seems everyone has taken a sudden interest in dragons these last few months, so I figured I'd try for it myself. This here is one of my newest pieces. It's a solid blade, and a unique design to boot. Go on, give her a few swings."

Elaethia reached out to the greatsword and lifted it off its rack. The smith seemed taken aback by how little effort she seemed to exert. She felt its weight and balance, and took a few steps back to try it out. After a couple of experimental swings, she realized she wasn't familiar with swords. She shrugged it off and returned it to its stand.

"So, uh, whaddya think?" the smith asked.

"It is well balanced, and the grip feels comfortable. I felt rather awkward with it, but I am sure that was due to not being used to it."

"Oh not a problem, not a problem at all. I enjoy constructive criticism, so any adjustments or ideas you'd like to mention, by all means, let me hear them."

She thought for a second. "As far as combat ability, I see no immediate issue. But the design is rather misleading."

"Misleading?"

"Dragon heads are not that long. The jaws are also a bit thicker. This one appears to have very large eyes as well."

He made a face. "What are you, some sort of dragon historian?"

"Not exactly. I am just speaking from experience."

"I, uh … I see. Anyway, I suppose if I were to adjust the engraving, would you be willing to strike a price?"

Elaethia shook her head. "I already have a weapon of my own. I was merely admiring the merchandise while I wait for a companion."

"Ah, shame. I think that greatsword suits you. It would be a real addition to the intimidation factor you have."

"I have been told my weapon is already very intimidating," she said.

"Is it? What do you use?"

"A large, deep blue twin-bladed battleaxe that stands as tall as I. It is a little wider than I am as well."

His eyes widened. "Say, you wouldn't happen to be with the guild, would you?"

"I am, yes."

"I thought those markings around your eyes seemed familiar! You're that dragon hero people are talking about!"

She tilted her head. "People are talking about me?"

"Of course they are! Haven't you heard the rumors?"

"I pay no attention to mindless gossip."

"Never mind that, you're famous! Practically a celebrity! Are you sure you don't want to consider one of my weapons?"

"Do you have something stronger than or equal to dragonite?" she asked.

The smith faltered. "Well I … it's not like we can … No … I don't."

Geran appeared next to them. "Elaethia, quit leading the poor guy on."

She tilted her head. "Leading him on?"

"I'll explain later," he said, and he then turned to the smith. "Sorry about her. We're not here to add to her arsenal."

The smith's face fell. "I see. I was really hoping to strike some kind of deal. Is there anything I can make for you? Anything at all within my capabilities? I'll even give you a massive discount."

Elaethia thought for a second. "I am perfectly content with my current equipment. However, should I feel the need for additions, I will consider it."

His feline ears perked up. "I suppose I can live with that. If you ever want something made custom to order, just come back here and ask for me, Simon Grommet. I'll make you a priority."

"I will, thank you," she said. She turned to Geran. "Was your dagger all right?"

"Yeah, just a little warped in the teeth. Nothing that couldn't be taken care of in a few minutes. Let's head back, shall we?"

"What did you mean by 'leading him on'?" she asked as they turned back toward the guildhall.

"Adventurers get fame and fortune by going out and doing quests. Smiths get theirs from famous adventurers using their equipment. The best only use the best, so aspiring adventurers will try to get the same gear as famous ones. If people know you use equipment from that Simon guy, he'll get more business. That's why he was so eager to make you something."

"That would explain his severe disappointment," she said.

"You actually noticed that?"

"Does this surprise you?"

"Well usually those social cues go right over your head."

"I do not understand that phrase."

He stared at her. "Where is your baseline?"

"A standard stance with sideways sweep from my dominant side. It takes little effort with a broad range of—"

Geran slapped his forehead. "No, no. I mean … Ah, never mind."

Elaethia looked at him with a hint of a smile. "You truly are acting strange today."

"I don't wanna hear that from you," he chuckled.

"It is true, though."

"Well, unless you think you're the normal one, and everyone else is weird."

She tilted her head. "How did you know?"

"That's how most people see the world. Everyone thinks they're right and everyone else is wrong. But most of us can identify the weird ones."

She shifted her weight. "Many find me strange, I suppose. Even you."

"Yeah, I won't lie to you," he said. "But I think it's a good kind of strange. It certainly got me out of my shell. I lived a lifestyle that practically *everyone* considered boring. Of course *I* found my job interesting, but people rarely appreciated it or cared. I was in a routine: Take a quest, complete it quietly, come back, cash in, take a breather—rinse and repeat. That's how it's been for ten years now. But then you popped in. Just appeared, outta nowhere. And before I knew it, my day-to-day was absorbed by you."

She felt a lump form in her gut. "Is this change … a negative one? I am sorry; I did not realize my appearance would affect you so. You do not have to adventure with me if you do not want to."

Geran's face twisted a little. "When have I ever made that impression? I asked to join you, remember? At first I said something about making sure you didn't act in a way that would give the guild a bad rep, but now? Hell, I can't really imagine going back to how I used to run. These last couple months have changed me. For the better. Up until recently, Maya and Liam were the only ones I really considered friends. But now even Shiro's fish-out-of-water demeanor and Lilian's antics have become somewhat of a comfort."

Elaethia smiled warmly. "Perhaps I am strange, but that is fine. Do you find those two strange as well?"

"Well, everyone's weird somehow. Don't know anybody who isn't."

"Even you?"

"I'm sure I am. I just don't know how yet."

"Such as the way you criticize minutiae and formulate a step-by-step plan that tends to fall through on contact? Or perhaps how you mutter to yourself when thinking."

Geran shot out his hands. "Hang on, those aren't weird! They're necessary steps in planning. And I don't mutter to myself!"

Elaethia laughed. It was short and relatively quiet, but it was also genuine and full of warmth. The ranger tried to laugh with her, but his breath hitched. His face flushed immediately after as well. She wasn't sure why, however.

"If you insist, Geran. But you do mutter to yourself," she said, still smiling. "Shall we commence our day's second task once Lilian and Shiro wake?"

Geran cleared his throat. "Yeah, sure. They should be up by now. Shiro's probably going to apologize left, right, and center to you, so prepare for that."

"Why would he apologize?" she asked.

"Consider it a ranger's intuition."

Sure enough, Shiro was waiting for them outside the guildhall when they returned. He was in his full armor, sword strapped to his waist. The samurai stood as stiff as a board as they walked up—eyes straight, face dead serious.

Geran rubbed his fingers into his eyes. "Shiro, what … What are you doing?"

The Osakyotan suddenly plunged to his knees in front of the dragon hero. "Forgive me, Elaethia-sama!"

"Called it," Geran stated.

Elaethia tilted her head. "I do not understand the need for such a display."

"Because of my actions!" Shiro barked. "I humiliated myself last night and was incapacitated in such a manner that I could not have defended you if the situation arose! My negligence to maintain my posture and honor within your presence is an affront to my code and surely an embarrassment to you. I will humbly accept whatever punishment you deem necessary for my inexcusable actions. I can assure you I will never drink alcohol again! Please, Elaethia-sama, do not cast me aside for being so careless!"

His voice wavered, and his body was shaking. Tears began to drip to the ground beneath his face.

Elaethia knelt in front of him. "Shiro, I was intoxicated as well. Besides, your actions were far from anything deserving reprimand, let alone removal from the party."

Geran knelt as well and put a hand on his shoulder. "We were celebrating, man. Getting drunk like that is part of the process. Don't even worry about it."

Shiro looked up, eyes red and nose running. "E-Elaethia-sama?"

"You are not at any fault," she assured him. "No harm came from last night. If you and Lilian are ready, Geran and I would like to carry out today's events."

"Of course!" he shouted, and he slammed his head into the ground again. "Thank you ever so much for your generosity and patience with me! Truly you are a most gracious master! I will be ready to leave as soon as you all are!" He jumped up, swung the door open, and sprinted inside.

"Well," Geran stated after a brief silence. "That wasn't as painful as I thought it would be. You handled that way better than I imagined."

"I am becoming used to Shiro's personality," she said. "And you did give me fair warning. That being said, I was not sure how he would act."

"Either way, it's over now. Let's go wait for Lilian. Hopefully all the shops will still be open by the time she's ready."

Rychus flexed his fingers along the arms of his golden throne. It was these moments that he longed for and savored the most—moments of solitude and silence in the peak of his domain, within his throne room, in his imperial palace, at the center of his capital city of Paragon. It was the space that was the epitome of his power and control. Everything he had worked and strived for led to these moments where he could bask in the presence of his own glory.

Rychus's appearance was unique among brehdars. Though he was 166 years old, his human face and body were those of when he was thirty-one. He was clean shaven, ripped with muscle, and had short, snow-white hair. But what set him apart was his almost golden skin and bloodred irises that seemed to pulse with power.

It was a shame he couldn't begin to experience this pleasure sooner in his reign. Perhaps he devoured too many slaves in the process of building his throne room. But to call the space a throne room would be a gross understatement, as it was larger than most courtyards. The massive ceiling was held up by twelve pillars, each four meters in diameter. White marble supports matched the white marble floor. The only other color in the room was on the enormous banners that draped between the pillars and behind the throne. These were bloodred with golden lining all around, and the emperor's sigil in the middle: a black hellflame with the head of an eagle in the center. A single carpet in the same colors ran from the grand double doors to the elevated throne. Gigantic stained-glass windows bathed the room in a golden light.

The room was empty besides the throne and a pair of two-meter-tall altars blazing with deep crimson flame. Chained to his throne were two terrified young women that were barely clothed. One was an elf, the other a demiwolf. Bruises and scrapes appeared on their torsos and legs, but their faces were left untouched. The only sounds in the grand room were the crackling of the fire and the occasional whimper or rattling chain from the slaves. He was hungry, and it was time for the evening report. As he expected, there was a knock on the great doors.

"Enter!" the emperor boomed.

"Yes, Your Majesty," came a dry voice. The elf that stepped in was old, nearly eighty. Clothed in a bloodred robe with black lining, he stepped forward and knelt before the raised throne with a parchment in his hands.

"I, chief advisor Nurelon, come bearing the evening report."

"Report, Nurelon."

"Yes, Your Majesty. No citizens have been identified as having an active magic trait today. A citizen distributing propaganda speaking against your rule was rooted out, and he and all his property were burned. Two households were caught with weapons in them; the adults received the standard punishment of removal of their dominant hands. Lastly, we found a potential source of the human trafficking circle in the ports that expedite fugitives out of the country. I have him outside, ready for questioning."

"Send him in," Rychus commanded.

"At once, Your Majesty." The advisor stood and shambled to the door. He opened it and revealed a teenage boy. He had short brown hair and wore plain garments accompanied by shackles around his wrists and ankles. "Approach the throne, knave. Do not even set your disgusting eyes upon him."

"Y-yes sir," he whimpered. He stumbled to the bottom of the steps and dropped to his knees in front of the golden tyrant.

"I'm going to ask you a series of questions," Rychus began. "Lie to me, and you will find yourself in unimaginable agony. If you cooperate, you will not suffer for long."

"Yes, Your Majesty," he said, trembling.

Rychus extended his hand. A red-and-black energy flowed from it, enveloping the boy. Its spectral tendrils surrounded his head and body as it flowed around him.

"You are one of my citizens that warns the smugglers when my legionnaires are nearby, correct?" Rychus asked.

"Yes, Your Majesty."

"You have done this fully knowing it is against my will?"

"Yes, Your Majesty."

"Were it stupidity, your actions would be pathetic. However, were it courage, this would be almost commendable. Which one was it?"

"I-I don't understand," the boy said shakily.

"I see. Then I take it you had no idea of the purpose of your task. A cloaked individual handed you a few coins or some food, along with a note telling you to give a certain sign if soldiers came?"

"How did you—" The boy looked up and was immediately kicked in the back by Nurelon.

"I told you not to look at him!" shrieked the elf.

"Don't think you're the first we've brought in here, boy," Rychus continued. "The organization you worked for is very discreet in their contacts. It appears you won't be able to provide any information I don't already know." He paused as the boy began to shake violently. "Tell me, do you have a family?"

"Y-yes, Your Majesty. My p-parents and a little sister," he stammered.

"You would not want any harm to come to them, would you?"

"N-no, Your Majesty!"

"Should you choose to serve me, and give me your life, I would spare them. Does that sound like a fair bargain to you?"

"Yes, Your Majesty! I will devote myself to your service."

"Then rise and approach me," Rychus commanded.

The teenager looked shakily over to Nurelon, who motioned to obey with an impatient grunt. Warily, he stood and approached the throne. Rychus extended his arm the boy and placed the palm of his hand on his head.

"I will now release you," he said. Instantly, the chains on the boy's wrists and ankles shattered. He stood dumbfounded and dropped to his knees.

"Thank you, Your Majesty. I will serve you in every way I can!"

"I only need one way." Rychus's hand moved from the top of the boy's head and covered his face. "You are now free of bonds—both your shackles and your burden on this earth."

"I don't understand—" The boy suddenly gasped, but no air came to his lungs. The emperor's hand began to pull on him—not just his body, but his mind and soul as well. The red-and-black energy began to pulse on his face. Desperately, the boy tried to pull himself free. His skin began to grow taut to his bones. His hair became longer and turned gray, until it fell out completely. His eyes rolled back and were sucked into his head as his flesh turned pale and wrinkled. The only sound that escaped his lips was a strained moan, no longer in his youthful voice. As his muscles and body deteriorated, he was left dangling helplessly in the emperor's hand until all that was left was thin, ashy, mummified skin that clung to dry bones. Rychus inhaled deeply and released the lifeless skeleton, which clattered to the ground. His red eyes began to pulse as he stretched. The emperor slowly brought his hands to his face and exhaled as a shadowy voice whispered in his mind. The red-and-black energy churned around him until it dissipated within his body.

"Is all well, Your Majesty?" Nurelon asked.

"Yes. He was weak. The surge was easily controlled."

"Is there anything His Majesty would like brought to him?"

"Yes, a light meal of fish, and a jar of wine. My appetite is not sated."

"At once, Your Majesty."

"And dispose of this corpse. Then find where his family lives so my legionnaires can pay them a visit."

"Of course. Is there anything else?"

"No. Leave me be for a while." He reached down and fondled the chains attached to his throne. The young women inched away in fear. "I have a sudden burst of vigor that I should make use of while I still have it."

Chapter 8
Hearts and Minds

Sixth Era. 139. Mertim 24.

Elaethia walked out of her room in the midmorning. She had become increasingly bored of merely sitting in her room, waiting for something to happen. Today she had decided to venture within the guildhall. She sat near the far corner and observed the day-to-day happenings of the guild. It was a different spectacle than the evening. Adventurers—some of whom she began to recognize—would prepare for their selected quest, receive their provisions, and head out. Listening to conversations provided her with a lot of information that she had never before known.

At first she concerned herself only with the classes of warrior, mage, and ranger. Soon after, she learned of priests, monks, duelists, druids, alchemists, and paladins. All sounded fairly self-explanatory except for monks, who used a certain type of anatomy magic. Anatomy mages overall were apparently a controversial sort. They could manipulate a living body—either their own or a target's—and the ability to alter another being was outlawed. Monks were the only class allowed to use it and were required by law to specialize in self-alteration in front of a court.

Much to her surprise, there weren't three guilds, as she first thought, but seven. Besides Breeze, Westreach, and Clearharbor, there was also Sprigganwood, Dinkerage, Frostshire, and even one in Apogee. She was about to go find Geran to ask him about them when Shiro appeared next to her.

"Good morning, Elaethia-sama," he said.

"Oh. Good morning, Shiro," she replied.

"May I take a seat?"

"Yes, but it is unnecessary for you to ask. You may simply join me whenever."

The samurai pulled back a chair and sat down. "Geran tells me the same thing, and so does Lili-chan. But I feel uncomfortable not asking for your permission. You are my master, after all."

"You know I do not claim that title over you, Shiro. But know that you do not have to request permission to join me. I enjoy your company."

He smiled a little. "I understand, and thank you. How did you spend your bonus money, Elaethia-sama? We got similar amounts."

"I have not purchased anything noteworthy. Only daily necessities."

"Oh. Well I bought a face mask!" he announced as he proudly held up a black cloth with a fixed divot. "This is made out of a material that's strong enough to protect against slashes! My helmet doesn't cover my face, and I don't like getting dust or blood in my nose and mouth. That divot goes over your nose so you can breathe easily!"

"A cloth that can stop a sword slash? That is difficult to believe."

"It's true! They proved it to me at the shop. He handed me a sharp dagger, and told me to slash it a few times. It didn't tear! Although he said it wouldn't hold against a thrust or a stronger attack."

"I have seen similar designs on assassins and cutthroats."

Shiro's eyebrows furrowed, and his voice became muffled as he put the mask on. "I'd rather not be compared to those kinds of people."

"Then perhaps rangers? I understand that at times they need to keep their identities protected or wish to cover their faces so as not to be seen. Perhaps we should ask Geran?"

"That would make me feel better. I tried talking to him earlier, but he was busy speaking with some other rangers."

Shiro motioned toward the adjacent corner, where Geran was still talking with the rangers in question. After a few minutes, Elaethia was able to catch his eye and wave. He gestured for them to wait a moment, took another minute to wrap up his conversation, and joined the two.

"Whaddya got?" he asked as he took a seat.

"Shiro purchased a protective face mask and would like your input," Elaethia said.

The ranger gave it a look over. "I mean, I suppose it's a good investment. The color is tactical, and it does a good job of covering the softer parts of your face while giving you maximum visibility. But if it's protective, that means it's thick, so it could restrict breathing. I wouldn't use one unless I expected to get up close and personal with an enemy. How much did that cost?"

"Thirty-seven gold," Shiro said.

Geran spat out a laugh. "Yeah, forget that! I hope that thing is worth the money for you. Don't tell me you blew all your cash on it."

"I … uh … should have enough to last to the end of the week."

"It's Thursday."

"I know."

Geran rubbed his face. "By the Moon, Shiro. That is not a smart way to live."

"It is wise to save whenever possible," Elaethia agreed. "Unforeseen events are common in this world. It is wise to be prepared for the worst in every occasion."

"Awwwww, don't listen to them, Shiro!" Lilian called from above. "If you find something cool, you should get it while you can. Whatcha talkin' about, anyway? I'm bored! Let's go on a quest!"

Geran groaned. "Stars above, Lilian, one thing at a time! And has it ever occurred to you that some of us aren't willing to go on a quest at the drop of a hat?"

"You don't have to come if you don't want to, Geran," Shiro said.

Geran sighed. "Nah, it's fine; we can go. Only a short one, though. I've got a ranger meeting tomorrow."

"*Sweet!*" Lilian jumped and pumped her fist, and she then turned to run to her room. "I'm gonna go get ready. I should be down in, like, thirty minutes! Just pick any one; I don't care!"

"Ranger meeting?" Shiro asked.

"It's where we all get together and exchange information found on quests and current events from the surrounding areas. We try to do one once every quarter year."

Elaethia inclined her head toward him. "Is that what you were talking about with the other rangers?"

"Yeah, that was Byron and Roderick. Roderick is Razorback's ranger, for what it's worth, and Byron usually runs solo. The three of us are the most active rangers in Breeze, so we coordinate these things. In the meantime, you two can go get armored up. I'll see if I can find a good quest."

"Are we ready to take a V quest yet?" Shiro asked as he eagerly scanned the quest board.

"Not yet," Geran said. "I'd like to get more synced with the group. Besides, we're looking for a day job. You show me a V-level quest that takes only one day, and I'll show you an expertly masked trap."

"Are we looking for any type in particular?" Elaethia asked.

"Don't think so. Our criteria are that it must be short and offer decent pay—although those quests aren't common and always get snatched up quickly."

"None of the A quests seem like they would work," Shiro muttered. "I don't think any of the ones we could do would take one day or less."

"Lemme take a look," Geran said, and he joined him to study the board. "You're not wrong. Maybe we should lower our standards and go for an I."

Elaethia exhaled heavily. "But those hardly pay to the standard we need."

"Not to mention they're a little beneath us. High-level party of four taking a low-level quest? Not something to write home about."

"Shiro could always go solo. I would not mind."

"Yeah, but I'm not sure if he'd want to go alone yet. Lilian would also pitch a fit."

"She did seem quite eager to go out," Elaethia agreed.

Shiro suddenly cut in. "Hey, what about this one? It was hiding beneath some other flyers." He exposed a covered A-level quest and motioned the other two over.

Geran stuck his face up to it. "This one looks familiar. Yeah, this is that kill-type quest for a troll we saw a few days ago. This one's been up for almost two weeks now."

"Read it aloud for us," Elaethia prompted.

"A troll has been seen around the plains, roads, forests, and communities to the west of Breeze. It has been wandering aimlessly, smashing anything and everything it comes in contact with. Property has been damaged, livestock eaten, and caravans halted or attacked, and there have been reports of four brehdar deaths as of posting. Kill the troll."

Shiro's eyes hardened. "Why hasn't this been taken yet? This seems urgent."

"Trolls are rather hard to kill. They're one of the biggest monsters out there, and they don't go down easy. The only reason this is an A-level is because they're the dumbest things to walk the earth, after slimes. Like the quest indicates, they just meander around aimlessly and smash stuff. It's not uncommon to see one outside the Titan's Forest, but not exactly an everyday occurrence."

"And you believe this would only take us a day?" Elaethia asked.

"With you? Yeah. The hard part would be finding it. Shiro and I wouldn't deal much damage to it. We could whittle it down after a while by dancing around it and slashing its legs. I think he and I could serve as a good distraction while Lilian knocks it down with offensive spells. We'll use your strength and battleaxe to finish it off."

"Helloooooo! Did we find one yet?" Lilian pranced down the stairs and up to the group. The demicat was donned in her questing gear, as well as some black markings on her face. The markings were two inward-facing triangles painted beneath both of her eyes, one on the cheekbones and one on the cheeks themselves. The other party members stopped and stared at her.

"Lilian," Elaethia asked, "what is on your face?"

"This? Oh, this is my war paint. Pretty awesome, don'tcha think?" The mage chuckled smugly, twirled her staff, and flashed a hand in front of her eyes.

Shiro blinked. "Are they supposed to resemble whiskers?"

She flushed and tapped her index fingers together. "Well, it, uh … I started putting it on, and it kinda, I guess, turned into that. Maybe?"

Geran gave her an odd look. "Why're you wearing war paint?"

"'Cause we're going on a quest and it looks cool! You guys do it too, so I thought I'd give it a try!"

Everyone went silent.

"When have we ever worn war paint?" Elaethia asked.

"What do you call that around your eyes?"

"These markings are a part of me. They appeared after I received Frossgar's power."

"Wh-what?" Lilian stepped forward and peered at the blue scales that melded with the dragon hero's skin. She reached out a finger and touched them, to find that Elaethia was telling the truth. The mage turned pink and whipped her head to Geran.

"B-b-but what about on the goblin quest when you put that green-and-brown stuff all over your face?"

Geran rubbed his temples. "For the last time, that was camouflage paint. I only wear it when I'm trying not to be seen."

Lilian slowly turned to the samurai. "Shiro …?"

He looked away. "S-sorry, Lili-chan. I can't say that I have."

"So … none of you have ever done war paint …?" Her voice became small as her ears drooped. The others all shook their heads. Lilian turned bright red and reached up with both hands to pull her wide-brimmed hat over her face. She shrunk into a squat, whimpering in embarrassment.

"I-it's not that it's weird or anything!" Shiro stuttered. "We just weren't expecting it! It looks good on you!"

"It's like something an overly motivated newbie would do," Geran stated flatly.

Elaethia pondered for a moment. "In Svarengel, the usage of war paint is intended to strike fear into the hearts of your opponents. I do not see yours as intimidating."

Shiro piped in. "It's also useful for keeping glare out of your eyes. She's got the placement down. Well, for the top two. But the shape's all wrong."

Lilian stuffed her hat back on top of her head. "Would you all stop! I didn't go to all this trouble just for you to—"

She was cut off when Maya burst through in the front door.

"*Emergency quest!*" she shouted into the hall. "Suppression, A level, uprising in the northern farming village! I need at least one party of three or more to get there *now!*" She noticed Elaethia and her party in front of the quest board. "You four—can you take this one?"

"We were just about to take the troll one," Shiro started.

Geran cut him off. "This is an emergency quest. We're not engaged in anything at the moment, and we're ready. We have to go. Maya, any details?"

The elf shook her head. "Practically nothing. The description is very vague, but the payment is all here, *plus* the emergency fee. It arrived via carrier falcon, so it's probably highly urgent."

Elaethia stepped up. "If it is urgent, then we will do what we can to help."

"Perfect! I'll start filling this out; you guys get over there as soon as you can. You know where it is, right, Geran?"

"Yeah, I was born in the next town over. Let's move."

"*Wait!*" Lilian shouted. "Lemme go wash this stuff off!"

"We don't have time, Lili-chan," Shiro said.

"I can't go walking around like this! This'll take five minutes, I promise." Lilian had started heading for the stairs when Geran's hand shot out and snagged her tail. She yelped and started to rattle off rapid-fire high-pitched objections as the ranger dragged her to the door.

"Ow! Ouch-ouch-ouch, Geran, stop! Leggo! Seriously, stop! Leggo-my-tail-I-gotta-get-this-stuff-offa-my-face-*owie-ow-ow-stoppiiiit!*"

"What part of 'emergency quest' did you not understand? We don't *have* five minutes, and nobody's gonna care if you have paint on your face. We gotta get to the village *now*, before someone gets killed. Elaethia, Shiro—you mind getting the door for me?"

The two of them stepped forward to open the double doors as Geran pulled Lilian outside. The demicat whined and objected the whole time, clawing at the door frame as she was yanked through.

"Pleeeeeeaaase Geran-let-me-go-I'll-only-take-five-no-*four*-minutes-to-wash-this-stuff-off-I'm-begging-you-by-the-Moon-this-is-so-embarrassing-would-you- take-three-minutes-I-can-do-three-minutes-I-don't-wanna-gooooo!"

The doors slammed shut, and her voice was cut off.

Elaethia read the description as they jogged to their destination. She had seen requests for suppressions before, but nothing like this. All the others required locating the group or individual in question and removing them from the area—that or forcing them to submit so the local guard could arrest them. This one mentioned none of that. In fact, it didn't mention much at all. It simply read, "Quell the uprising in the district without any casualties." There was no mention of who they were quelling or who had submitted the request.

How curious, Elaethia thought. "How much farther until we reach the village?" she called back.

"Three minutes at this pace, maybe four," Geran estimated. "It's just over that hill."

"Shall I go ahead? If your assumption regarding the time is correct, I would be there in twenty to thirty seconds."

"I doubt that very much, and we need to stay together," he said. "If you just show up and start swinging, who knows what will happen."

Elaethia found herself feeling rather indignant at the remark. "My full sprint would easily get me there within the minute."

"Giving your speed the benefit of the doubt, I still say it's best we arrive together."

"As you wish."

Lilian's ears twitched as they crested the top of the hill. "Gosh, the people are *not* happy down there."

"What do you hear?" Geran asked her.

"Can't make anything out 'cause we're running," she wheezed. "I don't know if I'll have the energy to do anything after this. By the Sun, I wish we had horses."

Sure enough, as they entered the gate into the village, Elaethia saw a mob of civilians with assorted farming tools outside the central building. It was a large stone-and-wood manor with green-tinted windows. A wrought-iron gate surrounded the property. It stood out very easily, as all other structures were made of thatch and wood. The manor obviously belonged to a wealthy family. Geran stepped ahead to address an onlooker: a middle-aged demiwolf in a plain dress.

"Pardon me, ma'am," he said, and he steadied his breath. "We're with the guild, sent here on an emergency quest. Do you know who submitted it?"

"I don't know," she said. "Could have been either side, really."

"Can you tell me what's going on?"

"Something about the village nobles pocketing income from trading caravans, but I've heard multiple stories. I'd ask one of the people trying to break into the mayor's house."

"Okay, thank you," he said. He then turned back toward the party. "It's probably the mayor who sent the request, asking us to deal with the mob. There's also a small possibility that it was a villager asking either the same thing or to help the protestors. Let's ask around the crowd, try to get a straight answer. Hit back hard if they get violent, but use nonlethal techniques. I'm not risking one of us getting hurt or having to do paperwork over this. Try to stay near the center so we can all regroup easily."

Everyone nodded and spread out into the masses. Geran weaved his way through in a fluid manner to approach calmer individuals. Lilian walked casually with her hands behind her back and tapped the shoulders of the younger people. Shiro excused himself as he made his way around, asking everyone he came in contact with.

Elaethia strode right through and looked around at the swarm of villagers. She had never had to do anything like this before and was completely at a loss as to how to approach the situation. Everyone who saw her backed out of her way, warily eyeing the heavy armor and massive axe. Her hard, expressionless face alone was enough to turn them away. It was as if she were a wolf among a flock of sheep. She sighed deeply. This was not her field of expertise.

A shout from one of the protestors broke through the crowd. "What's that supposed to mean, ya guildy? You think we can't handle our own problems? Who the hell sent you!"

The mob turned their attention toward the new commotion. Geran was the center of the outburst.

"We're just trying to figure out what's going on," the ranger explained with his hands up. "We got called, and we need information about the situation before we act. We're trying to get this solved as calmly as possible."

"Bullshit!" the dwarf spat back. "I bet the mayor called for you and you're here to beat us all into submission!"

The crowd began to shout out arguments in support of both sides.

"No way, they'd have acted by now!"

"They're just trying to get melded in before they attack!"

"We don't know that! The guild wouldn't harm civilians like us!"

"You think they'd send heavy hitters like them just to drag that rat bastard out of his mansion? They're here to shut us up!"

The man that engaged Geran shouted into the sky in frustration. "I'm not just gonna stand here and take this crap! We're here to set things straight, and I won't let you guildies ruin that!"

He wound up and struck Geran across the face. The ranger staggered back, glared at his assailant, and fired a wicked right hook into the protestor's jaw. The dwarf crumpled to the ground in a heap.

All hell broke loose at that instant.

The protest turned into a riot. Lilian quickly darted out of the slugfest as the rest of the party engaged. One elven woman in her early twenties slammed a rake into Elaethia's side. The dragon hero wasn't affected, but the attacker dropped the tool from the shock. The villager tried again, this time giving Elaethia a push-kick, which made her stumble backward and fall. Before she could get up, Elaethia planted her boot on the rioter's chest and knocked the wind out of her. Elaethia then raised her boot again for a stomp.

"Elaethia, stop!" Geran's voice shouted from her right. "Nonlethal! *Nonlethal!*"

She turned to look at him and set her foot down, unaware of the elf that banged desperately on her leg. "I had no intention of killing her. She attacked me first with a harmful intent. You said to hit back hard."

He growled in frustration as another rioter tackled him. "I've seen what you're capable of; that could kill her! You've got—*oof*—heavy armor, and you're the—*ow, damn!*—strongest one here. Just keep her on the ground!"

"Very well." She reached down to grab the elf's face. She lifted it up and then slammed the rioter's head back into the cobblestone ground.

"*Elaethia!*" Geran cried out. He twisted himself out of the grapple, striking his opponent on the temple. He rushed over to her to check on the woman.

"That was not enough to kill her," Elaethia said. "I have done that maneuver before. She is merely unconscious."

"That was a heavy slam! Keep them off of me while I make sure she's still breathing," Geran said as he ran his fingers under the back of her head and down her neck. "Her skull's intact, and she's still got a pulse. I guarantee she's got one hell of a concussion though. By the Sun, tone down your power! We can't risk doing this kind of damage to civilians!"

"I understand. I will adjust my tac—" she was cut off as a large demicat slammed into her side and wrapped his arms around her torso. Again, she didn't move. The dragon hero shot her left arm up and struck her elbow into his forehead. She turned to face him and thrust a kick into his chest that sent him flying into a wooden cart. The wheel splintered as he impacted, and the straw that was in the cart began to fall over him.

"What did I just tell you?" Geran shouted. "Stars above, I … That's it, you're on timeout!"

Elaethia tilted her head. "Time … out?"

"Yes! Timeout! You're putting us all in a bad light! Go stand off to the side. Shiro and I will finish this!"

Elaethia realized she was being scolded. It seemed to have been a long time since that last happened. The warrior stiffly turned and walked toward where she had seen Lilian escape to. The dragon hero was met with no resistance as she strode in a straight line through the melee. The villagers all paused or disengaged their brawling to get out of her way.

Elaethia met up with Lilian, who was leaning against the side of a tavern. Elaethia leaned against the wall as well and folded her arms in front of her chest. For the first time in over a decade, she found herself trying very hard not to pout.

Lilian cocked an ear at her approach. "What are *you* doin' here, Elaethia?"

"Timeout, apparently," came the sullen reply. "It appears I do not possess the tact or ethic for this kind of work."

"Gosh, I've never seen you make that expression before. Did Geran yell at you or something?" she asked.

Elaethia nodded. "How about you? Why did you run as the fight started?"

"I'm a mage. All my attacks are lethal, have long-term effects, or would hit friendlies. Even my air spells would get in the way of everyone else. I don't know who's on what side, so I stay out of it. And I'm no good in a fistfight."

"Perhaps you should invest in some armor."

"Metal gets in the way of using magic, and leather is so bland."

"I see."

Elaethia watched as Geran maneuvered around the fray. His fighting was almost acrobatic as he tumbled over opponents, flipped them over his shoulder, leaped onto their chests, and rolled to and from his targets. Shiro had strapped his sheath to the hilt of his sword so he could strike with a blunt object instead of the blade. He lashed and struck his targets with pinpoint precision and unnatural speed. The samurai maneuvered around the mob, flowing like a river in constant motion. Each step was smooth and deliberate. It seemed that he planned two to three strikes in advance before he executed them. Shiro was equally elegant and savage as he effortlessly dispatched the rioters. Elaethia knew little about swordplay, but she did know that Shiro was not one to cross blades with.

After a few minutes, the brawl was over. Only Geran, Shiro, and a few villagers who sided with them were still standing. Everyone else was on the ground; bruised, unconscious, exhausted, or a mix of all.

"All right!" Geran shouted, now out of breath. "Which one of you hicks filed an emergency request for a submission?"

The front door of the mansion opened. An old, nervous-looking nobleman stuck his head out. His blond hair was receding to the middle of his head, and his tweed mustache was giving in to gray.

"I-I sent the request," he said. "Are you the adventurers with Breeze?"

"Yes, we are. Who're you?"

"I am Samuel Heath, the mayor of this little farming town. Thank you very much for taking care of that unruly mob. Would you mind staying here until the guard shows up? I would certainly hate for any more fighting to occur over a simple misunderstanding."

"*Misunderstanding?*" exclaimed one of the villagers. "You stole from us, Sam! All that nonsense about caravan taxes and handling fees? That money was going straight to your pocket!"

"Now, now, I would *never* do something like that with ill intent. I merely … *exaggerated* the fees solely for the betterment of the community!"

"For the betterment of the … We haven't seen a single benefit since you started this scheme! Hey, ranger, you're not believing this crap, are you?"

Geran folded his arms and exhaled heavily. "From a personal standpoint, this sounds like fraud and theft. But I don't know the details, and I'm no lawman, so I can't pass judgment. However, from a professional standpoint, we have to follow through with what the customer requested. There's no proof what you said is true, so we have no basis to refuse his request."

The villager threw up his hands. "I don't believe this; the guild is siding with corrupt politicians!"

Elaethia walked over. "Surely we are not going to let this man go. If what the people are saying is true, these actions are inexcusable."

"He filed a request and paid the guild for it to be posted," Geran said. He then turned to the nobleman. "You *did* pay, right? Otherwise Breeze wouldn't have accepted it."

The mayor nodded fervently. "Yes, yes of course! Your sum of gold and silver is waiting for you at your guild!"

"Good, good. Then our quest is complete."

Samuel stared at him. "I'm sorry?"

"Yep. You specifically asked for a suppression mission. We have suppressed the mob, with no casualties. On the professional level, our business with you is complete. If you wanted more from us then you should have put more than one sentence in the quest description."

Elaethia caught on to Geran's implication. "Which means we have no obligation to defend you anymore."

"Close," Geran said with a point. "If the mob reformed before the guard got here, it might be considered a negligent quest. The same applies if he's found wounded. But nothing's stopping us from teaching him a lesson about greed."

The mayor's face blanched. "Now hold on; I'm sure we can strike a deal here, hmm? You're all soldiers of fortune, are you not? I'm sure we can strike some sort of deal that benefits all of us."

Shiro stepped up with his hand on the hilt of his sword. "Don't take us for some sort of mercenaries! We aren't so without honor as to take any job just for money, and we *certainly* have no interest in your ill-gotten gains."

Samuel sputtered. "I … You can't … This isn't … I am the *mayor* of this town, dammit! Your guild will pay if something happens to me!"

Elaethia stepped forward and cracked her knuckles. "We will take that chance."

All of the color drained from Samuel's face. The nobleman fell backward and kicked away from her with a terrified whimper.

"Rip off his ugly mustache!" a voice called.

"Hang him on the flagpole by his britches!" a random villager encouraged.

"Throw him on the roof of his fancy mansion!" another added.

Elaethia gleamed. "An excellent idea."

"Wait!" Lilian shouted, and she bounded up beside her party. "You guys have had all the fun. Let me have a turn!"

Samuel pointed at her. "If you so much as lay a finger on me, girl, I'll have you—" He cried out in surprise as he was suddenly lifted off the ground by an air spell. Lilian thrust her staff at his feet and then straight up, blowing him onto the roof. The mayor landed on top of his estate, scrambled to keep his footing, and started shrieking obscenities at the cheering people below.

"What was that?" Shiro asked her.

She gave a thumbs-up. "An air spell called *updraft*. I didn't lay a finger on him, he's safe from harm, and he's not going anywhere anytime soon! It's a win-win-win!"

Elaethia looked up at the frantic, screeching man. "I was rather looking forward to doing that."

"Whoops, sorry!" Lilian giggled, and she flashed her signature grin. "Geran, do we gotta stick around, or can we go get the reward now?"

He scratched his stubble beard and turned to the villager next to him. "You guys gonna cause trouble when the guard shows up?"

The human shook his head. "Nope. We'll keep an eye on Samuel up there, but we won't make any more of a ruckus. I'll make sure the guard knows you guys didn't do anything wrong. You're the party leader, right? What's your name? We'll put in a good word for you guys."

Geran pointed a thumb at the heavy warrior behind him. "Elaethia's the party leader. I'm just the strategist."

The villager blinked. "But … Didn't you put her in … timeout? Anyway, thanks for helping us. You guys are pretty powerful people, but I've never seen this group before … although I think I recognize your mage. Do you guys have a name?"

"No, we're a fairly new party. Thanks for offering to clear things up for us with the guard. If you don't mind, we'll head back and report to the guild."

"Shouldn't be an issue. Thanks again, adventurers."

As the party went over the hill and down the road back to Breeze, Geran's brow furrowed at the comment that villager had made. The more he thought about it, the more he realized he was assuming the role of party leader. He didn't like that. It wasn't that he didn't want to take charge, but more so that this was Elaethia's party, not his. Sure, Geran came up with most of the plans and strategies, but it was Elaethia who had brought them all together. Not to mention that she had final say in everything they did. If Elaethia wanted something to happen, they made it happen. If she didn't want to take action, they wouldn't. And yet, he seemed to be calling most of the shots. This was by far the most confusing hierarchy he'd ever seen.

"What happens to the people now, Geran?" Shiro asked. "Will they be okay?"

"They ought to be. They're in a position where they'll get what they want, so there's no reason to believe they'll form another mob. As for us, it's as simple as heading back and getting the reward. We'll take that troll quest in a day or two. No telling what will result from the meeting."

"Could I sit in on it with you?"

Geran made a sound of uncertainty. "You'd be bored out of your mind, but sure. Keep in mind you probably won't understand eighty percent of what we talk about."

"I'm sure I'll learn something. Besides, I have nothing else to do tomorrow and … What is *that!*"

Shiro froze in his tracks and pointed in front of them into the distance, just off the road. Geran followed his finger, and his jaw dropped. A lumpy, ten-meter-tall humanoid figure trudged around in the open field. It was dragging what appeared to be a tree behind it.

Geran shot his hand out. "Everyone freeze! That's a troll!"

Lilian stopped midstride, her left foot still poised in the air. "Oh, hey, so it is."

"That wouldn't happen to be the same troll from the quest board, would it?" Shiro asked.

"That one was supposed to be to the west. We're still north," Geran noted.

"Yeah, but it's been two weeks," Lilian pointed out. "It coulda wandered anywhere."

Geran nodded with a grunt. "Well, guys. Fight or run?"

"Excuse me," Elaethia stated as she donned her visored helmet. She drew her axe and held it high in her right hand. The warrior burst off like a shot toward the hulking monster. Dirt, grass, and air pressure kicked up in the faces of the other three. Dumbfounded, they watched her close the two-hundred-meter gap in about ten seconds. Her thundering footsteps grew quieter as she got farther and farther away.

"We didn't take that troll quest, did we?" Lilian asked.

"Nope," Geran replied.

"So no reward for killing it. Oh well. Good luck stopping her."

Shiro squinted. "I think she's doing this to release some pent-up aggression, or maybe out of instinct. I doubt money or quest completion has anything to do with it."

The dragon hero leaped into the air, her battleaxe poised for an overhead strike. The troll began to raise its makeshift club to swat at her but was too slow. She drove her feet into the chest of the massive creature and slammed the weapon into its face. A blast of ice spikes burst through the other side of its head, and its face was split and frozen over. The monster listed backward and fell stiffly to the ground. An audible boom pealed while a frosty mist enveloped the scene.

Lilian's staff clattered out of her hand. "Did she just one-shot a *troll?*"

Geran rubbed the back of his head. "Y'know, somehow I'm not even surprised. I've just come to realize we hold her back in all-out combat."

They all watched as the dragon hero emerged from the fog. The frosty mist seemed to cling to her as she strode through it.

Shiro rubbed his chin. "Lili-chan, didn't you one-shot a troll before? With that *lightning strike* spell?"

She let out a sheepish chuckle. "Well, it wasn't the only spell I used. To be honest, I just cast it to show off for the villagers. I blew out half my magic on the thing before it started to rain, so I kinda popped my potion and let 'er rip."

"Should we ... meet her halfway, or are we gonna keep standing here?" Geran asked.

"Let's catch up," Shiro suggested.

The three of them continued along the path until they met with Elaethia. Her hair was blown around and covered in debris, but other than that she seemed unaffected.

Geran addressed her first. "I thought I had you all figured out, and then you pull this. Now what am I supposed to make of you?"

"I do not understand what you mean. Are you looking for a specific answer?" she asked.

"Don't worry about it. I'm just thinking aloud, I guess."

"Kind of like your muttering?"

"Stop it." He grinned at her with a glint in his eye. "If it makes you feel any better, I now believe what you said about being able to run to the village in less than a minute."

She smiled at the response. "It does. Shall we send a verifier to the location?"

"Yeah, but we won't get a reward if that's the troll that was posted," Lilian explained.

"I was not considering the reward. I had felt unfulfilled after the recent quest, and I did not want to let the creature wander around and harm more people."

"I figured as much," Shiro said.

"Oh well," Lilian sighed. "Guess we'll have to take a different quest now. I hope Sammy boy paid us good."

They entered the guildhall in the late afternoon. Elaethia stepped inside and went to the reception desk to turn in their quest. Expecting Maya, she was instead greeted by a dwarven woman about the same age. She wore the receptionist uniform and had long brown hair in a single braid that cascaded over her shoulder.

"Evening, Bridgit," Geran greeted her. "Where's Maya?"

The receptionist gave him a pouty look. "Aww, you're not happy to see me?"

"Well, all things considered, you could say I am. Sorry about asking for her first, but she *is* the one who sent us on this emergency quest."

The dwarf pulled out the quest flyer. "She's upstairs talking to Master Dameon. Something regarding your party, actually. Lucky for us, she happened to leave the details behind. So your party can go rest up while you and I stay behind here and … talk business."

"Well," he said, stepping back, "if all you need is the party leader, then I'll let her take over. Elaethia, you're up!"

He turned and walked away from the counter, leaving a confused Elaethia and a very disappointed Bridgit.

Elaethia stepped to the desk. "I understand you have the paperwork to complete our mission. I am ready to fill it out."

"All right," the dwarf sighed, and she rested her cheek on her arm. "This isn't too different from a normal completion form. Just sign at the top next to Samuel's signature, as well as at the bottom like normal. Write out the names of all who took part on the lines in the middle. Put down the estimated time of completion, and I'll take care of the rest."

"Very well." Elaethia took the pen and filled in the designated spots. Bridgit brought out the tray of coins as she did.

"Here you go—fifty-five gold and nine silver. Please verify the amount."

The warrior took off her right gauntlet and measured the coins. "I accept the amount. I should inform you that I killed a troll that we believe to be the one currently posted, but we did not accept it here. Is it true that the payment will be voided?"

"Correct. We'll take it down and send out a verifier. Once they confirm, we'll discard the quest. Why'd you go after it?"

"It was in our way on the return. It is no longer in the western areas, instead along the northern path to the farming village."

"I'll make a note of that. You're Elaethia, right? I don't believe we've met."

"I am. You are one of Maya's associates? It is a pleasure to meet you."

"Likewise." Bridgit smiled warmly until her expression began to shift at the corner of her mouth. "So. You're Nightshade's new girl?"

"New … girl?"

"Never mind, that wasn't a fair question. I've heard enough about you to know better. Then again, the rumors are consistent."

"I do not understand."

Bridgit nodded. "I figured as much, but it was worth a try. Geran's a nice guy; he just needs his space. Be patient with him please. For me?"

"I … see. Thank you for telling me." She turned away and walked to meet her party at their usual table, placing the tray in front of them. "Here is our payment. What was that business with the receptionist, Geran?"

He tensed slightly and looked away. "Bridgit? Oh. She and I have … history. It wouldn't have lasted. At least we were able to part ways on good terms."

"What does that mean?"

"Aww! Gerry's shy!" Lilian sang as she jumped up and leaned over his shoulders. "He's too bashful to say it straight."

"Lilian!" the ranger protested.

"Geran and Bridgit dated for almost a year, breaking up a few months before you showed up. At first they were really cute, but she wanted to make things permanent. Geran here wasn't ready for that kinda relationship and didn't want to do all the fruity stuff she did. Eventually he broke it off, but she *totally* wants to spark it back up!"

"No account for tact as always huh, Lilian?" Geran mumbled.

"Tact shmact. You always pull the cute ones, anyway!"

"I told you I'm done with that stuff! It gets in the way of work. I can either keep a woman happy or I can do my job correctly. I can't manage the time for both."

"Oho?" she grinned smugly and then motioned at Elaethia. "Well, looks like neither of those would be a problem if you would just hurry up and go for it."

"Cat, I'm going to skin you and wear you for socks," he growled.

"Fine. Have it your way, Mr. Grumpy Pants. I'll have you know I'd be the most fabulous pair of socks you'd ever own."

"I'd be sad if you turned Lili-chan into socks," Shiro said shyly.

Lilian wrapped her arms around the samurai. "Aww, look, Gerry. *Somebody* loves me! Shiro knows how to make a girl fall for him, doesn't he? Maybe he can give you a few tips."

Geran suddenly banged his head onto the table. "Gaaaah! I don't have to listen to this! I'm turning in for the night!"

He stood and stomped his way to his room. Lilian sat in her chair and leaned back. She let out a girly cackle and kicked her feet in the air. "By the Moon, that was great! I haven't seen him make that face in *years!*"

Elaethia tilted her head. "What were you talking about?"

The demicat flashed her signature grin. "Aw, I can't tell you! That'd ruin the whole fun! I'm gonna take a bath. See ya guys later!" She twirled out of her seat and pranced upstairs.

Shiro scratched his head. "Why is Geran going to bed? It isn't even dark out."

"I do not know," Elaethia said. "Whatever Lilian said certainly made him upset."

"I hope he isn't mad at Lili-chan. I like her very much. A-and Geran! I certainly like Geran too!"

"Do you enjoy being in a party with them, Shiro?"

"Absolutely! They're both very nice and cool! But you're my favorite, Elaethia-sama! I see both of them as very good friends, but I'd follow you to the end of the earth if you'd allow me!"

"Where I choose to go, you may not wish to follow."

"To go back to your own homeland, right?" Shiro asked, and then he hesitated for a moment. "Forgive me, Elaethia-sama. I know it's not my place to ask about my master's personal life. But since you know *my* cause, I'm curious as to what yours is."

"To kill the tyrant emperor that rules Armini. I swore to Frossgar and my father I would see that man dead. Everything I do is done to improve and prepare myself for that time. I have been set on this path for as long as I can remember. Once I fully understand my magic, and feel I am physically ready, I will embark upon my final steps."

Shiro froze. "An emperor? Elaethia-sama, this may not be my place to say, but you won't just be fighting *him*. He has an empire: armies, allies, resources, and assets beyond what we can imagine. You want to fight against all that?"

"I do," she replied solemnly. She looked up to see Shiro staring at her. "You are silent. Do not worry; I would not ask you to accompany me."

He shook his head. "No. I would never abandon you. Not in the face of monsters, not in the face of an empire, not in the face of hell itself. I am your samurai, and you are my master, Elaethia-sama. Your enemies are my own. I will see this through with you to the end and beyond."

She smiled weakly. "That is very admirable of you. But I could never ask you to do that. None of you. I hold no intention or expectations to bring you all with me. Do not think that the time I spend with you is of no significance to me. I am very grateful for all of you—more than I know how to express. I hope you understand."

"What can I say to convince you that this is what I want?" Shiro insisted. "My family name would be restored, and I could spend my days making the world a better place with the most noble warrior the country knows. You have been kind to me, accepted me as a friend, and allowed me to fight at your side as an equal. I can't imagine myself in a better place. The others think very highly of you as well. We know you don't see us as simply tools or allies. I believe they're almost as honored as I to be at your side."

"Truly?"

"Absolutely," he nodded firmly and held a hand to the sheath of his sword. His hand suddenly curled and jerked up. "Oh, excuse me; I should go clean my sheath from today's quest. Some of those villagers had soft faces and dirty limbs."

Elaethia's smile grew. "I did not know you felt this way. Thank you, Shiro."

Shiro stood and pounded his right fist against his chest in a salute. "I am your sword, Elaethia-sama. Wherever you go, I will follow."

Sixth Era. 139. Mertim 25.

Elaethia was once again reading the book Lilian had loaned her. It was a story about a knight in armor who rescued a princess from a tower owned by an evil enchantress. It was one of the few Lilian owned that wasn't sappy or too complicated for her. Thinking back on it, Elaethia recalled that Lilian had indeed mentioned it was a book written for children. Suddenly a rapid knock sounded at her door. She got up to open it and saw a familiar young blond duelist in front of her.

"Good morning, Dylan. That is your name, correct?" she asked.

"Yes ma'am!" the teenager replied. "You and your party gotta come downstairs right now! Shiro's already there."

"What is it?"

"You'll see! You're gonna love it!"

"Very well. Would you be so kind as to fetch Lilian? I will let Geran know."

"Already got her! She'll be down soon. Tell Geran to hurry!" With that, he dashed off down the stairs.

Elaethia peered over the railing and saw a swarm of adventurers crowded in the massive hall. They all were grouped around the center of the bar, where Master Dameon stood on top of the counter. Shiro nervously stood next to him.

"Elaethia, my girl!" Dameon boomed. "Get you and the rest of your party down here on the double! I got something for all of you!"

The guild members all looked up and shouted their approval in accordance. Elaethia strode over to Geran's room and knocked sharply. The door opened quickly afterward.

"What's happening out here? What's with all the noise?" the ranger asked.

"I do not know," she said. "But nearly the whole guild is waiting for us. Master Dameon said he has something for our party."

"Are they all surrounding the bar, with Master Dameon standing on it?"

Elaethia blinked. "Yes, how did you know?"

Geran's face lost a little color. "Ooooh no. I think I know what this is." He sighed heavily. "Hold on, let me get my shoes. Did someone get Lilian?"

"Yes, she should be the last one."

"Typical," he muttered. "All right, let's get this over with."

Five minutes later, all four of them stood atop the bar with Master Dameon towering behind them. His hands rested on Elaethia's and Geran's shoulders, while Lilian and Shiro stood on the ends. Seemingly pleased with the scene, he inhaled and bellowed into the hall.

"All right, you rascals!" he began. "You all know what this is! Well, except for two of these kids up here!"

The ensemble laughed at his remark.

Dameon continued. "Now I know this is one of the newest parties we have in our little family. But nobody here can deny their effectiveness or strength. Hell, they managed to both pull in the reclusive Geran Nightshade and contain our potent little Lily! Now, you four! Each of you has decided that this is your permanent party, right? If any of you have had any thoughts of splitting off, now's the time to do it!"

"I trust and depend on everyone standing here," Elaethia stated.

"I will follow Elaethia-sama wherever she goes," Shiro pledged.

"You people couldn't *pay* me to leave these guys!" Lilian laughed.

Geran sighed. "Now that I've become a part of this group, I honestly couldn't see myself going back to how I was."

Dameon grinned. "That settles it! All of us have heard the stories of this party! Elaethia single-handedly took out a bandit hive and rescued five hostages. She, Lilian, and Geran took care of a sorcerer with sabercats in the nearby woods. Shiro joined up with them as they did a *textbook* clearing of a goblin cave. Yesterday they successfully suppressed a mob in the northern village *and* gave that nobleman what-for. And now I hear about this monster of a woman charging a troll head-on and taking it out in *one blow*."

The crowd whooped and growled in approval while banging on whatever surface was closest to them.

Master Dameon put a hand up to silence his adventurers. "All these actions and your attitudes toward your work, as well as your dedication to the guild, has been recognized. The city and guild have decided to make you four a named party!"

Shiro's jaw dropped, Lilian struck a pose, Geran shifted awkwardly, and Elaethia blinked.

"From this point on, Elaethia Frossgar, Geran Nightshade, Lilian Whitepaw, and Shiro Inahari, in light of your outstanding methods, strength, effectiveness, dedication, and downright *absurd* capability, you are now officially known as *Cataclysm!*"

The guildhall erupted into applause. Adventurers jumped up and down, banging their fists against the tables and chairs, whooping and hollering in celebration of the newly named party. Master Dameon turned the four around and shook the hand of each member.

"Congratulations, you rascals. Or should I say congratulations, Cataclysm. Now get out there and bring more death and destruction to the enemies of Breeze!"

Chapter 9
Sunbeam

Sixth Era.139. Mertim 25.

The revelry lasted over an hour, and Elaethia bore it for almost thirty minutes. Lilian immediately basked in her new source of attention and became the center of the party right away. Shiro at first was uncomfortable with the celebration, but he quickly warmed up to it. Geran got pulled to his ranger meeting, leaving Elaethia alone. She looked around the scene, and much to her concern, the staff had brought out alcohol. She decided to retreat outside to wander around the city, as there was only one way this could go.

Of course, several adventurers had other ideas. Whether the alcohol had clouded their judgment or they thought Elaethia was now accustomed to the guild lifestyle, they decided to block her path. They were very quickly reminded of who she was. Not wishing to harm her annoying compatriots, Elaethia simply walked in a straight line. At first, the members stood their ground. Their drunken laughter ceased as they realized she was still moving at the same speed, despite them attempting to physically hold her back. The adventurers then resorted to more gentle pleading to convince her to stay. They quickly gave up and moved out of her way once the temperature around them began to drop.

Once outside, Elaethia realized she didn't have a destination in mind. The frost dragon in her just wanted to be left alone. However, the human part of her wanted to have some company. It was a rather frustrating combination. Geran said his meeting could take a while, so she decided to visit Cathrine at her family's business. She arrived at the restaurant and realized there was a rather long line. Elaethia began to make her way toward it when she stopped. She wondered if it would be considered cutting in line if she simply wished to talk. After a conflicted moment, she decided it probably would be rude to attempt conversation, so she sat down at a table to wait.

"Elaethia! Hi there!" Catherine called as the last customer was served.

"Good afternoon, Cathrine. Are you well?" Elaethia asked.

"Yep! Even better now! Gosh, we've been so busy lately. I think it's because people figured out this is the only place they can see you besides the guildhall."

"My presence has drawn people to your business?"

"Kinda."

"I hope I am not causing your family some trouble by this."

"Oh, heavens no! If we sell out every day, that's a good thing! Papa's actually been telling me to find a way to keep you coming back here. But I don't know if that's a very fair thing to do."

"What do you mean?"

"I don't want to do something dirty or cheap; you're my friend!" Catherine said.

"I see. Regardless, your business seems to do well."

"I think so too. Although a few extra hands around here would really help. I wouldn't mind another person at the counter to sort orders during lunch and dinner hours. Papa could definitely use someone to help make the food too. When my sister gets old enough, she should be able to do more. But then there's talk of the younger of my brothers joining the guild. He's thinking about being a ranger."

"A ranger's work is very sensitive, and their efforts often go unnoticed," Elaethia said.

"You think so?"

"That is what Geran says. He would certainly be better able to explain the job to your brother than I. If you would like, I can bring him here next time."

"Maybe. Are all classes in a guild so complicated?"

"Perhaps not as difficult and meticulous as a ranger, but each has its levels of complication."

"I figure being a warrior is the hardest," Cathrine said.

"In a sense. The warrior's task is the simplest, but we are the first ones in the fight. My mentor, Jörgen, held a form of engagement known as 'berserking.' He would leap into the midst of the worst fighting and overwhelm the enemy with aggression and devastating strikes. He had a saying regarding this style of fighting: 'Your job is not to charge headfirst into hell, but to make sure it is crowded once you get there.'"

Cathrine winced. "That sounds … brutal."

"It is a brutal way of life."

"I guess. But speaking of Geran, I haven't met anyone else from your party besides Lilian. I've seen you all leave town a couple of times, so who are the other two?"

"The one with the cloak and bow is Geran. The young man in the odd red armor is Shiro, a samurai who has proclaimed his services to me. He is from Osakyota and seeks to make a name for himself here."

"What's a samurai?"

Elaethia thought for a moment. "There is no Linderrian equivalent to his title, but think of it as a cross between a warrior and a duelist."

"Oh, okay. I think I know what you mean. Maybe I can meet them someday. It sounds like they both have plenty of stories."

"Indeed. Geran is far more experienced than any of us, and Shiro comes from a foreign land."

"I can tell just from overhearing conversations here and there. People talk about you guys a lot! You guys got popular fast. How are you handling it?"

"Lilian certainly indulges in her fame. Geran and I, however, do not care for it. I now realize why he was so reluctant for us to become a named party."

Cathrine's mouth fell open. "*What?*"

Elaethia tilted her head. "Did I say something odd?"

"You became a *named party?*"

"Just this morning. The celebration became too boisterous for me, so I retreated to find more suitable company."

"B-b-but you've only been here, what, not even three months!"

"About that, yes. Why?"

"Elaethia, I may not be savvy about guilds and adventurers and whatnot, but even *I* know how awesome a party has to be to get a name! I mean, I know of Breeze's top three, plus a couple others. What'd they name you?"

"Cataclysm."

"What kind of name is *that?*"

"Apparently they see us as causing death and destruction everywhere we go. It is fitting, I suppose, as I suspect we will only get stronger."

"So, are you, like, *stronger* than Razorback or Earth Shatter? Are you guys the new ace?"

A certain female voice cut in before Elaethia could respond. "Hellooooooo! I *thought* I'd find you here!"

"Ah, hello, Lilian," Elaethia greeted the mage.

The demicat came to a halt next to her with a bounce. "Now why'd ya disappear on us like that? It's *our* celebration!"

"Such activities are not my preference. Surely you know this."

"Sure, sure. But you could've told me where you were going! I had to hunt you down myself!"

"You said you knew I would be here."

Lilian waved the comment aside. "Anyway, I'm glad to see you're catching up with your friend here. How ya doin', Cathrine?"

"Hi, Lilian," the serving girl greeted her. "I'm doing well. Elaethia was just telling me about how you guys just got named. Oh, uh, congratulations on that, by the way."

Lilian's ears perked up. "How much did she tell you?"

"Just the name, and that you got it today."

A mischievous grin spread across the demicat's face and quickly disappeared. "Well gosh, I oughta tell you how we got the name before ol' Elaethia here messes it up! So we were already pretty awesome, right? How we took out a sorcerer, wiped out a nest of goblins, suppressed a riot, y'know. Normal stuff for us. And then we have this troll comin' at us, right? Y'know, big, blubbery, lumbering … Anyway, this gigantic mass of muscle and stupidity comes bearing down on us, ready to smash us to paste, when we all—"

"That is not how—"

"Shushshushshush!" Lilian waved a hand in Elaethia's face and turned back to Cathrine. "This massive lump of fat is charging us, with a tree as big as ship mast raised above its head, when we leap into action. So Geran, being a total brainiac, rolls out of the way and dashes off to a safe distance and starts crunching numbers while flipping through a notebook. He starts shouting out useless things like 'battle formations' and 'skirmisher tactics.' Shiro then draws his sword, stares the monster down, and says something like 'For the honor of my family and as a testament of my warrior spirit, I will strike you down, foul beast.' And then he *cuts* the tree in *half!*"

Cathrine's mouth and eyes were wide open as Lilian dramatically carried on.

"So while the troll is staring at this useless chunk of wood in his hand, Elaethia leaps in the air, does a backflip, and *lands* on its head! A blizzard of ice and snow completely envelops her, and she *slams* her axe into the monster's face! The troll goes *sailing* backward and rolls to a stop almost a hundred meters away! But it isn't done yet. When it tries to stagger to its feet, I realize I need to put it down for good. I bathe the battlefield in an aura of pure energy as I prepare to unleash my elemental fury! I call down a lightning bolt so bright and powerful you would have thought the Sun himself came down to smite the monster! After the dust cleared, there was nothing more than a sizzling pile of ash at the bottom of a crater. Cataclysm had struck again!"

Catherine was dumbfounded. "That … that's normal for you?"

Lilian fluttered a hand. "Well, that was a little more hectic than usual. We've been ramping it up. But you bet your britches we'll have crazier tales for you in the future!"

A local man suddenly appeared behind them. "'Scuse me, that was interesting and all, but if you ladies aren't gonna order, mind if I step up?"

"Oh! Gosh, sorry mister! Didn't see ya there! We'll stop by again sometime, Cathrine. See ya!"

Catherine smiled warmly as they turned away. "Please do! It can get boring sometimes. Bye, Elaethia! Good luck on your adventures!"

"I like Cathrine," Lilian hummed as she and Elaethia turned a corner. "She's fun. Nice and gullible, too."

"I enjoy her company as well, but I do not approve of calling her gullible. Was it necessary to embellish the story so?"

"Duh! How else are we gonna get popular? I know you and Geran don't care, but I wanna be famous! People are gonna exaggerate our stories anyway, so we might as well get it out of the way."

Elaethia tilted her head. "Truly? I never would have thought of it that way."

"Well, I mean, for the most part. As long as the stories have the same baseline, it's fine."

"Would Geran play along as well?"

Lilian's tail stiffened. "Aw crap, I forgot about him. That modest stick-in-the-mud would probably *downplay* the story. Man … would it kill the guy to let himself be famous?"

"He often mentions the opposite about you," Elaethia said.

They returned to the guildhall shortly thereafter. Elaethia opened the large double doors and braced herself for the inevitable onslaught of cheering and hollering adventurers. Surprisingly, the noise had settled down to a normal level, as they had all either gone off in their own groups, returned to their rooms, or left. Lilian bounced in ahead of her, skipping her way up the stairs and over to her room. Elaethia remained in the entryway, pondering what to do with herself. She decided to return to her room and continue reading the book she'd been loaned.

"Hey, Frossgar," a man's voice called to her from her left. She turned to see Peter Stone leaning against the wall.

"Good afternoon, Peter. Is there something you need?"

"Yeah. Come over here real quick," he crossed his arms and stared at the ground as she approached. "Look. I'm gonna be straight with you. I don't like you. I didn't the second you walked through those doors that first night."

She regarded him coldly. "If you only wish to express your distaste for me, I suggest you keep it brief."

He put a hand up. "That being said, I can't help but have a good amount of respect for you. You walked in here, kicked my ass, became a favorite to Master Dameon on day one. Then you formed a party with some of the guild's most prominent members. Now you've got yourself a name."

"What are you trying to say?"

"I'm saying it pisses me the hell off that you show up and outshine me in a couple months, after I worked for eleven years to get to this point. I was the star here, and now everyone seems to be forgetting about me. But despite all of that bullshit, I can't bring myself to hate you. I mean, despite everything, you haven't let any of it go to your head. You don't flaunt yourself or your power. You just go around, do your job, and lie back like the rest of us. Both you and your party. Well, except Lilian, but none of us really mind that from her."

"I care not for fame or popularity."

"Right, right, just …" He heaved a sigh. "I've got a feeling you're about to take my title. You four are going to do things that will put Earth Shatter to shame, and I don't like that. Most of my party doesn't. But Christoph raised a good point. Everything you guys do is for the betterment of someone else. Whether it's for the people or the guild. As long as you're making Breeze famous, and not being cunts about it, I've got nothing to say."

Elaethia's face softened a little. "I suppose this may be difficult for you—that you feel that you are losing face to me."

He nodded. "That's part of it, but some of my party is feeling it worse than me. Look, if you find yourself short on hands for a quest, do me the favor and call on Earth Shatter for help. They've come to need the spotlight to drive them."

"I will take your request into consideration. Is there anything else?"

Peter stood and rolled his shoulders. "No. No, I'm done. Just don't lose your modest attitude is all." He paused and spat on the ground. "Else you may have to start asking yourself who's really on your side."

Sixth Era. 139. Abris 14.

"Gaaaah, none of these are any good!" Lilian groaned from in front of the quest board. "Bandits, another goblin nest, a bunch of tasks—all things we've done before!"

"We are looking for funding and to assist the people," Elaethia stated. "Not to mention it has been over a week since our last quest. It does not matter if we have done a similar task before or if we have to do a custom chore through a civilian."

"'Course it matters! We can't just take the same kinda quest over and over. We need experience! People gotta see that we can handle any situation!"

Geran made a face. "Any situation? We don't even have a healer."

"That's what potions are for!"

"Those only help with lacerations, burns, and frostbite. I think Michelle is starting on general antidotes, but all that's just simple mending. Good luck trying to get a limb reattached or a bone fixed."

Lilian waved a hand. "Bah, we shouldn't need one. We're good enough at what we do. Besides, we all know basic first aid!"

"There are literally three classes that can use healing properties, and we choose two fighters, a mage, and me. First aid ain't gonna grow your tail back."

"If we aren't happy with the A quests, maybe we can look at the veteran ones," Shiro suggested. "That giant slime we killed last week was definitely harder than an A."

"I concur," Elaethia stated. "It is undeniable that we have improved from when we first came together. Let us raise our standards as a group."

Geran sighed. "All right. Let's hope there's a decent one for us."

Shiro and Lilian scrambled over to the V section. Elaethia and Geran stood behind them. Elaethia noticed V-levels were certainly more challenging than A-levels: goblin hordes that had gone unchecked, a bandit camp that needed to be cleared, another troll quest. The veteran section was the first place she saw quests for the eradication of sorcerers. Most of the V-levels were kill quests or clear quests. The rest were entirely ranger quests, and a single escort quest.

Elaethia peered at the escort flyer. "A prospector is looking for a group of highly experienced adventurers to guard him as he charts out an unexplored sector of an ore mine. Details will be given by the individual behind the request, but expect to fight giant insects, goblins, grauergs, and possibly spriggans."

"Hard pass," Geran said. "I can't work very well underground. Hard to track, grauergs have stony, snakelike bodies that only Elaethia could crack, and giant insects give me the willies."

Lilian slapped a finger on one of the flyers. "Ooh! Ooh! How about this one! A sorcerer who has been using fire spells on passersby and adventurers."

Shiro leaned over her and read it aloud. "One day's ride west by wagon in the hilly forest, there is a sorcerer who is presumed specialized in fire magic. His name and origin are unknown, but he is a former adventurer from somewhere in Linderry. Until recently, he has been living in seclusion, and he now mercilessly attacks any brehdar he encounters. Kill the sorcerer."

"Two red Xs," Geran muttered as he scratched his stubble beard. "This guy managed to take out two parties already. We'd be the third group to try out for this one if we take it."

"What happened to the other groups?" Elaethia asked.

"Dunno. Let's bring it to Maya and ask." The ranger pulled the flyer off the cork wall, and the party walked over to the reception desk.

Maya looked up expectantly at the party of four. "Well, well. Looks like Cataclysm is ready to go out."

"Indeed," Elaethia said. "Do you have any information on this quest? Specifically regarding the previous groups?"

"Let me check." Maya bent over, pulled out a file drawer, and shuffled through it. After a moment she pulled out a sheet and scanned it. "Okay, found the reports from the previous attempts. First group was three A-level adventurers and an I; they were completely wiped out. No survivors. Second group was three A-levels and one V; one KIA, one permanently disabled, the other two are still in the infirmary."

"Holy shit," Geran muttered.

"No kidding. This one is one of the harder veteran quests we still have posted. I'm wondering if this shouldn't be a raid."

"Can we talk to one of the three survivors?" Elaethia asked. "They are downstairs, correct?"

Maya shook her head. "They won't be able to see anyone besides family and party members for another week at least. The disabled one is at the church. Apparently she may not survive."

"What happened to them?" Shiro asked.

"They were in no condition to talk when a recovery team found them, let alone give any kind of a report. But they all had only one kind of magical injury."

Lilian's tail twitched. "What kind of spell?"

"Our medical staff couldn't make heads or tails of it, but the injuries are all definitely some type of burn. I'm no mage, but I heard they were some extremely hot flames. In fact, it's almost like their bodies were melted and even disintegrated."

"What the *what?*"

Maya shook her head. "I haven't seen them myself, so I can't verify, but apparently this might get brought up for the Arcane Sages to investigate."

Lilian pounced on the desk and shoved her face into Maya's. "We'll take it!"

"Lilian!" Geran protested.

"C'mooon! We're perfect for this! Elaethia may be specialized in frost, but she's *Elaethia!* He won't be able to counter her magic forever. You're the best shot in the country; you can outrange him. He's probably not wearing armor, so Shiro can cut him up. On top of that, I *love* fighting other mages!"

"We're talking about a V-level quest here, where *multiple* groups have failed," Geran stated. "Five of our people, and countless others, are dead from this *one* guy. Never mind the strategy and prep work I'll have to do; everyone here besides Elaethia could get annihilated by him in an instant."

"We're a higher-ranking group than both those other ones. We have two A-levels and two V-levels in ours!"

"Who else besides me is Veteran here?"

"Elaethia. Sure, the highest missions she's completed are A, but you can't tell me she's not stronger than that!"

"Well, yeah, but … Elaethia, what do you think?"

Her face was solemn. "This man has killed many innocent people, and several of our compatriots. He must be dealt with immediately."

Shiro put his hand on the hilt of his sword. "I agree with Elaethia-sama. We must destroy this sorcerer."

The ranger sighed and picked up the flyer. "Sun and Moon help us. Maya, are we clear to take this?"

She looked at the report and then slowly to the party. "Well, I'm authorized to clear you for it. But for heaven's sake, if you come back burnt up, I'll never approve you for a V quest again."

Elaethia furrowed her brow. "That would be problematic."

Shiro put a hand on the counter. "Don't worry, Maya-san! I know that sometimes it is better to run and admit defeat than fight to the death. We all do. If nothing else, we can come back with better information."

"All right, all right," Maya said. "Go and give this guy a taste of Cataclysm."

Elaethia observed the landscape as they rode in the back of a cargo wagon, though there was not much to observe. They were in the heartlands of Breeze: wide, open, empty tundra and plains of long grass and marshland. Farms and villages dotted the landscape in nearly every direction. The soil here was rich and fertile—perfect for cultivation. Elaethia had heard that Breeze's agriculture was its main export. Much of Linderry's food came from the region. Crime, monsters, and beasts were all constant threats to the communities. Perhaps that is why Breeze's guild was so large.

She looked to her companions. Geran scribbled and muttered strategies to himself, Shiro fidgeted with the hilt of his sword, and Lilian was asleep on Geran's shoulder. It would still be nearly half a day until they reached their destination. This was the first time Elaethia had traveled so far with companions. Any other time, she had been either alone or with a wagoner. Waggoners rarely tried having a conversation with her. She was always very grateful for that. But somehow, being with close companions made the silence almost uncomfortable. She felt perhaps she should attempt to initiate conversation.

"Did you learn anything interesting from the ranger meeting, Shiro?" she asked.

The samurai blinked. "Huh? Oh, uh yes. I think."

"You think?"

"Well, Geran was right. I was so bored, and I didn't understand most of what they were saying. But I think it's fascinating how much they do. They were discussing things I don't think even nobles back home would talk about: crime in other regions and villages, taxation rates, civilian approval, road safety—topics I didn't think the guild would care about."

"What of the discussions did you understand?"

"Apparently there's a crime faction in Breeze known as Blackwolf. I don't remember much of what they do, but they're bad people with ties and assets everywhere. Breeze's new elected representative has been working on eradicating them, and from what I could tell, Geran played a part in driving them out of the main city. Then he mentioned our last quest with the farming village and their mayor, also expressing concern about how long it took for the troll to be taken care of. Something I found most interesting was discussion about named parties of other guilds."

"Any worth telling about?" she asked.

"One, but I was more interested in the individuals."

"I venture there would be several worthy opponents for you in the country."

"None compared to you, Elaethia-sama. I mean, not that I see you as a rival, but there were a few that sounded incredible. There's this ranger in Dinkerage that single-handedly uprooted a drug cartel. Another is a party in Sprigganwood that's famous for defeating, well, spriggans, and they're called Wood's Bane. They mentioned a few mages as well, and a paladin in Apogee who is apparently so strong he has a national title! The High Church has named him Sun Hammer."

"I have never heard of him."

"Me neither, but he sounds awesome! We'll have plenty to watch out for in the annual tournament."

Elaethia tilted her head. "Annual tournament? You mean other guilds will be involved in it?"

"Didn't they tell you? It's held in Apogee. Every guild enrolls its best members, and they all compete in games to be determined the strongest in their class!"

"No, I was unaware. This sounds interesting to you?"

"Of course! I'm *beyond* excited for it! Geran said all four of us would most likely be representatives—even me, since I'm foreign with a unique style!"

"I care not for competition and sport," she stated flatly.

"I know … but I also know you'll do great! You'll certainly make our guild proud. For the last few years, Earth Shatter has been the star party. Master Dameon said Cataclysm would take the spotlight for Breeze this time!"

"I see. I am beginning to understand Peter's frustration."

"He mentioned this to you?"

"Not in this way, but I believe he knew what was going to happen. I trust you to not let the sense of being portrayed as one of the best go to your head."

Shiro pounded his fist across his chest. "I am your sword, Elaethia-sama, and am but a humble servant. Your modesty and humility are surpassed only by my own."

"That is good to hear. I have come to not tolerate those who think themselves higher than those around them."

He gripped his hilt and looked firmly into her eyes. "Humility is the true mark of a warrior. I will never forget that."

She smiled at him.

He faltered. "I uh … Did I say something odd?"

"No, Shiro," she assured him. "I am just happy to be with company such as you."

"Th-thank you. Elaethia-sama." He turned slightly red and looked away into the distance.

Elaethia frowned. It seemed she had upset Shiro. But he didn't seem irritated. His face turned red, as the faces of brehdars tend to do when they are uncomfortable, but he was smiling. The conversation seemed to be going well. Then again, he was doing most of the talking. Elaethia hardly contributed. Either way, their talk seemed to be over. Her eyes shifted to Geran's, which were already locked to hers. His mouth was partially covered by a hand, as he was leaning into it, but there was an odd glint in his expression.

"What?" she demanded.

The ranger only snorted with a smile and shook his head.

It was dark when the party reached the closest point of civilization. The town they arrived in was small—only about a dozen buildings. Elaethia could tell it was a lumber town; it had been built on a river and boasted a large sawmill powered by a waterwheel. A couple of the structures seemed to be houses, with businesses run within them. The stores were set on the ground floor, while the shopkeepers lived upstairs.

The inn was nearly the largest building in town, second only to the sawmill along the river. Inside, the first thing Elaethia noticed was the front counter, which had an elderly dwarven woman standing behind it. She smiled warmly at the visitors as Geran returned stepped up to arrange rooms. A warm hearth crackled comfortably in the center of the room. It was a double-sided fireplace with a brick chimney going straight up through the roof. Three rooms ran along either side of the inn, making a total of six. A seventh room was behind the front counter, presumably belonging to the innkeeper. Aside from a pair of round tables with four chairs each, the inside was empty.

"All right, people, gather 'round," Geran called. "I got us two rooms: one for me and Shiro, the other for Elaethia and Lilian. Go ahead and set your stuff up for the night, then meet in my room. We'll go over everything one more time, and I'll get another map to see what we can expect for terrain and location."

They headed off into their rooms, which were the farthest down on the left. Elaethia and Lilian picked the one closest to the entrance, went in, and dropped off their travel gear. Lilian plopped her bag on the floor and dropped into the bed.

"Ahh," she sighed. "So glad to be able to take that thing off."

Elaethia tilted her head. "You have hardly even worn it, Lilian."

"I haven't used a rucksack since I moved to the guild! All that weight on my back makes my shoulders hurt."

"But you wore it for less than five minutes. What do you have inside?"

The demicat's eyes shifted as she pushed it under the bed. "Nothing. Don't worry about it."

Elaethia dropped her own ruck and began to separate her gear. "I hardly believe 'nothing' weighs enough to cause your shoulders to ache. But if you insist I do not need to worry about it, then I will not."

"Hey. Are you cold?" Lilian asked suddenly.

"Frost dragon blood runs through my veins. I do not feel the cold."

"No, no, I mean ... is your *body* cold? Like, is sharing a bed with you gonna make me freeze?"

Elaethia paused. "I do not believe so. Magicians do not radiate their magic unless they intend to. Then again, I would not know, as I would not be able to tell."

"'Cause if you do, one of us is gonna end up getting a different room from now on. I'm not gonna share a bed with someone's cold feet. Dana always had cold feet, and I *hated* it!"

"Then we shall see. When you are ready, we shall meet with Geran and Shiro."

The two of them finished their prep work and left to go meet with their party members. Shiro was kneeling next to the bed, while Geran had a large map spread out across it. He was comparing it with the map on the back of the quest flyer.

"You really gotta hand it to our cartographers," Geran mused. "The quest map is nearly identical to the area map the innkeeper had. The biggest differences are that this local map is topographical, with marked areas of relief, and it has a pretty good scale. Consistent color coordination, too. There're no grid lines, coordinates, or detailed descriptions of structures, but you won't find any maps with those anywhere besides the military."

Lilian's tail twitched. "In English, Geran."

The ranger pointed to some faint curvy lines on the area map. "See these gray lines everywhere? Those aren't roads or paths; they're contour lines. They indicate the elevation of that spot. The closer together they are, the steeper the terrain. That's what makes this map 'topographical.' The really detailed ones even follow the exact terrain and landmarks. That solid black line at the bottom corner with the number one hundred next to it is a scale. One of those lines is approximately one hundred meters according to this map. Don't worry about 'grids' or 'coordinates.' It'll be a *long* time, if ever, before you see a map with those."

Shiro leaned forward to look closer. "What does it tell us?"

"Well, by looking at the spot indicated on the request and transcribing it onto the area map, I can tell the landscape of the area we'll be in. With that I can formulate the best plan of approach, what to expect in the area, and the best areas of escape or advantageous positions. I'd like to go ahead and scout the area out, but it's a good walk from here."

"How should we prepare in the meantime?" Elaethia asked.

Geran scratched his beard. "You guys? Not much. Just set up all your gear for the approach, attack, and withdrawal. This map helps me out a great deal, but it's not perfect. I'll come up with the proper formations, contingencies, and order of movement once we get to the engagement zone."

Lilian stamped her foot. "Geran! Say things so we can understand them!"

He heaved a sigh. "Just prepare yourselves for the fight and go to bed. I'll think about the best ways for us to attack and the order in which we move and do things in. I'll make a final decision once we get there."

Shiro nodded. "Is that all?"

"For now. I've only been to this area once, maybe twice. There're gonna be a lot of on-the-fly decisions. Then again, that's standard for a quest. Elaethia, anything you want to add?"

She was about to decline but stopped herself. Geran had said that she was the leader, so it would be appropriate for her to act as such. But she didn't know what else could be covered, since Geran had already laid out the plan. It was up to her to set it in motion.

"It is best to begin at sunrise, but I understand some of us do not wish to be awake that early. Let us be out ready to move no later than seven o'clock."

Geran grunted. "That means awake, packed, fed, and dressed … *Lilian!*"

The mage stuck her tongue out at him.

Lilian and Elaethia began to disrobe in silence and prepare to go to sleep. As Elaethia readied her undergarments, Lilian couldn't help eyeing her body up and down as more of it was revealed. The dragon hero was the most muscled woman Lilian had ever seen, and yet, also the curviest. Her chest was surpassed only by Maya, but that wasn't much of a contest since the elven receptionist was in a league of her own. Lilian glanced down at her own sleek figure and made a face. She poked at her chest a few times and blew out a sigh. Lilian had always been proud of her body, but standing next to Elaethia? Forget it.

"Have you ever split a bed before?" she suddenly asked.

Elaethia shook her head. "I have not. But I do not move much, so I doubt I will disturb you."

"I don't move much, either, but Dana and my sisters were a bit … smaller."

Elaethia slid under the covers. "We shall see. If it truly bothers you, I am accustomed to sleeping on the ground."

"Oh no, I wouldn't ask you to do that. We'll just have this as a test night."

"Indeed. If you are ready, I will put out the light."

"One sec," Lilian said, and she shimmied under the blankets as well. "'Kay, I'm ready. G'night, Elaethia."

"Good night, Lilian," she responded, and she blew out the light.

The two of them lay in silence for several minutes. Soon after, Lilian could hear the gentle pattern of Elaethia's breathing. The earlier question of whether or not the dragon hero produced cold energy instead of warm body heat reappeared in her mind. Overwhelmed by curiosity, the demicat reached over to feel her companion. It was too dark to see where her hand was going, so she was rather surprised at how quickly she made contact.

Elaethia was warm. There was no indication of the unrelenting frost she held within. Lilian wondered what she was holding on to, as that might have had something to do with it. She squeezed a little to get a reference and found she was holding something large and squishy. She instantly regretted giving into her curiosity, as two bright-blue eyes shot open to meet hers.

Lilian tried for a smile. "Aheh … uh … has anyone ever told you that you've got a nice set of—"

A rather hard smack cut her short. Lilian whimpered and rubbed her head as Elaethia rolled over and went back to sleep.

"Elaethia-sama, Lili-chan," Elaethia woke to the sound of Shiro's voice coming from the door with a knock. "It's six o'clock. Geran is already suited up. He said to meet us at the front desk when ready."

"Very well. Thank you, Shiro."

Elaethia rolled out of bed and began to get dressed. Lilian sat up, rubbed the sore spot on her head, and stretched. She pushed the blankets aside to let her furry tail pop out from under the covers. The two of them pulled out their rations, ate, and got ready with five minutes to spare. Geran and Shiro greeted them at the front desk, and they headed out the door to take on the quest.

"How did you both sleep?" Shiro asked.

"Quite well," Elaethia responded. "With the exception of one mishap in the night."

Geran chuckled at Lilian. "I was wondering what that red spot on your forehead was about,"

She grumbled and stuck her lip out. "Was an accident … But she didn't have to hit me that hard!"

"I did not strike you, Lilian, it was a simple flick." Elaethia said

"That was just a *flick?*"

"Anyway, let's go over the plan," Geran said. "We're gonna walk along the main roads in a patrol. Myself first, then Lilian, then Shiro, then Elaethia. We'll maintain a staggered line, keeping about five to ten meters of dispersion between us. This way if a fire spell comes flying, it should only hit one of us. We'll keep up this patrol for a while and hope he engages us first. The best chance of engagement is on a popular road."

Elaethia took over. "It is reasonable to believe that this sorcerer depends on range for his attacks. If Geran and Lilian keep him pinned with arrows and spells, Shiro and I can get close to deal the final blow. Geran, I trust you have already devised contingency plans?"

He gave a thumbs-up. "Right on."

"Very well. Let us set forth."

"Uuuugh! What's taking so long!" Lilian shouted into the sky.

"This is a big area," Geran called back. "The odds of us bumping into this guy aren't very high. We've only been out here for a couple hours."

Shiro looked up at the hills around him. "Maybe we should get to the high ground and search from there."

"You want to walk up and down this steep terrain all day? Be my guest."

Elaethia looked around the rocky and forest-covered hills. "It would be unwise to continue our search in the dark. We should return to the inn before nightfall."

Lilian leaned on her staff. "I've only got the patience to do this for maybe another hour; my feet are killing me!"

Geran's tone began to shift. "We're not going back early on the account of 'too tired.' You really think that's how veteran quests oughta be handled?"

"You can't tell me you guys aren't tired either! Shiro! Back me up here!"

"I feel fine. The walk from Clearharbor to Breeze was a lot worse than this."

She mimicked his voice with heavy sarcasm. "The walk from Clearharbor to Breeze was … C'mon, Shiro, you're supposed to be on my side!"

"Well … uh, then I think we should take a break. I'm suddenly feeling a little hot from walking around in this sun."

"Kiss-ass," Geran muttered. "Fine, we'll take five. I'll climb this hill and take a look around; you guys just do whatever."

For the duration of the five minutes, Geran climbed the hill, looked around, came back down, and climbed it again out of restlessness. The other three sat patiently and took out their provisions to eat silently.

"Did you see anything?" Shiro asked as the ranger descended for the second time.

"Nope. Just trees, rocks, sand, rocks, a river, and some more rocks."

Lilian leaned over. "Didja see any rocks?"

"Shut up. Are you done being lazy yet?"

"I'm still deciding."

"What's that supposed to mean? Either your feet hurt or they don't."

The demicat folded her arms. "Well, I guess that depends."

Geran folded his, too. "Yeah. It depends if your feet hurt."

"No. If you decide to stop being rude."

"To stop being … Are you serious right now?"

Elaethia stood. "Now is not the time for hostilities between us."

"Bawwww, we've done so much walking! I haven't gotten to blast anything yet!"

"Lili-chan, it's okay. We'll find this sorcerer soon."

"We'd better! Geran! Can't you track him or something?"

"We've been over this before!"

"Please. We must not fight among ourselves."

"This is so stupid! Whose idea was it to take this quest anyway?"

"Y-yours, Lili-chan."

"No way! Geran was the one who took it off the wall, and Elaethia's the leader!"

"I fail to see how I could possibly be responsible for this."

"Oh for the love of …" Geran growled, and he threw his hands into the air. "Dammit, Lilian! I'm sick of listening to you bitch all the time! The reason I never wanted to party up with people for ten years was so I didn't have to deal with obnoxious brats like you!"

The demicat's eyes welled up, and she started to whimper. "G-Geran …"

"Stars above, it's this kind of shit that really gets on my nerves. By the Sun and Moon!"

"By the Sun and Moon indeed," an ominous voice said, resonating around the landscape.

Elaethia looked up the hill in front of her as she saw a figure approach. He loomed nearly fifty meters above them in a dirty white robe and a red hood. In his hands he held a large, strange-looking object at his side. The device was over a meter long and two feet thick. Tubes, magnifying glasses, and crystals were arranged down a single glass barrel in the center of the long object. The aging sorcerer had to strain to lift it.

"The Sun and Moon gave me their blessings," he began.

He pointed the muzzle at Cataclysm.

"But their blessings fell on ungrateful hands."

Light shone from the sky into the top of the object

"I once swore to spread their light for them."

The object began to glow.

"But it's not what I want anymore."

The air hummed with energy as he aimed the device at Cataclysm.

"My foolish youthfulness brought me to believe that I was destined to give life to this world."

The muzzle at the end of the object shone brightly.

"But now I only wish to see it *burn*."

Geran made a face. "The hell's with *this* guy?"

A flash of blinding light erupted from the device and traveled just above their heads. Searing heat emanated in proximity to the beam that barely missed them. The adventurers dived to the ground as the single burst of light began to lower toward them. Suddenly it dissipated.

"What was *that?*" Shiro shouted to Elaethia.

"I do not know! Run for cover! I do not wish to be touched by that light!"

"Elaethia, Shiro, get out of there!" Geran had dived to safety in a ditch behind him with Lilian. He suddenly emerged from his cover to fire an arrow at the sorcerer as Elaethia and Shiro dashed behind a large boulder.

"Weapons of the Sun cannot harm the Sun himself." The old man pulled out a wand that caused a wall of bright light to appear in front of him. The arrow clattered off it and fell to the ground.

"Wait a second!" Lilian shouted as she jumped up to send a *fireball* up the incline.

"Weapons of the Moon cannot harm the Moon herself," the sorcerer called. With his wand still up, the bright light was replaced by a pale one. Lilian's spell passed through it and disappeared.

The mage's eyes bugged. "That was *sun wall* and *moon wall*! I thought this guy was supposed to be a fire mage!"

Shiro turned around. "That's what the request said. What's wrong, Lili-chan?"

"Those weren't fire spells! They aren't even elemental spells; this guy's a priest!"

"I've never heard of a priest using magic like this!" Geran shouted.

The sorcerer priest spread his arms and addressed the adventurers below. "Beloved children of the heavens, I will purify this earth of your tainted presence."

He took a hold of the weapon, and another beam of light burst forth to strike the boulder Elaethia and Shiro were covering behind.

Geran stood up and aimed his bow as it dissipated. "Now, Lilian!"

An arrow and *icicle* flew up the incline, and the sorcerer pulled his wand out again.

"Weapons of the heavens cannot harm the heavens themselves."

Both walls of light appeared. The arrow clattered to the ground, and the *icicle* disappeared.

"Did he just cast *two* spells at *once?*" Lilian shouted. "That's impossible!"

Geran scowled and shrank back to the ditch. "He's weaponized sunlight! By the Moon, Elaethia, Shiro! Look at your rock!"

The samurai and warrior peered around. They looked down to see molten lava flowing downhill from the face of the boulder.

"What *is* this, man!" Shiro yelped, and he kicked away from the trail of hot, glowing liquid. Elaethia stepped out and made a gesture at the ground. A wall of ice began to construct itself between her and the sorcerer.

"Shiro, we will use *ice wall* as cover until we may get near enough to him to strike. Stay wi—" a beam of light pierced the wall and struck the dragon hero in the chest. She tumbled backward and crashed down onto the path below.

"Elaethia-sama!"

Shiro dived to aid her but was cut off by the beam of light, which passed right in front of him. He could not bear the heat it radiated. Obviously blinded, he staggered back behind the boulder.

Elaethia hadn't felt this much pain since she became a dragon hero. Her dragonite armor had saved her from the blast, but the heat still was still very much present. Her body burned, and it felt as if she were being cooked alive inside her armor. She tried to breathe, but the heat robbed her lungs of air. The dragonite plate was not breached, but it glowed from the immense temperature. Her frost could not withstand him.

She dragged herself to a knee and leaned on her axe. She felt there had to be something she could do. Her dragon strikes would be dissipated by the holy walls. She could not run faster than light itself. Her normal frost spells were easily melted by the sorcerer. Elaethia racked her mind for something, *anything*, she had learned or seen in her time with Frossgar. The dragon had different magic than brehdars. He had to have known more spells than she did.

Her memory shifted to when she was with Frossgar again. Tall grass and mountain flowers had burst forth from the ground to take advantage of the brief summer months during which they could bloom. It was her fourth year with the dragon, and one of the few times she was outside with him. As they returned to their cave, she pointed at the tall blue formations that protruded from the ground outside the cave.

"Mr. Frossgar," the girl asked. "What are those? They're shaped like crystals or gemstones, but they're as cold as ice. Did you make them?"

"Indeed I did, little one," he answered. "Long ago when I came to this area, I erected them to label my territory. Wiser creatures would recognize the potent magic, or smell my scent, and retreat. The few that were either braver or duller than that would pass by them. They were the ones that became my occasional meals."

"Wow, so they've been here just as long as you have?"

"Correct. They have stood for approximately two thousand years."

"Two thousand … How big were they when you made them?"

He tilted his head. "What do you mean?"

"Well if this is how they look two thousand years later, how did they look back then?"

"The very same as you see them now. It is *unyielding ice*. No means, be it might or magic, can alter them from their current state."

"You should teach me that!"

"You pose neither magic nor a dragon's affinity to make such a construct. Although their creation is nearly instant, it takes an incredible amount of magic to do so. It took four days to create the ones you see in front of you."

"Can any other dragons make something like this?"

Frossgar thought for a moment. "My earthen and forest kin could do something similar. However, nothing such as this. *Unyielding ice* is a spell only frost dragons can cast."

"Did you ever see them do those spells?"

"I did, once. An earth dragon whose name I cannot recall. She deformed the earth in a manner to uplift a wall of stone to protect her hatchlings—a much larger construct than what I can make, but not as durable."

"So she was a friend of yours!"

The dragon tilted his head. "Friend? You are quite fond of that term, but I do not believe it is applicable to dragons. However, there was one whose company I learned to enjoy. Somewhat. He came to visit me every dozen years or so after my seclusion."

"Wow! Who was he?"

"An air dragon named Thereous. He was like you in a way. I suppose that is what led to my taking you in at first."

"Why did he stop coming? Did you have a fight?"

"He died," Frossgar said solemnly. "He was pursued to my mountain by dragon hunters. A single ballista bolt made of dragonite pierced his underside. I had the means to avoid this outcome, but I faltered in my choice to not kill brehdars. It was since that day that I revised my decision. For a time, I blamed myself for his death. But knowing Thereous, he would not want me to feel this way."

"Well, I'll be here all the time!" Elaethia beamed. "I'll always be with you, so you don't have to be lonely anymore!"

Frossgar smiled fondly at the young girl. "I was never lonely, little one. But nevertheless I am grateful for your presence."

Elaethia's mind returned to the present. She remembered them—the blue ice crystals outside Frossgar's cave! In the years she saw the snow and ice retreat from and return to the mountainside, they stayed ever present when the rest of the frost had disappeared. Even when she joined with him and the landscape was ravaged by the surge, the *unyielding ice* remained unbroken.

The sorcerer again aimed his weapon at her as it glowed with energy. Tears began to form in her eyes again at the memory of the beloved dragon as she called to the power he gave her. Elaethia motioned again for an *ice wall*, this time calling to it not as a human but as a dragon.

Her eyes began to glow. She thrust a fist upward, and a light blue crystal erupted from the earth, taking the full blast from the superheated light. It did not falter. The formation of cleaved ice didn't even show signs of melting.

"Impossible …" the old sorcerer murmured.

"Shiro!" the dragon hero called to her samurai companion. "Use the *unyielding ice* as cover. I will make a path for you to get to him!"

"Understood, Elaethia-sama! I will be in your care!" He sprinted from the melting rock to the pillar of ice. The sorcerer tried again to hit him.

"The heavens will shall not be left undone!" he shouted.

"Shiro! Elaethia!" Geran called. "He can't fire consecutive blasts. Wait for the cooldown!"

"The light of the sun will purge you," he yelled as he fired again.

Elaethia erected another pillar, and Shiro ran behind it.

"The higher you climb to reach the heavens, the more you realize they are beyond your grasp."

The dragon hero and her samurai repeated the steps.

"One can never touch the sky. You shall be no different!"

The sorcerer's voice betrayed his panic as the swordsman and the bursting formations drew nearer.

"I will ascend this accursed life as a priest! The Moon will give me new life in the elements! You shall not stop me!"

Shiro was less than ten meters away.

"Begone! Leave this realm and myself alone!"

The sorcerer stumbled from the terrain, and Shiro seized the opportunity. He drew his blade and charged directly at the old priest with a terrifying war cry. The sorcerer lifted the glowing machine directly to Shiro's face and poured his magic into it.

"Then you will burn in hell with me!" the priest roared.

He was too late. The katana impaled him through the gut, and he looked down at the blade that pierced his body. He coughed. A spurt of blood flew from his mouth and trickled down his chin.

"M-mercy …" the old sorcerer gurgled.

Shiro brought the sorcerer to his knees. "Then use your final moments to repent. The heavens may grant mercy, but I will not."

Shiro tore the blade free. The samurai twisted his grip so he held the blade underhand. The old man looked up as Shiro lunged forward and slashed the blade across his neck. His severed head flew off, bounced on a rock, and rolled down the hill. His lifeless body fell forward, watering the dusty ground with blood. Shiro flicked the blood from his sword and returned it to its sheath, and then offered a silent prayer to the heavens before turning to his party.

"The sorcerer is dead. He won't attack anyone ever again."

"Are … are you sure?" Lilian's voice quavered from behind her cover. "I'm not poking my head out until I know for *sure* he's dead."

The priest's head bounced down the hill, across the path, and into the ditch on the other side. Lilian's shriek could be heard for miles.

Geran winced as he clutched the side of his head. "By the Sun, cat! Did you have to do that right next to my ear?"

"What gives, Shiro? You did that on purpose!" she yelled.

"I-I'm sorry, Lili-chan! I was so concerned about making sure he didn't get away!"

"Nevertheless, the deed is done," Elaethia said as she returned to the path. "This odd feeling in my head—is this magical exhaustion?"

"Right behind the eyes?" Lilian asked. "Kinduva pulsing beat that's slowly going away?"

"Correct."

"Yep. That's magic fatigue. It'll go away soon. How've you never felt that before?"

"What now, Geran?" Shiro asked as he descended the hill.

"Same thing as usual. Collect the loot, go home, cash in."

"What loot?" Elaethia asked.

"I don't know about you guys, but that weapon he was using? I think it collects sunlight and projects it into that beam. It'd fetch a good price."

Lilian rubbed her hands together and slinked toward the weapon. "Ooooh, you're right! To think of all the stuff I could buy if we sold that to some shop or enchanter." She gagged suddenly as Geran caught her by the cloak.

"Ah-ah-ah! Paws off. I don't trust you to hold something like that; you'll probably drop it and break it. Besides, I give it two minutes before you decide it's too heavy and dump it on Shiro. Elaethia, you mind carrying that while I keep an eye on greedy-guts here?"

"Very well," she said, and she picked up the device. "Let us return to the inn. We shall catch the next wagon, or walk until we find one."

"Sounds good to me. Everyone check your stuff. Let's go home."

Chapter 10
Mage

Sixth Era.139. Abris 16.

They took only four steps before the world around them erupted into a writhing cyclone of flame. The fiery walls encased the party in a twenty-meter diameter and traveled eighty meters into the sky.

Shiro stumbled back from the flaming wall. "Holy Sun and Moon!"

Geran staggered away and pointed at the dragon hero. "Elaethia! We need your frost magic, *now!*"

"I cannot! My magic has not returned!"

"I don't wanna be burned alive!" Lilian wailed.

"Guys! Guys, wait!" Shiro put his hands up. "Do you feel that?"

Everyone stopped and glanced around.

Geran blinked. "No ... it's not hot. I mean, I can feel the heat, but it's not *hot*."

"What does this mean?" Elaethia asked.

"I don't know; let me think." Geran began muttering to himself. "I don't know. I've never even thought this kind of thing was possible!"

"You don't have a plan?" Lilian objected. "You always have a plan! You can't go dumb now!"

"I just said I never thought this could happen! I mean ... who can even do something like this?"

"That would be me," a man's voice stated from the other side of the torrent of flame.

A silhouette appeared in front of them. It began to walk forward, directly into the blaze. Unscathed, the magician revealed himself from the inferno. He wore a crimson cloak with white-and-yellow markings and embroidery. He was a dwarf in his early thirties, with a bald head and a pointed black beard and mustache. His mahogany staff was elegantly carved with a single orange gemstone. He stopped a few meters in front of them and glanced at their insignia.

"Well, well, well. Fancy meeting you guys here. Hello there, Geran. Haven't seen you in over a year."

The ranger's jaw dropped. "Mordecai?"

The swirling flame dissipated. As the ash and embers scattered into the wind, they revealed Breeze's strongest mage. Cataclysm found themself in partial shock. Mordecai was shorter than Elaethia had imagined. Then again, she had only heard of him once, and he was a dwarf. He stood maybe five feet six inches, but his presence made him seem much bigger. He didn't seem as ominous or mysterious as she was led to believe, either. His opening introduction actually appeared friendly. But that didn't excuse him from the action he had just performed.

"You are with Breeze's guild, correct?" she asked. "What is your reason for encasing us in that spell?"

Mordecai raised an apologetic hand. "Ah. Sorry if that scared you; it's a precaution of mine. I didn't know who you were, and I certainly wasn't going to let you walk away without finding out. I heard there was a dangerous fire sorcerer in this area, so I came to investigate. You were never in any real danger."

"That doesn't exactly fill me with reassurance, Mordecai," Geran interjected.

"Come on, Geran. I know you're no magician, but surely you can recognize *pillar of fire*. It's one of the most common."

"*What?*" Lilian shouted. "That was *pillar of fire*? How? That spell's cyclone is nowhere *near* that wide, and it's *way* hotter than that!"

"Oho? Is that Lilian I see? It looks like you found your way out of the I levels—and grew a couple of inches, too! A lot happens in two years, doesn't it?" He tousled her hair with a laugh. "Last I saw you; you were up to my chest and making slick spots on the kitchen floor with frost magic."

Lilian shooed his hand off her head. "Mordecaaai! Stooop! I haven't done that in forever! Tell me how you did that fire thing! Is that something that comes with specializing?"

He ignored her. "Geran, my buddy! You won't believe how surprised I was to hear that you were in a party. I just *had* to come see for myself!"

"Yeah, about that. How'd you find us? And don't say it was a coincidence!"

Mordecai waggled a finger. "First things first, my dear ranger; you're being awfully rude. I come all the way out here, happen to bump into you and your party, and you don't even have the decency to introduce me. I want to know all about the group that reined you in."

"Fine," he sighed. "Well, you already know Lilian. This guy next to me in the weird armor is Shi—"

"My name is Shiro Inahari! I am a samurai from Osakyota. I came to Linderry to seek fame and redemption, and to prove my worth and usefulness to Elaethia-sama. I am her sword and will follow wherever she may lead me. She, Geran, and Lili-chan were generous enough to allow me into their party. It is a pleasure to meet you. And my armor is not weird."

"Fascinating," Mordecai mused. "A man far from home, traveling with a dragon hero, all to find his worth. You're not timid at all. Your family will certainly be proud." He turned to Elaethia. "Now, who might *you* be?"

"I thought you did not know who we were," Elaethia stated.

He blinked. "Eh?"

"You said you wished to be introduced to us and indicated you did not know our identities. Yet you knew I was a dragon hero and that Shiro was here to regain his family honor. Those were not mentioned in the introduction."

"Uhh …"

"Mooor-deee-*cai!*" Lilian sang as she stepped closer to him on her toes with each syllable. "Did you *reeeeally* come all the way out here just to say hi to Geran?"

"Well—"

"And how'd you know exactly where we were?" the ranger pressed.

"I hardly—"

"You also knew we were taking on a dangerous sorcerer," Shiro pointed out.

"I … you see … I may have been visiting the guild, and heard some rumors, and saw you were on a dangerous quest with a dragon hero. I wasn't worried about you or anything; I just figured you might want some help … or something!"

The fire mage started to turn red and looked away. Geran and Lilian glanced at each other and burst out laughing. Elaethia and Shiro looked at the flustered mage; to Geran; back at Mordecai; down at Lilian, who was rolling on the ground; and then at each other.

"I fail to see the reason for this reaction," Elaethia stated.

Mordecai shot out a hand. "Hold on; let me explain!"

"Fat chance!" Geran wheezed. "By the Moon, Mordecai. You haven't changed a bit! You're such a bad liar that *Elaethia* saw through you! You came out here just to meet Elaethia alone? You should have waited at the guild!"

"And you all wonder why I stay away so much," the fire mage muttered.

Lilian sat up. "Aww, Mordie! I always thought you were all big and scary. You're a bigger softie than Geran!"

"All right, all right! Enough out of you two! You have thoroughly botched my entrance. I had so many questions I wanted to ask Elaethia without this looming over my head."

Elaethia sighed. "If our introductions are over, let us return to the village. I care not for standing idly by for something such as conversation."

Mordecai nodded. "Good to see your reputation precedes you. You bring up a good point, however. Let's be on our way then, shall we? Ah! But first, you should dispose of those icy formations. It's unwise for a magician to leave remnants of his or her magic behind."

"I'm afraid I do not know how," she said.

"Very well, then allow me to. Fire is frost's greatest weakness, after all."

"You will not be able to melt or destroy them."

"You say this very confidently. I thought you knew who I was."

"That particular form of ice cannot be altered by any means known to me. It will likely remain there until the end of time."

"What exactly is it?" Mordecai asked.

"One of the few dragon spells I know. It is called *unyielding ice*. It cannot melt or be shattered."

"But it can be dispelled. You cast it, correct?"

Lilian shot a hand up. "Hold on! You can't cancel magic!"

"You can *if* you're specialized and it was your spell. Observe."

Mordecai thrust his staff upward and launched a massive sun-blocking fireball into the sky. He then swiped the staff to the side, and the flames disappeared. Everyone's mouths fell open.

"How did you do that?" Geran asked.

Mordecai waggled a finger. "Ah-ah-ah. Secrets. This should be common knowledge for a specialized magician, and I ought to charge you for such information. But for the sake of the moment, I will explain it to Elaethia in private."

He pulled the warrior aside and whispered in her ear. "In the same style that you call upon magic, you can dissipate it. By putting your will back into your cast and dispersing it into the area around it, you effectively cancel it. But it takes just as much magic to destroy as it does to create."

Elaethia's brow furrowed. "That is unsettling. Casting the ones you see fatigued me for the first time in my life. I cannot say I will have the strength to do as you say."

"For the first time, you say? Your *unyielding ice* certainly uses a lot of magic. I would suggest taking a potion before you attempt."

She nodded intently and turned back to her party. "Lilian, would you gift me your magic potion? I will need it."

"Sure, I guess. But you'll owe me one." The mage tossed her potion over, and Elaethia caught it.

Elaethia popped the cork out of the vial and drank its contents. It was an odd sensation—not pleasant, but not horrible either. The thick herbal liquid had a slightly metallic taste as it oozed down her throat. It made her insides tingle as it dispersed through her body. After a moment, she noticed a significant change in her magical energy.

"It did not replenish me entirely," she said, "but I feel I will be ready soon."

Lilian cocked an ear. "Seriously? That was a pretty potent potion. That one's always been more than enough to recharge me after a full blowout. How much magic do you have to tap into?"

"I do not know. I have always had this much, so I cannot give you an accurate scale."

Geran scratched at his beard. "Well, give it a whirl whenever."

"I believe I am prepared. Mordecai, if you will guide me?"

The dwarf shook his head. "There's no way I can. It's your magic. I told you what you needed to do; it's up to you to do it."

"Very well."

Elaethia looked at the ice protrusions on the hill. She focused on the nearest one and held a gauntlet to it. The dragon hero focused her power into it and willed the *unyielding ice* to disperse into nothing. However, instead of simply disappearing, the formation shattered and exploded. Shards of crystal-blue ice flew in all directions and peppered the adventurers, who flung their hands over their faces. The chunks bounced and rolled about, melting away as they scattered around the landscape.

"My word," Mordecai said, his mouth gaping. "I've never seen *that* reaction before. That is one powerful spell. How much magic did it take to make those?"

"I do not know. But those five alone were enough to deplete me."

"That's insane!" he shouted. "I could feel the amount of magic you just used! Are you using the same amount to destroy them as you did to create?"

"I would say so, yes."

"By the Moon … I'd venture you have higher magic reserves than me."

"*What!*" Lilian's squawked.

Shiro pursed his lips. "Will you be able to clear the others without hurting yourself, Elaethia-sama?"

"I may feel a bit more of that magical fatigue, but yes."

She repeated the process with the four remaining structures, having noticeable difficulty with the final one. The last *unyielding ice* grew stress fractures and crumbled slowly as opposed to bursting in an instant. Elaethia could feel the indescribable sensation behind her eyes more prominently than before. Her hands shook. She put a gauntlet to her brow and exhaled heavily as she felt the world churn beneath her feet.

"Hey, you good?" Geran asked as he walked over to her. "Damn. What happened to your eyes? Lilian, can you take a look?"

The demicat strode over and peered into Elaethia's dragon-like eyes. Their once vibrant, azure color was now a dark blue—nearly the same color as her armor.

She made a face. "Gosh. That's a bad case of overcast. You sure you're all right?"

Elaethia tried to nod. "I feel mostly fine, physically. But this sensation is very unpleasant in its own regard. What is overcast?"

Mordecai, too, looked at the dragon hero's eyes. "It's when a magician uses more magic than he or she has on reserve. The spell then takes the life force from the caster's body to compensate.

I've seen it this bad before. You should not even be able to stand, let alone have cognitive function. Your condition is bad enough to kill an inexperienced magician."

Elaethia wobbled slightly. "Is that so?"

Shiro stepped up to support her. "Is there any way to treat this?"

Mordecai pulled out a magic potion of his own. "Only by getting magic back. Waiting, magic potions, or a priest casting *moonlight* on you are the most common methods. Here, take my potion. You need this more than me. Don't worry about repaying me; I've gathered enough information here to make up for it."

"Thank you," Elaethia murmured. She took the vial and drank its contents. This one was considerably thicker, and the tingling sensation was more akin to a jolt. Her eyes snapped open and returned closer to their natural color.

Mordecai's eyes bugged. "Not even *that* was enough to give you a full recharge? What *are* you?"

"A dragon hero," she responded plainly.

"Yes, I know; it was a figure of speech."

"If you were looking for a more specific answer, you should have asked a more specific question."

Mordecai turned to Geran. "Is she always like this?"

"Pretty much," the ranger said.

"And yet you grouped up with her. I'd love to hear about how that came to be, and even more about your magic, Elaethia. You can tell me all about it on the way back."

"I will answer what I can—that which I am comfortable answering. However, I know very little about dragon magic."

"Then let's hear it from the beginning. I want to know everything you can tell me about dragons and dragon heroes."

"Now hold on, you stingy bastard," Geran intruded. "That was the first time I've ever heard of you sharing about your research and discoveries. You tell Elaethia one piece of common knowledge, and you think you'll get unique information from her for free? I don't think so."

"Vigilant as always, I see," Mordecai sighed. "All right, I'm willing to strike a deal. You give me that weapon the sorcerer was using, as well as telling me what you know about dragon magic—"

"This is sounding awfully one-sided," Geran muttered.

"And in return, I'll answer any questions you have about magic and specializing. Within my own knowledge, of course. As well as a few exceptions to specific details."

Shiro raised a hand. "This doesn't sound very beneficial to Geran or myself."

"All right, fine," Mordecai groaned. "I will also give you half the money I receive when I eventually sell the thing."

Geran scratched his chin. "Maybe. Elaethia, Lilian—your thoughts?"

Lilian eyed the bald man. "What exceptions do you mean?"

"I won't give you step-by-step details or processes of how to do things. Then there would be little point in your growth from this transaction."

"Okay, yeah, that makes sense. I wanna get stronger by my own work!"

"You understand? Perhaps I misjudged you, Lilian. You've grown quite a bit. And you, Elaethia?"

"I accept. I am curious to learn about magic and my own specialization."

Elaethia regaled on her times from when she first met Frossgar. She told the fire mage all she could remember from her childhood, but Mordecai showed little interest in her upbringing. He seemed more intent on hearing about the dragon himself and the magic he wielded, and he expressed much disappointment that Frossgar rarely used his magic around her. The only pieces of information Mordecai latched onto were the description of the dragon and the few spells Elaethia knew.

"Well," he stated. "That was a letdown, but not entirely. So it sounds like you, as the hero, take in the dragon's power. Then it gets dispersed into the brehdar so it becomes highly versatile. Same power, but more precise and compact."

"How did you come to that conclusion?" Elaethia asked.

"Transferal of energy and thermodynamics. What you just described confirms my suspicions. There had to be some sort of spell he used to combine the two of you, correct? That spell transferred all of his power into you. Magic, like all other forms of energy, can't be created or destroyed, just transferred. Only the heavens can create matter and energy by will. So: by putting everything into you and committing to the spell, you had to absorb all the power. It couldn't go anywhere else. If your body hadn't been able to take it, you probably would have been destroyed."

"But his mind did not accompany me. It was lost in the process. All I took was his strength, soul, and magic."

Mordecai waved a hand. "Then maybe there were parts he could control. Maybe he forgot to or didn't know how. Maybe the spell malfunctioned. Either way, his magic and strength made it into you, and your brehdar form can manage and control the magic more precisely than a dragon. That's why dragon heroes were considered the earth's apex species. Though that has been highly disputed when taking leviathans into account, but those monstrosities never attacked dragons despite being several hundred meters long."

Shiro perked up. "Apex species? That means Elaethia-sama is stronger than a dragon!"

"Well … From my own research and discoveries, the only thing that could defeat a dragon was a dragon hero or another dragon. Elaethia is nowhere near that capable. Not yet, at any rate.

History unfolds dozens of incidents where entire kingdoms waged war on a single dragon and were ultimately brought to ruin. That was actually the start of the second war."

Elaethia brightened. "You know of the dragon wars?"

"A fair amount more than most, yes."

"Tell me, please."

"Very well. I'll consider this a bonus for what you've told me thus far." Mordecai dug a thin brown leather book with metal edges from his satchel and handed it to her. The cover was embroidered in the rough outline of a golden dragon.

"For me to verbally recap even the most basic rundown of the dragon wars would take all day," he continued. "I hope this book will suffice for you. This is the Draconic Codex. It contains the combined knowledge of the history of the dragon wars."

Lilian stuck her face in. "Kinda small to hold thousands of years' worth of war in it."

"It's not a complete encyclopedia," Mordecai explained. "Those are held in the Moon's Pillar and stand taller than all of us combined. This is only a small booklet holding quotes, anecdotes, and entries from during the wars. It was mostly written by volunteer dragon heroes, actually. Think of it as a mass diary."

"Very well," Elaethia said. "I will put this to good use. Thank you."

Geran scratched his chin. "This is nice and all, Mordecai, but how does this come around to Elaethia?"

"Because now that we know her potential, we only need to figure out how to reach it."

"Easier said than done. How does she do this?"

Mordecai shrugged. "No idea. The authors of the codex hardly spoke of their training or transition. I'd ask one of the historians or archivists at the Moon's Pillar."

Lilian narrowed her eyes. "The Moon's Pillar? What kinda connections do *you* have with the Arcane Sages?"

"They seemed keen enough to let me into their ranks. But they want me to be out in the field, gaining experience and knowledge."

"*That's* what you've been doing this whole time?"

"Indeed. I should be indoctrinated in a year or so."

"You're gonna be a *book-sniffer?*"

"Is that jealousy I hear, Lilian?" Mordecai goaded.

She scoffed. "Fat chance! You can get dust mites in your bushy eyebrows all you want. I'm gonna be out here making history."

"Mordecai," Elaethia continued. "Could you access those records for me? Or bring me to them?"

He shook his head. "Unfortunately not. I myself am not a Sage or one of the historians. I have no authority to bring in guests, let alone allow them to look at records. There is very sensitive and dangerous information kept in the libraries. Your best bet is to get on the good side of a current Sage, who can get that information for you. It'll likely be several years before I can do that much."

"That is too long. Rychus must be destroyed before then."

Mordecai's eyes twinkled. "So that *is* your goal. Hmm. I'll tell you what. The next time I find myself in Apogee, I'll ask around the tower. There may be some interested in studying a living dragon hero in exchange for knowledge of the former ones."

"I thank you, Mordecai."

"Oh, don't thank me yet. Who knows which ones may be interested? Some of the Sages are fanatic, and their demands would be … Well, let's just say you may prefer to live in ignorance than agree to their terms."

"We shall see."

"Indeed we shall."

"Enough of the dragon stuff," Lilian groaned. "Let's talk about elemental magic. You said you'd answer my questions, and I got a lot!"

"All right, ask away. Bear in mind I won't tell you everything by definition."

"Whatever. How did you adjust the temperature and size of that *pillar of fire*?"

Mordecai gave a sly smile. "I altered how I channeled it."

"Yeah, I know. What did you do?"

"Hmmm … I adjusted the temperature and width of the blaze."

"By the Moon, Mordecai!"

"Sorry, Lilian. I can't help you find the answer without giving it away. Although what I've said should be enough for you to figure it out."

"That doesn't make any sense!" she wailed.

"It will if you think about it. Unfortunately, you already know beyond the basics of elemental magic. I can't hint to you anything you don't already know."

"So you duped me!"

"I suppose I did." The fire mage winked. "However, I will say this: You do not need to be specialized to alter a spell like I did."

Sixth Era.139. Miyan 16.

Lilian's appearances became very scarce over the following month. Every day, she would disappear midmorning with her questing gear and a plethora of magic potions. Elaethia would watch each time as her lively companion ventured out for the better part of the day and returned physically, mentally, and magically exhausted. The demicat was not taking any quests, as they had received a sizable reward from the previous one, so what was she doing?

"Have you noticed Lilian's odd behavior?" she asked Geran one day.

He looked up from a pile of ranger flyers. "Yeah. I asked her about that, but she didn't want to say anything yet. She told me something about not being sure how it would work out, whatever that means. Honestly, I could trail her if I felt like it, but she'd get mad if she found out. Besides, with the exception of the most serious, she's terrible at keeping things to herself. She'll tell us eventually."

"Whatever it is, she is most dedicated to it. I have never seen her put forth so much effort before."

"I have. When Lilian gets into something, she *really* gets into it. Despite everything else, she's a hard worker. That cat can get downright obsessive over something if it hits her right."

"Perhaps it was something Mordecai said," Elaethia pondered aloud.

Geran shrugged. "Most likely. But that fiery recluse went and disappeared on us as usual. Michelle is the only person Lilian's been talking to recently. Not sure how anyone can stand daily interaction with that crazy alchemist, but *nothing* stops Lilian when she's on a roll."

"Perhaps Michelle will know what Lilian has been up to."

"I highly doubt it. But if you wanna ask, go right ahead. You may bite off more than you can chew without even opening your mouth, though."

"What do you mean?" Elaethia asked.

"You'll find out. Just don't expect me to bail you out like usual."

"Very well. I will exercise caution if that is what you believe necessary."

"Something like that. Anyway, have fun."

Elaethia blinked a few times at his words. Geran chuckled to himself as he sorted out a couple of papers. She thought nothing else of it and made her way into the enormous pantry that was the provisions line. She was greeted by the field cook, Brodic. The bald dwarf was putting together a line of sandwiches and misting them with an opaque liquid. He looked up as she walked through.

"Be right there, lass. I'm touchin' up th' preparations on this batch."

"I am not here on a quest, Mr. Brodic."

"Hmph. Shoulda known. Never seen ye back here outta yer armor. What can I do ye for?"

"I am just passing through. I simply wish to speak with Michelle."

"Ye placed a special order?"

"I did not. I only wish to ask a question regarding one of my companions."

"Yer gonna talk with frazzle-brain? Heh. Good luck to ye."

"You are not the first to mention something of that sort.

"An' I won't be the last. Hold on a sec. Lemme get outta sight."

The dwarf pulled down some hanging shutters and went quiet. Elaethia stood baffled in front of the now-closed station. She shook her head, walked past the canteen, and halted in front of the counter to the potions station.

Michelle was in her standard outfit: a white lab coat, black pants, black shoes, and gray turtleneck. Her brown hair was a curly mass pinned behind her head in a ponytail. Steel-rimmed spectacles sat on her pointed nose. She muttered to herself while she twisted her wand at several multicolored liquids in beakers, vials, and tubes. The station hissed and bubbled and popped as the alchemist altered their components. Elaethia rang the service bell on the counter.

"One moment," the alchemist announced.

After a few seconds, there was a poof followed by a small cloud of green vapor pouring out of a vial. Given the color, it seemed that a stamina potion had been completed. Michelle turned around and walked to the counter, kneeling to sift through her shelves.

"What kind do you need?" she asked. Michelle seemed normal, if not distant. Elaethia wondered why everyone was telling her to be careful.

"I am not going on a quest. I—"

"Special order?"

"No. I have a question, and I believe you are the best to answer it."

The alchemist stopped. She stood up to look Elaethia in the eye. "A question? You request knowledge? From me?"

"Indeed. Is now not a good time?"

Michelle looked down and tapped her fingers together rapidly. "A question … She wants to learn …"

"It should not take a moment." Elaethia wasn't sure if the woman was paying attention anymore. Michelle turned her back to the warrior and began to mutter to herself.

"Finally. Oh, happy day *finally*. Oh, how long I've waited for this moment. It's always the ones you least expect, but that matters not. Oh, how fortunate am I. What could it be? What could it be indeed? How intriguing, I simply cannot *contain myself!*"

She wheeled around, half-diving over the counter to press her face into Elaethia's. The dragon hero flinched back and instinctively raised her hands in a guard.

"Miss Michelle …"

"So! You've come to learn of the fascinating and prosperous arts of alchemy? Well, well, well, I assure you that you have come to the right place!" She leaped over the counter with dexterity Elaethia didn't think possible of the middle-aged woman. "Come! Come! I will gladly share with you the *bountiful* and vast knowledge that I have for this incredible art! Don't be shy! Don't be shy at all. Follow me; come, come!"

Michelle grabbed onto Elaethia's arms with hands shaking so violently with excitement that she visibly vibrated. Elaethia could not free herself without harming the alchemist, so she followed along. Michelle started to push her over the counter, despite there being a door a few meters to the left. Elaethia thought best to comply. Once both of them were in the lab itself, Michelle pulled Elaethia along to the station.

"It's truly a miracle from the Moon that you came when you did. Such great fortune for you! You see, I have been working on a more compatible flux for the plasmatic infusions that help with the viscosity of the crude base product. I made a breakthrough using kingsfoil as a stabilizer for most basic potions. However weak, it proves consistent in the lower states of the concoctions! *But!* Once I added crushed nightshade berries to the flux, I canceled out more of volatile corruption occurring in the transmogrification."

The door opened behind them. Elaethia turned to see a chatty intermediate party enter. They took two steps, saw Michelle rambling, and scrambled over each other back out the door.

"*However!*" The wild alchemist waved a finger in the air. "By diluting it with water, I can increase fluidity! Although it isn't quite perfect. But! Through research of slimes, I found their digestive bodies can be deactivated by having two mages simultaneously charging them with electricity as well as freezing them! Then, by continuously discharging electricity into them through the flash thawing procedure, they become more gelatinous and concentrated."

"Michelle, I do not see how this is—"

"I can then take that substance and line the inside of the vials with it! Now, as I'm sure you're aware, slimes are resistant to all liquid from the outside. Their hydrophobic properties are perfect for lining the inside of my bottles, guaranteeing every last drop of the potion makes it out in rapid fashion! My research has been at a consistent need for slimes. Adventurers bring me some, I pay them. *Oh*, being in a guild is so convenient! But I'm sure you aren't here to talk about quests and adventure. You wish to hear more of my discoveries and progressions, hmm?"

It took a moment for Elaethia to find her voice. "I only had a question regarding my companion. She seemed to be only talking to you these last couple days."

"Companion? What companion? No one else has come to gather information like you. How unfortunate that you've been the only one in recent memory to care."

"Her name is Lilian. She is a demicat elemental mage."

"Lilian … Lilian … Nope! I don't know anyone named Lilian! Now take a look at this vial I have in the freezing chamber."

"Please, Michelle, I simply have questions of whether or not you know what she has been doing with so many potions as of recent."

"Potions? Who's buying potions? Are you? Certainly! After our revisions, of course. But that does remind me. I simply must make more magic potions. This same girl has come in every day this month and purchased several. Nobody has blown through so many in such a long time."

"What was she using them for?" Elaethia pressed.

"No idea! Now take a look at this vial in my centrifuge. I call it 'distillation zero-four.' It can be used to alternate the disposition of a compound, which in turn assists in the aeration process! We can deduct from this discovery that …"

Michelle rambled on for two more hours about the states and properties of alchemy. Elaethia finally escaped the social hostage situation by feigning hunger, and she made her way to her room. The dragon hero opened the door, shuffled to her bed, and promptly passed out on the spot until the following morning.

Elaethia decided to simply give up and wait for Lilian to approach them. Once again, she was bored. Cataclysm had agreed to take quests either alone or all together, so the option of the remaining three of them to take a quest together was non-existent. Geran had taken two ranger missions since the battle with the sorcerer priest, and Shiro had taken his first solo just the other day. Elaethia kept herself to low-level quests, as she didn't want to be away for more than a day at a time. She acted as a wagon guard earlier in the week, and the other day she killed a bear that was damaging honeybee apiaries. She walked downstairs to see whether Lilian had made an appearance today. Instead she noticed Geran and Shiro at their usual table.

"You would have been proud of me, Geran," Shiro said, bouncing in his seat. "I had been sitting in that loft for more than six hours. I even covered my scent the best I could with the surrounding straw and dirt!"

Geran scratched his beard. "When trying to conceal myself from animals, especially ones with strong noses like wolves, I try to use musk or urine if I really need to. Oh. Hey, Elaethia."

She sat down to join them. "Good afternoon, Geran, Shiro."

"Good afternoon, Elaethia-sama. Geran, did you really cover yourself with … urine …?"

"Occasionally. And it's not like I took a bath in the stuff—just a splash or two. That was mainly for making sure guard dogs didn't catch a whiff of me if the wind changed. I hardly went after wild animals, though. My specialty was people and organizations."

"What are you talking about?" Elaethia asked.

"Just about Shiro's first solo quest."

"I see. How did it go?" she asked the samurai.

"It went well! I met up with the rancher, and he explained how this wolf kept going after his animals. He brought his stock as well as fresh meat into a barn and tied them up while I hid in the loft. I could tell when the wolf had entered because the animals started acting distressed. I drew my sword and perched myself right on the edge above the entrance and waited. Once it appeared underneath me, I leaped down and drove my blade through its head. The rancher came out and saw that I had completed the quest and that none of his animals were harmed. He insisted on putting me up for the night instead of having me walk home at such a late hour. I just got back and turned it in."

"How are you feeling?" she asked.

"Rather disappointed, actually. All that waiting and preparing, just for it to be over in an instant without a fight."

"You'd hate being a ranger," Geran chuckled.

"How often did you do something like this, Geran?"

"I set up ambushes and stakeouts for people all the time. Espionage and hunter-killer missions were some of my best works. But I was not at the same caliber as Jacklyn Meyers. When it comes to covert missions, her party's top-tier."

"I have never heard of her," Elaethia stated.

"That's the idea. Jacklyn is the leader of Breeze's black-ops team, Nocturnal. They're a three-person party that exists for the sole purpose of taking care of missions and quests that don't technically exist."

Shiro leaned forward. "So they're like ninjas."

"What? No. Why are you bringing up ninjas? Nocturnal isn't like that. They're a search-and-destroy team. They get clearance directly from the church and state. The kind of stuff they do would be illegal if they weren't granted special authorization. If you've done something to have Nocturnal called on you, you're beyond redemption. No one has ever crossed them and survived."

"You have ties with such a secretive group?" Elaethia asked.

"I've got ties just about everywhere."

Shiro clenched his knuckles and looked around. "Are you sure it's okay to tell us this?"

Geran waved a hand. "Their existence is more or less public knowledge. I know a bit more than most because I've worked with them a couple of times. They're a very hush-hush group. It's best not to try to learn about them."

"So why are you telling us?" Elaethia pressed.

"Well, because I trust you guys. Shiro especially ought to know since they've recently stopped spying on him."

"They've been spying on me!"

"Obviously. You're practically nobility from a country that Linderry doesn't have the closest relations with. Naturally politicians would be suspicious. But they've deemed you a nonthreat, so you're fine now."

"Wh-what?"

"Well, only one of them watched you at a time. They wouldn't have all three members keeping tabs on you simultaneously," the ranger chuckled. "I bet Jacklyn's even managed to spy on us during our quests, and I didn't even notice."

Shiro scratched his head. "You make it sound like Jacklyn-san is a better ranger than you. I thought you were the best."

Geran laughed. "Oh, she'd kill me in a heartbeat. But overall? I mean, I guess I am for now. She's better than me in a couple of aspects, but supposedly I'm the most well-rounded in Breeze. Maybe all of Linderry. I don't know for sure, though. I'm just basing that on the annual tournament. But everyone's special in their own way, you know? There are some adventurers there that can blow even *my* mind."

Shiro began to bounce in his seat. "This tournament sounds incredible! Don't you think, Elaethia-sama?"

"Perhaps," Elaethia agreed. "However, I have little interest in partaking in sport."

Geran shrugged. "You may not have much of a choice. If you're selected as a contender, you're obligated to go. You can bet your battleaxe that Breeze is gonna want their own dragon hero at the head of it all."

"They wish to have their strongest members away from where they may help the people for three days? This does not seem at all well thought out."

"Over a week, actually. Four or five days for travel, two or three for the events and preparations. The people love it, however. Not to mention the revenue it generates for the country. And it's not like the entire guild will be gone. At least thirty or so from here will stay behind because they feel the same as you, and the local guard picks up the extra slack. But you're right in a sense. There's always extra work to take care of when we get back. It's the busiest time of the year for Nocturnal."

A dwarven waiter suddenly appeared next to them and approached Elaethia. "Excuse me, Miss Frossgar. You have a visitor."

"I do? Who is it?"

"A young demiwolf lad from Westreach. He says his name is Michael Finway and he knows you personally. Would you like me to bring him in or send him away?"

Something about that name seemed familiar. "You may bring him here. I will take care of it should it turn problematic."

"Very well, I'll send him over."

The waiter walked over to the receiving desk and disappeared behind the quest wall. After a few seconds, a teenage demiwolf with black-and-white hair bounded over to them with a wagging tail. He grinned widely at Elaethia as he reached the table.

"Hiya, Miss Elaethia! Remember me?" he asked.

Elaethia froze for a second. She *did* remember him. "Michael? What are you doing here? Did you come all the way from Westreach?"

"Yes ma'am! I've known it for a while, but after you rescued me from those bandits, I *knew* I wanted to be an adventurer. Westreach has a guild and all, but I wanted to come over here and be with Breeze. You guys are way nicer and cooler."

She tilted her head. "Cooler?"

Geran interjected. "Elaethia, you wanna introduce us to your … friend?"

She nodded. "This is Michael, one of the civilians I rescued from the watchtower several months ago."

"The watchtower hostage situation? So you *are* from Westreach?"

"Yes sir!" Michael said. "But I came here. Miss Elaethia was really awesome, and I was hoping she could train me!"

"Train you?" Elaethia asked.

"Yeah! I wanna be a warrior just like you!"

Shiro puffed out his chest. "Elaethia-sama doesn't really have the resources to take another under her wing. Although she is great, I don't think she can spare much time."

"Now, Shiro." Geran winked. "No need to get jealous. I don't think Michael here wants to take her away from us."

Michael put his hands up apologetically. "Oh no, not at all! I-I didn't mean to intrude or anything. If you're too busy, I … I understand."

Elaethia shook her head. "I would have no problem teaching you to fight. After all, you came all this way and sought me out with a clear heart. Unfortunately, Shiro does speak some truth. I do not have time allotted to teach; nor do I have the ability to do so. I am still learning myself and would not make an adequate mentor."

The demiwolf's ears drooped. "Oh …"

"Nothing is stopping you from joining the guild, however. There are plenty of able-bodied warriors who could instruct you."

"All right. Who should I talk to?"

"Well that depends," Geran said. "How old are you? What kind of experience do you have? What kind of weapon and armor are you used to? The more we know about you, the better we can get you in the right direction."

"I'm fifteen. And weapons and armor? Well, I don't do much fighting like that. Just scraps and fistfights. I've always been a hunter."

"You have to be sixteen to join, but you might be able to start an apprenticeship. And I'm going to assume you're good with the bow and knife?"

"Yes sir, and I'll be old enough in seven months. I'm good at trailing and tracking too! I always followed people to see the best way to learn about them. If I can find their weaknesses, I can figure out how best to fight them!"

The ranger scratched his stubble beard with a twinkle in his eye. "Hmm. Well, most of the warriors I know that could spare the time to train you are out. Have you eaten anything yet? It's about lunchtime."

"No sir, but I'm too excited to be hungry!"

"Tell you what. While we wait for some of the meatheads to get back, let's you and I do a little hunting. I'm feeling hungry myself, and I already spent money on food today."

"Hunting? With you? Right now?" Michael sent a concerned look over at Elaethia, who urged him with a nod.

Geran grunted. "Right now. You did bring your bow and knife with you, right?"

"Yes sir. But I had to leave them next to the door."

"That's standard. Let me get my gear, and we'll head out. Let's get a good score for Miss Elaethia."

"I … I guess." The demiwolf took a step back. He looked from Geran to Elaethia, back to Geran, and behind him to the door.

"Do you not trust Geran? He is most reliable," Elaethia assured.

"Well, not really. I'm sorry, sir, but I don't know you."

Geran nodded and stood. "Caution is good. And I figure you would be hesitant to trust a stranger, considering you're from Westreach. Don't worry, bud. I don't get any sick kicks out of screwing kids over. Besides, I've got a good reputation here. You can ask around if you want."

"It's fine, I guess. If Miss Elaethia says you're okay, and if this'll help me get into your guild, I'll do it."

Chapter 11
Ranger

Sixth Era.139. May 18.

Elaethia and Shiro looked on as Geran and Michael left. The samurai exhaled softly and leaned on the table with his head resting on his arms. Elaethia tilted her head. She had seen Shiro act this way before. Something clearly troubled him.

"Is something the matter, Shiro?" she asked.

"No, Elaethia-sama. Well … I mean, I'm not surprised that others would seek you out. After all, traveling with you is the highest honor I can imagine. I just … there's something inside me that dislikes the idea of that demiwolf training with you as well."

"You do not trust him?"

"It's not that. I suppose he seems good-hearted and loyal, but he may think of himself as one of your companions."

"Is that so bad? Lilian and Geran do as well, but you harbor no feelings such as this toward them, do you?"

"No, of course not! Geran and Lili-chan are my wonderful friends. I would never think ill of them!"

"Then why do you feel this way about Michael?"

Shiro's brow furrowed "I don't know. I guess I fear that he might take on your fighting style and spirit. I only wish to be your sword, but he wants to be just like you. Maybe he will become strong and powerful, and you may forget about me."

Her eyes softened. "Shiro, I could not forget you. Even if I were to find the time and knowledge to take him under my wing, he would only be my student and friend. Michael may become a strong and trustworthy ally, but never a companion so committed and dependable as you. You have fought well at my side, and my friends throughout my journey have been very few. I am glad that you were one of the first."

Shiro blushed and looked into his lap. "Your words honor me, Elaethia-sama."

"As do your loyalty and spirit to me, Shiro."

He smiled. "I'm acting selfish, aren't I?"

"Perhaps. But that no longer matters."

THE ELAETHIUM

The guild's front door burst open before Shiro could respond. Standing in the doorway was a very out of breath Lilian. The mage wildly looked around the guildhall until her eyes landed on the two sitting at the table.

"*Guys!*" she shouted, and she sprinted over, scrambling around the other tables and chairs. "Guys-guys-guys! I think I got it!"

"Got what, Lilian?" Elaethia asked.

"The spell thing! The thing Mordecai was talking about!"

"What spell thing, Lili-chan?" Shiro asked. "I don't remember much of what he said."

The demicat panted heavily and took a second to regain her breath. "Remember when Mordecai said that you didn't need to be specialized to alter the details of a spell? I might have figured it out!"

"You were able to make a *pillar of fire* like he did?" Elaethia asked.

"*Nope!* Not even close! But I *think* I got the premise! I've been casting spells all day every day this month, trying to figure out how to adjust their properties. I blew myself out three or four times a day, and my magic reserve has *spiked!* By the Moon, I'd feel like I could take on the world right now if I wasn't so tired and thirsty!"

"Maybe you should get a drink. This is something worth celebrating!" Shiro said.

Lilian sat down and slumped in her chair. "Funny thing—I blew through a *lot* of potions this month, and consequently all the money we earned."

Elaethia sighed. "So once again, you are—"

"Flat broke!" Lilian stated. She laughed softly and heaved a sigh. "We need a quest …"

"You need a bath first, Lilian. Plenty of rest as well. Geran is out hunting with a young man who wishes to join our guild. Tomorrow we can discuss a quest."

Lilian looked up and made a face. "Geran? Hunting? With a new guy?"

"Correct," Elaethia said.

"Do they know each other?"

"Not before today. His name is Michael, a demiwolf who will be old enough to join in seven months. He is looking for a warrior to take him as an apprentice."

"And *Geran* agreed to go out with him for a little hunting?"

"Geran was the one who offered," Shiro said.

Lilian blinked twice. "We're talking about the same Geran, right? Like, *our* Geran? Not some other Geran that I don't know about."

Shiro blinked back. "Yes. Geran Nightshade."

"Is he sick or something? Did you guys check his temperature before he left?"

"What's so wrong about what he's doing?"

215

Lilian scratched her ear. "Well I wouldn't say *wrong*, just weird. Geran taking an aspiring warrior out for some one-on-one time sounds just as likely as Elaethia deciding to be a diplomat."

"I hardly see myself doing something so tedious and rudimentary," Elaethia said.

"Then you see my point," Lilian responded.

"Do you truly see this as strange behavior for Geran? He is a rather open man."

"Well yeah, but mostly to us, and only since you got here. Before that? He was what I call a 'social introvert.' He had people skills, but if he had the choice of being with others or being alone, he'd always choose to be alone. The thought of him inviting a new guy out for man-to-man time doesn't sit with me. Especially since this Michael kid wants to be a meathead. No offense, Elaethia."

"None taken."

"I mean, what were they even talking about before they left?"

Shiro tapped his chin. "Something about bows and tracking. A little bit about apprenticeships and how there weren't any warriors here right now that could train him."

Lilian's tail flicked. "*Huh?* There're *plenty* of warriors here that could get him started. He doesn't even have to be an apprentice; he just needs to find someone to get him started down the right path. Liam is literally right there. Geran wouldn't talk about apprenticeships or bows or tracking or lie like that unless he …"

She stopped.

Elaethia tilted her head. "What is the matter?"

Lilian's mouth fell open. "Noooo … He's not thinking about … Is he gonna … Hey! When did he say they'd be back?"

Shiro raised an eyebrow. "He didn't."

"Oh, come on! He *totally* did this while I was gone on purpose!"

Elaethia shook her head. "I hardly believe that Geran did this just to irritate you, as he just met Michael. What are you going on about?"

"I don't wanna say anything until I know for sure. When did he leave? How long do you think he'll be gone?"

"Just now, and you would know better than I."

"*Aaaaauuughh!*" Lilian slammed her head onto the table and groaned into its wooden surface. "This is so not fair!"

Shiro shifted in his seat. "Putting Geran and Michael aside, what have you been doing all this time?"

The demicat sighed and leaned back. Her arms dangled freely, and her tail curled above the floor. "There's not much to say. I spent the first week casting my tail off, trying to figure it out. The following week and a half, I chased a red herring. For the last few days, I was finally able to adjust the temperature of *torch*, and I spent the rest of the day trying to do the diameter change to *tornado* until I ran out of potions. This morning I could *swear* I started to do it. I held it for almost a minute before I ran out."

"Why did you stop and come back? Surely you wanted to keep going."

"Of course! Except I didn't have any potions today. I couldn't afford them. But I got on the right track, so I'm more or less satisfied for now."

"Fascinating …" he said, and he rubbed the back of his head.

"I know, right? Anyway, do either of you happen to have some food? I literally only have enough cash for breakfast tomorrow, and I am *not* going into a quest hungry."

Shiro piped up. "I can come get you when I go down for dinner tonight! I can pay for your meal!"

She sighed in relief. "Thank the Moon, Shiro. This is why I like you so much."

The Osakyotan blushed. "I, uh … I like you a lot too, Lili-chan."

The demicat's ears perked up. "Y'know, I don't think anyone's ever said it to me like that before."

"I-I'm sorry if that came off as inappropriate or rude! I don't want you to think badly of me!"

"No, no, Shiro. You're fine. I just"—she laughed—"wasn't expecting that."

They looked at each other. Lilian smiled almost sheepishly, while Shiro turned pink and looked away.

Lilian chuckled quietly and stood up. "Hey. I'm gonna go bathe and take a short nap. Come find me whenever you want to get some dinner."

"O-of course, Lili-chan! I'll see you then!"

He watched Lilian as she walked toward the stairs and gave him a gentle wave. Once she disappeared from sight, Shiro jumped up and began to pace around in front of the table.

"Oooooh, now I've done it! I don't know where to go from here. I've never done anything like this before! Elaethia-sama, what do I do?"

"What do you mean?" she asked.

"I think I just asked her on a date! I don't … by the Moon, I'm so stupid! You're a woman; how should I act? What should I say!"

"I do not know if that is how she feels, and I have no knowledge regarding courtship. Perhaps you may ask Geran when he returns, as he has had romantic affairs before."

"But I don't know when he'll be back! It might be too late!"

"That is a risk you will have to take."

Shiro groaned and put his head in his hands. "I am so bad with girls."

"Bad with girls, eh?" a man's voice suddenly asked.

Elaethia and Shiro looked up to see Liam Barron standing over them with a tankard of ale. Elaethia realized this was the first time she had been so close to the demiwolf. Liam was tall, around six feet two inches. His body was rippled with muscle—so much so that Elaethia held no doubt that he was the third-strongest warrior in the guild. He had sharp features, a clean-shaven face, amber eyes, and a scar that traveled diagonally along the bridge of his nose. His black hair was rather long, and he kept it gathered behind his head in a choppy ponytail. The bangs above his eyes rose a little and draped down directly above his left eyebrow.

Elaethia nodded a greeting. "Hello, Liam."

"'Sup, Frosty, Inahari?"

"My dragon's name was Frossgar," she corrected him coldly.

The demiwolf put his hands up innocently. "I know. I wasn't bein' disrespectful or nuthin,' just givin' you a nickname."

"I have no need for names other than my own."

"Ahhh, don't be like that! I got names for all my buddies. It's a sign of friendship, y'know?"

Elaethia tilted her head. "Friendship?"

Liam turned to Shiro. "What's the problem, Inahari? Some lady giving you more attention than you know how to handle?"

Shiro gave a slight bow. "Hello, Liam-senpai. No, I just finally got the courage to ask her for … I don't know if it's even a date."

"Well, that depends," the large demi wolf said, and he spun a chair around to sit backward on it. "What're you doing?"

"We're having dinner here tonight. I offered to pay for her."

"Sounds simple. A nice, easy start. What kinda questions you got?"

"Just … What do I wear, what do I say? I-I don't want to mess up! I don't know what I would do if I made her hate me!"

Liam laughed and took a swig from his tankard. "Take it easy, bro. Relax. She already agreed, so it's obvious she's interested. Not many girls in this guild would lead a guy on just for free dinner, and none of 'em would pull that stunt on *you*. Especially since you've got Geran, Lilian, *and* Elaethia to back you up if she did. Who is it, anyway? I didn't know any of the curious ones got the courage to even talk to you yet."

"No others have approached me. It's just with Lilian."

Liam choked on his drink mid-gulp. He erupted into a coughing fit and pounded on his chest as he choked out his words. "I'm sorry, you said what? Lilian!"

"Y-yes?" Shiro stared at the coughing warrior and waited for him to regain his composure. Liam caught his breath and stared at his mug. He shook his head and set it on the table.

"Lilian agreed to dinner … with *you?*"

"Is that so hard to believe?" Elaethia interjected coldly.

Liam put a hand up. "No, no, I wasn't sayin' it like that. I can see how, I guess. You guys *are* in a party after all. But she's letting you treat her?"

Shiro nodded. "She's almost out of money, and I offered. She seemed happy to eat with me tonight."

The demiwolf scratched his ear. "Huh. Well I don't wanna say she agreed only because she's broke, 'cause that's not like her. Lilian's independent, y'know? Wants to be self-sufficient. She always turned other guys down in this situation, including Dylan when they ran together. *I* even offered once. But hell, I guess you're special."

"So what advice can you give me?"

Liam clicked his tongue. "Welp. Can't say for sure. She's unique, y'know, and has her own criteria. My best bet? Don't force yourself or pretend to be something you're not. Remember: you're the first guy I know of who Lilian's let treat her. She probably said yes because she likes what she's seen. Since you're in her party and around her a lot, she'd see right through any act or persona you put on. Just be yourself."

"Be myself. Okay. Yeah, yeah, I just … Have to be me. I can do that …"

Liam stared at him. "You're somethin' else, you know that, Inahari?"

"I'm sorry …"

"Don't be sorry," the warrior grunted as he grabbed his drink and walked away. "Just have some confidence in yourself and put your best foot forward."

"My best foot forward." Shiro tapped at his chin. He started to bounce on his toes and snapped his fingers. "I think I got it! Elaethia-sama, I'm going to get ready."

"You are not meeting until tonight, Shiro. It is still early afternoon," she noted.

But the samurai had already bolted upstairs.

"See?" Geran said to Michael as the two of them returned. "I wasn't gonna pull something on you.

"That was actually pretty fun, Geran," Michael said. "That breathing technique made *way* more sense once I actually did it. And that thing about my scent getting carried by the wind? I don't wanna *know* how many times that's screwed me over! Those stories you told me are pretty awesome, too! Breeze rangers sure are something else."

"I'm not gonna tell you to do something if it isn't useful. Otherwise it's just a waste of time for both of us. And thanks, I think."

"You're welcome!" Michael beamed. "So do you think any warriors are back yet?"

"Probably. But are you sure you want to be a warrior?"

"Yes sir! I think so. Elaethia was so cool, and I want to be able to help people just like she does!"

Geran shrugged. "It's true the warriors get a lot of the glory. But Elaethia isn't fully brehdar like you and me, in case you hadn't noticed. Don't try to get to her level. Besides, are you looking for fame or looking to help people?"

"Well … I want to help people. Being famous would be kinda cool, though."

"Anyone can be famous if they play their cards right, no matter what their class is. Most of the warriors here are rough-and-tumble. If something can't be swung over their heads and used to clobber an opponent, they want nothing to do with it. The job of warriors is to be the first ones into the fight and soak up the majority of the hits. If you feel up to getting constantly battered around while wearing heavy armor and a heavy weapon, I'll find someone to get you started."

Michael's tail stopped wagging. "Wait. First in the fight and taking all the hits?"

"Well not *all* the hits. Just most of them. Making sure the enemy is focused on you and not your allies. You have to listen to your party, too, and do what they say. They're counting on you to keep the enemy off of them."

"Is that really how it goes?"

"In A-level quests and below? Yep, that's what eighty percent of your fights are gonna be like. But you're up there in the thick of it, getting battle scars for equal pay and bragging rights."

Michael looked at the ground. "Maybe I oughta wait a while before I go into this. Get a bit bigger first."

"Now's the best time to start," Geran said. "Get the training out of the way and you'll get used to being slapped around faster."

"I-I didn't know that's what warriors really did."

"Hey. If you're good, and you survive long enough, you'll definitely start seeing the bonuses of being a well-known warrior."

"What's *that* supposed to mean!"

Geran pointed to a veteran adventurer near the bar. "Oh hey, perfect timing. I see Liam Barron over there! He's our third-strongest warrior and will definitely whip you into shape in no time! The last apprentice he had was delayed a few months because of a broken collarbone he got while training. Buuut I'm *mostly* sure Liam has toned it down a notch after that. Let's go talk to him."

"Wait!" Michael froze and twiddled his fingers. "I don't think I'm actually ready to do this. This sounds way different than I imagined. I guess I'm not cut out to be an adventurer. I'm sorry for causing you all this trouble."

Geran rested a hand on the demiwolf's shoulder with a gleam in his eyes. "Now hold that thought. Maybe warrior isn't the best pick for you right now, but there're other options for you if you'd like to be an adventurer. There're multiple classes after all."

"What do you mean?"

"You're pretty good with a bow, you know how to track, you've got the basics down for remaining inconspicuous, and you seem pretty smart. Ever give much thought into being a ranger?"

Michael blinked. "A ranger? I don't know anything about being a ranger, though."

"You didn't know anything about being a warrior, either," Geran said. "The difference is, I know a ranger here that has ten years of experience in the field, has done every type of mission, and is regarded as one of the best in the country. On top of that, he's been considering an apprentice."

"You do? Who is he?"

"You're looking at him."

Michael stared at him with big eyes. "So this whole time you were …"

"Testing you out."

"Did … did I pass?"

"I'm offering, aren't I?"

"Well, you keep dancing around the subject."

"All right," Geran walked him over to the reception desk and looked Maya dead in the eyes.

The elf looked up. "Geran, what are you doing?"

Geran grinned and turned back to Michael. "Michael, you show a lot of promise for being a ranger. You're a bright kid with a good heart and an open mind. It's been a long time since I've seen a youngin' come in here with as much potential as you, and I've reached a point in my career where I think it's best I bring up the next generation. So … how would you feel about being my apprentice?"

"I …" the demiwolf stuttered. "You mean I'd work with you? And you'd train me?"

"Yep."

"I would be a ranger here. In Breeze."

"In seven months, when you're sixteen. But you'd still be my apprentice until I felt you'd learned all you needed to be set up for success. You can back out anytime you want."

"Y-yeah! Okay, I'll do it!"

Maya suddenly took off her glasses and held her hands in a T shape. "Hold on! Time out! Geran, are you … did you just … *what?*"

"Surprise." He grinned.

Maya threw her hands in the air—and, consequently, the papers she was working on. "That's not fair! You've been nothing but antisocial for as long as we've been here. Then one day Elaethia shows up and you join her out of the blue, and now you're suddenly taking an *apprentice?*"

"What can I say? That woman changed me."

Maya rubbed the sides of her head and adjusted her glasses. "No kidding. I suppose you want an apprenticeship form to take to Master Dameon?"

"If you would, please."

"One second." The receptionist dug around in a filing cabinet and pulled out a couple papers. She stamped the top page and handed the short stack to Geran. "Like everything else we have, this is very self-explanatory. Take it upstairs when you're done. In the meantime, I'll send a runner to see if Master Dameon is available to review it."

"Thanks, Maya. What would I have done all these years without you?"

"Probably still be stuck in a tree somewhere."

Geran sighed. "You're never gonna let me down from that, are you?"

"Nope, and neither will the bear that chased you up there. Now shoo; go fill that out. Good luck, Michael."

"Yes ma'am! And thank you!" The demiwolf grabbed the papers and started to bounce with excitement as Geran walked him over to a table. "Bear? Tree?"

Geran chuckled. "Long story short, Maya and I came in on the same day, so we've been close friends for twelve years now. She went administration, and I went adventurer. She had to save me from an angry bear that chased me up a tree when I was a little younger than you."

"What did she do?"

"Threw the first thing she could grab out of her satchel at it. A half-full inkwell. Smacked the bear right in the face and got ink in its eye."

"That's so cool! But you're *just* friends?"

"That's what I said, right? Maya's definitely been my closest buddy all these years."

"Ah, darn. She's real pretty. Also has a *huge* pair of boo—" He cut himself off as Geran's eyes turned dangerous. "By the way, where do we start on these forms? What do I gotta do?"

Geran snatched the papers. "I'm starting to feel glad that Liam didn't take you. What's with demiwolves around here being pervs? As for the forms, most of this stuff is for me. You only have to initial a few statements and sign at the bottom of the last page."

"What kind of statements?"

"Just making it clear that you're not an adventurer yet so you have no official authority or weight in the guild. Also you don't have the right to speak on the guild's behalf. There're others, but you'll read them." Geran stopped writing and looked up at the teenager. "You *will* read these carefully, right?"

Michael nodded furiously. "Yes sir!"

"Wouldn't be much of a ranger if you couldn't follow simple instructions and pay close attention. Take a look at this page here. It gives you the basic rundown of what's expected of you. It's almost your turn to write."

Soon after, Geran and Michael were seated in Master Dameon's office. The huge demibear scratched his thick beard and looked over the forms. He frowned as he got to the last page.

"So, Mr. Finway. You're from Westreach?"

"Yes sir!" Michael responded. He held his clenched hands between his legs and sat stiffly on the large couch.

"And you want to become an apprentice, and eventually an adventurer, here in Breeze?"

"I do, sir."

"Do you have any contacts within the guild that referred you here instead of your own region?"

"Yes sir. Miss Elaethia did. She saved me from bandits that kept me locked up in a watchtower a few months ago."

Dameon sighed. "Elaethia? Damn. You've got two of my star kids vouching for you. If it wasn't for Geran offering to mentor you, I wouldn't even consider this apprenticeship. Woulda taken you for a spy or just a dumb kid. But since it's Elaethia that pulled you, I guess I've got little choice."

Geran leaned forward. "So you'll authorize it?"

"Yes—for now, because we're down a few members thanks to that sorcerer your party took out. Don't make me regret this, Nightshade. If anything goes down because of this kid, your ass is mine."

"Understood, Master."

"And you!" Dameon said, pointing a massive finger at Michael. "If I hear so much as a peep about you acting suspicious or causing trouble, I'll throw you out of this city by the tail in a heartbeat. Do I make myself clear?"

"Y-yes s-sir!" Michael stammered.

"Good. Now get your training started. If you're not an asset to me in seven months, I'm shipping you back to Westreach. You're both dismissed."

"Yes, Master," they both sounded off, standing up to leave the room. As they left, Michael tripped on the carpet and stumbled forward. The demiwolf crashed into the door and fell out into the walkway outside.

"I'm sorry!" He called back as Geran quickly shut the door. Michael picked himself up. He looked at the ground with his tail between his legs.

"I'm sorry, Geran. I totally made a fool of you there."

Geran smiled at him and tousled his black-and-white hair. "Don't worry about that. You can make up for it by working hard for me and Master Dameon."

"He's so scary," Michael whispered.

"Yeah, but he's the best guild master we could ask for. His number-one priority is taking care of us, and that includes making sure outsiders don't have the chance to cause problems. It's not a job that you can be gentle and lax with, and I certainly couldn't do it. He cares about every single one of his members and will fight tooth and nail for our well-being."

"Would he do the same for me?"

"If he accepts you into the guild? Absolutely. He'll treat you like one of his own children, but take that how you will."

Michael's tail started to wag. "All right! Let's get started!"

"That's the spirit. It's a little dark to start any field training, but we can go over knowledge while you mop up and clear dishes with the rest of the apprentices. I'll even help."

"Wait. Clean? I'm gonna be doing chores around here, too?"

Geran smirked. "You don't think the guild's gonna let you freeload, do you? You gotta get money somehow, and the guild needs to benefit from you. This is a good compromise."

"You didn't tell me about that!"

"Well, we're in the learning process, aren't we? Rule number one of being a ranger: always expect the unexpected."

Michael made a face. "That doesn't make any sense."

Geran laughed as he escorted his new apprentice into the kitchens. Geran grabbed two washrags and handed one to Michael. They began to scrub dishes and silverware in a basin of hot, soapy water.

"Basically, always be on your toes," Geran continued. "And be ready to deal with any situation that comes at you. Think ahead, and use reason for everything you do. The only time something is guaranteed is after it's already happened."

"So roll with the punches," Michael said.

"Roll with them until you learn to dodge them. Once you know how to dodge them, you can learn to counter them. Once you learn to counter them, you can keep the punch from ever being thrown."

"You're so cryptic, Mr. Geran."

"Am I?"

The demiwolf laughed. "Yes sir. You say things so seriously. Almost like some wise old hermit."

"I'll take that as a compliment."

"Uh, sure. What's the number-two rule?"

"Well, there isn't a set amount of rules like that, but if there was one, I'd say it would be walk softly, speak humbly, be professional, and have a plan to kill everyone in the room."

Michael's ears perked up. "Like, always? Even here?"

"It's good practice. It trains you to always be thinking."

"Are you doing it right now?"

Geran nodded. "Of course."

"Woah. How would you do it?"

"In this scenario?" Geran took a quick look around. "First things first, take care of anyone within arm's reach, then go after the biggest threat. So I'd stab you in the neck, then throw the knife at the head cook over there."

Michael inched away from him and looked at the fat chef. "Why him?"

"Everyone here except you, me, and the other apprentices are kitchen staff or waiters. They aren't combatants. That being said, the head cook is wicked with that wooden ladle. He gave me plenty of bruises on my head when I was a youngin' trying to sneak in here."

"You learned your lesson pretty quick, huh?"

Geran laughed. "Of course not. I just got better at not being seen."

"You must have had a lot of fun back then sneaking in and out."

Geran winked. "Still do."

The demiwolf gave him a bewildered smile. "You sure have a lot of crazy stories, Mr. Geran."

"You haven't heard anything yet. I've been here for twelve years, remember? And I thought I told you to just call me Geran."

"I know, but it doesn't feel right. You're teaching me and all, and my mom would smack me upside the head if I didn't give you the proper title."

Geran sighed. "I suppose you've got a good reason. Besides, that's what apprentices are supposed to do with their mentors. I did that with Adrian until I completed my first ranger quest alone."

"What was your first quest like?" Michael asked.

"My first *real* quest was a scouting mission. A party went missing, and it was my job to find them so a recovery team could bring them home. My first quest ever, as is the case with most people, was a task. All I did was run a delivery from the guild to a client."

"Well that's lame."

"What? You thought you'd be preventing wars or taking down gangs and smuggling organizations right off the bat? You're probably gonna be keeping your meathead warrior from walking off a cliff while your mage decides to spontaneously set everything on fire."

"So impulse control. It sounds like you're speaking from experience."

"I am. All of that's happened. That's why I went solo for most of a decade."

"What was your party like back then?" Michael asked.

Geran thought back for a second. "It was me, a druid named Mary Simpson, and a warrior named Peter Stone. We all became adventurers around the same time. I currently hold the title of best ranger, and Peter became our best warrior for four years until Elaethia showed up."

"What about that Mary girl?"

"She was killed in action a year after I split from the party. They got cornered by a troll on the way home from a quest. Peter blamed himself for it, believing he should have been strong enough to take it down. Of course that wasn't true, but that's why he's pushed himself so hard all these years."

Michael's tail went still. "Sounds like coming in with friends is the best way to find a group. I came in alone, though."

"It is, and you certainly did. Tell you what, go help the other apprentices deliver orders, and make your acquaintance with them. The dinner rush is about to hit, so I'll finish up here. We can talk more after they let you go for the night."

"You sure? All right, Mr. Geran, thanks a lot!"

The demiwolf put his rag down and went over to where the other apprentices had gathered. Geran finished on the last stack of plates and began to walk out from the kitchens. Then he noticed a stack of pastries cooling on the windowsill. Geran casually went over, slipped one under his cloak, and calmly walked to the door.

Unfortunately the fat, aging chef was eyeing him. "Nightshade! You better put that back!"

Geran whooped and dashed into the hall, while the ensemble of apprentices cheered.

Shiro had been lying topless on his bed for a couple hours. He had already bathed, combed his hair twice, and written a letter home, and he was now reviewing his plan over and over. His clothes were washed and neatly hung so as not to wrinkle before dinner. Should he get some cologne? No, no, that was too expensive. He didn't even know where to find it. Then maybe he should bring out his yukata. No! That was for ceremonies and formal events; it was only for the most serious of times. But he was serious about looking good for Lilian. *Wait, this is an informal dinner! I'll look foolish! Everyone will laugh, and then Lilian might hate me!*

Shiro rolled around on his mattress and groaned in frustration. *Oh no! I'm messing up my hair.* He shot up and ran to the mirror to make sure the tight bun was still in place. He hand-brushed some loose hairs over his head, sighed, and slumped into the chair at his desk. His eyes drifted to the pen and paper on the surface—another letter home, this time about his excitement and nervousness for tonight's events. There were so many questions he wanted to ask Mother and Grandfather.

Shiro wished his grandfather were still alive. He always had been able to help and guide Shiro through anything. Elaethia had given him a new sense of comfort and purpose, but she wasn't Grandfather. Shiro buried his head in his arms. Elaethia was so level-headed and confident. It seemed there was nothing she couldn't do. This was the first time she couldn't help him come to terms with his feelings. Liam was a little helpful, but he didn't know much about Lilian in this regard.

Shiro's thoughts returned to his family. The last of them he saw was Father as he distracted the shipyard with his presence. Shiro could only watch as the great man known as the northern shogun caused a scene to draw attention away from his eldest son so he could sneak aboard the diplomat's ship. Shiro had always wanted to live up to his image. He once swore to bring pride to the Inahari name. He held himself to that promise now more than ever.

Shiro sighed with a small smile as he remembered that Elaethia had promised to help him achieve this. As long as he was by her side, he had nothing to fear. He scratched his head and chuckled. It felt very odd at first, working under a female warrior. Part of his samurai code, and something his mother always told him, was that it's a man's job to protect women. But that didn't seem to be the culture here. Mainland women, especially Elaethia and Lilian, were very self-sufficient. He wondered how they would react to a girl as delicate and gentle as his sister.

Tears started to form in his eyes. Mitsuki, his beautiful little sister, was sixteen when that cursed noble came and took her life, right in their very home. Shiro's memory was a blur from the moment the blade left Mitsuki's throat to when he pinned the assailant to the ground. He remembered rage he had never felt before, the shrieks from his dying sister, and the darkness of the room as he clashed with the murderer. The memories of his Mitsuki always returned to the mutilated state he last saw her in. Drops fell from his cheeks to his desk and patted on the surface. He should have been faster. He should have been with her. Why was she the one that had to die, why couldn't it have been him?

"Dammit!" He slammed his fist onto the desk, rattling the lamp and knocking the letter to the floor. Before he could do anything else, a knock came from his door.

"Shiro?" Lilian's voice came through. "Are you okay in there? I know it's early and all, but I'm feeling kinda hungry if it's all right with you."

"L-Lili-chan! Yes, I'm fine! One moment, please, I'll be right there." He wiped his eyes with the back of his hand and checked his hair one last time before walking to the door. He opened it to see a somewhat surprised Lilian.

She raised an eyebrow while looking him up and down. "Everything all right?"

"Yes, fine, thank you. I just, uh, stubbed my toe."

"Musta been a bad stub to make your eyes red like that."

"Of course, it was awful. It was probably the worst one I've ever had."

"Do you wanna take a minute to … sort yourself out?"

"No, no, it's fine. I just need to walk it off."

She nodded slowly. "I see. Hey, is it just me, or is it kinda cold in here?"

"I feel perfectly fine. If you would like, I can loan you my winter coat, but that would be a little warm for inside use."

"Thanks, but I'll pass."

"Ah, all right," Shiro said. "Are you ready?"

She nodded again and stared at him in silence for a moment. "So, uh, where's your shirt?"

He put a hand on his chest. "It's right—" Shiro froze. He looked down at his bare torso, turned red, and slammed the door shut.

Lilian doubled over, howling in laughter. Shiro hastily fumbled to get his top on and opened the door again to see the demicat leaning against the railing while clutching her side. Lilian's spastic gasps made her whole body shake as she struggled for breath between outbursts. She slumped into a sitting position and slowly regained herself, giggling every couple of seconds.

"Sun and Moon, Shiro," she said, and she wiped a tear from her eye. "I thought you did that on purpose!"

"N-no," he stuttered. "Why would I do that?"

"Maybe to try to impress me with that nice bod of yours. I shoulda known better."

He looked down and turned red again. "I'm so humiliated."

"Stars above, Shiro." She got up and hugged him fondly. "Don't ever change."

Shiro and Lilian sat together at a table next to the bar. Even though Shiro promised her she could order anything, Lilian insisted she wanted a simple meal of rabbit stew and water. Shiro decided to get the same thing. He had never heard of stew before, so Lilian explained it was like "hard soup." This made no sense to him, so he figured it was similar to the soups from Osakyota. He soon found out how misinformed he was.

Both of them ate in somewhat awkward silence and talked mostly about Lilian's magical discoveries. The mage also asked a little about Michael's appearance, but Shiro was able to tell her only about the brief moment he had with the demiwolf. Lilian was clearly racking her brain to piece it all together. She stared at the food in front of them and suddenly dived into a deeper topic.

"Hey, Shiro. I know you're here more or less to keep peace between your family and a rival one, as well as gain a name for yourself. But that's all I really know about your personal life or where you came from."

He nodded. "That's mostly correct, yes. What else do you want to know?"

"Well, everything really. Just like I was the first demihuman you talked to, you're the first Osakyotan *I* talked to. You already know all about demihumans and have a pretty good grasp on magic, but I don't know thing one about where you come from. What's it like over there? Is everyone just like you?"

Shiro made a face. "I don't know what you mean by 'like me,' but I guess I'm a very traditional Osakyotan. Grandfather Ryuuki always said I was more serious about my views than most. But all Osakyotans hold the same values and traditions. Honor and family come before all else. That and repaying all debts in full."

"Sounds a lot like you." She smiled. "I'd love to visit it someday."

"And I'd love to bring you, Lili-chan. You'd look wonderful in a kimono at a summer festival."

She gave him a smug look. "Are you imagining me getting dressed, Shiro?"

He flushed. "N-no! I didn't mean it like that! Just that I think it would suit you very well! My sister had a deep blue one that would match your hair and eyes! I wouldn't have any kind of impure thoughts or actions whatsoever!"

She laughed. "It's fine; I'm just teasing! Gosh, I figured you'd get used to it by now!"

"I don't want to get used to you, though," he replied sheepishly.

She cocked an ear. "Whaddya mean?"

"Well, you're always so positive and full of life. Every time we talk, I see some new part of you, and I find it wonderful! If I get used to it, that means I won't ever see another side of you."

"Wow, I …" she stammered, and she leaned back. "I don't know what to say to that."

"You don't have to say anything! I've wanted to say something like that for a while."

Lilian went quiet and looked at him. Shiro bashfully looked up and met her eyes, and both of their cheeks began to change color. Her expression quickly shifted into that of her usual mischievous self. The demicat suddenly leaned forward and gave him a little punch on the shoulder.

"C'mon, Shiro! It's *my* job to make *you* feel all flustered, not the other way around!"

"I'm sorry, Lili-chan."

"Ahhh, don't worry about it, you big dork."

They both smiled as they turned back to their food.

Lilian piped up again after a minute. "What was she like?"

Shiro looked up. "What was who like?"

"Your sister. You talk about her just as much as your granddad. I know she was … murdered and … and that's the main reason you're here, but"—she exhaled through her nose and her brow furrowed—"I've only ever heard you say good things about her when the subject came up. Like you absolutely adored her, or she was the best thing in your life."

Shiro stopped eating and looked down. "I suppose."

Lilian gasped and her eyes widened. "Hey … hey I'm really sorry; that was really insensitive of me to ask. Forget I said anything."

"No, it's fine. I'm just not sure where to begin." He thought for a minute. "Her name was Mitsuki, and I guess she was a bit like you, actually. Although she didn't love blowing things up or anything. I rarely saw her frowning. She was very much an optimist, always looking for the good in things. She did everything with a smile, and she could find fun in anything. Life was almost a game for her, and we played along whether we wanted to or not."

Lilian's face brightened. "We could almost be sisters! Lookit you, smiling now."

He realized she was right. "That Mitsuki. Even in death, she can make me smile when I don't want to. You know, when I would come home from a hard day or I humiliated myself in any fashion, she would *always* pop up out of nowhere to brighten my mood. There were many times when I lashed out at her for her playful personality when I was trying to be serious or reflect on my mistakes. But it was impossible to be mad at her for long."

The demicat slowly leaned forward with a cocked ear. "Why not?"

"The first thing she'd do was run up and give me a big hug. Mitsuki would give me a lot of praise—too much, really. But she was always there to reassure me and urge me on. She's the one who convinced me that I really was strong … that I had a fighting spirit no one could see but her.

"On my darkest days, when unimaginable thoughts crept into my head, she would stay glued to me. Mitsuki would refuse to let go until I swore on my honor that I would never hurt myself out of shame or humility. She would talk the entire time. Nothing came out of her mouth more than 'Big brother, I love you.' No matter how long or hard I tried to stay in self-loathing, she would be with me. Even when it lasted for days."

Lilian's eyes glazed. "What a wonderful sister. I woulda loved to meet her."

He nodded. "You would have been great friends. Just like you, it was impossible to be sad about anything around her. Because of her, I try to smile as much as I can. I miss Mitsuki very much, but she wouldn't want me to be sad. She would be quite disappointed to see how often I'm in a state of self-pity."

"Well, that settles it then," Lilian stated firmly with a smile. "I'll make sure she won't be disappointed!"

Shiro looked up. "What do you mean?"

"Well, to be honest, I can't even pretend to understand how you feel or what you've been through," Lilian began. "I don't understand disputes between nobility. I've never been thrust into a world I know nothing about. Nobody in my family has died, let alone been murdered. I just don't think I could handle this anywhere near as well as you have. So I'm gonna pick up where Mitsuki left off. I can't understand your hardships like Elaethia, or relate to you man-to-man like Geran. But I can promise you that no matter what, I'm not gonna let you be sad anymore."

Shiro's lips began to quiver. "Lili-chan …"

"That's right! You don't get to make those sad faces anymore. I'm gonna make sure every second we have together is gonna be a good one. There's a whole world out there waiting for us, and we're gonna see it all together!"

"T-together? The whole world?"

She leaned over and hugged him fiercely. "Only if I have any say in it, and I do! We're gonna get in trouble and *like* it!"

Geran suddenly materialized next to them. "Well. You two seem to be getting really chummy."

Shiro nearly jumped out of his seat "Ah! Geran! It's not what it looks like! Lili-chan and I were just—"

"Just what? Hmmmmm?" she said, batting her eyelashes at him.

Shiro began to stutter helplessly until Geran sighed. "Jeez, Lilian. What'd you do to him?"

"Nothing evil, I promise. But forget that! What's the deal with that Michael kid?"

"I don't think you can call him a kid. You're barely three years older than him."

"That's beside the point! What're you doing with him?" she demanded.

"Making him my apprentice."

Lilian leaped out of her chair and thrust a finger at him. "I *KNEW* it! I *knew* you weren't gonna just take a random meathead out for some quality time! When did you decide on this? How long are you gonna mentor him for?"

"About four hours ago, and until his birthday in Davilisk. Or as long as he needs the help."

"*Why are you so nonchalant about this?*"

"Jeez, Lilian, no need to shout; I'm right here."

"Gera-a-a-a-n!" the demicat whined, stamping her feet like a child having a tantrum. "You can't just do this outta nowhere! What's gotten into you?"

"You can probably blame Elaethia for that. What I still wanna know is why you were all over Shiro."

"Don't you turn this around on me! I'm the one asking questions here!"

"What is all the yelling about?" Elaethia's voice asked from the stairwell. "You have drawn quite a considerable amount of attention to yourselves."

"Geran's taken on that Michael guy as an apprentice!" Lilian shouted.

"I see. That explains his interest in the young man."

"*Why are you all accepting this!*"

Geran grinned. "Neither of them have known me as long as you, Lilian. If it's of any consolation, Maya had a pretty good reaction."

"No! Because I didn't get to see it!"

"So that's what he was doing," Shiro said as he regained his composure.

Elaethia turned to Geran. "Will you be able to train him properly by the time he comes of age?"

He gave a thumbs-up. "No problem. He's already got the basic skills, so all I have to do is teach him how to apply them. I'll probably take him on an easy quest at some point to boost his confidence."

Lilian sighed in resignation and sat back down. "All right. Well, what's he like?"

"Bright, cheerful, optimistic, eager to learn. Overall, a good kid."

"So you're replacing me."

"Don't flatter yourself, cat," Geran said, pulling a pastry out from his cloak. He took a bite as he continued. "He's from a poor family in Westreach and came here because Elaethia saved him. He's with the other apprentices, but he'll be able to come meet you guys soon."

Lilian's tail flicked. "Westreach? And Master Dameon let him join?"

"He wasn't exactly happy about it, and he gave some pretty harsh criteria. But Michael's determined to join Breeze, so I'm not worried. Hold on; I see him right there. Michael! Over here!"

Geran waved down the demiwolf. Michael saw him, set down the stack of dishes at the window, and bounded over to them.

"Yes, Mr. Geran?" he asked.

Lilian raised an eyebrow and looked at the ranger. "Mr. Geran?"

"It's customary," Geran replied. "Michael, this is our mage, Lilian. She's the last member of my party you haven't met."

Michael gave a small nod of greeting. "Hi there, Miss Lilian."

"Oh, hello there," she said with a flirty look while she fingered a lock of his hair.

Shiro inhaled sharply. Elaethia-sama had *just* helped him come to terms with his jealousy of this newcomer, and suddenly he found it coming back. For once he wished that Lilian didn't act like Lilian.

Michael leaned away from her hand. "Can I help you?"

"Well aren't you a cutie?" she asked. "Your hair is *just* adorable."

"Thanks," he responded plainly. "My mom has white hair, and my dad's is black. I'm the only one out of my siblings to be mixed like this."

Lilian pouted and slumped back down. "Hmph. He's *your* apprentice, all right."

Geran slapped the demiwolf on the back. "Atta boy."

Michael's ears cocked, and his tail wagged a little. "What'd I do?"

Lilian stamped her foot. "Gerry! You didn't tell him about me, did you?"

"Nope. Just your name and class."

"Hmph. Whatever," the mage sighed.

"So," a gruff voice said from the side. "I come down to check on you, and I see you slacking on the job. You're not looking too hot already, Finway."

Shiro turned to see Master Dameon leaning on the bar.

Michael stiffened and faced him. "M-M-Master D-Dameon! I-I'm sorry, sir; it won't happen again, I—"

Geran cut him off with a hand. "I called him over, Master. I wanted him to meet my party so he could understand that I'd be busy frequently. This way he knows he needs to focus on his training and knowledge in his free time."

"Hrmph," the massive demibear grunted, and he walked over. "Well, boy? Are you satisfied with your introduction?"

"Yes sir! I'm honored to be an apprentice in a really powerful guild."

"You should be. This guild has the best rising story out of all seven regions. You know what I'm talking about, right?"

"N-no sir."

"You're telling me you want to be a part of *my* family and you can't be bothered to learn one of the most important moments in history for it?"

"I'm not sure what you mean, sir."

Master Dameon folded his arms. "All guild crests mean something. Westreach's insignia is just that pine tree with a hilt. Where do you think ours came from?"

Lilian raised her hand. "Master Dameon, I'd hardly call that history. It was only, like, ten years ago."

"Still long before you joined, girl. Every one of my rascals knows the story, and to bear the insignia, you need to know what it stands for."

Elaethia tilted her head. "Are you referring to the event when the entire guild was called upon to stop a behemoth?"

"Exactly. The only G quest to happen this century in the entire country."

"I apologize. I have heard of the event, but I am unfamiliar with the story."

"As am I," Shiro added.

Master Dameon looked at Geran and Lilian. "Th' hell have you been telling these two that's more important than the behemoth quest?"

"Kinda forgot about it." Geran said. "Even though I was here, I wasn't actually present."

Lilian shrugged. "I was told it once when I first showed up, but I couldn't recite it if I needed to."

The guild master sighed and pulled up a chair. "Well then, I suppose it's time for a little history lesson."

Chapter 12
Behemoth

Sixth Era.129. Setibim 3.

Dameon sat in his small office at the guildhall. Things were starting to get back to normal after the annual tournament, with Breeze taking third overall. The demibear had been the guild master for fourteen years now, and it had begun to show. His rich, brown hair and beard were beginning to speckle with patches of gray. Were it not for the fact he was a monk that used physical enhancement magic, his eyesight would also have begun to slip

Dameon sighed and leaned back to look at the insignia draped over the door: three swirled lines to represent the windy plains the city and region was built in and named after. Breeze wasn't as big or strong as Westreach or Clearharbor, and they barely scored higher than Apogee. Their popularity mainly came from their central location in the country—and a plethora of work. There just wasn't much to bring talented adventurers to Breeze. That was a shame, as more experienced individuals would mean a higher rank.

He grunted and brought himself back to reality. Dameon realized he didn't care that much about their placement in the tournament. All that mattered to him was his rascals going out to help the region and coming back alive. That and keeping pompous bigwigs and rich assholes off their backs.

Dameon picked up another apprenticeship form for a new warrior, Liam Barron. He was fifteen, a demiwolf from southern Breeze who was to be mentored by Quaid Sterling. That was a good pairing. Quaid was patient, and Liam was beyond eager to start his apprenticeship. The kid was adamant about sticking with his spear. No matter how much the other warriors taunted or clobbered him for using such a basic weapon, he kept with it. This pup was either very passionate or very thick. It was almost admirable, in a way. Liam showed promise, but he was eyeing some of the female adventurers a little too much. Dameon would have to instruct Quaid to keep him on a short leash.

There were now three youngins that showed a lot of potential. Peter Stone had been an official adventurer for almost year now, but he and Liam were already butting heads. Somehow, the new demiwolf was able to keep up with the cocky human. They both showed promise but would easily turn into a handful. Thank the heavens that Geran Nightshade was a mild and reasonable kid. But that young ranger was a curious little bugger who stuck his nose into anything and everything. Especially the kitchen.

Dameon stacked the papers and clapped them on his desk so they lined up in his hands. The guild master stood up and walked outside to hand them to his head receptionist. The brunette demicat looked up as he approached.

"Got an apprenticeship form for you, Brittany," he said as he handed them to her. "Any update on that party of three that went missing two days ago?"

"Yes sir," Brittany said. "Jaime came back from the scouting mission in the late morning. I'm working on the flyer for a recovery team."

"Good work. Get those rascals back home."

"Yes sir," she said. She then turned around to call for her assistant. "Maya, you know where apprenticeship forms go, right?"

"Yes, Miss Brittany. I'll put it there right away!" The young elf took the form and scurried over to the filing cabinets. She fingered her way through the folders and deposited it in the proper one.

"How's Redbranch doing for you?" Dameon asked Brittany.

"Just fine. I think she'll be able to handle more advanced forms soon. She's a little slow with reading, though. I think she might need glasses."

He hummed and scratched his beard. "We'll set her up with an engineer. If you think this'll benefit her performance, the guild will cover half the expense."

"Noted, sir. Anything else?"

"That's all for now. It's quieter now that the buzz from the tournament has died down, but people are still motivated to up themselves after our final placement. I think a couple are taking quests out of their league to try to prove their worth. Feel free to exercise your authority to deny a quest if you see fit."

She nodded. "Will do, sir. I'll pass the word to my receptionists."

Dameon grunted and took a walk around his guild. The building was a fairly large one-story structure in the center of town, right at the edge of the main square. This was good placement that allowed citizens and officials to find and get to it easily. The bar stood at the far back wall, and the dorms lined the outer walls on either side. Adventurers and civilians mingled and socialized in the big center hall. Morale seemed to be high as the members greeted the guild master while he made his way toward the bar. He stopped at it and ordered a half-gallon jar of mead to take to his office.

For the first time in a month, he had some down time. The demibear lumbered back to his study and took a look around. His guild had a nice, homey feel to it. It reassured him that the outcome of the tournament wouldn't affect day-to-day life. Dameon sat down at his desk and poured himself a mugful. He gulped some down, placed it back onto the table, and sighed deeply.

The sounds of the guild flowed through the doors, as did the sounds of the city through the window. He looked at the mug in front of him, pondering whether he wanted to take another drink.

The liquid inside rippled. Dameon raised an eyebrow. He felt nothing that would have caused that and didn't hear anything inside or out. In fact, he didn't hear much of anything at all. It rippled again. He leaned forward and peered down, wondering whether it was his imagination. It wasn't. Another ripple trembled inside the mug. The guildhall and the bustling streets grew quiet. He tuned his ears to the surroundings and watched the mead intently for another shockwave. There it was, and it was accompanied by a distant boom. Thunder? No, too brief, and it was a clear day. He realized the magnitude and intervals between ripples were consistent. It couldn't have been some sort of magic. These deep vibrations seemed almost like footsteps.

Dameon stood sharply and walked quickly to his door. He opened it and gazed into the hall. Everyone had frozen as well, looking around and listening to the distant thundering sounds.

"What's going on?" he asked no one in particular.

"Don't know, sir. We thought it was you," a dwarven priest responded.

"I haven't done anything to cause this kind of commotion in years. This ain't anatomy magic."

Suddenly, bells tolled throughout the city from the massive cathedral. Their deep, resonating ringing made the air hum as their clangs traveled through the city and over the countryside.

"What the hell?" Dameon shouted. "Those are the alarm bells. We're under attack?"

Brittany shuffled through some files. "I don't think so, sir. There haven't been any reports of organized forces plotting against Breeze."

"I want my rangers out there getting to the bottom of this! Civilians, get the hell outta my guildhall! Noncombatants and anyone not fit for a fight, get downstairs. If you're intermediate level or below, you're staying back here on standby. The rest of you, suit up! I don't know what's going on out there, but we need to be ready *now!*"

"Yes, Master!" The chorus of guild members sounded off as they scrambled to their appointed places.

Adventurers darted to their rooms to prepare themselves while administrative members and injured personnel went downstairs. Dameon darted to his office and made his way to his wardrobe. He shed the official outfit of the guild master to don his old questing gear from when he was an adventurer: a tough jerkin, baggy linen shorts, fur shoes, and absolutely nothing else. Monks wore no armor or fitted clothing, as it got in the way of their bodily enhancements. Weapons were impractical for them too, considering the individuals changed size and strength at will. The guild master rifled through his shelves to find a record about possible assailants that could pose a threat to the city. He gave up with a growl after several minutes of anxious searching. Dameon burst out of his office to check on his adventurers. Only a few stood ready.

"*Let's go!*" he thundered. "Hurry up! Get the hell outside, formed up right now!"

"Yes, Master!" the chorus called back in growing panic.

"On the Sun, if every last one of you isn't ready in the next two minutes, that alarm is gonna be the *least* of your problems! I'm gonna make the dragon wars look like a playground scrap if I don't see every single one of your worthless hides out there!"

"Yes, Master!"

Those that were ready made a beeline for the front door. As they neared it, it burst open. A very out-of-breath ranger stood panting in the doorway.

"Adrian!" Dameon called to him. "What in heaven's name is going on out there?"

"Beh …" he gasped. "*Behemoth!*"

Dameon froze. "What did you say, boy?"

"Behemoth, sir! It's on a warpath straight for the city! The church and city have issued an emergency quest, level G! They'll support us with siege equipment when they get it into position!"

"Where? How big? How far? How much time do we have?"

"From the west, twice the size of the cathedral, a little over a kilometer away. I don't know how long we have."

He glanced at his members, who were all looking up at him. "Sun and Moon preserve us … All right, rascals! Looks like Breeze is up shit creek and we're the only paddle! Everyone get to the western wall!"

"Sir, that thing is way too big for our weapons to kill it!"

"Who said that? Miriam? Unless you want to stay behind with the rest of the weaklings, I suggest you figure it out! You've fought giant enemies before!"

"Y-yes sir."

"Adrian! You've read about killing these things, right?"

"A little," he said. "Just old tomes and stories."

"That'll have to be enough. I want you up front with us! Point out its weaknesses and blind spots."

Adrian nodded. "Yes sir!"

"Johnathan!" Dameon called into the masses. "You and the rest of Gale Break are taking the lead! We need our ace up front. make sure civvies don't get in our way!"

The warrior beat his axe into his shield in response. "Count on it!"

"Everyone else follows behind! We're gonna take off with our war cry, and I want every milk-drinking civilian to feel it in their bones. Here we go! Bang 'em!"

The adventurers started pounding their weapons and feet against the ground in a steady beat. The metallic clang sounded throughout the courtyard as Dameon raised his voice to the heavens.

"Breeze! Today we show the country what we've got! Let's knock that dumb mammal back into the dirt! Give 'em hell!"

"Ah-*ooh!*"

"Give 'em hell!"

"Ah-*ooh!*

"Give 'em hell!"

"Ah-*ooh!*"

The combined shout from the entire guild reverberated throughout the city. Dameon turned around and led his adventurers to the front gate, jogging in formation. Onlookers and soldiers cheered and shouted encouragement as they passed by. All of them made way as Dameon led his guild out of the city and toward the approaching threat.

The guild halted a few hundred meters off the western wall. Everyone froze and balked at the monstrosity that lumbered toward them. Its footsteps sounded as clear as day as the ground shook from each impact. Less than six hundred meters away, the enormous mammal drew nearer. Dameon understood firsthand how these things could be mistaken for hills. From the distance he could see live trees and grass growing along its back. Its tan fur was stained brown and green from the dirt and moss that clung to it. Two great tusks protruded forward from the corners of its mouth; these were used for uprooting the forests that it would eat. Watery, unintelligent eyes stared forward; its mouth hung agape. Two rows of yellow molars ran along its maw.

"Sun and Moon," a duelist breathed. "How the hell are we gonna stop *that?*"

"Just as I explained," Dameon said gravely. "Every second we waste standing here is another step it takes closer to demolishing the city. Let's go!"

The army of adventurers moved toward the behemoth, slowly increasing their speed until everyone was at a sprint head-on to the animal.

"Mages and druids! Light it up!" the guild master commanded.

The collection of magicians wound up their conduits and thrust them at their opponent. A volley of spells flew from the guild and impacted into the behemoth. *Fireballs, icicles, lightning bolts, and stone blasts* struck its massive head, embedding in and scorching its fur. The great beast let out a skull-shaking groan but didn't slow down. It pushed through the barrage of elements that battered its face, seemingly unaffected by the attack.

"Focus fire between the eyes! Try to blind it and breach through its thick skull! Priests! Use *moonlight* on our mages to keep them going, but save yourselves for healing if we need! Paladins, I want some *smites* coming down on that thing's nose!"

As he commanded, pale light from the priests shone onto the mages to steadily replenish their magic. Paladins sheathed their weapons and pulled out their conduits. The sky above the beast glowed as blasts of pure sun energy struck it like hammers of light. The behemoth groaned again and shook its head, listing slightly to the side.

"Warriors and duelists, start getting close! I want all of you swarming that thing as soon as you can get on it! Mages, cease fire as they do. Paladins and monks will join them in close quarters. Ranged magicians, aim to the legs as that happens. Rangers, keep your eyes out for breaches in its hide so we can shift fires to them. Prepare to get fallen members out of there!"

Adrian turned to his guild master. "This thing's not slowing down; where the hell is the army with the siege engines?"

"Ballistae and trebuchets take time to move and set up, and we're probably still out of range! We have to somehow buy time until they get into position."

"Understood. Do you have any other ideas on how to stop it?"

Dameon scratched furiously at his hair. "Dammit, Adrian! I'm not the only one who has to think here! If you've got ideas, spit 'em out!"

"If all our mages focus a single high-power spell onto one spot, that should be enough to halt it for a short time."

"I don't want them blowing themselves out this early!"

"Our current plan isn't working!" Adrian insisted. "They'll run out of magic quickly at this rate, so let's give that thing one massive hit so we can get on it!"

Dameon looked at the ranger, to his mages, and then at the ever-approaching behemoth. It was only two hundred meters away. He swore.

"Mordecai, Dorothy, Terrence! Get all of the mages ready for a single blowout! I want you to knock that thing's face into the dirt! Merrick, are you here?"

"Right here, sir!" Merrick sounded off.

"You're the only strong druid we've got. If it slows, I want you and the rest of the druids to channel vines and roots around its tusks and legs. Keep it on the ground long enough for everyone to climb on! Mages, are you ready?"

"We're set!" Mordecai called with a thumbs-up.

"Now!" Dameon bellowed. "Fire! Knock that bastard down!"

The collective mages thrust out their staves, and the air in front of the behemoth glowed orange. A sudden burst of blazing inferno erupted from its nose, immediately followed by another, and the rest combined into one surging column of smoke and vapor. A bright flash and a massive wave of heat rolled over them from the gargantuan mushroom cloud that billowed to the sky. A single blinding bolt of lightning cracked the bridge of its nose.

Dameon turned to the group to see Terrence crumple to the ground and turn pale. "What the hell! He cast *lightning strike*? Someone help him! That idiot could have killed himself!" He wheeled back to the behemoth to witness it bellow as it collapsed into the ground, its tusks digging into the dirt.

"That's it! Druids! Pin it down! Mages, stand back. Once you have enough magic, use frost on its legs. Keep it sluggish for our front line!"

The melee adventurers charged forward as plant life grew along the fallen appendages. Warriors, duelists, monks, and paladins scrambled up onto the face of the monster, hacking, pounding, and stabbing at the charred skin and exposed bone. The behemoth groaned as it tried to pull itself free. Dameon looked to his druids, most of which were beginning to falter from the exertion. Some, who had already burnt out, sat on the ground, out of breath.

He clenched his jaw. "If you're out of magic, get back toward the city and stay out of the way! Come back when—" He was cut off buy the sound of ripping vines and sod.

The behemoth tore itself free from the earth.

Vines, dirt, and rocks flew in every direction and impacted into the guild members. Most managed to dive clear of the raining earth, but an unfortunate few were crushed beneath the flying debris. Some adventurers on the beast were thrown clear in every direction and landed heavily on the ground.

"Dammit, no! Rangers, get them out of there! Priests, save who you can. If you can still fight, slow that thing down! Aim for the eyes!"

The cloaked group of scouts and archers sprinted ahead to aid their comrades as the behemoth began to move again. Several of the adventurers that were thrown lay lifeless on the ground. A few managed to crawl or stagger away from the massive marching legs. A single paladin that fell forward from the face of the monster tried to get out of the way, but his broken leg prevented him from standing. The young man threw up an arm and screamed as the massive foot came down on him. Unable to stand by anymore, Dameon leaped forward to race to the aid of his guild. Merrick sprinted up behind.

"Thatcher, stay back!" Dameon called.

"I can help, Master!" the druid insisted. "My spells are more effective the closer I am, and I can heal a little with forest magic!"

"I need you back there slowing it down!"

"I'm the only druid left standing! I can't do it on my own!"

Dameon gritted his teeth. "Fine! But don't you dare get killed!"

"That's not my first choice either!"

They came alongside the rangers who were aiding the ones thrown from the behemoth. They fanned out to collect anyone that was still alive, and started to move back as fast as they could toward their line of priests. Merrick and each ranger carried one, as Dameon draped the remaining four over his shoulders. The demibear enhanced his legs with his anatomy magic and sprinted with incredible speed to the main group.

The guild master reached his waiting priests and set the survivors down at their feet. He checked the pulses of the other two and swore in a soft whisper. He gently lowered them to the ground a few meters away. They were Sylvia and Mark, one of his top duelists and a newer paladin. He doubted the two ever even conversed, but yet the brotherhood they stood for joined them together through the bitter end, side by side alongside their sibling.

Merrick had slowed down, barely able to move under the weight of the armored compatriot he carried. Adrian sprinted back to him and took the other shoulder of the limp warrior.

"Man are you a sight for sore muscles," the druid panted.

"We gotta work on your stamina, Thatcher. All that magic you got doesn't amount to much if you can't keep up with the rest of us." The ranger stopped and turned grim. "Merrick, why are you carrying this guy back? I know you want to help, but he's already dead."

"I'm sorry; I didn't think to check," Merrick helped Adrian lower their fallen brother to the ground and continued to run back. He lowered his head, sucked in a deep breath, and noticed a huge shadow. The druid looked back to see the behemoth wind up to swipe the two adventurers aside.

"Oh, shit—*get down!*"

Merrick threw himself to the ground as a gargantuan tusk barreled overhead, barely missing him. The ranger was not so lucky. Adrian was caught by the full impact of the behemoth's swipe. Blood splattered the druid's face as he watched his mangled friend rag-doll through the air.

"No!" Merrick cried.

He tried to pull himself to his feet and run to where the ranger had landed, but he was slammed back down by a crushing weight that pinned his legs. He twisted his body and saw that a tree had fallen off the back of the monster when it lashed out. The druid started to manipulate the log with forest magic but stopped as he realized he couldn't feel or move his legs anymore. The same shadow reappeared above his head, and the behemoth's tusk fell down on top of him once more.

"Get off my kids, you bastard!"

Master Dameon had fully empowered his body. He leaped forward and slammed a fist into the exposed bone of the behemoth's face. The rampaging monster staggered back from the impact, nearly halted in its tracks. The demibear was already big as he was, but his full power made him appear beyond brehdar. Merrick looked up at his guild master with equal amounts of awe concern. *What is he thinking? Growing that much that fast could kill him!*

Dameon was glowing, and his whole body had more than quadrupled its standard size. All that covered him was a draped cloth around his waist as he pounded the monster's face again and again. The behemoth bellowed in pain and lurched to the side. Over and over, Dameon struck the beast. A loud crack erupted from the brawl, as the monk fractured its skull with his fists. Blood gushed from the face of the monster as it whined in agony.

"*Die, damn you!*" Dameon roared as he clobbered the behemoth with everything he had.

But the behemoth still pushed forward. Merrick could only watch as his guild master threw himself head-on to the beast. There was no sign of siege engines, the magicians were depleted, and the warriors had all jumped or been shaken off. The monster was less than two hundred meters from the city wall.

He let out a strained chuckle. *So this is how it's gonna end, huh?* Even if he did manage to survive, he'd be paralyzed for life. The church could reattach limbs and seal gaping wounds, but they couldn't repair nerve damage. That was no way for a man like him to live. No, he was done. He let his head drop while the monster loomed over him, its pink underbelly directly above him. The druid turned his head to look at the main group of the surviving adventurers. There was a look of defeat, panic, and hopelessness engrained on their weary faces. They probably thought they were all going to die too.

No. To hell *with that.*

He wasn't going to just lie here and die like a dog with its foot in a trap. Every single one of those adventurers were his family, and he'd be *damned* if they didn't go back to the guildhall today in one piece. He clenched his staff and cast the biggest spell of his life.

Merrick thrust his conduit straight up, and a single spike of rock erupted from the earth—a *stalagmite* so massive it blasted straight through the belly of the monster and out the other side, piercing it completely. He gasped sharply. His vision turned blurry as blood poured down on him like a waterfall. The behemoth wheezed as it tried to move in its straight path despite being impaled. Merrick laughed weakly and coughed. He'd done it. It stopped. If it didn't bleed out, the battery from the city should finish it off.

His relief was cut short as a massive crack pealed from the rocky spike. He wiped the blood from his eyes. The behemoth still pulled. The strain on the rocky formation caused it to crack and crumble while the gargantuan beast staggered forward. At this rate it was going to break free.

Merrick Thatcher gritted his teeth and made the ultimate choice.

"This one's for Adrian, you son of a bitch."

It was an enormous overcast, and he knew it. Again he thrust his staff forward to cast another *stalagmite,* But before his vision blurred and darkened, the second giant spike erupted from the earth to impale the beast again in a cross. Merrick's staff fell to the mossy ground, and his hand fell limp, his body shriveling and disintegrating from the overcommitment of energy. The beast inhaled sharply and coughed. Blood poured from its mouth. It let out a single, final groan and collapsed to the ground with an earth-shaking boom.

There was no celebration that night in the center of town. The surviving members of the guild and the population of Breeze stood solemnly around a great funeral pyre. The thirteen fallen adventurers lay side by side, dressed in their formal wear or armor, weapons in hand, and insignia draped over their bodies. All lay waiting to be sent home to the heavens by their mourning friends and family. Most of them had to be fully covered because they were barely recognizable.

Master Dameon stood on a platform next to the elevated wooden stack with a torch in his one good hand. He himself was one of the most injured. The overcommitment of anatomy magic had nearly torn him apart from the inside out. Had it not been for the church's rapid response, he might have died. Dameon Greatjaw would never again be able to grow more than twice his current size. He inhaled deeply to collect himself and began to speak.

"Fourteen years ago, when I accepted the role of guild master, I never would have dreamed something like this would happen. I thought I was just going to be the one to knock heads together, maintain order within the guild, and protect my members from anyone or anything that wanted to do them harm. Well, not to this extent, anyway. I always expected a lot from my guild. Never settled for anything less than one hundred percent from these rascals. I came in fully expecting to lose a few along the road, some biting off more than they could chew, others panicking and making the wrong decision, maybe even a couple to dumb bad luck. If I was told then that I would be standing up here right now sending off thirteen of the ones I swore to protect, hell, I don't think I could have taken the responsibility.

"There are no words, no accolades, and no rewards that could ever amount to or compensate for what happened today. We've lost thirteen of the best damn men and women this city had to offer, and thirteen of the finest adventurers any guild master could have asked for. Some of these brave souls lying before you have been a part of this guild for almost a dozen years. Others, only a few months. But at the end of the day, that doesn't matter to me. Every single one of them had family, friends, maybe a lover. Heavens know what I wouldn't do to get these rascals back to the arms of their loved ones.

"But we can't go back. We can't change the past. I knew every single one of these men and women, and I know for a fact they wouldn't want us to grieve for long. We are *adventurers*, dammit. We knew, day one, that we'd be ready to face Hell itself for the sake of the brothers and sisters to our left and right, *and* for the people of our region. They all may not have been ready, but they were willing to give their lives for everyone standing here tonight. Their sacrifice will never be forgotten. Not so long as Breeze and her guild stand intact.

"And to my rascals lying before me: What you've done today has more than saved a city. It's built a legacy and an example of what it means to be an adventurer, both in my guild, and across the country. I am *damn* proud to have been your master."

A single tear fell from the face of the great demibear. He wiped his eyes and gave the command to the adventurers that stood in a circle around the pyre.

"Bang 'em."

In response, dozens of weapons and boots stamped the ground in a steady beat. The sound grew louder and louder with each hit, until it became more intense than he had ever heard. Dameon looked into the crowd and choked. He saw not just his rascals but every soldier, civilian, and church member keeping the beat with them. Soon the whole city shook with the sound of wood and steel striking against stone in salute to the fallen. Master Dameon found his voice again, and reached it to the heavens to give the call.

"Rascals! We live because you paid the ultimate price. We will not waste this sacrifice you gave us! Thank you! For your honor. For your courage. And for your commitment! Give 'em hell!"

"Ah-*ooh!*"

"Give 'em hell!"

"Ah-*ooh!*"

"Give 'em hell!"

"Ah-*ooh!*"

As the last shout sounded off, the marching beat ceased with it. The echo of voices and banging metal resonated throughout the countryside. Tears streamed from Dameon's face as he spoke the final words and lit the great pyre.

"Give 'em hell, rascals. Wherever you go."

Sixth Era.139. Miyan 18.

The guildhall was quiet as Dameon finished. What had started as a lesson for three newcomers quickly turned into a mass storytelling. The entire guild had gathered around to listen to their guild master retell the tale. It wasn't often that he himself came down to tell it. The staff and veteran adventurers nodded and turned back their original activities. Some of the younger ones stayed a little longer to listen to the follow-up. Elaethia, Geran, and Lilian sat back in silent honor of the story. Shiro and Michael both had tears forming in their eyes.

"So, boy," Dameon said to Michael. "Now you know what it means to be in my guild. Do you understand the weight and depth of what you're asking to be a part of?"

The demiwolf cleared his throat and ran a hand under his nose. "Yes sir. I understand."

"That day and those lives lost are the reason you see everything around you here today. This guildhall was granted and built by the city, paid for by the church and other guilds. All the things this guild provides and owns are because of those who fought that day. Don't you dare come in here thinking you can dishonor their sacrifice. You too, Shiro. I won't tell you that you have no reason to cry about your own situation. But I hope you can have the dignity to honor this guild's history."

The samurai cleared his throat. "Of course, Master Dameon. I am beyond moved by this city's tragedy."

"Don't call it a tragedy. They knew what they were getting themselves into, and we completed our mission. That's what it means to be an adventurer. What about you, Elaethia? Anything you want to say?"

The dragon hero thought for a moment. "We carry events such as this with us our whole lives. They define who we are, almost as much as the people involved in them. It is important to remember them and everything that happened, so as to be sure their memory lives on. However, time moves ever forward. Our lives are not defined by those we've lost but by how we live for them. Frossgar and my father forged the path I walk today. I will follow it ever forward to honor them, as opposed to mourning them. We should do the same for Merrick, Adrian, and the other eleven that died that day."

Lilian looked to Geran. "I guess it must have been hard on you. Y'know, with Adrian's death."

The ranger sighed and nodded. "It was, but Master Dameon and Elaethia are right. I grieved for a time, but he would have knocked me over the head if he saw me going on about it for too long. I still make sure to visit his grave every year to let him know I'm doing well. He was a good mentor, and an even better man." He paused and looked over to his apprentice. "Guess now I've got more reason than ever to carry on his legacy."

Michael clenched a fist. "I'll be sure to make both of you proud!"

"All of us, kiddo," Dameon said, looking at the demiwolf with a softer gaze. "We're a family here. Everything you do is for us. Everything that burdens you is a burden your brothers and sisters share. We share our lives with each other. Even you, Nightshade. No matter how hard you try not to."

"Not that I have a choice now," Geran chuckled. He then looked at Elaethia. "Guess some people are worth sharing your life with."

Elaethia only tilted her head with a softened brow.

Lilian poked her head in and grinned smugly. "What's that supposed to mean, Gerry? You thinkin' about spending your days with the woman you lo—"

The ranger pounded on the top of her head with a fist. The demicat recoiled backward and clenched her mouth.

"Ow!" she slurred. "Ow, I bit my tongue! Ow-ow-ow-ow-*ow*!"

Dameon burst out in laughter. He set a meaty hand on Geran's shoulder and wiped his eyes. "By the Moon, Geran. I figured it at first, but this party has worked wonders on you."

"I'd like to argue, but I don't think I can. But speaking of parties, Michael, tomorrow you and I are going on a low-level ranger quest. Finish up your duties for the night and get ready."

Michael cocked an ear. "But Mr. Geran, I've only been here one day."

"I said what I said. We're going on a quest tomorrow. I've only got seven months to get you up to speed, and during part of that time I'll be gone on quests and whatnot. We have to make every day count."

"Yes sir!" Michael gave a salute and dashed back into the kitchens while Geran made his way to the quest board. Elaethia and Dameon watched them leave from the table.

"How are you really feeling about my guild?" Dameon asked.

"Exactly as I have stated," Elaethia responded.

"I've never heard your statements."

"It is a fine place. I have met good people and have been able to rid the land of evil while maintaining a source of income. It is a great opportunity to train and grow until I am ready to continue with my journey."

"Well, whenever that day comes, just know you'll always have a home here. Besides, I don't think Mr. Nightshade would last very long after you left."

She tilted her head. "What do you mean?"

He laughed. "You really are naive. Oh well. Just keep in mind that everyone here has their own life goals, too. I think Geran has changed his a bit to accommodate for you. It'd be a shame if you left him behind."

"I would never leave him behind. But I also could not ask him to join me."

"You don't have to. Inahari's been more upfront about it, and that may have overshadowed Nightshade's resolve. But he'd stay with you through thick and thin just the same, y'know. Think a little about what kind of relationship you'd like with Geran over time."

"I ... I see ..." she said.

"Do you?" Dameon pressed.

Elaethia pondered for a moment, unable to answer his question.

"Geran is a good man, and a great partner in many ways," Dameon continued. "Both of you could greatly benefit from each other. Now. I think I've slacked from my own duties long enough. Give some thought to what he and I have said."

With that, the demibear lumbered away to leave Elaethia alone with her thoughts.

Sixth Era. 139. Miyan 19.

Geran stood at the quest board, flyer in hand. The ranger was in civilian clothing with his swordbreaker sheathed on his belt. With a green linen shirt and a brown leather vest, he wore simple tan hide pants and black leather shoes. Geran had put a lot of effort into his unassuming outfit and couldn't help but laugh at the irony. He turned his head as he heard his young apprentice bound up the stairs from the apprentice quarters.

"Got everything?" Geran asked him.

Michael gave a thumbs-up. "Yep! I have my bow, knife, pack, and apprentice insignia."

"Good, but you won't need all of that. Put your bow and arrows back; same with your insignia. They'll get in the way."

"Yes sir!" The demiwolf unslung his bow and quiver and ran back downstairs. He emerged again shortly in his normal clothes: a white undershirt and his gray cloak, along with long black pants that blended into his black leather boots. His hood was pulled over his head, but his wolf ears poked through it.

"Are we ready to pick a quest?" Michael asked.

"Already got one. I'm choosing this time, but after today you'll be the one to decide which ones we do. Take a look."

Michael took the flyer and read it. "A potential narcotic distribution source has been reported in the southeast part of town. A scouting mission is needed to identify locations of the distributors or buyers. Report any information to the guard."

Geran took it back. "Don't think of this like the times you stalked bullies back home. Scouting is a little different. First we have to find the general area, and then we set up a listening and observation post, or LOP for short. This is a common phrase you'll hear in ranger-talk, so I hope you're good at remembering acronyms."

"I can get the hang of it."

"Good man. I'll get us started and in the right spot, but I want you to be doing the looking and listening as well. It's up to both of us to keep an eye out for suspicious behavior, understand?"

"Yes sir!" Michael said.

"Then follow me," Geran replied, and he led his apprentice to the receptionist desk, out the door, and through the city toward the southeast quarter. "Can you think of why we aren't bringing our bows and insignia?"

"You said they'd get in the way, so maybe they'd indicate to people we're on a quest and they might get suspicious?"

"Perfect. Do you know why we do it this way?"

"If they knew we were there to spy on them, they'd attack us."

"Unlikely. Local gangs or dealers that just sprouted start their business in secrecy. The last thing they want to do is stir a hornet's nest like the guild or guard. If our cover's blown, they'll scatter or maybe leave the city completely."

"That's bad?"

"That's bad," Geran confirmed. "Sure, we've solved the problem short-term. But they'll be back, even more cautious than before. If we don't snuff it out on the first try, it gets increasingly harder."

"Got it," Michael said. "This seems pretty high-stakes for my first quest."

"It isn't your quest, it's mine. You're just a tag-along. This is an intermediate quest, and I'm a veteran ranger. All this is, is just a scouting mission. We set up in our LOP, watch for a while, and then go report. We aren't even engaging the people we're scouting for."

Michael nodded as they turned down an alley into the southeast quadrant. Geran walked calmly along as they made their way through an open square. It was a normal, sunny day in the main city. Birds chirped and fluttered from the cobblestone streets and low-hanging trees. Shops had their front doors open, with the store owners displaying their wares. Children laughed and chased one another around a fountain in the center of the square. Geran smiled and led his apprentice to an outdoor café. They both took their seats and watched the peaceful city.

Michael looked around with his ears perked up. "This is a nice part of town. I wouldn't have guessed there was a drug problem here."

"There isn't," Geran said.

Michael made a face. "But I thought—"

Geran held up a hand for him to wait as he flagged down a server. "Two daily specials. Ale for me, water for the kid."

"Two daily specials, a water, and an ale. Coming right up, sir." The demibear waitress turned and walked inside.

Michael continued. "I thought we were here to set up a drug bust."

Geran put a finger to his lips. "Don't say that stuff so loud. You never know who's listening. Anyway, there isn't a drug problem. We're here to prevent one from happening."

"But they're here, aren't they?"

"That's what we're finding out. There have been reports, and we're investigating."

"So what's our first step?"

"We're doing it," Geran said. "In order to chase something, we have to find it first. This right here is our LOP."

"Wait, here? We're just sitting at a café, in the open."

"Kinda hard to listen for clues if you're up a tower or in a dark alley. Practice eavesdropping onto passing conversation for key words or phrases. At the same time, maintain a conversation with me."

"Okay. Any tips or pointers you can give to help?"

"You may not realize it, but your emotions show very easily. Control your tail and ears as best as you can. Keep your expressions in sync with our conversation. Don't get excited when you hear something of value. That said, don't be surprised if we don't find anything. It's very common to have to set up multiple LOPs over multiple days."

"Got it. So uh, where are you from, Mr. Geran?"

"Me? Nowhere interesting, really. I was born in a tannery northwest from here. My family was one of the two that hunted and collected hides for the treaters. It was an experimental community village, and it did pretty well. Maybe not as much as a farming or milling town, but it worked out all right. Tanning isn't a profession that takes a whole village, so I got bored easily. Not to mention it smells awful. I spent most of my time outside and in the woods."

"That sounds an awful lot like *my* childhood," Michael said.

"Maybe that's why I latched onto you. I'm the middle child, with an older brother and a little sister. Once I turned thirteen, I convinced my dad to let me go to the guild and help there instead. Pretty soon after, Adrian took me under his wing and trained me on and off for the next three years."

"You trained for three *years?* I've only got seven months!"

"Needless to say, I hit the ground running when I turned sixteen. I was already on par with the advanced rangers skill-wise. I lacked real experience, but I had the know-how."

Michael looked into his lap. "You're giving me some big shoes to fill."

"Don't worry about who you think you need to be. Worry about making yourself the best you can. Don't get so preoccupied looking up that you forget to look straight ahead."

Michael laughed. "There you go, being cryptic again."

"What? What'd I say?"

"Quite a bit. Some parts about your childhood and your apprenticeship, and some words of wisdom."

"All right, you little smartass, when did you get so sarcastic?"

Michael shrugged. "About four seconds ago."

"I'm gonna smack you," Geran muttered with a twinkle in his eye.

The waitress suddenly appeared with their orders. The two thanked her and dug into their sandwiches, listening more intently to their surroundings. After a minute, a group of young men walked by.

"You hear about that spice shop down Finch avenue?"

"They're kinda new, right?"

"About a month, yeah. You hear about their back room?"

"Oh, so they're the ones with the mellow?"

"I think so. My kid brother said he saw some dopey-looking people around there."

"You aren't thinking about tryin' it out, are you?"

"Hell no. My old man will rip my tail off. Never touched the stuff, anyway."

They walked out of earshot after that.

Michael slowly looked to Geran. His tail wagged under his seat. "Did you catch that, Mr. Geran?"

"I did," he said. "All we have to do now is report to the guard. Our job's done."

"That's it? All right! Let's go!"

"Woah, woah, woah! I've still got some food left. And control that tail of yours."

Michael looked down at his flailing appendage. "Oh, sorry, hold on." He closed his eyes and started to breath slowly. His tail relaxed and stopped after a few seconds.

Geran grunted. "Better. But you need to learn to keep it from doing that in the first place."

"I'll work on it, sir. Why don't we go down and investigate ourselves? We can save the guard the trouble."

Geran shook his head. "Not our job. We aren't getting paid for that risk; they are. If the request asked us to take it down, and had some more cash for it, we would."

"But don't you want to help and solve problems?"

"Normally you'd be correct. But we don't have the authority to conduct a raid, level accusations, or warrant an arrest. Technically we're still civilians. Think of adventurers as private contractors with church and government regulation. If we kicked down that shop's door—even if there *was* mellow in there—we could get arrested for trespassing, and breaking and entering. This is what the guard is for. They deal with peacekeeping and maintaining law and order."

"Oh. So what now? What'll the guard do?"

"Conduct their own investigation and then do a search and seizure. They'll take the dealer into custody and find out who the provider is. All the mellow will be destroyed, persons involved arrested, and the operation uprooted. They may or may not ask for our help down the road."

"Would I be able to join you again?" Michael asked.

Geran finished the last bite of his sandwich and drained his beverage. "Even if it was me, most likely not. The stakes and risks would be a bit higher than I'm comfortable bringing you along for. But now that that's out of the way, let's head to the guard station. You're gonna report your findings, and then we'll head home to collect the reward."

"How much is it worth again?"

"Ten gold and eight silver. Not much, but it was an easy quest. I'll take seven gold, and you can get the rest."

Michael's ears drooped. "Oh. Okay …"

Geran laughed and tousled Michael's black-and-white hair. "I'm kidding. We'll take five each, and I'll let you have the silvers. You're allowed to speak up if you don't like something. This ain't the guard, remember? Just 'cause I'm your senior doesn't mean I'm infallible. You need to think and speak for yourself."

Michael laughed softly. "Okay, Mr. Geran! Thank you!"

Geran laughed and set some coins on the table. "Don't mention it. Here, take the flyer. You're gonna talk to the guard on duty and give them the rundown."

"Yes sir!" Michael took the paper and bounded excitedly alongside Geran.

At first Geran had his doubts. But after today, something else bubbled inside him. It was a new feeling: pride in someone else. For the most part, when it came to ranger duties and cooperation, he was silently competitive. Whether it was his party that softened him up or his memories of his time with Adrian, Geran couldn't remember why he was so uncertain about this apprenticeship. With a new smile forming on his lips, the ranger and his apprentice walked out of the southeastern quadrant to turn in their quest.

Chapter 13
Escort

Sixth Era.139. Miyan 19.

Elaethia, Shiro, and Lilian crowded around the quest board, straining to get a closer look at a unique quest that had just been posted. They and dozens of other advanced and veteran adventurers swarmed the corkboard to get a glimpse of it. Elaethia was surprised, but not perturbed, by the amount of physical resistance she was receiving from her guildmates. They would push or bump against her as they tried to get closer to the flyer. But this didn't bother her. After all, she had already read most of it.

The shouting and growling of the men and women around her were starting to grow loud. Many were butting heads and shoving each other to get a closer look at the special flyer. She turned to see the front door of the guildhall open and Geran and Michael step through. She was about to call to them when Lilian suddenly flew toward them.

"Geeeeeraaaaaannn!" Lilian shouted, and she screeched to a halt in front of the ranger. "Where have you *been!* We gotta take this quest now, 'cause I'm *totally* out of money!"

Michael looked back and forth from her to Geran. "Mr. Geran and I just got back from a quest. He might want a break."

Geran waved a hand. "It's fine. That was more like a walk around town with lunch in between. What did you have in mind, Lilian?"

"There's this limited-time quest out right now that pays *super* good! Some official lady from Apogee needs an escort, and she's being *real* picky about who takes her. She won't accept any parties lower than A level, and wants at least two to accompany her!"

"So it's a raid?"

"You could call it that, but it's just an escort. That's hardly a raid-style quest."

"Who is she?" he asked.

The demicat shrugged. "I dunno. Ask Elaethia. She and Shiro got a better look than me."

"Figures," Geran muttered. "All right. Let's go talk to them."

He followed Lilian to the quest board, where the crowd had grown larger around the decorative paper that bore the information. Elaethia and Shiro stood at the rear of the pack and acknowledged their approaching party members.

"Geran, did Lili-chan tell you about this escort quest?" Shiro asked.

"She gave me a bare-bones explanation. Could you explain it to me? Looking at the forming crowd, I'm not sure I'd get a good enough look."

Elaethia tilted her head. "You would choose me explaining it rather than looking at it yourself?"

"I'm sure you'll give enough to form a basis. On top of that, the client will undoubtedly go further into detail than the request would."

"Very well. The client, Emily Hatchfield, is a politician from Breeze—a representative for the capital city. She is to return to Apogee today after conducting business here in Breeze. Due to recent events, she feels her own guard would not be enough and wishes to have hired help from adventurers."

He made a face. "A representative not trusting her own guard? What kind of attacks is she expecting? Unless she's shorthanded from a previous attempt on her life."

"I do not know. However, as you say, she will most likely answer these questions should she accept us."

Geran scratched his beard. "Hmm. And you said we'd be going to Apogee?"

"Correct."

Shiro put a hand to his chin. "So close to the tournament. Would this make us lose our positions? Or maybe we would not be allowed to take it, as it would interfere."

"That matters not," Elaethia stated plainly.

Lilian's jaw fell open "Of *course* it does! You don't wanna miss out on the tournament, do you?"

"I do not care for competition or spo—"

"Yeah, yeah, yeah, you gotta be all Miss Stoic and bland. But come *on,* the tournament is the best opportunity for the rest of us to get our names out there! This kinda chance only happens once a year *if* you get selected."

"My being there will improve your chances of becoming famous?"

"Well, actually, you're probably gonna steal the spotlight. Being a dragon hero and all, so … no."

"Then you agree it would be best for me to stay uninvolved."

Lilian silently looked to Geran for help.

The ranger sighed. "Maybe. But there are always incredibly strong opponents at the tournament. Adventurers with strength, power, and abilities you haven't seen yet. It'd be a great opportunity for you to practice against a skilled combatant. It'll help condition you for your battle with Rychus."

Elaethia pondered his statement for a moment. "There are those there who could challenge Emperor Rychus in strength?"

"Maybe. I don't know him, but you never know."

"That is reasonable. I will consider the matter more seriously. However, this is all secondary to the current situation. Do we all wish to try out for this escort?"

Her companions agreed in unison.

"Then let us speak with the client. We shall then see whether or not this quest will interfere with the tournament."

Maya was the only one standing outside Master Dameon's office. An A-level party of adventurers trudged downstairs, clearly looking defeated. Elaethia realized they had been turned away.

Geran stepped ahead. "Maya, what's the deal with these interviews?"

"I can't say for sure, but Madam Hatchfield has a certain criterion she's looking for. She's already accepted one party and is being rather picky about which others she chooses."

"Who'd she accept?" Lilian asked.

"Heaven's Light. Madam Hatchfield found them 'adorable,' as she said."

Shiro raised an eyebrow. "I hope she didn't choose them solely on their appearance."

"No, they actually function very well for what she needs. Anyway, those last guys just got turned away, and they left the door open, so just go on in."

"Very well. Thank you, Maya," Elaethia said.

"Good luck!" Maya called after them. As they approached, Elaethia heard the middle of a conversation between Master Dameon and one she assumed was Emily.

"Guild Master," Emily huffed. "I have already given in to your policy of paying half the money before and the rest upon arrival. But I simply will not budge on no-name parties. This trip down to Apogee is potentially highly dangerous, and I will not take such a risk because you don't want to pan out more experienced individuals!"

"It's *my* guild, so I have more say on which of my rascals go out on this quest," he growled. "You've already selected one well-known party, so why are you trying to get another? That last group was perfectly capable of protecting you. Nathan is one of my top duelists, and his party is equally competent. Just because the city hasn't recognized them to the point of naming them doesn't mean they're weak!"

"And I have told you I simply am not willing to take that risk! As a guild master, I expect you to speak highly of your members. I know none of the adventurers here, save a few, so your pride in them might overshadow their actual skill."

Dameon's eyes turned cold. "Are you accusing me of embellishment, madam?"

"Not at all, Guild Master. Your guild has a good reputation, as do you. Trust but verify, as I say."

"A lot of these kids were banking on you to see them in action so they could get names for themselves. Turning them away because they don't have fancy titles does *not* earn you any favors."

"I do feel bad for them, but if Nathan is one of your top duelists, he will certainly compete in the tournament. He'll earn more fame there than with me."

"Only the top three in the country get any noticeable attention. Nathan is seasoned in duels and combat, but to pit him against twenty others and expect him to make the top three is unreasonable."

"Then perhaps your confidence in my protection is not as sound as you have tried to explain," she said.

"You don't even understand what a guild does for a region! Nathan and his party have fought numerous bandits, monsters, and beasts before. They've handled anything that would attack you on your trip!"

Emily returned his cold stare. "Mind your tone, Guild Master. This may be your guild, but I am still an official in its city. You will find that I am not as easily intimidated by your demeanor as some others in the region."

The two regarded each other with growing heat until Geran coughed and knocked on the open door.

Dameon looked up. "Well. I shouldn't say this; but I was hoping you four wouldn't try out."

Emily sighed and turned around. "More lack of faith? If this is your initial reaction to their appearance, then I see little reason to intervi–"

She stopped.

Elaethia looked at the woman who sat on the couch in front of Master Dameon's desk. Emily was a dwarven woman in her late forties, maybe early fifties. She wore an official blue dress with pink and white detail. Jewelry hung from her round ears and thick neck, as well as around her plump fingers. She was certainly eating well. The madam looked more like nobility than a city official.

"My, my," Emily breathed. "What an interesting group of individuals. Perhaps I can hear them out at least. What do we have here, hmm? A handsome man, an adorable girl, what appears to be an Osakyotan, and *you*, my dear," she said to Elaethia. "Aren't *you* simply a conversation starter?"

Elaethia tilted her head. "I do not understand."

Emily chuckled with a patronizing tone. "Oh, you are fascinating. All right, very well, all of you come in, come in. Let me have a look at you."

The four of them walked in and stood in a line next to Master Dameon and Emily.

"Well, Guild Master?" Emily continued. "Normally I want to hear from them first, but your comment has me curious. I would like to hear what you have to say about these young adventurers, and why you hoped they wouldn't try out."

"This is Cataclysm," Dameon sighed. "From left to right we have Geran Nightshade, Lilian Whitepaw, Shiro Inahari, and Elaethia Frossgar."

"Cataclysm? So a named party then? What an interesting title. Go on."

"They're arguably my best party. They've only existed as a team for a couple of months, but they're giving my current ace a run for their money. Personally, I know they'd thrash Earth Shatter, but they haven't been working together as long."

"Let's introduce them then, shall we?" Emily prompted. "Now, Mr. Nightshade. You and I are already acquainted. You are still Breeze's top ranger?"

He put a hand to his chest and gave a short bow. "So I've been told, Madam. I've been an adventurer for ten years and been active in my ranger training and duties for thirteen. I'm the only one in the guild to have completed every type of ranger quest, as well as standard quest, alone. It will be a pleasure to work for you again."

"Of course. You did such a splendid job against Blackwolf when I first came to office. You have my absolute confidence! I approve unconditionally. And you, my dear. Lilian, is that right?"

The demicat spread her arms and curtsied with a cheerful grin. "Yes, Madam. I've been practicing elemental magic since I was a kitten and have been an adventurer here for three years. I'm already in the top three!"

"Oh, you simply are just precious. I couldn't turn you away if I tried! And now the young man from Osakyota. Do forgive me for not attempting to try to repeat your name, but I don't want to offend you and mispronounce it."

He doubled over in a deep bow. "Shiro Inahari, Madam! I am the son of Hanzo Inahari, a revered general in Osakyota. Grandson of Ryuuki Inahari, a samurai master. My skill with the blade is unmatched in combat, while my loyalty and service to those who have entrusted me with their care is second to none. If Elaethia-sama wishes to protect you, I, as her sword, will do the same to my utmost capability. I look forward to working for you!"

Emily put a hand to her chest. "What … a … *charmer*. Such exquisite manners and posture are nearly impossible to find in your profession. I am looking equally forward to being in your care. Finally, you, my dear. With the curious markings."

"I am Elaethia," she stated expressionlessly, holding Emily's gaze blandly. "I am a dragon hero who fights with magic and weaponry gifted from Frossgar. My party and I will see to your protection as a client."

The representative wrinkled her nose. "What a crass young woman. Did this Frossgar character teach you how to bow?"

"I bow to no one. Especially to one who sits in comfort before those willing to risk their lives for one's safety."

"How *rude*!" Emily gasped. "You are a citizen of my city, and you *will* give me the respect I deserve. Your mentor has clearly failed you if this is how you treat your superiors."

Elaethia's expression hardened. "Respect is earned, Emily. Never given. Your words with my guild master and posture to my friends make you undeserving of it. I will not stand here to offer you my services should you speak ill of Frossgar again."

Emily inhaled and was about to stand up when Elaethia's eyes flashed and the room grew cold. Emily shrunk back down and began to shiver as she shot a look over to Dameon, who had a gleam in his eye.

"G-G-Guild Master! What is the meaning of this? I *demand* an explanation f-for your subordinate's b-behavior! And what is wrong with the t-temperature in this office!"

Dameon chuckled quietly, his misty breath flowing into the air. "You should have paid more attention to fairy tales and history, madam representative. Your first mistake was forgetting what a dragon hero was."

"D-dragon heroes? What do those old st-storybook legends have to do with any of this?"

He gave her a wicked look. "Didn't you hear her when she introduced herself? She *is* a dragon hero. That Frossgar character you insulted? He was the world's last dragon, and Elaethia's his champion. She shares his soul. There's only one thing I know that gets under her skin in an instant, and you found it immediately. All your time parading around the country has left you unaware of current events. If you want a bow, you're gonna have to get up and fight her for it."

"What?" Emily looked from Dameon to Elaethia, and then to the other three adventurers in the room. Their expressions showed that Elaethia was serious. "Y-you? A dragon hero? H-how? I th-thought they went extinct hundreds of years ago. You c-can't expect me to just sit here and believe that!"

"Then stand," Elaethia stated. "Unless you will continue to plead for protection from those you insult while set upon a cushion."

Elaethia held Emily's unblinking gaze. Instead of retorting, the representative froze. Her bottom lip quivered, and her whole body trembled. She blinked hard and gripped the arm of the couch with white knuckles as mist flowed from her mouth.

"Frossgar, my girl"—Master Dameon smiled—"I think you've made your point. Now, if you wouldn't mind, the rest of us are starting to feel a little cold."

Elaethia regarded him, as well as the shivering woman in front of her. "Very well. However, I am still most displeased with the representative's words. If this is how she will treat me and my party throughout the duration of the quest, I will not offer her my protection."

"Might be as well," he chuckled. "I don't think the madam wants to be around you any more than you do her. Razorback is out right now, but Earth Shatter might be game to take this."

"I understand. We shall take our leave then."

"That's a bummer," Lilian sighed, and she folded her arms behind her head. "This was gonna set me up for a while. Guess we'll pick a low-level quest to get me through the day."

Shiro nodded firmly. "I agree with Elaethia-sama. I will not work for one who insults her."

"Can't say I agree, but I understand," Geran muttered. "Oh well. Let's go look for a normal quest."

The four of them turned to leave the room when a small voice called after them.

"W-wait …"

They turned to see Emily Hatchfield standing in front of the couch.

"I will humbly accept Cataclysm as a part of my guard."

Two hours later, Cataclysm, Heaven's Light, and a dozen of Emily's guards stood in front of the guildhall. A wooden stagecoach with ornate decorations and a comfortable interior was led by two brown horses. Two identical stagecoaches were lined up behind it. Behind them was a cargo wagon for everyone's equipment.

Elaethia looked at her party. Geran and Shiro stood a few meters to her left, while Lilian talked excitedly with the mage from Heaven's Light. The monk and priestesses from the second party leaned against the stagecoach just next to them. Elaethia tilted her head. She could have sworn she heard Geran say Heaven's Light had four members.

"I don't know much about escort quests, Geran," Shiro started. "But even I can tell this seems excessive. Is all of this necessary?"

Geran seemed to mull the comment over in his mind for a moment. "She hasn't said outright, but I'm pretty sure I know why the representative's so paranoid. I think she's concerned they might attack her outside the city walls, and wants all of us to be a deterrence."

"That explains the other stagecoaches. They're probably decoys."

"Exactly. Blackwolf knows the representative will be traveling by stagecoach along the main road over the next few days. If it were up to me, we wouldn't leave for another day or so, as well as take an alternate route to throw them off. But the representative is bent on arriving in Apogee on time. The coaches are armored and enchanted with a decent magical defense system. Even if Blackwolf *did* attack, she should be safe. But we don't want them knowing exactly where she is either way."

"Hope for the best, prepare for the worst," Shiro agreed.

Elaethia turned away from the conversation. She shifted her interest to the guards and guild staff who were loading everyone's equipment, belongings, and rations into the cargo wagon. She felt somewhat useless just standing idle while others worked. However, she was told otherwise—something about their already having the job to protect and watch out for the madam, and their not being able to ask her to assist further. It made no sense to her, but she did not want to interfere with established procedures.

Suddenly an armored human woman approached her. She wielded a mace and shield, and had a wand sheathed at her hip. This style of heavy armor and magic could indicate only one type of class. It would seem Elaethia was about to meet the fourth member of Heaven's Light.

"Good afternoon, Elaethia," the paladin said politely, extending a gauntlet. "We've seen each other around, but I don't think we've officially met. My name's Angela; I'm the leader of Heaven's Light. I look forward to working with you."

The dragon hero grasped the gauntlet in her own. "Likewise. It is a pleasure to meet you."

Angela was tall—almost as tall as Elaethia. Fair skin and long, flowing blond hair highlighted her white-and-yellow steel armor. The paladin's armor was plated but was nowhere near as thick or heavy as Elaethia's. The metal pieces were almost form-fitting to the woman. Like Elaethia, Angela was toned, but she very much had a feminine form. She was curvier than Elaethia, but not as muscled. The paladin drew quite a bit of attention to herself. Even Elaethia couldn't help but realize how beautiful she was.

"Girls! Front and center!" Angela called to her party. After a moment, the other three women walked over. "Well, now that everyone is here, let's do a formal introduction. Geran and Lilian already know us, but you and … Shiro, I think … should probably get caught up. Could you call him over?"

Elaethia nodded. "Shiro, would you come over here?"

"Yes, Elaethia-sama!" The samurai instantly jogged over to her and stood firmly at her side.

"Obedient, isn't he?" Angela remarked. "All right, ladies, let's reintroduce ourselves. My name's Angela Bright. I'm the third strongest paladin in Breeze, as well as the leader of this party."

The elf next to her waved. The bouncing girl had bright crimson hair in a ponytail and held a long, simple staff. She had circular steel glasses and wore white clothing with a long red cloak.

"Hi-hi-hi! I'm Suzanna. Suzanna Mist! I'm the mage! I don't know how strong I am number-wise, but Lilian helped me get pretty good. Let's all become really good friends, 'kay?"

The tall demibear next to her walked up and rested a hand on her muscled bicep as she flexed it. She had short brown hair and wore baggy white-and-green clothing. She flexed her muscular arm and gave a slightly broken toothy grin.

"Wassup! The name's Sammy Shoemaker, and I'm this party's monk! I've taken after Master Dameon, so I know my martial arts! Show me someone who's givin' you trouble, and I'll knock their lights out! Your turn, Cassie!"

"Uh … I, uh … My name is …" The small demiwolf girl shifted uncomfortably and clutched her white wooden staff. Her black hair was collected in a braid and curled inside a hood that covered the top of her head. The hood had two flaps on the top so her ears could be covered but not pinned down.

Sammy patted her on the shoulder "Aw, c'mon, Cas! You can do it! Just like we practiced!"

Cassie whimpered and brought her hands to her face. The white robe with pink embroidery was a little too big for her, so her floppy sleeves covered her eyes and draped in front of her face. She mumbled something into the fabric.

Angela sighed and smiled. "A little louder, sweetheart."

"I … I'm Cassie Luca. I-I'm a p-p-priestess and, and …" She looked up at Elaethia, who had tilted her head in confusion. Cassie whimpered again and pulled her hood down to cover her face.

Angela chuckled and shook her head. "Well, that's about as good as we're gonna get for now. Don't worry; Cas is a solid priestess. Just give her some time to warm up to you. How about you two? Care to introduce yourselves?"

Elaethia sighed at having to explain herself again. "My name is Elaethia. I am Frossgar's champion, and I fight with axe and frost magic."

"I'm Shiro Inahari. I am a samurai and Elaethia-sama's sword. Wherever she goes, I will follow. I look forward to working with you!"

Angela looked back and forth between them. "Well that was … enlightening. Are you guys gonna be ready when Madam Hatchfield comes out?"

Elaethia looked at her other party members. Geran was discussing the route with the coachman, and Lilian had nuzzled up to one of the younger guards to poke his chest and grin at him.

"I would say so."

It was at this moment when Emily Hatchfield walked out the front door with a guard on either side of her. Everyone halted to courteously bow and acknowledge her. Elaethia stood as she was. The representative froze at the sight of the dragon hero in her armor. Her jaw went slack as she looked the thick blue plating up and down. Her face lost all color when she saw Elaethia's battleaxe. She cleared her throat and regained herself, and she waved for everyone to carry on as she approached her stagecoach. The coachman stepped down to help her into the carriage and closed the door behind her.

Geran hopped up onto the driver's seat. "Everyone listen up for the order of movement! The first squad of the personal guard will take point; the second squad will be in the rear. Both parties of adventurers will walk on either side of the carriages. The guard will stay in their respective squads; the adventurers will alternate to best compensate for our abilities. It's not a long trip from here to Apogee, but we'll still be taking frequent breaks both to rest the horses and escorts, as well as to allow the representative to change coaches. Nobody gets to ride in the cargo wagon or decoy coaches unless you need medical attention, *Lilian*."

"Baaaaaaw …"

Angela continued. "If you have any questions, bring them to me, Geran, the head coachman, or one of the two squad leaders. Do not bother the madam unless she asks for you. We expect to arrive no later than four days from now, and the enemy knows this. It's imperative that we all keep our eyes and ears peeled. We aren't expecting to engage the enemy, but we need to be prepared to. Let's roll out. Coachman, she's all yours."

The head coachman took the reins and snapped them to urge the horses forward. The decoys and cargo wagon followed behind. The guard got into their positions as the two parties surrounded the convoy. Cataclysm and Heaven's Light walked along either side.

Elaethia looked around at the city as they set off. This was the most she had ever been looked at—even more so than her first day in the city. She suspected it was due to the citizens expecting this large departure. She frowned. A display such as this was very conspicuous. If the representative was preferring to not be engaged at all, this was not the method to achieve that goal. Only time would tell if the idea of such numbers acting as a deterrence would suffice.

They departed the city in the late afternoon with the sun still high, but setting. As they traveled, the escort stopped three to four times a day to let everyone rest, as well as to allow the representative to change coaches. For two days they kept to this pattern with no encounters, save a trader caravan and a returning group of adventurers.

Elaethia was sitting under a tree with the rest of her party on the third day during the afternoon rest period when the head coachman approached her.

"Excuse me, Miss Frossgar, Madam Hatchfield wishes to see you."

"Did she give her reasoning?" she asked.

"She did not. She merely asked if you could come talk."

Elaethia sighed. She did not want to merely talk, but she had no excuse not to go. If Emily was going to be insufferable, Elaethia would simply leave. She rose to her feet and walked toward the stagecoach that was parked beneath the shade of a tree. She knocked at the door.

"Who is it?" the representative's voice called from inside.

"Elaethia."

"Ah, do uh … do come in."

Emily opened the door for her. Elaethia stepped up and tried to step through. However, the massive axe strapped to her back became caught in the narrow entryway.

"Oh, you can leave that outside," Emily offered.

Elaethia shook her head. "This axe and armor are gifts of Frossgar. I will never leave them behind unless it is in my room back at the guild."

The warrior unsheathed the axe and fed the massive twin blades into the carriage. She propped it against the wall, climbed in, and sat down. The stagecoach groaned under the weight as Emily watched, bewildered, throughout the process.

There was an uncomfortable silence.

"That is a very beautiful necklace," Emily said after several seconds. "I must say it surprises me that a woman such as yourself wears something so elegant."

"Thank you," Elaethia replied flatly.

"You're welcome. Where, uh, how did you acquire it?"

"It was a gift from my father."

"Fascinating. Where is he now?"

"He was murdered when I was a girl."

Emily gasped. "I'm sorry; I had no idea!"

"It is all right."

"I … see. Are you sure it's all right to travel and fight with it? You might lose it."

"I am not concerned. I have not removed it in over ten years."

"Such a long time. I suppose there's no point in politely requesting to admire it more closely?"

"Correct."

The dwarf shifted. "As you wish."

Elaethia sighed heavily through her nose. "I hope you did not request my presence simply to engage in light conversation."

"No, no, my dear, I assure you I didn't."

"Then may we proceed to the main topic?"

"Of course." Emily swallowed and inhaled to steady her breathing. "I fear we may have gotten off on the wrong foot. I asked your guild master a little about you and your past. It never would have occurred to me that a dragon hero could still be possible today. I grew up in a world of politics and current affairs. History has always been a weak subject for me, and I never took interest in the stories of dragon heroes like most children do. Master Dameon informed me on their existence and impact. He also mentioned to me that your conjoinment with Frossgar ended … poorly. I am, truly, sorry for your loss."

Elaethia's brow furrowed. She opened her mouth, but closed it again after a moment. "What all did Master Dameon say?"

"Nothing too detailed. He insisted that it was up to you to make yourself known. All he said was who you were, where you came from, and what you are."

"What I am?"

"Well, being a dragon hero. He knew a little based on his own research and time around you, but I thought I would ask you yourself. What is it like being a dragon hero?"

Elaethia thought for a moment. "I do not know how to explain. Nearly my whole life I have trained to become one, and from that day on I simply was. I do not know what I do not know, so I cannot explain the difference between you and me."

The dwarf nodded. "I see. So what was he like? Frossgar, that is."

"Firm, caring, encouraging, and wise. He cared for company less than I but raised me with compassion and kindness all the same."

"And what of your magic?"

"I was not born with the ability to use magic. It was only after we joined that I could wield it. He only ever showed me a few spells, but I have heard there are records of the rest somewhere."

Emily folded her hands. "That's what I had heard as well. Which is why I would like to strike a bargain with you."

Elaethia tilted her head. "A bargain?"

"Yes. Your guild master informed me that everyone from your party is partaking in the tournament, which will be a week after our estimated arrival. If you were to act as my personal escort around the city until then, I would give you unlimited access to whatever tomes and records I can get for you. Everything regarding dragon hero knowledge and abilities, as well as any historical records I am authorized to access."

They sat in silence for a moment until Emily spoke again. "Of course, I would not require you to regard me as everyone else. I would hope that you and I could become some sort of friends. We have much we could gain from one another."

"It sounds like you plan to use my strength to increase power for your personal goal," Elaethia said.

The large woman waved a hand. "Oh, heavens no! Perish the thought! I work purely for the well-being of the region I represent. While I certainly appreciate the benefits of being a country official, I am quite content with how things are. I have no need or desire to further improve my comfort at the expense of the region."

"Forgive me if I cannot bring myself to trust your word," Elaethia said. "I was given another offer in regard to access to the knowledge I seek. But the price offered then would prove less tiresome. If the cost for identical knowledge is your exploitation, then I have no intention of giving you such leverage."

Emily blanched. Her eyes sank to her lap, where her hands wrung together between her thighs. Her lips pursed and relaxed. Her brow wrinkled as stuttered syllables came from her mouth, but no words were constructed.

Elaethia continued. "That being said, there is no reason for me to believe you are like that. At the same time, you have not given me a reason to believe otherwise."

Emily forced a laugh and wiped the sweat from her forehead. "I see your reputation precedes you. You truly lack any sort of filter."

Elaethia's eyes turned cold. "Was that a form of insult?"

"No, no, no; that's not what … I … it's a figure of speech meaning you say exactly what you think with no regard for how others may feel. But I, as a woman who believes herself an honest politician, can't help but respect that about you."

Elaethia remained silent.

"I see this isn't really getting me anywhere," the representative sighed. "Do you know why you are all on this quest with me? More specifically, why I requested such heavy escorts?"

"I do not."

"Let me back up a bit then. Over a year ago, I was elected to be the new Breeze representative for the Linderrian Council. The old representative was impeached for collaborating with a region-wide crime faction called Blackwolf."

"I am aware of them," Elaethia said.

Emily nodded. "The old rep would turn a blind eye, and they would alter the ballot box to keep him in power. After a while, Blackwolf started lobbying for him in exchange for them to operate freely within the city and set up a base of operations. Blackwolf began dealing in smuggling, trafficking, slaving—you name it. They became overconfident and subsequently were quickly found out. Geran Nightshade played a large role in that discovery and upheaval, which is why I continued to use him after my election.

"My first and foremost priority was eradicating Blackwolf. My entire time and resources since then have been dedicated to that. Last month, we finally purged them from the main city. But Blackwolf is far from gone in the region. They know I must return to Apogee around this time. My next step is to begin a campaign against Blackwolf, and they will stop at nothing to keep me from doing that. I am terrified that they will ambush and kill me."

Elaethia nodded. "So by having me constantly with you, they will be dissuaded."

"That is one reason. The other is so by being in close relations and proximity with me, you will get many benefits originally unobtainable as you currently are. I would declare you my thane. Your national status and reputation would increase, and you would be highly respected. It would be much easier for you to access what you needed to achieve your own goal."

"I see," Elaethia said. "Perhaps I, too, have misjudged you then. If you have been after a good cause during this time and are concerned for your life, I think you would not always be in a calm state of mind."

Emily smiled. "Oh, my girl. I'm realizing it is nearly impossible to get a read on you. But I do believe we can learn to get along."

"Indeed. I have no love for nobility or those in power who do not know what it is like to live a difficult life. But your cause is noble, and I feel no ill intent from you any longer. I will consider your bargain."

Before the dwarf could answer, sounds of harsh voices and movement came from outside. Guards shouted, horses whinnied, and weapons were drawn. Geran's voice cut through the noise.

"Elaethia! Get out here; we might be under attack!"

"Stay in here, Emily," Elaethia said. "I do not wish for harm to come to you."

The representative shook and gripped her dress. "Oh, Moon, please let this be a misunderstanding. I put myself in your care, Elaethia!" Elaethia nodded at her and left to rejoin the escort.

She approached them to see Geran looking over the horizon from a tree while Angela stood still with her wand in front of her. A glowing sun with a pupil hovered in front of her closed eyes. The other members of Cataclysm and Heaven's Light were equally dispersed with the guard on standby.

"What is the matter?" she asked Geran.

"I was taking a look around the area when I noticed movement in that tree line across the field. The captain of the guard used a spyglass to take a closer look and saw a large group of brehdars. Whether or not it's an attack for us is being determined right now by Angela."

Elaethia looked to the paladin on the side of the road. "What is she doing?"

"A holy spell. *Sun eye*, I think it's called," Geran said. "The large group in question is concealed by a thicket, so she's only getting bits and pieces. Don't talk to her until she's done. From what she said, this spell takes a lot of magic and concentration, as well as leaves her completely vulnerable."

"Very well. In the meantime, we will prepare for an attack. We should consolidate the wagons in one location to maximize protection and reduce friction between us."

"That's the plan. We also need to come up with a formation and skirmisher engagements. We're defending, not attacking, so we need to hold this position."

"Very well," she said.

"The key phrase is 'hold this position.' We aren't chasing them down."

"I am aware of this."

"That means stay put."

"I understand, Geran; you do not need to explain further."

"Well, you never know," Geran said. "We've always been the ones to initiate, and I'm not sure if you'll be able to keep yourself from charging off and taking them all on by yourself."

She tilted her head. "Is that such a bad tactic?"

"Blackwolf may be criminal, but they're still an organized force. They probably have a plan of their own, and I want to keep all of us nearby to adjust for it."

"I will be highly restricted."

"I know, just …" He sighed in contempt. "Can you hold off on going ballistic until we can get a feel for the situation? I want time to read the fight without excess variables."

"If you insist. However, should there be a need, I will disengage."

"I guess that's as good as I'm gonna get, isn't it?" he muttered.

"Geran! You were right!" Angela called. "That's definitely Blackwolf, and they know they've been spotted! It looks like they're moving into position. We've got a large group of them coming our way!"

Geran looked at the approaching horde and then to their surroundings. "This is not an ideal defensive position. Sheer face going up to our rear, downhill where we came from, open field ahead, flat forest further up the road. What kind of magical protections do we have?"

"The wagons are still operational. As for us; I'm sun specialized, so all I can use is *Sun wall*, but Cassie has both defensive spells. Does anyone in your party have a sun or moon ring?"

Geran made a face. "A what now?"

"Some new rings imbued with holy properties. Enchanters are getting rich off making them."

"Those are new to me. Elaethia's armor is impenetrable to physical and magical attacks, but the rest of us are entirely dependent on Cas for magical protection."

"Understood. Tell your magicians to act sparingly. I don't want to dry Cas out by keeping them going with *moonlight*."

Geran nodded. "Rodger. Lilian! Did you hear that?"

"Whaaaaat?" the mage called back

"Don't blow yourself out! All you have for replenishment is whatever you brought."

"I'm broke, remember?"

He gritted his teeth. "Dammit. That reduces our firepower."

Angela tapped her cheek. "Suzanna might have an extra potion. If it comes down to one of our mages being depleted, I'd rather it be her."

"We'll cross that bridge when we come to it. How many did they have?"

"From what I could make out, over fifty. Most likely more because my vision was obstructed."

Geran's mouth fell open "*Fifty!* We only have twenty! Not including the madam and drivers."

"They have magicians and archers, too. We're outnumbered probably three to one, and they may have more firepower than us."

Geran looked at the dragon hero to his left, who tilted her head at him. "Well. Luckily for us, we have a juggernaut. Elaethia, looks like you're on point."

"As to be expected. I will be sure to stay within hearing range." She donned her visored helmet and strode out into the field. Shiro, too, put on his open-face helmet and equipped his tough face mask. He stepped forward to follow Elaethia.

Geran stopped him. "Hold on, Shiro. We need you back here."

"But ... I belong at Elaethia-sama's side."

Elaethia turned back. "I do not wish for you to be swept up in my attacks. Lilian would be most grateful for your protection. Do not worry, Shiro. I will retreat if I need to."

The samurai rested a hand on the hilt of his blade. "I will be by your side the moment something goes wrong. I'll see to Lili-chan's care until then."

Geran nodded. "Good man. Lilian! Shiro's gonna watch your back as usual. Focus on your magic!"

"Okeydokey!" she chirped, and she gave a thumbs-up.

Angela called to her party. "Suzanna, get on the opposite side of the formation as Lilian. If she runs dry, give her your potions. Sam and Cas, stay in the middle behind the main guard. Cas, you're on defense. Intercept the big spells with *moon wall*, and keep some in reserve for healing. Sam, stick with her. Elaethia is taking the front."

"O-okay!" the demiwolf said.

"Aw what? I gotta let Elaethia have all the fun?" the monk groaned. She sighed and clapped a hand on Cassie. "All right, priestess, it's you and me. Just like old times."

The twelve guardsmen formed a defensive line in between the small approaching army and the stagecoaches. Lilian and Suzanna took positions near either flank. Cassie and Samantha stood behind in the middle. Geran climbed atop a stagecoach and drew his bow. Angela stood in front of the formation; her shield attached and her mace rested on her shoulder. She wore her own steel helmet, a burgonet with a visor that covered the lower half of her face. All watched as Elaethia stopped fifty meters ahead. Her great battleaxe was drawn and held at her side. The dragon hero stood alone, staring down her approaching opponents.

Angela turned to Geran. "Nightshade, are you sure she's gonna be okay?"

"I've seen her serious before. If Blackwolf is receiving the same look she gave that troll, they're already dead."

She nodded grimly. "May the Sun guide her."

Elaethia watched the small army get closer and closer. Though her helmet reduced her vision, her dragon eyes could easily make out the horde. They were all fighters, no magicians—an even mix of duelists and warriors. Their weaponry ranged from simple daggers to heavy hammers and axes. They were running now, seemingly unimpressed with her lone stand. All fifty-some men and women bore down on her and formed into a more condensed formation. They were fifty meters away now. Elaethia took a stance. Forty meters. The warrior poised her battleaxe behind her head. Thirty meters and closing. The dragon hero swung and slammed the massive blade into the ground.

A rift of jagged ice crystals exploded from the earth. The erupting spell traveled in a straight line and crashed directly into the charging mass. The attackers attempted to stop or dive out of the way. Many were too late. The frozen crystals plowed into them, the toothy icicles piercing their bodies. The afflicted Blackwolf found themselves hoisted off the ground, impaled by the attack. Nine of them were killed or fatally wounded in the opening spell. The group of criminals halted in their tracks and fearfully eyed the strange, magic-wielding warrior. Elaethia glared at the stunned aggressors and uttered a single word of challenge.

"Come."

The force split. Half attempted to charge around her left, the other to her right. The group on the left side was slightly larger, maybe twenty-five. She leaped to intercept and slammed the battleaxe down again into the nearest man with a burst of ice and blood. A few others fell from the attack. The remaining assailants surrounded the dragon hero with their weapons drawn and raised. They struck and shouted at her as their blows ineffectively landed on her dragonite armor. Elaethia swung the axe around at waist height, cutting four more in half with the single swipe. She brought it around behind her, which caused the axe to snag another assailant. The dragon hero heaved the blade down on a different enemy in front of her. The unfortunate Blackwolf that was caught on it was thrown clear from the skirmish and crashed to the ground fifteen meters away.

Still surrounded by a dozen or so opponents, she wound up and swung in a full circle that took down three more. Maintaining the momentum, she performed her flourish. Mist enveloped the scene as the attackers attempted to push through or retreat. Those that approached were cut down. Those that ran were impaled by flying ice spikes.

The man that was thrown recovered from his excursion and looked back. His face lost all color as Elaethia marched toward him with unmistakable intent. He frantically grasped a horn from his belt and blew three sharp notes before another ice spike lodged itself into his head.

Another swarm of enemies charged from the woods up the road. This time they numbered around thirty, and they poured onto the dirt path, headed straight for the stagecoaches. At the same time, the other half of the first charge came directly from the front.

"Angela!" Geran called. "You and the guard take the ones in the front. The rest of us will deal with the flankers!"

"Understood! Where are the enemy mages? These are all fighters!" Angela shouted.

"I don't know! Cassie, stay close to me. Sam, keep her up." The ranger turned to his right as the two demihumans complied and stood ready. Cassie nervously gripped her staff while Samantha eagerly bounced on her toes.

"C'mon, c'mon, bring it!" the monk roared. "I've gotten real bored these last two days, and you guys are gonna entertain me! Come over here and make my day!"

"P-please don't come over here," Cassie whimpered.

The forces clashed. Angela and the guard engaged the charging enemies head-on. Each soldier was faced with one or more assailants. Their training was high-tier, but being outnumbered was evidently too much for them. Each soldier fought valiantly against the enemy and struggled to hold the line. Angela, however, was in her element. The paladin whirled her mace around to clobber the attackers, blocking with her shield and counterattacking whoever struck at her. The paladin bashed with shield, mace, and smites, and soon began to glow. By the end of the skirmish, only Angela and eight of the twelve guards remained.

The other adventurers fared better. Lilian engulfed the enemies in a billow of searing flame while her elven counterpart shot lightning bolts into the mass. Much to their surprise, several burst through the elemental torrent, poised to run them down. Suzanna shrieked and scrambled backward, while Lilian sighed with a smile and calmly stepped aside. A flash of red flew past her. Shiro had drawn his sword and intercepted the enemies that survived the mage's attack.

The samurai parried a thrust from the first man, slashed his side, and then drove the blade into his torso. Shiro kicked the dead elf off his sword and stepped back to dodge an overhead slam from a greatsword. Shiro planted his foot on the steel tip and ran up the heavy blade to drive his knee into its wielder. The demicat let go of his weapon and toppled backward to the ground. As he tried to rebound, he was slammed back down by a blade that drove him into the dirt. Shiro rolled forward to slash at the ankles of another that charged him, and completely severed the dwarf from his feet. The samurai twisted with lightning speed to thrust his sword up while kneeling. The Blackwolf, with no feet to stand on, fell face-first onto the waiting blade.

A shadow flew over his head. He looked up and saw Samantha leap into action. The demibear's body glowed with self-imbued energy as she drop-kicked the first man she came across. The monk pounced on his chest and battered his face until his struggling ceased. A human with a one-handed hammer ran forward and swung down to clobber her off his ally. The monk's left hand shot up and caught the heavy hammer head. The man froze. Samantha sneered with a wicked gleam into his shaking eyes. She ripped the weapon from his hand and fired a heavy uppercut to his stomach that lifted him fully off the ground. There was an audible crunch as blood spurted from his mouth. Before he could fall, she lashed a push kick into him that sent him flying.

"Who's next!" she bellowed to the survivors. She paused as she realized there were none. "Tch. I'm not even warmed up yet. Cas, Suzy, you two good?"

"Just peachy!" Suzanna called.

"I-I'm okay!" Cassie said in like.

Cassie knelt next to the fallen soldiers to heal whichever ones she could while Lilian and Shiro walked into the group of Blackwolf that had charged them. The demicat reached down to one of the men that had seemingly ignored her attack. She saw nothing of interest and was about to go back until she noticed an odd ring on his left hand. She bent over to pull it off. "What's this?"

Lilian turned it around and slipped it on. Energy briefly hummed from the ring and dissipated again. At the same time, she noticed a pale light appear and disappear around her figure. It was *moonlight*. Her eyes widened, and she immediately got up to search the others for the rings. Shiro decided to look with her, but they were burnt out or damaged beyond usage.

Lilian grinned smugly. "Score. Hey, Angela! I think I found one of those moon rings you were talking about!"

"Seriously? Let me see!"

"Okay, but finders keepers, so it's mi—"

She and all the other magicians froze.

"Cas! *Moon wall*, now!" Suzanna shouted.

Cassie held her staff forward to cover the main group behind a pale wall of light. A volley of spells rocketed toward them and dissipated as they passed through the priestess's spell.

Lilian and Shiro dived to the ground as several elemental and druidic spells flew overhead. Shiro peered up to see a *fireball* fly into Lilian. He was about to scream her name but stopped. Instead of scorching her, the fireball dissipated as it hit her. The ring on her finger glowed with each spell that struck her. He met her eyes to see that she had realized the same thing. Lilian instantly shot up to shield her samurai companion until the barrage ended. The sleek demicat held her arms out to the side as she knelt in front of him, absorbing each attack that came near. Within seconds, the barrage of spells came to an end.

Shiro stood up to see how the main group had fared. Cassie lowered her staff and fluttered to the ground. Suzanna dug out her last magic potion and gave it to the depleted priestess. The weary demiwolf gulped it down and instantly continued her treatment of the wounded.

Shiro turned his attention to Lilian. "Lili-chan, that was amazing! I never thought you'd be the one to protect me!"

Lilian gave him her signature grin. "C'mon, Shiro, we're a team! It's what we do!"

"Of course!" He beamed. "Let's get back to the others. There might be another attack."

As they started to walk back, they heard a low whistling. Thin, spotty shadows darkened the area. They looked up to see a rain of arrows falling onto the main body.

Angela ran up with her wand and cast *sun wall*. "Shiro, Lilian, stay away! Everyone else, get behind something!"

Shiro watched as the storm of arrows clattered off the bright light and fell to the ground. Angela's spell was effective, but she couldn't hold it for long. It didn't help that her wand and armor made it so she had to strain to maintain such a large spell. The paladin kept it active until everyone could get to cover. Angela threw up her shield to cover herself from the relentless rain of wood and iron as the wall of solid light flickered and disappeared.

The Blackwolf archers ceased fire once they realized their attack held no effect. But then they spotted the two alone off to the side, and the archers nocked the remainder of their arrows. Seemingly determined to inflict some level of casualties, they fired their last volley at Shiro and Lilian.

Lilian frantically started to pull Shiro toward the main group. "We have to run!"

Shiro halted and grabbed her wrist. "No time, Lili-chan! Get behind me!"

"No! I'm not gonna sit here while you get turned into a pincushion! It's our best chance!"

His expression was solemn. "Lili-chan, do you trust me?"

"What kind of question is *that?*"

"Do you trust me!"

She faltered. "Y-yes, but what are—"

"Then get behind me!"

Her eyes softened and her mouth twisted into a snarl as she crouched behind him. "On the Sun and Moon, Shiro. If you die, I'm kicking your ass when I join you in the heavens."

Shiro silently turned and drew his sword to face the volley of arrows.

They impacted. Wooden shafts sprouted from the ground around them like flowers. Lilian trembled behind him as he focused on the storm. A glint caught his eye, and Lilian saw it too. Her breath hitched as the arrow fell straight toward them.

"Shiro!" Lilian cried.

Time slowed for the samurai. His mind cleared and went calm. It was as if a single drop of water had fallen into the center of a rippling pool and smoothed the troubled surface. Shiro exhaled long and slow, and he shot his arms forward. There was a sharp ting—the sound of metal striking metal. Lilian gasped from behind him.

Shiro had deflected the arrow with his sword.

Standing steadfast, the samurai again flicked his blade to the side to strike another arrow to the ground. Again and again he maneuvered his katana to intercept the deadly rain of metal. *Ting, ting, ting.* He could hear only two things: the sounds of his sword meeting arrows, and the thuds of shots impacting the dirt.

Finally, it was over. Shiro inhaled slowly and sheathed his sword. A tug on his right thigh prevented him from fully standing. He looked down and noticed an arrow had lodged itself in between the gaps of his armor. He found it odd that he didn't feel it, but passed it off as part of the adrenaline rush. He gave it a gentle pull, only to realize it hadn't made it to his skin. Shiro broke it off and dug out the dented arrowhead. He shrugged and tossed it to the ground.

"Lili-chan, are you alrigh—"

He froze. She was not all right.

Lilian lay on her back and strained to hold herself up. Blood trickled from her mouth as she weakly grasped the shaft of an arrow that had pierced her torso on her right side. The demicat gurgled and choked, obviously struggling to breathe.

"*Lili-chan!*" Shiro screamed, and he dropped to the ground. "I'm sorry; I'm so sorry I wasn't diligent enough. Please, can you breathe?"

"I … I can't …" She coughed, sending blood flying from her mouth.

"No, no, no, don't speak, just relax. Geran! Elaethia-sama! Lili-chan is hit!"

Geran sprinted over to them and slid next to his wounded companion with Elaethia behind him.

"By the Sun, she's punctured a lung," the ranger murmured. "We have to get that arrow out and close the wound or her lung will collapse. Cassie! Get over here!"

"How bad?" Angela asked as her party arrived.

"Bad. Where's Cassie?"

"H-h-here," the priestess whispered. "B-but I'm already overcast. We used our potions, too. I'll be ready in m-maybe five minutes."

"We don't even have one minute! Shiro, you bought a healing potion, right?"

"I did, let me …"

He reached into his pouch. All he pulled out was a single arrowhead and a shattered health potion. Its contents poured from his shaking hands and into the dirt. Lilian coughed weakly and began to turn pale.

"*Shit!*" Geran shouted, and he slammed a fist into the dirt. "We have to get this arrow out. Shiro, hold her tight; this is going to hurt like hell."

Shiro nodded grimly and put a hand to her shoulder. Geran placed one hand on Lilian's chest around the arrow, and the other around its shaft. He exhaled steadily and gently wriggled the projectile free. The mage convulsed and cried in agony as the arrow was slowly removed. Her body writhed so badly that Shiro and Elaethia had to forcibly hold her down. She gasped sharply and screamed the moment Geran pulled it free.

Geran was turning frantic. "Shiro! Put your hand on her wound! Get some pressure on it!"

"Alright!"

"I'm going to make a makeshift bandage. Someone pour some water on that wound; don't let it get infected! She's gonna have to survive on one lung until Cas can get enough magic back."

Shiro's eyes widened. "Geran, she's not breathing! Her heartbeat's getting faint!"

"No, no, no, no, no! The other lung is overinflating. We're gonna lose her! Anyone, does anyone have any potion that can help?"

All of the onlookers shook their heads. Suzanna and Cassie began to cry. Angela stood behind them with a hand over her mouth. Geran rifled through his pouches for something unknown.

Elaethia didn't seem to know what to do with her body. Samantha's hands clenched to her baggy pants with white knuckles. Everyone was at a loss or in shock.

Elaethia spoke with a trembling voice. "She has lost too much blood and is unable to breathe. She will not live long. Is there truly nothing we can do?"

Geran paced back and forth. "I don't know, I don't know. Dammit, what do I do!"

"Lili-chan …" Shiro whispered.

Tears fell from Shiro's face as he looked into Lilian's dim and watery eyes. He had sworn to protect her. He'd had one job, and he had failed. He couldn't stand it. Why? Why did it have to be Lili-chan? Why must he lose everything he loved and cared about? Hadn't he suffered enough? How much more would he have to lose before his sin was forgiven?

Though these doubts plagued his mind and Lilian's heartbeat grew faint, he bowed his head and prayed with all he had.

"Please …" he whispered shakily. "Please let me help. I want to save her; I want her to be healed. Please don't take my friend from me. I can't lose someone I promised to protect—not again. I don't care what it costs; I'll do anything …"

A gentle surge welled within him, and his hands started to glow.

Geran froze. "By the Sun and Moon …"

"Sh-Shiro! That's *healing touch*!" Angela sputtered. "I don't know how, but you're doing it! Don't stop; keep concentrating!"

She didn't have to tell him. The samurai poured everything he had from this source into Lilian. He could feel the hole in her body close until it was fully sealed. Shiro's hands began to dim as he felt the source of energy disappear. It was strange; he had always felt it there. The samurai shakily removed his bloodied hands. Everyone looked in shocked awe as Lilian gasped sharply and the color began to return to her face.

Elaethia helped her sit up. "How do you feel? Are you all right now?"

"Y-yeah I'm … fine. I …" Lilian murmured. She looked up at Shiro.

"Lili-chan. Thank the heavens; I thought you were—"

He was cut off as Lilian leaped onto him and wrapped her arms around his chest. The demicat inhaled deeply and let out several long, heaving sobs into his neck. Her fingers ran up through his hair and gripped shakily. Shiro was stunned only for a moment before he embraced her as well.

"I'm sorry," he whispered. "I tried. If only I was better …"

She only shook her head in response.

Geran stood and wiped his eyes. "Okay … we can't stay here, all right? We need to remember our mission. Let's get out of here before they regroup and try again."

The adventurers nodded and stood. Geran, Elaethia, and Angela walked in front toward the stage coaches. The other members of Heaven's Light held on to each other while wiping their noses and clearing their throats. Shiro and Lilian followed from the back. The demicat's tail sagged to the ground, and her legs shook so badly that she could hardly walk. Shiro scooped his arm under her legs and picked her up, clutching the trembling girl to his chest and carrying her the rest of the way.

The representative opened the door of the rearmost stagecoach and nervously peered out as they approached. "Is everything all right out there?"

"Madam, get back inside!" Geran shouted. "We don't know if they're gone yet!"

"Can we please get away from this place? I can't stand seeing any more of you suffering at the hands of these abominable people."

"We're on it, Madam," Angela insisted. "Just stay hidden so we—"

She stopped. The air tingled and smelled of ozone. The hair on everyone's arms and necks stood on end.

Suzanna's eyes bugged. "Oh no, they aren't serious! Everyone get down!"

They all threw themselves to the ground as a massive charge of energy hummed in the air. A blinding flash followed by a deafening boom rocked the landscape. It was over the instant it started, and everything went dark.

Elaethia looked up from the dirt with ringing ears and blurry vision. She slowly pushed herself up and assessed her surroundings. She was the only one standing. Geran, Samantha, and Angela crawled to a kneel. They clutched their heads and rubbed their eyes from the effects of *lightning strike*. Cassie was still on the ground, shaking violently and holding her head. Suzanna was slumped on her hands and knees while staring at a puddle of her own vomit. Shiro was huddled over Lilian, who was clutching her ears. Everyone was alive.

Elaethia realized that was because they weren't the target. In front of her stood the shattered and smoldering remains of the madam's stagecoach. A single charred and skeletonized hand adorned with blackened rings rose from the wreckage. Representative Emily Hatchfield was dead.

Chapter 14
Apogee

Sixth Era.139. Miyan 22.

Cataclysm and Heaven's Light scoured the battlefield. Lilian and Cassie stayed back, as the both of them were still recovering. The other adventurers pushed farther into the thicket the crime faction had burst from. They came across only one body—that of a single mage, pale and shriveled in the symptoms of overcast. Elaethia turned to look at Geran as he stood and shook his head.

"What have you found, Geran?" Elaethia's expression stayed neutral, but a dangerous fire burned in her eyes and voice. "Can you track them down?"

"I could," the ranger replied. "Although there's no point."

"There is very much a reason. Blackwolf has killed Emily, a good woman we promised to protect. They cannot be allowed to escape with their lives."

"Those cowards," Shiro growled. "Murdering the representative and then running away like the dogs they are. Spineless wretches didn't even have the honor to stand and fight."

Geran faced them. "Why would they?" His voice, too, was steady. However, his mouth was twisted into a repressed snarl. "They got what they came for. Blackwolf only had one goal, and that was to kill Madam Hatchfield. It would've been pointless to try to fight the rest of us. They'd likely kill themselves before being captured by us."

"I'd be happy to hear it if they fell on their own swords. Although I'd rather kill them all myself."

"Indeed," Elaethia agreed. "If you are able to track them, let us. We will slaughter them all and finish what the representative started."

"Can't," Geran stated. He clenched a fist and inhaled slowly to steady his breathing. "Even though she's dead, we still have to finish the escort. Then we need to give a report to the National Guild Department. The Circle of Representatives will also want the body. On top of that, we have a week and three days to spend in Apogee until the tournament is over. After that, we can do whatever we want for hunting them down. If we're lucky, Nocturnal will have gotten a head start."

Elaethia's eyes hardened. "That is unacceptable. There are criminals loose in the region, and you choose not act upon it? I expected better from you, Geran."

His expression turned hostile. "What do you want me to do? They've scattered. You want me to follow every single set of tracks individually like a dog? They'll kill me before then."

"They will not stay dispersed for long. Once they regroup, we can find them."

"And how long do you think that'll take? They have to go into hiding, regroup, reconvene, and then make a footprint large enough for me to track. That kind of organization takes weeks. The best we can do is send word back to Breeze, and they'll launch their own initiative."

"But we are here with a fresh trail. Instead of acting, you wish to proceed as though nothing happened?"

"Don't mistake my calmness for apathy, because I'm just as pissed as you are. We're not moving on like nothing's happened; we're moving on how we're *supposed* to."

Elaethia's tone grew hot. "We are to carry on and ignore this event?"

"No, we have to report it and take Madam Hatchfield to where she can have a proper funeral," he growled back.

"This is idiotic," she declared.

"This is politics!" Geran finally snapped. "This is what happens when you involve the guild with the government! That's how we have to follow through! You think I like it? *Hell* no! But we don't have much of a choice!"

"There is *always* a choice!"

"Sure! Either we follow protocol or we go off on our own and lose support from both guild and country! So you can go back to being a lone vagabond or suffer in silence with the rest of us!"

Had it been anyone but Geran who said that, she would have knocked the speaker's teeth loose. Stunned by her companion's harsh words, the warrior turned and stormed back to the wreckage site. As she passed through the grove, she slammed a fist through the closest tree. The tall pine splintered and groaned from its new gaping hole, and it slowly fell over with a crash behind the heated dragon hero.

The rest of the day was spent burying the dead and reorganizing. The fallen soldiers were given semi-proper burials in the field. Makeshift headstones of wood and rocks marked their final resting grounds, while all the Blackwolf members were stripped and left to rot.

The remaining members of the escort rode in the surviving stagecoaches and cargo wagon to the nearest village, where the adventurers and guard were able to recuperate and resupply. Heavy rain began to fall that night, and the escorts were offered to stay the night inside the church. The guards passed out in the pews, while Elaethia sat alone along the far wall. Geran and Samantha had allegedly gone to the tavern.

Shiro sat leaned against the wall. Angela and Cassie took similar resting positions, but Lilian had fallen asleep on his lap. The mage was lying next to him with her cheek pressed firmly onto his thigh. It was almost strange. The demicat had hardly left his side since the incident. Anywhere he went, and anything he did, Lilian was right next to him. On the surface, he was almost uncomfortable with how close she clung to him. But deep down, he wanted her close—though he didn't understand why.

"Hey, samurai," the paladin started. "What happened back there?"

Shiro looked up. "Back where?"

"The *healing touch*. How did you do that? Geran told me Osakyotans didn't have magic."

"We don't," he said. "Or … I thought we didn't. I don't know, actually."

"What happened right as you did it? What was going through your mind?"

"I just … I wanted Lili-chan to get better. I prayed to the Sun and Moon that I could make her well again, and it sort of happened."

Angela frowned. "That sounds like a roundabout way of the normal spell. But you were praying? And then it just … happened?"

"That's right. All I wanted was to heal her."

"That's the strangest awakening I've ever heard."

"Awakening?"

"A magician's first spell," Angela explained. "It's the moment you confirm you have active magic, as well as lock yourself into your school. It's usually done in a very deliberate and controlled environment, and the magician has to know exactly what they're trying to do. I didn't think what you did could be possible, unless …"

She looked over at Cassie, who sat cross-legged to watch the conversation. The demiwolf cocked her ears.

"Divine intervention?" she asked quietly.

"You were thinking that too?"

Shiro rubbed his head. "I've never heard of divine intervention."

Angela grunted. "It's the idea—or more like the myth—that the heavens directly imbue a brehdar with holy magic to act upon their will. I personally think it's all a bunch of crap. Allegedly, there were some priests and paladins in the dragon wars that claimed this happened to them. There was no way to prove they were telling the truth, but at the same time, there was no way to prove they were lying. According to the church, though, divine intervention is a very … flashy … event. As amazing as your awakening was, I don't think it fits the bill. Did you, or do you, feel any different?"

Shiro shook his head. "I felt an odd surge when I did it. Like a well or a spring of some sort of energy. But after a few seconds, it started diminishing, and I couldn't keep it up anymore."

"And this energy source, is it gone?"

"No, strangely it came back after about an hour. I've always felt it there, though. It was just my first time using it."

"You just described having a magic reserve. Now *that's* odd."

Cassie shuffled forward on her knees. "Can … Can you do it again?"

"Maybe, let me try." Shiro held out his hand and prayed again, straining his mind to the heavens so they might hear him. After a few seconds, he put his hand down.

"Nothing. I can't seem to call on it again."

The priestess sat on her heels. "You're trying too hard. Or you're thinking about it the wrong way. What are you doing when you try?"

"I'm attempting to reach the heavens again. It's their magic, after all."

Cassie shook her head. "It's not their magic. It's yours. Think about what the spell is and what it does. Focus on what you want to happen, and it will."

"What I want to happen …" he muttered to himself. Shiro thought about *healing touch* and willed it to happen. His eyes widened as his hand began to glow with the same light as before.

He gasped. "Look! Look, I'm doing it!"

Cassie smiled. "Yeah, you're doing good. If you keep practicing, you'll be able to hold it for longer, and you'll recover faster."

"Thank you, Cassie-chan. You're a wonderful teacher."

She blushed and looked down. "I-I'm not all that great …"

"Of course you are!" he insisted. "I wouldn't have been able to figure it out if it weren't for you!"

The demiwolf mumbled something and buried her face in her sleeves.

"Well," Angela continued. "Either way, we can all attest to your saving Lilian with your little swordplay and sudden awakening."

"Yeah, I guess."

He looked down at Lilian, who was still asleep on his lap. He couldn't help but smile at her gentle face. He had made comparisons between her and his sister before, though they were nearly polar opposites. But like this, Lilian bore quite a lot of semblances to Mitsuki. Shiro gently reached over and touched the tip of her furry ear. It twitched slightly at the contact, but she didn't wake.

"Well?" Angela asked, eyes glinting.

"Well what?" Shiro responded.

"Aren't you going to hold her?"

"Am … am I not?"

She laughed. "Oh, Shiro, you really are naive. Were you around *any* girls back home?"

"None as close as Lili-chan."

"Really? I'm surprised you've even gotten *this* far."

Shiro rubbed the back of his head. "Liam-senpai *did* give me a couple pointers."

Angela blinked. "Liam? Hoo boy. I'm breaking a couple unspoken rules here, but for Lilian's sake and yours, I'm gonna help you out."

"What do you mean?" Shiro asked.

"Here, put your arm around her. No, your other arm. The one closest to her. Around her back … no, under*neath*. By the Moon, Shiro, rest your arm across her back. *There!* There you go."

"My hand is just hovering in the air, though."

"Right, but now relax. Breeeaaaathe out. Just relax. Set your hand on her waist, and just let it sit there naturally."

Shiro did as instructed. Nervous at first, he tensely rested his arm on the sleek girl. Although still asleep, Lilian apparently felt the contact and sighed deeply, nuzzling deeper into his thigh. Shiro stiffened and turned pink for a moment, and then he smiled. Slowly, he relaxed and leaned against the stone wall behind him with his arm gently resting on her hip.

Angela smiled. "There, see? Not so bad, is it?"

"No, it's not," he said as his chest filled with a pleasant warmth. "Is there anything else you can tell me some other time?"

The paladin chuckled. "I could, but that would ruin the fun. Besides, Lilian would be pretty cross with me if she found out."

"I see. Thank you, Angela-senpai."

Angela stood and stretched her legs. "No problem, Shiro. If you ever have any issues, come and talk to me. I'll help sort 'em out as best as I can. Don't go talking to Liam again, though. That meathead spearman's no good when it comes to delicate girls like her."

"You think Lili-chan is delicate?"

"You're right. Poor choice of words. Unique, maybe? I don't know. Lilian's special in more ways than one. I think you're damn lucky to have what it takes to keep up with her. Anyway, I'm gonna go lie down, too. C'mon, Cas."

The blonde human walked over in between the aisles and laid out a bed mat. Cassie stood up and grabbed her own belongings. She gave Shiro a shy look, glanced sadly at Lilian, and shuffled over to join her party leader.

Shiro rested his head against the wall behind him. So much had happened to him over these last few months. Half a year ago, he never would have imagined he'd be here right now—especially with a girl so wonderful as Lilian by his side. He looked down at her quiet form. Her furry tail was curled around her legs, and her gentle breath lifted and lowered his hand with each respiration. He smiled and blushed again as he thought on her promise to him. He began to nod off as he pondered his own goals and journey. He had sworn himself to Elaethia and couldn't imagine a more worthy place. But maybe, just maybe, traveling the world with Lilian would be a more wonderful experience.

Sixth Era.139. Miyan 23.

Elaethia figured each city was sized comparatively to its guild. Since Apogee had a fairly small guild, she figured it was a fairly small city. While that may have been true for the region overall, she was woefully misinformed when it came to the city itself. To put it lightly, Apogee was enormous. Elaethia froze in her steps at the mere sight of the capital. To call it a city was to call a sabercat a kitten. The entire horizon from the elevated road they walked along was enveloped by the country's capital.

She recalled as much information about the city as she could. Apogee was divided into three terraces, all in a ringlike pattern. The outermost ring was the largest and appeared to be residential. Straight streets and canals ran in a neat grid pattern for kilometers. Although she was at a distance, Elaethia could tell the buildings were larger and more complex the closer they were to the center. Even among the elegant houses, manors, and apartment buildings, there also seemed to be farms of some sort within the massive walls.

The middle ring was the industrial, business, military, college, and overall official terrace. While the outermost ring was the largest in surface area, this one was the most complex. Large buildings, factories, offices, and other various structures popped up all throughout the terrace. There didn't seem to be any rhyme or reason to the layout or spacing. Everything simply existed where it could. The most prominent structure in the ring was a colossal stadium—a circular structure with seating all along the outside and a very large field in the center. It could easily have fit a behemoth.

The innermost ring was the smallest but the grandest. From the distance, Elaethia could see the ornate structures. The elegant capital building, the breathtaking High Cathedral, and some other assorted, equally glamorous buildings. One in particular made her forget to breathe. It was a pale white tower that pierced straight up with a glowing peak. It protruded so high that it seemed to dwarf even the cathedral.

"That's the Moon's Pillar," Lilian said. "It's where all the book-sniffers live and research. All those buildings around it are annexes for certain things."

"The Arcane Sages have many things locked away, do they not?" Elaethia asked.

"In the pillar? Yeah, or so I'm told. Stuff none of *us* will ever get to see. But all those little annexes are mostly open to the public, I think. Kinda like museums."

"What is a museum?"

"You've never heard of a … No, I guess you haven't. It's like a place that holds and collects priceless pieces of equipment or ancient artifacts—really anything that people would pay to see or study."

"One must pay to look at things?"

"Well, yeah. They're supposed to be really rare or unique. Like the staff of some legendary mage, or a tome from the dragon wars."

"And these items hold use in today's world?" Elaethia asked.

"Some of them, maybe," Lilian said

"What prevents people from stealing or using them?"

"Well they're locked behind really thick glass or enchanted cages. Only certain people can get to them."

"They are not used?"

"No. It's a museum. They're there to just study or admire."

"I do not understand the desire to simply admire them. What purpose does it serve to display old or broken items? But if some are functional, should they not be used?"

"Gaaaah, Elaethiaaa! You're so—"

"Anyway," Geran interrupted, "one of those museums is dedicated to the dragon wars. There's also a section just for dragon heroes, although we'd be pretty limited on what we'd learn from it."

Elaethia tilted her head. "Go on."

"That's it, really. We might be able to learn something about ancient dragon heroes, but it's more likely we'd just see epitaphs, scrolls, and statues of them. Our best bet for learning about what *you* can do is Mordecai getting us into the Moon's Pillar. According to him, they have records and scrolls all over their libraries."

"What is our immediate responsibility once we enter the city?" Elaethia asked.

"Reporting into the NDG, as well as giving our condolences to the Circle of Representatives."

"That could take a while," Shiro noted.

"Easily the rest of the day. Why, what's on your mind, Shiro?"

"It's such an amazing city. I have never seen anything like it. I want to explore it and see what it's like!"

"That'll take months."

"I would wish to see the museums," Elaethia stated firmly.

"Really singing a new tune about them now, aren'tcha?" Lilian goaded.

"I am not singing. I have been given more insight into them and have adjusted my views. I am now interested in what they have to offer."

Geran smiled. "That'll have to wait until tomorrow. Sometime in the afternoon."

"Hopefully after we can drop off our equipment," Shiro added.

Lilian scratched her ear. "That'll probably be in the tournament dormitories. All of us are participants, so hopefully they'll let us move in early."

Shiro wheeled around. "Wait. *All* of us? Including me?"

Geran made a face. "Did nobody tell you? You've been classified under 'duelist' so you'll be facing off against light weapons and armor. You can get a better description from the other two from Breeze when they get here with the rest of the participants."

"I don't know any of the duelists very well …"

"It's also probable they won't tell you much, considering it's entirely possible you might go up against them. You afraid to get knocked senseless, samurai?" Geran prodded.

"Not entirely. But the thought of raising my sword to an ally is unthinkable."

"In all honesty, Shiro, I'm not sure if you'll make it as far as them."

"Way to knock the wind out of his sails, Geran," Lilian said with a glare.

"No, he's right," Shiro said. "This is all very unfamiliar to me. I'll try my hardest, but I'm unversed in combat against the seasoned fighters of Linderry. I have utmost confidence in my blade and body, but my lack of knowledge and experience will cut me short."

"Aw, c'mon, Shiro! We've all seen you fight!" Lilian chirped. "All those dainty fencers won't be able to make a dent on you. Besides, this is Elaethia's first time too!"

"But she's Elaethia-sama and has the strength of fifty men."

"Is that accurate?" Geran asked the dragon hero.

She shrugged. "I do not know. I have never tested it."

"Well, one thing's for certain. We can definitely guarantee that Elaethia will bring the warrior trophy home for Breeze."

The entourage passed through the second wall into the middle terrace in the late afternoon. The adventurers split up from their guard counterparts as they passed the High Cathedral. The royal soldiers escorted Emily's remains to the nearest chapel to be prepared for burial. Cataclysm and Heaven's Light took their own gear out of the wagon once they reached the National Department of Guilds. Lilian stared woefully at her rucksack. She always hated wearing it, and this time was no different. With a deep inhale the girl grabbed it, braced herself, and heaved the bag onto her back before turning around with a stagger.

Lilian made a face at the two-story wood-and-stone office building. This was her third time seeing it, and every time she did she could swear it was supposed to be bigger. Maybe this was because it stood quite literally in the shadow of the massive coliseum. She glanced at Shiro and Elaethia, who also seemed confused at the lackluster building

Angela took note of their confused expressions. "You guys might be confusing this for Apogee's guildhall. The NDG is more like a meeting place and counsel for the seven guilds whenever they have to meet. There's a permanent staff inside that creates regulations and rules, but there're hardly ever any reps from the guilds here. It's kind of like a free bed and meeting room for overnight business as far as adventurers like us are concerned."

Lilian's mouth dropped as she lugged up her pack. "Wait, we get a free bed? They never did that for contenders before!"

"We never came here on a quest before. We'll see if we can crash here, report the quest, and then ask if we can move into the dorms early."

The paladin pushed the door to the office building open as the seven other adventurers followed behind. Everything was just as Lilian remembered. The front was fully reception style. A very large gated desk with three tellers was enclosed with an even larger back room. From what she could see, there were filing cabinets and safes going all the way to the back wall. A few civilians stood in line. To the left was a hallway with three office doors on each side. A flag with each guild insignia, with the exception of Apogee, was draped above them. To the right was a staircase going up as well as down, and a short hallway to wooden double doors.

"Hey!" Angela called from the desk. "We're good to stay the night here or walk down to the dorms. We can move into them tonight or tomorrow. You're choice."

The group almost unanimously agreed to stay in the NDG. Everyone except Angela and Geran began to pick up their gear and head upstairs. Lilian hefted her backpack higher onto her shoulders with a strained grunt and trudged after everyone. She got up a few steps before she leaned back and groaned.

"Everything all right, Lilian?" Geran asked as he came up behind her.

"Yeah … I just gotta … get up there." She ambled up the first set of stairs, huffing and puffing the whole way. She finally reached the first landing and leaned against the wall with a groan. "Baaaaaaw, this suuuucks."

"You had problems with this the last time you wore a rucksack too, right? I figured you would have packed more appropriately this time."

"Yeah, but … this time … we're here for … two weeks," she wheezed.

"Jeez, all right, lemme drop my stuff off; then I'll come help you." He disappeared around the corner up the stairs and then reappeared a minute later and reached for her pack.

"I feel like I've said this before, but all that magic you've got doesn't amount to much if you can't carry around the basic—" He grunted in surprise at the weight of the mage's ruck. "Son of a … What do you *have* in this thing?"

"Everything I need to get me through these two weeks," Lilian said

"I thought mages were supposed to travel light!"

"Where'd you hear that kinda nonsense?"

"Never mind that, just open the door for me when we get there."

Lilian walked up the rest of the stairs to open the door for Geran and watched as he dropped the ruck on the wooden floor with an audible groan. The pack made a loud thud as it met the ground. A couple clinks and tings accompanied it.

Geran raised an eyebrow. "What the ... Lilian, what's in there?"

"Hmm? Oh, nothing. Don't worry about it. Thanks, Gerry, you're such a sweetie. I think I can handle it from here."

"Not very reassuring, cat. What's in the bag?"

"I tooooold you, just the things I need to get through the weeks." She gave him an innocent smile, which he obviously didn't buy. He reached down and pushed the rucksack over. "Geran, wait, *no!*"

The pack fell over. The top flap burst open, and its contents spilled into the room. Inside were bottles, brushes, combs, pouches, purses, canisters, makeup kits, mirrors, clothes, loose change, and other bits and baubles the demicat had decided to bring along. Lilian tried to make an innocent smile, but even she had to admit that the pack looked as if it belonged to a small horde of goblins.

The ranger gave her a hard look. "Are you kidding me?"

"Whaaaaaat? I told you it's everything I need!"

"Everything you need? You're the only one who has this much crap!"

"Hey! It's *not* 'crap'! It's necessary!"

Geran threw his arms out. "How? How is even *half* of this stuff necessary?"

"Because I need it! How am I supposed to maintain my image and presence without them?"

"Image and presence ... *what?*"

"Yeah! I have to be in top condition and appearance at all times! I can *not* afford to be looking shabby in front of hundreds of thousands of people at *any* point in time!"

"The arena is huge! They can't even see you from the bleachers!"

"They still have that huge enchanted panel that displays everything going on in real time!"

"You're still being ridiculous," Geran insisted.

Lilian stamped her foot. "Hey! Not all of us are okay with looking like a beached trash barge like you, Geran!"

Lilian's face blanched as the ranger's eyes went ablaze. Her eyes suddenly widened, and her tail bushed out as her voice became small.

"I'm sorry ..."

Lilian shrieked as Geran lunged after her, chasing her around the small room. She scrambled around the floor, furniture, door, walls, and anything she could clamber across. The demicat rattled off apologies and objections in her rapid-fire style as they crashed around the room. The entire time, Lilian frantically tried to escape the ranger in the impromptu game of tag.

"I'm sorryyyyy!" she wailed. "I-didn't-mean-it-like-that-it-just-came-out-all-wrong-I'm-sorry-you-don't-actually-look-like-a-trash-barge-please-forgive-me-*ack-no-not-the-tail*-no-no-no-no-no-okay-okay-I'll-make-it-up-to-you-I'll-do-anything-I'll-polish-your-sword-I'll-wash-your-cloak-I'll-give-you-a-nice-haircut-just-please-leave-me-alo*ooonne!-oh-my-gosh-no*-you're-gonna-make-my-tunic-flap-up-Geran!-*Geran-my-panties-are-showing! Geran!*"

"Excuse me," Elaethia said from the doorway.

She was greeted with an odd spectacle. Lilian was face down on the wooden floor; arms flung out in front of her. Her eyes were watery, and her lip blubbered. The mage's butt was hoisted in the air in a very unladylike position, while her tunic had flapped up, exposing her rear end. Geran, his eyes still partially ablaze, looked up. Both his hands were wrung tightly around the demicat's poofed-out tail, and his leather boot was planted firmly on her behind.

"Is everything all right in here?" Elaethia asked.

Geran growled and let go. "Yeah. Just had a little spat is all."

He trudged out of the room. Elaethia shrugged and followed him. The members of Heaven's Light quickly ducked back into their own rooms as the fuming ranger passed by. Shiro suddenly poked his head into Lilian's room. She had partially recovered and began to adjust her clothing. The demicat knelt on the floor and sniffled as she repacked all her items.

"Are you okay, Lili-chan?" he asked tentatively.

"Huh? Oh, yeah, I'm fine." She cleared her throat and looked up at him. "Just, uh, cleaning up a little."

"Let me help." He strode in and picked up assorted bottles and beauty products. "What did you do to make Geran so mad?"

"Hmph," she pouted and rocked back to sit cross-legged while holding her sore tail. "Grumpy-pants doesn't understand thing one about appearance and aspiring legends. Hard to believe he actually managed to keep some of his girlfriends for as long as he did. I oughta teach him a lesson about relationships."

"But Lili-chan, you've never had a boyfriend."

She glared at him.

"S-sorry …"

"It's fine," she sighed. "Besides, you haven't had a girlfriend, either."

"That's true. I've always been so involved in my family and training."

"Same with me, for the most part. I guess you and I have that much in common."

"Yeah, we do." He looked at her, blushed, and looked away. "Say, Elaethia-sama and I were discussing looking at the museums tomorrow after we move into the dorms. Would you like to join?"

She nodded as they finished repacking her bag. "Yeah, of course."

"Great! I'll let you know when we go! I'm going to clean my gear and then find somewhere to eat tonight. Would you … like to join me?"

Lilian smiled. "All right, but *I'm* paying this time!"

"If you insist. We can take turns from now on."

She beamed. "Deal."

Cataclysm moved to the dorms the following morning. Later that afternoon, they decided to venture up to the third terrace to see the Moon's Pillar and its annexes. The third tier was significantly less busy than the other two, but there were still plenty of people around. Every single building was magnificent in its own regard: the towering spires of the cathedral, the massive dome of the senate building, the crenelated walls of the college, but especially the magnificent pale tower that was the Moon's Pillar.

"How …" Shiro breathed. "How has the mainland gone so far ahead of Osakyota? Such ingeniousness and beauty. How were such wonders built?"

"Magic," Geran stated plainly.

"Duh," Lilian followed in suit.

"That is logical. It is impressive nevertheless," Elaethia said.

She looked up at the ornate structures looming above them as she followed Geran in the direction of the Moon's Pillar. As they neared the base, she saw the annexes that Geran and Lilian had described. In fact, it seemed they were passing them the whole way. She wondered how many buildings and sections were a part of this museum.

"Geran, where are we going?" she asked.

"A little surprise for you, actually. I figured we'd start with something that'd pique your interest."

"What does it entail?" she asked.

"Well I *could* tell you, but then it wouldn't be a surprise anymore."

"Is there a need for it to be?"

He sighed. "Just humor me, all right?"

Cataclysm rounded a corner and began ascending some short steps to a very intricate building. Murals and tapestries were on prominent display at the front entrance—murals and tapestries of dragons.

Elaethia took it all in. "Geran. Is this …"

"The dragon museum," he stated proudly. "Inside is everything that's public knowledge regarding dragons, dragon heroes, and the dragon wars. Luckily for us, I was able to seal a private tour with the chief expert."

"You just keep proving yourself more and more resourceful, Geran," Shiro said.

"This wasn't too hard. I just asked for a personal favor. I was escorting the guy with some scrolls a few years back, and we got attacked by some thugs hired to steal them, presumably from a competitor. Long story short, I got him and the precious cargo here intact. He's been a good friend ever since."

Lilian gave him a bewildered look. "How many people do you know?"

Geran shrugged. "I've got contacts basically everywhere."

The front door opened, revealing a man in his midthirties. Clean shaven with brown hair, he wore a duster jacket and rimmed spectacles. "Aha! There's the man of the hour. Geran, my dear friend, how *have* you been?"

"Frederick!" Geran ran up and grasped his friend's hand in a hearty shake. "It's been a full year since I've seen you! How've you been?"

"Wonderful, my dear ranger! I say, I am quite chuffed at your arrival! Always a pleasure to welcome an old friend."

"The feeling's mutual. Let me introduce you to my party; they're all good friends of mine." Geran began to introduce Frederick to Cataclysm, the historian shaking each hand at the introductions. "Guys, this is Frederick Borough. He's a historian who's written encyclopedias and books about dragons. Right here is Shiro Inahari, an Osakyotan. This is Lilian Whitepaw, although I'm sure you've heard of her. Finally, this is—"

"Elaethia Frossgar, the dragon hero," Frederick finished. "Absolutely no introduction needed. My dear, your unique markings gave it away in a heartbeat. Fascinating. Absolutely *fascinating!* You cannot believe how honored I am to meet you. Forgive my demeanor, but you must understand how tickled I am to see a live dragon hero in person."

Elaethia tilted her head. "You do not appear to be laughing."

He tilted his head in like. "Beg pardon?"

"I thought people laughed when they have been tickled. Or at least showed signs of discomfort."

Frederick looked at Geran. "Is she well?"

Geran chuckled. "Healthy as a horse. She just takes a little getting used to. You'll warm up to her."

"I do not understand," Elaethia continued. "Does Frederick not have the capacity to laugh?"

"Let's find out, shall we?" Lilian said, and she wiggled her fingers with a devious look.

Geran rubbed his eyes. "Lilian, don't tickle the man who's about to give us a personal tour. Elaethia, should you be asking that? You laugh the least out of all of us."

"There has hardly been time for folly," she said.

"I forgot about how much of an ice queen you can be."

Shiro lit up. "I like that! Elaethia-sama, the ice queen! Or frost queen. Or frost … dragon … queen? Maybe?"

Frederick gave Geran a bewildered look. "This is the company *you* keep?"

"I'm still coming to terms with it myself. Can we go inside now?"

Frederick led the four adventurers into the museum. "To get to the dragon room, we first walk through the hall of heroes. To either side of you are exhibits displaying armor, weapons, and other various equipment used by dragon heroes from all factions. There are very few intact pieces of dragonite equipment these days, as most were destroyed during the wars. On top of that, while nearly impenetrable, dragonite is still organic matter. It is subject to breaking down and decomposing over time if not properly treated and maintained. Scales become flaked and disintegrate, while the bones turn brittle and shatter. The specimens you see around you have been kept here in Apogee for hundreds or thousands of years or were discovered in the condition you see them in. We have more, of course, but they aren't fit for display.

"There was no doctrine, baseline, or uniform for dragon heroes and their equipment. It was purely on the individual's preference. Even organized dragon hunting groups encouraged their members to make their armor and weapons as they saw fit. Looking around, you'll see this wide variety of styles and versions, from basic to extravagant, light to heavy, full body or partial. Dragon heroes prided themselves on their individuality. On the right you'll see the heavy armor and war hammer of Gerard Arcious, a lightning dragon hero who was also a cofounder of the dragon-hunting group Hell's Maw. On the left, you'll see the light mail and daggers of Olivia Hyedra, a water dragon hero who served as a peacekeeper for a city where Clearharbor is today. Arcious's deep purple armor seems to resemble Osakyotan style from the era, while Hyedra's light blue looks very similar to the stone and wooden growths one would see on a spriggan. After all, dragon heroes could afford to have exposed skin, since their bodies become significantly tougher after the conjoinment.

"Now take this one at the end of the hall, our most prized set. This was the ceremonial armor of Falk Listhgun, the dragon hero of the sun emperor. He was the champion of the sun dragon's king and had the title of high paladin. I will be quiet for a moment so you may observe in silence."

Silence was indeed what was needed. Elaethia was dumbfounded by the dazzling set of armor in front of her. The golden plates of dragon scales accompanied by pearl-white bone was a beautiful enough combination. But the gemstones, intricate plating, metalwork, infused gold and silver, and hand-carved designs of the shining set of armor made Elaethia forget to breathe. With such a dominating presence of regality, this was truly armor fit for a king of dragons. Elaethia felt almost inadequate with her own simple dark blue heavy plating and battleaxe. But the moment only made her even more prideful of her armor. It was made to her design, and of her own beloved dragon.

"Gosh," Lilian murmured. "Falk actually wore this?"

"Listhgun was the high paladin," Frederick explained. "He was *always* in armor: The heavy set for war, the light set for travel, and this one for public events."

Shiro tore his eyes away from the case. "You keep referring to them by their last names."

"In those days, heroes took the names of the dragons they conjoined with. In most cases, it was a show of respect and recognition for the dragons who gave up their own earthly lives. Other times it was used as bragging rights to show off one's status. But it was all started by the dragons themselves. Still very much alive and aware inside their brehdar counterparts' minds, they referred to one another as dragons. The tradition stuck. By all accounts, Elaethia, you should be referred to as 'Frossgar' instead of your given name."

She shook her head. "It was enough that I changed my family name. Frossgar saw little need for his name to be known, let alone used as a symbol of status."

"How curious. But it makes sense when I think about it. Now, follow me to the dragon room." Frederick led the adventurers into a dome-like room filled with tapestries, murals, carvings, scrolls, scales, bones, and even an enormous intact skeleton of a dragon.

Shiro glanced around. "There isn't as much in here as I thought there would be."

Frederick nodded. "Yes, our collection is rather small, but it is still the largest in the world. Keep in mind that dragons were killed and harvested for thousands of years. To be able to find much of them is astonishing. Think of this as more of a place of insight as opposed to one of display. Here we have tomes and recordings of each of the nine species of dragons and how they lived. We have nearly complete information regarding each faction's way of life."

"Dragons had lifestyles?" Geran asked.

"Oh yes. While appearing beastlike, they were still sentient. All of them were unique, and I have vast knowledge of them all—save one, of course, but nobody ever knew much about that species to begin with. In fact, I was asked to write a section inside the pocket guide to the dragon wars titled *The Draconic Codex*. Inside this little book is—"

"You mean this one?" Elaethia said, and she pulled out the small leather-and-metal book from her satchel.

Frederick froze. "I … Yes, actually. What a coincidence. How did you come across a copy?"

"Mordecai gifted it to me in return for assorted knowledge of my own."

"Regarding frost dragons, I presume?" he asked.

"Correct."

"Bah," the curator scowled. "That man. He hordes knowledge no matter the type, regardless of whether or not he can even use it."

Shiro raised a hand. "We can still share with you the information we gave him."

Frederick shrugged. "That seems fair. But you should have told me that you read my encyclopedia. I would have been quite pleased to know that the world's only dragon hero studied my work."

Elaethia shook her head. "I apologize; I did not know you were the author."

Frederick raised an eyebrow. "But you read it, did you not?"

"I have."

"Isn't the author's name just as important as the book? Were you never curious to know the name of the individual who provided the information?"

"I was not. Should I have been?"

"Anyway," Geran stepped in as Frederick's face began to shrink. "I think you should tell us what you already know about frost dragons. We'll fill in anything we know that you don't afterward."

"Ahh. Frost dragons," Frederick sighed. "I apologize in advance and mean no ill intent when I say they were an uninteresting species. They were completely reclusive, found only in Svarengel and northern Linderry. Frost dragons were the only species to choose to live their entire lives in absolute solitude. The only time they ever interacted with each other was for mating, and then they would immediately return to their own territories. As a result of this behavior, frost dragons were *highly* territorial, attacking anything and everything that came too close. I can count on one hand how many frost dragon heroes there were, including Elaethia. Two were desperate for survival after being hunted and lived short lives thereafter. The other dragon was forced to conjoin with a hero by a dragon-hunting group."

Elaethia's eyes hardened. "Forced to? I thought a brehdar could not take a dragon's power by force."

"They can't. They captured and tortured the young frost dragon to insanity, until it finally gave in. This group, whose name was purposefully forgotten, wanted at least one of every type of dragon hero in their ranks. The insane dragon joined with the decided hero, but it didn't last. Two minds in one head was taxing enough as it was. It didn't help that the young dragon's own mind was broken. The hero didn't function very long, and not well while he did. He killed himself after only two weeks of conjoinment."

Geran winced. "That's ... disturbing."

"So now you see my fascination with Elaethia," Frederick said. "Somehow a frost dragon, Frossgar, agreed to make you his champion after ... how many years of life?"

"He was around thirty-four hundred years old," Elaethia said.

Frederick shook his head. "It simply boggles the mind. It goes against everything my research has led me to believe about frost dragons. His age is also astounding. Frost dragons had the longest lifespans, even outpacing their earthen cousins, who were known to hibernate. The longest-living dragon on record was a little over two thousand. Frossgar was a millennium older than that. Such a long life to spend only in seclusion."

Elaethia nodded. "In his younger years, he longed and fought to be alone. It was not until the wars that he allowed another dragon to visit him with information—an air dragon named Thereous. It was not until long after the wars that Frossgar and I met."

"Thereous ... Why does that name sound familiar to me? Maybe in my notes?" Frederick fumbled into one of his pockets to pull out a notepad with a watch attached to it. "Oh! By the Moon, I'm late for an appointment! I apologize, everyone, but I must go. Feel free to continue to look around, and I will root for you all in the tournament!" With that, Frederick Borough ran off in the direction they came from.

"Did you learn anything noteworthy, Elaethia-sama?" Shiro asked.

She shook her head. "No. I had hoped to learn of magical abilities or special skills I may use. He left before I was able to ask."

Geran folded his arms. "Well, we can catch him again before we return to Breeze. There may be something of use written around here, too."

"We shall see. However, I would like to know about them before the tournament."

"Finally warming up to it, aren'tcha?" Lilian goaded

"I still have little interest in placement or winning. I wish to practice what I have on strong opponents, as Geran mentioned."

Lilian shrugged. "Suit yourself, but you know you won't be allowed to use magic in there."

"I will not?"

"Of course not. It's a warrior fight, not a mage fight!"

Elaethia frowned. "Unfortunate."

Rychus stood alone on his balcony. The sun was setting over the tropical coastal city of Paragon. Disturbing news had been coming to him nonstop. Trafficking was more prominent. Magicians had become more and more scarce. Word of uprisings had become more frequent. Now there was news of Linderry getting stronger and stronger as time went on. Something about this year was different. His contacts kept hearing of a single warrior that had unimaginable power, potentially as strong as his own. The voice in his head began to whisper again as Rychus rubbed his temples. He needed more information about this warrior. All he had to go on was a name—"Elaethia."

What troubled him most was not that this was a capable warrior but that her name was Arminian. That meant she may have been one of his subjects. She needed to be found and returned. Elaethia would undoubtedly have information regarding how she had managed to escape. She would prove either a useful tool or a threat that needed to be exterminated. The voice whispered again. Yes, that was another option. Maybe her power would sate his own and he could regain control.

Chapter 15
The Tournament

Sixth Era.139. Miyan 25.

"All right, everyone," Angela began as Cataclysm and Heaven's Light met in the dorm. "Here's what we know of the three events for each class so far. With the exception of the rangers, all classes have a one-on-one elimination-style bracket. The goal is to defeat your opponent by the means and methods allowed. If you win, you progress to the next stage. If you lose, you're out. There's no consolation bracket except for third place. Points are assigned to the guild depending on what places we finalize in."

"Why don't the rangers have a bracket?" Shiro asked.

Lilian leaned back in her chair to sneer at Geran. "'Cause nobody'd want to watch 'em slap at each other like schoolgirls. They just shoot targets and tackle deer."

The ranger glared at her. "It's called 'fawn wrangling.'"

"Pfft. Fawn wrangling. It even *sounds* dumb."

"Anyway," Angela interjected. "Besides the bracket elimination, everyone else has a power or skill competition. Warriors, mages, and paladins have a single strike measurement. The duelists will compete over speed as opposed to power. Rangers will have their traditional archery event. That's all we know about them."

"And what of the final events?" Elaethia asked.

"They change every year, but we have some insight thanks to Geran's snooping."

Geran nodded and pulled out a notebook. "Warriors, duelists, and druids will be fighting atronachs. Duelists and druids fight a brehdar-sized one alone, while all three warriors from each guild will team up to fight a single large one. Rangers and Paladins will have a battle royal, where all of them are put in the arena and fight each other until there is only one left. Monks have some sort of shot put–style competition, but the points are decided both on the weight of the object and how far they throw it. I couldn't find any more detail surrounding these events."

Lilian's hand shot in the air. "Hold up! You forgot the mages."

"Nope. I just couldn't find anything on them."

"No, no, no I saw something written about 'em in your little notebook. What do we have?"

"Did you? You oughta get your eyes checked. Whatever you have, it's probably more interesting than rangers slapping each other and tackling deer, right?"

"Geraaaan!" Suzanna moaned, and resting her chin on his arm. "You're hiding something! Can't you tell us? Pretty please?"

Geran looked down at the red-haired elf. "Suzanna, you're not even competing."

"But Geran …" She touched her fingers to his wrist and tapped them slowly. The mage gave him big eyes and a pitiful whimper.

Geran sighed and put his palm to his face. "Fine. The mages are also fighting a single large atronach."

"*Yippee!*" Suzanna jumped in the air with a few girly twirls. She sat back down and hummed in excitement while she rocked side-to-side.

Angela continued. "Just as a heads-up, these atronachs are a new generation made by the Arcane Sages. We can expect them to be tough."

Shiro nodded with a grunt. "I eagerly anticipate any worthy opponent."

"The Arcane Sages assist in the tournament?" Elaethia asked.

Samantha raised an eyebrow. "You kidding? They make it possible. The NDG organizes everything, but the Sages actually put it all together. They're the backbone of the recovery and medical teams, and to top it all off, they have this massive screen thingy that shows everything happening in real time. Spectators can watch the events as if they've got front-row seats!"

"How is such a thing possible?"

The demibear shrugged. "I dunno. Moon knows what combination of magic and engineering they use to power the thing."

"Back to the point," Geran interjected. "Make sure to use this downtime to prepare yourselves. Do individual drills, and keep yourself in shape. We're all different classes here, except for Lilian and Suzanna, so it's not like we can practice on each other."

"Understood," Elaethia said. "Perhaps we can spar with our fellow guild members when they arrive."

Samantha laughed. "Good luck finding someone whose willing to train with you."

"I don't need a partner," Lilian announced. "I'm gonna keep practicing my spell alter … I mean concentration!"

"I'm gonna practice too!" Samantha said, joining the excitement. "I plan to blow myself out every day with enhancement magic! Cas! Think you can keep me goin'? You can practice your spells while we're at it!"

The demiwolf looked up. "I don't mind."

Angela sighed. "Well, you can drain our little priestess dry all you want. I'll alternate my holy magic and fighting techniques."

Cassie shook her head. "I ... I can help you too, Angela."

"Not a chance, sweetheart. That's your biggest problem, remember? You've got to stop trying to help everyone at once. You push yourself way too much."

"But ... I just want to ..."

Angela set a hand on the priestess's shoulder. "I know, Cas. You're really strong for being just sixteen, but you don't have the magic or skill to do all that. We'll get you there, though."

The demiwolf mumbled something and buried her floppy sleeves in her lap.

Lilian's face lit up. "Oh yeah! Shiro! We need to get you a conduit! You can have Cassie teach you *moonlight*, and you can keep me goin' too!"

"Of course, Lili-chan! I don't know how well I can fight with this magic, but I want to use it as best I can."

The demicat shot up and dragged him out of his chair. "Perfect! Let's go shop for a new conduit!"

They were out the door before anyone, including Shiro, could say a word.

"Well"—Angela blinked—"those two certainly get along."

"Almost *too* well," Geran noted. "Have you seen how all over each other they are?"

Samantha fluttered a hand. "Ah, c'mon, they aren't doing anything juicy. Yet."

"Mm-hmmm," Suzanna hummed. "Lilian's got him wrapped around her finger. I can't wait to see how far they go."

Cassie looked down and mumbled something.

"One more time, sweetheart?" Angela soothed.

"I ... I don't want t-to talk about these kinds of th-things ..."

"I have little desire for such conversation myself," Elaethia agreed. "Although I do not entirely understand what you all are referring to, I believe Shiro and Lilian's business is their own. If you are not bold enough say it in their presence, you do not deserve to speak about it behind their backs."

Geran stood. "Fair enough. But I think we've lost focus. I'm gonna go for a run."

Angela stood as well. "I'd like to join you if you don't mind. Could you wait for me to get my armor on first?"

Sixth Era.139. Jinum 10.

Finally it was the day of the tournament. All of Breeze's competitors and Master Dameon gathered in a large preparation room beneath the arena's bleachers. Elaethia recognized most of the twenty contenders in the room. The warriors were simple; it was her, Liam Barron, and Peter Stone. The rangers included Geran, Roderick Griffith from Razorback, and a dwarf she barely recognized as Byron. Besides Shiro, for the duelists there was also Nathan Beckett, the one who had been turned away for the escort; and a trim elf Elaethia didn't recognize. From conversation, she learned her name was Erin.

Lilian, Remus Lichen from Earth Shatter, and another unknown named Charlie were the mages. Angela Bright, Micah Roth from Earth Shatter, and a man named Derrick represented the paladins. The druids consisted of River Cartwright from Razorback, Daniel from a party called Back Blast, and an unknown named Trevor. Finally, the monks had Samantha Shoemaker from Heaven's Light and two unknowns named Jarrod and Mikaela.

Master Dameon looked up from a roster. "All right, rascals, get with your respective class members. Now that we're all accounted for, this is your last chance to let me know if something's wrong with you. If you're feeling sick or hurting, we'll get you looked at. If you're broken and trying to act tough, you'd better tell me. I'm not gonna be happy with you if you get damaged beyond repair. And for the love of the Sun, if you're thinking of chickening out, tell me right now so you don't embarrass us by doin' it in the arena in front of half of Linderry."

Elaethia turned to Liam. "Half of the country is in the city to watch?"

"Nah," he responded. "But a good amount of 'em. Although I did hear rumors of the Sages fiddling around with hologram mirrors in the region capitals. Civvies can watch everything we do on them. But occasionally a couple officials from Armini and Osakyota watch too."

"Curious. None from Svarengel?"

"You kiddin'? Those northerners don't care about us. The western ones are too busy sea-raiding and yak-herding. Last I heard, the eastern ones are in the middle of a civil war."

"I see."

Master Dameon looked up. "If you two are done socializing, I'd like to get on with the itinerary and events. How it's lookin' for today is as follows: First off is all the warrior, monk, duelist, and paladin events. The finals regarding the one-on-one fights will be held tomorrow at the very end. Tomorrow starts in the forest, where the druids will kick it off with all their events, followed by the rangers. Once those are wrapped up, there will be an intermission to move back to the arena. The mages will go, and then the tournament will finish off with the finals of all one-on-ones. The points will be tallied, the winners and prizes will be announced, we dance, we drink, we cry, we go home. Any questions?"

Shiro raised his hand. "Um …"

"No questions. Great! Stone, Barron, Frossgar, you're up first. Are you ready?"

The three of them nodded.

"Good. The one-on-ones are first, and so are you, Liam. You're fighting some hick from Dinkerage named Eli. You've got five minutes to get out there. Make sure those enchanters get that dulling enchantment on your stick there. If they find out your weapon is still sharp, both of us are in deep shit."

"Ohoho!" the demiwolf grinned and flipped his heavy spear. "It's on now, fellas. See you in the semifinals."

Liam stepped into the arena for the third time in his adventuring career. The demiwolf's thoughts drifted back to the previous years. He'd been number two every time except this one, but that was fine with him. Elaethia definitely deserved that number-one spot, and Peter right behind her. Liam chuckled. *Blondie was pretty pissed that Frosty took his spot. But it was kinduva bummer how quickly he got over it.* Liam was ready to send verbal jabs at him all week. But now it was time to send real jabs at some opponents.

The enormous crowd exploded into cheers and roars as the two warriors stepped up to each other. Their weapons enchanted, the referee stood ready, and the overhead screen followed their every step. Liam flashed a grin and hefted his spear to the crowd. He got exactly what he wanted, as the deafening roars of the spectators pumped hot blood through every vein. Number one, number two, number three—it didn't matter. He had only gotten stronger since last year, and he'd kick anyone's ass to prove it, starting with this Dinkerage guy.

The shaggy-haired human named Eli had plain steel armor with a sword and shield. He was heavyset and definitely looked like he could take a hit. Liam looked at Eli's stride and form. Taking hits was obviously all this guy was good for, considering how weak his footwork was. Liam guessed this would be over before he knew it.

"Gentlemen, touch weapons!" The elven referee commanded. Liam and Eli connected blades in the sign of good sportsmanship. "The warriors are ready. Gentlemen, fight!"

The ref threw his hand in the air and backed up as Eli barreled toward the demiwolf. Liam sized him up and threw a fast jab at his opponent's unguarded shins. Eli threw his shield down to intercept the blow and succeeded, at the cost of halting his charge. Eli glared, flung his shield up to knock Liam's spear away, and charged again.

Liam smirked. "Dumbass."

The spearman pulled a maneuver he was very fond of. He drop-stepped back and balanced his heavy weapon across his shoulders with the momentum Eli provided. Liam whipped around to heave his arm across his body, directing the spear in an unnaturally fast side-slash. The spearhead slammed into the side of Eli's helmet and sent the human crashing to the ground, the helmet popping off and rolling through the dust. Still conscious, but just barely, Eli tried to stand, but he was slammed back down by Liam's boot. The crowd roared in approval at the sheer one-sidedness of the first battle. Liam rested the spear tip on the back of his opponent and turned to the ref.

"Pin," Liam announced.

The referee threw his hand up. "Barron has pinned his opponent! This fight goes to Breeze!"

The crowd erupted again as Liam hefted his spear into the air to urge them to cheer louder. He bumped a fist to his chest and pointed at the screen as he walked back to the standby rooms. He had advanced to the next bracket.

Elaethia watched as the first round of warriors clashed with each other. She didn't fight in the first bracket, as her spot was a bye. She had no idea what that meant. Either way, she had to wait until the next round, which, of course, she was late for. She found this out the hard way as Dameon came charging into the preparation room nearly out of breath.

"*Frossgar!*" he gasped.

"Yes?"

"What are you doing? You're up! If you aren't out there in thirty seconds, you'll be disqualified!"

She tilted her head. "Why would I be disqualified?"

"Forget that! Just go! Get out there!"

"Very well. Although you do not need to shout. I am perfectly capable of hearing you at such a distance."

She stood up, donned her helmet, grabbed her battleaxe, and walked toward the arena as the announcer's voice boomed throughout the stadium.

"Breeze's third warrior has still not shown! If she doesn't appear soon, this match will go to Apogee by default! If my watch is correct, she has … Ten! Nine! Eight! Seven! Six! Fi— What's this? Someone's coming out from the east wing! Could it be? Yes! Our second fighter, and fashionably late, Elaethia Frossgar!"

Cheers and boos alike resulted from the warrior emerging from her tunnel. It was an uncomfortable setting for her. There were so many people. She wondered how on earth some of her compatriots enjoyed such a thing. Elaethia walked to the center, where the referee and her supposed opponent were waiting.

The elven judge looked at her. "About time. You got all the requisite enchantments on your weapon there?"

"I do."

"Good. Warriors, touch weapons," he commanded. Elaethia extended her massive axe, while the opponent from Apogee clanged against it with his two-handed sword.

"I'm gonna beat your ass for making me wait so long," he said.

Her reply was steady. "We shall see."

This large, brown-haired demiwolf was well built and seemed quite competent given his form and stance. Perhaps he would give her the challenge and experience she was looking for.

"Warriors, fight!"

As the referee threw his hands down, he began to glow. It seemed this elf was a monk and used his enhancements to disengage from the fight quickly. *How curious.*

Her opponent seized the opportunity.

"Eyes front, moron!" He lunged forward and slammed the blade into her left thigh. She didn't even flinch. "Wh … what..?"

He, the ref, and the crowd were all stunned.

Elaethia looked down at her leg, which appeared to have had a two-handed sword bounce off of it. She cursed at herself. What would Jörgen say if he saw her forget about her opponent like that? She sighed, both at her own carelessness and at her disappointment at this man's strength. She wound up and swung the massive axe upward, catching the demiwolf in the ribs. The warrior was lifted off his feet and sent through the air; he crashed to the dusty ground twenty meters away. The arena went dead quiet.

Elaethia looked around and then at the referee. "Have I won?"

The elven referee stared in shock for a few moments and then remembered how to speak. "A-Apogee's warrior is unable to continue fighting. Frossgar wins!"

The arena exploded into cheers. The deafening roar became beyond what she could handle, so she turned and escaped back to the tunnel as the announcer spoke again.

"What an incredible display of strength! I don't think I've ever seen anything like this in the warrior competitions! This woman is insane! She's unbelievable! She's absolutely on a whole other level and she's … already gone … Very well! Once the medical team has cleared the field, we'll continue on with the second bracket of the warrior fights!"

The rest of the brackets were nearly identical for Elaethia. The next fight she was assigned ended before it started, as her opponent forfeited as soon as she saw whom she was going to be up against. The elven woman got halfway into the arena, saw the dragon hero, froze, and promptly turned around without a word.

Liam approached Elaethia after the fourth round, hobbling along with a bruised face and a little grin. "Jeez, Frosty. You're really tearin' it up out there! I'm almost glad I just got knocked out, else I might have to fight you."

"That would be unfortunate. Your company is less enjoyable than what I currently keep, but you are a good man, as well as one of my compatriots. I would not wish to hurt you."

"I'll take that as a compliment," he groaned as he slumped into a chair. "That crowd is really something, huh? They sure like you."

"I cannot express mutual feelings. It is quite an annoyance."

"Really? They don't get your blood pumping like crazy?" Liam asked.

"They do not. It is important to keep a level mind and a calm approach. Such masses of people interfere with my concentration."

"Huh. Oh well, guess I shouldn't be surprised. You heard about Peter yet?"

"I have not."

"He's killin' it. Blondie's crushing his way through almost as easily as you are. We're getting to the semifinals, so don't be surprised if you have to clobber him a little."

"It would not be the first time," she recalled.

"Hah! You're right; I forgot about that!" He laughed again and winced. "Ah well. I'm gonna take a load off while I wait for one of our priests to come down here. Those medical teams on the field are really stingy."

"Very well, I will leave you to rest. It is nearing my turn to fight again."

Elaethia easily won all the way to the semifinals. She emerged again from her tunnel into the accursed cheers and roars from the crowd. Her opponent appeared after her, a dwarven man about her age. His armor was thick, and his weapon—a halberd—was taller than he was. That didn't amount to much, since he was hardly five foot four—seven inches shorter than she was. Elaethia hadn't fought many dwarves from a warrior standpoint. They were a stocky race, and very sturdy. But their height inhibited their combat effectiveness in certain areas. She figured he chose a polearm to compensate for his lack of reach. All these things considered, he was certainly not an opponent to take lightly. He had gotten this far; therefore, she knew he must be skilled. Following the prefight customs, the two warriors touched weapons and stood ready to fight.

The referee gave the signal.

Instead of charging straight for her, the dwarf stepped back and aimed the tip of his halberd to level the hook at her at neck height. She understood now. Like her, he was accustomed to his opponent launching an immediate attack in a show of brute strength. Given his footing and the way he held his weapon, she realized he intended to hook her from behind the neck and throw her down—a difficult, but very effective, maneuver. It would not have worked on *her*, but she was impressed nonetheless.

Seeing that he would not initiate the attack, she took matters into her own hands. Elaethia could simply run him down, but that was not the reason she was here. This was a learning experience, and he had provided her with a new situation. No matter how she could deflect it, the dwarf could still maneuver his weapon back into position to defend himself—that is, unless she came from above.

Elaethia leaped into the air over his head and raised her massive axe to bring it down on top of him. The dwarf was surprised, but not stunned, by her inhuman leap. As she predicted, he maneuvered his halberd to intercept her as she came down. She clashed her axe into it to deflect it and thrust a kick downward to his chest. At the last moment, the dwarf leaped backward out of the way. Elaethia impacted the earth where he once stood, billowing up a cloud of dust.

The dwarf leveled his halberd to lunge back at the spot where she had landed. He was about to charge when a flash of dark blue flew toward him at a speed he could not visually comprehend. Elaethia body-slammed the dwarf and sent the stout warrior careening backward, causing his weapon to fly out of his hands.

Dazed, he attempted to rise until he looked up. Once again Elaethia was airborne, poised to strike. She landed, slamming the axe into the dirt, which shook the ground and created another massive cloud of dust. The audience went quiet. Once the area cleared; it revealed Elaethia standing over her opponent. Her axe lay embedded in the sand over his shoulder.

"Sprigganwood's warrior has been pinned! Frossgar wins!" the referee declared.

The crowd went wild. *Sprigganwood?* Elaethia had thought that guild was fairly weak. She looked down at the coughing dwarf, who began to brush the dirt from his beard.

She extended a gauntlet. "Thank you."

He took it as she helped him to his feet. "Hrm? For what?"

"For an enlightening battle. You are the most experienced warrior I have fought with in a while. I learned much from you."

"That makes me feel a bit better. By the Sun … that really knocked the wind outta me."

"I apologize. I did not wish to harm you," she said.

"You were goin' easy on me?"

"Yes."

"And just like that, I feel less better."

Elaethia's guild members greeted her with enthusiasm as she entered the common room. Even Peter's somewhat hostile attitude toward her gave way to a hint of a smile.

Master Dameon laughed and put an enormous hand on her shoulder. "Well done, my girl! We've got someone in the finals, and I dare say we've won the warrior brackets!"

She looked at Peter. "Only one?"

"Yup." The blond human nodded. "I lost. The dude from Clearharbor is insane. He's got a party named Maelstrom, and it revolves completely around him. That shield and flail are a pain in the ass to deal with."

"Flail?" She tilted her head. That was interesting but troubling. The flail was a clumsy weapon and hardly practical. Unless used proficiently, a flail was almost as deadly to the wielder as it was to the opponent.

"Can you tell me how he fights? What technique does he use?" she asked.

"That's tough to say. The fight didn't last long. His flail has spikes on it, and when it wrapped around my greatsword, it swung back over and nailed me in the face. I got put on my ass and pinned by his shield after that. Only other piece of information that could help you is that he keeps the ball and chain constantly moving. If you interrupt his pattern, you get an opening. Or *you* could just bowl him over. Whatever works."

"I see." She nodded. "Thank you."

"You can thank me when you win tomorrow. Take the trophy home for us."

After a short break, it was time for the second event. This one was called the "hit measurement." Master Dameon explained that this was a show of strength, but this didn't answer any of her questions. She thought this entire event supposed to be a show of strength. Her brow furrowed as she, Peter, and Liam exited the tunnel and emerged into the sunlight. She looked around to see every other warrior from the other guilds enter as well, from their own tunnels. All that was in the enormous arena was a metal pedestal in the center. *How confusing.* There was little she could infer from this.

Liam bumped a fist on her shoulder. "You good, Frosty? Can't say I've ever seen you make that face before. You ain't afraid you'll lose, are you?"

"What is this line we are forming?" she asked.

He pointed to the pedestal. "See that gemstone at the front? That thing turns your hit into a number. Your number gets turned into points."

"How do we get this number?"

He gave her a confused look. "Hit it."

"That is all?"

"Yeah, this one's really straightforward. I can go before you if you wanna see how it's done."

"We are the last three in line."

"Well, yeah, but I thought I'd help."

"I see. If you wish to go ahead of me, I have no issue."

He grinned and stepped ahead of her. "Well, if you insist."

"I made no indication of insistence," she stated. Liam smacked himself in the face.

The twenty-one-person line slowly made progress nearer and nearer to the center of the arena. Elaethia watched, intrigued, as the numbers were displayed above their heads as the warriors struck the pedestal. 234. 192. 257. They all seemed to average around the low two hundreds. The highest number she saw was 381; the lowest was 79.

Finally it was Breeze's turn. Peter stepped up first and hefted his greatsword. He glared at the clear gemstone and brought the blade down with a yell. The giant weapon struck its target and bounced off onto the sandy ground. His number appeared: 366—the second-largest number they'd seen today.

"Tch!" he spat as he sheathed his large sword and looked to his guildmates. "Looks like we're only gonna have two of us place. You got something up your sleeve, Barron?"

The demiwolf flipped his spear. "Nothin' fancy. Just gonna try a running start."

He took several steps back and checked his grip and footing. He inhaled deeply and charged forward at the gemstone, growing a shout as he got nearer. Once he approached it, he thrust his spear forward with all his might. The heavy metal blade clanged just off center and ricocheted to the left.

"Aaahhhh, shit ..." His ears drooped as he looked at the screen, which displayed a score of 269. "Welp. I obviously gotta work on my aim. Better than what I expected, though. You're up, Frosty."

"The goal is only to strike it as hard as one can?" she asked.

"Yep. Hold nothin' back."

"Hold nothing back?"

"Exactly. Clobber it. Full power. Give it everything you've got." He waved good luck and started to walk backward.

Elaethia looked at the gemstone in front of her and tilted her head. She didn't know how this object worked, but if she simply needed to strike it for it to function, that was enough instruction. She unsheathed her battleaxe and hoisted it above her head. *Hmm ... Hold nothing back?* Elaethia had never tried to swing the battleaxe as hard as she could before. The dragon hero inhaled deeply, paused, and swung with all her might with an inbrehdar yell.

From the crowd's perspective, there wasn't even a swing; there was simply a warrior poised to strike, and then suddenly an explosion of dust filled the arena. Bits of earth, stone, and sand flew in every direction, even going so high as to hit the screen hundreds of feet in the air. Once the dust settled after several minutes, all that remained in the center of the arena was a crater and a dragon hero wrenching her axe from the stony earth. The gemstone and the solid metal pedestal it sat on were completely gone. Everyone's eyes fixed on Elaethia as she yanked her weapon free.

The announcer's voice finally came over the speakers. "Ladies and gentlemen, we had a uh ... *slight* technical difficulty with the gemstone reader. The enchanters have the last recorded numerical value before they lost contact and are putting it up now. Bear in mind this is not the actual score, just the final number before the malfunction."

Everyone's eyes shot over to the screen as the number appeared. Gasps and murmurs enveloped the stadium. The number grew staticky and glitched until the screen turned white.

999.

Elaethia inspected her axe. There didn't seem to be any damage—no cracks, bends, warping, or the like. Were it not for the enchantment, she was certain, it would at least have been dulled significantly. However, the dragonite battleaxe didn't seem worse for wear. She looked up to the screen. It was blank. *Disappointing.* She had been curious to see what would happen. She waved the dust away from her face and turned to the silent crowd, who were entirely fixated on her. She looked around, tilted her head, and sneezed.

The final event for the warriors consisted of all three members from a guild going up against a single atronach. It came as no surprise that Breeze was selected last for this event. Elaethia watched keenly as the other six guilds battled against their mechanical foes. Clearharbor and Apogee defeated the metallic monstrosities with ease, while Frostshire was the only guild to fail. Elaethia, Liam, and Peter stood in the tunnel, awaiting the signal to enter the arena.

"Okay, brain buckets on, people," Peter instructed as he put on a white steel close-faced helmet.

Elaethia tilted her head. "Brain buckets?"

"That means put your helmet on," Liam explained as he donned a dark barbuta.

"I understand. Is there a method you wish to use in this battle, or shall I simply go ahead?"

Peter looked back. "Yeah, actually. Let's try this …"

Two minutes later, the three warriors from Breeze emerged. Once again the crowd erupted into cheers, louder than ever at Elaethia's presence. However, she didn't realize she was the center of attention. The trio stopped in the center of the arena and looked around at the wild audience. Liam and Peter were obviously riled up, as they encouraged the crowd with gestures and flexes. None of this made any sense to her, but they seemed to be enjoying themselves.

Finally, the announcer's voice sounded. "It's time for today's final warrior event! Let the last battle against the atronachs begin! Warriors, are you ready?"

Liam and Peter pounded their armor and whooped into the air. Elaethia simply raised her gauntlet.

"The warriors are ready! Enchanters, release your atronach!"

Peter pulled out his greatsword. "Here we go. Just as we planned."

Liam gripped his spear. "You sure you've done this before, man? This seems kinda … crazy."

"How do you think my party got its name? 'Course I've done this before. It's only crazy if it doesn't work."

The three stood side by side as the tunnel on the other end began to rumble. A glint caught their eyes as the atronach emerged into the sunlight. Elaethia realized it was crouching as it moved through the tunnels. The humanoid creation of magic and metal stood fully upright as it marched into the arena with thundering footsteps.

Peter stepped back a bit. "Woah …"

"Big fella," Liam commented.

"Is it just me, or is this one bigger than last year's?"

"I think it's bigger than the rest of 'em *this* year."

"Does this affect your plan, Peter?" Elaethia asked.

"Nah. Same as we went over. Although it's a little more dependent on Liam now."

The demiwolf flipped his spear. "A'ight, pressure's on."

"Okay, Let's go!"

The three charged head-on to the enormous atronach. Liam in front, Elaethia directly behind him, and Peter several meters back. As they got closer, Elaethia got a full appreciation for the machine. The others seemed about five meters tall, while this one was the size of a small troll—nearly seven meters.

Peter shouted up at his compatriots. "Elaethia, you gotta be spot-on with that block! Liam's gotta get there in one piece!"

"Understood," the dragon hero called.

Liam turned. "Frossgar, on the Moon, if that thing pancakes me I'm gonna haunt you."

"I have no intention of allowing such things to happen," she called back.

"Glad to hear it! Here I go!"

The atronach raised its clubbed right arm to smash down on Liam. The demiwolf dropped on his back to slide between its legs as Elaethia swung her axe to intercept the massive, metal limb. With a quick glance; Elaethia noticed that the atronach had to kneel to land its strike.

"Liam!" she called. "Attack the right leg while it is on the ground!"

"Thaaaank *you!*"

He leaped up, aimed his spear, and drove the heavy polearm into the back of the atronach's right knee. He jammed it between the plated joints and wrenched it further in. The machine buckled and started to turn toward him.

His ears flattened. "Uh, guys? If you're gonna do the thing, now's the time to do it!"

"Frossgar!" Peter sprinted up behind her as she wheeled around and offered the flat of her axe to him. Peter leaped onto it and jumped as Elaethia stood to launch him like a springboard. Peter flew nine meters in the air, floating above the giant machine as it turned to face him. Before it could raise an arm, Peter landed on its head and drove his greatsword through its face. The atronach lurched backward, and collapsed to the dusty ground with an earth-shaking boom.

Liam dived out of the way as Peter leaped off and rolled to his feet. All three turned to see the lifeless, defeated atronach.

"*Yes!*" Peter screamed into the air as the crowd went insane. Whooping and hollering, he and Liam high-fived and slammed their heads together.

Liam grabbed Peter's shoulders. "Did we just set a record?"

"By the Sun, I hope so!"

"Hell yeah! Elaethia, up top!" The demiwolf put a hand up for her.

The dragon hero looked up. "Where?"

"No, I mean give me a high-five!"

"I see." She had seen them done before but had never tried it. She bumped the palm of her gauntlet against his open-handed bracer.

Liam made a face. "You gotta work on that."

"Hey, Elaethia?" Peter called from the atronach. His helmet was removed and he had a hand on the hilt of his greatsword, which was still lodged in the machine's face. "Mind, uh … giving me a hand?"

Liam sneered. "Pfft! C'mon, blondie! Use them muscles, put your back into it!"

"Can it, dog-breath! Unless *you* can pull it out."

"Excuse me." Elaethia walked over to Peter and effortlessly removed his greatsword.

"Thanks. For … a lot of things."

She tilted her head. "What do you mean?"

"Jeez, you're gonna make me say it? I guess … Everyone knows you coulda just one-shotted that thing by yourself. But you let me take the glory instead. I know it doesn't mean much to you, but for whatever it's worth"—he extended a gauntlet—"I'd say you're all right, Frossgar."

"Likewise." She shook his hand as their eyes met. For the first time, they regarded each other with a smile.

Liam's tail suddenly drooped. "Well, I'm glad you two are finally getting along. Not to mention your gear's all right. Those eggheads better compensate me."

"Why the face, Barron?" Peter asked.

Liam held up the splintered shaft of his spear. "Stupid trashcan broke my favorite stick."

Shiro thought he knew what he had walked into. He was sure he understood the environment, tasks, events, rules, and overall order of things involved in the tournament. He thought he was ready and prepared to face the challenges ahead.

Shiro was very, very wrong.

If it hadn't been for the fact that he was able to observe the warrior events before his own class, the crowd, noise, and overall size of the event would have sent him into shock. He expected an orderly and friendly competition in a show of force and honorable combat, all in front of an audience of respectable and tradition-driven people.

This was anything but.

Thank the Moon he was surrounded by his guildmates, with Lilian and Geran on his right and left. The ranger showed both discomfort and acceptance toward the atmosphere. Lilian, on the other hand, was not providing much comfort. The bubbly demicat hurled jeers, slurs, and incitements alike into the arena, and jumped up and down to shake Shiro whenever she got excited. She truly had become one with the crowd.

The loud and boisterous mob of onlookers were sometimes on such levels of vulgarity and unruliness he thought they might be adventurers themselves. While some of them were, the civilians certainly got swept up in the heat and passion of the environment. Fights even broke out in the stands among civilians and adventurers alike. Just when he thought it couldn't get any worse, vendors began to sell alcohol. What was *wrong* with Linderrians?

By the time it was finally his turn to battle, he was already at his social limit. He wearily trudged into the arena, sending a silent prayer for it to be over soon so he could go to bed. A brief thought of intentionally losing so he could leave more quickly fluttered through his head. He instantly banished it. What would his father, grandfather, Elaethia, and all of his friends think of him? What would *Lilian* think of him? By the heavens, he was ashamed of having such a thought for even a moment. That was the *opposite* of his code! If he performed well here, his goals would be one giant step closer to becoming fulfilled. Honor awaited, and thoughts of surrender were a cancer to him.

The samurai slid a finger along the edge of his katana. He didn't like the idea of having a dull blade and was very hesitant to allow the enchanters to apply it. But they wouldn't let him enter the arena without it, despite explaining he could strap the sheath over it. At least they had sworn to remove it after the events. He looked up as he reached the center, and he saw his demicat opponent impatiently flourishing his sabers.

"Hey!" the opponent called. "If you're done moping over your sword, can we fight already? What gives, man? You really gonna walk up here with your head down? C'mon, you're not supposed to give up until I beat you!"

"Are you trying to forfeit to Westreach already?" The referee asked Shiro. It was a different ref than the warriors, as this one was a demiwolf.

"N-no sir. I'm ready," he replied, and he put on his face mask.

"Very well. All right, gentlemen, you know the rules. You fight until one of you gives in, is disarmed, or I stop you. No ifs, ands, or buts. Ready, set, duel!"

The duelist from Westreach immediately stepped forward and slashed directly at Shiro's face. The samurai flinched back to dodge the attack as the demicat continued his advance, slicing the air in unbelievably rapid and continuous strikes. Shiro dodged and blocked with precision and concentration as the whirling storm of metal flashed again and again in unnaturally quick succession. This was nearly as difficult as deflecting the storm of arrows during the escort. Such a technique was designed to overwhelm an opponent, and anyone less experienced would have fallen to it by now. He was fast. Very fast.

But Shiro could see through it. He figured it was designed to wear an enemy down with dozens of cuts before he or she could be finished off. That being said, they were far from heavy. In the split-second that Shiro shot his arms up to strike, he absorbed two blows to his torso. The samurai ignored them. He rammed the hilt of the katana into his opponent's face, causing the demicat to double backward and clutch where he had been struck. Blood trickled from his nose and dripped to the sand. The crowd winced and groaned in empathy.

With his sword still poised to strike, Shiro lifted it up and brought it down in a single, devastating arc to the top of his opponent's head. The demicat's sabers flew from his hands, and he dropped to the ground with a thud.

"Hold!" The ref stepped between them. "The duelist from Westreach has been disarmed! Breeze wins!"

The defeated duelist clutched his head and groaned as he rolled onto his back. Medical teams rushed to render aid as the ref held up Shiro's arm for the roaring crowd. The samurai blinked. *That was it? I defeated my opponent after only two strikes? Do all Linderrian duelists have such weak conditioning?*

The demicat suddenly bolted up and ran to the ref. "Now wait one damn minute! He's wearing heavy armor; how is that allowed? My weapons can't do anything against that! This is completely backwards to how duelist fights are supposed to go!"

The referee gave him a hard look. "If you had a problem with it, you should have said so before you readied up. I don't see anywhere in the rule book that states what you can and can't wear in duels. The only rules are regarding the weapons. You could come out here in full plate or stark naked for all I care."

"This is bullshit! No one's ever done that before! I didn't win the last two years in a row just to get knocked out in the first round!"

"Save it for someone who cares. Both of you get out of here; you're holding up the next match."

"Master Parson's gonna give you a mouthful," he growled. He then turned to Shiro. "You got lucky, foreigner! Watch your back next time you're near Westreach!"

"I said beat it, cat!" the ref barked. He then turned to Shiro. "You too, weirdo, what're you standing there for?"

"R-right! Sorry!" Shiro wheeled around and jogged out of the stadium as briskly as he could. As he entered the tunnel, he let out a long sigh. Stars above, his heart was pounding. Once he got to the ready room, he sat down to take off his helmet and face mask. The demiwolf priestess from Heaven's Light peered around the corner as he took his seat. Once Shiro relaxed, she shuffled up to him.

"A-are you okay? Do you need healing?" she asked.

"Oh! Cassie-chan! No, thank you, my armor took the hits just fine."

"Oh, and you could have healed yourself. I-I forgot; I'm sorry for asking."

"No, it's okay, thank you for thinking of me! And I forgot too. Lili-chan and I meant to get a conduit for myself, but we kept getting sidetracked. I've been so focused on refining my swordsmanship these last few days."

"You really like Lilian, don't you?" she asked shyly.

He nodded. "Lili-chan is wonderful. She can be too much to handle at times, but I think that's what makes her so great. She's not afraid of who she is and won't pretend to be something she's not."

Cassie's ears drooped. "Oh, okay. Y-you fought really bravely out there."

"Thank you. I was a little overwhelmed until I figured it out. It was a new situation for me. The atmosphere is really uncomfortable, too. I much rather prefer quieter company such as yourself, Cassie-chan."

"Oh. I, uh, mh …" She blushed and looked down. "I-I'm not all that great."

"But you work so hard and care so much for others! It's no wonder you're in a named party! They're lucky to have you!"

The priestess buried her face in her sleeves and mumbled something. She jumped with a start as Geran and Lilian suddenly burst into the room.

"Shiro! That was amazing!" Lilian ran over and pounced on him, rubbing her cheek on his. Cassie's tail instantly drooped to the floor, and she looked away.

Shiro blushed and placed a hand on her head. "Lili-chan, w-what are you talking about?"

Geran stepped up to speak over her giggles. "Dude, didn't you hear? That was the duelist two-time champion, and you beat him in round one!"

"He did say something like that," Shiro noted.

"You don't understand! He opened with his signature move, and you took it like it was *nothing!* I don't think anyone's ever pushed through his 'steel ultimatum' like that before!"

"Steel what now?"

"That's the name of that flourish he used!" Lilian chirped. "He's famous for it!"

Geran continued. "He's considered the top duelist in the country as far as the tournament goes! He's taken first in the bracket and strikes-in-ten the last two years."

Master Dameon stepped into the room with Elaethia behind him. "He's weak stuff as far as quests and adventuring go, however. Britton's just an A rank and seems to only train for the tournament. As Shiro proved firsthand, that cat's as squishy as he is cocky. All this aside, boy, you're good and lined up for the finals. We weren't sure how you'd do against western fighting, but seeing how you handled Britton, it's as good as in the bag. Elaethia's already in the finals, Geran's been an ace for years, and now you're on the winning path for the duelists. I was right to put you guys in."

Lilian shot up. "Hey! I'm here, too!"

"Right, right," Dameon sighed. "You're damn good too, girl. But you've never taken first before."

"We'll see about that!" she huffed.

"When is Shiro's next fight?" Elaethia asked.

"He's got a bye next round, as they expected Britton to take it all the way. It'll be a little bit."

"Awesome!" Lilian cheered. "C'mon, Shiro! Let's go watch so you can try to learn a bit about your opponents!"

"Great idea, Lili-chan! Just … no more shouting please?"

"Aww, c'mooon! That's part of the fun!"

"I really don't think so!" he insisted as they ran back upstairs.

Geran shrugged. "Well, it's not like I've got anything better to do. Guess I'll join 'em. You coming too, Master?"

Dameon grunted. "Nah, I'm gonna sit with the rest of the guild masters. Rub it in their faces a bit more. You'd better not disappoint me tomorrow, Nightshade. You're already being talked about."

"Wonderful," he grumbled as they left.

Elaethia turned to the small priestess next to her. "You are not with the rest of your party, Cassie?"

She shook her head. "I-I wanted to make sure Shiro was okay."

"He fared well. I do not believe anyone else was concerned for him."

Cassie shuffled. "I j-just wanted to be sure."

"You simply wished to see him?" Elaethia asked. The demiwolf blushed and nodded. "Shiro is not one to turn away pleasant company. I am sure you are welcome to visit him at any time."

"Well … but … Lilian …" the girl trailed off.

"Lilian would not prevent you from speaking with him. I do not see her doing so."

"No it … it's not like that; it's …" She stood and pulled her hood over her face. "I'm going to sit with my party. I'm sorry; excuse me."

She quietly shuffled past Elaethia and out the door.

Shiro pushed his way through the semifinals. This was not without difficulty, however, as he struggled to overcome each type of fighter he encountered. Whether it was due to his armor, his style, or the underestimation factor, the samurai was able to win his way through the bracket—although not without a notable amount of controversy. Twice the tournament officials needed to pull out the rule book to prove there was nothing illegal about the Osakyotan's equipment. Apogee's guild master even tried to demand an alteration of the rules just for this situation.

The one-on-one battle with the atronachs was next. Shiro understood very little of what they were supposed to be. Magic metal men, maybe? The samurai entered the arena as his metallic foe lurched and turned to face him. Shiro froze. The carved eyes that met him were totally void of life and emotion. This was no brehdar, beast, or monster, just a metal-filled body in the shape of a human. This was absurd! How was he supposed to test his mettle against an opponent that knew no drive! This enemy had no purpose or passion, let alone anything resembling honor! This foe—no, this *thing*—was unworthy to be considered a combatant!

Shiro's thoughts were interrupted by a blast of steam that hissed from the atronach's joints. Two dull blades extended from its arms. In a burst of speed Shiro could barely comprehend, the atronach launched toward him, poised to strike. His katana sang from its sheath as he slashed it across his body to strike the neck of the atronach. His blade connected, and chunks of metal fell off the enemy and clanged to the dust. Shiro held his pose, frowning at the waste of time and skill he had put forth on an unworthy opponent. He jumped as another hiss of steam and grinding of metal whined from his left. He whipped his head toward the noise, and his eyes bugged. The machine was not so easily defeated.

Before the samurai could retaliate, the atronach lunged again with its blades poised. Shiro tried to leap back and raise his own weapon to defend himself, but the machine was too fast. Its arms pumped back and forth in alternating jabs, bashing and digging into his body as it continued to advance, despite Shiro standing steadfast. He attempted the maneuver he pulled on Britton and rammed the hilt of his sword into the atronach's face. The machine was not fazed. It collided into him, causing him to stumble backward and fall on his back. Shiro lashed out a savage kick to the machine's thin knee. His attack was successful; the atronach lurched forward and toppled over as its leg was kicked out from under it. Unfortunately, it didn't seem to be bothered by this.

The metallic foe crashed forward directly on top of Shiro, still jabbing and striking painfully at his bruising torso. The samurai gasped as the wind was continually knocked out of him over and over. In a desperate attempt to free himself, he chopped his hand along the side of the machine's neck. He immediately regretted this, as not only did the machine not have nerves, but it was also very hard. Shiro cried out again and clutched his throbbing hand as the event referee rushed over to deactivate the atronach and roll it off of him. Through his teary and dotted vision, Shiro could have sworn the demiwolf was stifling a laugh.

The final event was quite straightforward, but Shiro still felt very uneasy. In a slight difference to the warriors, instead of a single heavy strike to the pedestal, they were given ten seconds to hit it as many times as they could. Shiro was at a disadvantage for this event, since he wore heavier armor and a single heavier sword. The lightly equipped duelists had free range of motion and very little weighing them down. Shiro stood with his guildmates and watched the officials place a new gemstone in the arena's center. He recalled Nathan Beckett from the interviews for the escort quest and had talked with him a few times since he had arrived. He had never interacted with the other girl.

"Excuse me, Erin-san—that's your name, right?" he asked her.

She turned. "Hm? Oh, yes, hi! Shiro, right? Sorry, I don't think we've met."

She was a rather plain elven girl but was attractive in a fairy or pixie kind of way, thinly built with wavy brown hair and freckles, a sense of elegance in her posture.

Shiro nodded. "I'm sorry, I don't think I saw your fights. How did you do?"

"Ah, that's 'cause I got knocked out in the first round. My opponent from Frostshire had a buckler that he used to perfectly block my rapier, and then he bonked me over the head with it. This is my first tournament, so I was pretty nervous going in."

"Hey, not like I did much better," Nathan joined in. "I got to round three before that dwarf kicked my feet out from under me. Luckily you've been taking the spotlight off of us, Shiro."

"Yeah, how'd you do that?" Erin asked. "I thought this was your first year, too."

"It is," Shiro said. "I've actually only been in this country for a few months. You've done this before, though, right, Nathan-senpai?"

"Once, yeah. This is my second year. We're all a new generation of duelists."

"Oh well," Erin sighed. "We won't be at the bottom forever. This is our last event—except for you, Shiro. You've got the finals tomorrow."

"Oh yeah, I do, don't I?" he recalled.

Shiro turned to the overhead screen to see the current scores. The average was around forty-five hits in ten seconds. He was going to have a hard time beating that, not to mention the highest score, which was seventy-three. That one was Britton using his steel ultimatum flourish. There were several noticeably low scores in the upper twenties, but those came from duelists using heavier single weapons like his. This did not instill much confidence in him.

Finally it was Breeze's turn. Nathan was first. He stepped up and drew his dual short swords. They were not as light or fast as the sabers or daggers Shiro had seen. Like him, Nathan chose his weapons for combat, not sport. The human poised his blades at the ready while staring down the red gemstone. Suddenly it turned green. In that moment, he lashed his blades forward, twisting his arms over one another in a fluid traditional flourish. He kept the motion going until the gemstone turned back to red. Nathan exhaled and panted heavily while sheathing his blades with shaky arms. He looked up to the screen to see his tally, which read forty-four—an average score. He sighed and pushed the sweat from his brow as he turned to Shiro.

"All right, Osakyotan, your turn. Don't get disheartened if you score low. Your equipment isn't built for speed, anyway."

"We'll see. I think I know what to do."

Shiro took off his face mask and placed it in his belt pouch. He stood at the ready and poised his blade, waiting for the gemstone to turn green. The moment the color changed, Shiro had already landed his first strike. Twisting and rolling his wrists, his katana slashed the gemstone in consecutive strikes with a speed nearly unimaginable for a blade its size. His single longsword moved as fast as some of the short sabers had throughout the event. Though his heart pounded, his lungs heaved, and his muscles screamed, he pushed through what seemed like the longest ten seconds of his life. Finally the gemstone turned red. The samurai dropped to his knees, gasping for breath.

The crowd wowed in astonishment at the display of speed from thick armor and heavy sword. With spots in his vision, Shiro stared up at the screen to see his score. He had slashed his katana forty-eight times in ten seconds. Through his exhaustion, he felt equal amounts of disappointment and satisfaction. While his score was barely above the average, it was probably the fastest he had ever moved.

Erin suddenly helped him to his feet. "Holy hell, Shiro! Where'd you learn to do *that?*"

"I liked to … practice on … falling cherry blossoms," he wheezed. "I wanted to see how many times I could cut one before it touched the ground. I think my record was nine."

"Nine! You cut a flower *nine* times midair?"

"Not a flower, more like a single petal."

"Stars above. I'd hate to fight you."

"I wouldn't do it in a fight. It was for conditioning and form. A bit for fun as well."

"Still, that's crazy. Are you gonna be all right going back?"

"Yes, actually, come to think of it I just remembered something Angela-senpai taught me."

He closed his eyes and inhaled deeply to call upon the magic inside of him. He willed it back into his own body, and channeled *sunlight* to reinvigorate himself. Shiro exhaled slowly, relaxed, and rolled his shoulders.

"Much better. I keep forgetting I can do that now."

"Hey!" a voice shouted from behind. They turned to see one of the opponents Shiro had defeated earlier storm up to them. He recognized the demibear as the one from Clearharbor. "There! Right there! Ref! Did you see that? That was magic!"

The demiwolf cocked his ears. "I saw it. It was a little hard not to since he was glowing. What of it?"

"Are you kidding? You can't use magic for duelist events! And don't give me that 'I never said you couldn't' crap; it's been a base rule for as long as the tournament's been around! I'm still not convinced that armor isn't cheating, but you can't talk me out of saying that's somehow okay!"

The referee scratched his chin. "It does say magic and potions are not allowed during events, but nothing states you can't use them *after*. We do it anyways as medical treatment, and I never saw him using it during any of his events. Don't get me wrong; I'm just as shocked as you are. But he didn't break any rules."

The demibear wheeled away in frustration. "Oh come *on!* Why won't you can this guy already? He's completely taking advantage of the rules!"

"You're just butthurt because he's coming at you with a style you've never seen before! If you don't like it, watch him and learn how to beat it next year!"

"*What!*"

Erin began to push Shiro back to the tunnel with a harsh whisper. "Go, go. Get out of here; I'll take care of this."

"Will you be okay?" he asked back in the same tone. She winked and turned around.

"Hel*loooo*!" she intervened in an intentionally obnoxious voice. "Can I *go* now?"

The demibear glared at her. "Oh now don't *you* start!"

"Well *excuuuuuse* me, your highness! If you're done *gracing* us with your *presence*, I'd like my turn!"

"What'd you say to me, you little twig? I'll have you know I graduated top of my class in …"

Shiro darted back to the ready room before it could heat up further. As he raced out of sight, he sent another silent prayer to the heavens that the rest of the tournament would go much more smoothly.

Chapter 16
The Finals

Sixth Era.139. Jinum 11.

The tournament continued on the second day, starting in the forest outside the city walls. While the events took place far away, the spectators were still able to watch from the arena through the overhead screen. They also had the option to make the walk and watch in person.

The druid's forest was something out of a storybook. Vines and trees grew everywhere in all shapes and directions. Flowers bloomed in sizes and colors unimaginable. Pools of crystal-clear water were everywhere. Fields and thickets enveloped their own portions of the land that was used for the events. It was as though every possible ecosystem was combined into just a couple of acres. In case it wasn't already obvious, this place wasn't naturally occurring.

Whether Lilian was joking or not, there was considerable truth in what she said. The ranger events were quite dull. Her words kept sticking in Geran's mind as he completed his events, starting with fawn wrangling. The rangers went one at a time, starting with Dinkerage. A terrified adolescent deer would be released from a cage and was allowed to dash into the constricted woods with a fifteen-second head start. The ranger's goal was to chase it down and bring it back. Points were deducted based on time and the condition the animal was returned in. If they did not bring it back within ten minutes, they received no points. Needless to say, fawn wrangling took the longest of all the events in the tournament.

Geran looked at the current scores and calculated the average. It seemed to be around the midthirties, meaning it took the average ranger seven minutes or so. Every ranger started with one hundred points. Every minute that passed deducted ten points, and every minor wound on the deer deducted one point. Serious wounds took away five points each, and if the deer was beaten to unconsciousness, fifty points were deducted. A dead deer resulted in an automatic zero.

Several failed to meet the time requirements, and there were a couple that killed their deer. One woman managed to get her animal across the line at the last second, with several abrasions. She got two points out of the one hundred. In contrast, another contestant's deer got tangled in some bushes right after being released. The lucky ranger from Frostshire only needed to tie it up and bring it back to receive ninety-four points. While several complained, it was dismissed as "luck of the game." Apparently this phenomenon had happened several times over the years.

Finally it was Geran's turn. The ranger from Breeze stood behind the line, anxiously waiting for his quarry to be released. With the sudden click of the gate being flung open, his deer burst from its cage. Geran watched with fixed eyes as his quarry dashed to what it thought was safety, until his fifteen seconds were up.

The clock was ticking.

Geran took off from the line and flew into the small forest after the deer. Under normal circumstances, he would have waited for it to tire and tracked it through standard means. But he didn't have that kind of time. Deer tracks were all over the place. He made a note of its tracks as it shot out of the gate: average impressions, average distance between sets, average dig from front to back of each print. This animal was utterly and frustratingly average. That is, until he noticed something different with its gait. This animal had a wider stride than most. He had the means to follow it if it crashed out of earshot.

Geran leaped over a stream that ran through the constricted forest. He looked at the enormous *sun wall* that encased this section and could tell he was near the center. According to the timer above his head, he had nine minutes left. Deer were not known for their stamina, but they would run in panic until their hearts stopped. He didn't have the time for this; nor could he afford for it to happen. Midstride, he drew his bow and nocked an arrow with some cord tied around the shaft. The ranger leaped through some brush and came into sight of his quarry. The terrified animal saw him, bolted, and smacked full-speed into the *sun wall*. The deer stumbled backward and tried again to scramble away.

The ranger aimed at a tree in front of the animal and released. The arrow embedded itself into the trunk just as the deer tripped over the cord attached to it. Geran wasted no time in sprinting forward and tackling the animal before it could stand. With a flash of his swordbreaker, he severed the cord from the arrow and immediately tied the squirming hind legs together. With the same piece, he wrapped them with the front legs.

All was going flawlessly until one hoof came loose and struck him in the ribs. Geran inhaled sharply and gritted his teeth from the impact. He quickly took a third length of cord and tied the four legs together, immobilizing the animal in a hog-tie. He pushed through the sharp pain in his chest, grunted, and hoisted the animal over his shoulders to sprint back to the starting point.

Geran tore across the finish line with his quarry. His muscles ached, his lungs burned, and his chest stung from the animal's strike. Geran gasped for breath and forced himself to stand straight. Sweat dripped from his brow and stung his eyes as it trickled into them. The ranger wiped his eyes and checked his time. Three minutes and fourteen seconds. This ensured him a maximum of eighty points. With only a few minor abrasions to the animal, his final score was seventy-seven. Geran landed himself in second place.

Second was archery. Twenty-one archers lined up in front of twenty-one targets and were allotted five arrows each. At a distance of fifteen meters, the top nine scorers would advance. As had happened in previous years, several archers, including Geran, hit the center ring of their targets all five times. Anyone that missed the four-centimeter circle even once was eliminated. This year, eight rangers advanced. The final elimination was an unforgiving process, as any miss meant the archer was out. All eight took turns one at a time to take their single shots, this time from twenty meters. All eight hit the center. They backed up another five meters and repeated the process. Seven advanced this time.

This continued until only two archers remained at fifty-five meters: Geran and a ranger from Sprigganwood. Back and forth they took their shots, hitting the bull's-eye every time and then backing up five meters. Again and again the two rangers battled out the title for the best marksman in the country until they hit ninety-five meters. Exasperated at this point, Geran snatched his arrow from the event assistant.

He trudged to the 125 mark, faced his target, nocked his arrow, tested the wind, and fired. The shot was airborne for several seconds before it hit, splitting his opponent's previous arrow clean down the center. A collective gasp emerged from the crowds. Geran turned to his opponent and crossed his arms. The ranger from Sprigganwood simply looked at Geran, scratched her head, chuckled, and walked off the field.

Finally it was time for the rangers' most anticipated event: the battle royal. All twenty-one rangers returned to the same sectioned part of the forest as before and were assigned random starting locations. Once all the rangers were in their positions, a horn sounded and the battle royal began. The event was simple. Twenty-one would enter; one would leave. All of the rangers were given sun rings that locked their bodies down inside a shape-forming *sun wall*, very similar to the moon ring that Lilian had obtained. The difference was that instead of absorbing the damage, these rings would intercept it. In turn, the wearer would be immobilized, indicating he or she had been eliminated. Every two minutes, the area would be restricted by *moon wall*, until the zone had only a five-meter diameter. If the moon wall touched a competitor, the ranger would be locked down.

At the sound of the horn, Geran made a beeline for the outer circle. There were no points awarded for eliminations, so there was no reason to actively engage enemies and risk getting "killed." He noticed another ranger as he dashed to the edge of the play area. Still running, he fired a quick shot at her. The arrow impacted the dwarf's leg and bounced off as she fell over, paralyzed by the activated sun ring.

He very quickly reached the outer edge, as it had already started its first phase of contraction. Keeping a ten-meter buffer between him and the shrinking wall, Geran crept along while the zone got smaller and smaller as time passed. He glanced up at a counter above the arena to see that only nine rangers were left. That was fast—much faster than in any other year. It was a good thing he had decided to play the long game, as it seemed this year's competitors were more focused on eliminations. His concentration was broken by a quiet rustling to his left. In a flash, he drew his bow and trained it on the sound. From the brush emerged Roderick Griffith, one of Breeze's other rangers.

"Psst! Rod!" Geran called out to the demicat in a harsh whisper. Roderick nocked an arrow and whipped to the sound of Geran's voice. At the recognition of his guildmate, he laxed the bow and crept over.

"Nightshade, what are the odds of bumping into you here?" he asked.

"'Bout twenty-one to one," Geran said.

"Funny. You see how many are left already? The wall isn't even on phase three yet."

"I know; there're seven others out there besides us. I plan to ride the wall all the way to the center."

Roderick nodded. "Same here. You take anyone out yet?"

"One. You're literally the second person I've even seen. How about you?"

"Saw a few, took one of 'em out myself. You're not gonna believe this, but By got knocked out. It's just you and me from Breeze now."

Geran's eyes widened. "They already got *Byron?*"

"Crazy right? He shoulda outlasted me, maybe even you. That dwarf might as well be a phantom with how quiet he is. Too bad he got a shit starting point."

"No kidding. Either way, we're in a good spot right now. If we play it right, we'll get both of us in the top three, maybe top two."

Roderick rubbed his chin. "We've got a bigger footprint, though. My plan was the same as yours—just stay low until we hit the middle. You got any bright ideas?"

"Nah. Let's just stick with that. Keep quiet; the wall's moving."

Together the two of them stayed low all the way until the zone was thirty meters wide. Roderick looked up at the counter just as the number went down one.

"Four left. It's you, me, and two others," he whispered.

Geran nodded. "Stay quiet; stay down. Wait for them to make the first mistake."

"Got it."

The zone began to shrink again, forcing the remaining four into a fifteen-meter area. They crawled along the ground and silently inched their way to the middle until Roderick forgot to look where he was crawling and put his weight on a dry twig. The branch snapped sharply, instantly giving away their position. Roderick's eyes widened as he held his breath. Geran could tell what he was thinking. He was contemplating either making a break for it to draw the attention away from Geran or staying still to see whether they didn't hear it. He didn't have time to choose.

The Elaethium

The sound of an arrow nocking directly in front of him sprang him into action. A bowstring strummed as an arrow shot through a bush, straight toward Geran's face. In a flash, Roderick leaped in front of it to intercept the shot. His ring activated, and the demicat was encased in the form-shaping light. The number above their heads went down to three.

"Geran, trace it!" he mumbled through the spell.

Geran shot to a knee, nocked his own arrow, followed the path the arrow came from, and fired back. A whack followed by a frustrated yell indicated he had hit his mark. It was just him and one other. Before he could load another shot, the final opponent charged through the brush, sword poised to strike. Geran reached out with his bow and kicked back to narrowly avoid the thrust from the enemy ranger. The enemy slashed to the side and ripped the weapon from Geran's hands. Geran rolled to his feet, drew his longsword, and stood at the ready, eyeing his opponent down.

He recognized him as the top ranger from Apogee. The elf eyed him in turn as the two rangers sized one another up while slowly circling each other. Geran's bow was stripped, and his opponent was out of arrows. They would have to settle this with their blades—the human's longsword versus the elf's falchion. With his longsword at the ready in his right hand, Geran placed his left hand on the hilt of his swordbreaker, which was still in its sheath.

The elf saw that Geran was unsteady and clearly not going to initiate the attack. The ranger from Apogee lunged forward with a straight thrust, poised to take him out instantly. In a flash, Geran's swordbreaker flew from its sheath and intercepted the falchion. The dagger's teeth met the blade and guided it in between the jagged ridges. In the same instant, Geran twisted the swordbreaker, biting down into his opponent's blade and locking it in. Geran immediately thrust his longsword forward and struck the elf in the chest. The sun ring activated, and the ranger from Apogee was locked down within the enchantment. The sounds of distant cheering echoed through the forest as Geran looked up to see the number above his head go down to one.

Back in the ready room at the arena, Lilian stood with the other two mages from Breeze. She sat down on a bench and looked intently into one of her makeup mirrors. The demicat grabbed a pen to even out her eyeliner and popped her lips to make sure the lipstick would stay in place. Remus Lichen paced eagerly around the room behind her. The elf walked over to a mirror to gather his long blond hair into a ponytail and brushed off his silver-and-yellow cloak. The third mage, Charlie, sat on a stool in the corner with his legs crossed and chin resting in one of his hands. His black hair drooped over his sleepy, indifferent eyes.

"Oy, Charlie," Remus said. "Hurry up and get ready; we're about to go."

"I've *been* ready," Charlie mumbled in response.

"Are you serious? C'mon, what's with that getup? You look like you're going to a funeral."

Charlie lazily glanced down at his all-black attire. "What of it?"

"Stars above, you're gonna be mopey for the tournament, too? You ought to be more excited like everybody else. This is your second year in the guild, and Master Dameon selected you!"

The pale-skinned human blew a lock of hair out of his eyes. "And?"

"No wonder you can't find a party; you're so depressing. You look more like a necromancer than a mage."

"Are you done talking yet?"

"You sassing me? Just 'cause you got selected doesn't mean you're hot stuff. I've been Breeze's number-one mage in this tournament for four years now. Keep up with the attitude and I'll show you how I got that title firsthand."

Charlie rolled his eyes. "Whatever."

"Awwwww, leave poor Charlie alone." Lilian said as she put her kit away. "This is totally new to him; he's probably just as nervous for his first tournament as we were!"

"I'm not nervous."

"Yeah, you're probably right," Remus sighed. The two of them continued their conversation, seemingly unaware of Charlie's interjections. "I was kind of obnoxious my first year too."

"You're still obnoxious."

"Don't discourage him, Remus! He needs to have confidence!" Lilian pressed.

"I *am* confident."

Remus shrugged. "Yeah, but he *is* a newbie. I can't say I've even seen him in action."

"I'm right here. I can hear you."

"He's still selected!" Lilian said, and she waltzed behind the human to give him a hug over his shoulders. "Master Dameon saw potential in him! He's gonna do great!"

"Please get off me."

Remus shook his head. "I'm just saying, I've heard nothing from him. Guess we'll find out soon. I don't remember much from my number-two days, let alone number-three."

"What does that even mean?"

"Don't worry, Remus; you'll find out soon enough after today." She winked.

"You two sound ridiculous."

Remus's eyes gleamed. "Oho? Tough talk, cat. We'll see if that attitude sticks around after I set your tail on fire."

"You can't. The rings stop that."

Lilian gave the elf a wicked grin. "I'd like to see you try. I'll blast those pointy ears right off."

"Will you stop shaking me?"

The one-on-ones began immediately after. Breeze wasn't scheduled to fight until near the end of the first round, with Charlie being the first of the three. Lilian would go next, and Remus's was the final battle. The demicat sprawled out on a bench and kicked her feet in the air while she studied the enchanted ring the officials handed her. It was a different moon ring than hers. The one she had looted simply dissolved whatever spell hit her. This one would lock the wearer down. As an added bonus, they could hold the ring hand out to channel a ward to block an incoming spell. All she would have to do was hit her opponent or make him or her run out of magic first.

The mage fights were a crowd favorite. Magic was always regarded as epic, and civilians found little more entertaining than a battle between elemental magicians. Druid officials would alter the earthen terrain so there were mounds, pillars, and girders all around the field. The most epic of battles would leave the entire field completely leveled by the finish. Lilian grinned as she imagined the ways she would demolish them in spectacular fashion.

Master Dameon interrupted her daydreaming by appearing in the entryway. "Whitepaw, you're up next. You got your ring and equipment ready?"

"Yessir!" she chirped, hopping to her feet.

"Good. You're up against some girl from Clearharbor. Might have your work cut out for you right off the bat."

"Hm-hmm," she hummed smugly. "We'll see about that."

"Indeed we will. Geran mentioned you've been training your tail off and have a secret weapon up your sleeve."

"Aw, he's been blabbing already? He hasn't even *seen* it yet! Besides, I'm not using it until the very end."

"Awful presumptuous of you, girl. Don't hold yourself back for the sake of a dramatic reveal; that's how you get knocked out early."

"Don't worry about me, Master! I never said anything about going easy on 'em!"

"Hrmph. Whatever you say. Just do your best."

Doing her best was indeed what she did.

Lilian was somewhat known as a well-rounded mage around the country to begin with, but this year she really blew that standing out of the water. During the first several rounds, her opponents went in expecting a tough fight. What happened was closer to a thrashing. Lilian's power and reaction times were off the charts as she blasted her way up the ranks. As promised, she held nothing back save her newfound secret abilities.

Every round, she would strut confidently into the arena and decimate her opponents with overwhelmingly powerful elemental attacks. In the beginning, she needed only to batter them with spells until their magic depleted from holding the ward. In the midlevels, the demicat let loose with unrelenting spells from multiple angles until they gave up or were overwhelmed.

Remus was no different. The elven mage cast and channeled spells in rapid succession in a torrent of elemental fury, dominating his fights with equal ease. From the VIP box in the stadium, the guild masters' mouths fell open at the raw destructive force that came from the sleek demicat and blond elf. Master Dameon leaned back and folded his arms in smug satisfaction as the ground shook from their explosive battles.

"Take a good, long look, ladies and gents," he said with a grin. "My monks and druids might not be much to look at compared to some of yours, but my warriors and rangers compensate. Now we've got some heavy-hitting mages, so expect to see my Remus and little Lily clear the board."

The guild master from Sprigganwood glared. "Don't act so high and mighty, Greatjaw. You're still in hot water with me because of that foreign duelist of yours."

The big demibear waved a hand. "Cry me a river, Schaefer; we didn't break any rules. You just have to be ready for him next year."

"Tch," the human spat.

It was time for the semifinals before anyone knew it. Lilian heard that Charlie got knocked out in the third round, but she heard nothing from Remus. She figured he had either been eliminated or would be in the fight immediately following hers. All she had to focus on was the fight ahead and then get into the finals. Her last two battles were tough, but she'd made it farther than she ever had before. No matter who she was about to fight, she was fired up.

She emerged from her tunnel into the massive arena and was greeted by the deafening roars of the audience. Lilian had easily become a crowd favorite, and she knew it. She twirled and skipped into the center, waving and blowing kisses into the wind. Her girly and idol-like demeanor halted only for a moment as she saw her opponent enter the arena. Silver cloak flapping, blond ponytail bouncing, pointed ears twitching, she met the eyes of her fellow guildmate.

"Well, well, well," Remus crowed. "How about that noise, huh? They certainly know a legend when they see one."

Lilian sighed dramatically. "Sorry you had to come into the same spotlight as me, Remus. I really do feel bad about outshining you."

"And that's where you're wrong. Sorry, Lilian, but this is as far as you go."

"Mages!" the announcer called through the speaker. "The semifinals are about to begin! Are you ready?"

"Ready," Lilian stated, giving the screen a wink.

"Ready." Remus grinned and flourished his ebony staff.

"The contenders are ready! Mages, fight!"

Remus opened with a hefty *air blast*. The relentless air spell forced the demicat back several meters until she tripped over one of the earthen protrusions. She stumbled backward but quickly sprang back up as a *fireball* exploded right where she had fallen. Lilian thrust her own staff out and sent a *thunderbolt* directly at him. Remus saw the gesture and held out his ring hand, dissipating the spell in his ward. Lilian thrust her staff out again, this time casting a colossal *torch* that billowed directly into the elf. He made the smart decision to not try to absorb it. Instead he quickly dived behind cover and channeled an *arctic wind* over himself to bear the immense heat. Lilian cut the *torch* and stood ready. Remus took advantage of the break to peer over the edge and immediately shot back down as another *thunderbolt* blasted the top of his cover.

Remus didn't appear for a moment, and Lilian knew why. That cocky elf was definitely confused out of his brain. She wasn't this strong the last time he sparred with her. He suddenly rolled over his cover and thrust his staff at Lilian. Instinctively, she put up her ring to intercept. But what came was not something she could dispel. A bright flash followed by a deafening crack erupted in front of her. Remus had hit her dead-on with *flashbang*.

Lilian covered her ears and shrank down behind the cover. Her vision was reduced to nothing but pure white while her ears were robbed of all hearing save the high-pitch ringing in her head. The demicat shook her head and inhaled slowly to try to clear the spell.

Her senses weren't returning.

Panic began to rise in her chest. It had been several seconds now. If she couldn't get back in the fight *now*, Remus would get an angle on her and finish her off. In that moment, she could start making out the surroundings in front of her, though they were very blurry. Still deafened, and with only part of her sight returned, she realized she had to pull out her secret weapon early.

She pointed her staff straight down and cast a hefty *updraft* that sent her rocketing into the air. This was just as well, because Remus had launched a *fireball* at the place she had been standing less than a second before. The crowd gasped at the sudden and desperate escape maneuver as she rubbed her eyes, now twenty meters above the ground. She could see more clearly now!

Lilian thrust her staff to the side to cast a high-speed *straight wind* to careen herself to the opposite side of the arena, and another *updraft* as she was about to hit the ground. Flipping and twisting as she touched down, Lilian slid on her feet and one hand to face her opponent as her vision returned to her. The roar of the crowd going wild came in as her hearing went back to normal as well. She was back in the fight.

"A cute trick, Lilian!" Remus applauded. "But that fancy flying won't save you."

"Don't need it to!" she retorted, thrusting her staff forward to engulf him in a powerful pillar of fire.

Remus crossed his arms in front of his face to keep the sparks and flames out of his eyes. He gritted his teeth and thrust his own staff out to counter with *blizzard*, but he found his cyclone was wider than the one he was in. Somehow hers was thinner and more powerful. The elf yelled in frustration as he canceled his spell and thrust his ring out to shut down Lilian's *pillar of fire*. His irises dimmed, as the maneuver undoubtedly sapped him of a considerable amount of magic. Panting and sweating, he glared at the smug demicat as she twirled her staff.

"How …" he breathed. "How the hell did you do that?"

"Hm-mmm," she hummed. "That's a secret."

"Why you little—"

"I'm actually kinda mad at you now, Remus. I was gonna save these techniques for the finals, but it looks like I gotta pull them out early or I might not even get there."

"We'll see about that!" he shouted, and he held his staff up while building a massive *fireball*. "Let's see you fly out of *this!*"

"Too slow!" she called, and she thrust her staff out to channel *electric drain* at him. Remus roared in frustration as he was forced to abandon the enormous fire spell to intercept the attack. The elf glared at her, his eyes now considerably dim. He was starting to run out of magic, while she had more to spare.

Lilian gleamed. It was time to end this. She launched herself into the air again and aimed her staff down at Remus from the sky. This technique was her pride and joy, and she was well pleased with herself for coming up with it. The demicat altered the properties of *icicle* and fired off a volley of small, rapid-fire *icicles* in a succession so fast they nearly touched each other in the air. The stream of ice shards impacted and shattered into Remus's ward until they broke through and peppered him square in the chest. His ring activated its second function and locked him down.

Still airborne, Lilian cast another *updraft* to buffer her landing. The moment she hit the ground, she slammed the butt of her staff into the dusty surface. An enormous *flame burst* erupted from her landing, with the purpose of doing absolutely nothing but showing off. As the flames dispersed, the demicat slowly looked up with a devious gleam in her eye.

The arena went absolutely ballistic. Medical teams rushed onto the field to deactivate Remus's lockdown while Lilian flourished her staff. The demicat struck a sassy pose, winked, and blew a flirty kiss for the screen. The crowd somehow went even wilder—so much so that she couldn't hear her own jubilant laughter. Once Remus was released from the enchantment, he simply sat back down and leaned against a charred bit of earth. The elf ran a hand through his disheveled hair. All he could muster was to mouth the word "woah."

Flapping her cape with one hand and gripping the wide brim of her pointed hat with the other, Lilian spun on her heel to exit her stage. As she made her way back to her tunnel, she enthralled the crowd once more as she strutted out of the arena with a flirty catwalk.

The next mage event was the blowout, and surprisingly, Elaethia found this event rather boring. She guessed that once she had seen one explosion, she had seen them all. She watched as the mages lined up to unleash their spells on the enchanted gem, and see a numerical value appear above their heads. The average was around 450, with high scores being around 700. Lilian scored a 671, which finished her off in fourth place. That surprised Elaethia. Given how well Lillian had done during the previous event, she thought the demicat would have at least placed in the top three.

The atronach battles provided a little more entertainment. While having no magical offensive capabilities, the giant machines had a *moon wall* forcefield around them that dissipated only while they attacked. If a mage was strong enough, he or she could overpower the forcefield, which took it out permanently. Needless to say, Lilian did exactly that.

The demicat was perfectly capable of timing her spells and managing her techniques to outsmart the machine. But she wasted no time as the mechanical monstrosity thundered into the arena. The moment it came into range, she channeled a high-powered *electric drain* on the atronach until its forcefield was depleted. In another display for the purpose only of showing off, she thrust her staff again to channel a *torch*. But this was no normal billow of fire. Instead there came a glowing stream of flame so compact and hot it could have been mistaken for a beam of light.

The machine shuddered as the precision spell melted through its metal hull and erupted out the other side. The atronach went rigid and crumpled to the ground. The metal on its chest was melted and boiling. Searing heat radiated off of its lifeless body so strongly that it could be felt from the stands. A burning metallic stench filled the air. The spectators craned their necks to look into the glowing hole that was the atronach's chest. The insides were completely unrecognizable. Gears, wires, crystals, and liquids that once were interwoven had all been welded and fused together into a single black-and-brown sludge.

Murmurs and befuddled statements arose from the crowd.

"Woah, hold on a second; what spell was *that?*"

"I dunno. Maybe something nobody's used in a while?"

"Not a chance. I've been watching these tournaments for forty-three years, and I've never seen that one once."

"That's not the first time she's done something crazy today."

"Yeah, I'd like to get a closer view of what she's doing. The screen's mostly on her face, though."

"I don't know what you're complaining about; look at her! She's as cute as they come!"

The bystanders' comments reignited the question Elaethia had raised before. She thought about it for a while but couldn't come up with a solution on her own. Elaethia's understanding of magic had improved significantly over these last few months, but it appeared she was far from well-versed. She would have to ask the mage herself.

Elaethia was used to Lilian drawing a crowd. She was always popular and relished any form of positive attention. Elaethia expected to have to wait her turn to speak to her companion. Then she rounded the corner to the tunnel hallway and was halted in her tracks. People had poured into the ready room—adventurers and civilians alike. This puzzled her, since there was no way Master Dameon would allow such a mob to form in his area. Elaethia contemplated on whether to wait for the mass to diminish or to push through. The warrior had only a moment to think before Geran materialized next to her.

"Elaethia! Thank the heavens! Lilian's getting swarmed in there; we gotta help!"

"Where is Master Dameon?" she asked. "Surely he is not allowing this."

"He's being held up by the Arcane Sages. Something about Lilian. There's no way in hell he'd let something like this happen. The rest of us can't even get in there!"

"Yes, I had noticed that. I, too, wish to speak with her, but I have little intention of joining this … pandemonium. However, I would also like access to our common room."

"You're telling me. I couldn't do much on my own, but both of us together should be able to drive a wedge in."

She tilted her head. "You have a plan?"

"I always have a plan. You have your helmet on you?"

"I do." She felt for her helmet, which sat strapped between her shoulder blades.

"Good. Put it on and walk through them."

"That is your plan?"

"If I tell you any more, it won't work as well."

"If you believe so, then I will trust your judgment. Let us go."

The duo made their way toward the ever-growing mob. The gatherers from outside the room saw the heavily armored woman approach with what seemed to be intent, and they reluctantly backed away. The people in the entryway and inside, however, were completely unaware of her presence. She could see that the room was utterly packed with brehdars. Curious onlookers of every race, class, and occupation had flooded Breeze's common room to completely surround Lilian.

Normally the cheerful demicat would have basked in the attention, but she appeared very uncomfortable. The crowd of ecstatic fans and adventurers pressed closer and closer to her, forcing the sleek girl into the corner. Shiro was valiantly trying to hold them at bay but was being drowned out by their vast numbers. Lilian backed farther away as her tail began to poof out. Her eyes darted around the room, looking for breathing room. Despite her obvious signs of growing panic, the mob showed no signs of giving in.

Then the room became cold.

After a few seconds, the overwhelming mob became quiet and began to shiver. Vapor flowed from their mouths as they turned to meet the dangerous gaze of a now-angered Elaethia. Mist enveloped the warrior. Her blue-green dragon eyes glowed ominously through the visor of her deep-blue helmet. Silence filled the common room. All eyes were now fixed on the plated woman standing menacingly in the doorway. Elaethia slowly looked over the room, viewing a near-panicked Lilian; Shiro, who was now knocked to the ground; and then the unruly crowd around her. After what seemed like an eternity, the dragon hero spoke one word.

"Leave."

The command left no room for debate. With fearful mumbles and chattering teeth, the room was very quickly cleared of all brehdars, save the members of Breeze. Elaethia released her spell once the last had left. Lilian seemed to be breathing normally again, but her tail was still bushed from the ordeal.

Geran stepped up and looked at his guildmates. "If you guys wouldn't mind, could our party have the room for a few minutes?"

He was given no objection. The adventurers from Breeze nodded respectfully and filed out as well. Elaethia removed her helmet as Geran closed the door. Shiro pulled up some chairs and gently guided the shaking demicat into one. After a minute, Lilian inhaled and looked up.

"Thanks, guys. Really. Thank you."

"Absolutely," Geran said, and he sat down in his chair.

Elaethia sat as well. "Take whatever time you need, Lilian. We will not allow anyone to enter until you are ready."

She shook her head. "No, no I'm fine. I just ... wasn't ready for that. Gosh, it all happened so fast. I didn't even have time to blink before they swarmed in here. I woulda blasted them back out, but I'm still recharging after that atronach battle."

Shiro placed a hand on her thigh. "I'm sorry, Lili-chan. I tried to keep them back. But who knows what would have happened if I had resorted to violence? I wanted to find Elaethia-sama, but I couldn't even leave the room. Nor did I want to abandon you,"

Geran raised an eyebrow at the samurai's action, but returned his thoughts to the problem at hand. "That was the smart move. Good thing we got here when we did. Fame comes at a price, doesn't it, Lilian?"

"Hence why I never cared for it," Elaethia stated. "You say you depleted your magic in the last event. Given your performance in the battles and atronach fight, it surprises me that you placed only fourth in the blowout. How is this so?"

Lilian slumped into her arms on the table. "That boils down to technique versus power. Sure, my magic reserves have more than tripled since we met, and I have my unique style. But a blowout's a blowout. It doesn't matter how advanced my tactics are. If someone has more magic, they can make a bigger spell. But hey, this shows I've got the fourth-highest magic reserve in the country. Well, for mages anyway … And, uh, not taking the Sages into account … Or Mordecai …"

"What were you last year?" Shiro asked.

"Eleventh."

Geran's jaw dropped. "You bumped up seven places in a *year?*"

"Well, closer to half that. I've had more time and opportunity to work on it since being with you guys."

Geran sat back and folded his arms. "All thanks to that tip you picked up from Mordecai, huh? Something about altering a spell?"

"I had intended to ask about that," Elaethia continued. "You had what you considered a partial success in your experiments not too long ago. Am I correct in saying you have made significant strides since then?"

Lilian shifted in her seat. "Hey, we're all friends here. Can I trust you with something?"

"That is a strange question to ask," Elaethia said.

"Yeah, of course; why the uncertainty?" Geran agreed.

"You're my wonderful friend, Lili-chan," Shiro declared. "I wouldn't ever do anything to make you think otherwise."

"All right," Lilian sighed. "Yeah, I figured out how to alter spells."

The room went dead quiet. Shiro's mouth fell open. Geran nearly fell out of his chair. Elaethia simply tilted her head.

"Go on," Elaethia prompted.

Lilian continued. "For as long as elemental magic has been used, people believed it was cut-and-dried. Magic fanatics like to rip on it since it's flashy but not as flexible or practical as the other schools. There's only one way to cast the spell, and only one way to make it more powerful—by putting more magic into it. All the fancy research and techniques were focused on enchanting, druidic, holy, alchemy, and anatomy magic.

"It's one thing to alter things *with* magic, but to alter the magic itself is totally unheard of. But that's what Mordecai found out, and me as well. I guarantee a lot of sorcerers figured it out too, and that's why they went rogue. To protect their knowledge. I'll bet my ears and tail that a lot of people died because they discovered this."

"So why are you telling us?" Elaethia asked.

"Because I know you guys won't say anything. This is a *huge* breakthrough, and I seem to be the only one who uses it! For *thousands* of years, mages thought that the only way to get stronger was by getting better at the available spells. I've found out that's not true at all! Learning all forty elemental spells isn't mastery; that's just the beginning! The possibilities are endless! The sky's the limit! This is *beyond* groundbreaking and … and …"

Shiro finished for her. "And you want to keep it secret so your advantage doesn't become public knowledge, but you're terrible at keeping secrets."

"Bwaaahhhh, it's so *frustrating!*" She reeled back, grabbing her hair and kicking her feet around. "How am I supposed to brag about how awesome I am if I can't afford to explain why!"

"So much for instilling us with a sense of awe and wonder," Geran sighed.

"So what is your next step, Lilian?" Elaethia asked.

"Same as before," she sighed. "Keep experimenting with spells and finding ways to tweak them however I can."

"I imagine this takes a significant amount of magic to execute."

"Not really. I just blew myself out every day trying to figure it out and then working with it. Some of the tweaks I do take even less magic than the base spell."

"Like what?" Shiro asked intently.

Lilian made a face. "All right, now we're getting into details you don't need to know. Ugh. I gotta keep this stuff on the lowdown for the rest of the day. Elaethia's final battle is after mine, so hopefully that'll soak up most of the attention. I've had enough of people scrambling all over me."

Geran snorted and grinned.

"What?" The demicat demanded.

"Who are you, and what have you done with Lilian?"

Her green feline eyes rolled heavenward.

All that remained in the tournament was the final battles. It would be paladins, monks, duelists, mages, and warriors, in that order. The contenders from Breeze that made it into the finals were Elaethia, Lilian, Jarrod for the monks and Micah Roth from Earth Shatter. Unfortunately, Micah was up against Apogee's top paladin, Aaron Lahoskie, who was more commonly known as Sun Hammer. Shiro recalled the information he had learned about this man. Apparently his skill with the war hammer and proficiency in sun magic was so incredible that the High Church granted him a title. He was an R-level adventurer and apparently even more famous than Elaethia. But he didn't care about that.

What he *did* care about was the condition his guildmate was carried out of the arena in. As strong as Micah was, he was no match for the country's most famed holy warrior. Aaron had been holding back through the whole tournament and went all-out for the final battle. Micah tried to stand against him but couldn't last more than half a minute. He would need to be taken to a church to make a full recovery. Shiro put that concern aside for now, as it was time for his final.

The Osakyotan made his appearance first and received an equal amount of cheers and boos. He turned red from the crowd pressure and shuffled awkwardly to the center. His opponent appeared soon after—Sarah Middleton, a human from Dinkerage. Seemingly floating into the arena, the short-haired woman faced Shiro. Tall and muscular, she wore thick leather armor in the vital areas. Her weapons were two stiletto daggers—weapons he had never seen before. He later learned that was because they were Arminian in origin.

The demiwolf referee put a hand in the air. "Duelists! Are you ready?"

Shiro drew his katana. "Yes sir!"

"Ready," Sarah acknowledged, and she got into a stance.

"The competitors are ready! Commence the finals for the duelist one-on-ones!"

Shiro made the first move and slashed across his body to strike her in the side. The light-footed woman read it and leaped back to dodge. Shiro pivoted on his heel and spun around with the blade to strike again from the same side while still advancing. Again she dodged. He twisted a third time with a leap and slashed the blade toward her face with inhuman speed and precision. Sarah was not impressed. She bent backward from the waist and watched calmly as the katana slashed millimeters above her face.

She righted herself and lunged forward to thrust the long, fine point of one dagger into his gut. While it couldn't pierce his armor, the impact still winded him as he stumbled back. She took advantage of his falter and lunged into the air to drive the other dagger into the top of his helmet. The samurai crashed back and saw stars from the blow. His countless hours of training saved him. Shiro rolled back with the impact and brought himself to his feet as he watched Sarah drive both daggers into the sand where he had fallen.

The crowd became deafening. This was the kind of duel they wanted to see.

Shiro slashed again at her, but her reaction time was too quick. By the time his sword was above his head, she was already in his face and jabbing at his armor. He found himself being pushed back by the light-footed woman. Every time he prepared an attack, she was already in position to counter it. She was too fast. He was completely on defense. He needed a shorter reach to keep up.

Shiro was forced to revert to the other style of katana fighting he knew, iaido. He had used only the traditional style since coming to Linderry, as it was his preferred style. However, he was out of options. He dive-rolled back, turned to face his enemy, detached his sheath, and put his blade inside it. The action stunned the entire arena. Instead of at the ready in front of him, Shiro held his sword at his side in its sheath. Left hand holding the blade in scabbard and right hand poised over the hilt, the samurai stared down the duelist from Dinkerage.

The ref stepped between them. "H-hey … is that a sign of surrender?"

"No," Shiro responded. "I'm still fighting."

"Did the dulling enchantment wear off or something? Why are you putting your weapon away?"

"No, it's still on. This is how I will finish the duel."

"What gives, ref?" Sarah glared. "You just paused the finals."

He put his hands up apologetically. "All right, all right. Carry on,"

Sarah charged at Shiro, blades ready to strike. Time slowed down for him. He inhaled deeply through his teeth and relaxed his entire body.

"Grandfather, guide me," he prayed.

As the right-hand stiletto neared his throat, Shiro stepped forward and swiped sharply to the side with the sheathed blade to deflect her strike. He pivoted and planted his stance while thrusting the scabbard toward his opponent. The light metal sheath smacked into her face so hard it stopped her completely. As she stepped backward, Shiro whipped around and thrust the open end of the sheath at her face, launching the sword hilt-first at her. The heavy handle slammed into her forehead and deflected into the air, knocking her backward and off balance. Shiro leaped after it with all his might. He caught it midair, grabbed the hilt of the sword in an underhand grip, and brought it down with all his weight and strength into the stunned opponent. The stiletto blades flew into the air as Sarah slammed down to the ground, knocked out cold.

"Hold!" The referee dived in and took one look at the unconscious duelist. "Dinkerage's contender is unable to continue fighting. Breeze wins!"

He held up Shiro's wrist, just as he had for all the other fights. The audience went completely crazy as the bewildered Osakyotan processed what he had just heard. Medical teams appeared on the field as the samurai looked around, now understanding what was going on. He had won.

If Lilian was to be perfectly honest, she felt nervous right now. She'd never even placed in the tournament before, let alone made it to the finals. Yet here she was. Talk about pressure. And to make matters worse, the whole crowd was looking directly at her. Normally that would be great, but they were studying her magic, not her.

As much as she wanted to win, Lilian wasn't ready to go all-out with her alteration techniques. Not to mention she was up against the alleged number-one mage in Linderry. If she won here, she'd be the top mage not only in the guild but also in the whole country. Was she ready for that? Yes. Were her spells? No. She had a lot of fine-tuning to do before she was ready to claim that title.

Her mind began to race ahead of her, but the mage quickly overcame it. Her confidence was far from shot. As she emerged into the light, the demicat strutted her way into the arena for the last time. Her opponent, a dwarven man in his thirties, stood already waiting. The crowd went wild at her appearance and chanted her name.

"Li-li-an! Li-li-an! Li-li-an!"

They were happy to see her. She supposed she could afford to give them another show. Geran and Elaethia would be at her side instantly afterward anyway, since they expected a mob to form again.

The announcer came over on a loudspeaker. "This will be the final mage battle! Lilian Whitepaw from Breeze and Joshua Torvin from Westreach! Mages, are you ready?"

The dwarf kicked up some dust around him with a spin, stopping as he slowly leveled his staff at Lilian. The demicat responded by flourishing her own staff, flapping her cape, gripping the brim of her pointed hat, and beaming at him from under the edge.

"The contestants are ready! Mages, fight!"

Joshua thrust out both his staff and his ring hand. A controlled burst of *thunderbolts* struck Lilian's ward as she threw her own ring hand out and dived for cover. She shot up to fire a *thunderbolt* back, only to understand why he held his hand up as well. He was both attacking and defending at the same time. That was so clever! How had nobody done that before? She didn't have time to marvel as an *icicle* flew past her face.

Lilian stood and copied his stance. With her staff leveled in her right hand and her left hand held out in the ward, she concentrated on her attacks. First she fired a small *fireball* as a quick test. Sure enough, the orb of flame launched from her staff and into the dwarf's defenses. He retaliated with another *icicle* that dissipated in her ward while a *lightning bolt* arced from her staff simultaneously. Lilian grinned. She figured it out. This was cake compared to alterations.

The two continued to launch spells at each other. Not a single one landed on its target as their wards served their purposes. She now understood why this technique wasn't common. It took a surprising amount of magic to maintain. It was gonna come down to who ran out of magic first, and everyone knew he had scored higher than she had in the blowout. Talk about boring! Lilian's tail flicked, and she cut her ward to take cover again. The demicat racked her mind for a way to get around his combo. For a moment she considered using *flashbang* as Remus had against her. She snarled. Maybe in a real fight. But she was not gonna copy a technique like that in a tournament. She was gonna do what she had been practicing.

She was gonna outmaneuver him.

Lilian had already demonstrated her agility and precision with the air spells. But for the same reason she didn't want to borrow Remus's tactic, she was reluctant to use the same trick twice.

Her thoughts were interrupted as a huge explosion demolished her cover and sent her airborne. Her pointy witch hat flew off her head and was blown away into the wind. The crowd gasped as the demicat was flung into the air and tumbled back toward the ground, and then cheered as she buffered her landing with *updraft*.

Hair disheveled, face sooty, and eyes ablaze, Lilian glared at her opponent until she noticed something from where she generated the air spell. The flames had been blown away. Could she use wind to deflect fire spells instead of absorbing them with the ring? She could save a lot of magic that way. Unfortunately, it didn't seem that Joshua would comply. With the area in front of him clear of cover, he thrust his staff out and enveloped it with *arcing tendrils*. Lilian had no choice but to hold out her ring and absorb the multiple channeled lightning bolts.

She gritted her teeth, pointed her staff down, and launched herself into the air. She aimed her staff and rained several *fireballs* down at the dwarf. He dodged a few and absorbed the others. He tried to knock her out of the sky with more large, offensive spells, but she was too nimble in the air.

Lilian landed and rolled to absorb the impact. Joshua aimed again, this time blowing a hefty *arctic blast*. Lilian channeled a narrow *firewall* to try to counter it. While it didn't totally negate the frost spell, she used the flaming torrent as concealment as she darted to the side to launch a sneak attack. But every time she tried to get an angle, Joshua would react quickly and absorb her spell.

The elemental battle raged on for another minute, and Lilian realized she was running low on magic. All the high-tier spells they were both using were leaving them sapped. His ward would continue to absorb all her spells until she ran dry, but this gave her an idea. Maybe the rings could absorb only something that was projected. Joshua couldn't negate something that wasn't a launched attack! There was a series of elemental spells that she could channel without using her staff. While it was a gamble, she had to take it.

Lilian pointed her staff down again and launched herself directly at her opponent. While surprised, Joshua still was able to thrust his staff at her. Instead of an attack, however, he cast a spell quite uncommon in a mage fight. A dense mist enveloped the arena. It was clammy, but not chilly like Elaethia's. This spell had *very* little in common with the warrior's dragon magic. This wasn't cold or intimidating; it was just obnoxious. Everything around her was covered in the frost spell *fog*. Lilian couldn't see two feet in front of her.

To make matters worse, she was airborne. She couldn't even see the ground! The only reference she had was where Joshua was once he cast his spell. She didn't know whether she had the reserve to absorb the *fog*, but she certainly wasn't going to take that risk. Lilian's hand began to glow with *burning touch* as she sailed toward her target. A break in the mist right in front of her caught her attention. It could only be movement from her opponent. She had him! She reached forward as she touched the ground, lunging out to grab him.

The world around her suddenly flashed and turned blurry. Pale glowing light enveloped her as icy spikes exploded at her feet. She blinked. *That was weird.* She couldn't move. She also couldn't feel anything. Her heart sank as she realized that this could only mean one thing.

As the *fog* dissipated, Lilian was able to see a little bit of what happened from the corner of her vision. Joshua may not have known her plan, but he knew she was launching at him. Using the *fog* to cover himself, he had placed a *frost rune* right where he knew she would land. The second her foot stepped over it, it activated and hit her. He played her perfectly. She laughed quietly through her paralyzed state.

Well that was clever. I'm gonna have to try that sometime.

Lilian was suddenly in control of herself again, as the medical team had deactivated the ring. The demicat stretched and rolled her shoulders. She gingerly took off the moon ring and handed it to one of the medics. A hand suddenly appeared in front of her.

"That was a good match," Joshua applauded. "I'm surprised you copied my technique so fast. That kind of maneuver is usually unheard of, since it's impossible to cast more than one spell at a time."

"Hmm?" Lilian hummed. "But you *weren't* casting more than one spell at a time. Your staff was launching attacks while your ring was absorbing them. You made use of its automatic system."

"Well, well, you nailed it right on the head. You're smarter than you look."

Her ear twitched. "What's that supposed to mean?"

He laughed. "Just that you're obviously more than a pretty face. Your tactics are nothing to scoff at either. You obviously have a higher grasp on magic than most. I feel we can learn much from each other."

"Oh?" she took his hand as he helped her to her feet.

He kept it as she stood. "Absolutely. Two powerful mages with advanced technique? I think we can get along quite well. Why don't you consider coming to Westreach sometime? Or maybe I could come over to Breeze. There would be quite a lot of benefits to us getting to know each other."

She chuckled and dropped his hand. "Ohhh, I see. Sorry, Josh. I'm not looking to be tied down."

Something about how she said that felt wrong. Lilian turned to where her guild was sitting in the stands and focused on Shiro. The Osakyotan waved fervently with a big smile as she looked at him.

Okay, maybe there's one dork out there I'd consider.

Joshua rubbed the back of his head. "Ah. Shame. Well, I suppose I can thank you for letting me down gently. Either way, good fight, but don't expect me to take it easy on you next year."

"You won't have to," she said with a wink. "In a year, I'll be strong enough to end it in an instant."

"I never figured you for a sore loser," he said with a grin.

"No, I lost fair and square. But the techniques I used today? I've only been working on them for two months. With this new information and more practice, imagine me in twelve. See ya around, Joshie!"

She flitted a hand in farewell and strutted out of the arena. Lilian may have lost, but the crowd roared and cheered for her all the same.

There wasn't much to be said about Elaethia's final battle. It went exactly the same as all the others: over in seconds.

The menacing warrior from Clearharbor was exactly as Peter had described. He wore green-tinted heavy steel armor, with spikes on his shoulders, knees, elbows, and helmet. A heavy shield strapped to his left arm accompanied the morningstar flail in his right. She had to applaud him a little, as he showed little to no sign of being intimidated by her. The two sized each other up, and the match began.

His first strike was an overhead swing. She raised her battleaxe, and the ball and chain wrapped around the handle. He attempted to use this maneuver to rip it from her grasp but found very quickly she was immovable. Instead the dragon hero wrenched the ball and chain backward, yanking the entire weapon out of his hands. The battle ended very predictably after that.

Elaethia went through the tedious process of being announced the winner for the warrior one-on-ones and patiently waited to be told she could leave the arena. Elaethia was rather disappointed at the outcome of it all. She had not been able to battle someone who could give her the challenge she had hoped for. She shrugged. At least she had been able to gain information regarding other techniques and styles. She thought that perhaps this wasn't as fruitless as she once considered it to be. Elaethia considered this one more step in her readiness to face Rychus. A small step, anyway.

"Hold!" a voice boomed over the thundering crowd.

The arena quieted down to murmurs. They very quickly built up with excitement as they saw the owner of the voice. Elaethia turned her head to see Aaron Lahoskie enter the arena.

The referee stammered as the legendary paladin approached. "I uh … what seems to be the problem?"

He was ignored.

"You there. Elaethia, is it?" the Sun Hammer called.

She faced him. "That is correct."

He stopped a few meters in front of her. Aaron was immensely tall. Whether it was because of his stature or posture was unclear, but he seemed to tower over everyone else. Elaethia guessed he was about six foot five. His shining white-and-gold armor was thick and elegant, very sturdy and very intricate. His face was firm and full of pride, verging on levels of arrogance. Elaethia couldn't tell whether or not the blond man was attractive, as the expression he wore made her unconsciously snarl.

"Are you really content with this?" he asked.

"I do not understand."

"Your battles. All your opponents felt lacking, didn't they? None could match your strength, and now you're overcome with unfulfillment? I feel the same. It's shameful to put weaklings like them in the same arena. They do not deserve the honor to face us."

The audience began to murmur. Quiet hisses and boos sounded and quickly silenced themselves as the Sun Hammer glared at them from down his nose.

"I feel no such emotions," Elaethia said. "A moderate amount of disappointment, but that is all. I have brought pride to my guild, gained knowledge, and seen the capabilities of this country. I have no need to speak ill of my opponents."

Aaron crossed his arms. "Hmph. I expected more of a fire from you."

"My frost affinity speaks for itself. Internal flame means nothing to me."

"So I've been told. But I've heard rumors. People have told me that you are a being of legend. A warrior forged for a different era. Ancient power and strength the world has all but forgotten. You are a dragon hero. You have magic abilities. Abilities that you couldn't even use during your fights. You have hardly even been trying this entire time."

"What of it?"

The entire crowd murmured and gasped at her response.

"That's something you and I have in common," Aaron continued. "My fights with the other paladins of the country were disappointing as well. So I have a proposition for you."

Elaethia sighed. "I will hear it. But I have no obligation to heed it."

"Well then. I want a fight," he announced.

The crowd began to grow louder in excitement. The air felt entirely different than it had at any other time. The atmosphere was alive with tension and excitement. The arena buzzed and shook with the sensation of anticipation so thick that Elaethia could nearly taste it.

She raised an eyebrow. "A fight?"

"One-on-one. You and me. The power of the sun against the power of a frost dragon. I've heard the legends surrounding you and your inconceivable power. Seeing just a fraction of it these past two days has set my soul ablaze."

"I decline," she stated flatly.

He froze, and his face fell flat. "What?"

"You said you had a proposition for me. I have little to gain from this fight. I will not waste time on pointless tests of mettle."

"I have never challenged someone so directly in front of such an audience! You are the only one here worthy enough to stand against me, and I you! How can you choose to walk away from such a glorious fight!"

"Glory is meaningless to one such as myself. It gives nothing but troublesome distractions as I work toward my own goals."

"Are you so scared of fighting me that you hide your fear behind a pretty little speech?" Aaron jeered. "I never knew there could be a coward under dragonite armor."

"Your words of provocation are hollow. I am not as easily goaded as other warriors you have encountered."

She turned to walk away. The crowd groaned and even booed at the warrior's words. Mugs, plates, food, and other various objects were hurled into the arena. None landed anywhere near her, but she was perplexed all the same. The once-excited taste in the air turned sour and bitter. These people were obviously displeased with her. But this was of no bother to her. She had no reason to please them. So what was this lump in her gut and burning sensation in her face?

She was halfway out of the arena when she heard what sounded like a unique round of applause from the stands. Tuning her ears, she could tell it was not applause but the steady beat of metal on stone. She turned her head to see that the sounds were coming from her guild. Master Dameon had begun to lead Breeze in what she realized was the guild's war cry. This would be the first time she heard it aloud. The audience went quiet as they, too, turned toward the section of the stands that had started the beat.

Elaethia stopped. She gazed up at her compatriots. Her dragon eyes could make out the individuals in the stands. There were the eager faces of Peter and Liam, the determined ones of Geran and Master Dameon, and excited grins from Lilian and Angela. And then she saw Shiro and Cassie.

The usually quiet girl also rapped the butt of her staff on the stone bleachers. Her face was both nervous and encouraging. Shiro, however, was the one who sealed it for her. Standing stiff, heels together, the samurai had donned his helmet and held his sheathed sword in his left hand. His right hand was in a fist, pounding across his chest with the beat in his sign of salute.

She sighed. It seemed once again that her guild was influencing her to act in a manner discordant to her own way of life. Elaethia turned to the paladin in the center of the arena. For the first time in her life, she would accept a direct challenge. The crowd began to hum and buzz again at the possibility of the fight. The ambient noise was quickly drowned out by Master Dameon and the guild of Breeze with their iconic shout.

"Frossgar! Bring fear and honor to our name! Freeze the sun and give 'em hell!"

"Ah-*ooh!*"

"Give 'em hell!"

"Ah-*ooh!*"

"Give 'em hell!"

"Ah-*ooh!*"

The final shout reverberated throughout the arena. The stands roared in anticipation of the fight to come. There was a moment of clarity for Elaethia. She had felt unfulfilled by those she had battled in this tournament. There was none that could give her a challenge. Yet this human had felt the same way. If they were to battle, perhaps his power would condition her to defeat Rychus.

Elaethia walked back to the middle and faced her opponent-to-be.

"It would seem my guild has ideas other than my own," she declared.

"They know a good match when they see one." Aaron grinned and put on a decorative helmet. Then the paladin began to glow. "The rules remain the same as always. We battle until one of us gives in or is unable to continue fighting. Magic is fully allowed. Let us see what is stronger, Frossgar. Your frost or my light."

"I accept your challenge and understand the rules. I am ready."

Elaethia pulled her helmet over her head, letting her dragon eyes glow through the dark visor.

Aaron laughed with vigor. "Then it has begun! A legendary battle between the Sun Hammer and the dragon hero! This will be a battle to remember for decades!"

Aaron hefted his white war hammer. His bright armor was now definitely shining with almost blinding light. Elaethia realized that was because he had already activated his magic. She had heard this man was specialized in sun magic, just like Angela Bright, but he was very clearly on a different level.

Aaron's left hand shot to his waist and pulled out what Elaethia could barely make out as a wand. With a thrust, a flash of solid light struck her on the head. He had hit her with a *smite*. She staggered back. The structure of her armor could withstand the blow, but dragonite resisted mostly elemental attacks. Holy strikes did not glance off so easily.

Aaron laughed heartily. "You're still standing after that? This will be a more interesting fight than I thought."

The Elaethium

Elaethia gave no response. Instead she inhaled deeply. As she emptied her lungs, the air around her turned chill as a burst of freezing vapor and crystals erupted from her mouth to envelop the paladin. A brilliant beam of light cascaded from the heavens and shone on Aaron. The *frost breath* that entered the light melted and showered him. Light shone through the water droplets, and a rainbow glistened over him. The specialized spell *sun beam* was hot enough to melt the ice to water.

Elaethia raised her battleaxe above her head and slammed the great blade into the earth. A trail of jagged spikes erupted from the ground toward the paladin at an astounding speed. Aaron could not move fast enough to dodge the attack, but he stood steadfast. The paladin slammed his hammer into the approaching burst and shattered it to a halt.

His aura of satisfaction was cut short, as Elaethia cancelled the spell just as she had with *unyielding ice*. The remnants of *burst trail* exploded into shards and shattered against him, peppering him with sharp icy fragments. His armor prevented him from being cut, but the impact alone made him stagger. Elaethia took advantage and charged.

Aaron recovered just in time and pulled out his wand. A blinding flash of light burst from the wooden conduit as Elaethia was forced to halt her swing to cover her eyes. She had nearly been blinded by *holy light*. Aaron gripped his hammer and heaved it into the warrior's side. The impact was the heaviest she had ever felt from a brehdar. The giant hammer slammed into her torso, staggering her a few feet to the side. The paladin charged to strike again while the warrior was blind, but her dragon ears still worked. She heard his approach and slammed the spearhead of her axe into the ground to cast an *ice burst* to intercept him.

Aaron stopped just in time and doubled back to avoid the ferocious spikes. He halted. He was clearly in conflicted deep thought. His once arrogant demeanor gave way to critical thinking. It was as if he was not used to such heavy resistance. But in his few seconds of gathering his thoughts, Elaethia regained her vision.

She slammed her body into his with all her might, sending him careening back several meters. Elaethia leaped into the air as he rolled through the sand, her axe raised for a cleave. But he was not as stunned as he seemed. Aaron shot to his feet and pulled out his wand to hit her again with a flash of *holy light*. Elaethia expected this and had closed her eyes in the approach. Aaron swung his hammer to meet the side of her battleaxe, deflecting it to the sand on his right. Once again an *ice burst* erupted from the impact and struck him in the side. The paladin was lifted off his feet once more and crashed to the ground a few feet to the left. He thrust his wand out in a flash, and Elaethia was struck by another heavy *smite*. She stumbled back, this time falling to a knee.

That was his key. Her frost was unrelenting, but she couldn't keep up with the light. Aaron stood and willed into his magic, calling upon a specialized spell. Light shone from the sky and engulfed the paladin. Blinding energy encircled him and began churning faster and faster, getting brighter and brighter until he was enveloped in the holy energy.

The Sun Hammer had transformed.

The audience had to shield their eyes to prevent themselves from going blind. Now at full strength, Aaron appeared to be little more than a silhouette inside a supernova. Fully engulfed in the holy brilliance, Elaethia was forced to shut her eyes. Even then the light broke through and dotted her vision. She was completely caught in Aaron's *sun envelopment*. Unable to tell where her adversary was, she rose to send her dragon attacks in the direction she thought him to be in. However, every time she wound up, she was struck down by a *smite*. Each hammer of solid sunlight pounded her harder than the last. She now understood how he had obtained his title.

She had to think. What did she know about specialized magic? What were its weaknesses? How could one counter a transformation spell? Aaron's specialization seemed to give him the upper hand. But Lilian had said that Elaethia was also specialized, instead in frost. She had just as many capabilities as he did, if not more. The only way she could think to counter a transformation was with another transformation. Elaethia felt the spell around her to understand its properties. She reached within to call on the power Frossgar had granted her as she, too, transformed.

At once, the air turned cold—well beyond the chill she emitted at will. Elaethia enveloped herself in a freezing torrent so cold it froze the melted water around her in an instant. While her *frost envelopment* was beyond brutally cold, it was not as large as Aaron's of light. She would have to get closer, but every time she rose to her feet, a *smite* struck her back down. His years of practice and experience with the transformation spell seemed to overtake hers, which was small compared to it. She had to make it bigger while being mindful not to harm those who watched. But how was she to do it? She had no experience with this spell, and she was only human. Then again, so was he.

No. No, she wasn't human. Not anymore. Even though Frossgar could not be with her into this transition of her life, his soul and power lived on through her. Aaron may have had years of experience. He may have had the battles to practice, as well as the church and guild to support him. He was a man who had the whole world at his back, while she had it all in front of her. While he had mastered the power of the sun, he was not the Sun himself. He was still just a man. But she—she was a dragon in every way but physical form.

With an inhuman roar, the dragon hero willed her transformation to get stronger. The torrent of unfathomable cold expanded and overlapped the dazzling blaze of light. After only a single second, the paladin's transformation cut off and her vision was returned. Elaethia immediately released her own spell and gazed with dots in her vision at Aaron Lahoskie. His ring had activated, encasing him in the paralyzing form of holy energy—holy energy that, in turn, was encased in ice.

Elaethia braced herself for the onslaught of cheers and shouts that always followed one of her battles. But nothing came. Curious, she turned to look at the audience to see every single one of them huddled together. Teeth chattering, beverages frozen solid, and visibly shivering, the crowd was completely covered in frost.

Chapter 17
White Shepherd

Sixth Era.139. Jinum 16.

Breeze placed second overall, barely losing to Clearharbor. While the warriors and mages dominated, the monks, paladins, and druids were mostly average. The duelists and rangers had a few good members, but none noteworthy beyond Shiro, Geran, and Byron. Breeze had powerful members, but Clearharbor proved more well-rounded. Disappointed, but not disheartened by their placement, the twenty-one contenders and all who had come to watch returned home.

A monstrous celebration was had upon the return to Breeze. The building itself shook from the chaotic partying. Alcohol flowed like an unending spring, while every single adventurer and civilian that entered the great hall danced and sang and ate and reveled well into the late hours of the night. Even Shiro found himself swept up in the chaotic mass of celebration. Lilian wasn't sure if it was because he had become more accustomed to Linderrian traditions or because he was already three mugs deep in alcohol.

Lilian looked around to see where her party members were. It was no surprise that Geran was nowhere to be found, and she soon learned that Elaethia had gone to a local inn to spend the night. Apparently she couldn't sleep amid all the noise. Lilian felt bad for a moment but instantly forgot about it as the local bards began to play her favorite song. A ton of guys—including Liam and Dylan—danced with her, but they weren't the partners she wanted. Lilian found herself disappointed that Shiro hadn't asked her.

Shiro was still around, but he wasn't in the thick of it—not for long, anyway. He started out in the middle of the mob and slowly migrated his way to the edge. He ended the night alone at the bar to watch the celebration continue. Lilian considered following him, but she wasn't ready to give up the spotlight. The sidelines would be there later.

The demicat's eyes soon caught his. Lilian couldn't help but think about how kind and brave Shiro was. He somehow always pushed through, despite having such a sad past. Lilian knew that the death of his sister and grandfather still hurt him after all this time. He just hid it behind a brave face and a wide smile. Shiro was the first man that cared about her for who she was and wanted to know more about her. He was honest, gentle, caring, passionate, confident, strong, had a nice body, and was a total dork. On top of that, he had a face and eyes she just couldn't say no to.

Then Lilian remembered the promise she'd made to him. She had sworn he would never have to make sad faces ever again, just as Mitsuki had done for him before. Besides, Shiro always worked to make her smile too. In a moment of clarity, Lilian suddenly halted her dancing and subtly floated toward the front door.

Shiro craned his neck to see where she was going, as if he were wondering whether it would be all right to follow. His question was answered, as she again met his awed gaze and gently beckoned to him with a single finger. As the celebration raged on, the two slipped alone together into the night.

For the first time in a long time, Elaethia was visited by a vision of her past. Once again in the mountains of northern Svarengel, Elaethia was a young woman, now eighteen years of age. Frossgar had often spoken about continuing to grow until the day they were ready. But she didn't know what it meant to be his champion. The subject of conjoinment for a brehdar and a dragon was a cloudy one for the both of them. She never knew what to ask. Today, however, she would try.

"Frossgar, what does it mean to be a dragon hero?"

The dragon tilted his head. "That is an odd question, little one."

"We have been preparing for the conjoinment, but I do not know what that means for us. What shall become of us? What shall we do? How shall we do it? How do we carry ourselves?"

Frossgar pondered her questions and scratched his chin.

"All of that depends on who you wish to be. I have no legacy to leave behind, as well as little desire to begin one. I have stood idle in solitude as time passed me by. This is no longer my world we live in, but yours. What we do, when we do it, and how we do it is up to you. Do not concern yourself with what it means to be a dragon hero, or even my champion. I have raised you in my image, and I will always be with you. If you bear these things in mind, you need not worry about how to act for me."

"But what of your power? You say I will inherit it, but I do not have magic. How will I learn to use it?"

"I shall guide you. I understand it must be troubling to not be able to learn, but I cannot teach you something you cannot practice. Once the process is complete and we are able to make war against Emperor Rychus, we will explore the depths and capabilities of my magic in your body."

"What are they though?" she pressed. "Could you show me now so I may better understand them when that time comes?"

The old dragon groaned and shifted. "I have not used my magic in a long time, little one. I would even go so far as to say that I have forgotten the extent of my spells. It would seem that two thousand years of solitude has its drawbacks. My memory is strong, but parts of it that remain unused tend to drift beyond recollection. Perhaps as you use what I can teach you after we conjoin, they will return to me."

"There is not one you can show me now?" she asked.

He sighed in resignation. "If you are so insistent, perhaps I can demonstrate the simplest for you now. It takes little magic and is easily controlled."

Frossgar raised his head and drew a deep breath. He opened his mouth to exhale with a steady, controlled, breath that sent a billow of freezing vapor into the vast cave. The dragon spell wafted into the air and slowly floated back down around them like glistening snow. The air around them chilled as the remnants of the spell spread around them. Several glistening particles that touched the floor sprouted into small icy formations.

"That is the most basic attack for a dragon," he said. "*Frost breath* takes no practice or skill. It is something even hatchlings can do. You should be able to use it even without my guidance."

"I see." Elaethia nodded. "I will use it well. Is there anything else you can remember that can be shown here?"

"Your curiosity never ceases, does it?" Frossgar asked in mild exasperation.

"No sir. I am sorry. I realize it was selfish of me to ask for more after you granted me what you did."

"That is all right. It is only natural for the young to seek knowledge. I suppose I should commend you for your eagerness to learn. Nevertheless, that is all for today. Perhaps when I feel up to the task, I can show you more. Until then, continue on your path to build your strength. Magic can wait."

"I understand. Thank you, Frossgar. I will learn everything I can from you when the time comes."

"Indeed you will. There will be much to learn, and seemingly very little time to learn it. But for as long as we are together, it will be simple. A journey begins with a single step, little one. This is step one."

She awoke the next morning with tears in her eyes. It had been nearly two years since she left that cave, but the dream was so vivid that it seemed as though she had just been there. But the question still lingered. What other magic was she capable of? Lilian had told her she could use any spell a frost mage could, but Elaethia was more concerned about the spells Frossgar had given her. The old dragon hardly demonstrated any, save the one from her dream, and she had taught herself *unyielding ice* as well as *burst trail*. The museum in Apogee was disappointingly uninformative as well. It seemed she was doomed to live in ignorance of her true capabilities unless she could figure them out or there were individuals who held such knowledge. Elaethia sighed deeply, gathered what she had brought to the inn, and departed back to the guild.

A comforting spectacle greeted her. Instead of the obnoxious noise and chaos from the night before, the great hall was quiet and nearly empty. Staff members and a few adventurers, many of whom she now recognized, were all that occupied the immediate interior. She looked over to their usual table to see that Geran was already there. He ran a hand over his stubble beard and appeared to be looking over several documents. She found herself eager to speak with him again, as they had not been able to converse normally since before the tournament. The ranger saw her approach and pushed a chair out with his foot so she could sit down.

"Mornin', Elaethia," he said.

"Good morning, Geran. I see you also are taking advantage of the calmness."

"It's nice, isn't it? That's the *one* good thing about massive celebrations like that. The next morning is always nice and quiet."

"Indeed. Have you seen Shiro or Lilian?" she asked. "They stayed longer than I."

"Nah, I haven't. I knocked on their doors this morning but didn't get an answer. I didn't stay much longer than you, so I assume Lilian drank both of them under the table. Their heads have to be hurting, as well as their purses."

She nodded. "A likely assumption. What is it that you are working on?"

"A couple things actually," he said as he spread the papers out. "Michael's been working his tail off since we've been gone. I'm filling out reports on his progress to the guild, as well as writing something called 'counselings' for him. Basically I jot down all the good and bad things I see from him so he can read it and work on what he needs to. This other stack is a follow-up from the tournament. Master Dameon wants reports and training regimens for improving every class. I'm the top ranger, so I'm making the reports for rangers. He *would* have had you do the one for warriors, and Shiro for the duelists buuut …"

"We would not know what to say or how to improve the others."

"Exactly. Anyway, he's got Peter working on that one, and Nathan for the duelists. Lilian's supposed to do the ones for the mages now that she's officially our top mage, but nobody trusts her to do it right. Remus is gonna fill in for her, but he's obviously not happy about it. Next time she may not get off so easily."

"I see. What is that third stack you have?"

Geran looked at the largest stack to his left. "Well. Something you said during our escort got me thinking. Emily entrusted us with her life, and we couldn't protect her. Now, I understand there wasn't much we could have done, as none of us would have imagined they'd cast *lightning strike* in clear skies. Either way, it doesn't sit right with me for letting those Blackwolf bastards go."

Elaethia leaned forward. "So you are ready to track them down?"

"I'll do you one better." He handed her a few of the papers, which turned out to be quest flyers. "We're ready to start hunting."

She scanned each flyer intently. "This is incredible. From what you said, it would take time to get even this much."

"It did. I told you, Nocturnal is always busy this time of year. Our failed quest gave them some extra motivation. The three you're holding are just small-fry quests for hideouts and fences. The rest of what I have here are collaborative reports. Jacklyn and her team are working damn near round-the-clock to find the rest of them."

She nodded intently. "We shall be sure to put their hard work to good use. Once Shiro and Lilian recover, we shall set out immediately."

Geran leaned back. "Works for me. Although it's still fairly early by hangover standards. We might have to wait until tomorrow to—" He stopped as the front door opened. Elaethia turned to follow his gaze, seeing Shiro and Lilian walking in together.

Elaethia tilted her head. "Fascinating,"

"The hell?" Geran raised an eyebrow and called to them. "Hey, Shiro! Lilian!"

The two froze and turned to Geran and Elaethia. They looked briefly at each other until Lilian grinned and made her way over to them with Shiro close behind.

"Well hiya, guys!" she chirped. "Fancy meeting you here. What's up? What's with all the paperwork?"

Elaethia greeted her companions. "Hello, Lilian, Shiro. Nocturnal has found the locations of a few Blackwolf bases, and Geran has obtained the quest flyers to act upon them. We have decided to set out at once, after you and Shiro have recovered."

Lilian turned a little red. "R-recovered from what?"

"Last night," Geran answered.

Her ears started to turn back. "I uh … don't know what you're talking about."

Elaethia continued. "The last time we celebrated like this, both of you felt sick the next morning. Geran and I had assumed both of you were recovering in your rooms."

"Oh!" she perked up. "Oh yeah! Nah, we didn't drink much, y'know? We had to save up for Shiro's wand!"

"Wand?" Geran asked "I thought you guys got one in Apogee and just got back from shopping. I didn't see you leave; how early did you get up?"

"Well, we had to be sure to get a good spot in line! Didn't want them to sell out!"

Lilian's face was full of innocence, but Shiro's eyes darted all over the place. He didn't seem to know what to do with his hands, and he kept shuffling his feet. Elaethia doubted they were being completely truthful, but she didn't sense any malicious intent.

"Whatever," Geran sighed. "Did you guys get a good one?"

"Oh totally! Well, it's not the *best* wand we could have bought, but Shiro's more of a swordsman than a magician, so we stayed cheap."

"I'd like to hear about this from Shiro," he said with a glance at the Osakyotan.

"Huh? Oh! Uh, yes, it's a nice wand," the samurai fumbled to pull out the short wooden conduit. "It's made of birch and has a single gemstone core. Lilia-… I mean … Lili-chan has been showing me how to use magic the best she can, and in return I'm showing her how to use a sword."

"That is most wise," Elaethia said. "While we all have our roles; it is important to maintain a level of flexibility should there be a need for it."

"I kinda hate to admit it, but I agree," Geran said. He turned to the mage. "What made you interested in swordplay all of a sudden?"

Lilian put her hands together and swung them around as if she were holding an invisible sword. "You saw how cool Shiro was in the tournament! Those moves were badass! I don't think *I* could ever do that, but I'd like to learn a little bit!"

"Fair enough. Well, now that we're all here, are we ready to start exterminating Blackwolf?"

Shiro jumped in. "Absolutely! I haven't forgotten about them, and I certainly haven't forgiven them. It's the heavens will to pass judgment on them, but we will be the ones to send them to their fate."

"Right on!" Lilian gleamed. "Lemme get ready, then we can go blast some Blackwolf!"

As she said it, the two of them charged upstairs to prepare for the quest ahead.

Geran turned to Elaethia. "Well, that should give me enough time to finish Michael's last counseling. Are you gonna be ready by the time they are?"

"I will. I have been ready since that *lightning strike* killed Emily." She suddenly paused. "Thank you, Geran. And I am sorry."

The ranger looked up. "Huh? For what?"

"The words I said to you in the thicket were rash and spoken without thought. What I said about you was wrong. I understand you were just as infuriated as I, yet you maintained composure and a level mind, while I lashed out in anger. You did what was right and best for all of us. You are a good man, Geran, and I cannot say I trust any other as I do you. I have had my doubts in my abilities as leader, and your decision then gave me a clear example of how I should conduct myself. If there is anything I can do to return this sense of gratitude and properly apologize for my actions, please let me know."

Geran waved a hand. "I don't fault you one bit. Keeping one's cool in those kinds of scenarios is something that takes years to master. A couple years or so ago, I would have done exactly what you suggested. But if it's really going to eat at you if I don't think of something"—his eyes crinkled with a smile as he looked into hers—"you could let me buy you dinner sometime."

She tilted her head. "Buy me dinner? As in how Shiro does for Lilian?"

"Yeah, a bit like that."

"I see." She smiled, now beginning to understand what Master Dameon once told her. "Then I will gladly accept. In the meantime, I shall get ready for the day's events."

Elaethia stood and began to walk up the stairs. The same smile still clung to her lips for several minutes, and her heartbeat was slightly faster than normal. She didn't understand these feelings in her chest, as they were entirely new to her. One thing she was sure about, however, was that she was quite happy.

Geran watched as Elaethia ascended the staircase and entered her room. As the door closed, he let out a long, ecstatic sigh. He grinned widely and pumped his fist under the table in celebration. A cough to his right took his attention as he met the eyes of Liam Barron. The spearman was also grinning, and he flashed a thumbs-up to the ranger. Geran eagerly returned the gesture and laughed.

Sixth Era. 139. Otoril 25.

Maya sat behind her desk in the guildhall. Ever since the end of the tournament, Cataclysm had been taking Blackwolf quests nearly every other day. It seemed that as soon as Nocturnal found enough information and the receptionists could put it on the board, Elaethia and her party would snatch it up immediately. There weren't many of these quests coming in anymore. Something told Maya that this was the last one.

Representative Hatchfield may have been dead, but the campaign she started certainly wasn't. These quests for ridding the region of the crime faction paid rather well, and Cataclysm always took them. Subsequently, they had made a small fortune between the four of them. Any other party would have cashed in and taken a break, but Maya knew Cataclysm wasn't taking these for the money. This was personal. It seemed the other adventurers in the guild also understood this, as no one argued with them for taking all the Blackwolf quests. Heaven's Light was the only other party to join the campaign.

Maya watched as the iconic quartet left the guildhall to embark on their now thirteenth clear quest. At first, she was nervous to let them go out. They were her good friends, after all. But now she felt very little concern. They had more than proven that they could handle anything thrown at them. With that thought in mind, Maya filed their flyer under "active quests" and shut the drawer.

"Maya, are you busy at the moment?" a very familiar female voice asked from behind.

She turned to greet the head receptionist. "Not at the moment, Brittany. What do you need?"

"If you have about an hour to spare, Master Dameon wants us in his office."

Maya adjusted her glasses. "An hour? What kind of meeting is this? What materials do I need to bring?"

"Nothing," the middle-aged demicat stated. "Just yourself."

Maya stood to brush off her blouse and adjusted the insignia brassard around her arm. "I'm not in any sort of trouble, am I?"

"Nope. Something of the opposite, in fact. Just follow me."

Brittany led Maya upstairs to Master Dameon's office and walked over to the grandfather clock along the far wall.

"Lock the door behind you," the head receptionist instructed.

Maya thought this was odd but complied.

Brittany faced her in full. "All right, I need you to answer with full honesty. Nothing held back. I swear to you that whatever you say will not be held against you should it not be what we want to hear."

Maya blinked. "What does that mean? Who is 'we'?"

"Just answer the questions and you'll find out. Are you happy working with the guild as a receptionist?"

"Yes," Maya said.

"Are you considering making a long-term career out of it?" Brittany asked

"I am; you know this."

"Can we trust you to maintain confidentiality and keep sensitive information about the guild to yourself?"

"Yeah, that's something I agreed on when I signed up."

"Last two—and these are the hard ones." Brittany paused. "Are you ready and willing to die for the guild, its members, and its information?"

"Of course."

"If you agree to the contracts about to be presented to you and then violate the agreements, the punishment is death. Do you understand?"

Maya gulped. "C-contracts? What contracts?"

Brittany's eyes hardened in a manner Maya had never seen. "Yes or no, Maya."

Maya finally nodded. "Yes."

"Then we're ready."

Brittany opened the case to the clock and pulled on one of the chimes. A metallic click came from the corner wall. The head receptionist walked over to a bookshelf, pushed on it, and opened a concealed passage to a secret room.

"Come on in," she said. "Full disclosure: until we say otherwise, you can back out at any second."

"All right," Maya said, and she stepped through.

There were no windows to the room. Inside was a plain circular table with five chairs, a single oil lamp, several walls of filing cabinets, Master Dameon, and all three members of Nocturnal. Maya froze as Brittany shut the entrance behind them and walked in. Master Dameon sat at the table with Jacklyn Meyers and Tyler Glass. Sebastian Timber leaned against one of the cabinets, while Brittany had taken a seat.

Each member of Nocturnal was just as Maya had heard. Jacklyn was a demiwolf with brown hair gathered in a lifted ponytail behind her head. She held herself with grace and almost elegance, but her eyes were so hard that Maya couldn't hold her gaze for long. Tyler was a well-built human with broad shoulders and a stout jaw. His head was shaved, and his hood was pulled up, but he seemed the most relaxed out of all three. Then there was Sebastian. Rumor had it that no one had ever heard his voice, with the exception of Jacklyn and Master Dameon. The black-haired elf was so inconspicuous that Maya almost didn't notice him when she entered the room.

Master Dameon looked at her. "So. You made it this far."

"What ... What's going on?" Maya asked.

"Let me back up a bit," Brittany responded. "Do you remember my husband?"

"Yes, he's an officer in the guard, right?"

The demicat nodded. "He was offered a promotion to major, but only if he changed his station to Apogee."

"An officer in Apogee? He'd have to be crazy to pass that up!"

"Exactly. He accepted, and we've been in the process of getting ready to move ever since. Which means I'm retiring."

"Retiring? But you're the head receptionist! Who would take over?" Maya looked around to see everyone else in the room staring at her. "M-me? B-but what does ... I don't ... Why, Miss Brittany?"

"He's my husband. I swore to be with him through sickness and in health, thick and thin, for better or for worse. Besides, my children are of an age where they can be adventurers, and me working in a guild is influencing them toward it. It's not the life I want for them. Master Dameon and Nocturnal sympathize with this."

"I don't understand. I can see why you would need Master's approval, but why Nocturnal's?"

"Because," Jacklyn said as she stood, "there's more to the head receptionist's duty than meets the eye."

Master Dameon eyed the brown-haired demiwolf. "I can explain for her."

"It's fine," Jacklyn insisted. "We'll be working together from now on, so it's best we get accustomed to speaking with each other. As you know, Maya, no action can be taken by guild members without a receptionist approving it. Nocturnal is no different. As I'm sure you've noticed, neither you nor your peers have ever seen a form from us. We need to keep our work secret while still maintaining a two-point check system with the guild master and a receptionist. That's the duty of the head receptionist."

Maya's head swam, but she managed to keep up. "So with Brittany retiring you need someone to step in for her … so Nocturnal can keep operating?"

"Exactly."

"But … Why me? I haven't been here the longest."

"Doesn't matter," Tyler said. "Ever since Brittany announced her resignation, we've been discussing the best replacement. You're it. We know a lot more about our receptionists than you think, since we keep tabs on *all* members of the guild. You're smart, reliable, trustworthy, quick on your feet, you have good composure, and you would never betray the guild. She won't say it, but Brittany's the proudest of you over any of her other subordinates."

"Tyler …" Brittany grumbled, putting a hand to her face.

Jacklyn ignored them. "This is the biggest responsibility of the head receptionist. You record and document all of our missions, as well as manage their history and reports. You will be handling top secret information that in some cases you will be required to die before revealing. This is your last chance to back away, Redbranch. Are you in or out?"

Maya was struck by a sudden sense of closure. She had been with this guild nearly half her life. The friends she had made and lost here, the stories she had acquired, and the chaotic but charming atmosphere of this guild—*her* guild—were everything to her. This building, the people in it, and everything it stood for were her life. She had always been willing to go the extra mile, and that's what this was. With a sense of finality, she stood firm and faced the covert group.

"I'm in. I accept the position of head receptionist."

"Then we accept in return, and there's no going back now. The only way to be relieved of this position is if all of us and Master Dameon allow you to, or you're killed."

Maya glanced around nervously. "I don't like how you keep saying that …"

"Good. Then it's setting in how high the stakes have become."

Brittany stood up and walked behind Maya. "Don't worry. I've been doing this for thirteen years and haven't been killed once. This part of the job isn't hard at all. Just the most sensitive. We'll get to the rest of the duties you take over later."

Maya looked to Nocturnal. "Thirteen years? How old *are* you guys?"

"Nocturnal's been around for a long time," Tyler explained. "We aren't the first. Jackylne's a second-generation member; Sebastian and I are third."

The silent elf in the corner nodded.

"I founded it thirteen years ago," Master Dameon said. "I was tired of having to circumvent the church and state to get matters of security and information through 'legal' means. Once Jacklyn came in, Nocturnal turned into the covert operations specialists they are. We have to get permission from church and state again, but their grip on the guild isn't as tight as it used to be."

Maya nodded. "Okay, so what does our business entail for your quests?"

Jacklyn pulled out some papers. "You're about to find out. Grab a pen; take a seat."

"W-wait. You're about to go out? Now?"

"Tonight, but we're all here now. We've been tracking down the remaining members of Blackwolf since we got word that Emily Hatchfield was murdered. The most recent quest that you posted regarding them was the second to last holdout for them. Cataclysm took that one just now, as we expected them to. The final one is Blackwolf's last bastion. But it requires a certain tactic and engagement that we can't entrust them with.

"Blackwolf's founder, Quinton Forbes, needs to be taken alive. Forbes is almost guaranteed to kill himself rather than be captured. Geran's the only one in Cataclysm that could handle this, but this task is too big for him alone. He has the tact but not the numbers. So Nocturnal will be seeing to this one personally."

Maya held her hands up in a T shape. "Woah, hold on; I'm not prepared at all. I'm sure you guys need some special forms or pens or seals or … or something!"

"Nope," Brittany assured her. "For the most part, it's exactly as you would do for a normal adventurer quest. It's the follow-up that's a little hard. That will be a full-blown written report of everything that happened during the operation. Every detail they relay to you *must* be put in writing and then filed according to date."

"Operation? You mean quest?"

Master Dameon shook his head. "Nocturnal's missions aren't undertaken the same as the rest of the guild. They aren't quests because they're usually privately assigned by the church and state. We only refer to them as quests to the public for simplicity's sake, as well as to help keep their work on the lowdown. We tell the church and state when they act and, more or less, what they do, and give them code names to distinguish each mission. All of Nocturnal's missions are given these code names instead of descriptions and types. The details are written in the top secret portions, which we keep entirely to ourselves."

Maya picked up the description up and read it.

Mission: Approach designated location prior to sundown. Objective is to locate and neutralize all hostile forces within the compound. All unknowns are hostile. Any individuals that surrender must be rendered unconscious for retrieval. If the operator is in doubt of an individual's sincerity regarding the surrender, accepting the surrender or eliminating the individual is at the operator's discretion.

Parameters: None.

Exceptions: HVT Quinton Forbes must be taken alive.

Allied units: None.

Methods: Any.

Contingencies: Operator survival takes highest priority.

"All right, what do we do now?" Maya asked.

"Fill it out normally," Brittany instructed. "The only difference is that Master Dameon has to sign too. Once you're done, close the folder and leave it on the table. That means this operation is active."

Maya did as instructed. The elf closed the folder and set it down. On the front of the folder she saw a large, solid black line that had the word "Operation" written on it.

"What's this for?" she asked.

"That's where you title the mission, giving it its code name," Tyler answered.

"What's the code name?"

Jacklyn stood and looked Maya in the eye. "Operation: White Shepherd."

It was past midnight in the westernmost parts of Breeze's region. The three members of Nocturnal had lain as still as stones to stake out their target since the sun began to set. Blackwolf's last holdout was an old farm with dry fields and decayed buildings. Through information gathered by observing the location, they had confirmed that Forbes was in the basement of the central building. A total of fourteen hostiles had been confirmed, with potentially more underground or in hiding.

Armed with standard small arms and armor, as well as three magicians, the compound was on moderate alert. Blackwolf knew their outposts had been systematically taken out and this location would likely be next. Blackwolf was expecting a guard platoon or a raid group of adventurers, not a small, covert team. Donned in their all-black attire with hoods and masks that exposed only their eyes, Nocturnal began the operation.

Silently, the three specialists rose to a knee, bows drawn. Jacklyn motioned her team to their targets and blew three quiet breaths in steady succession. On the fourth breath, their arrows flew simultaneously and struck their targets. The three enemies crumpled to the ground without a sound. Jacklyn and Tyler instantly reloaded and fired again as Sebastian dashed to the nearest building. The elf reached the barn and drew his dual falchions. He stood ready in the entryway as his team silently appeared behind him. He felt a bump on his shoulder. It was an indication that they were ready to move. Sebastian flowed inside and moved into the center. The duelist saw no immediate threats and stepped out of the way so the archers behind him had an unimpeded shot at any hostiles. There were no other enemies in the barn. The building was clear.

The next target was a lone outhouse. Nocturnal had seen one enemy enter but had not seen her leave. They crept up to the wooden stall to hear the sound of rustling clothing. Sebastian handed Tyler one of his swords and motioned for him to neutralize the enemy in the locked stall. Sebastian took Tyler's bow and trained it on the main house. He and Jacklyn stood watch as Tyler placed his left hand on the handle. The monk imbued strength into his left arm and poised his right to thrust with the falchion. With a mighty pull, Tyler ripped back and tore the lock off the wooden door. In the same motion, he thrust the sword forward into the face of the woman inside. The mage didn't have time to make a sound before the blade was torn back out and the door closed again. Tyler flicked the blood off the sword and guided it into the sheath on Sebastian's back. He took his bow back out and bumped his team to signal he was ready. Together the three glided forward in silent darkness, trained on the house in front of them.

Nocturnal reached the front of the house. Sebastian slung his bow and hid in the shadows next to the door with his blades drawn. Jacklyn and Tyler turned in opposite directions and trailed around the perimeter of the house. After a minute, they reappeared on the opposite side from where they had started. The two archers floated up the wooden steps to stack behind Sebastian, who had pulled his sword from the neck of a dwarf that had stepped outside. He gently lowered the corpse to the ground and held up one finger to show he had killed one enemy. Tyler responded by holding up two; and Jacklyn, three. Their current count was twelve enemies down. Nocturnal stacked again on the front door, with Sebastian in front. He received the bump, opened the door, and flowed inside.

The two enemies in the entryway were instantly dropped by Jacklyn and Tyler's arrows as Sebastian slid on the ground to intercept the falling bodies. They carried the two corpses outside, entered again, and slowly crept up the stairs. Bows drawn, the two archers ascended at the ready. The old boards creaked beneath their weight, so they moved to the edge of the staircase, where there was less tension. As Jacklyn reached the top, she popped up and aimed into the single room. A watchman sat in a chair in front of the window and looked out into the yard. It was apparent he had not seen their approach. Jacklyn loosed her arrow into the back of his neck, and the elven watchman slumped forward to the windowsill. With the top floor clear, Nocturnal returned to the ground level.

The team moved through an empty kitchen and heard voices in the next room. Jacklyn halted them by holding up a fist. She motioned for Sebastian to stay with her, while Tyler went around to look for another entryway. The human disappeared for a few moments and reappeared with an okay sign. Jacklyn signaled for him to breach through when ready. The demiwolf held two arrows in her hand to be speed-nocked for close quarters, while Sebastian held both swords at the ready. After a moment, the sound of Tyler making an entry signaled them to engage.

Sebastian slashed and thrust his dual falchions with lethal precision, killing three Blackwolf members before they could reach for their weapons. Jacklyn loosed her first arrow into the nearest target, following up with the second shot in one fluid motion. Tyler leaped forward with inhuman speed and agility, and planted his boot on the arrow lodged in the chest of one enemy to secure the kill. He switched targets to the last Blackwolf adherent that had not been affected in the opening attack. He lunged forward and broke the enemy's knee backward with a savage kick and snapped his neck, cutting off his cry.

Jacklyn collected an unbroken arrow and moved her team toward the stairs that led to the basement. She crept down them to see that they led straight into one large cobblestone-floored room. Jacklyn suddenly halted them as she noticed the light behind them cast their shadows along the descending stairs. She crept back up and extinguished the flames of the lanterns and candles.

A female voice echoed from the basement. "What the hell?"

It was given no response. She was alone.

The moment the Blackwolf touched the bottom stair, Sebastian leaped down them to drive both swords into her as he landed. He rolled through with his blades poised and then froze and looked around. The room was not empty, as they first thought. A couple dozen bunks were aligned against the walls, all occupied by sleeping Blackwolf members. This place was truly meant as a final stand, ready for an army. Tyler and Jacklyn appeared behind him to assess what was in front of them. Somewhere in this mass of sleeping brehdars was Quinton Forbes.

Jacklyn pulled out a black hood and made the signal to search. The covert ops team inspected every bed, looking for the leader of the criminal organization. Tyler made it all the way to the very end, where he confirmed the identity of the demibear in the last bed. He held up a hand to signal for Jacklyn to give him the bag. The demiwolf handed it to him as he sprinkled a potent sleeping potion on it. Tyler put it over Forbes's head as the demibear began to stir from the movement. With the black hood fully over his face, Tyler pressed it down on Quinton's mouth and nose until he lay still again. Tyler tightened it so it was snug on his neck and gave a thumbs-up. Jacklyn nodded, motioned at the remaining beds, and gave the signal to kill.

Sixth Era.139. Davilisk 18.

Michael Finway was now one day from his birthday and deadline. For the past seven months, Geran had given him classes, instructions, demonstrations, fieldwork, homework, workbooks, workouts, work, work, work. The human was relentless in his mentorship, and every second not spent completing a quest or recovering from one was spent whipping the young demiwolf into shape. Michael staggered downstairs to his bunk after a session with Geran and collapsed onto the cot with heaving breaths. The other apprentices watched as the black-and-white-haired demiwolf pulled out his waterskin and took several short sips.

It was another ruck run today. The two of them would put on their backpacks and equipment and go for a jog. Michael thought his own pack was heavy at twenty-five pounds, not including his bow, dagger, and leather armor. Then he tried on Geran's after accusing him of skimping out on the weight. The ranger's own pack was easily twice as heavy. Michael couldn't figure out how the hell Geran could run seven kilometers with that thing and be only a little out of breath.

Michael rolled over, sat up, and started getting changed for a bath. Geran had told him to meet upstairs again in one hour for some more classwork. He had to bathe, change, and eat before that. He didn't have time to lie down.

"Jeez, Finway," a duelist apprentice piped up. "What's Mr. Geran *doing* to you out there?"

"The better question is what *isn't* he doing to me," he replied.

"I still can't believe he took you out when it's this cold. It's below freezing out there, and the snow's only getting deeper."

"The enemy doesn't care if you're cold; so neither should you."

"Another one of his phrases?"

"Bingo." The demiwolf nodded

"That blows. Mr. Nathan doesn't do any of that stuff with me. He trusts me to stay fit on my own. Guess you pulled the short straw, huh?"

Michael shrugged and grabbed a towel and a clean set of clothes. "Maybe. But Mr. Geran never does pointless stuff like some of your guys' mentors. He doesn't haze or berate me, and I can tell everything he does has a reason. I've soaked up everything he's put in me, and it hasn't failed me yet."

The other apprentice shrugged. "Either way, I think you're just as crazy as he is for doing all this crap. Thank the heavens you'll be an official adventurer tomorrow."

"Yeah, but that doesn't mean I'll stop being his apprentice."

"That's rough stuff, man. You'll never be able to get away from him."

"Honestly, I think that's a good thing," Michael said while heading upstairs. "It's nice to know he'll always be there if I need him."

Now clean and in a fresh set of clothes, Michael realized he was *very* hungry. The guild food was good, but he'd have to spend a lot of money to fill his stomach. He decided to risk going out into town for a cheaper meal. Michael grabbed his boots and coat, and he dashed outside. He nearly slipped on the ice once he saw who was out there. Sitting at one of the snow-covered patio tables were Mr. Geran and Miss Elaethia.

"Oh, Michael," Elaethia noted.

"M-M-M-Mr. Geran!" he stammered. "I-it's not what it looks like! I'm just going out for some cheaper food!"

Geran laughed. "I gave you a timeline, Michael; I don't care what you do until then. You could take a nap for all I care."

"Although it is unlikely he would wake in time for your lesson," Elaethia noted.

"Speaking of which, how much time do we have left?" Geran asked his apprentice.

"Thirty-five minutes."

Geran scratched his stubble beard. "Tell you what … I'll give you an extra half hour. Your legs gotta be feeling like jelly right now, and I don't want you killing yourself on the slick ground. Is that coat warm enough for you?"

"Yeah, but should you be asking me that? Yours is even thinner than mine," Michael noted.

Geran looked at his ranger cloak, which was inverted so the gray side was out instead of the green side. He then looked over to Elaethia, who was only in her casual wear. The dragon hero was completely unaffected by the freezing temperatures.

"I'll be fine," he said. "The conversation's good, and we have decent privacy out here."

Michael looked back and forth at them and got the hint. "*Oh!* Oh, I gotcha. All right, Mr. Geran, thank you!"

The demiwolf flashed a grin at his mentor and headed out into town. Michael pulled his hood over his head and wiggled his ears until they comfortably poked through the slots in the cloth. He took a deep breath and released it slowly, sending a thin cloud of vapor from his mouth. He twitched slightly as a snowflake softly landed on the tip of his reddening nose and melted.

A smile cracked his lips. He looked around the city as he made his way through it, taking it all in. It was his favorite time of year. The winter solstice was here, and the Evergreen Festival was only a week away. Wreaths, holly, mistletoe, and assorted coniferous bows lined the streets of Breeze, covered in a thick blanket of soft, powdery snow. It was the time of year for the citizens to reflect on the gifts and blessings they had received, and this year had given him *plenty* to be thankful for.

As he passed by the usual food stands and restaurants near the guild, he noticed they were all quite full. Even though he had a little over an hour, Michael didn't feel like waiting in line. He decided to go a bit farther, and he soon found himself at the town square. Michael had seen a few places here, so he figured he'd try them out. He strolled up to the counter of a small restaurant and rang a little brass bell that hung from it.

"Coming!" a female voice called from inside. Moments later, a brown-haired human appeared. "Hi there! What can I get for ya?"

"Hey, I've never eaten here before, and I don't see a menu. What do you got?"

"Our daily special is seared trout," she said. "We have some venison, but that's getting a little harder to come by, so it'll cost a bit more."

"I'll go with the fish then. Can you make that a double order?"

"Sure thing. That's gonna be five silvers." the server said then paused. "Say, I've seen you around before."

"Huh? Where?" Michael asked as he handed her the coins.

"Going in and out of the city every now and then, sometimes with Geran. Your hair makes you easy to recognize."

"Yeah, I get that a lot. Wait, you know Geran?"

She gave a half-shrug. "Well I don't *know* know him. I've talked to him every now and then, but he only comes here when Elaethia visits me."

"Yeah, he's my mentor. I'm gonna be a ranger and am in an apprenticeship with him until then. I didn't know you were friends with Elaethia. Do you know everyone from Cataclysm?"

"Well, mostly Elaethia and Lilian, and a bit of Shiro, too. I helped those two get to the guild when they first entered the city. Elaethia is one of my closest friends."

"That's pretty cool," Michael said. "Elaethia saved my hide from some bandits, so I came here to be her apprentice. But I decided being a ranger would be a better pick for me, so I trained with Geran instead."

The girl's mouth dropped. "Wait, that was *you!*"

He cocked an ear. "What was me?"

"Elaethia told me about that when she got back. It was her first quest—and our first real conversation. I remember it clearly. What are the odds you were one of the kids stuck in that tower?"

"Hey, I'm not a kid. I'm probably the same age as you!"

"Oh yeah? How old are you?"

The demiwolf puffed out his chest. "Sixteen tomorrow,"

"Nuts," she grumbled, and she folded her arms on the counter. "I'll be fifteen for three more months."

"Well, if it makes you feel better, I thought you were a little older than me at first."

"Really?" Her eyes lit up and met his. They stared at each other for a second and blushed.

Michael scratched the back of his head. "Yeah … Hey, uh, what's your name?"

"Cathrine, Cathrine Wilhelm," the girl replied. "What's yours?"

"Michael Finway," he said, and he held out a hand. "Nice to meet you."

"Nice to meet you, too."

She grasped it, and they shook hands for a few seconds. They locked eyes, flushed, and quickly pulled their hands away.

"So, uh … What are you gonna do for your birthday?" she asked.

"Well, tomorrow I'm gonna apply for the guild to be an adventurer," he said. "I've been training for seven months, and hopefully Master Dameon will let me in. He's kinda suspicious of me since I'm from Westreach, though."

Cathrine handed him his order as it finished. "Oh. But you're staying here in Breeze … Right?"

"Oh, for sure! I'm gonna be making a career out of this city, anyway. Geran's gonna give me a final lesson tonight for the application process, and then I'm gonna give it my best tomorrow. Oh! I gotta hurry 'cause that's starting soon!"

"Oh, okay. Well, good luck tomorrow! I really hope you get in!"

"Me too, Cathrine! I'm really excited. Thanks for the food!" He took a bite and swallowed. "Hey. This ain't bad at all. I wish I had more time to actually enjoy this."

Cathrine laughed. "I'll tell Papa you liked it; he loves hearing that."

"Please do," he said as he inhaled the rest of it. "Man, I'd really love to stay and chat, but I gotta go."

"That's okay!" she assured him. "But hey, if you get in, why don't you come back here to celebrate?"

Michael looked up as he set the wooden plate back on the counter. He noticed that she had frozen the moment the words came out of her mouth, which was still half-open. Cathrine's face began to turn pink as her hands slowly came up to hold her cheeks. She quickly cleared her throat and looked down to straighten her apron.

Michael blinked a few times until he found his voice again and started back for the guildhall. "Oh yeah, for sure. I'd love to come back and talk some more. Both you and your dad's cooking are worth it."

His last words of farewell came back to him as he jogged back and rounded a corner. *Did I really say that? Why did I say that? Stars above, that was an embarrassing thing to say. Sure, she was cute, and seemed nice, but I don't even know her. Maybe it was her soft, brown eyes, or the way her braided hair fell over her shoulder, or her innocent voice that made me want to …* He shook his head back and forth. *No, no, no. What am I doing? Now is not the time to think about girls; I have bigger things to worry about! I have to get ready for tomorrow so I can—*

Michael's thoughts were interrupted as he collided head-on with a sign outside a café. He crashed over it, rolled with the fall, and sprang back up. He paused for a second and let out an excited chuckle. *Hey, that was a pretty cool recovery. Geran's drills are finally paying off.* The sound of a window slamming open snapped him back to reality. Michael scrambled back to pick up the sign and right it to where it belonged.

"Hey!" A man's voice yelled from above. "Watch where you're going! You better not have broken my sign!"

"I didn't! It's all good! Sorry, sir!"

The dwarf closed the window. "Hmph. Kids."

Michael shook his head, clapped his hands against his cheeks to focus himself, and continued back to the guild.

Chapter 18
Blood

Sixth Era.139. Davilisk 28.

Elaethia sat frowning at her usual table in her casual attire. Her mind was plagued by conflicting feelings. Blackwolf had been exterminated by their hands, and Emily was avenged. So what was this negative emotion that floated around her head? Cataclysm had spent all this time doing nothing but taking quests to hunt down the crime faction. Now that they were all gone, it seemed as if there were nothing left to do.

Of course that was not true, as there were always quests to be had. The foremost part of her mind didn't care what they did as long as it aided the people. But there was something so fulfilling about the campaign they had undertaken. She just couldn't bring up the same motivation she had then. Unsure as to what to do with these feelings, she approached the first member of her party that she came across. Unfortunately, it was Lilian. However, the flaky mage had been known to show signs of deep thought before.

"Lilian," Elaethia called to her as the demicat came downstairs. "Do you have a moment to talk?"

"Yeah, sure!" she said. "I was just getting a drink anyway. Be right there."

Lilian waltzed to the bar to order a mug of her usual sweet-tasting mead and joined Elaethia.

"What's up?" Lilian asked as she took a large gulp.

"How has the last month felt to you?" Elaethia began.

"Whatcha mean? A lot happened."

"Concerning the conquest we held against Blackwolf and how you feel now that it is over."

"I haven't really thought about it much. Yeah, I was more than happy to wipe them off the face of the earth. But after a while, it got kinda dull."

"Dull?" Elaethia tilted her head. She'd had quite the opposite feeling as they progressed.

"Don't get me wrong. I didn't get bored of blasting the bastards, just more or less of taking the same kind of quest over and over and over again. I mean, that's all we did. Three, sometimes four days a week. No diversity at all."

"But they needed to be destroyed as soon as possible. Do you believe we should have gone about it a different way?"

Lilian rocked back in her chair. "Nah, not really. You and Geran were right in saying they needed to be dealt with ASAP. I just woulda been more into it if we could have thrown in some different kinds of quests here and there. Overall? I'm glad we're done with it. Blackwolf is all but exterminated, and we can go on different kinds of quests now. Shake up this boring routine we've gotten into."

"All but exterminated?" Elaethia asked. "Was their last bastion not recently destroyed by Nocturnal?"

"Oh yeah, they completely ghosted the place. Maya told me the reason they got that last quest instead of us was because they had some special way they needed to do it. I wanted juicy details, but she wouldn't spill. Something about 'confidentiality.' She's been using a lot more big words like that since becoming head receptionist."

Elaethia tilted her head. "What is the head receptionist?"

Lilian made a face. "You're asking that *now?* How long have you been in the guild again? Ah, never mind. Basically, she's now in charge of all the admin responsibilities and logistical stuff. If it's on paper or deals with the facilities, she's in charge of it. Super boring, in my opinion, but she seems happy with it. The only part of it that sounds fun is that now all the staff answer to her."

Elaethia nodded. "I see. So if Nocturnal completed their mission, then all of Blackwolf is dead, yes?"

"Not *all* of them. There's one left. They captured the ringleader, and the city's gonna have him put on public trial, then executed."

"Why would they do that?"

Lilian rolled a hand. "Something, something, send a message, something, something, enforce the laws and demonstrate the consequences. I think it's like showing all the bad guys what'll happen if they do this kind of stuff."

"No, I mean why would they bring him back alive if they intend to kill him regardless?"

Lilian slumped. "I dunno. It's all politics. Doesn't affect me in the slightest."

Elaethia shook her head. "I will never understand their way of thinking."

"Don't even bother. It's not worth it."

"You understand them?"

"Feh," Lilian spat. "I *hate* politics. Buncha old people sit in a room and argue about how not to fix something until it expires, and then they move on to ignore the next problem. Those overpaid windbags only ever unanimously decide on something if it has to do with getting more money. The only time they get serious is when reelection season comes up, and then it's back to blowing smoke up each other's asses."

"How do you feel about the church then?" Elaethia asked.

"I don't mind 'em. They don't tell us how we should or shouldn't live, and they at least do something for the public on a daily basis. The high priest of the Sun and high priestess of the Moon both make frequent trips around the country to spread health and comfort."

"I do not know much about them."

Lilian shrugged. "Not much to tell. If you know about the followings for the Sun and Moon, you can get a good feel for them. The high priest preaches and guides for strength and courage, and the high priestess teaches wisdom and magic. They both speak about the heavens and how we are their beloved children. It's nice to know there's someone up there looking out for us."

"I have never relied on the heavens for strength or wisdom. All I have is gained through my efforts and the teachings of those who have guided me."

The demicat pulled out a brush and began to groom her tail. "You'd be surprised. The heavens work in mysterious ways, often through other people. I'd say it was a sign from the Sun with you getting Michael out of that tower, and the Moon working through Geran to make him his apprentice."

"You seem keen in your religion."

"Maybe. If the Moon gave us magic, then I have her to thank for getting me this far. A lot of people lean on the heavens for everything that's good and then curse them for everything bad. I don't think that's very fair. You gotta have the bad with the good to balance it all out. If everything that ever happens is good, is anything good at all?"

Elaethia stared at her. "Are you sure you do not wish to pursue a career in the church?"

"What are you, nuts? I'm a mage, not a priestess! They can't even blow stuff up!"

"I apologize if I offended you. That was meant as a joke."

Lilian's jaw dropped. "*You* told a *joke?*"

"I have tried a few before, but none of you seemed to notice. Did this one work?"

"Oh man, forget *this!*" Lilian downed the last of her beverage and shot up. "I gotta tell Geran; he'll never believe it!"

"I believe he is with Michael. They should be trying out for the guild."

"Nah, that finished up this morning. Michael totally nailed it! Geran's probably in his room being an introvert right now."

"Truly? I have not seen either of them since."

Lilian started upstairs. "Oh yeah, Michael should be out back with Dylan's party right now. He's gonna fill in for the opening I left."

"But he is a ranger, and you are a mage. How could he fill your role?"

"You *know* what I *meant!*" the mage called down.

Elaethia rubbed her chin until it dawned on her that Lilian meant that Michael would fill in the empty spot in Dylan's party. The warrior shrugged and stood to go outside and see for herself.

It was a chilly afternoon—not that the dragon hero could tell on her own, but by looking at the few people outside, she could see they were rather cold. She moved to the outside training area behind the guildhall and saw the intermediate party of four practicing on some dummy targets. The young group was obviously engrossed, as they didn't seem to notice her approach. Dylan performed his strikes and flourishes on one target, while Horst hacked at another with his axe.

Dana stood shivering off to the side with her white robes wrapped tightly under a thick wool coat. Her dim eyes suggested she used her magic to keep the two fighters going past any exhaustion. Michael stood next to Dana, peppering a dummy with arrows. The straw-and-wood target stood thirty meters away, its face completely turned into a pincushion by the young ranger's shots. Elaethia's boot crunched on the snow as she approached. The demiwolf cocked his ear and turned to the noise. He seemed startled for a second, but then his face lit up.

"Oh, hey! Miss Elaethia!" he called, and he bounded over. Dana and Horst turned to look, while Dylan halted his flourish, saw her, and slipped on the ice.

"Good afternoon, Michael," she greeted him. "I heard your application went well."

"Yes ma'am! Master Dameon's still is a *teeny* bit wary of me, but he seemed pretty happy with my progress. It's all thanks to Mr. Geran's training."

"He is quite capable in his field. Given his patience and knowledge, it is no surprise that he is an excellent teacher as well."

"All the field time helped, too. We went on a couple of intermediate kill quests, and I even made up a strategy for one of 'em! It's so satisfying watching something you planned out come together. I'm really glad I chose to be a ranger. No offense to you, Miss Elaethia."

"None taken. And you do not need to refer to me as 'Miss Elaethia' anymore. You are an adventurer of this guild now, just as I am."

"Aw, but it feels so weird. I've only ever called you that. Besides, I'm just a B level. You're an R level, and it doesn't sit right talking to you casually."

She tilted her head. "Raid level? When has this been decided?"

"Sure, the highest you've done are V level, but it's universally accepted that you're stronger than that. I mean, you're a frickin' dragon hero! *And* you single-handedly beat the Sun Hammer, who is close to gaining the legendary G level! If you got a new guild tag with an *R* on it, nobody'd argue one bit."

"That matters not to me. If the guild sees fit to alter my status, so be it. I do not pursue titles or stature. Nevertheless, I will insist you refer to me by name. It makes me feel odd to be called 'miss.'"

"All right, Mi … uh, Elaethia. Thanks for checking up on me!"

"You are my friend, Michael. It is only proper to do so," she said. Michael beamed as his tail wagged.

Dylan stepped up. "Hey, uh, ho-how's Lilian doing?"

"She is well. Her magic abilities get stronger every day. Why do you ask? Does she not come to visit as she promised?"

"No, no, she does. I just … feel she's holding something back from us."

"How so?" Elaethia asked.

Dana spoke up. "Like, she's not the same anymore. She's not as goofy or compulsive. She's still very much Lilian, but it's like she's grown up a lot. Not sad or serious, just …" She shook her head. "I don't know how to explain it."

"I do not understand complex feelings like this very well," Elaethia admitted. "But I know she has been working very hard in her studies. She holds no ill feeling toward you; nor does she say negative things about her time in your party. Lilian has discovered a new beginning in the world of magic, as well as the path she will take to reach her own goals. Do not fret for the relationship you have with her. She is not so shallow as to leave you behind on her journey."

"Thanks, Elaethia," the priestess sighed. "That makes me feel better."

"All of us," Horst grunted.

"I am glad to hear that," Elaethia said with a smile. "Have you all taken a quest together yet?"

Dylan's eyes widened. "What? Are you serious? It's Michael's first day; why would we jump right into a quest?"

"Is that so strange?"

Michael's ears cocked. "Oh yeah. Elaethia went out on her first day. Did an A-level by herself, remember? She'd probably think it's normal."

Dylan shook his head. "Yeah but she's *Elaethia*. We aren't all juggernauts like her."

"Juggernaut?" The dragon hero tilted her head. She had been called that before but didn't know what it meant.

"It's fine, though," Michael continued. "I've gone on quests with Mr. Geran before. It's not like I'm a *total* newbie."

"Still," Dana insisted, "we like to plan our quests a day in advance. We can go in now and pick one out for tomorrow. But it's not safe to just jump into one. I don't know anyone who can just get up and go on a dangerous mission like it's nothing."

Shiro suddenly trotted around the corner. "Elaethia-sama! The rest of us have decided to take a quest. Geran and Lilian are looking at the board right now; you should join us!"

"Very well, thank you for finding me. Let us go." She followed him inside as Dana's mouth hung slack.

"What are we considering?" Elaethia asked as she and Shiro joined their companions. Lilian had her face up to the corkboard, while Geran stood behind and scanned the available flyers.

The ranger shrugged. "I figured I'd let you guys decide. It's been nine months, but the last ten years of solitude still has my scope way off from what you guys want. I'm not saying I'm fine with *anything*, but I'll be okay with going off what you all decide. Although Lilian seems pretty bent on the V section again."

"As if we'd go back down!" the mage scoffed.

"Do you see anything yet, Lili-chan?" Shiro asked.

"A couple. There're a lot of sorcerer ones, but that's normal this time of year. These all pay pretty good, but that's not a big concern for once."

Shiro rubbed his chin. "So sorcerers are more common in the winter …"

"Well not more common, but more prominent. Same with bandits, but those usually stay in the I and A levels. Sorcerers like to experiment on people and occasionally animals. But this time of year, everything goes into hibernation or doesn't wanna leave the house. So they venture out or get crafty with their tricks. It wasn't too long ago that the guild stopped taking anonymous requests. Some sorcerers would send them in just to lure low-level adventurers right to their lair."

Elaethia took a flyer off the board and read it aloud. "In the advances of monster taming and trading of rare goods, a trapper has asked for the delivery of twenty pristine griffin feathers to be delivered to the location provided below. There will be a bonus five times the current reward for each griffin eggshell, and twenty times the current amount for an intact griffin egg."

"Does it say where there are griffin nests we could go to?" Geran asked

"It does not."

"Then that's a no-go. I can think of only one place we *might* find a griffin nest, and that's in southern Westreach. I'm not going on a wild egg hunt like that. I'm *especially* not willing to get clawed to ribbons by a pissed-off mama griffin."

Lilian turned around. "Hey, Geran. You've never suggested a quest for us before. Why don't you pick?"

"I just said I don't think I'd be the best to choose for us."

"Aw, c'mon! My standards are pretty low right now; you should take advantage while you can!"

"Yeah, Geran," Shiro agreed. "You've always followed us on fighter quests, why don't you take us on a ranger quest?"

Geran raised an incredulous eyebrow. "You guys wanna go on a ranger quest?"

"That's a great idea!" Lilian chimed. "Then we can brag even more about how capable we are!"

"I do not see why not," Elaethia joined. "I imagine a ranger would like allies in case of emergency, especially in the higher-ranking quests."

"You're not wrong. There've been times where I'd have appreciated some backup. All right, I'll take a look."

Geran stepped forward and scanned the high-ranking ranger flyers. Elaethia, too, read along, seeing mostly overwatch and espionage quests. Her study was cut short as Geran pulled a flyer off the board.

"This one would work," he announced.

Shiro craned his neck to see. "Read it for us, Geran!"

"There have been disappearances one day's walk northwest of Breeze. People approaching the area around the ruins have been reported to enter but not leave. Individuals that venture into these ruins have not returned; nor have their remains been found. Scout the area for the reason behind these disappearances."

Lilian scratched her ear. "Spooky."

"Those who enter never leave?" Shiro asked. "Is this the work of evil spirits or demonspawn?"

Geran flipped the flyer over. "That's what we'd be finding out … although there's no such thing as spirits, and I don't think a demonspawn is likely at all."

"What are those yellow circles next to the red *X* in the top corner?" Elaethia asked.

"You guys already know the *X* means someone failed. A circle is something only for suppression, scouting, and cure missions. It means the suppressors couldn't locate the threat, the scout couldn't find anything, or the priest couldn't identify the ailment in the patient."

"So two circles indicate two rangers investigated and came back with nothing."

"Correct," Geran said. "The *X* is what's bothering me, because that means the first and third came back empty-handed. But the second never returned at all. Let's get ready and meet back down here."

Cataclysm suited up and approached the reception desk with the flyer. But instead of only Maya at the counter, the elf was accompanied by a human girl they had never seen before.

Maya looked up as they approached. "Ah, perfect timing. I'm training the new receptionist. We're short one since Brittany left. I was just explaining the procedure for authorizing quests, even though she won't be able to do that until I think she's ready."

"Hello, I'm Sophie Stone," the girl greeted politely.

Sophie's eyes shot around to look intently into the face of each member as if she was studying them. She shifted in her seat and looked back up at Maya, and she then quickly looked away and glanced randomly around the room. Despite that, her expression was calm, even friendly. Her hands sat tightly clasped, yet still, in her lap. Sophie was a tall girl that looked to be about seventeen. Her blond hair, blue eyes, and facial structure struck Elaethia as somewhat familiar.

"Have we met?" the warrior asked her.

"No ma'am, I don't think so. You probably know my brother, though."

"You have the same family name as Peter," Shiro said. "Are you his sister?"

"Yeah, that's me—Peter's little sister," Sophie sighed. She tensed and glanced up at Maya, who gave a gentle smile with dark, burning eyes. "I-I mean, yes sir. We are related. I apologize for my attitude."

Geran waved it aside. "So you've got an apprentice too now, eh, Maya?"

"Kind of, but not quite," she said. "We call them trainees, which is a bit different from the apprenticeship. Instead of her following me around and helping me, I follow her around and give her instructions. She's been good at keeping things organized so far, and her memory is unnatural. We're still working on manners, however."

"Sorry," Sophie mumbled sheepishly. She then tensed up again. "I mean, I'm sorry for giving off a bad first impression. I'll be sure to help you however I can. What can I do for you today?"

Geran put a hand up. "Don't worry about the formalities for a minute. You seem like you've got something you'd like to get off your chest. It's okay to tell me."

Sophie looked up at Maya, who nodded her approval. "Well, I actually am sorry for coming off like that. I'm just tired of being bunched up with Peter. Everywhere we went, it was 'Peter this' or 'Peter that.' Even when we're around family, everyone just flocks to him. It's like I don't even exist when he's home. Every time the subject comes up that we're related, the conversation switches right to him. I don't want to sound selfish or anything, but I'm just so over it."

"Harsh," Lillian said sympathetically. "Why'd you join the guild then?"

"At first I thought I could be an adventurer too and make my own legacy. But we aren't magicians, and I don't like getting hit. I don't have any other life ambitions, so I thought I'd become a receptionist. I'm more or less used to the adventurer lifestyle anyway."

"Do you harbor ill feelings toward your brother?" Elaethia asked.

"Oh, no ma'am! I mean, no. He's a good big brother. He's always provided for the family when we are in need, and defended us from anyone or anything. We all love each other, but we need our space."

"Well," Maya interjected, "I don't mean to cut you guys off, but we do have some other things to get to. Not to mention I've got my own new responsibilities on top of that. Sophie, you can feel free to finish this conversation with them once your shift is over. In the meantime, we need to get down to business."

"Absolutely," Geran said, and he pushed the flyer forward. "We'd like to take this one."

Maya picked it up and read it. "Cataclysm is taking a ranger quest?"

"Well, it's a notably difficult one. I'm pretty sure I'd be fine alone, but they insisted. I know the request already says so, but you wouldn't happen to know anything about the previous three attempts?"

"We've got nothing. Even Byron couldn't find anything, but he and the first didn't even enter the ruins. We suspect the missing ranger did, however."

"I hate going in with no leads," Geran muttered.

Maya smiled. "But you're used to that."

"Doesn't mean I have to like it. This might be the first quest we don't complete."

Lilian grinned and flapped her cape. "Fat chance of *that*! If those ruins are making people disappear, I'll turn 'em into a crater."

Maya laughed nervously. "I believe you, but please don't. The client is trying to resettle that land, and that can't happen if you burn it to the ground."

"Hmph. Lame."

"We'll be careful, Maya-san!" Shiro promised. "Can you approve it for us?"

"Can do," the elf said, and she stamped the flyer. "Be careful out there, guys."

Cataclysm reached the ruins a day later. Geran had studied the map prior to their arrival and had chosen a position on a hill that could see into most of the ruins. The area was not too far off a main road, but it still seemed to be in the middle of nowhere. A thin forest surrounded the landscape, which was covered in an ever-growing sheet of soft snow. The ruins themselves lay at the base of the hill and sat on the mostly flat terrain that spread beyond it. A couple other hills rose here and there, but the frozen forest was mostly level.

Geran observed everything through a spyglass, which he passed around to his companions every hour or so to keep them engaged. Shiro and Lilian eventually got bored and ducked off to warm themselves with the mage's *burning touch*. Elaethia, completely immune to the chill, stayed with Geran the entire time. Though her dragon eyes could see farther than a normal brehdar's, she inspected with the spyglass as well. The ruins appeared to be an old fort or maybe a small castle. Mossy stone structures crumbled around moldy and decrepit wooden stables and sheds. The courtyard was empty, save for a shambled well in the center.

Geran collapsed the spyglass as the sun began to set. He shook the snow from his cloak and rolled his shoulders. The ranger reached to his side pouch to deposit his spyglass. With reddened fingers, he closed the flap and stuffed his hands into his armpits. A small cloud of vapor wafted from his mouth.

"Nothin'. There's no sign of any life whatsoever. Any tracks or imprints from before have been covered by fresh snow."

"What do we do from here?" Elaethia asked.

"If it was just me, I'd set up camp and keep watch for another day or two. But I doubt any of you are game for that."

"I do not wish to sit idly by and do nothing. What will we do instead?"

"One moment." Geran turned and let out a low, distinctive whistle. Moments later, Shiro and Lilian appeared.

"Didja find anything?" the demicat asked.

"No. We've got a decision to make. Option one: we go back to the guild and add another yellow circle—"

"Screw that! I didn't walk all the way out here, freezing my tail off, just to go back! What else you got?"

"Option two: we go down there for a closer look."

"But hasn't anyone who's entered never come back out?" Shiro asked.

"Correct. We'd be taking a huge gamble, but it's our best option for finding anything in a reasonable amount of time."

Elaethia tilted her head. "Do you believe this course of action to be worth the risk?"

"Since there's four of us? I'd say so, yeah."

Shiro scratched his head. "So we'd be entering an area that may consume us, which would result in no one ever hearing from us again and our remains never being found."

Geran nodded. "Basically."

Cataclysm sat in silence for a few moments.

"I love this plan!" Lilian suddenly burst out. "I'm glad to be a part of it! Let's go!"

The mage hopped up and began parading down the hill.

"Lilian, wait!" Geran stood to stop her but was too late. "Gaaaah, that damn cat. Everyone stay close; don't go off on your own without warning!"

"Here's the plan," Geran began as they reached the courtyard. "Let's split up into two teams: Shiro and myself, and Lilian and Elaethia. You ladies will keep watch here. Shiro is the only one of you three who is good at stealth, and I don't want any of us to be alone. He and I will scour the area, and if you don't hear from us within five minutes, follow our tracks. From there you guys can make the call to go back for help or attempt a rescue."

Lilian flicked her tail. "Well, obviously we'd try to get you back."

"That may not be the best course of action," Elaethia corrected. "Depending on the case, we might not know where they are, or they may already be dead. Though it would pain us so, it would be wiser to retreat than to die with them."

"Bold of you to assume they could kill us."

"If our adversary is clever enough to get the better of Geran and fast enough to overwhelm Shiro, I would not doubt they have capabilities against you or I."

Lilian shrugged. "If you say so."

Elaethia took note of their surroundings as Geran and Shiro departed. The decaying structures loomed and crumbled all around them. Dead silence enveloped them. The area was still enough as it was, but the fresh snow dampened all noise except for the sound of the crunching footsteps the samurai and ranger made as they disappeared. Elaethia and Lilian leaned against one of the snow-covered structures and tuned their senses to their surroundings.

"Hey, Elaethia," Lilian said after a minute. "What do you think the cause behind these disappearances is?"

"I do not know," she said. "I have not encountered anything like this in my travels. Disappearances tend to lead somewhere, while these do not. Be it beast, monster, or brehdar, there has always been a trail to the culprit. I believe that is the reason Geran is willing to take such a risk. It is most unusual to have a scenario like this, and he knows it."

Lilian blinked. "That was a fairly deep analysis. Since when have you been able to read people like that?"

"I do not understand your question."

She grinned smugly. "Well, to be fair, you have been spending an awful lot of alone time with him."

"Indeed. You and Shiro have spent considerable time alone together as well."

"W-well, it's because you two are hoggin' each other! We gotta keep ourselves entertained somehow!"

"Geran and I have kept each other's company so much because you and Shiro would often go off alone when not on quest," Elaethia noted.

"Gosh, if you don't like being alone with him that much, you could just say so."

"I …" She faltered. "I never indicated such feelings."

"It was starting to sound like you were only with him because you had no other choice."

"Of course not. Geran is a dear friend. He is one of the few that I feel I may speak freely to, and vice versa. All of you are my good friends, but Geran puts me at a sense of ease that I have not felt before. Is this unnatural?"

"Hm-hmm." Lilian flashed her signature grin. "You're blushing."

Elaethia touched her face to see it was true. "What … What is this?"

"Oho?" Lilian's grin turned dangerous. "Have I finally found a way to tease you?"

"I feel no shame in regard to my views on Geran."

"I don't think that's it at all. I think you're cutting yourself short."

"What are you saying?" Elaethia demanded.

"I think you feel a little bit deeper than just friends with Gerry-berry."

"You are not making sense, Lilian."

This was not the time to have such a conversation, but the way Lilian goaded her got the better of her judgment, and Elaethia found herself unable to turn away from the situation.

Lilian stood and waltzed in front of Elaethia. "I think your heart goes pitter-patter when you think of him. I bet your face gets all warm when he crosses your mind!"

"What of it? And what of your time with Shiro?"

"Ohoho, you're changing the subject! I have you right where I want you."

"If this is one of your games, I am not entertained!"

"You're turning red!" Lilian crowed.

Elaethia was about to retort when her dragon ears heard a short, muffled cry on the other side of the ruins. Lilian's perked ears indicated that she, too, had heard it.

Elaethia drew her battleaxe. "It came from the other side of the main building."

"That was definitely Shiro's voice. Let's go!"

Elaethia traced the imprints left by her companions, with Lilian hot on her tail. The demicat's eyes were wide and dilated, and her tail began to bush out. Less than a minute later, they came to the end of the tracks. They had stopped just along a stone wall, halfway across the length of it.

Lilian paced around. "What the hell? They're gone! Where did they go?"

Elaethia knelt where the last boot print rested. Instead of a normal imprint, the indentation was distorted to the side. It looked as though either Geran or Shiro had slid, but there was no indentation of a body in the snow. There was no blood, no equipment, no tattered clothing. The only trace indicating that the ranger and samurai had been here was their fresh tracks. Elaethia returned her attention to the warped print. She rested the butt of her axe on it and pushed down. Instantly the ground beneath it lowered. A rectangular panel, two meters in length and width, opened downward into the ground.

"A trapdoor," she announced. "Whoever set this has lined the edges with a substance that conceals any crevices or indentations. It is hidden perfectly."

Lilian knelt. "They must have fallen in! We have to go after them!"

"We do not know what is down there." Elaethia stated. Her words were true, but her tone betrayed her. She, too, wanted to rush to their aid.

"We can't just leave them!" Lilian insisted. "Shiro wouldn't abandon us, and Geran would find some way to get us back! All I'm good for is blasting things; I'm not as smart as you or Geran! By the time we get back up, they'll be dead!"

Elaethia shakily gripped her battleaxe. "Very well. You are correct; we must see that they are well. Do not call down to them. Whoever or whatever has them captured may be hastened to act if alerted. I will go first. Hold on to me so that we are not separated."

"O-okay …" Lilian gripped the leather sheath for the enormous axe and clung tightly to the dragon hero. Elaethia put her weight on the trapdoor once more and dropped down the slide.

They slid for several seconds down the steep, slippery slope. The fall brought back memories of when she first entered Frossgar's cave. The same dread that gripped her heart then began to rise again—not for the fear of what lay beneath, but for the safety of her companions. Like then, she knew not what she would meet at the bottom of the slide. She knew only that it was up to her and Lilian to save Geran and Shiro.

The two women shot out of the slide and into a wide, open room. Its walls reached and melded with the ceiling dozens of meters above. How far had they fallen? Similar chutes led into the room from nearly every direction. Only one wall was devoid of one of the trap slides. Instead, high above the ground, there was a single balcony with a stone railing. There was no visible way out. Torches lined the inside of the ominous room, lighting it up in its entirety. Someone definitely lived here.

Her study of the surroundings was cut short as she saw what lay in the middle of the room. Skeletons and corpses were strewn around the floor. Decaying bodies and dried bones lay in mutilated and twisted positions. Beast, brehdar, and monster alike lay desecrated in the underground dungeon. Their mangled bodies were contorted into stomach-churning positions around them. In the center of it all was Shiro and Geran. The samurai knelt over the unmoving ranger with tears forming in his eyes. He whipped his head around as Elaethia and Lilian fell into the room.

"Shiro!" Lilian cried. "Thank the heavens. What's wrong? Please tell me Geran's okay!"

"L-Lilian … Elaethia-sama," he whispered in terror. "You shouldn't have followed us."

Elaethia stood and hurried over to them. "What is wrong, Shiro? Is Geran all right? How can we help?"

"No! Stay back!" he cried. "I don't want to hurt you too. Get out of here. Hurry! Before Morgan returns! I knocked him unconscious, but it didn't work! He can't control himself; she won't let him! Run! It's too late for us! Get back to the guild! We need a raid to defeat her; she's too powerful for us alone!"

"Fat chance, samurai!" Lilian growled, brandishing her staff. "We're not leaving without you two. Elaethia, grab them! I'll *air blast* us all back up the chute!"

Elaethia had just begun to rush toward her friends when an evil cackle echoed throughout the room. It was the smug laughter of a woman who knew she had won.

"No, no, no …" Shiro whimpered and trembled as his eyes rolled upward. His fingers clenched, and his wrists rolled. The samurai's usual stance turned clumsy and awkward, as if he were fighting himself to stand. A strained gurgle flowed from his throat as he clenched his jaw with bared teeth. The once graceful and dignified samurai seemed little more than a rabid puppet on strings.

Footsteps echoed from the balcony above. Dry chuckles of satisfaction resonated around them as the owner made her appearance. An elven woman in her late fifties emerged from the darkness. Stringy white hair flowed down to her chest. A bloodred cloak and hood hung over her frail shoulders. A face with crimson eyes and an unnerving cruel grin gazed at Cataclysm below.

The elf spread her arms out, wielding a carved wand of human bone embedded with gemstones. Elaethia gripped her axe as the woman threw her head back in laughter again.

"Good evening, my little dancers!" she taunted. "My name is Morgan Blackthorn! And you—you will be tonight's entertainment! Tonight you will know pain. Tonight you will know misery. Tonight you will show me the agony I desire! The beautiful, melodious cries of your suffering will be the lullabies that rock me to sleep. How boring this society is. How dull and unoriginal their pathetic excuse for entertainment is! False feelings and emotion, staged drama and predicaments. All I yearn for is the suffering and torment of others, but no stage on this earth can bring forth true terror and desperation! No stage other than my own. That is where *you* come in, my little dancers. And tonight you have brought me a grand performance!"

Lilian's eyes went ablaze. "What are you on about? What'd you do to Geran, you old sack of bones!"

"Nothing, my adorable little kitten. Nothing at all. Turn your gaze to your armored friend with the sword, for *he* is the one who has harmed your precious Geran."

The elf flicked her wand over the room. Elaethia braced herself, but nothing happened. She turned her head to see that Lilian, however, was both wide-eyed and trembling. Her whole body shook as her fingers curled and her veins bulged under her skin.

"What …" Lilian stammered. "What's going on? What did you do! I-I can't …"

Morgan cackled in wild laughter. "Marvelous! Oh how wonderfully marvelous! You're blood churns with such passion! Such burning emotion! It tells me all I need to know. Your heart beats like a rabbit's! All the ambition and hopes you have! The passion and love you hold for your swordsman companion! How tragic! Oh, how deliciously tragic!"

"Shut up!" Lilian screamed. "Let me go. What did you do?"

"Leave her alone!" Shiro sobbed. "Please, please don't hurt her!"

"Yes, *yes!*" Morgan sighed. "Scream! Scream for me! Your anguish only excites me more! How tragic for you, little mage. How unbearably sad that your love for your swordsman is returned by his blade!"

The elf flicked her wand at Shiro. The samurai shuddered and rose to his feet with a strained yell.

"I can't stop her, Lilian!" Shiro wailed as he stumbled toward her. "I'm sorry! I'm sorry! My limbs are moving on their own!"

"What will it be, mage?" Morgan taunted, releasing the girl, who collapsed to the bloody ground. "Can you bring yourself to destroy your love and survive, or will you let him live as he carves your pretty body to mangled pieces? Choose, my little dancer! Entertain me!"

Elaethia had had enough. There was no more time to gather information about their foe. All she knew was that this elf was a sorceress who could control the bodies of others. Morgan intended to have her friends kill and maim each other for her own entertainment. Elaethia inhaled deeply and exhaled with all she had at the sorceress. Her breath billowed up to the balcony and covered it in the lethal dragon spell.

But Morgan was more agile than she seemed. The sorceress stepped back a few paces into the shadows as the spell dissipated. In turn, Morgan's influence also seemed to be broken. Shiro dropped to the ground, shaking and panting violently.

Morgan reemerged to look below in wonder, pointing her wand at Elaethia. "What is this? What is this indeed? Your blood. It does not sing to me. I cannot hear its voice, but I can feel its splendor! Its power! Its vigor! The emotion of hundreds of lifetimes, coursing through your sturdy body! The pain and sorrow of millennia in every delicious drop. Why? What makes you different from the other humans I have ensnared? What do you have that they didn't? No matter. I must have it. I *must* obtain the crimson surge within you! I thought I had it all, but you, my little dancer—you are something new! Something inbrehdar! The one I have waited for all these years! You will be the one to quench my insatiable thirst."

Elaethia's eyes began to glow. "I know not what you are saying; nor do I care. But you have harmed my friends, as well as countless others. It is your blood that will flow tonight, not mine."

"Ah, ah, ah!" Morgan waggled a finger and flicked her wand.

Lilian and Shiro cried out with a strain as they were thrust to their feet again. Even Geran's unconscious body rose from the sticky floor.

"I have my hand gripped around their hearts, my precious warrior. One false move and I will tear them apart from the inside. I *will* have your blood tonight. But first you will dance for me."

Elaethia donned her helmet as Morgan flicked her wand again. Shiro growled in strain as he lurched forward with his sword raised above his head. The samurai took another step and brought it down onto her in a clumsy arc. But as the blade struck her armor it simply recoiled off.

"Forgive me, Elaethia-sama!" he cried. Tears flowed down his face, and his body seemed to tear at itself under Morgan's control.

Elaethia didn't respond as her mind raced for a way to save them from the spell. She shoved Shiro away and stepped back as Geran's longsword slashed in front of her. Elaethia grabbed his arm to wrench the sword from his hand, as well as the swordbreaker from its sheath. She pushed him away as well as she cast the weapons aside. Shiro and Geran were forced to their feet, and the samurai slowly approached again.

"Elaethia!" Lilian shouted. "She can't make them both move at once! You can—" she screamed as her body twisted and fell to the floor.

"Now, now," Morgan chided. "No talking among yourselves. That is not a part of the play, my dear. You don't want to ruin the show, do you?"

Morgan flicked her wand again to force Shiro forward. With his sword raised once more, the samurai strained with a cry to try to stop himself. The katana was brought awkwardly down, only to be caught by Elaethia's gauntlet. She reached up to disarm him, but the blade suddenly shot back as Shiro was pulled away.

"I wouldn't do that if I were you," the sorceress taunted. "Else I will turn him inside out before your eyes. You must dance as I command, little warrior. Nevertheless, that meddlesome armor is in the way. No matter. If I can't have him cut you, I'll have him cut himself!"

Shiro raised the blade and paused. Sweat beaded on his brow. As he shut his eyes and clenched his teeth, his arms were brought inward.

He screamed. His sword thrust straight down into his left leg above the knee, piercing through his thigh. The blade was torn out again, with blood spurting from the wound. Lilian tried to call out to him with tear-streaked eyes, but she was cut short as her stomach retched and emptied itself onto the ground in front of her. Elaethia's eyes widened in rage as the samurai was forced to stand on his crippled leg.

"The swordsman and his lover's cries are beautiful!" the elf moaned euphorically. "But you, my warrior, have not entertained me enough! I see I must go deeper to hear your wonderful anguish!"

"Elaethia! Hold me!" Lilian's voice choked through her convulsions. Elaethia saw the determination in her eyes and slid to her.

"Yes. Yes!" Morgan sighed, and she gripped at her robes. "Embrace your pretty companion once more before she dies by the hand of her beloved swordsman! Let the tears and grief flow through as you say your final farewells!"

Lilian whispered into Elaethia's ear as the sorceress taunted from above. "There's a frost spell called *petrify* that can freeze the water wherever you channel it. I'll give you an opening by hiding you from her vision. The second I do, you have to—" She was cut off as she seized and gargled. Lilian choked on her own breath as the veins on her neck pulsed and writhed.

The sorceress cackled wildly. "How terrible. Oh how *terrible!* To have your touching good-bye wrenched apart! Show me your tears, warrior! Show me your anguish! Let me see the sorrow that overcomes you once her pretty head is severed from its shoulders!"

Morgan flicked her wand to Shiro, who moved toward Lilian with his sword poised.

"No! Please! I'll do anything!" the samurai cried out, straining to stop himself.

Lilian gritted her teeth and looked at Elaethia with intent, trying desperately to explain the last bit of her plan.

She didn't have to.

The air grew cold. The three other conscious brehdars in the room began to shiver as the dragon hero chilled the room with her presence. The brief interruption in the sorceress's concentration was enough, and Lilian tipped the head of her staff at Elaethia. In that instant, the warrior was enveloped in a writhing torrent of searing flame that spiraled to the ceiling. Lilian had concealed Elaethia in a *pillar of fire*.

"How heroic!" Morgan grinned over the roaring spell. "You think you can save your warrior friend from the pain and rob me of her blood by burning her to ash! How brave! How clever! How totally naive! One drop is all I need to be satisfied. You cannot possibly destroy her in time. But I warned you. You haven't danced for me, as I demanded. Now stand in helpless agony as I rip you apart vein by vein."

Morgan raised her wand and aimed it at the mage. She slowly turned it upward and began to flick. But her hand wouldn't respond. She looked at her arm to see the color drain from her hand. Her fingers began to tremble. Her wrist strained but wouldn't budge. Morgan's eyes widened in horror as vapor began to flow from her agape mouth. Her trembling hand began to freeze over as the wand fell from her grasp and clattered to the ground.

"No … No, it cannot be!"

The dragon hero extended her gauntlet within the flaming tornado to find the water in the demented elf, and she froze the sorceress's body from within. Morgan wailed in terror as the frost traveled up her arm and to her shoulder. She clutched desperately to her torso to try to stop the spreading frost, but the ice grew from inside her body.

Morgan cried out in a strained shriek and tore at her throat to interrupt the spell in any way. Her torso froze over as *petrify* seized her from the neck down. Her flesh crackled and popped and her skin tore along the veins as they expanded from the freezing. The elf gargled weakly one last time as the skin around her face turned a sickly shade of blue. Her lips split, her eyes shattered and popped, and she moved no more.

Lilian cut her spell off as she, Shiro, and Geran collapsed to the ground. The mage and samurai gasped and shuddered as they began to sob in relief. Elaethia removed her helmet and ran to their sides. She quickly checked Geran's unconscious body for injuries but found nothing except a bump on the side of his head, presumably from where Shiro had struck him. She then went over to Lilian. The girl braced herself on all fours with her face drooping toward the ground. Her tail sagged and draped between her legs, lying in a puddle of blood and bile. Behind her, Shiro winced and began to use *healing touch* on his leg.

"Are you all right?" Elaethia asked Lilian. "Are you injured in a way we can heal?"

"I-I'm fine, I think," she sniffed, and she wiped her nose clear of snot and vomit. "I'm just scared. Holy shit, I was scared. To have your body moving without control of it … Stars above, I'm glad that's over."

Elaethia handed her a healing potion. "Regardless, drink this. You may have some internal bleeding. The way that sorceress spoke indicated she was an anatomy wizard who specialized in body alteration. That is how she made you all move without your will."

"Elaethia-sama …" Shiro called shakily. "I'm so sorry. I raised my blade to you. Even though I could not control myself, that is unforgivable."

Elaethia said nothing and rose to her feet to walk swiftly toward the samurai.

Shiro continued through his tears. "I understand if you can't see me as trustworthy anymore and wish to cast me aside. Striking one's master is a blatant affront to the samurai code, and violating it has left me unworthy of—" He was cut off, embraced by the dragon hero. He stammered with a choke as Elaethia held him tight while her own breath turned shaky.

"I would never dream of doing away with you," she stated firmly as she clung to her friend. "All that matters to me is that you are alive and well."

The samurai only took another uneasy breath and returned her embrace with a sob.

Cataclysm returned to the surface less than an hour later. Geran had regained consciousness, while Elaethia built a series of *ice walls* in such a way that the party could walk up a set of frozen stairs to the balcony. Elaethia and Lilian wouldn't even look at the blood sorceress, but Shiro couldn't take his blazing eyes off of her. The samurai glared into the terrified face of the frozen statue and promptly slashed his sword across her torso. Shards of frozen blood and ice were sent flying as both halves of the severed body fell to the ground with a thud.

Geran searched the remains inside the pit before he followed his companions. On one of the mangled corpses was a single metal tag with Breeze's insignia on it. He wiped the tag clean to identify the adventurer. It was Douglas Clark, an intermediate ranger. Several emotions overlapped each other in Geran's heart, anger and sorrow being the most prominent. He had known Douglas fairly well—maybe not as well as some of his closest friends and party, but enough that tears formed in Geran's eyes at the discovery of the name.

The cheery demiwolf did not deserve this. Douglas was as pacifistic as an adventurer could be. He never wanted to hurt anyone. Douglas was known among rangers for being one of the best at recovery missions. He had joined the guild to save lives, not take them.

Geran clutched the tag and looked at the mutilated corpse before him. Morgan had made him cut himself in half with his own dagger. Geran's gaze rested on the demiwolf's left hand, and he instantly tore his eyes away. With a shaky breath, he felt the fallen ranger's hand and gingerly removed a gold band from his ring finger. Geran sent a soft prayer to the heavens and placed the ring and tag in his pouch. He wrapped Douglas's remains with his own cloak and gingerly carried him upstairs. He swore under his choked breath. He had done this too many times in his career.

He looked to the stars as he got outside. A cloud of vapor billowed from his breath and dissipated into the air. It was too dark and cold to return to the guild tonight. It would be best to spend the night in the ruins.

Geran was awakened the next morning by the sound of a large group of brehdars arriving at the scene. Several tarp-covered sleighs pulled by draft horses drew alongside the adventurers as they watched in curiosity. The entourage of strangers eyed the party as well but didn't seem surprised to see them. Each sled and wagon came to a halt next to the debris and crumbled structures. Workers began to jump down from them and unload tools, papers, tents, equipment, lumber, and cut stone.

A middle-aged dwarf approached the adventurers. "I suppose you're the adventurers from Breeze? I'm Paul, the head foreman. Thanks for clearing this place out for me, but you didn't need to stick around for so long. Your guild should have told you we'd be here in a week or so."

"A week or so?" Geran asked.

"Well that's when we put in the request. My company plans to use this site for production, but our surveyors and contractors kept disappearing. Apparently other people and adventurers had gone missing around here too. That's why we called on the guild for help. We knew someone would sort it out within a couple of days."

The adventurers looked at one another.

"We got here last night," Shiro said.

"Last night? The request has been active for over a week."

"Yeah, but no one was able to complete it in the lower levels," Geran stated. "It worked itself up all the way to V level. Do you even know what was down there?"

The dwarf shook his head. "Not a clue. But that's what I paid you guys for. Frankly I don't even care, so long as it doesn't come back. All that matters to me is that I get the land and none of you died getting it for me."

"One of our rangers *did* die," Elaethia told him. "And many other unfortunate souls."

Paul shifted uncomfortably. "Oh. Well, I, uh … I'm sorry to hear that. I'd pay you more in compensation to give to his family, but I'm barely making ends meet as it is. Making a brewery isn't cheap. And since everything here is decrepit, I've got to clear this area of all the existing structures and then rebuild from the ground up. What makes matters worse is that most of the materials here are unusable, so I have to spend even more on fresh stone and lumber. I'm not sure if I can afford to pay my workers to clear all this crap and get more building material too."

Lilian's ears suddenly perked up. "You gotta level this place first?"

"Sure do. That alone will probably take us until spring. I hate to start a project in the winter, but my time constraints are immovable."

"What if you could have all that done today? Could you afford it then?"

"What kind of nonsense is that?"

"I'm just asking!" she insisted.

The dwarf crossed his arms. "Huh, well … Hypothetically speaking, if I could possibly get all or even most of this cleared by today, I could definitely afford to compensate for that dead ranger. I don't know why you're asking, since that's impossible. Even if I blew all my blasting powder, I could only knock down a fourth of this stuff."

Lilian's wicked grin returned to her once somber face. "Tell your crew to get all the junk they want out of here. I'll take care of the demolition."

Paul looked her up and down. "Look. I can tell you're a mage, and I know Breeze has some pretty powerful ones. But you must be crazy if you think that I'd believe you can blast this place apart in one day."

"What've you got to lose?" she pressed.

He sighed. "All right, fine. I'll have my boys clear it out for a few hours, then I'll let you try. *If* you manage to knock it all down, I'll give you that compensation."

"Sweet." She grinned as the dwarf turned to give the word to his workers.

"Are you sure about this?" Shiro asked the mage.

"Course I am!" she said, puffing out her chest. "I haven't been able to blow myself out since the tournament! We can get money for Douglas's family, they get the demolition out of the way, and I get to blow something up! This is a win-win-win!"

"If you say so, Lilian," Shiro said.

"All right, I *thought* something was fishy about you two," Geran said, and he looked at the pair. "Since when have you been referring to her so casually, Shiro?"

The samurai shifted his weight. "I, uh … Maybe a week now?"

"I noticed this as well," Elaethia said. "Although I thought it was a coincidence at first."

"Hey, things change!" Lilian piped up. "Shiro's decided he's comfortable enough around me to call me by name. There's nothing wrong with that, right?"

"I suppose not," Elaethia agreed.

Geran shrugged. "I guess. Well, no point in standing out here and freezing our toes off. Let's go inside while we wait for the crews to finish."

He and Elaethia headed for the door. Shiro and Lilian glanced at each other with a grin. The two flashed a thumbs-up and went inside as well.

The crews were decidedly satisfied with their sweep after a couple of hours. They got a full understanding for the reason behind the delay. Unlike the adventurers, the craftsmen were not so desensitized as to be willing to go into the basement where the horrors had happened. Entirely avoiding the rooms the sorceress had occupied, they scrounged through the rest of the ruins to collect all the weapons, armor, and items that could be resold. Soon after, they gave Cataclysm permission to begin their attempt. Lilian, eager to begin, led everyone to the top of a very distant hill.

"I understand elemental magic is potent and all," Paul said as they reached the hilltop, "but is this distance really necessary? We can hardly see the ruins! And why did we have to move the wagons so far back? What do you think you're about to do?"

"Watch, and be filled with awe," Lilian said with a grin. "I plan to blow myself out, and little beyond. I've still got a magic potion, so I'm not afraid of a little overcast."

Shiro put a hand on her shoulder. "Don't hurt yourself."

"It's fine, it's fine," she said, and she fluttered a hand as her eyes began to flash. "Just hold on to your teeth."

"By the Moon, she's serious," Geran murmured.

The workers all glanced at one another as Lilian took the stage. The mage flapped her cape, gripped the brim of her hat, and inhaled deeply. With a dramatic windup, the demicat thrust her staff at the distant ruins. For a second, nothing happened. Then the hazy white air began to turn orange.

There was a blinding flash, and then a sight that would never be believed by anyone who hadn't seen it firsthand. The mushroom cloud that billowed up from the ruins was so immense that it broke through the low-hanging clouds above. Then the sound hit—a rumbling clap of raw power so potent it shook the very ground they stood on. The workmen all yelped and gasped in surprise, and some even cowered to the ground. A shock wave raced along the earth outward from the explosion, kicking up the snow and melting it to water. Everyone turned and looked at the sleek demicat in awe, trying to comprehend how such a small girl could make such an enormous explosion. Lilian had entirely captivated her audience.

Until the shock wave raced its way up the hill they stood on and blasted through them. All of them managed to stay on their feet except Lilian, who began to tilt backward. Unfortunately, everyone else was still in partial shock and only watched as Lilian toppled backward into the snow. As the exhausted demicat struck the ground, the only noise that escaped her lips was a sound one would expect from a cat falling over.

The ruins were entirely decimated. Rubble and chunks of the stony structure were blown clear of the blast site. All other pieces were reduced to dust and gravel. There were no hints or indications that any structures made of wood had existed there at all. It took several minutes for the area to be cool enough for the workers to begin their project. As promised, Cataclysm was given a bonus in compensation for the increase of difficulty, as well as some set aside to give to the family of the fallen ranger. Paul even assured them that he would see to Douglas's return via wagon. With all business complete, the adventurers returned home.

Unfortunately, Lilian's potion was smashed when she fell backward. The glass vial had struck a rock and shattered inside her pouch. Viscous blue liquid stained the snow as the demicat grumbled and pouted from the snowy ground. While Elaethia was perfectly capable of carrying her all the way home, Lilian complained that the warrior's armor was too hard. Geran's cloth-and-leather outfit was more comfortable, but Shiro was determined to aid his feline companion as well.

The three of them switched on and off with the duty of piggybacking the girl for nearly half a day. Geran was sure it wouldn't take this long for her magic to recover, but the demicat moaned and complained whenever the subject came up. Shiro and Elaethia soon after became suspicious as well. Lilian drew out her special treatment for as long as she could, until it was Geran's turn to carry her again. After taking a few steps with the sleek girl on his back, the ranger swiftly shot his arms straight up and plopped her on the cold and dirty ground. For once, it was Geran who had to run away from Lilian after that.

They were heartily greeted on their return. Elaethia and Geran went to the front desk to finalize the quest with Maya and Sophie. Shiro went out back to clean his gear, and much to his surprise, several adventurers had followed him to ask about his quest. Geran raised an eyebrow at this, since normally they'd all flock to Lilian. But since she had already made a beeline for the baths, Shiro was their only option.

"Mr. Geran! Elaethia!" Michael called from across the room. The demiwolf bounded over to him in his questing gear. Michael wore his grey ranger cloak, brown leather armor, and had his weapons slung at his side. He even had an insignia, which was a grey band wrapped around his left bicep.

"Hey, buddy," Geran greeted him. "Looks like you guys got back from your first quest. How'd that go?"

"By the *heavens*, you were right!" Michael said. "Being in a party is a lot safer and all, but stars above! Do you have *any* idea how frustrating that was? I thought goblin quests were supposed to be easy stuff! I tried to give them the rundown and formulate a plan, but they completely blew me off! Not to mention we got lost getting there because Dylan insisted on holding the map because, oh, he's 'the leader'! Dana blew herself out in the first fight, Dylan kept charging in alone, and Horst stepped on *every single trap!* Every single one! There was a pile of leaves and branches lying on the ground of a stone floor, and he didn't understand how that could be a pitfall! Please tell me it gets better over time!"

Geran chuckled. "No amount of skill and training will save you from the luck of a chronic dumbass. I can't help you on this one, Michael. You're gonna have to smarten them up. It'll take them getting banged up a few times, but eventually they'll be tired of getting slapped around. Don't jump them into the ranger ways right off the bat. Work it into their style."

"I guess. Man, I need a drink."

Elaethia tilted her head. "Are you not sixteen? You still have two years before you are of legal age in this country."

His tail drooped. "Sorry; it was a joke."

"I see. Perhaps I will try that next time."

Geran sighed with a smile. "Elaethia, the day you understand humor is the day I start laying eggs."

"That is impossible. You are brehdar, which bear live young. You are also a male, which does not birth the offspring regardless."

"I shouldn't be surprised that that one went over your head."

Elaethia looked up. "Where?"

Michael blinked. "How can someone have changed so much and yet not at all?"

She tilted her head. "Whom are you referring too?"

Geran and Michael looked at each other.

"I ask myself that a lot more than I care to admit," Geran replied to his apprentice.

Lilian's voice sounded next to him. "Care to admit to what?"

"Woah!" Geran jumped. "Where the hell'd *you* come from?"

"Upstairs. Baths are full. I'm waiting for them to clear out. Didn't you hear me coming?" She looked at him, then at Elaethia, and then back at him. "Well, I see a certain someone's got you all distracted. Elaethia's really mellowing you out, hmm?"

"Cat, on the Sun and Moon, I'm gonna—"

"Oh be quiet, you. You know you love me!"

"I'd sell you to Morgan for half a pint."

"Yo! Fellas! Long time no see!" a familiar man's voice called from the bar. Everyone turned their heads.

"Ah, Liam," Elaethia said in acknowledgment of the demiwolf. "It is good to see you. I agree it has been a while since we last conversed."

The spearman laughed. "You've got that right. I don't think we've had a proper catch-up since before you all went on that Blackwolf conquest. Where've you guys been these last couple days? I thought you mopped up that crime faction over a week ago."

"On quest," Geran replied. "Got back just now. Some nasty business with a blood sorceress. We'd actually be dead if it weren't for Elaethia and her dragon lineage."

"I've been meaning to ask about that," Liam said. "So are you half-dragon, half-human? Or some sort of dragon in human form?"

"I cannot answer that question honestly, as I do not entirely know myself," Elaethia responded. "All I know is that I have taken Frossgar's power, soul, and magic into my own human body. As for how that alters my structure genetically, I do not know."

"That actually answers my question pretty well." Liam shrugged. "But you guys just got back from another quest? I thought you were pretty set up from the last month. Did Lilian blow all her cash again or something?"

The demicat's tail flicked. "Hey! I'm doing just fine, thank you very much! We were bored is all!"

"Then you guys are making some serious bank. Sounds to me like the next round's on Cataclysm."

"Fat chance of that, Barron," Geran laughed. "You're a V class too. Go get your own cash."

"Aw, c'mon, Shady, we're best buddies! You can't spare a drink or four for your old pal Liam?"

"You still owe me about a dozen drinks yourself."

Liam groaned. "Jeez, you're *still* keeping count?"

"One of us has to. Not my fault you can't count higher than your own fingers. I've got my own finances to manage too, y'know."

Liam grinned and put his hands up. "Hey, c'mon now! No need to be like that. Although, come to think of it, you do have more gifting and spending you ought to be managing for."

Geran raised an eyebrow. "What're you on about?"

Liam gave him a wicked grin and motioned to Elaethia. "I understand you may have to set gift money aside to keep your lady happy. On the other hand, she's pretty smart and low-maintenance."

Elaethia tilted her head. "I beg your pardon?"

Liam turned to walk back to the bar. "In any case, I'll go order a round for the rest of Razorback. You don't mind if I put it on your tab, do ya, Geran?"

The ranger's hand shot out and snagged Liam by the tail. "What was that?"

"*Ow!* Damn, Nightshade! What's with you and grabbing tails!"

Michael scratched his head. "Wait, so it's not just me?"

"I have noticed that you are the only person who does this," Elaethia noted.

"Oho?" Lilian grinned wickedly. "Have we discovered a fetish in Mr. Gerry?"

Geran's eyebrows twisted as he let Liam go. "What? No, it's just convenient. It's like you guys are built with your own leashes."

Everyone went quiet for a moment until Lilian's mouth fell open.

"Oh you did *not* just ..." She stomped toward the ranger with ears back and tail lashing. Geran stood there while Lilian pounded her fists on his chest.

"What? What'd I do? Did I strike a nerve or something? What's the deal?"

Liam pointed a finger at him and walked back to his party. "You win this round, Shady, but I'mma remember that next time."

"I don't … Michael, help me out here." He turned to his apprentice, who had his arms folded, ears back, and mouth twisted into an irritated snarl.

"It's nothin'," he growled. "I just remembered I have to go wash my gear." Michael turned and stormed off as well.

"Elaethia?"

"Do not ask me," she said. "I do not have a tail."

"Ah, whatever. I'm gonna go take a long soak." Geran shrugged and made his way upstairs, with Lilian punching him in the back the entire time.

Chapter 19
Enchanted

Sixth Era.140. Juery 8.

Elaethia awoke with a smile on her lips. She had been gifted with another dream from the past. The visions of her time with Frossgar were becoming more common and even more vivid. She sat up in her bed and reached down her shirt to pull out her family amulet. The gold-and-sapphire necklace clicked as she turned it over in her hand. It had been four years since she left Frossgar's cave, and nearly eighteen since she had fled from Armini. She was twenty-four now; her birthday had passed last month.

As a girl, Elaethia had loved her birthday. Her family would celebrate it with gifts and sweets, and let her invite all of her friends to have a special dinner. Even when she fled with her grandfather, Celus would somehow find the compassion in his heart to put something together for the occasion. But such frivolous activities promptly ceased once she came into Frossgar's care—not that she minded the absence of these birthday parties anymore; she was simply far too old to feel giddy at the sight of a cake or doll.

Elaethia understood why the great dragon cared very little for the anniversary of his birth. After being around for millennia, he lost count of not only his exact age but the day of his hatching as well. In turn, Elaethia lost interest in hers. In the grand scheme of it all, her birthday meant nothing. It merely signified that she had lived one more cycle on this earth as it traveled around the sun. Such a day held no significance to the world, so it held no significance to her.

She had decided within the last couple of years to avoid announcing it to those around her as well. At the mention of it to Ingrid, the old demiwolf had literally jumped with shock at Elaethia's apathy. The warrior vainly tried to explain her views, but Ingrid would have none of it. The housewife dragged both her and Jörgen into the kitchen to prepare a special feast and sing for the allegedly very special woman. Elaethia smiled at the memory—not because of her special treatment, but because of how awkwardly she and Jörgen sat while Ingrid sang and prattled on.

Come to think of it, it had been Geran's birthday not too long ago as well. He held similar views as she did regarding it but gladly accepted a few drinks from his friends. The introverted man had no interest in fanfare and had attempted to have a quiet celebration with a peaceful day. He had his wish until Lilian caught wind and made an appearance. The demicat ordered several drinks for the ranger—most of which she drank herself—and began to poke fun at him by calling him an old man. Once she was thoroughly intoxicated, the mage jumped onto his back and began to yowl "Happy Birthday To You" at the top of her lungs, yowling very, *very* off-key. Elaethia was no vocalist herself, but Lilian could not carry a tune if her life depended on it. Elaethia believed it was best her lively companion stuck to magic and dancing.

She chuckled softly at the recollection as she got in front of the mirror to fix her hair. She nearly jumped as she met her own eyes in the reflection. She hardly recognized herself with that expression. *How curious.* However, her keen study of her own face caused the smile to disappear. She tried to bring it back. This smile wasn't quite the same, but it held almost the same impact. It wasn't often that she smiled, but she was doing it more frequently. Her moments alone with Geran were the most common times her smile appeared, and he seemed to enjoy bringing it out of her. Come to think of it, Geran was the only man she knew who always tried to make her happy. She noted to herself that she would have to ask him about that sometime.

A sudden rap on her door broke her reminiscence. She let her hair fall loose and walked to the door. She opened it and came face-to-face with a guildhall butler.

"May I help you?" she asked the elven man.

"Yes, Miss Elaethia. I'm sorry to intrude, but you and your party have a visitor."

She tilted her head. "A visitor? Have you informed Lilian yet? She takes a very long time to get ready."

He nodded. "Yes, of course. Mr. Geran suggested it when I retrieved him nearly an hour ago. Mr. Shiro should be ready as well."

"An hour ago? Nobody has come to find me in that time?"

The elf shifted and looked to the floor. "I didn't want to wake you and cause a bother."

"It has caused me more of a bother now that I am rushed to meet with my companions," she stated coldly.

A bead of sweat trickled down from his brow. "O-of course, I apologize. I will be sure to remember that and will prevent this from happening again. Good day!" With that, he turned sharply and walked rather quickly back downstairs.

Elaethia sighed and shook her head. She quickly prepared herself and walked downstairs to join her party. She looked at their usual table to see them seated around it, presumably waiting for her. But there was also another man with them.

He was a dwarf in long gray cloak and trousers. A floppy wizard hat of the same color sat on his head with a pair of leather goggles resting around the cone. The wide brim covered the top half of his face, but she could tell by the white beard and wrinkles that he was elderly. What caught her attention the most was the insignia on his cloak—a dazzling comet surrounded by swirling patterns. She recognized this design. It indicated not that he was an adventurer but an

Arcane Sage. He turned as Elaethia approached. The elderly dwarf's milky eyes narrowed and then widened as he recognized the dragon hero.

"And there is the woman of the hour," he announced as she took a seat.

"Good morning," she greeted him. "I assume you are the one who is here to see us. I apologize for being late."

The dwarf waved a hand. "It is no matter. I understand it is still early in the morning by adventurer standards. Not to mention I came unannounced. It has also come to my attention that you were not alerted to my arrival until just a few minutes ago, so worry not. Though I will say that I was surprised at how quickly your ranger and swordsman got prepared."

"Hey, I'm here too!" Lilian protested.

"Yes, yes, my dear, so you are," the Arcane Sage sighed. "Now that we are all here, allow me to properly introduce myself. I am Arthur Veldwig, an enchanter of the Moon's Pillar. I'm sure you are all full of questions, but give me a moment to explain a little before you ask. The reasoning behind my visit is twofold. The first is to ask for your services. You see, I am the inventor of the moon rings, and I created them at first for usage during the tournament. Of course, however, the technique got out, and it is being sold to wealthy magicians. While that tidbit is neither here nor there, it serves a good baseline for my impact on the country.

"Now, as for what I want with you. For a while, I have been looking for adventurers with outstanding reputations. Needless to say, I was *very* impressed with all of your performances in the tournament. I originally prepared to make my quest a raid, but once I learned that all of you were in a party together, I realized you four should have little difficulty. Admittedly, it is also very convenient for my wallet.

"The quest I have for you is a simple retrieval, but don't get my verbiage confused for the idea that the quest itself is easy. No, no, no. The *instructions* are what is simple. Go to the place in question, retrieve the item by any means necessary, and return it to me intact—preferably with all of you alive and still in one piece.

"The catch is that this is a distant, ancient location long since forgotten until recently. The area it rests in hasn't been charted in over a millennium. We have no accurate maps of the place. We call the location in question the Enchanters' Imperium. As the name implies, this place was the pinnacle of enchantment studies at the time. Unfortunately, it was razed in the second war. All studies and artifacts were stolen or destroyed, except for one. There was allegedly a treasure in a secret chamber—a marvel of enchanting ingenuity that shook the world of magic as we know it. As one of the top enchanters in the country, you can understand my interest in it.

"So. I want you, Cataclysm, to venture to this ancient place, delve into the secret room, see if this artifact exists, and bring it to me. Your reward, should you find nothing, will be an amount of gold that could allow a man to retire at a young age, divided among the four of you. If the artifact is retrieved, I will add on a second reward of nearly equal value. However, the second reward will be yours only on another condition."

Lilian's eyes were wide open, and she was visibly drooling. "What? What is it? Tell us!"

"A chance to study Elaethia."

Her ears fell flat. "Oh no …"

Elaethia tilted her head. "I am sorry?"

Shiro reached for his sword. "I don't care who you are or what title you claim. If you intend to defile Elaethia-sama, you will lose your hands."

"Now, hold on," Geran said, raising a finger. "Define 'study'."

Arthur laughed. "What a variety of reactions. Stay your blade, master swordsman, I don't intend for Elaethia to disrobe or to allow me to become physically familiar with her. All I ask is to study her armor and observe her dragon abilities. I intend to see if I can copy dragon magic into an enchantment."

"How can you copy dragon magic?" Elaethia asked.

"That's what I intend to find out. How much do you know about enchanting?"

"Very little, if any."

"Then I will give you a basic explanation: Enchanting is the art of imbuing inanimate objects with magical properties. It is the only school that can assimilate all forms of magic. That being said, enchanters cannot cast or channel. We cannot manifest magic into an attack or spell. As I said, we imbue other things with our magic. And so we are not combatants—not magically, at any rate. If I were to take your samurai's sword and imbue it with fire magic, it would burn anything it touched."

Geran raised an eyebrow. "Why would anybody want that?"

"Exactly. No sensible person would. The blade would be practically useless. However, through study and practice, the enchanter could make it so the sword would only burn what it strikes. If I delve deeper, I could make it so Shiro could launch a fireball from it as well."

Shiro rubbed his chin. "How come I've never heard of a weapon like that? Everyone would be scrambling to get their hands on one of those."

"Because only the best enchanters are capable of doing that," Arthur said. "Not to mention that anyone who could afford it wouldn't even consider using it. People with that kind of money don't do their own fighting."

"Does it have to be a weapon?" Shiro asked. "Could you do it for clothes or armor?"

"Clothes? No. Armor? Some kinds, yes. If you imbue something organic with magic, it becomes a conduit. Since it's impossible to cast something with clothing and very impractical to cast with leather, it's not done. But full plate armor can be enchanted, although it takes a considerable amount of time and effort. The only exceptions are gemstones. They are unique in that they can enhance the conduit's function. We're still researching how that works, although we suspect it's a result of the crystalline properties."

"Could you enchant ice?" Lilian asked.

"You could," Arthur began. "But what happens when that ice melts to water?"

"It flows everywhere and evaporates."

"And with it the enchantment."

"But what if the ice never melted?"

"While impossible, yes, the ice would retain the enchantment," Arthur said.

Everyone looked to Elaethia.

"What?" she asked.

"Elaethia has a unique dragon spell," Geran explained to Arthur. "It creates ice that can't melt."

Arthur's cloudy eyes gleamed. "Fascinating. I am now more curious than ever. So on that note, and returning to the business at hand, do you accept my quest?"

The members of Cataclysm turned to each other again.

"Well, if a Sage asks for us specifically, who are we to decline?" Geran said.

"I see no issue," Elaethia concluded. "If Arthur wishes to study my magic, perhaps he can give me insight I do not know myself."

Shiro nodded firmly. "I have no issues either. Wherever Elaethia-sama goes, I will gladly follow."

Lilian thumped her fist on the table. "Hell yes! Study shmudy; if Arthur's word is as good as his gold, you bet your britches I'm taking this!"

Arthur beamed. "Excellent! Now then, you will want to know where you're going and what to expect to find there. On to the logistical side and planning."

Lilian's huge grin slowly faded away as Arthur and Geran took out scrolls and maps and began to talk about the details of the quest.

The entire trip took five days. Arthur took them as far as the border of the Frostshire region in his own wagon before dropping them off and wishing them luck. From there the adventurers went from town to town to the northeast corner of Linderry, where the ancient location was said to be. Before he departed, Arthur gave them a very detailed map and a general location. But they would still have to traverse around a three-kilometer diameter to find the entrance. With a mixture of walking and wagon riding, Cataclysm left the last town on the fourth day and began their final search on the fifth.

As the party of four scoured the landscape, Elaethia inhaled deeply and smiled. It was her favorite time of year. The air was clean and crisp, the sky clear and vast. Bright sunlight made the snowy hills and forests around them glisten as if thousands of shining silver coins dotted the landscape. The gentle wind smelled of salt and pine. It reminded her of the Svarengel village and her time with the Sterkhand family. With her friends at her side, her father's pendant around her neck, and Frossgar's armor around her body, she felt very much at peace.

"So lemme get this straight," Lilian started, clinging tightly to her coat. "We're supposed to just *wander* around this area that has been remote and unexplored since the dragon wars. Then *maybe* we find some sort of entrance to this Enchanter's Imperium. Then we try to go in, potentially find the magic ancient artifact, and hopefully bring it back."

Geran shivered and looked up from the map. "Wow. It's almost like you actually paid attention to the meeting,"

"Hey! Don't give me that look! There's a ton of cash on the line here, and I am *not* missing out on this opportunity."

"I wonder what kind of treasure it is," Shiro wondered aloud as he shielded his eyes from the glare of the snow.

"Arthur gave no indication of its appearance or ability," Elaethia stated. "The only unique identifier this item has is that it is contained in a room of its own."

"This is still a very simple quest for the amount of money he's paying us."

Geran blew a cloud of vapor into the dry air. "That's how I felt at first too. But Arthur said the amount was for anticipation and travel expenses. But we also have to take into account that we have no idea what's in there. Those ancient enchanters could have some nasty surprises waiting for us."

"Wasn't there something else about incentive for not taking the item for ourselves?" Lilian said as she huddled next to Shiro.

"Partially. Although he says he has a lot of trust in us. I guess I've been branded as one of the more trustworthy people in the region. Elaethia is also highly reputable, as is Shiro."

"What about me? What do they say about me?"

"Quite a lot. Like, way too much to keep track of."

Lilian's tail flicked. "What's that supposed to mean?"

Geran shrugged. "Let's just say that if I were to keep a personnel file on everyone in the guild, yours would be the thickest."

"I'll take that as a compliment," she replied indignantly.

"I will too," Shiro said. "There's a lot to Lilian, and I think it's all wonderful in its own way."

Lilian purred and hugged him fiercely. "Aw, Shiro! You're such a sweetie I can't handle it!"

"Li-Lili-chan …" The samurai blushed furiously, as Lilian had pulled his face right below her chin.

She pushed him away and crossed her arms. "Whaaaaat? Why're you going back to that name! C'mon, say my name again!"

"L-Lilian."

"One more time!"

"Lilian!"

She scooped a finger under his chin with a wicked smile. "Good boy."

Geran groaned into his hand. "Stars above, Lilian, he's not a dog."

"One would think the two of you have an odd relationship should you act this way in public," Elaethia agreed.

Lilian scratched her head. "Man. If Elaethia's giving me a lecture in public decency, I must be doing something *really* wrong. What do you think, Shiro?"

"It … doesn't bother me greatly. But could you please not do that again in front of people?" He swallowed hard. "Especially in front of … Elaethia-sama."

"Fiiiiine. I'll add that to the list."

Geran wheeled around. "Wait, there's a *list?*"

Lilian blanched. "No, no, no! I swear it's not what you're thinking at all!"

Elaethia tilted her head. "What do you believe us to be thinking?"

"It's not like that, it's—" She smacked herself in the face. "I'm trying to learn about his culture! Osakyotans are a squeamish bunch, and I wanna make sure I don't go overboard!"

Geran eyed her. "With the way you two disappear and go on with each other, you have to understand how we got to this conclusion. I'm still not entirely convinced."

Shiro's face turned the same color as his armor. "We don't do anything indecent! Lilian and I are perfectly moral people!"

"Uh-huh. Sure."

Lilian pulled her wide-brimmed hat over her face. "Oh my gosh, Geran, please believe us."

Geran was about to respond when his eyes suddenly latched onto something in the valley. Elaethia followed his gaze and focused her dragon eyes. Her brow furrowed as she could make out decrepit remnants of a stone structure in a draw in the hills. It was tucked away between the fingers of the mountain range and thick coniferous vegetation. The shape and placement of the stones could not be natural. She turned back to Geran, who was darting his eyes back and forth between it and the map. The ranger let out an exasperated breath and looked at the demicat.

"You and I are gonna have a long talk when we get back, Lilian. Elaethia, you should do the same with Shiro."

"What do you mean?" she asked

"I'll explain later. In the meantime, I think we've found our destination."

A closer inspection revealed that what caught their eye was undoubtedly an old, ruined entrance to a buried sight. Whether or not this was the Enchanter's Imperium would remain to be seen. The majority of the entrance was covered by snow, rubble, and large rocks, all of which Elaethia was able to lift or pry free. With their standard formation of Geran in front followed by Elaethia, Lilian, and then Shiro, Cataclysm descended into the darkness, guided only by Lilian's *torch*.

They leveled out after a couple of minutes. The adventurers carefully eyed their surroundings to realize they had entered one giant room. Lilian channeled more power into her spell and illuminated the entire cavern. A massive ornate dome hung over their heads, adorned with detailed and intricate carvings. The designs were definitely ancient. As masterfully carved as they were, they had weathered away into unintelligible depictions. Marvelous as the place was, its age showed. Flakes and cracks appeared all over the ceiling and walls, while soot and dust clung to every inch of each surface. Clinging and rotting vines sprawled along the ceiling and down the walls, where they dangled into the open air, stopping several meters above their heads. Drops of cold water trickled from them on occasion. There were four other passages from the main room, each leading in a cardinal direction. With their weapons at the ready, the four of them strode into the middle of the room.

Everything suddenly lit up. Bright blue flames erupted from fixed sconces on the wall and filled the giant room with pale light. The stony floor was revealed to be nearly as intricate as the ceiling above it. Massive tiles of smooth blue and white stone were laid perfectly level on the ground. A dim blue glow grew from the grout between them. It shone in hollow beams of light that reflected through the dust. Crumbled leaves and clumps of barren sod were scattered here and there along the ancient floor.

Above the four hallways were four icons. Each was a different design that glowed with a different color: one of red, another of amber, a third of green, and the last of orange. Undoubtedly this place would have been even more of a marvel thousands of years ago. The party was taken aback by the sudden display of magic around them. Lilian and Shiro were completely awestruck. Even Geran's ever-watchful eye was captivated by the room. Only Elaethia managed to bring her party back to reality.

"How truly fascinating," she said. "Is this what enchanting is capable of?"

"By the Moon," Lilian said, gaping. "It's beautiful. I don't even feel cold anymore."

Shiro sighed. "It makes the journey worth it. I could spend hours here looking at it all. To think what it must have looked like in all its glory before it became decrepit."

"If there even is a treasure, it's gotta be here," Geran said, looking to the four hallways. "I suppose we could start by checking out these four annexes. Do any of you recognize these symbols?"

Lilian looked around. "Nope. They look like just random designs to me. Actually, wait a minute." She trotted up to the glowing orange one off to her left. "Say, this one looks an awful lot like the arcane symbol for elemental magic."

Elaethia joined her. "Magic has symbols?"

"Yeah. If you ever look at texts or scrolls about magic, they most likely have a symbol on the cover. That's how you know what school of magic they're talking about. I wonder if these are all the ancient symbols for each kind."

"There are only four symbols present," Shiro noted. "But there're six schools of magic. There should be two more hallways."

"This whole place is dedicated to enchanting, so we can rule that one out," Geran reasoned. "Also, if Lilian believes this one's elemental, that also accounts for it. That leaves us with holy, druidic, anatomy, and alchemy."

"Alchemy is special in the same way enchanting is," Lilian said. "So maybe the other three are for druidic, holy, and anatomy."

Elaethia stepped past with her battleaxe drawn. "There is only one way to find out for certain. Let us investigate each of these rooms."

The warrior led them down the hall marked with the ancient elemental symbol and halted as it opened into a room. As the four entered, it, too, lit up in the same way the main entrance had. Orange flames burst from lifeless torches on the wall to reveal dusty tables, chairs, desks, and counters arranged evenly around the room. While mostly in shambles and falling apart, some of the furniture was still intact—that is, until Shiro tried to sit in a chair and promptly broke through it before crashing to the dusty floor. The samurai jumped up and instantly doubled over with innumerable apologies to both his friends and the surrounding furniture. Geran dusted the prostrating man off while Lilian and Elaethia studied the walls. Instead of stone and pillars, the four walls were composed of shelves—shelves entirely filled with books.

Lilian's mouth fell open. "Oh my *gosh* ... Is this all stuff about elemental magic?"

She dashed over to the nearest shelf to grab a book. The mage instantly turned it open and beheld its contents. She got less than a second of study before it disintegrated and fell to the floor.

Geran turned at the sound of the commotion. "Hey! Be careful! This stuff is over a thousand years old!"

"Aw, man. Crummy old book fell apart on me. I got gunk all over my coat." She patted herself off and reached for another.

"Don't do it again!"

"Relax; I'll be more careful this time."

The mage picked a different book and gingerly opened it. She scanned the first few pages and nodded intently while mumbling quietly to herself.

"I see, I see. That's what I thought," she muttered.

Shiro walked behind her to look over her shoulder. "What? What is it?"

"Yep! I can't read it!"

She slammed the ancient book shut. Its pages crumbled instantly and floated lifelessly to the ground as she tossed the leather spine and cover over her shoulder. Shiro had to duck to avoid getting hit in the face by it.

"Lilian!" Geran dashed over and snatched her wrist as she reached for another. "The hell are you doing! Do you have any idea how priceless this knowledge must be?"

She snatched her hand back. "You can't even read the stuff. It's worth about as much as the paper it's written on."

"Someone can probably translate it!"

"Translate what? The language hasn't changed much between now and the dragon wars. All the ink's faded and smudged. If you wanna try to play historian, be my guest."

"Maybe it's enchanted or something! Maybe you need a special light or lens to comprehend it."

"You can't enchant paper, dummy; it's organic material. Remember what Arthur said?"

Geran stared at her aghast. "I can't believe someone so dumb can remember something so unrelated to her field of expertise."

"You're just mad because I proved you wrong, Mr. Know-It-All."

"You still can't just trash the place. The Arcane Sages would want to study everything they can!"

"Oh yeah. Those book-sniffers would have a field day in here. Oh well. There're still plenty of things for them to stuff their noses into.

"Unbelievable," Geran muttered as the mage waltzed around the room.

"Everyone should look around," Elaethia interjected. "As fascinating as this room is, it is not our priority. We should try to find an indication as to where this treasure is. This room is clearly designated for the study of elemental magic. The item we seek would not be here, since it is supposed to have its own room."

Shiro nodded. "You're right. But everything here is illegible."

"Regardless, we must conduct a thorough search and check the other rooms. Do not overlook anything."

As Cataclysm investigated, they discovered that the three other rooms were nearly identical. Each appeared to be dedicated to a certain field of magic, as they had thought. The green room was for druidic magic, the gold for holy, and the red for anatomy. None of them, however, equaled the grandeur of the middle entryway. The annex's size and construction didn't lead the party to believe that this ancient structure was as important and spectacular as Arthur had implied. None of the four wings gave any clue or indication of this alleged room that held the treasure. After several hours of methodical searching, they came back to the center area empty-handed.

"Well this was a bust," Lilian said as she pouted and flopped down to the hard, dusty tiles. "I'm gonna give that Sage a piece of my mind when we get back. If he wanted us to get something, he shoulda sent someone to scout it out first."

Elaethia sighed and closed her eyes. "That is why we are here, Lilian."

"This wasn't even a scouting mission."

Geran glared at her. "It was a task. It's whatever the client wants us to do."

Shiro looked around. "Why doesn't Arthur come here himself if he's so interested in this site?"

Lilian rolled her hand while she stared at the ceiling. "He's a book-sniffer. Who knows why they do anything?"

"Not like he has the time or strength, either," Geran added. "He's one of the top magicians in the country, but he doesn't sound like much of a combatant."

"But he seemed willing to pay an incredible amount of gold for this item," Shiro said. "If he's never been out here himself, he wouldn't know what would or would not be here."

"Not to mention I highly doubt he'd lead us on with some sick joke."

Elaethia looked down and folded her arms. "Do we believe the best course of action is to return to the guild? Or perhaps there is something else that we may have missed. We might have been looking for the wrong things."

"Maybe," Geran murmured as he scratched his stubble beard. "I don't know what else to keep an eye out for, though. But if the people that used this place were as smart as we were led to believe, they could have any number of secrets or fail-safes that we would never figure out."

"You're right, Geran!" Shiro said. "There may be secret passages or hidden alcoves. Take those magic torches for instance. They lit up just from us entering. Already these ancient enchanters have shown that they could bend magic to ways we couldn't imagine. There has to be something that we can't see."

"But how would we see it?" Elaethia asked.

Geran shrugged. "Not like any of us are enchanters. Hell, none of us are familiar with any. Even *I* don't have close contact with one. The guild has a couple novice ones for our enchanted door locks, but that's it. We're completely out of our element."

"Hey guys," Lilian called from the floor. "Is it just me, or do those engravings on the ceiling look almost like something in particular?"

"Any way you can be more specific on that?"

The mage pointed up. "Like, that bit right there in the center looks like a pedestal or something. Those wavy lines look like water, and that group of shapes surrounding it looks like people or soldiers."

Shiro squinted at it. "I think Lilian is right, but we saw nothing like that. That pedestal looks like it's coming out of the water. There's no lake or pool around here."

"The oceans on the other side of these hills though," Geran said. "Maybe it's over there?"

Elaethia shook her head. "No. If we look farther up, we can see that there is a stony cover above the pedestal. This may indicate it is in a cave."

Lilian's ears perked as she sat up. "That's it! It might be underground! Maybe there's some trapdoor or a hidden staircase."

"Let's look for a switch or a lever!" Shiro said as he bounced on his toes.

The four of them spread out. Geran and Shiro checked the crevices and walls for any sign of said lever. Lilian and Elaethia stayed in the center of the room and tapped the ground with their weapons. Both had their ears close to the ground to listen for the hollow resonance that would indicate a hidden cavity. It wasn't too long before Lilian found exactly that. She followed the sound and found herself moving in a wide circle around the center of the large room.

"Found it!" she called cheerfully.

Shiro ran over, followed by Elaethia. "You found a lever?"

"Nope, but there's definitely something right below us. All we gotta do is figure out how to get down there."

"And that bit's gonna be a problem," Geran announced from the other side. He stood in front of a hidden panel that he had found on a pillar. He moved aside as everyone came over.

"What is this, Geran?" Elaethia asked.

"I think it's a code. There're a bunch of those small tiles with glowing symbols on them that seem to be buttons. I pushed a few of them, but nothing happened. However, looking at the glow from this panel, and the glow from the floor, it seems the two are connected."

Shiro rubbed his chin. "So by pushing these buttons in the right order, we might be able to open the floor."

"Exactly."

"Welp, let's give it a whirl!" Lilian approached the panel and started pushing the buttons randomly. The buttons turned red for a moment, and then back to blue. "Well that didn't work. Let's try again!"

"Hey, hey, hey, hey, hey!" Geran said, intervening. "I already tried that once. And you just pushed a random pattern. Let's try to remember the order so we can narrow it down."

"There're nine buttons. You wanna keep punching in combinations over and over until you get it right?"

"Unless you have a better idea," he stated.

Lilian looked him up and down, blinked, and shot her hand out to push all of them again.

"*Seriously?* What did I just say?" Geran shouted.

Lilian laughed. "I'm just messing around, Geran, no need to get your britches in a bunch. You can do your method all you want once the buttons turn blue again."

"Are you gonna be able to keep your paws off while I am?"

"Yeah, yeah, yeah, just go. Those buttons should go back to normal any second now."

They stared at the panel for a few seconds.

"Hey," Geran said. "They aren't turning blue."

"Just give it another minute; I'm sure it's fine," she insisted.

Nothing happened after a minute.

Geran tried to push the red buttons, but they wouldn't move. "Great. Just great. Look what you did."

"What? Like you were magically gonna get the right combination this time anyway?"

"Stars above, I hate you."

She shrugged. "Looks like you were wrong twice today, Gerry. Don't get mad at me for pointing it out."

"Cat, I'm gonna …" He started for her until Shiro stepped between them.

"Hold on, Geran, I don't think Lilian meant it that way. I'm sure she's just as frustrated as you, but she expresses it differently. Maybe she needs a little—"

"Maybe she just needs my boot up her ass!"

Lilian spat out a laugh. "You're welcome to try! I'm a *lot* stronger than I was when we first partied up. I'll blast your grumpy pants right off!"

"Lilian, please don't make Geran madder!"

"No, No! Go ahead Lilian, by all means, make me madder! Piss me all the way off; see what happens!"

"Or what, hmm? You gonna rip my tail off? Real original, Gerry!"

"Oh, that's it!"

Geran threw Shiro aside. Lilian was about to raise her staff when Elaethia shot a gauntlet out and grabbed her by the collar of her cloak, yanking her back. Elaethia stepped forward and planted a hand on Geran's chest.

The dragon hero's voice was dangerously cold. "The cause for such a distasteful disagreement is our inability to open the floor, is that correct?"

"That's part of it," Geran growled. His eyes still flashed at the mage, but his voice was more controlled.

"Then you three will stay here. I will take care of this. I trust you two will refrain from further conflicts, yes?"

"Hmph. Only if he apologizes," Lilian grumbled.

"If you do not agree to be civil, you will remain outside while the rest of us finish this quest. Have I made myself clear?"

The demicat looked in Elaethia's eyes, opened her mouth, but then shut it after thinking better of it. "All right, all right. I promise I won't talk about this anymore."

Elaethia released both of them. The ranger and mage glared at each other but said nothing as they stood against the wall. Elaethia nodded and huffed. A small billow of chilly vapor poured from her nostrils as she turned and strode to the center of the room.

"What do you think she's going to do?" Shiro whispered to Geran.

"Dunno. She seems to have a plan, though."

Lilian looked on keenly. "She's gotten a lot smarter and more methodical since we met. Maybe she saw something we didn't."

The three of them watched intently as Elaethia stopped where Lilian had discovered the hollow floor. The warrior tapped it with her battleaxe to verify there truly was empty space beneath it. She stopped, nodded, and raised the axe above her head.

Her companions saw what was coming and tried to stop her. It was too late. Before any of them could utter a word, the dragon hero brought the massive blade onto the ground with earth-shattering force. An eruption of dust, light, and fragmented tile blasted up and around the room. The three of them stumbled back, coughing from the particles and debris. By the time they stood up and the dust settled, all that was in front of them was a massive hole in the ground. Elaethia was nowhere to be seen.

"Elaethia!" Geran called out.

He was given no response.

"Elaethia-sama!" Shiro called in like. He, too, was greeted with silence.

Lilian gripped her staff. "Guys … you don't think she—"

"Don't say it!" the samurai was shaking. "I don't want to think about it."

Lilian started forward. "We can't just stay here, though!"

"Wait!" Geran caught her arm. "The floor is unstable! One false move and you could follow her. We have to be very careful and watch where we step. Only one of us should try."

"I'm the lightest! I can also blast myself back up with air spells. I'm the best one to do this."

"Okay …" Geran's voice turned shaky. "Okay, just be careful, all right?"

"I will." She nodded and started onto the cracking floor. "I'll be fine, I promise."

She hadn't made it two steps when another explosion shook the room from their right. The mage stumbled backward into her companions as the ground beneath her gave way and fell into the darkness. A large, dark silhouette rose ominously from the floor toward them. The three adventurers scrambled to their feet, weapons ready, as the figure emerged.

It was Elaethia.

They sighed in relief and sheathed their weapons.

"Elaethia-sama, thank the heavens!" Shiro breathed. "When we didn't see you, we feared the worst."

"Do not worry, Shiro, I am unharmed," she said. "As Lilian thought, there was a staircase hidden beneath the floor. I fell only a few meters before landing on it. All I needed to do was follow it up and burst my way through again."

"Wait, so you were right there the whole time?" Geran demanded.

"Correct."

"Why didn't you respond to us? We were worried sick!"

"You seemed to be having a more pleasant conversation with Lilian than before. I did not want to interrupt."

Lilian scratched her head. "I don't … What?"

The four of them walked for what felt like ages. The spiraling staircase lit up beneath their feet as they stepped further down into the earth. The descending passageway was bland stone, but the outer walls themselves were far from that. Detailed carvings ran all the way down the corridor, depicting stories and discoveries of enchanting and magic. Presumably this was the history of the location. Lilian's eyes never left the murals that told the story of this place. The demicat's fascinated interest in the etching work slowly diminished to sadness. This section portrayed the construction of the Imperium. According to the carvings in front of her, the momentous place was built not by magic but by slaves—more specifically, demihumans.

The demicat ran her fingers over the depictions of her ancient kin being whipped and beaten while carrying large stones and tools. Elves, humans, and dwarves all commanded and supervised the work the new species partook in. Elaethia took note of Lilian's falter and nodded quietly to herself. Apparently demihumans had not achieved their freedom by this point in history. It seemed they would not be on equal status with the other brehdars until well after the dragon wars.

Finally they reached the bottom. Cataclysm passed through an ornate archway and entered an underground cavern whose size put the entryway above to shame. After walking down the stairs for so long, one should have expected the location to be big. However, the adventurers were completely awed once again. Even with the light that shined from the stairs, they couldn't make out the entirety of the gargantuan cavern. The dim blue light diminished in the distance along the wet, stony walls of the cave.

After another pause, Lilian thrust her staff out and launched a moderate *fireball* into the darkness. They all watched as it passed through the air and hit the wall on the far side. In the glimpse she saw from the spell, as well as her dragon eyes adjusting to the lighting, Elaethia could get an appreciation for the size of the place. Frossgar's own cave paled in comparison. In fact, the dragon could have spread his wings and taken flight inside the massive cavern.

She could see more clearly now. The mural above the entryway upstairs was correct. There was a pool down here, although it was more akin to a small lake. The smell of salt and brine indicated it was seawater from the ocean outside. In the middle of the body of water was a single, meter-tall pedestal on a small island. There was no path or bridge to it.

"Holy Sun and Moon," Geran muttered. "How long did it take to build this place? Is this cavern even a natural occurrence?"

"Perhaps it is a mixture of both," Elaethia said. "The structure in the middle of the lake is certainly artificial."

Shiro squinted. "You can see it?"

"I can. I believe our objective is on that small island."

"Okay, so how do we get to it?" Lilian asked. "Want me to fly over?"

"I have an idea." Elaethia walked to the water's edge. She placed a gauntlet finger above the still surface and poured frost magic over it.

Geran raised an eyebrow. "Is she about to do what I think she's about to do?"

Lilian raised her own. "Depends what you're thinking."

"Oh, I see! Elaethia-sama is so cool!" Shiro said, and he bounced in anticipation as the dragon hero stepped over the water. The liquid surface turned to ice as her plated boot came down on top of it. With every step she took, the calm waters froze over to guide her to the center of the lake. Elaethia walked across the ever-growing bridge of ice to the pedestal before her.

The room began to light up once she got halfway. She stopped in her tracks. Elaethia and her companions looked around the massive cave as it was fully illuminated. Enchanted stones along the walls glowed brightly enough for them to see everything clearly: the glistening blue walls, the mossy ceiling far above, the quartz pedestal in the middle of the crystal-clear lake. From the shore, Shiro stepped forward to peer breathlessly into the translucent water. He suddenly inhaled sharply and scrambled back, knocking Geran over.

"Ow! Shiro! What gives?" the ranger growled.

He was only greeted by a shaking hand that pointed to the saltwater lake. Geran walked to the shore to peer down, and his knees buckled. Ignoring the sheer drop-off of several hundred meters, his balance was robbed of him as he saw what lay at the bottom. He inched back and looked right to see that Lilian, too, was paralyzed. The demicat's eyes were wide and affixed. Her tail was bushed out further than any of them had ever seen.

"E-Elaethia ..." she stammered. "Whatever you do, don't look down."

"What do you mean?" Elaethia asked as her eyes tilted straight down. She, too, seized, but only for a moment before she regained control of herself. Directly below her at the bottom of the lake was a living mass she never thought possible. The monster's pure-white serpentine body was curled around the rocky growth that towered up to the surface. Even though it was lying over itself in a coiled slumber, she could guess it was a little less than fifty meters in diameter and three hundred meters long. Its eyes were closed, but the lids told her they were the size of the cathedral's stained-glass windows. The sleek, triangular head held a toothless mouth that could have swallowed Frossgar whole. Elaethia wondered whether the great dragon could even have fought this monster.

Geran swallowed hard. "Is … Is that …"

"A leviathan," Shiro said shakily, finishing the sentence for him. "And it's still young."

"That's just a little one?" Lilian's voice was small.

"Fully grown they're supposed to be anywhere from five to seven hundred meters long. The biggest one ever recorded was over a kilometer."

The mage began to shake. "Why … Why would the heavens create such a thing?"

Shiro put a hand to his head. "How did it even get in here? Maybe it swam in here as a hatchling and got too big to get out?"

Geran shook himself. "I don't care to take the time to think about that. Elaethia! Grab whatever's on that island and let's get the hell out of here!"

"I wholeheartedly agree," she said.

Elaethia turned and hastily continued her walk across the water. She did *not* want to linger. For the first time since becoming a dragon hero, she felt fear of the monster before her. She did not believe she had the power to compensate for her lack of size. Elaethia reached the island and walked briskly up the short set of stairs to the pedestal. On it was a small, ornate metal chest.

She attempted to open it. It seemed to be locked. She tried to pick it up, but it was fixed to the stone it sat upon. Growing quite impatient with the scenario, she gripped the metal box and wrenched it from its stand. Bits of rock shattered and fragmented to the stone floor and into the water. She turned the box over in her hand and saw no hinges or lock on it. Not knowing what else to do, she shook it.

"Elaethia! What is it?" Lilian called from the shore.

"A metal box. There appears to be something inside!"

"Well, open it!"

"I cannot! It is sealed shut!"

"We'll worry about that later!" Geran hurried. "Just bring it over so we can get out of here!"

Elaethia nodded and began to walk forward. A glow and hum from the box stopped her. She turned back to see that the pedestal it rested on was also glowing. The hum grew louder, and the box started to vibrate. Elaethia debated between putting it back or ignoring it. Her thoughts were interrupted by the booming sound of stone falling on stone. She shot her gaze to the shore to see eight stone slabs burst from the wall. An ominous green glow resonated within as eight atronachs emerged from the spaces. As her companions drew their weapons and closed together, Elaethia prepared to charge to their aid.

She stopped. The box. The small box was the reason for this activation. These atronachs were clearly a defense mechanism set in place by the ancients who had made them. She dashed back to return it to where it belonged, but the humming didn't stop. She turned around to see that the atronachs hadn't ceased their advance either. Shiro, Geran, and Lilian had defensively backed themselves into the stairway that led upstairs. Lilian channeled her condensed *torch*, which only ricocheted off the foes. These atronachs appeared to be resistant to magical attacks. Shiro and Geran thrust and slashed at the enemy to keep them at bay, but their longswords couldn't deal a fatal blow to their metallic green bodies.

"Lilian!" Geran shouted. "Is there any way you can freeze these things?"

"There's no moisture in them; *petrify* won't do a thing!" she responded.

"It doesn't have to be that spell; is there any other that can work?"

"I could try using a *frost rune*, although I don't know if that'll do the trick!"

"We're out of options until Elaethia gets here; just try it!"

"All right, try not to move around until it's placed!"

Lilian made a circle with her staff at her feet and backed away. Nothing happened.

"What was that, Lilian? Are you out of magic?" Shiro called back, shoving away one of the green metal creations.

The mage rubbed her head in panicked confusion. "No! I don't know what happened! The only reason that wouldn't work is if …" She faltered.

"If what? Geran yelled as he parried a strike from an atronach.

"If I already have a rune somewhere! I can't have two runes placed at once."

"*What!*"

Shiro spoke again. "Where is it? You can just detonate it from anywhere at any time right? If you do, you can make a new one!"

"I don't remember where I put it! I could seriously hurt or kill someone!"

"What kinda mage slaps a lethal spell on the floor and forgets about it?" Geran roared.

Elaethia gripped the box in her gauntlet. Her friends were in need of help. Once again resorting to force, Elaethia smashed the box. She fingered through the fragments and pulled out a single ring. She took only a moment to study the immense magic that radiated from it, and slipped it into the leather pouch around her waist. The dragon hero donned her helmet, planted a foot against a sturdy rock, and shot off from the island across the icy bridge.

A deafening toll rocked the entire cavern. The deep alarm, like that of a church bell, shook the room as pieces of rubble trembled and fell from the walls. As Elaethia halted on the shore and drew her axe, all eight atronachs turned to her and began to glow brighter.

Shiro took immediate advantage of this. He gripped his katana underhand, raised it above his head, and drove it into the back of the nearest atronach. The metallic creation shuddered, grew dim, and collapsed to the ground. Geran quickly copied the tactic and destroyed another. The other six ignored their partner's fall as they advanced on Elaethia. They charged forward, brought to life by the deafening alarm, intent on retrieving the object they were commanded to protect.

She was ready for them. Elaethia wound up and swung with all her might across her torso. The ancient atronachs may have been constructed by master enchanters, but no material or magic could save them from the devastating blow of a dragon hero. With a burst of green light, the six machines exploded into shrapnel, all felled by the single swing. Chunks and fragments of their green-tinted bodies flew into the air. The pieces slammed against the wall and splashed into the water. The adventurers looked warily around. The alarm suddenly ceased. The loud tolling had stopped, but the cavern still shook.

"The pedestal!" Lilian pointed. "The pedestal's still glowing! If you break that too, maybe it will stop!"

"It's worth a shot!" Geran agreed.

"Stay here; I will take care of it!" Elaethia called.

Elaethia got into position to charge across the lake again. With a slow exhalation, she burst forward and tore over the ice bridge at astounding speed.

She got only halfway.

The rumbling was not from the alarm or the defense systems left by the ancients. Elaethia quickly learned what the true cause of the earthquake was. One moment she was sprinting over the lake, the next she was launched hundreds of meters from the water's surface. An unfathomably enormous explosion of white water and flesh erupted from below. The dragon hero was hurled into the air and slammed into the ceiling above.

The leviathan had been awakened from the alarm.

The enraged monster burst through the surface, poised over the three adventurers. The leviathan glared at the brehdars below, which seemed to be mere insects in comparison to it. The gargantuan sea monster let out a shrill roar. Seawater flowed from its head and rained down onto them like a torrent. The three adventurers wiped their eyes to see it coil its neck and strike at them with blinding speed.

It suddenly lurched straight down into the water, and its wide mouth slammed into the shore. Geran, Lilian, and Shiro were lifted into the air from the sheer impact and crashed to the ground. They looked up to see a burst of ice crystals atop the monster. The leviathan's head was nearly the size of the guildhall, and the jagged burst had covered it completely. Elaethia appeared moments later and made her way to the edge of the monster's head. The dragon hero leaped to the stony floor, cracking it as she landed.

Geran staggered to his feet. "No way …"

Lilian pulled herself up as well. "That's the biggest burst I've ever seen her use."

Shiro stayed on his knees. "She … she just—"

The leviathan's eyes shot open.

Geran scrambled back. "Nope! No she didn't! *Run!*"

Elaethia charged at the side of the leviathan's face, again slamming the giant battleaxe into it with another burst of dragon magic. The monster lurched to the side and struck the wall of the cavern with enough force to shake the ceiling above. The leviathan recoiled into the air, screeching in pain. It was enraged; the blows from the dragon hero had not been enough to kill it. The white sea monster rose above them again, towering one hundred meters above their heads. The leviathan shrieked again in a reverberating roar that shook the air itself. Rock and debris burst from the wall and ceiling and continued to fall to the lake below.

"It is no use," Elaethia panted as she fell to a knee. "I hit it with two of the mightiest blows I have ever dealt, and it is only angered."

Geran slid next to her. "Woah, woah, are you okay?"

She shook her head as blood dripped from her visored helmet. "I hit the ceiling of the cavern when I was thrown. By the Sun, I have never felt such a blow. I used nearly all of my magic in the attacks on the leviathan. I am sorry, but I do not have the strength to fight."

"This is bad." Geran gritted his teeth as he looked up. The leviathan thrashed around, slamming into the stone walls to dislodge the icy growths from its head. More rubble fell from the cave and crashed into the water below. Each piece that fell splashed into the lake, raining saltwater droplets onto them.

"We must retreat!" Elaethia said, and she put a gauntlet to his shoulder. "We have what we came for; there is no reason to try to fight such a foe."

"You can say that again. Lilian, Shiro! We're running!"

The samurai looked over his shoulder. "No. No we're not."

Everyone followed his gaze, and their hearts dropped. Debris and boulders had fallen into the lake from the leviathan's spastic thrashing. But the destruction was not limited to within the cavern. The entryway—the only way in and out of the underground area—had caved in.

"That's not good …" Lilian's eyes contracted and shakily darted around. "That's not good at all. Geran, what do we do!"

"Hold on, hold on!" Geran muttered, and he ran a hand through his hair. He began to mumble under his breath. "Shiro, is there enough room for all of us in the archway to take cover?"

"There is, yes!"

"Elaethia, how much magic do you have left?"

"Very little."

"That'll have to do. Lilian, what about you?"

"I-I'm almost full!"

"All right, everyone get to the arch. Elaethia, prepare some unyielding ice. Lilian, I need you to hit that ceiling with a heavy *explosion*! Bring it down!"

"*What?*" she shouted.

"Elaethia's ice will keep us from being crushed; we'll be fine for the time being!"

"But we're in here; are you crazy?"

"Don't start arguing with me, dammit, just do it!"

"Moon help me," the mage whispered as she wound up.

Lilian thrust her staff up and detonated a sizable *explosion* in the middle of the ceiling. The leviathan shrieked from the flames, thrashing and flailing even more from the searing heat. Steam hissed and billowed around its glistening body. The cavern shook from the detonation, sending rocks and earth in every direction. However, it didn't break.

Lilian's mouth fell open. "How thick is that ceiling?"

"Geran!" Shiro called. "Elaethia-sama collapsed! She made two constructs of unyielding ice and fell unconscious!"

Geran joined them and felt her neck. "Stars above, no! She's breathing, just overcast. Dammit this is *not* good. I hate to say it, but if this goes south, it's been an honor working with you all."

Lilian gritted her teeth. "All right, fine! To hell with it! You want that ceiling brought down? I'll knock that shit down!"

The mage dashed to the middle of the floor, inhaled deeply, wound up, and thrust with everything she had.

"No, Lilian, *wait!*" Geran called out to her, but it was too late.

The demicat poured everything she had and then some into another *explosion* that rattled the cave with earth-moving force. The spell was enough. Beams of sunlight burst through the high ceiling and flames as the earth caved in from above. Trees, boulders, snow, and pieces of earth rained down through the inferno, smashing into everything below. The leviathan shrieked and squirmed as it was crushed beneath the literal weight of the hill above. Lilian smiled in grim satisfaction as she lost all feeling in her body. Sighing deeply, she collapsed to the ground from overcast.

"Lilian!" Shiro cried out and ran from the cover of Elaethia's spell.

Geran reached out to grab him but was too slow. "Shiro, no! Get back; we can't have you getting killed, too!"

The samurai ignored him and sprinted out into the falling rubble. He slid to the ground, threw the demicat over his shoulders, and scrambled back. He started to glow. Geran realized he was using *sunlight* to keep himself from being exhausted, but the avalanche was crashing down all around him. With a roar of desperation, the samurai dived under the unyielding ice as the earth fell and encased them underground in complete darkness.

Lilian woke to the feeling of a glass bottle touching her lips. Other than that, she couldn't feel much else. The familiar sensation of a magic potion flowing down her throat increased as she started to regain feeling through her body. A hand was holding the side of her head, and she could tell she was leaning against something hard—several hard things, actually. She opened her eyes and began to make out the fuzzy silhouette in front of her.

"Geran?" she asked weakly.

"Well. Looks like your brain works after all," the ranger sighed. "How are you feeling? Can you sit up on your own?"

She nodded and leaned forward to take the bottle. She drank the rest of the contents and set it on the stony ground next to her with a clink. Lilian inhaled deeply and sighed as she looked around. Small beams of light shone through the cracks in the rubble that had them trapped. It seemed Elaethia's spell held up to its reputation. Two crystalline blue growths were holding up the weight of the earth above them. There wasn't much room in the pocket of cover that Elaethia created, but it seemed to be enough for the four of them.

Geran was still kneeling next to her. She looked around to see Elaethia propped up against the wall across from her. The warrior was breathing, but her eyes were closed and her skin was paler than usual. Lilian tried to lift a hand to fix her hat, but something held it back. She looked to her left to see that Shiro was passed out on her arm. The samurai clutched her hand in his own, breathing gently. She smiled. They were all alive.

"He wouldn't leave your side after the collapse," Geran said. "All three of you were overcast. As soon as Elaethia went under, he tried to bring her back with *moonlight*. Damn fool put everything he had into her and then some. Couldn't even make a dent. Elaethia's magic reserve is astronomical compared to his, and she used all of it attacking the leviathan and making this shelter."

"So you brought me back with my own potion?" Lilian asked.

"Right. You were in worse condition than Shiro, and it wouldn't have been enough for Elaethia. She's sturdy, though. She'll be fine. On that note, what about you? Is everything all right up there?" He pointed to her head.

She nodded. "Yeah. I'm good now."

"Are you sure?"

"I'm sure. I'm not fully recharged magic-wise, but I'm good to go beyond that."

"Good."

The ranger reached out a hand and slapped her squarely across the face.

"Ow!" Lilian fell to the side, clutching her reddening cheek.

"You *idiot!*" Geran roared. "Do you have *any* idea how boneheaded that was? You were in the middle of a cave-in, and you just … turned yourself into a rag doll!"

"Geran …"

"Forget the fact you didn't even have the brains to get to *cover* before you brought the world down on top of you! Did you even stop to think about how the *rest* of us would react? You gave us a damn heart attack! Shiro's dumb ass went panic mode and charged out into that shitstorm to grab your stupid tail! Not only did you almost kill yourself—you almost took him with you! Now you've got an *active rune* somewhere out in the wild that *anyone* could step on! How could you possibly forget about that? Stars above, Lilian! What have I been saying all these months? What have I been trying to get through your pea brain? You have to *think!* Is this what it takes? Does one of us have to *die* before you finally get all that fur out from between your ears? Or are you so stuck in your own little agenda that the rest of us come second to your bullshit!"

Lilian was in shock. Tears streamed down her face as she held her stinging cheek. He was right. What was she thinking? She had been so caught up in trying to prove her point and act that she hadn't thought about her friends. This wasn't the first time everything was her fault. Upstairs with the buttons, she should have held herself back. In the arrow storm with Shiro, she shouldn't have strayed so far away. Against the blood sorceress, she should have blasted Morgan before she could take control of them. Countless times before with her old party, similar events had happened because she was too impatient or selfish.

And now here. Every single time she screwed up, her party had to cover for her. *Damnit.* What was *wrong* with her? Was it really even worth it having her here with them? They were all so capable and able to reason their way through every situation. They could think anything through. All she was good for was blowing things up and creating problems.

A shadow fell across her face. She looked up to see Geran's hand reach for her. She flinched and tensed for the impact. Instead of striking her again, his hand cupped the back of her head and pulled her into his shoulder. The ranger wrapped his arms around her and drew a shaky breath.

"Don't you ever—*ever*—do that to us again."

His fingers wrapped around her black cape as he held her tightly. Choking out a sob, the demicat buried her face into his chest and bawled.

Elaethia and Shiro awoke a little over an hour later. While still exhausted magically, the dragon hero still had her inbrehdar strength. Carefully testing the pieces of rubble that encased them, she dug a way out back into the cavern. The sight that met them was an homage to their name. The only word to describe the spectacle was "cataclysm." Light from the setting sun illuminated the entire collapsed cave. Everything that had been above ground hours prior was now scattered and broken in front of them.

"In all my life, I have never seen such a spectacle," Elaethia murmured.

Geran pushed his hair back. "I gotta say, I've seen some crazy things before, but this takes the cake."

Lilian poked her head out from their cover. "Did … Did *I* do that?"

Shiro nodded. "Yes, although I think that leviathan helped a bit."

Everyone nodded, paused, and lit up.

"The leviathan!"

The four of them dashed over the broken and rocky landscape to get to the water's edge. Halting on a single, large boulder, Cataclysm looked into the lake. The once crystal-clear water now held an opaque crimson hue. Bits of soil, ice, plant life, and blood swirled around the underground lake. All around the body of water was the broken and decimated corpse of the leviathan. Lilian's staff clattered to the ground. Elaethia and Shiro were stunned. Geran reached both hands to the top of his head and was the only one to speak.

"Ho-ly shit."

"We … we killed it," Lilian murmured. "We killed a leviathan. We've gotta be the only ones to do something like this in centuries, millennia … maybe even ever!"

"We may just be the first," Shiro said.

After a minute of stunned silence, Lilian suddenly perked up. "Oh yeah! Wasn't this all to retrieve some sort of enchanted item?"

"Way to kill the mood," Geran muttered. "Elaethia, were you able to secure whatever was in that box?"

"I was," she said, and she reached into her pouch. "All that was there was this ring."

Shiro leaned forward and eyed it. "Just a ring? I mean, I can feel an awful lot of magic radiating from it. But did those ancient enchanters really set up all this for one ring?"

"Let me see," Geran said. Elaethia placed the ring in his palm as he began to inspect it. "Huh. It's shiny and silver colored, but it's too hard to be actual silver. It's in near perfect condition for being over a thousand years old, too, but that could be the enchantment. Judging by the brightness and hardness of it, I think this could be platinum."

"Whaaaaaat?" Lilian's mouth fell open as drool started to flow from it.

"Yeah, I'm pretty sure. We'd have to take it to a jeweler or a smith to be sure, though."

Lilian wiped the spittle from her lip and reached out shakily. "Can … Can I hold it? Please?"

Geran looked her up and down and sighed. "Fine. But give it back to Elaethia when you're done slobbering over it."

The demicat let out a fervent, euphoric moan as the priceless metal ring was placed into her shaking hands. She twisted it over in her fingers, holding it up in the light to get as familiar with the ring as she could. Elaethia promptly took it from her once the mage started giggling and muttering something about "precious."

Shiro asked the obvious question. "So what does it do?"

"Let us find out," Elaethia stated. She removed a gauntlet and slipped the ring on her finger. Everyone tensed as she did. Nothing happened.

"Fascinating," she stated. "I did not feel a surge or change in either the ring or myself."

"Try putting some magic into it," Lilian urged. "Just a little bit to see if it'll activate."

Elaethia nodded and did just that. She poured a little of her magic into the ring, and it suddenly began emitting an ominous red glow. Everyone gasped and backed up, but the red disappeared as quickly as it had appeared. In its stead, a gentle blue glow came to life. Elaethia poured more of her magic into it, and there was a second reaction. As the ring glowed, she began to rise into the air.

"Do not be alarmed by my words," Elaethia began, "But it seems you are all getting smaller."

Shiro balked. "We aren't getting smaller, Elaethia-sama. You're getting bigger!"

Geran's mouth fell open. "Wrong on both accounts. Elaethia, you're floating!"

Lilian started to bounce. "Oh my gosh. Those old coots figured out *flight magic!*"

Elaethia tilted her head as she slowly rose higher. "Does such a thing exist?"

"Beats me! Hey! Everyone grab on! Elaethia's gonna give us a ride outta here!"

"Do you believe this ring to be strong enough to carry all of us?"

"We're about to find out!" Lilian leaped up with a girly giggle and wrapped her arms around Elaethia's waist. The warrior didn't show any signs of stress or slowing down. "C'mon, guys! You don't wanna miss out on this!"

Geran stepped back. "I think I'll get out the normal way."

"The stairs are blocked, remember?"

"Gaaaah, fine. Elaethia, take my arms."

"C'mon, Shiro! You don't wanna be left behind, do you?" Lilian beamed at him as Elaethia continued to slowly climb. Shiro said nothing. Instead, he shuffled up underneath Elaethia's open side, jumped, and clung on for dear life.

"Is everyone ready?" Elaethia asked. "Hold on to me very tightly. I wish to be out of here as quickly as possible."

The dragon hero flew up with greater speed. Getting faster and faster, she rocketed up to the open ceiling. Lilian whooped with glee as they flew through the air and the chilly wind whistled through their ears. Geran looked around as if he were still trying to wrap his head around what was happening. Shiro, however, made the mistake of looking down.

"I don't suppose this is the best time to mention I'm *terrified* of heights!" The samurai yelped as they emerged from the sinkhole and outside to meet the setting sun.

Cataclysm spent the weeklong return mostly in silence. Lilian, being the usual conversation starter, was quiet the entire time. She wasn't distressed or exhausted, just choosing to be quiet. Her party members frequently asked whether she was okay, but she always responded with insistence that she was perfectly fine. Even at their long-anticipated return to Breeze, she stayed mellow. Citizens all noticed their entrance and cheered with waves and hollers at the famous party. The demicat only gently waved at her fans instead of engaging in her usual fanfare.

It wasn't until they reached the guildhall that she came back to life. As the adventurers reached for the door, Lilian suddenly shot her staff out. A sudden and potent blast of air burst forth, flinging the heavy oak doors open. The spell was so powerful it even knocked one of the doors off of its hinges. Everyone was stunned. The entire guildhall went dead quiet and froze as they looked, bewildered, at the sleek girl posed dramatically in the open doorway.

"Guess what, bitches!" she taunted into the hall. "We just killed a fricking leviathan!"

Chapter 20
Advancement

Sixth Era.140. Juery 22.

The entire guildhall made a beeline to hear the story. Adventurers, civilians, servers, receptionists, apprentices, and anyone else that happened to be there surrounded Lilian as she began the tale. The demicat stood atop the bar and walked up and down the length of the long counter. She waved her arms and flapped her cape in dramatic fashion, somehow managing to embellish the story further beyond what was already believable. Elaethia was sure that Master Dameon would burst from his office to quell the commotion. To her surprise, she spotted the massive demibear leaning over the railing, listening intently to the mage's story. Elaethia shook her head and turned to assist Geran and Shiro, who had begun reattaching the front door.

Lilian chose to leave out the details regarding the platinum ring and replaced their escape with her flying them out one by one with air spells. While grateful for the choice, Elaethia found the ease with which Lilian could lie unnerving. The mage's fabrications flowed from her mouth as easily as she breathed—so much so that Elaethia began to question her own recollection of that day.

Once Lilian finished, Elaethia heard Master Dameon grunt with satisfaction and then call out to one of his members below. "Finway!" he shouted.

The demiwolf raised a hand. "Right here, Master!"

"I know you are; I'm looking right at you! Run over to the inn near the capitol building and fetch that Arcane Sage. Arthur Hedwig's his name. Tell him that Cataclysm's back and they've completed the quest."

"There're a couple inns, Master, which one?"

"I think it's the Beauregard. Ask at the front desk to be sure."

"Th-the Beauregard?" Michael stammered. "That's the fanciest inn in Westreach!"

"There's one in every region capitol, and three in Apogee. It's the kind of fancy-schmancy luxury that all the rich people dump obscene amounts of money into. Don't even think about touching anything in there. The cheapest decoration they have is worth more than you. Get in and out as quick as you can before some aristocrat calls the guard on you. Wash your hair before you go, too!"

"Right away, sir!" Michael called, and he dashed upstairs toward the baths.

Dameon pointed to Cataclysm. "You four! As soon as you're done fixing my door and finishing up with the receptionists, I want you in my office for an initial debrief, pronto! No bath, no drinks, no socializing—nothin'! You can drop your gear off, but that's *it!* Arthur's already wasted enough time waiting for you to get back. You're gonna be ready to talk to him the *second* he walks through that door!"

"Baaaaaw!" Lilian whined as she trudged toward the stairs. The other three looked at each other, shrugged, and continued fixing the entryway.

Michael stood agape in front of the grand marble building. The Beauregard was as the young demiwolf predicted. Pure-white pillars held up an intricately carved mural above a glass-and-wood entryway. An iron gate with twisting bars and pointed tips ran all around the property. Even though it was midwinter, a lawn of neatly trimmed grass enveloped the grounds around it. It was so lush and smooth that Michael mistook it for carpet at first. A beautiful garden of trees, flowers, and shrubbery led to the rear of the marvelous hotel. Guests in lavish suits and dresses paraded around the grounds and interior. *How much did all of this cost to make? Were there really more of these in the region?*

The ranger shook himself back to the task at hand and stepped inside. The interior was somehow even more grand than the outside. Carved statues and bubbling fountains lined the entryway of polished granite and quartz. Magnificent upholstery and flooring filled the lounges and foyers. Smells of mouthwatering dishes wafted into the air from a kitchen around the corner. Michael felt very inadequate in his ranger garb and hood.

A posh man's voice interrupted his thoughts. "What are you doing in here? Beggars are not allowed on the premises!"

Michael looked up to see a suited man with a black hat and monocle. The young ranger pointed to himself. "You talkin' to me?"

"Yes, you. This area is for paying customers only, and you certainly are not one of them. Hurry up and leave, or I shall call for security."

Michael held out his guild tag. "Keep your pants on; I'm just here to grab someone."

"Excuse me? Do you know who I am!" the man demanded.

"I really couldn't care less," Michael said, and he walked to the front desk, leaving a sputtering aristocrat in his wake.

"'Scuse me!" he called, and he showed his tag to the receptionist. "I'm looking for one of your guests, an Arcane Sage. The name is Arthur Veldwig."

The demibear woman gave him a look and sighed. "I'll check the directory and send someone to get him if he's here."

"Don't worry about that; I can get him myself. Just tell me where to find him."

She stood and turned around with her nose in the air. "I don't want you walking around. Commoners are not welcome beyond this point."

The demiwolf raised an eyebrow. "Well, damn."

Michael was shocked at how quickly the staff retrieved Arthur. He was almost as shocked at how fast they herded both him and the Arcane Sage off the property. The elderly dwarf and young demiwolf were politely, yet firmly, escorted out through the front gate and onto the boulevard.

"I *knew* I made the right decision sending you four!" Arthur said, bouncing in his seat in Master Dameon's office. Cataclysm sat on the couches, while the guild master stood to the side.

Lilian gleamed. "Darn right you did! One ancient ruin discovered, one magic artifact retrieved, four adventurers returned alive!"

"All as I asked, to the letter! You still have the artifact on you, do you not?"

Elaethia pulled out a small pouch with the ring in it. "Yes. Right here."

Arthur gingerly took the pouch and undid the drawstrings.

"Oh my …" he breathed. "Oh my oh my oh my. I … I can't find the words to describe what you have brought me. The power radiating off it alone is something I have never felt in all my years. The pristine condition, the strength of the enchantment, the value of the ring. This … this is priceless! Enchanters would unhesitatingly give away their life savings to study this artifact."

"So there is no known value for it?" Shiro asked.

"We have already been given a set amount for the completion," Elaethia said. "There is no need to further discuss the value of the item."

Geran raised an eyebrow. "Hey now, we *were* offered a bonus depending on what we brought back."

Lilian started to drool again. "How much more do you think we'll get for retrieving a ring that can make the wearer fly?"

Arthur shot up. "What did you say? Flight? This ring can make you *fly?*"

Elaethia nodded. "Yes. We discovered this once I put it on."

"You *wore* it?"

Lilian cocked her ears. "Duh?"

"Never mind how potentially dangerous that was. What happened? How does it activate? What were the initial properties? Were there any side effects? Is it continuous or manual?"

Shiro blinked. "I didn't understand a word you just said."

"Just tell me everything that happened when you put it on," the Sage pressed.

Elaethia explained the event of her donning and using the enchanted ring.

"Fascinating," Arthur breathed. "It seems it only needs a set amount of magic to start, and it stays active until removal! The ancients managed to make an item that lasts indefinitely and doesn't drain the wearer during use. The only thing that bothers me is that red glow you described upon activation. Nothing I know of reacts like that. I have to get this to my lab as soon as possible!"

"What about our bonus?" Lilian asked.

"Of course! There is only one thing I can offer you all that comes even close to the value of this ring. Shiro, before you left, you asked why no adventurers had enchanted weapons, such as swords that launch fireballs."

"Because it's extremely expensive, right?" he recalled.

"Exactly. So, in addition to your payment, and as a reward for this ring, I shall grant any enchantment that I am capable of to any one item of your choice. For all of you."

The room went quiet. The five of them stared at each other in absolute silence. After a moment, a massive boom to their left shook the room. They jumped in their seats and turned to see that Master Dameon had fainted.

Only Shiro was able to speak after a moment. "I still don't understand magic very well, and even less about enchanting. What could you do for us?"

Arthur's opaque eyes gleamed. "The better question is, What *can't* I do? Think of any problem you've encountered in your battles—something that has always been a consistent inhibition that shows no physical way of being corrected. With my enchanting, I can overcome those hurdles and give you a permanent and unique edge."

"I get it now," Geran said. "I'm always looking for better ways to be hidden, or to understand what others are thinking. Any way you can help with that?"

Arthur thought for a moment. "While mind-reading is out of my current capabilities, I do have a solution for the former. You have no magic reserve to tap into, so invisibility is out of the question. But with a ring or necklace, I can imbue an enchantment that makes it so people simply ignore your presence when you wear it."

"How would that even work?"

"Ah, now that's a mind trick, you see. Think about your nose."

"My nose?"

"Yes. Isn't it odd how you can't see it? Despite it being right on your face?"

"I guess," Geran mumbled as he crossed his eyes.

"The thing is, you actually *can* see it. Your mind simply chooses to ignore it because it knows it's there. In the same way, once you wear the item, you are enveloped in an enchantment that makes people's minds tell them to ignore you when they look at you."

Geran shook his head. "That's nuts."

"Wait and see, dear ranger. Now you, miss mage. You seem keen to go next."

"You bet!" Lilian was bouncing with excitement. "You said you made the moon rings for the tournament, right? Well, I want one of my own, but with a twist!"

"Interesting. Go on."

"I want a ring that not only absorbs the incoming spell but also turns that spell into magic that goes right into my reserves! Just like *electric drain*! I'll recharge myself with their own magic!"

Arthur grinned and scratched his beard. "I've already toyed with that idea before but decided against it considering how powerful it could be in the wrong hands. But you've proven yourself. I'll make an exception for you."

Lilian cheered. "All right! Your turn, Shiro! Tell him what ya want!"

"Well …" the samurai started. "My sword is nearly unmatched in its cutting capabilities, but it's almost useless against armor. Can you give it something to fix that? Make it so it's as if the armor isn't even there?"

Arthur sat back. "This isn't the first time I've been presented with this issue. I've never given much thought in regard to how swords work in battle, as I've never given melees much thought or care. But the way you worded that almost gives me an idea. I'll have to research this, but it shouldn't take me more than a day or two. Same with you, Lilian. Geran's should take me less than a day—only a few hours, in fact. Now, how about you, Elaethia? You've been very quiet."

"I am sorry, but I do not believe I have something for you," she replied solemnly.

"Why do you say that?"

"There is nothing that has proven a roadblock for me in combat other than my own mind. Regardless, my equipment is dragonite. It is made from living matter, so it cannot be imbued with magic."

"I see …" The old enchanter frowned. "Yes, this could be quite the issue. I intend to leave as soon as the enchantments are done and after I am allocated some time to study your magic. It would be very difficult to find me after, should you think of something in hindsight."

Shiro raised a hand. "Wait! What about your necklace, Elaethia-sama?"

"My necklace?" She reached down her shirt and pulled out the gold-and-sapphire pendant—the only relic she had from her family.

Arthur suddenly leaned forward. "A perfectly cut gemstone embedded in pure gold. I could work wonders with that material."

"But what could she use?" Shiro asked. "She is nearly perfect."

Elaethia shook her head. "No one is perfect, Shiro. All I yearn for is to see those I have held dear to me again and to rid my homeland of Rychus. Were I perfect, I would have done so by now. And I cannot bring back the dead."

"If I may make a suggestion?" Arthur said. "The only flaw in your combat I have been able to see is your difficulty holding back. Many times, it seems, you don't wish to kill your targets, but only subdue them or knock them back. You are hyperlethal and seem to need something in your arsenal that grants restraint. If you would be willing to entrust your necklace to me for this time, I could give it a property to drive back any adversary or dominate an area with a presence more intimidating than what you already have. All without seriously hurting anyone."

"I …" she started, looking at the necklace she had so fiercely guarded her whole life. It had come off only a handful of times since it was put around her neck by her mother when she was a little girl. Her hand shook as she held the beloved jewel. Suddenly a wrinkled hand placed a platinum ring in her open palm. She looked up into the soft, milky eyes of Arthur Veldwig.

"Elaethia," he began gently. "I know how hard it is to give up something you love dearly. You know loss, and you cannot bear to meet it again. The pricelessness of this ring to me matches that pendant to you. Take this ring. You will hold on to it as long as I hold on to your necklace. We guard each other's treasure as if it were our own."

Elaethia inhaled with a shudder, gently grasping his hand, then the ring, and then her pendant. Then she whispered in a voice none of them had ever heard from her before.

"All right."

After shakily taking the pendant from her neck, she placed it in Arthur's gentle hands. She gripped the ring in her own and clutched it to her chest. Arthur stood straight and guided the clinking metal into the leather pouch that had held the ring before.

"Forty-eight hours," the Arcane Sage announced. "Exactly two days from now at this time, we will meet back here. I will provide the items for Geran and Lilian, and will be able to perform the enchantment on Shiro's sword on the scene. I cannot do the same for Elaethia, since the enchantment requires additional tools and fluxes. Well then. Without further ado, I shall begin my work. Until then, brave adventurers. In the meantime, I strongly suggest you visit the baths. I can tell how treacherous the quest was by your scent alone."

With that, he strode out of the office and down the stairs.

Lilian's ears went flat. "No regard for our feelings on *that* one, huh?"

"He's right, though," Shiro said. "What we need most right now is to clean off."

Geran's stomach growled. "And eat a solid meal, too."

Shiro jumped up and walked out the door. "Absolutely! Lilian! It's my turn to pay tonight. I'll meet you downstairs at the usual time!"

"Okeydokey!" she chirped, and she stood to stretch. She yawned widely, exposing her fangs and curling her fluffy tail.

Geran stood as well. "That sounds like a good idea. You want to get a bite to eat tonight too, Elaethia? I'll treat you to my favorite restaurant."

She nodded and tried to smile. "I find myself wanting for comfort. I care not where we go as long as you are with me. Thank you, Geran."

"Anytime, darlin'." He smiled as he left.

Elaethia inhaled a little and blushed.

The others could see Lilian's grin without even looking at her. "Well I'll be. He outright went and said it."

Elaethia responded only by touching her cheek. She looked up to watch the man she felt so fondly for walk away. Something in her mind wanted him to say that again. Before she knew it, a giggle escaped her lips. She suddenly gasped at the outburst and covered her face. She parted her fingers to sheepishly look out to see if Geran had heard. Unfortunately, he had. He stopped and turned to look at her again and smiled warmly. With a chuckle that made her heart skip a beat a second time, he reached down to open his room.

A loud blast and sudden burst of air erupted from the ground under his door. The ranger was lifted off his feet, over the railing, and sent tumbling to the floor below. He landed with a crash on top of a round wooden table that splintered from the impact. Geran flopped to the side and rolled to a stop at the feet of some bewildered adventures. The entire guildhall was stunned in silence as the only sound that escaped Geran's lips was a pained groan.

"Oh," Lilian said suddenly, scratching her head.

With a slack jaw, Elaethia looked over at her feline companion, who seemed more relieved than shocked.

Lilian met her bewildered gaze with a small grin. "Hey, I just remembered where I put that rune."

Two very long days later, they all were back in the exact same spots. Master Dameon was not present, however, presumably being on business regarding Nocturnal. Arthur Veldwig sat down and pulled out a leather hip pouch with a lock on it. The old enchanter took his wand out as well. He tapped it to the metal lock, which popped open with a click. He opened the flap and rummaged around inside for a few moments. The Sage then smiled and looked up at the anxious adventurers.

THE ELAETHIUM

"I suppose none of you are interested in the process and difficulties I went through to make these enchantments. The eagerness in your eyes gives it away. So, moving past the tedious formalities, I believe we should start with Elaethia."

Arthur took out her gold-and-sapphire pendant and placed it in her waiting hand. "While the base enchantment is not unique, I added a little something to it. It is called *force burst*. At its core, it is a very low-level enchantment. That is because it is neutral magic. Depending on the power you will into it, it shall send a shockwave of raw energy in all directions. You can use it to push someone away or to knock all those in the area off their feet. Given your magic reserve, you could spend a whole day keeping an army on the ground. That or level a forest in a single blowout.

"The twist that makes yours special is that it not only accomplishes everything I just said but also omits a secondary wave in succession that dispels all magic. Elemental, druidic, holy—it matters not. It goes even so far as to interrupt anything an anatomy mage, enchanter, or alchemist is doing. Actually, low-level enchantments or potions that are hit by this burst are nullified. It is the ultimate self-defense weapon. I am quite proud of this, and even more so to let you be the one to wield it."

"Thank you, Arthur." She took her family heirloom to place it back around her neck and in between her breasts. She sighed deeply as her father's gift was returned. Elaethia then took out the platinum ring from her pouch and placed it in his own hand. Arthur gripped it and dropped it into his satchel.

"Now, Lilian!" the dwarf stated. He took out an etched gold ring. "I can see you're beyond eager for your item, so you shall be next. As you requested, I have a moon ring that not only absorbs incoming spells but also converts the energy from them back into magical power. It then transfers that power and diverts it to your own reserves. Simply put your power into it and aim its ward in the direction of the attacks. Be warned, however, as it will drain you more than the moon rings from the tournament. I advise you to use it only for large or sustained spells."

"Not a problem!" Lilian grinned as she took the gold ring and slid it onto her left finger. "Ohoho. Oh, there won't be a mage alive that can defeat me!"

Arthur scratched his head. "Hmm, yes. Perhaps this wasn't such a good idea. Oh well, I'm sure it will be fine. If worse comes to worse, Elaethia's enchantment will nullify your ward. Now, Geran! In light of your nature, I have provided you with an inconspicuous silver necklace. As you see, it is nothing but a thin chain designed to go around your neck. As I said, put it on and everyone will simply ignore that you are even there. Keep in mind that once someone notices you, it will be very hard to make them forget about you again."

Geran took the chain and slid it into his pocket. "Luckily I'm good at that. This will really come in handy. Thank you, Arthur."

"And now for the last!" Arthur stood and walked toward Shiro. "Master swordsman, if you would, may I see your blade?"

The samurai drew his katana. "Yes sir. There is no other like it in the country, and it is a gift from my grandfather. But I entrust it with your care."

"I do not even need to touch it. Simply hold it steady for me."

Arthur drew his wand and slowly ran the tip along the metal blade. The wand glowed, which lit up the sword as well. From hilt to tip, the enchanter imbued the sword with magic for over five minutes. Once he reached the curved point, he instructed Shiro to turn the blade over, drank a magic potion, and repeated the process again. Once it was done, Arthur stood and exhaled slowly and sheathed his wand.

Shiro held the sword up and studied it. "It doesn't feel any different. What did you do?"

"I gave it an enchantment that is entirely new to this world. Well, as far as I know. You mentioned you wished you could use your sword effectively against armored opponents, so I invented an enchantment just for that."

Lilian leaned forward. "Invented an enchantment? For Shiro?"

"Oh yes. Simply put, the blade now ignores armor—more specifically, inorganic material. His sword will now only cut living or once living things, meaning it will glide through metal and rock as if it isn't even there. The katana will pass through steel and shingled armor like an illusion, striking the vulnerable flesh underneath with uninhibited force—unless your opponent is wearing leather or gambeson."

Shiro shot up. "A-a-amazing!"

"The drawback is that you cannot use it against atronachs or elemental familiars. I suggest you acquire a second weapon that can do so."

The samurai plunged to his knees, bowing on the ground to the Arcane Sage. "I understand, but nevertheless I am beyond grateful for your gift!"

Arthur chortled. "Come now, no need for that! This was simply a payment for a service you provided. Think nothing of it. However, such a weapon should have a name. As a part two for your sword, I will engrave the name you bestow upon it into the blade itself. Choose wisely, young samurai."

Shiro stood and studied his sword. "A name for a unique blade?"

"Let's piece this together," Geran started. "A sword used by a samurai who uses holy magic."

Elaethia caught on. "A weapon that passes through an opponent's defenses as if they aren't even there."

Lilian rubbed her chin. "A sword that kinda ghosts through armor, huh?"

Shiro closed his eyes and thought for a moment. "My grandfather would tell me stories of the heavens. The holy entities he revered the most were spirits that waged war on hell and brought divine judgment upon the wicked. In honor of my grandfather, I'll name the blade after these spirits."

Arthur's eyes glinted. "I believe you have made a decision. And if I follow your thoughts correctly, you have chosen an apt name."

"Seraph," Shiro proclaimed. "My sword shall be named Seraph."

Rychus scratched sharply at his neck, digging his nails into his golden skin. Grinding his teeth and wrinkling his eyes, he sat upon his throne in anxious frustration. More and more households were being found empty, with no clues or valuables within. Magicians were starting to become increasingly scarce. The citizens that had not fled his country were less like people and more like livestock—mindless, thoughtless, emotionless animals. Now he was destroying his own fields and towns outside the walls to prevent possible uprisings. The facts were evident. He could deny it no longer.

He was losing control.

That damn smuggling organization. Rychus scratched harder at his chin as rage began to build within him. He had snuffed out countless groups like them before; what was so different about this one? He asked himself this question, but in reality he knew the answer. This one was fast. They never showed signs of warning. They passed out no propaganda. They left no trails or hints behind. They struck at seemingly random times and households. This group held no campaign or motivating goal. They didn't even have a name. All they ever could find of this group were mere echoes of their actions.

The Echo—that is what his legionaries had started to call them. No matter how swift or spontaneous his attacks, they were always one step ahead of him. Any hideouts he thought they had were only the now-empty houses of families that had managed to contact the Echo. It was beginning to feel as if they didn't even exist. Had he not been able to capture lookouts they used on occasion, he would have believed these citizens had simply disappeared into thin air. Rychus had begun to pull his best minds from not only his counsel but also his engineering and military branches to stop them.

A knock on the grand doors broke his concentration.

"Enter!" he commanded.

The door opened as his voice reverberated around the enormous throne room. A dwarven woman in her midtwenties with caramel skin and curly brown hair stepped in. She was short even by dwarf standards. At just under five feet, she could almost be mistaken for a child. What prevented this misconception was her figure. She was well muscled, with stern and serious eyes.

She was not physically toned in the way a warrior or dancer would be, but rigid like a bodybuilder or workman. She wore a dirty tank top and thick leather pants, with steel-and-leather goggles resting atop her head. Her skin was smudged with grease and soot.

She knelt and bowed her head before the emperor. "You called for me, Your Majesty?"

"Chief engineer Hailey. What is your progress on the image-recording devices?"

"I have made it my priority, Your Majesty, though they're proving very difficult. But I can't abandon my other projects in the process."

"Your self-propelled wagon and two-way communication modules are important as well, yes. But we need the recording devices to get tangible evidence against the Echo. Speed and communication haven't been able to win us this war thus far."

"The wall-listeners and pocket explosives are also proving to be time and resource-consuming. If I may, Your Majesty, we need to balance a strategy of stealth and force. One alone hasn't proven effective; we should try a new approach with both."

"Damn it," Rychus growled as he dug his nails deeper into his skin. Blood began to flow from the self-inflicted claw marks on his throat. "Hailey Foot. You have served me loyally your entire life. You have earned my trust, and you know this. However, as a result you have become overconfident in how you speak to me. Don't treat my favor of you as a tool for arrogance."

She bowed deeper. "I am sorry, Your Majesty, but I do believe we should put more effort into our—"

Rychus shot up with a roar. The golden tyrant swung out with his right hand and struck the stone brazier next to him, shattering it to rubble. The enraged emperor began to emit an ominous, dark red-and-black aura. Unnatural voices floated in whispers around the room. He clutched his head and growled, and he then roared in seemingly two voices. "*Will your methods provide the results we need? Can what you say bring destruction to the Echo!*"

Hailey averted her eyes. Her fingers shook on the floor. "Yes, Your Majesty."

Rychus glared at her with glowing crimson eyes. "Then do what you must."

Shiro immediately found a flaw in his wonderful enchantment. Seraph, as promised, now faded through metal and stone as if it were thin air. Armor made of steel, iron, and slate were rendered useless against the unique blade. Unfortunately, so were other weapons. Shiro had practiced for years in the art of countering and parrying enemy strikes, only to find now that other blades simply passed right through his own. Any attempt to block an opponent's weapon with Seraph was now completely useless.

The samurai sighed as he guided Seraph back into its sheath. While he was now truly unmatched in his offensive capabilities, he was nearly useless in defense. He now had to adopt the other style of swordsmanship he was familiar with, which involved holding his sheath in his off hand, while using the sword in his main hand. Iaido style demanded he resheathe the blade after every iteration so he could successfully block with the scabbard.

He didn't like using the katana with only one hand. It wasn't as precise or powerful. He had grown much stronger this last year, and his holy magic could help compensate, but this felt so … off. He had been able to win in the tournament doing so, but that was mostly due to a stroke of confusion and sheer luck. It would take quite some getting used to.

"Having a rough time adjusting?" Geran's voice said from the left.

Shiro nearly dropped Seraph. "Gah! Geran? What? Where are you?"

"Right here," the ranger said again.

Shiro squinted and looked carefully at where the voice was coming from. It was definitely Geran, but something was off about him. There was a shimmering mirage in the shape of Geran's outline, and a set of tracks in the snow that led to it, but Shiro couldn't make out the ranger's features.

"Am I … Am I looking at you right now?" he asked tentatively.

"What? Of course you are. Why would you—" He stopped. "Oh. Hold on a sec."

Geran suddenly came into focus in front Shiro, holding his enchanted silver necklace.

Shiro doubled back. "Woah! By the Moon, that startled me!"

"Yeah, looks like I forgot to remove it when I was taking it out for a practice run. I completely forgot I was still wearing it. I was wondering why I couldn't get any service at the bar."

"At least your enchantment is working perfectly," Shiro sighed, looking at Seraph.

"Yours works perfectly too. Our lack of foresight has it so you gotta adjust on the fly, though. What's that other style you can do called? Iaido?"

"Yes, but I'm not as skilled in it. I can make it work, but … It's going to suck."

Geran shifted. "Are you thinking about just getting another sword?"

"Absolutely not!" Shiro sputtered. "This sword was made by my grandfather. It was his final gift to me before he died! On top of that, it was given a unique enchantment by one of the most prestigious magicians in the world! My pride for this blade vastly outmatches any regret!"

Geran put his hands up apologetically. "All right all right, jeez. At least you and I can practice, though. Lilian and Elaethia need a lot of space to work on theirs."

"Lilian, yes. Not so much for Elaethia-sama. She did a few of those burst things in the woods earlier and then went with Arthur Veldwig to study her magic. I haven't seen her since."

Geran nodded. "Come to think of it, Lilian didn't go charging off to practice like she always does. I guess that makes sense, though, since she needs someone else to throw spells at her. She's probably in her room or showing off to her mage pals."

They both nodded in silent thought.

"Does all of this bother you, Geran?" Shiro suddenly asked.

"Does all of what bother me?"

"A year ago, we were all just ordinary people. Now we're the strongest party in the country. We've destroyed crime factions, defeated powerful sorcerers, dominated the tournament, explored uncharted regions, and even defeated a leviathan. And now we all have *enchanted items*. Just one of these things is something people would spend their whole lives working to accomplish. We've done it all in just the time we've been together."

"Where did *this* come from? What're you on about?"

Shiro rested a hand on Seraph's hilt. "It just feels … wrong. We've done all these powerful things, and we show no signs of slowing down. Looking at Elaethia-sama's next step, we're only going to keep doing greater and greater feats. Where will this take us? How far will we go? What if we get so strong and ahead of ourselves that we forget what it means to be an adventurer? What if one of us goes down the wrong path? Maybe we'll be so caught up in our methods that we don't even realize the harm we might cause. I've seen what power does to people, Geran. And … and I'm afraid. I don't want to lose myself to it."

Geran sighed as he looked into the distance, sending a small billow of vapor from his nose. "You know, the fact that you have these thoughts is enough to know you won't lose yourself. It's not wrong to be cautious about power, but you shouldn't be afraid of it. As strong or skilled as you or I could get, we'd never be able to come close to Elaethia, even if she were to peak where she is currently. Something tells me Lilian's going to put her mark in history too. They've got the entire world ahead of them, and it's up to you and me to be with them through the whole journey. Never forget that there's always someone better than you and there's always someone who could use your help. Don't worry about unknowingly causing harm. If you want the world to change for the better, it starts with you. Just be the change you want to see."

"You've put an awful lot of thought into this, haven't you, Geran?"

"A little bit," he admitted. "Besides, even if we *do* go off the deep end, Elaethia will be there to bring us back to reality."

Shiro laughed. "You're right. There's no way Elaethia-sama would ever let her power go to her head."

"Speaking of which," Geran said, looking over Shiro's shoulder. "She's coming this way."

Shiro turned. "Lilian's with her too, and they're both in their adventuring gear. Do you think they found a quest?"

"That's the most likely reason. Let's go see what they've got."

Elaethia was the first to approach. Lilian was right behind her, bearing an expression none of them had ever seen before. Her smile was wide, but it tugged awkwardly at her cheeks. Her bright eyes were full of both excitement and anxiety. The demicat's tail flicked back and forth in an obvious sign of distress. Despite all this, the mage's voice was cheerful.

"Hiya, guys! Boy oh boy, do we have a predicament here!"

"What's the matter, Lilian?" Shiro asked.

Lilian didn't respond. Instead she looked at Elaethia. The dragon hero noticed her silence, and realized it was intended for her to speak. Elaethia inhaled slowly.

"I am leaving."

Geran stared blankly at her. "What does that mean?"

"The time has come for me to begin the final steps of my journey. As you know, I joined this guild to hone my skills and magic. I have become much stronger—strong enough that I have been considered the greatest in the country. While I pay no heed to these claims, it shows I have peaked my capabilities here. While I would not consider spending more time with the guild a waste, I cannot accomplish my goal of challenging Emperor Rychus here. It is time to face him."

"Elaethia-sama ..." Shiro's voice was shaking. "You're not ... you're not saying good-bye, are you?"

Geran shook his head and smiled grimly. "No. This isn't a farewell. It's an invitation."

Elaethia shifted awkwardly. "I could not ask you to join me, as this road is mine alone to walk. Not to mention the dangers that loom ahead. I had intended to leave quietly, so as not to drag you all with me, but ..." She looked to the demicat behind her.

"But she got busted," Lilian finished. "I caught ol' Miss Stoic here packing her stuff. She spilled the beans, and I informed her that there would be no way she'd be going anywhere without me. We had a nice, long chat about manners and friendship. Didn't we, Elaethia?"

The woman only grunted sheepishly.

"So!" Lilian continued. "Now that the cat's outta the bag, you guys better go get your stuff ready. The whole guild already knows what's goin' on, and if we stick around too long, they'll try to convince us to let them join."

"Lilian," Elaethia objected. "Please do not pressure them into joining us. I wish for them to choose on their own accord!"

Geran laughed. "You know damn well we'd tag along. Even if you *did* manage to sneak out, we'd be right on your heels. I'm coming, Elaethia. And there's nothing you can say or do to stop me."

The warrior flushed. With pink cheeks, she turned to her third companion.

"Shiro?" she asked the now trembling man.

The samurai looked down. He clenched the hilt of his sheathed sword and dropped to a knee. He made a fist with his right hand and drove it across his body, striking his chest over his heart in salute.

"I am your *sword*, Elaethia-sama," he proclaimed as tears formed in his eyes. "Wherever you go, I *will* follow. I am … hurt … that you would think to leave without me."

Elaethia's lips parted, but no sound came out. Her hands clenched and came up, but she didn't seem to know what to do with them. She closed her mouth and stared at her feet in silent reflection.

Lilian suddenly slapped her on the back. "See? Look what you did! You had them all worked up. Now c'mon! No more standing around being all sappy; we've got things to do! Places to be! Dictators to blast! Less talk, more pack! Let's go!"

The entire guildhall watched as the four of them emerged with their travel gear slung across their backs. Elaethia and Shiro were in their full armor, while Geran and Lilian had donned their travel cloaks, equipment, and harsh-weather gear. They looked just as they did whenever they would head out for a long quest. The only difference this time was that they wore no insignia. This was not a quest for the guild after all.

As they walked to the front door, they were halted by their friends. Liam Barron, Maya Redbranch, Michael Finway, Cathrine Wilhelm, Master Dameon, and even Peter Stone stood by the entryway. They looked up as the departing group approached, sad smiles enveloping their faces.

"So," Master Dameon started. "That's it, eh? You're off to the wild blue yonder, to bring death and destruction to enemies near and far. And you're taking all my star members with you. Don't give me that look, Elaethia; I understand what's going on. You've got a mad adventure ahead of you, and it's only natural that your friends would want to come along. This is a guild. You signed no contract saying when and how you could leave. None of you are grounded here. This is a place of family and friends, action and adventure, glory and sorrow, not some stuck-up government job. Besides, you're my rascals, aren't you? Every single one of you. What kind of parent would I be if I didn't let my kids spread their wings? This dragon is ready to fly, and who am I to stop her?

"That being said, you still have a home here. No matter where you go, how high you climb, how far you fall, or how big you get, you'll *always* have a place here. We're family. Even after you show that emperor the business end of your axe, there's a room and bed for you here. Right with your brothers and sisters."

Elaethia smiled. "Thank you, Master. You have all done so much for me, and I will never forget that. I will be sure to return once my journey is complete."

Dameon laughed. "*That's* my girl. Now, you three! Nightshade, Whitepaw, Inahari! You take care of her, eh? Watch her back out there. She might be able to knock down a mountain, but negotiation and diplomacy are still over her head. Keep her out of trouble for me."

"Yes sir, Master Dameon!" Lilian chirped.

"Easier said than done," Geran chuckled. "But we'll manage."

"Wherever Elaethia-sama goes, I will follow," Shiro stated. "Be it battle or peace."

"Damn right," the old demibear grunted.

"It's gonna be quiet around here," Maya sighed. "I won't be able to send you guys out for a while. But the same thing I say to you before every quest applies. All of you had better come back in one piece."

"She's right, you know," Liam said with a grin, and he grabbed Geran's hand in a hearty shake. "I still owe you a couple drinks. The second you get back here, I'mma pour them all down your throat myself. Don't think I've forgotten that rip you threw about my tail being a leash, either!"

"I'm gonna miss you guys," Michael said. His tail was drooping, but the droop turned into a wag. "But I know you'll be back! I've got some big shoes to fill, but I'll wear 'em! If I'm not an A-level adventurer by the time you get back, you can take me on as many ruck runs as you want, Geran!"

Cathrine smiled. "I still don't know too much about adventurer stuff, but I'll be waiting for you! My restaurant's going to be a lot quieter now, and It'll be sad without you coming to visit, but"—she looked at Michael and shyly took his hand—"I won't be lonely. You'd better stop by the first thing you do when you get back to Breeze!"

Peter crossed his arms and shifted. "Guess it's my turn, huh? Look, I'm not saying I'm *sad* you guys are leaving. It's gonna be pretty nice being the ace again. Don't think we'll be slacking, though! Earth Shatter's gonna be on the rise again, and you'd better be ready for us to take you on when you get back. You've got us as a rival, and there's not a soul alive that can—" He fumbled as Maya jabbed him in the ribs with her elbow. "Ow! Son of a … Gah, anyways, you better not take it easy on anyone out there. Kick ass and take names. We'll be waiting."

Master Dameon stepped up again. "All right, all right, enough with the chitchat. We aren't saying good-bye, and we all know it. Despite this, we're still a guild, and we need to act like one. Now, I've got one final gift for you rascals, and we need to head outside to do it."

The guild master led them outside to the front of the massive guildhall. The sky was clear, the air was fresh, a thin sheet of snow covered the city, and the town was bustling with everyday city life. Merchants called out their wares, guards walked their patrols, citizens milled about their business, and a horse nickered. Actually, the horse was directly in front of them. Attached to the brown animal was a small cart with just enough room for four adventurers and their packs.

Lilian's jaw dropped. "Master, is that … for us?"

"Yep," he said, beaming. "A little gift we all pooled together for you. It'd suck to have to walk or hitchhike all the way to Armini, so we got you your own horse and carriage."

"Yippee!" Lilian leaped into the old man's chest and hugged him fiercely. Before the demibear could react, she had already leaped off and dashed to the wagon. Hurtling her ruck into the bed, she trotted up to the very confused horse and hugged its face while giving it kisses and baby talk.

"Woooah!" Shiro said, joining Lilian. "Our own wagon! Thank you so much, everyone!"

Geran raised an eyebrow. "How much did all that cost?"

"Don't look a gift horse in the mouth, Nightshade," Maya said with a glare.

Elaethia looked to her guildmates. "I do not know what to say. Such kindness is difficult for me to return. How do I repay you?"

"You don't," Maya stated with a smile. "That's what makes it a gift."

Michael grinned. "But if you insist, I'll take a souvenir from Armini. A weapon or piece of armor in their style would be cool."

Cathrine glared at him. "Stop it."

"Then I shall thank you again." Elaethia smiled and walked to put her gear with the others'. "But I will also consider your request."

Geran was about to follow her when Liam suddenly put his arm around his shoulder. "You're gonna have a lot of quality time with Elaethia, buddy. If you two don't make some progress next we see each other, we're gonna have a loooong talk."

Geran grinned and jabbed the demiwolf. "Can it, Barron. I don't wanna hear relationship advice from a horndog like you."

A sudden shove from behind sent Geran stumbling toward the carriage. The ranger turned to see a grinning Peter.

"Quit thinking about us, Nightshade. Just don't keep your lady waiting."

Geran grinned back and flashed a thumbs-up. The gesture was heartily returned by both men.

"Liliaaaaan!" a girly voice called from out of nowhere. A bright-red flash of hair flew past Geran and landed on the demicat next to him.

"You didn't tell me you were leaving!" Suzanna Mist whined, clinging to her fellow mage.

Lilian smiled and hugged her back. "Gosh, Susie, there you are! I was looking all over for you!"

"We just got back when we heard the news; why couldn't you wait?"

Lilian scratched her cheek. "Ah, heh, well, it wasn't really my choice."

Samantha Shoemaker walked up. "You've got a lot of nerve, Whitepaw, thinkin' you could just up and leave on us like that. If everyone wasn't watching, I'd noogie you good!"

Lilian laughed nervously and put her hands on her hair. "I believe you, but please don't. Yours hurt worse than Geran's."

"That's because Geran's a bigger softie than we all give him credit for," Angela Bright said as she appeared. "And even more secretive. So much so that he thought he could leave without us noticing. Did you really think your other friends back here wouldn't have something to say about that?"

"No, but time was of the essence," the ranger said. "We've got a long road ahead, y'know."

"Make sure you come back to tell us all about it, eh?"

"Will do," Geran said, and he extended a hand to the paladin. "Looks like Heaven's Light is gonna be back in everyone's sights again with us gone."

The blond woman took it. "Don't think I'm exactly happy about that, Nightshade." She then turned to Elaethia. "Bring him back in one piece, will ya? And keep his nose where it belongs if you can help it. Oh, Cas, there you are, sweetie. I was just about to find someone to get you."

The black-haired demiwolf shuffled passed her and looked at Lilian and then Shiro. Suddenly the little priestess stepped up to her toes and kissed the samurai on the cheek. She quickly stepped back and buried her reddening face into her floppy sleeves. Silence enveloped the group as all eyes slowly shifted to Lilian. After a tense moment, Cassie peeked over to await the mage's imminent rebuttal.

Lilian looked at her; over to Shiro, who was also blushing; and back to Cassie. Surprisingly, she chuckled.

"Well, well." Lilian shook her head. "You totally got me there, Luca. I would never have guessed you'd muster the courage to do something so bold. I can't even be mad at you. I'll let it slide *just* this once. But you won't get off so easy if you try again. Remember: he's *mine*."

The priestess only nodded sheepishly.

"And *you*," the mage turned to Shiro. "Wipe that dumb look off your face. Don't make me scold you, too."

"Y-yes, Lilian ..." he fumbled.

Dameon chuckled. "All right, rascals, get out of here before anyone else starts trouble. Nightshade, I expect a full report on Armini from you when you get back. I wanna know everything you can tell me about them."

"Will do, sir," he promised as he stepped into the driver's seat next to Elaethia.

The ranger took the reins and led the horse down the frosty cobblestone road toward the city gate. They turned around to wave one more time to everyone. All of them faltered. Instead of the group that sent them off, the entire guild had made its way outside. With Master Dameon at the lead, all one-hundred-plus adventurers stood in front of the enormous guildhall with weapons in hand. Master Dameon raised his arm and gave the order.

"Bang 'em!"

As he commanded, the sound of wood and steel beating against stone filled the air. The steady beat of weapons striking the road grew louder and louder until the city grew quiet. Citizens, guards, and officials alike stopped what they were doing to watch the guild sound its war cry.

"Cataclysm!" Master Dameon roared over the deafening beat. "Live up to your name and shake the ground you tread on! Give 'em hell!"

"Ah-*ooh!*"

"Give 'em hell!"

"Ah-*ooh!*"

"Give 'em hell!"

"Ah-*ooh!*"

They rode out of the main city and down the snowy dirt road that webbed throughout the region. Cataclysm was instilled with a sense of purpose and overwhelming pride that they had never felt before. Shiro was even moved to tears by the raw comradery and motivation. The samurai tried valiantly to control his expression, but his trembling lips and leaking eyes gave it away.

"Ahhh, that was *great!*" Lilian said as she stretched. "I haven't felt this good since the tournament! What do you think, Elaethia? Was that one helluva sendoff or what?"

"It certainly filled me with more determination and purpose, yes. I would not use that exact verbiage, but I will agree."

Geran smiled. "That's actually the first time I've ever been on the receiving end of the war cry. I might get used to that."

"Whaaaaat?" Lilian taunted. "Is that *our* Geran enjoying the *spotlight?*"

"Got a problem sharing, cat?"

The demicat flicked her hair dramatically. "Pfft, you wish! You're still bottom-tier compared to me! The greatest success you'll ever accomplish will be *my* lowest. You just can't achieve the fabulous grandeur that I have."

"Uh-huh. Whatever."

"Elaethia-sama," Shiro began. "Was your study with Arthur enlightening? Were either of you able to learn anything?"

"It is strange," she said. "Many of the spells I knew are apparently able to be used by specialized frost magicians. The only ones I have that he could not replicate were my *frost breath* and *unyielding ice*, both of which I know are unique to frost dragons, so it would seem an enchanter could not replicate a dragon's magic."

Geran rubbed his chin. "Interesting … By the way, why am *I* driving? You're the one leading this mess, Elaethia."

She smiled. "I do not believe this is a mess yet, but you are correct. I do know where we should go."

Elaethia took the reins and turned north at the next intersection.

Lilian poked her head up front. "Um, Elaethia, you got your directions mixed up? Armini is the *other* way."

"I am well aware," she said with a nod. "But something Master Dameon said reminded me of a promise I made over a year ago. There is another family that has told me I will always have a home with them. I should pay them homage."

Chapter 21
Pilgrimage

Sixth Era.140. Febris 27.

Jörgen stood over the chopping block with a stack of firewood in the snow outside the village longhouse. The elder had fallen ill over the winter, and finally succumbed to the sickness last month. As he had predicted, the coastal village unanimously elected Jörgen to be the next elder. He and Ingrid moved into the longhouse, leaving behind their cabin on the other end of the village. It would remain empty until a new family was ready to move in.

The old raider grunted as he hefted the simple axe above his head. His age had definitely caught up with him. Whether it was because the winter had seeped into his joints or the position of village elder had some supernatural effect on him, Jörgen couldn't find the strength of his youth anymore. He sighed as he regaled over his glory days: his long, blond hair, his berserker armor, his axe that stood even taller than him … He had earned the title of "Sea Bear" back then. He had been the pride and terror of his clan. But those days were over.

The sound of a horse and wagon crunching through the snow from behind his longhouse brought him back to reality. That was odd. Wagons rarely came this far north. It was also too cold, and the snow was too deep, for merchants from Linderry to try to come barter. Easter Svarnengels wouldn't come over to the west for any reason either. And other western clans rarely used wagons to get from place to place. They lived by the sea, after all. Usually Jörgen would ignore those who passed through the village. But as the elder, he felt some obligation to see who they were.

He rounded the corner and saw four foreigners jump out of a small cart pulled by a single brown horse. Two of them were obviously adventurers; the third had odd armor and features he had never seen before. The fourth was on the other side of the horse, but Jörgen could tell he was in heavy armor. One of the Linderrians, a demicat, bared her small fangs in a wide yawn. She met his gaze and flashed him a grin that was equally mischievous and cheerful.

"Hiya!" she chirped. "You're the, uh, village elder, right?"

"Aye." He crossed his arms. What did this flaky young lass want with him?

"Hey, quit being rude," the other Linderrian scolded. This one was human—a man in his midtwenties, wearing a hood and cloak. Experience told Jörgen that there were many layers to this man, but somehow the old raider knew he could be trusted.

"Lilian meant no harm!" the other odd man insisted. His dark hair and slanted eyes were really throwing the Svarengel man for a loop.

Jörgen shook his head. "I don't know what ye want, but yes, I'm th' village elder. This is my village. If ye have business, out with it. Otherwise, keep movin'. My wife may love visitors, but I'm not so keen on strangers." The old raider remembered his position again and sighed. "Let me introduce myself. I'm elder Ste—"

"Sterkhand," the fourth man said. Although shockingly, it was a female voice. The woman rounded the cart. Her armor was instantly recognizable. Jörgen's axe fell out of his grip and thudded to the snow as he met her dazzling blue-marked reptilian eyes.

Elaethia smiled. "Hello, Jörgen."

The scene had turned nearly hectic inside the elder's longhouse. Ingrid, Jörgen, and several other villagers fawned over Cataclysm with no regard for personal space. Geran happily found himself alone in a corner by the fire after a few minutes, while the other three were promptly placed in the center of attention. Shiro was surrounded almost instantly by the large northern people, and he was rather intimidated. Luckily Lilian was able to pull the attention away from him and place it firmly on herself. Try as she might, however, she couldn't be the center of attention for long. That honor fell to Elaethia.

"Oh, my heavens!" Ingrid cooed as she touched the dragon hero's face and body, her canine tail wagging the entire time. "Let me look at ye. How have ye been? What have ye been doin'? It seems ye've been getting plenty to eat; what are these clothes yer wearin'? They very much highlight yer figure! Ye aren't tryin' to allure a suitor, are ye?"

"I am well, Ingrid." She smiled. "I joined a guild, just as Jörgen suggested, and met my good friends there. We were on our way to Armini when we decided to come and visit. I had promised to return after all. But no, I do not wear these clothes to attract suitors. Lilian helped me pick them out."

"So ye haven't found a man worthy of ye yet? Such a shame. A whole country of men down there, and none of 'em can hold a candle to ye."

Elaethia blushed and subconsciously glanced over at the ranger in the corner. "I never said anything such as that …"

Ingrid followed her gaze. "You! Young man with the hood! Come here!"

"Uh-oh," Geran mumbled as he stood up and walked over.

"Yes, yes, come here; come!" the old demiwolf commanded, feeling his face and body as she had done with Elaethia. "Hmm. Firm jawline, soft eyes, neatly trimmed hair and beard, well fed but not fat. Ooh! Plenty of muscle, surprisingly."

"Uh … thanks?"

"One final check!"

As she announced this, Ingrid reached around and firmly grasped Geran's posterior with unbridled invasiveness. The ranger jumped with a yelp and shuffled away. The entire longhouse erupted with laughter.

"Hmph." The old woman nodded. "Nowhere *near* as meaty as my Jörgen was back when he was yer age, but that's settin' the bar too high. Now, what did ye say yer name was?"

"Geran. Geran Nightshade," he said as he freed his trousers from between his buttocks.

"So ye've caught Elaethia's fancy, have ye? What do ye have to offer her besides nice features and a strong body? I know I taught her how to choose a man quite well."

His face turned pink. "What kinda question is that?"

"Aye!" Jörgen agreed. "A man's heart's not tested by his words! His actions hold his true intentions. We have a tradition here, lad. If ye want the honor of courtin' my girl, yer gonna have to show me yer worthy of her!"

"Wait, what?"

Elaethia stood. "Jörgen, that is unnecessary. Geran has been by my side for over a year and never led me wrong. I trust no other man better than him!"

"Well, I suppose I can believe ye, girl. But tradition is tradition. As the elder, it's my responsibility to see it through. How about it, Geran? Do ye think yer worthy of Elaethia? Would ye raise a blade for her honor, a mug for her name, and die for her soul?"

"Odd question, but yeah, absolutely!" Geran stated firmly.

Elaethia intended to protest again but found her heart began to flutter instead.

Jörgen grinned. "Then ye'll be followin' me outside."

"What the hell is this?" Geran's voice was incredulous and quavering as vapor flowed from his mouth. He stood shirtless and barefoot in the snow as he faced an equally naked Jörgen. The old raider laughed and flexed his muscles as steam rose off his large body. Even though he was in his sixties, Jörgen was seriously built. Easily twice the size of the toned Linderrian ranger. As the two got into positions, the village formed a circle around them, jeering and roaring in anticipation.

"Yer lookin' awful nervous, Geran. Ye aren't turnin' yer tail and runnin,' are ye?" Jörgen taunted.

"Fat chance, I just wanna know what's going on!"

"Didn't I tell ye, southerner? We have a tradition here! If ye want to win our approval for courtin' Elaethia, ye have to prove it with yer actions! It'll take too long to see yer personality, and ye can lie all ye want. The best way to see a man's heart is through combat!"

"So what, I have to fight you?"

Jörgen roared with laughter. "Now yer gettin' it! If ye want to take Elaethia's hand in marriage, yer gonna have to take mine in grapplin'!"

"Hey, wait a minute. I never said anything about marria—" Geran couldn't finish his sentence as Jörgen bore down on him. The nimble ranger dived out of the way as the huge raider barreled past him. The onlookers booed and groaned, disappointed at the outcome of the first move.

"What's the matter, boy?" Jörgen challenged. "Are ye *that* afraid of me? Stay on yer feet, and embrace me like a man!"

Geran gritted his teeth. What kind of rules were these? In fact, there were no rules—no guidelines, no goals, no restrictions; just take your shirt off and go. What kind of unorganized, backwards people were the Svarengel? Jörgen circled around Geran and eyed the ranger's footwork and posture. This meathead yak herder was sizing him up! Geran took the time to study his posture. It was clear that Jörgen knew what he was doing. Geran knew that if this was a tradition and he was the village elder, Jörgen would be more than formidable.

Geran was not a wrestler, nor did he like long fights. His grapples were all based on pressure points, throws, and holds. Even though he was still in his prime, he couldn't outmuscle the Svarengel raider. They wanted to drag him into their world and put him in their game? Fine. If that was the case, Geran was going to play by his own rules.

Jörgen charged.

Instead of diving to the side, Geran hunkered down in a defensive stance. Geran faced his shoulder toward the raider and held his arms out in preparation. Jörgen took the bait. The old raider went to grab Geran's hand, but instead of locking in as he was used to, the ranger flicked his wrist and grabbed the large man's forearm. Geran pivoted his waist, stepped into his opponent, planted his legs between Jörgen's, pulled the old man's arm, and threw him over his shoulder.

Jörgen hit the ground with an earth-shaking thud. The villagers roared in approval, finally able to see some action. Geran felt a moment of triumph and confidence and moved to pin the old man's arm. Jörgen didn't budge. The raider looked over his shoulder and grinned in satisfaction as he grabbed Geran's leg with his free hand and rolled. The ranger found himself flung like a rag doll and pinned to the cold ground by the heavy man.

Geran twisted and wriggled his body to try to free himself. He managed to kick Jörgen's feet out from under him and wheel around to wrap his arms around Jörgen's neck. The old man saw it coming. He caught the ranger's arm, twisted it behind his back with sheer force alone, and kicked him to his knees. Before Geran could try to retaliate, he found the weight of the world slam on top of him, and a thick, muscled arm wrapped around his neck.

"I'll give ye a lifeline here, lad," Jörgen grinned. "If yer lookin' to make this end quicker, all ye need to do is tap me with yer free hand. I'll let ye go, and ye'll admit defeat."

Geran couldn't respond. He was losing his ability to breathe as the old raider slowly constricted his blood flow. He growled in frustration and fought with all he had to free himself from the overwhelming strength of the raider. But it was no use. Jörgen couldn't be budged. The thick man had the ranger exactly where he wanted him, and there was no way Geran could force his way out. The roars and cheers from the crowd grew louder as they could see the fight nearing its end. A single familiar voice stood out to him especially. Shiro had his hands cupped around his mouth, shouting encouragement to Geran. The samurai bounced on his toes, anxious to see how Geran would find a way to win. The ranger felt a small burst of determination, until he looked over to Lilian.

She was laughing. That little shit was laughing! The demicat was doubled over in howling jubilation while she pointed at him. Tears formed in her eyes and flowed down her reddening cheeks. Geran swore that if he survived this, he'd put that stupid hairball in the exact same position he was in. Then his eyes met Elaethia's. At first they looked concerned, until he got a closer look. Her fists clenched and laxed, her jaw tightened and opened. She was rooting for him, although she didn't know how.

"Well, boy?" Jörgen taunted. "Yer not gettin' out of this. Ye'd better tap out before I squeeze yer head off! All ye need to do is admit to me that yer unworthy of Elaethia, and I'll let ye go."

Geran glanced once more at Elaethia. The look in her eyes was everything he needed.

"You're gonna have to kill me first," he wheezed.

"We'll see about that!" Jörgen flexed his arm harder and choked Geran again. The village elder crushed the ranger's neck so hard that dots formed in his vision. His head felt as though it were about to explode. Color began to drain from his face as the world around him turned dark and flipped. The hold Jörgen had him in could kill him within a few seconds. Geran still refused to tap. As the light faded from his vision and he felt his body turn limp, Jörgen suddenly let go.

Geran fell to the slushy dirt, gasping for breath and struggling to hold himself up. Elaethia appeared next to him in the blink of an eye. She wrapped her arms under his own, rolling the panting ranger on his back. The ground was freezing, but the woman that held him was warm enough that he could ignore it. Elaethia knelt while sitting on her heels and rested his head on her lap. His sight began to return to him, and he could make out the details of her concerned face: her deep blue eyes, her pale cheeks, her full lips. By the heavens, she was gorgeous.

"Are you all right?" she asked.

He smiled weakly. "Never better."

She smiled back. "You are a stubborn man, Geran."

"I don't wanna hear that from you." He coughed once and groaned. "Guess I lost, huh?"

Jörgen knelt next to him and rested a meaty fist on Geran's heaving chest. "Depends how yer lookin' at it. If ye mean the grapple, yes. Ye fell like a fawn to a wolf. But if yer askin' if ye got yer message across, then ye won. That's the kind of resolve and dedication I was lookin' for.

"Hooray …" he cheered faintly.

"Now put yer shirt on. We're havin' a feast tonight, and ye need to be there!"

"Can I take a bath first?"

"Th' hot springs are a good walk from here. Ye can do that tonight!" Jörgen stood and walked away to meet with the other villagers. They cheered and howled at their elder's approach, while Geran groaned and dropped his head back onto Elaethia's thighs.

"How are you feeling?" Elaethia asked.

"Like my head's about to pop," he wheezed.

She smiled and touched his cheeks. "I believe you. Your face is quite red."

"Don't stare at it too much, all right? I look like hell."

"Indeed, but it was for my sake, was it not?"

"Yeah," he smiled. "Yeah, it was."

"I am truly happy to know this. Would it make you feel equally pleased to know I would have done the same for you?"

He chuckled. "You would have tied him into a knot, but yeah. It does."

He met her gaze, and they looked into each other's eyes for a moment.

Elaethia's face turned red as well. "I … I am glad. Are you feeling better? Can you stand?"

Geran closed his eyes. "Just a little longer," he pleaded, and he nestled his head further into her lap.

The Svarengel feast, like any other party Geran had been to, was far too loud and boisterous for him. The clan's antics were on a level that would even contend with those of drunken adventurers. He guessed it didn't matter where in the world he was. Parties were parties. The ranger was able to excuse himself after a while and retreat to the hot springs to take a much-needed bath. Geran grabbed a fur towel and began the kilometer-long walk uphill through the frozen woods to where the baths were supposed to be.

They were easy to find. Bubbling and flowing, the hot springs gave off so much steam in the frigid air that he couldn't see the other side of the four-meter-wide pool. He sighed heavily, set the towel on the edge, and waded into the spring. The ranger groaned as the hot water flowed over his aching body. *Stars above, this is heavenly.* Geran found himself so relaxed by the soothing bubbles and steam that he began to drift off to sleep.

It could have been thirty seconds or thirty minutes before Geran woke to the sound of rustling fabric. He slowly lifted his head as he heard someone else get into the baths with him. He guessed it was probably one of the other men from the village, as they had told him this particular side was for the men. He was about to put his head down again when he began to make out a familiar shape through the mist. A sudden breeze blew by and cleared most of the steam. His cheeks flushed intensely as he realized who it was.

"E-Elaethia! Woah, woah, woah, I'm in here; I'm in here!"

"Geran!" The woman froze and lifted a hand to secure the towel wrapped around her body. "Wh-what are you doing here?"

"Taking a bath! I said I was coming up here! What about you? This is the men's side; didn't they tell you down below?"

"Th-they never said such a thing!"

His mouth fell open. "Wai-what?"

"They said that if I followed this path, I would come upon a hot spring suitable for bathing! They said nothing of a men or women's side."

"So … they lied to one of us?"

She shuffled awkwardly. "It … it would seem so."

The two stayed there in uncomfortable silence for nearly a minute.

Geran cleared his throat. "W-well, I'm almost clean. I can leave and let you have the bath."

"No, no it is fine." She looked down and pivoted a leg. Geran couldn't see her expression through the thin fog. "I do not mind waiting. You do not have to leave because of my presence. I should have called to see if there was anyone here. I … I am sorry for disturbing you."

"No, no it's okay." Geran's heart started to catch in his throat. Elaethia was acting surprisingly feminine. "It's my fault; I shoulda said something as you walked up. I'll hurry up; I don't want you to wait around like that."

"I … do not mind," she mumbled shyly. "I can simply sit while I wait."

As she said this, Elaethia removed her towel and walked to the edge of the pool to lower herself into it. Geran couldn't make out too much of her, but her figure was still very prominent. He swallowed hard and exhaled slowly as he shook his head.

"So uh … how about that party?" he asked.

She looked over. "The feast? It was rather loud for me. I was not very comfortable and allowed myself to retreat here."

"It's odd they let *you*, of all people, leave. It was meant to be for you either way. Sorry that it turned out so awkward here, too."

She pulled out a brush from a leather pouch and began to run it through her black hair. "That is all right. The calm and warmth of the spring are far more favorable than the loud and rambunctious longhouse. I thought only the guild was capable of such noise."

"Out of the frying pan and into the flames, huh?"

She looked up. "I understand that phrase. It means to escape one predicament and find yourself in another that is similar, correct?"

Geran smiled. "That's it all right."

Elaethia laughed, which made Geran's heart skip a beat. "How curious. Phrases like that used to confuse me so much, but I am slowly coming to understand them. Perhaps being around so many people has helped me learn so quickly."

"I'd say so too. If you find yourself around the right crowd, you learn a lot more than you realize."

Elaethia nodded. "Indeed. But whomever I am around, I must say I am glad you are with me, Geran."

"I'm happy to be around you, too, but what brought that up?"

She pushed a curl of hair behind her ear. "It is strange. Odd emotions have been increasing more and more from spending so much time together. It seems that whenever you are near, my heart feels at ease. Yet at the same time, it beats in excitement. I do not understand what this means, but I know it is a good feeling. A sense of belonging I have never felt before. But when you are gone, my heart feels almost as if it is in pain."

Geran stood and waded to the other side. She moved so he could sit next to her. Geran could see her more clearly now: the water glistening over her pale, smooth skin; her breasts halfway submerged in the bubbling water; the steam rising around her warm face as drops fell from her glistening hair and back to the pool below. She was absolutely stunning, and he surprised himself with how easily he could respond.

"A sense of fulfillment whenever they're nearby, and a sense that something is missing when they're away," he said.

"Yes, you understand?"

"Almost like an aching feeling in your chest that can only be cured by their touch, or them just being close. It doesn't matter where you are or what you're doing, so long as they can be with you."

She looked at him with bright eyes. "You know these feelings, too?"

He smiled and looked to the stars above. "Yeah. The chest kind of closes in on itself and does loops. The mouth just smiles automatically. The hands don't seem to know what to do with themselves. I feel almost uncomfortable around you, but"—Geran laughed a little and looked at her—"there's nowhere else I'd rather be."

She met his gaze, her eyes full of wonder, her hands slowly clenching on her lap. His body began to act on its own as he brought his face closer to hers. His heart leaped in his chest as she brought hers to meet his. As their lips touched, he felt a wave of closure and longing flow off his shoulders like a fog clearing from a hill. For the first time in his life, there was true fulfillment in his heart as he cupped his hand to her cheek. Elaethia placed a soft hand on his chest as she deepened their kiss while the steam rose to embrace them both.

Jörgen, Ingrid, and all of Cataclysm sat in the elder's longhouse the next morning. Lilian and Shiro dug heartily into their breakfast, while Geran and Elaethia ate more slowly. The two of them sat close to each other but also seemed to keep their distance. Ingrid raised an eyebrow, and when she met Elaethia's gaze, the woman shot her eyes back to her food. The old woman smiled and laughed into her bowl of stew.

"So!" Jörgen burped. "What's yer plans goin' forward? I can't imagine yer here for very long. Ye mentioned ye were only here to visit, after all."

"Indeed," Elaethia said. "I wished to see you again before I traveled to my homeland. I promised to return, and it is possible I will not survive this journey."

Lilian looked up from her plate. "Hey, c'mon! Don't be talking like that! We're gonna kick that guy's ass! Rychus won't know what hit him!"

"I wish to share your optimism, Lilian, but I cannot overlook the possibility. His true strength is unknown, as is the source of his power."

Shiro grunted. "You're not only strong, Elaethia-sama, but you have determination! Your spirit alone can overcome anything he may have!"

"Your mother and father will guide you, too," Geran said, joining in. "They say the heavens send the souls of your loved ones to aid you in battle when you fight for them."

"That dragon as well," Ingrid said. "Ye only got this far because of him. I'm sure he'll be there to guide ye along."

Elaethia looked down. "Indeed."

Jörgen looked at her. "His home was nearby, wasn't it?"

"A day's walk north of here," she recalled solemnly. "Although it would likely take longer to walk up there than down."

"It's good ye came up here to say hello to us. But don't ye think ye ought to pay homage to him too? It's only respectful."

"Jörgen!" Ingrid scolded. "Have some tact, will ye? She's obviously still upset about the incident!"

"As were we with our fathers, and with Erika. It's our tradition to honor th' dead, not mourn them. She's come all this way; it would hurt her more in th' long run if she doesn't!"

"And how can ye decide that for her? She spent a year in a tradition different from ours! She's a free woman and can choose what she wants! Not to mention she's not a member of this village! Elaethia doesn't have to—"

"He is right," Elaethia suddenly said. "I should go see him."

Geran put a hand on her shoulder. "Woah. Hey now, Elaethia. Don't force yourself to do this because you want to make Jörgen happy, all right? If it's too much, it's too much. I was the same way when Adrian died."

She looked at him. "But you visit his grave, do you not?"

Geran closed his mouth.

"Do you remember where his cave is, Elaethia?" Lilian asked.

"I do." She nodded. "What do you think, Shiro? Honor and family are both very prominent in your culture."

Shiro thought for a moment. "When my grandfather died, I was distraught. My father was always gone because of his position, so Grandfather raised me. He taught me the way of the blade, the samurai code, and how to be a man for my family. For a time after his death, I wanted to distance myself. The memories were too sad. But I realized I must honor him in death, as he honored me in life. This year was the first that I did not visit the shrine to pay my respects to him. If Grandfather Ryuuki were up in that cave, I would go to him."

Elaethia stood. "Then it is decided. We will go pay homage to Frossgar."

Cataclysm began the ascent up the snowy mountain the next afternoon. Thankfully, the wind was nonexistent. The snow was knee-deep and very soft. The four adventurers trudged up the incline, following the path Elaethia somehow remembered after all these years. They and Jörgen took the wagon as far as they could go, leaving it and him at the base.

Elaethia was quiet the entire way. She could not find the will to speak as they marched up the northern mountain. She turned to look behind at her companions, who kept up with her surprisingly well. Lilian was obviously tired, but she had grown either courteous or mature enough to not complain. Shiro and Geran fared better, but not as well as Elaethia.

The walk brought back memories of the first time she ascended the mountain with her grandfather. Celus was little more than a face in her imagination, but she sent a silent prayer to the heavens to thank him for all he had done. Another wave of sadness washed over her as she remembered he did not survive the ascent.

Finally she saw the iconic landmarks that entailed Frossgar's territory. Rock formations, divots in the terrain, groups of trees, and, finally, the constructs of unyielding ice. Her party marveled at the many icy creations that surrounded the mouth of the cave. All of them were bigger than anything they had seen Elaethia make. Elaethia looked around to take in everything she saw. The memories of the eleven years she spent here hit her like a battering ram. Tears flowed down her cheeks as a choked sob began to form in her throat. Words that Frossgar had instilled in her began to creep back into her head in whispers as she stood shuddering in front of the entrance.

"Elaethia," Geran's gentle voice said to her right. "Can you do this?"

Through her blurred vision, she saw his expression of worry and compassion. Before she could answer, she felt his hand slide into hers and interlock their fingers. She shakily held his grasp and squeezed it with gratitude. Shiro came to her left and cupped his fingers around her hand. Lilian walked up behind and rested her hands on Elaethia's trembling shoulders.

Geran spoke again. "We're all with you. You're not alone. Not anymore. Not ever. Let's go say hello to him together."

Elaethia could only nod shakily as she took the first step forward, and they descended into the darkness.

The area within held everything that Elaethia dreaded to see—the very sight that had plagued her nightmares and haunted her waking thoughts. The cave was exactly as she had left it. Animal bones lay on the ground next to the empty firepit she had used to cook her meals. The old pile of degraded weapons and armor in the corner sat untouched. The bedroll near the wall where she had slept was open, with the old furs still on top of it. In the center of it all were the hollow remains of Frossgar.

Elaethia collapsed to her knees. She wept without restraint, burying her face into her hands. Geran, Shiro, and Lilian halted their admiration of the enormous skeleton in front of them and wrapped their arms around their friend. Mournful sobs enveloped the cave, interrupted only by shaking gasps of breath. Tears formed in Geran's and Shiro's eyes as Lilian joined her friend in weeping. After some time, Elaethia finally looked up to her old mentor and friend. She reached out to place a hand on the dragon's bony nose as a gentle wind whispered throughout the room.

"I have returned, Frossgar."

"Indeed you have," said a deep voice that resonated through the cave. "Welcome home, little one."

Chapter 22
Frossgar

Sixth Era.140. Mertim 2.

The four of them froze. Lilian and Shiro darted their eyes around the room, while Geran looked directly at the skeleton in front of them. Elaethia remained motionless in her state of shock.

"Hey," Geran said. "I'm not crazy, right? You guys heard that too, didn't you?"

Shiro nodded fervently. "A voice! I heard a man's voice, but it wasn't brehdar! So deep and powerful that I could feel it in my bones!"

Lilian whipped her head around. "Someone's here! Where did that come from? That wasn't one of you guys, was it? Who's there? Come out!"

Elaethia's eyes were far away. "Frossgar …"

"That was him?" Geran asked. "That was his voice?"

Shiro trembled. "The voice of a dragon. In all my life, I never thought I'd hear such a thing!"

Lilian put her hands on Elaethia's shoulders and shook her. "But how? I thought he died! No, wait, he *did!* That's definitely him right there, isn't it? How is he talking to us?"

The voice spoke again. "If you would be silent for a moment, I would explain. Elaethia, I am beyond pleased that you have returned. But must you have brought company?"

"Frossgar …" she whispered again.

"Yes, little one, it is I. Your expression troubles me. Were you gone so long that my lessons disappeared from your mind? Did I not teach you that it is improper to mumble in the presence of your elders?"

She suddenly shot to her feet. "Y-yes, Frossgar. I apologize. Forgive me, I … I did not expect you to be here. I could not …"

"Did not expect to see me? Have you lived this time believing I was dead?"

She nodded through her tears. "Yes. I did. I thought I had lost you, too. The memory of you and my father pushed me through times of struggle and hardship. I never swayed from your teachings or forgot who I was."

"Hmm … Perhaps I have regarded you too harshly. Very well then, I am sorry for scolding you so. Now on to the matter at hand. You returned here very quickly. I must say I expected you to be gone longer."

"It has been three years, Frossgar."

"Has it? Then it was even less time than I thought."

"Three years is a long time."

"Ah yes. I forget that brehdars perceive time differently than a dragon. I wonder about the places you have been and things you have done. Have you advanced yourself in this time?"

"I have," she said. "I forged armor and weapon from your bones, honed my skill as a warrior, learned what I could of your magic, and even made friends."

"Friends?" the dragon's voice asked. "You were always fond of this term. Try as I might, I could never understand the desire for consistent company."

"They are admirable people with hearts and goals of their own. You will undoubtedly come to enjoy their presence as I have."

"That remains to be seen. Nevertheless, you are the one who will lead our life. Tell me more of your endeavors. I am curious about the current state of the outside wo—"

"Aaaaauuugghhh, enough already!" Lilian wailed. She grabbed her hair with both hands. "I can't take you two going back and forth like the rest of us aren't even here! What's going on? Where are you? I'm so confused!"

The cave went silent as her voice echoed throughout it.

"I take it she is one of your ... friends ...?" the dragon asked.

Elaethia smiled and wiped her eyes. "Indeed. The liveliest person I know."

"This will be more difficult than I thought."

"Oh, she's not *that* bad," Geran said. "Sure she's an annoying, whiny, self-absorbed brat. But she grows on you."

"She does not seem pleasant," Frossgar said curiously. "If your words are true, I do not see how I will come to grow fond of her."

Lilian stuck her tongue out. "Hmph. You say that now, Mr. Cold Bones. Just you wait!"

Shiro stepped forward. "U-um. Are you Mr. Frossgar?"

"I am," he stated warily.

The samurai suddenly plunged to the floor and prostrated himself in front of the giant skeleton. "My name is Shiro Inahari! I understand that you are Elaethia-sama's master! She has been gracious enough to allow me to travel with her and fight at her side! I am beyond honored and humbled by your presence!"

"Interesting," Frossgar stated. "I have never seen such a reaction from a brehdar. However, it seems there is one among you that is capable of civility."

Geran folded his arms. "I was being civil."

Lilian cut back in. "Wait a minute! Why are we all taking this so normally? What the *hell* is going on here? Where's Frossgar? Why can't any of us see him?"

Geran rubbed his eyes. "We've seen all sorts of crazy stuff so far. I think I'm just getting desensitized."

"Your reaction is rather eccentric, Lilian," Elaethia said with a smile. "But perhaps he is as perplexed as we are."

"Indeed this phenomenon is most curious," the dragon said. "I, too, thought that I had died. But my consciousness soon returned to me, and I was alone in the cave. Once I awoke, you were gone. Everything was encased in ice, and I was looking at my own corpse. I knew not how much time had passed since I jettisoned my mind from the conjoinment. But I knew we had failed. Given that my soul, magic, and strength had disappeared, I realized you had taken them and set forth."

"Why didn't your mind join her?" Geran asked.

"She could not bear it. Physically, she was a perfect host, as I had raised her to be. Her mind, however, was too shallow to comprehend mine. Instead of forcing it into her, I broke it off, expecting to die from the action. It appears I managed to live."

"Okay, but *how?*" Lilian pleaded. "How is your mind still here? Shouldn't it have passed on to the heavens?"

"That is what I believed as well, but it seems that is not how life works. The mind and soul are connected but are not one. Soulless creatures, such as beasts and monsters, prove this. Sentient beings like ourselves do not simply die. Our minds return to the heavens and are reborn to the earth, or kept to live forever among the stars. But in order for this to happen, our souls must leave the earth. Since mine went into Elaethia, my mind could not pass on. The mind and soul are connected, as I said, but they could not exist together within you. Instead my mind returned to the closest thing it could. And that was my body.

"But since my body was destroyed, and could not house a mind, my consciousness simply existed in the space of my demise. With no soul or body to use as a vessel, I could only stay here and wait for you to return or die. Once my soul departed from your body and into the heavens, my mind would most likely have followed. However, since you are here, I believe we may continue from where we left off."

Elaethia's eyes shone. "Truly? You can enter my mind, Frossgar?"

"I can. My soul calls to me, and it is only right that we stand united as dragon and hero."

"But is my mind ready?"

"You have traveled the land, learned many things, and broadened your horizon. There should be little hindrance in this."

"Then I am ready. I have always been ready."

"As am I. Come. Open your mind to me, little one, and let us finish what we started three years ago."

Lilian rubbed her hands together. "Ohoho. This'll be *good*."

Elaethia closed her eyes, inhaled, and relaxed. Her companions watched as she tensed in anticipation. The dragon hero suddenly twitched, and her eyes shot open. They glowed blue so brightly they illuminated the cave in front of her. Then they dimmed to her normal color and she inhaled sharply.

Geran rushed forward. "What ... What happened? Are you okay?"

"We are fine, yes," she assured him. "He has entered my mind."

Lilian's ear twitched. "That's it? That was lame."

Shiro nodded glumly. "I was expecting something more ... dramatic."

Geran waved them off. "How do you feel? What's different?"

I do not know." Elaethia paused.

Suddenly Frossgar's voice sounded in her mind. *Nothing much is different. I expected us to become one, but I do not share your thoughts or memories, Elaethia.*

What do you mean? she called to him with her thoughts. She was given no response. *Frossgar?*

Geran looked at her. "What's with that face, Elaethia?"

"He has gone silent. I heard him again, but he has not responded."

Because you have said nothing, little one.

"Wait, there he is. What did I do differently?"

Shiro's face began to twist as his eyebrows furrowed. "Elaethia-sama, what's going on? We don't understand."

Can you hear me, little one?

I can hear you, Frossgar, can you hear me? Again Elaethia heard nothing.

"This is most strange," she said aloud.

Indeed it is.

"You hear me?"

I can now. If you are trying to reach me with your thoughts, I cannot hear them. Only when you speak aloud can I understand what you are trying to say.

Lilian cocked her ears. "Elaethia, who are you talking to?"

"Frossgar," she replied. "He speaks through my thoughts but can hear me only if I talk. Do you not hear him anymore?"

"No we don't," Geran said. "Is it wrong that you can't talk to him in your head?"

It certainly is not right.

Elaethia shook her head. "I do not understand."

"I am so confused," Shiro murmured, and he ran his hands through his hair.

Geran slapped himself in the cheeks. "Okay, so if we're done here, can we go? I really don't want to sound rude, but there's no point in hanging around here, right? I know I said I was desensitized, but this is actually about to give me an aneurysm. We came here to honor Frossgar, but he's alive, and now inside Elaethia's mind; but somehow *that* messed up too, and that's about all I can process for the day. Let's just give this a bit of time to sink in and we can come back to it, okay?"

Your bearded companion is prudent; I will give him that.

"Frossgar agrees," Elaethia translated.

"Is it okay, though?" Shiro asked. "Isn't this hallowed ground?"

Hallowed ground? Why would it be?

"Frossgar was not a deity, Shiro," Elaethia said.

"But he was a dragon, wasn't he? This is his final resting place! It's sacred!"

He speaks as though I am dead. What a curious human. Is he not of this land?

"No, he is from a country across the sea, called Osakyota."

It does not surprise me that there is land across the ocean. It also does not surprise me that brehdars live and thrive there. They are uniquely capable of cultivating nearly anywhere.

"Shiro is a wonderful companion, but you two will not understand each other for a while." She said then turned to Shiro. "Shiro, Frossgar wished for a simple life away from tradition and civilization. He has no desire to be honored."

"W-well, if he insists," the samurai acknowledged.

Tell him that I do. I also am glad that you made good use of my scales. It would be wise to take more, should you desire to improve your equipment or create more.

"I will." She nodded and again addressed her friends. "Frossgar also wishes to depart but suggests we take more scale and bone for my armor and blade. Will you help me?"

Her companions agreed. Cataclysm scoured the dragon's body for usable scales and bone to be repurposed. Geran and Elaethia took the most preferable materials, while Shiro gingerly picked pristine scales and bones. The samurai's hands shook as he pulled off pieces of the dragon's corpse, muttering apologies under his breath every time he wrestled one loose. Lilian, however, climbed on the back of the skeleton and thoroughly inspected the large, black spines that protruded into the air.

Are you fond of your companions, little one?

"I am," she stated instantly.

"What?" Geran asked, turning to her. Elaethia tapped her head with a finger. The ranger nodded in understanding.

There is more here than you could use yourself. I do not see into your thoughts or memories as I should, but something tells me that these three brehdars hold a special place in your heart. Do you wish to protect them?

"We protect each other, Frossgar. They stand as equals to me."

I see. Then I will make a suggestion. I would feel better for my body to be used instead of left to decay. They may not have the strength to wear dragonite armor or wield dragonite weaponry, but perhaps they can make use of what is left. I will allow them to indulge if you believe they would like to.

"I understand," she said with a smile. "Everyone, Frossgar has something for you all. You may take some scales and bone for yourselves as you see fit."

Shiro's jaw dropped. "Wait, really? This whole time I've been thinking that I couldn't sharpen Seraph because it goes right through the grindstone. But if I can make a whetstone from dragonite, I could keep the blade keen!"

"I was thinking, too," Geran muttered, rubbing his chin. "I couldn't make padded armor out of this stuff since it's so heavy, but I *can* take one or two to cover my heart—keep something from slipping between my ribs."

It appears I was wrong regarding your companions. Perhaps they show signs of intelligence.

"Hey!" Lilian called from atop the dragon as she held on to one of the spines. "I want this one! Someone whack it loose for me!"

Then again, perhaps not.

Sixth Era. 140. Mertim 5.

"Remind me again why you want that thing?" Geran asked Lilian as they sat in the back of the wagon. "I'm not surprised you charmed one of those meathead Svarengels into engraving those tribal designs into it, but what is it supposed to be? A walking stick?

Lilian leaned against the spine and smiled. "Well I was thinkin' about conduits, right? Like how bone is more powerful than wood? You saw how much power that blood sorceress could put through a wand made of brehdar bone. She controlled *all* of us with just that tiny little thing!"

"You want to turn that spine into a conduit?" Shiro asked.

"I'll let you guys into the magical mind of Lilian," she said, beaming. "If that wand was about as strong as my current staff, just *imagine* what a *dragon-bone staff* could do!"

"Moon help us," Geran muttered. "You want to take that thing into combat when you can barely hold it in one hand?"

Lilian made a face. "Honestly, that's the only downside. Ugh. I don't want to have to start lifting weights so I can be stronger."

Shiro touched the five-foot black spike. "How would you turn that into a conduit?"

"I just gotta take it to an enchanter! I'm gonna use basically all my money to get a top-tier gemstone and staff-maker. I'll have the most powerful conduit in the world!"

They stared at her.

"There are over one and a half million words in the English language, and I can't string enough of them together to construct an appropriate response to that," Geran said.

Shiro bounced in his seat. "So cool! If you keep studying into your alteration techniques and then get a super powerful conduit, you could be the strongest mage in the world! You could even get a national title!"

"Hm-hmm," she hummed as she flashed her signature grin. "You hit the nail right on the head, Shiro. Looks like my dream of becoming a legend is starting to piece itself together."

Geran sighed. "Welp, if you end up going off the deep end, we'll know that Elaethia will be there to bring you back to earth."

"Oh hush, you. I'm perfectly sane, and that'll never change."

The ranger raised an eyebrow.

"What's with that face? Shiro! You too? Hey, Elaethia! The guys are being—" She cut herself off. The dragon hero was talking to herself in the driver's seat. Or at least it appeared to be so. In fact, she was talking with Frossgar.

"They've got a lot to catch up on," Geran said. "Leave them alone for a while."

"I wonder what they're talking about up there," Lilian murmured.

"Mostly what she's been up to these last few years," Geran said. "They're getting to the part where she met Shiro."

Shiro leaned forward. "Really? How can you tell? You've been talking to us this whole time."

The ranger tapped his head. "A little skill I've developed over the years. I'm starting to train Michael on it early. Takes a lot of concentration and discipline, so if he can master that, he can master almost everything else."

"Woah, could you teach *me*?"

"Oh, that could never happen."

Shiro's voice became crestfallen. "What? Why?"

"To put it lightly, it requires a certain kind of discipline you don't have."

"What's that supposed to mean?" Lilian asked.

Geran spread his hands. "Shiro just doesn't have the focus or mindset for it."

The demicat's tail flicked. "Are you calling him dumb?"

"Of course not. We don't have room in this party for *two* idiots."

"Hey!"

"Lilian's not an idiot! Look how far she's come with her magic! She's a genius compared to other mages in the country!"

"And yet she still has the common sense of a housecat."

"I don't know much about housecats, but I'm offended on Lilian's behalf!"

"That's kinda pathetic, Shiro."

"Geraaaaan! Stop being such a stinker!"

The ranger raised a finger at her. "You haven't seen the worst of it, Lilian. I'm still mad about you laughing your tail off while I was wrestling Jörgen. I've got a lot of embarrassing stories about you when you were younger, you know. I'm sure plenty of guys back at the guild would love to hear about how you found a peephole to their baths from the— Ow! Jeez, would you quit? *Ow!* Hey! Stop— Ow! Stop hitting me with that thing! Aren't you ... *Ow!* ... gonna turn it into a conduit or something?"

A sudden burst of energy rattled them from the front of the cart. The three in the back slowly turned their heads, and the color drained from their faces. They looked up not to see Elaethia staring back at them, but an enormous aethereal lizard whose eyes bore into theirs.

"G-ghost dragon!" Shiro screamed. He scrambled back and fell out of the wagon. Lilian's tail puffed out, and her ears shrank back. The mage could only cower on the cart floor with an undignified "Wa-wa-wa-wa-wa-wa-wa."

Geran stared blankly at the giant, translucent dragon. "Well, I'm glad I already took a piss not too long ago."

Frossgar exhaled heavily, but no air blew from his nose. "Elaethia has assured me that you all are pleasant company. At first I promised her I would not intervene but would simply observe the way you all interact with one another. However, should I be forced to listen to petty banter, I will not stand so idly by."

Shiro poked his head out from behind the wagon. "Y-y-yes sir. We'll be more civilized."

Lilian only quivered and violently nodded her head.

"Right. Yup. Not a problem," Geran said quickly. He then raised a finger. "One question though. How are you doing that? Is that a dragon spell or something?"

"Hmph." The ghostly dragon rose to his full height and looked down at them. "That was two questions, but I will answer them nonetheless. No, this is not a spell specific to dragons or dragon heroes. This is a spell unique to Elaethia and me. By using her *familiar* spell, we constructed a form that I communicate through."

Lilian sat up. "*Familiar*? That's *way* different than what you're doing. *Familiar* makes an entity out of whatever element you're specialized in, right? You should be some brehdar-sized wraith-looking thing."

"That is indeed what the base spell does. Through modification, we can alter the appearance. Elaethia told me that *you* discovered such a technique."

"I did? Oh! I did!"

"It fascinates me that one with such a capable mind can still be a simpleton," Frossgar said, shaking his head. "Elaethia transformed herself to cast this spell, which I, in turn, maintain. However, it is a flawed creation. While I can be seen and heard, I have no tangible effect on the world. This form can neither attack nor be touched."

Geran rubbed his chin. "That sounds almost like a waste of magic then."

"You are astute to believe so. Fortunately, it does not take much power to summon this form. The largest flaw is having to interact with those around me."

"Man, it's like I'm meeting Elaethia again for the first time."

Shiro scratched his head. "Elaethia-sama used to be like this?"

"Not as bad, but yeah."

"I am still able to hear you," the dragon hero announced from the front of the cart.

"Sorry …" Geran muttered.

"Hey," Lilian said, "besides this, have you two figured out any other dragon spells?"

"Ah, yes, about that," Frossgar began. "In our comparisons, it seems there are only three spells that a dragon is capable of that brehdars are not. I was most disappointed to hear that our intermediate spells only require a brehdar to specialize to achieve them."

Lilian leaned forward on her knees. "Let's hear 'em!"

"You are already aware of *frost breath* and *unyielding ice*. The third is a frost dragon's ultimate spell, though we do not have a name for it. In fact, it is the only dragon spell to not be named."

"Oh-ho-ho, go on! I wanna know why!"

"Partially owing to our seclusion, partially because it is incredibly rare for it to be channeled. It was the most lethal of spells in the world at its discovery. For all I know, it could still be. Dragons and brehdars fought and debated over many things during the wars. But one thing we all agreed upon was that this spell was never to be called upon in an act of war. I, for one, have never used it."

The mage threw her hands in the air. "You've been sitting on the world's most dangerous spell for over three thousand years, and you never used it *once?*"

Shiro bounced in excitement. "A forbidden spell? What does it do? Is Elaethia-sama able to channel it?"

"She is. It is similar to *frost envelopment* in function, but on a scale beyond mortal comprehension. It surrounds whoever transforms it in an aura of the coldest temperature possible."

Lilian cocked her ear. "That's a thing?"

"Indeed. While flame and heat may climb to temperatures infinite, coldness has a limit. Frost dragons are the only ones who may achieve this. It quite literally freezes reality. Life is ceased the instant it comes in contact with the spell. Nothing may move. Plants, animals, the earth, and even air itself cease entirely."

"Absolute zero," Geran announced grimly.

Frossgar tilted his head. "You know of this spell?"

"No, but I know what you're describing. I heard a Sage describe it on an escort quest once. Don't ask me to explain it; I could hardly understand what she was saying."

"Fascinating," Frossgar mused.

"Then that is what we shall name the spell," Elaethia decided.

"I concur," Frossgar agreed. "Though be warned, little one. *Absolute Zero* is not to be used lightly. It has been said to destroy the land it touches—permanently. We must never use it unless the outcome is more favorable than the consequence."

Sixth Era.140. Abris 16.

Elaethia looked around as they passed through Apogee. Buildings, shops, and markets lined the massive city region. Canals with docks and boats splashed and groaned, drowned out mostly by the noise of horses, carts, and merchants. The four of them made their way down the cobblestone road, guiding the cart down the center of the wide city street. People moved out of their way or glared at them as they pushed through the crowd. Occasional merchants approached the cart, pushing alongside to offer Cataclysm their wares. They quickly faltered and backed away when Elaethia locked eyes with them.

"We are here, Frossgar," Elaethia announced.

So this is the capital city of … Linderry, was it?

"Yes," Elaethia said. "Apogee. By far the busiest city in the country."

It is not to my liking. Far too many people, quite loud, and the presence of magic is so strong I can taste it.

"I understand, as that is how I felt when I first set foot here. I am still uneasy with such crowds but have learned to deal with it out of necessity."

Remind me once again why we came to this place.

"Information, Frossgar. That and it is the only place where Lilian can turn that spine into an ample conduit."

If you deem this a necessary visit, then I will refrain from further complaints. However, do not expect me to engage myself. In fact, I intend to fall deep within your subconscious until we leave. Wake me only should you need me.

"Very well. I will call to you once we leave, unless your presence is required."

Lilian poked her head up front. "Whatcha talkin' about?"

"Frossgar does not like such a crowded environment," Elaethia said. "He will remain dormant until we leave."

"Can you really blame him?" Geran said as he looked around the bustling middle tier. "He's lived by himself for thousands of years. He's gotta be experiencing some sensory overload."

"Will he be all right, Elaethia-sama?" Shiro asked.

"He will be fine," she assured him. "He is merely going into deep slumber for the time being."

"Must be nice," Geran grumbled.

"I hope those messages you sent ahead made it here, Geran," Shiro said.

"They should have. The postal service is really good. Letter-bearers almost never get attacked. Either way, we'll find out soon enough."

Lilian cocked an ear. "Messages?"

"Once I realized we were gonna take that detour through Svarengel, I sent some letters down here to let the appropriate people know we were coming."

"How many stops will we be making?" Elaethia asked.

"Three. Mordecai should get us hooked up with a staff maker, as well as someone with international affairs. While Lilian gets her staff made, the rest of us can do some research on Armini before we get there. Once that's sorted out, we'll meet with Frederick Borough again. He'll have more details regarding the combat prowess of dragon heroes."

"That last one isn't as necessary anymore," Shiro noted.

"Yeah, but it doesn't hurt to clarify. He'll be happy to see us either way."

Lilian's eyes grew bright. "Wait, you hooked me up with an *Arcane Sage* for my staff?"

"That depends on Mordecai," Geran corrected. "He doesn't know about that part since we didn't realize you'd have it until after I sent the messages. But I can imagine a Sage would be more than happy to work with dragon bone. How much gold do you have on you?"

"'Bout a thousand. A little more."

"You actually brought that much with you? No wonder the horse gets tired so fast, the poor animal. Either way, that'd better be enough. We all had about twice that when we started; where did it all go?"

The demicat shrugged. "Dunno. Money tends to disappear if I hold on to it."

Geran put a hand to his brow. "Stars above, Lilian."

The four of them rode through Apogee, passing through the walls to the innermost terrace in the midafternoon. Geran took the reins and led the wagon toward the Moon's Pillar. Elaethia recognized many of the buildings and annexes, and looked keenly to the domed building that was the dragon museum. She realized now that it was a bit smaller than she remembered.

A shadow fell over her vision. She looked up to see that it had been created by the pillar itself. The Moon's Pillar towered so high it broke through the clouds, and the base was thicker than the tournament arena. The pale building could be described only as a marvel of engineering and magic. Elaethia remembered that the construct was tall, but she still felt a wave of vertigo just looking at it.

Lilian joined her gaze. "Crazy, isn't it? That's the biggest building in the country, maybe the world. And it's chock full of all sorts of knowledge and materials. If I was a book-sniffer, this is where I'd want to be."

Shiro rubbed his chin. "Are you thinking any more on trying to be an Arcane Sage, Lilian?"

"Nah, not really. I mean, they'd probably take me if I tried out, but I don't like the idea of being cooped up in there. Kinda hard to become a legend by living in a library."

"I think the Arcane Sages are legends!"

"Yeah? Name one."

"Arthur Veldwig."

"That we *haven't* met."

"Uh …" the samurai fumbled as he scratched his head. "Frederick Borough?

Geran rubbed his eyes. "We've met him too, Shiro. And he's not a Sage."

"He's not?"

"No! He's a curator for the museum! Just because he's a historian in an annex doesn't mean he's a Sage! He's not even a magician!"

"Who are we fighting about?" a familiar male voice asked.

Elaethia turned. "Oh, hello Mordecai."

"Good afternoon, everyone," the dwarven fire mage responded. "Your predictions were nearly spot-on, Geran. How *do* you do that?"

The ranger shrugged. "Going to business, I've got an additional request besides looking at international affairs."

Mordecai raised an eyebrow. "Any particular reason you failed to mention it in your letter? This may cost you, Geran."

"It came up after I sent the letter. It's nothing crazy. Just wondering if you could point us in the direction of a staff maker who might want to work with dragon bone."

"Dragon bone, you say? I've never heard of a dragon-bone staff before. This will be most interesting." He looked appraisingly, almost covetously, at Lilian's spike. "All right, very well. Lilian, go on ahead to the visitor's center at the pillar. Tell them I sent you in regard to your staff. In the meantime, the rest of us will go look into Armini's current events."

Lilian rubbed her hands together. "Ohoho. This'll be *great!* Thanks, Mordie!"

"Um …" Shiro looked pleadingly at Elaethia as Lilian bounded toward the massive white tower.

"You may accompany whomever you wish, Shiro," she said.

"Thank you, Elaethia-sama!" Shiro gave her a brief bow and jogged off after his demicat companion.

Sixth Era.140. Abris 17.

"Well. That was rather interesting," Geran noted, studying their newly acquired map of Armini.

Elaethia tilted her head. "The term 'interesting' has many meanings, Geran."

"And every single one applies to this situation," he replied. "Civil unrest, lowering population and birth rates, almost nothing on magicians. In fact, if this information is correct, the whole country is nearly uninhabited outside of Paragon. Once we're done talking with Frederick here, I'd like to put together some plans."

"Paragon?" Shiro asked while looking at the map.

"The capital city, where Rychus lives," Elaethia said.

Lilian scratched her ear. "Sounds like good news, right? We can get in there without anybody trying to stop us."

Geran shook his head. "You'd think that, but we'd stand out. We're almost guaranteed to be apprehended by soldiers if we're discovered."

"Meaning we'd have to move with stealth and caution," Shiro continued.

"Mostly at night," Elaethia concluded.

Lilian folded her arms. "Hmph, lame."

"We'll probably end up ditching the wagon at some point, too," Geran noted.

"What!"

"Wagons draw a lot of attention, and the horse needs a lot of care. We won't be able to operate and maintain it once we're deep in Armini territory."

Lilian's tail drooped to the ground. "So … we're gonna have to … walk."

"Yup. Save your whining until after we're done talking with Frederick, 'cause we're here."

Lilian ignored Geran's request and groaned woefully as the dragon museum curator opened the door to greet them.

"My word." The middle-aged man raised an eyebrow. "I was under the impression that you were as happy to see me as I was you."

"We are," Geran assured him, clapping Lilian across the back of the head.

"Owww," the demicat mewled. "Meanie!"

"Thank you for agreeing to meet us again, Frederick," Elaethia said, and she extended a hand.

He grasped it firmly and led them inside. "No problem, no problem at all. You are always quite welcome. My work has me constantly busy, but there is nothing that I will not put on delay for a dragon hero. After I received Geran's letter, I gathered all information and tomes I could on frost dragons and all those who had encountered them. I have them ready and sitting on my desk. Unfortunately, it is a rather measly conglomeration. However, it is also more abundant than what I was able to provide last time."

Shiro approached the desk. "You weren't lying when you said there wasn't much about frost dragons. There are only a couple of books and papers here."

Lilian poked her head in. "Uh, guys? I think you're all forgetting an important detail here. We don't really need them anymore."

"What do you mean?" Frederick asked.

"Lilian …" Geran groaned and rubbed his eyes. "He already went through a ton of trouble getting this for us, the least we can do is let him have his moment."

"I don't understand; is all this somehow obsolete now?"

Elaethia shook her head. "Not entirely. There may very well be information that would still prove advantageous. It is unlikely we know everything."

The curator began to wring his hands. "I thought I had everything the world had to offer regarding frost dragons here, have you all found another source?"

Shiro glanced tentatively at Elaethia. "Well, in a sense …"

"So my time and research was for nothing? Did you not actually need my assistance?"

"No-no-no," Lilian said, waving her hands. "We did; we totally did. It's just that … something … came up."

Frederick's eyes hardened. "So in this discovery, you entirely forgot to inform me? Or at the very least let me know that I wouldn't have to go through all this time and effort?"

Geran rubbed the back of his head. "Hoo boy. That was one helluva blunder on our part. Hey, Elaethia?"

"Yes?"

"Think you could"—he tapped the side of his head with a finger—"do some negotiation?"

"You know as well as I that negotiation is not my strong suit."

"Not you, *him*."

She nodded. "I see. I will ask."

Frederick looked back and forth between them. "What are you on about?"

"Frossgar?" Elaethia called.

Frederick made a face. "What?"

"Frossgar."

"Yes, yes, your dragon, what about him?"

"Frossgar, can you hear my voice?"

"What in the …? If this is some addition to a joke in poor taste, I am not amused."

Geran raised a hand. "Just trust us."

Yes, little one, what is it?

"There has been a misunderstanding, and we could use your assistance."

There does not seem to be any sort of physical conflict. What assistance could I provide?

"We are hoping you may speak with someone. He worked to aid us, and we may have offended him. Your presence would clear our intentions."

I have little intention of speaking with other brehdars, let alone attempting to come to some sort of agreement. If you cannot gain what you seek through peaceful means, then I suggest you resort to force.

THE ELAETHIUM

"We cannot do that, Frossgar; he is a friend."

This is why I never saw the appeal to such relations. If you are unable to come to agreements with your ally, then how do you think I would be able to solve your predicament?

"He has devoted his life to studying your kind. It would please him greatly to see and speak with you."

So you intend to use me as an arbiter. That is what you wish, hmm? To parade me in front of him as a sort of appeasement?

"No, Frossgar, I do not wish to use you as a trick. This man aided me in my studies while we were separated. It would only be right to return the favor."

Elaethia stood in silence for a moment until she heard Frossgar sigh.

Very well. Take heed, Elaethia, as I will act in accordance of my own. Do not expect me to attempt diplomacy for a mere brehdar.

"Thank you, Frossgar. I will be sure to—"

She was cut off with a sudden burst of energy. The room grew chill as a misty shape began to take form. A frosty aethereal body formed in the center of the room. Its enormous scaly torso was the first to form, and a snakelike neck and tail soon followed. The dragon's limbs and head were now visible as the great wings stretched and enveloped the air above them. Frossgar gazed down at the five of them. His ghostly dragon eyes bored into those of Frederick.

"So," the spectral dragon began, "you are the one in question?"

Frederick fell back and stammered helplessly. "I-I. I, uh. Wh-what is—"

"I suggest you find your words quickly, human, as my patience has been tested enough. I was under the impression that you were a man of study regarding dragons, but your dumbfounded demeanor is enough to make me question the word of my champion."

"You … you are him. You're Frossgar!"

"Yes, I am he. If you are finished stating the obvious, perhaps you may carry on with whatever business has been interrupted by a petty misunderstanding."

"I … I …" the curator stared awestruck at the cold, misty form of the frost dragon. A bead of sweat flowed down his brow. A soft chuckle escaped his lips with a wisp of vapor from his breath. Frederick removed his spectacles and wiped them on his jacket. "I see now. Forgive me; I should have asked for an explanation as opposed to leveling accusations."

"An astute observation," the dragon agreed. "Now, if all has been made well; I shall return to where I was."

Frederick threw up a hand. "W-wait! Please, sir, if I may. This is a momentous occasion! The opportunity to speak with a dragon is an *astronomical* opportunity for someone such as I! My research has nearly nothing on your kind. Would you honor me with just a few minutes of your time? I have many questions!"

The dragon regarded him. His gaze shifted from the hopeful eyes of the curator to those of Elaethia. She may not have shared his mind, but Elaethia knew what he was thinking. He did not want to. He considered his presentation of himself to this human as graceful enough, but now Frederick wanted more. Frossgar sighed heavily and closed his eyes in deep internal conflict.

"So be it," he finally stated. "But if, and only if, you answer all questions from Elaethia and her allies. Unrestrictedly."

"Yes, yes, of course, I swear!" Frederick stammered.

"Take heed of your promise. You will fare a fate worse than ignorance should I hear of you withholding even the smallest piece of information. Now ask your questions, curator. Your minute of my time has begun."

Several hours later, Cataclysm wearily trudged out of the dragon museum. The entire time, Elaethia had fought with her own consciousness. Shiro and Lilian soon lost interest and practiced with their weapons until they got tired of that and traded with each other. Even Geran seemed bored. The ranger initially took notes of the conversation between Frossgar and Frederick, but even he couldn't feign interest for long.

That was beyond taxing.

"I know, Frossgar, and I am very thankful for your generosity," Elaethia said.

As you should be. I love you, little one, but I will no longer be doing such things for you or anyone. I am not an exhibit to be beheld; nor am I a bargaining chip. You will have to mend your problems on your own from now on.

"I … I understand."

Very good. While unpleasant, our conversation was at least fruitful.

"It was, Frossgar. We may have already known this, but we are unique."

"It's getting easier to understand your conversations," Geran noted.

Shiro raised an eyebrow. "You were thinking that too?"

"'Bout time you guys figured it out!" Lilian gloated. "I've been following their conversations for weeks!"

Geran's eyes hardened. "Yeah right."

"Hm-hmm, say what you want, Gerry. There's no way you can prove me wrong!"

"Besides you constantly asking what they were talking about whenever they conversed? Every single time?"

Lilian opened her mouth and raised a finger. After a moment, she clamped her lips together and drooped.

"It was quite bothersome," Elaethia sighed.

The Elaethium

"But this is so cool!" Shiro piped up. "You're the first dragon hero in known history to be able to project your dragon's form! *And* he can travel around the surrounding environment at will!"

"Yes, but he cannot stray far from me. While his mind may be cast, his soul and power are within me. He cannot engage in the world, only examine it."

Geran rubbed his chin. "That's pretty nifty in its own regard. He can scout ahead, call shots, observe the whole battlefield, act as eyes on the back of your head. The imagination's the limit with this ability."

Your bearded companion has rather lowly ideas for usage of my powers.

"Perhaps," Elaethia agreed. "But you cannot deny the plausibility."

I did not deny it. He has demonstrated remarkable critical thinking and unimpeded common sense. That being said, this companion of yours seems to think of me only as an asset.

"He has a name, Frossgar."

Yes, as all brehdars do. He is an ally of yours, and proves useful, so I respect your choice to keep his presence. However, do not think I must regard him as you do.

Elaethia's tone started to shift. "All dragons have names as well. My friends have addressed you by yours; would it not be polite to do the same for them?"

That would mean putting myself on equal terms with brehdars.

"You address me by name."

Of course. You are my champion. The carrier of my soul and power. The one and only brehdar I deemed worthy.

"And they are not?"

No. And it is unlikely that they will be. The bearded one demonstrates intelligence, the swordsman practices humility, and the demihuman shows power. All hold only one worthy characteristic that you do. They are, frankly, beneath you.

Elaethia stopped.

"I beg your pardon?"

"Uh, Elaethia-sama?" Shiro slowly stepped up and froze. The dragon hero's eyes flashed, her fist clenched, and her mouth twisted itself into a snarl.

I do not understand the reasoning behind your reaction.

Elaethia's voice alone was enough to make her companions back away as she addressed her dragon.

"Has your mind been cast so far from your soul that you have forgotten the words I wove into your heart as a child? I recall a precious memory of our first time leaving the cave together, walking through the brisk chill of our mountain. The spirit and demeanor you had were open and accepting, compassionate and caring. I told you of the world we live in and how we treat one another. *All* are equal. It matters not if you have fur or scales, two legs or four, are one meter tall or one hundred meters. If you have a mind and feelings, you are a person. If you will not treat them as the individuals they are, then they and I will refer to you simply as 'the dragon.' Have I made myself clear?"

Frossgar was silent for a moment.

I ... see.

"Is that all you have to say?" she demanded.

The dragon fumbled with his words for a moment before he addressed her.

Forgive me, Elaethia. I lost myself within my irritation at the previous situations. This is the world we live in, and we must adapt to it. You have told me before that you fight and live on equal terms with these individuals, so therefore they are deserving of respect. I promise to you that I will regard Geran, Shiro, and Lilian with more dignity. Have patience with me, little one, as this change will take effort. But I will work toward it for you.

"Then perhaps you will soon understand the impact and necessity of having others close at hand—others that you can trust and depend on with your life. Give them time. You will find they are more reliable and noteworthy than you first believed."

The dragon only grunted in response and departed into subconsciousness. Elaethia sighed and turned to face her friends. Geran and Shiro were white in the face, while Lilian had cocked an ear.

"So, uh ..." the mage said, "what were you talkin' about?"

Chapter 23
Armini

Sixth Era. 140. Miyan 17.

The information gathered from the Moon's Pillar was out of date. According to what they had researched, Armini should have been nearly empty close to the border and gradually more inhabited as they approached the capital city on the southernmost coastline. In reality, it was almost entirely uninhabited. For decades Arminians had fled the dictatorship that had them enslaved for over a century. Where they went, or how they got there, seemed to be a mystery.

The cool, mountainous landscape of northern Armini looked almost like a painting. Rolling hills and rocky outcrops dotted the luscious green countryside. It was beautiful—a paradise within a country of unfathomable evil. The adventurers began to fall in love with the scenery around them as they traveled through it. But they could not behold the landscape without seeing the remnants of what was left behind.

Among the flowing rivers and rocky hills stood decrepit farms and abandoned villages and cities, crumbling aqueducts, roads in disrepair, and untended vineyards and orchards. Once cultivated locations were now turning back to nature. All were solemn reminders of what had happened over the last century. A few days Further along their journey it wasn't just buildings and structures that lay barren and decayed along the path. Soon destroyed wagons and tents popped up. Rotted chunks of wood and cloth lay discarded to the side of the broken road. The stench of burning wood and flesh, along with the sound of buzzing insects, filled the air. Several of these wreckages had the bones of both brehdars and animals scattered around them. A few still had flesh clinging to them. It was only a week later when the landscape started to turn dangerous.

"Hold." Geran held out a hand and stood on the driver's seat. "I see smoke. Get the wagon behind something; I'm going to check it out."

"Should we expect you to return in the usual timeframe?" Elaethia asked.

"Nah, extend it to a half hour. If I'm not back by then, come get me."

"Should we be cautious in our rescue, Geran?" Shiro asked.

"No. The people on both sides here would work quickly. The civilians are desperate, so they'll do whatever they need to get what they want. The soldiers are tyrannical, so they'd have special plans for me. I've been captured before, but something tells me these guys would hold nothing back in their interrogations."

"Please do not say such things," Elaethia whispered.

Lilian gripped her dragonite staff. "That settles *that,* then. It wouldn't matter if you told us to be cautious or not. If those creeps get you, I'll … I'll …"

Geran smiled. "Raise hell and break shit."

The demicat nodded fervently.

He patted her head. "That's what I'm asking for."

The ranger pulled up his hood, put his silver necklace around his neck, leaped off the cart, and vanished into the tall grass.

"Do you want the bad news or the worse news first?" Geran asked as he returned.

Elaethia tilted her head. "What is the difference?"

"The bad news: that was a group of refugees that didn't make it. There are no soldiers nearby, but the bodies are still warm. From this point on, we have to be on high alert."

Shiro exhaled slowly. "And the worse news?"

"Meaning we have to abandon the wagon."

Lilian's staff fell out of her hands. "What!"

"We knew this was going to happen eventually. We got lucky as is in getting it this far, but this is a clear sign that we need to go low profile from now on."

"But I *hate* wearing a ruck!"

"All you're carrying is your own gear!" Geran snapped. "Elaethia was generous enough to carry all the cooking and travel equipment so the rest of us could focus on our own stuff. If you can't carry the basic clothes and equipment for this trip, what made you think you could fight an emperor at the end of it? You'll get over it."

Elaethia grunted as she hoisted what she could on her back. "We should burn the wagon so it does not stand out and cause reason for investigation. Preferably near those latest victims. As for the horse …" She trailed off.

"We'll have to kill it," Shiro finished.

Lilian's eyes bugged. "What! No. Not happening. Not Maple."

"This is why I told you not to name it," Geran sighed.

"Just cut him loose! Send him on the trail back home! Tie him up somewhere so we can come back for him!"

"All of those are reasons to suspect, Lilian," Shiro said. "There haven't been any other horses roaming around; he would stand out. We couldn't come back for him in time anyway, even if he wasn't found by someone or something else."

"He is not wild, either," Elaethia continued. "He was raised in captivity, so it is unlikely he would survive in the wilderness without a herd."

"But that is so unfair!" Lilian insisted. "Maple worked so hard for us all these months. We can't just up and kill him!"

Geran stared her down. "Lilian, he was dead the moment he crossed the border. This was a one-way trip for him. If we do what you're suggesting, he'll die slowly and painfully or give us away and botch the whole mission. The best we can offer him is a quick and painless death."

"But …" the mage rest a hand on the nose of the brown horse. It blinked with watery eyes and twitched an ear.

Shiro walked behind her and put his hand on top of hers. "Lilian. His sacrifice won't be in vain. He's fulfilled his duty and gotten us this far. Maple-san was a good horse, and he deserves a good death."

The girl sniffled and looked at him silently.

"I can make it painless," he promised. "I'll give him all the oats he wants and brush him down nicely. His last thoughts will be happy."

She only nodded and wiped her eyes with her other hand.

"We'll go on ahead, Shiro," Geran said. "Make it look believable. We've got a lot of road ahead."

Sixth Era. 140. Miyan 26.

"What the hell happened here?" Lilian whispered.

Cataclysm gazed over the now desolate landscape of Armini. The once beautiful countryside had gradually changed into a smoldering wasteland. The dusty and beaten road was full of potholes. Charred rock and bits of wood lay scattered around the uneven earthen surface. Fields and farms had turned into ashen and barren plains. Wheat fields and orchards had shriveled. Dry flakes of bark and stalks flew past the four adventurers in the wind.

It was dawn now. The sun began to rise, signaling to the party that it was time to stop again. Cataclysm had begun their plan of moving only at night. At first they tried to keep away from the paths and focus on staying hidden in the undergrowth and outcrops. But as the land around them turned dead and desolate, there was nothing to conceal them anymore. Now favoring speed over caution, they had taken to the main road.

"How close are we?" Shiro asked as he took the cookware from Elaethia's back.

"Closer. That's all I can tell you," Geran said. He unstrung his bow and pulled out some smoked meat from his hunt the previous day.

"Intuition tells me that we are nearing our goal," Elaethia said. "I would not doubt that the horrors we have seen this last week are from Rychus's rage. His influence does not reach far, according to the texts we studied. We are most likely in or nearing the outskirts of Paragon."

"I just don't get it," Lilian muttered. "Why? Why is he burning and destroying his own towns? He just kills everything!"

Geran shook his head. "I don't get it either. The towns and villages maybe because they revolted and he tried to make an example of them. But his fields and orchards? I can't wrap my head around it. If he's trying to grow and maintain a legion, then he needs the resources. How is he feeding his armies?"

"Maybe he couldn't get the resources from these locations," Shiro thought aloud as he filled a pot with water. "These communities may have refused to give him their crops, so he destroyed them."

"Just like a little kid," Lilian huffed. "'If I can't have it, nobody can,' huh?"

"So it would seem," Elaethia said, sadly looking over the terrain.

"There isn't much here, Geran," Shiro noted as he took the meat from him. "Wildlife is getting more and more scarce the further south we go. I'm afraid this stew won't have much to it. What kind of meat is this, anyway?"

"Dog," the ranger announced. "Mangey thing was scavenging the remains of a destroyed caravan. There was about as much meat on the animal as there was the people it was eating."

Lilian shuddered. "You didn't have to say that last part."

"How many bodies have we come across?" Shiro asked.

"I've lost track," Geran muttered grimly.

"Seventy-three," Elaethia stated. "Brehdars of all species. Men, women, and children. Rychus and those who serve him show no mercy."

"You kept count, Elaethia-sama?"

She nodded. "Every corpse we pass is another gouge I will carve into his body. Rychus leaves these scenes to deter and strike fear into the hearts of those who defy him. But all it has done is fill me with rage."

"We'll get him," Geran promised. "It'll take a helluva lot more than this to make me call it off."

"Nothing short of the apocalypse would turn me away," Shiro said.

"Tch," Lilian spat. "You talk about that as if it's not gonna happen. I haven't had a chance to test out the full potential of my new staff. Once I get to unleash, that bastard's gonna wish for the end of times over what I plan to do."

I empathize with Lilian's anger. But she must not forget our end goal.

"I agree, Frossgar," Elaethia said. "I am grateful for your dedication, Lilian. But I do not wish to destroy my homeland. Our goal is to rid it of Rychus and rebuild anew."

The mage gripped her staff. "I *hate* all this sneaking around. This isn't what a mage like me is meant to do. This isn't anything like an adventure!"

"It shouldn't be long, Lilian," Shiro said and handed her a wooden bowl. "If Elaethia-sama is right, we should be there in maybe less than a week."

Geran nodded. "Then we have to start phase two, which will be the hardest part. We have to find a way to infiltrate the city itself—without getting caught."

"I wish we could have interacted with some of the survivors," Lilian said. "They might have told us a way to get in."

"We could not risk that," Elaethia reminded her. "They are desperate and unpredictable. Not to mention almost certainly in an irrational state of mind."

Lilian sighed and lay down to stare at the withered tree above her. "But people are obviously getting out somehow. Maybe that's our ticket in."

"That's what I was thinking, too," Geran agreed. "One of my options was that we should lie in wait outside the fortifications until we see a group pass by. But who knows how long that would take, or even if we can spot them. Whatever method gets them out is clearly efficient enough that Rychus's forces can't detect them. No guarantee that I'd do much better."

He would fare better in that endeavor with our aid, little one. You can defend him while I can cast my senses to the area.

"That is plausible, but I still may impede his approach," Elaethia said.

"What?" Geran asked.

She relayed Frossgar's idea.

"You still aren't that good at sneaking, Elaethia," Lilian pointed out.

"You're not much better, Lilian," Geran countered.

"I never said I was!"

"Oh! The pot's boiling!" Shiro suddenly yelped, and he scooped some of the stew into his bowl. The others handed them theirs so he could fill them.

"Not much, huh?" Lilian noted as she took a spoonful.

Geran shrugged. "At least he makes it taste half-decent."

"Indeed," Elaethia said. "Although I find myself eager to have a meal from the guildhall again."

Shiro drank from his bowl and rested it in his lap. "I do the best I can. I made the effort to understand Linderrian cooking. The herbs there are way different from Osakyota's."

Geran chuckled. "I suppose you're missing home cooking more than all of us, eh samurai? You haven't had the comfort food you're used to in over a year."

"It's true that this land lacks many of the vital ingredients. But any meal shared with friends is comforting enough."

Elaethia smiled. "Agreed."

I find it odd, you being able to show such expressions in this environment.

"That is the power of companionship, Frossgar. Burdens shared weigh less on our shoulders. It is through this bond that we are able to stay positive and smile."

You have said before that you cannot rely on your strength alone. Is this what you meant?

"This is one of those meanings. In fact, I would say it is the bedrock of the phrase. You had always been interested in brehdar civilization and their knack for rapid and vast growth. Brehdars are weak, but together they can overcome nearly anything. I have learned that is what makes empires, legends, and stories. They are not made through an individual's strength alone"—she looked up at her friends and smiled—"but through the strength they have in others."

"Wha?" Lilian cocked an ear with her spoon halfway in her mouth.

I see. You gained your true strength through them, then?

"In a sense. I still cannot put it into words very well."

What does that make of our time together on the mountain?

"We were still together, were we not? We became strong through one another."

You are suggesting I became stronger as well?

"I am." She nodded.

Frossgar remained silent for a moment.

I believe I am beginning to understand your reasoning behind companionship. While I cannot fully bring myself to commit to it, it is beginning to form a picture in my mind. Do you believe I, too, can obtain this "true strength" you speak of, through your friends?

"It is possible. But if you think of it like that, it will be increasingly difficult. You will never see yourself growing. Only once it has happened can you see the result."

Intriguing. Tell me more.

"Hey!" Lilian cut in. "If you're gonna chat, then you can be the first watch. Somewhere where the rest of us can sleep."

"Go find a good spot, Elaethia," Geran called, and he flapped his bed mat out. "Come get me when it's my turn."

Sixth Era. 140. Miyan 30.

They awoke each night at dusk. Cataclysm packed everything and removed all traces of their presence from the day and continued down the broken road toward the capital. Ambient light alone guided them through the ragged terrain. Light came from both the waning moon above and the occasional fire from a destroyed caravan.

The Elaethium

They walked as the hours went on, stopping only to take a short break or hide as a group of brehdars walked past. Cataclysm would take cover behind whatever was available and lie in wait until the group traveled out of earshot. Usually they were soldiers or scouts from Rychus's forces. Some nights they would be refugees.

A week ago, they saw these groups only once every several nights. But refugee sightings became more frequent as they moved farther south, as did the remains of those who had been caught by the legion. The terrain had become steep and rocky, the road more beaten and worn—almost indistinguishable from the dusty ground around them. Elaethia looked up the long and uneven hill road that blocked their view of the horizon. She turned around to see how her companions fared. Lilian was visibly sweating from the effort of climbing the dusty hill. Shiro was attempting to hide his own fatigue, but his exhaustion was apparent. Even Geran was breathing heavily from the climb.

She looked back up toward the crest of the hill. This was undoubtedly the tallest one they had climbed. But it seemed they were near the top. After a moment of consideration, Elaethia pushed forward to reach the summit. She halted as she did. Breath was forced into her lungs from the shock and then stolen from her at the realization. This hill was the last thing between them and their destination.

Paragon stood on the other side.

Elaethia's final memories of her home bore almost no resemblance to the city before her. No light or life could be seen from the distance. In the night sky, the city seemed almost like jagged mounds and hills. The decrepit capital appeared more like a ruin than the greatest city in the country.

The massive wall that surrounded it was tall and in disrepair. The harbor was empty, and ships sat moored in the retreated water. Only a single dock remained standing. The botanical garden had decayed and withered into a dry and dusty plot of land in the center of the city. The grand cathedral was gone entirely. There was only the foundation and bedrock that lay flat where it once stood. Entire blocks of the residential tiers were decrepit and abandoned. All of the unique landmarks of the city were gone.

Save one. Elaethia's gaze turned the very southeast corner of the city and beheld the only structure that showed light and activity. Emperor Rychus's grand palace stood alone atop a natural arch of rock. Even in the darkness, she could see its detail: its polished quartz statues, the limestone walls, the flawless arches and domes that supported the massive and ornate building. It was sickeningly beautiful.

"He's in there, isn't he?" Geran's voice asked from her right. She hadn't even noticed his approach.

"Most likely," she said.

"How fitting for a tyrant," Shiro growled as he joined them. "Living in absolute luxury while his people struggle to survive."

Lilian appeared right behind him, panting as she leaned on her staff and growled. "I'm not gonna lie. I had my doubts about how bad it could be down here. But not anymore."

Geran exhaled and pushed his hair back. "Let's move. We're sitting ducks just standing on the crest in the open like this. Keep your eyes open for a way to get in as we approach."

Wordlessly, they began the descent. Cataclysm walked in silence down the packed dirt road. The only sounds were the crunch of gravel, the shuffling of equipment, and the whisper of the breeze that rustled the grass. Elaethia knew she was supposed to be looking for a possible entrance into the city, but she couldn't take her eyes away from the depressing view of her childhood home. She couldn't even make out the details of the few buildings she could see over the wall. She saw only the rough and ragged outline of the rooftops.

They reached the bottom less than an hour later. All Elaethia could see over the wall was the top half of Rychus's palace—a false beacon of hope and light in a city of empty darkness and fear. Though it was still several kilometers away, Elaethia felt as if it were right in front of her. She closed her eyes and inhaled slowly to steady her heartbeat. The warrior let it out and opened her eyes to observe the landscape around her. All she saw was dry grass and dusty soil. Rocks and divots sprouted and sunk around them.

A sudden creak of wood and hinges followed by the crash of stone on stone came from ahead. In a flash, the adventurers dropped into a ditch for cover and brandished their weapons. Geran and Shiro propped themselves to a knee, ready to lunge forward. Lilian leaned against a dirt mound, gripping her dragon-bone staff. Elaethia unclipped the traveling gear strapped to her back and drew her battleaxe. After a moment of silence, they all peered out over the plain.

They froze as a shaky group of brehdars emerged from the side of the road not fifty meters ahead of them. The three hooded figures turned back from where they came, spoke something in hushed whispers, and started along the path leading north. They quickly diverged from the road and went off to the opposite side from where Cataclysm was hidden. It was undoubtedly another group of refugees beginning their own journey north. Elaethia assumed the four of them would choose to wait until the refugees were gone, but Geran began to creep up. She moved a hand to catch his arm.

"What are you doing?" she whispered.

Geran whispered back. "Those three were definitely talking to someone as they appeared out of nowhere. We need to know who it was."

Lilian brushed against them. "Why now? We've passed several refugees like them before; what's different this time?"

"We saw where they originated from," Geran said, exasperated. "They looked nervous and unsure what to do with the situation from the recent interaction, which means they were now on their own. That, in turn, means someone or something was guiding them this far. I don't have time to explain this in detail; I need to get on this while the trail is warm!"

"Just send Frossgar!"

Geran glared at her with impatient eyes. "He can't interact with them; this requires a hands-on approach!"

"Does the same contingency plan stay if you don't return in time?" Shiro asked.

"Make it five minutes. If you hear my horn, come running."

With that he disappeared.

"How long has it been?" Lilian asked as she peered into the darkness.

"Two minutes," Shiro noted. "Almost three."

"I don't like this. Not one bit."

"We must remain patient and vigilant," Elaethia said. "Geran knows what he is doing."

Shiro nodded. "He's very clever and has done this before. We should trust him like he always trusts us."

"But he's never given us a time frame less than fifteen minutes," Lilian muttered.

"Five minutes is a long time when something goes wrong," Shiro agreed.

"You suggesting we go now?"

"No, let's wait until we reach the time Geran gave us."

"Gaaaah, it could be too late by then!"

"We say that every time Geran scouts ahead—and every time he returns."

Elaethia spoke. "And this time should be no different."

Your tone betrays your words; it seems as if you are trying to convince yourself that Geran is all right. Lilian may be apt in believing we should hasten in our actions.

"You are agreeing on this sudden action, Frossgar?"

I cannot answer that comfortably. Geran has always stayed true to his word, and his skill is refined. However...

"You feel it, do you not?"

I do. Something is amiss.

"Frossgar feels uneasy too?" Shiro asked.

"He does."

Lilian clenched her staff. "Then this can't be a coincidence. Something's about to go really wrong, and we can't—"

She froze and perked her ears. She shot her head above the tall grass and turned to Elaethia, who was also listening intently.

"What?" Shiro asked. "What is it?"

Lilian whipped her head over. "You heard that too, Elaethia?"

She gave a single nod. "That was his horn. It began to sound and was swiftly silenced!"

Shiro lunged forward. "That's a sign! Go!"

Seraph sang from its sheath as the samurai tore across the open plain. He was quickly passed by his female companions. Elaethia shook the earth as she thundered toward where she had heard the sound. Lilian flew behind as she heard one of her air spells propel her forward.

Elaethia reached the location first. She darted her eyes to the ground and saw the curved bone horn lying in trampled dirt. She followed the indentations in the dry grass and saw movement fifteen meters ahead. Four shadowy figures lowered themselves into the ground. Elaethia charged without hesitation. The figures turned and froze for only a moment before hurrying further down into the earth. As Elaethia reached them, the last figure pulled down a heavy rock covered in moss and vanished.

"Geran!" she shouted, and she pounded a fist into the rock.

It didn't even crack.

Lilian landed next to her. "What happened? Where is he!"

"They took him; he is underground!"

Shiro slid next to them. "Who are they? What did they look like?"

"It matters not. Move away from me, quickly!" Elaethia ordered.

Shiro and Lilian backed away as Elaethia raised her axe above her head. With a single swing, she slammed the blade down on the reinforced sheet of rock and broke through. The slab shattered and sent shards and debris of not just rock but also metal in all directions. In an instant, the dragon hero donned her helmet and jumped down. Elaethia flew down the dark and dusty embankment and saw a dim light further below. She heard Shiro and Lilian descend close behind her. As she reached the bottom of the slide, the light grew brighter and she could see clearly.

Four figures stood at the mouth of another tunnel. Now illuminated, she could make out their features. All wore hoods, but three of them had studded leather armor. The fourth was a limp Geran. She saw and smelled no blood. The three faced her and drew their weapons. Two had thick swords with no crossguards. The third, who held Geran, pulled out a long and thin dagger. Elaethia recognized it as a stiletto. Her assessment was cut short as the three enemies aimed their weapons. The two longswords pointed at the three adventurers, the dagger needling into Geran's throat.

"Drop your weapons!" one of the enemies with the longsword demanded. He had blond hair and stout features.

Lilian's tail lashed as she caught up. "Fat chance! Give Geran back or I'll blow this whole tunnel to kingdom come!"

"Do that and you kill all of us, mage!" the other swordsman retorted. This one was female, with brown hair and blue eyes. Lilian let out a low growl in response and leveled her staff.

"We won't tell you a second time!" the man holding a knife to Geran's throat shouted. "Drop your weapons or we kill this one. Do it now!"

Shiro leveled Seraph. "Kill Geran and you lose not only your one bargaining chip but also the only thing stopping Elaethia-sama from turning you all to *paste!*"

The three enemies turned their gaze to the armored woman. Her helmet hid her face, but her glowing dragon eyes burned through the visor. Cold mist enveloped the underground tunnel. Vapor flowed from the stranger's mouths as they shivered and looked at one another with uncertainty.

"Ember, something's wrong here," the blond stranger muttered.

"I know, but we can't just stand here!" the woman responded. "I told you we should have killed him right there!"

"They still would have followed us, and this way we could have interrogated him! We need all the information we can get!"

Ember faced him. "What information? None of the ones we've captured ever talked! And this one looks nothing like any of them before! This is weird, Anvil!"

Anvil shook his head. "The boss is not gonna be happy about this … Falcon, what's the call?"

The man holding Geran and the knife looked at the three adventurers. "I have only one thing to say to you: Bleed to Make the Grass Grow."

Lilian's tail lashed. "What?"

Elaethia's voice was level and as hard as steel. "Release him, or it will be *your* blood that waters the ground."

The three strangers faced one another.

"They're not the enemy," Ember said.

"They're not *our* enemy," Anvil corrected. "But they might still be hostile. Falcon, what do we do?"

"I don't know!" Falcon snapped. "Nothing like this has happened before; how the hell would I have a contingency for this!"

"You're in charge of this team!" Ember snapped back. "That's *your job!*"

"That's right!" Anvil agreed. "You're the one who demanded to lead this, so *you* can figure this out!"

"Gaaaah, I can't concentrate with you two boneheads yelling at me! Shut your mouths so I can think of a plan!"

Elaethia's eyes flashed. The pendant around her neck hummed and sent a pulse of energy all around them. The gentle but firm shockwave buffeted the dust into the air, as well as shook the dirt ceiling. She remained silent as all three strangers stared at her in shock.

Shiro's voice came low and steady. "Here's what the plan is. You're going to give us Geran. Then we're going to kill you quickly as a token of appreciation. And then we're going to go into your city and kill that bastard you call an emperor!"

Falcon's eyes widened and then hardened. "Bold words. But that only complicates the situation. On the other hand, I now have a plan. You three are going to follow us. We'll be keeping the hostage in front with me and Ember. The three of you will get in order as follows: swordsman behind Ember, warrior behind him, mage after her, and Anvil in the rear. If one of you so much as trips in the wrong direction, your ranger friend and mage are going to be breathing through holes in their necks."

"You think we'll just follow that!" Lilian demanded.

"They aren't trying to disarm us," Shiro said. "Elaethia-sama, what do we do?"

The dragon hero exhaled, sending a slow cloud of frost into the room. "We shall follow them for now. If so much as a drop of our blood is spilled, the three of you will meet a twisted fate beyond your comprehension."

Falcon's eyes hardened as he hefted the unconscious Geran over his shoulders. "And I'll say the same to you. Now get in line. And no talking if you want all four of you to get out of this alive."

For over an hour the seven of them trudged through the underground tunnel system. All along its length were alternate tunnels and passageways. This was undoubtably a maze to confuse potential invaders. Occasional shakes from the ground above showered them with dirt and dust. The dim torch held by Ember lit the way as they twisted and turned their way through the earth. At the end of the path, they emerged into a wider underground room the size of the office back at the guild. A single steel door stood embedded in solid rock on the far wall. A closer look showed that it was not rock but laid brick. Falcon stepped up to the door and rapped on it with a deliberate pattern.

"Are you sure about this, Falcon?" Anvil asked. "We should have blindfolded them!"

"Do you want to lower your weapon and get close to them? I don't think so. Now shut up and keep watching them."

Suddenly a panel at eye level slid open as another figure looked into the room. They spoke in hushed voices, but Elaethia's dragon ears could hear every word.

"The hell?" the figure asked. "Falcon? What's going on?"

"We had a complication, and plans changed. Get everyone with a weapon on standby; we're bringing these four in!"

"Have you lost your mind? One of the golden rules, Falcon. No one comes back in but us!"

"No one else has threatened to kill the emperor before!"

The figure on the other side faltered. "They did? Those four?"

"Yeah, they did. Get everyone on alert over here and open the door!"

"Stars above, Falcon. Give us a minute."

"For Moon's sake, Mousetrap, hurry up! I only made it this far with some quick thinking, and they could call my bluff any second! I've only got one hostage here!"

Mousetrap slammed the panel shut. Elaethia could hear indistinct shouting and rummaging from the other side. Though muffled through the metal door, she could hear weapons being drawn and people charging in from several directions. The faint shouts got louder and louder in a clear manner of argument. After a couple of minutes, the panel slid open again

"You've really got a screw loose, Falcon!" Mousetrap snarled and spoke into the room. "But we're ready. I'm going to open the door. Sprint past me with the hostage and get the other three in the center. The rest of us will surround them."

"All right, all right we get it!" Ember shouted. "Just open the damn door!"

"Tch!" Mousetrap spat.

A few grinding and scraping noises could be heard from the other side until the steel door opened. Falcon burst forward and lugged Geran with him. Anvil and Ember herded the three adventurers inside, who were met by over a dozen weapons pointed at them. Swords, spears, shields, and knives all stood at the ready. Elaethia got a quick analysis of the room around her as the door slammed shut and locked behind them.

The entryway was large. Stone walls, floors, and ceiling surrounded them, along with heavy white bricks held together by mortar, archways leading into adjacent rooms, and carved pillars holding up the ceiling above. Inside were stalls, carts, small rooms, a long table, and sets of provisions set aside. The small rooms had no doors and contained only straw beds and hooks for belongings. It resembled nothing like a military encampment or a prison.

"Well?" Anvil demanded. "We got them in here, now what?"

"We have to wait for the boss!" Mousetrap snapped. He was an elven man in his late thirties with short black hair.

"What?" Ember demanded. "That could take hours!"

"Luckily the boss hasn't left yet. Snake went to get her, so sit tight. It shouldn't be more than a few minutes."

"Thank the heavens," Anvil sighed. "I thought we might be stuck here until tomorrow."

Falcon let out a relieved chuckle. "We really did luck out. Once the boss gets here, we'll asse—"

He was cut short as the ranger he was holding suddenly twisted and struck him under the chin. Falcon dropped his knife and was about to fall back when Geran lashed out his right arm and wrapped it around Falcon's neck. Geran's left hand flew from behind his back and held his swordbreaker to his opponent's throat. He walked backward to join his companions near the entrance. The group of strangers only choked and froze in silence as they watched.

"All right, *my* turn," the ranger said, glaring. "If you guys want to keep your buddy's throat inside his neck, you'll do *exactly* as we say!"

The enemies around them looked back and forth at one another. Most of them shook nervously now that all four of the strangers in their base stood firm and confident. They had numbers on the intimidating foreigners, but not the skill. They had lost their only leverage, and with it all control.

"Falcon, you complete idiot," Mousetrap said as he quivered and held his sword shakily. "I knew I shouldn't have listened to you; now you've gone and killed us all!"

"You bastard," Falcon growled at Geran. "I knew you were asleep for an awfully long time."

"Should have paid less attention to my friends and more to my breathing patterns." Geran smirked. "Not that it would have mattered. I've trained for years to combat these situations. I hope you didn't think you were the first person to catch me."

Lilian grinned. "Look at 'em shake. This'll be easier than the time we wiped that goblin nest."

Shiro joined the satisfaction. "Is the entirety of this country's forces so timid? This will be *too* easy. This isn't war; this is sport."

Elaethia sighed. "To think I trained with the guild, Jörgen, and Frossgar for all those years to meet an enemy like this. I should have challenged Rychus sooner."

A woman's voice broke into the room. "What the hell is going on down here!"

Everyone turned. In the entryway stood a dwarven woman. At first she seemed only tall enough to be a child. But her dense muscles and pronounced figure told otherwise. Her caramel skin was covered in grease and soot. A grungy apron with overalls clung to her muscled body. Thick leather gloves covered her hands, while heavy boots connected with the overalls. Her curly brown hair was pulled behind her head, with steel-and-leather goggles resting on her brow. The once panicked group suddenly regained their composure at her arrival.

"B-boss!" Mousetrap stuttered.

"Can it!" she shouted. "I'm supposed to go report to Emperor Rychus about the development of the recording devices, and all of a sudden I hear about Falcon bringing in *hostages?* If you're telling me that in the time it took for Snake to find me and bring me down here you lot got completely overturned … stars above, that's pathetic. Ember, care to explain?"

The brunette human cleared her throat. "We captured that hooded one holding Falcon, and the other three chased after us. We almost got away, but they smashed through the Deadgate! We didn't have a choice but to negotiate!"

The boss raised an eyebrow. "They *smashed* the Deadgate? And what conclusion did you reach?"

"We haven't," Anvil said. "They said they were trying to kill the emperor."

The dwarven woman eyed the adventurers. "Kill Emperor Rychus? Are you four serious? Pick your answer carefully, as your life depends on it now."

Elaethia's eyes hardened. "I am not trying to kill Rychus. I *will* kill him."

"Really?" the boss held her gaze. "In that case, you'd better tell me your name."

"Elaethia Frossgar. I was born here as Elaethia Soliano. My father led an assault against Rychus but failed. I am here to avenge him and finish what he started."

The boss faltered. "S-Soliano? Your old man was Marcus …?"

"I have given you my name. Now give me yours, so I may tell Rychus who sent me to him."

The dwarf chuckled. "My, my. Well, in that case, the name's Hailey Foot. I'm the chief engineer under Rychus's command."

"B-boss!" Mousetrap gasped.

She waved her hand. "It's all right, doorman. After all, these foreigners might be the magic bullet we need."

"As if we'd help one of Rychus's toadies!" Lilian spat.

"Toadies?" Hailey laughed. "Oh, you guys don't get it! Does this really look like an engineer workshop to you? A hidden, run-down annex under the edge of Paragon? The chief engineer is my cover story. Well, for the most part. I *am* his chief engineer."

"Then what is your true identity?" Elaethia asked.

"Hailey Foot is the name I was given at birth, but I go by a different name when I'm working my real job."

"Get to the point already!" Geran demanded.

"And don't think you can pull a fast one on us!" Shiro added.

Hailey folded her arms. "You can call me Ash. And I'm the head of the underground resistance."

"How can she say that and just *leave?*" Lilian wailed, throwing her hands in the air.

Mousetrap put his sword in a barrel near the stairs. "Didn't you hear her? She's got a meeting with Rychus regarding her advancements. She'll be back tonight or early tomorrow."

"Yeah that doesn't exactly fill us with confidence," Geran said, eyeing the elf. "There's a lot not to trust here. But putting most of that aside, how do we know she didn't go to rat us out?"

"'Cause then we'd be found out and destroyed," Ember said from a stool next to a counter. "Rychus has been after us for over a year. We've lasted longer than any other of our predecessors, and he's hopping mad about it."

Elaethia tilted her head. "Predecessors?"

"Yeah. We aren't the first group to stand up to Rychus and smuggle people out. For as long as he's been a tyrant, there have been groups trying to overthrow him. After a couple decades, it dawned on us that that was impossible. So instead we decided to help citizens escape Paragon and eventually Armini as a whole. *Our* group only lasted this long because we learned from the mistakes of the previous ones."

Shiro's eyes widened. "And none of them lasted more than a year?"

"None of them lasted more than a month or two," Anvil said.

Geran held his hands up in a T-shape. "Woah, woah, time out! You mean to tell me you've lasted almost a year longer than any other resistance has for the last, what, *century*?"

Falcon nodded. "About that long, yeah."

Mousetrap took over. "We're the longest-lasting organization after Major Soliano led a direct assault against Rychus himself fourteen years ago. The fighting lasted only a day, but there was two months of prep work beforehand, and a week's worth of aftershock before everything was stamped out. Bottom line? Everything we have now is all thanks to the boss and her position. Without her, we'd be long gone."

"My father planned the attack for two months?" Elaethia marveled. "I never knew. He never gave any indication to us."

"Marcus was planning on it for almost a year. He didn't start working on it until two months prior to the assault. He took himself and every holy magician he could to kick down Rychus's door."

Shiro perked up. "Holy magicians? Why them? Why not also mages and warriors?"

"Couldn't tell you. Marcus was always thinking two steps ahead of everyone else. The only reason he lost was because Rychus was able to flat-out overpower him. But the holy magicians did some considerable damage to him. They hurt him more than anyone ever had before. That gave the rest of us a week to flee or go into hiding."

Lilian made a face. "A bunch of priests did a better job than every other class? That doesn't sit right; what'd they do? What even *is* Rychus?"

Falcon shook his head. "We don't know. At first we thought he was some crazy anatomy magician. But after Marcus's assault, we couldn't hold on to that notion. All I know is that Rychus flat-out banned holy magic after that, going so far as to killing all priests, with the exception of his chief advisor. Marcus caused a shift in tides that Armini hadn't seen in a century. Was he really your old man, Elaethia?"

She nodded and pulled out the golden pendant from between her breasts. The members of the resistance gathered around to look at it.

"Well I'll be," Mousetrap murmured.

"No kidding," Falcon agreed.

"What? What is it?" Anvil pushed past.

"That's the pendant Marcus always wore. Said it was an important part of his family that he refused to take off. I thought it was odd that he wasn't wearing it the day of the attack. I always wondered what happened to it."

Elaethia's eyes brightened. "You were there? You knew my father? What was he like? Was he as great a soldier as you say?"

Mousetrap nodded. "Damn right he was. Smart as a whip, too. Marcus came to us the day of the assault and took over like he had been in charge since day one. Frankly, without his plan, nobody would have survived. I don't even think we'd be here. On top of that, I think he was able to cut his way to Rychus by himself, with only the priests to back him up. Marcus was an imperial officer for a reason."

"My father …" Elaethia could only tremble with tears forming in her eyes. This was the legacy set in motion for her, founded by the man she adored, who had none of the resources she did. She could not fail him.

"How come you recognize it, Falcon?" Geran asked the pointy-nosed human.

"It's been the symbol of every resistance group since," he responded. "We're the first not to use it."

Shiro frowned. "So much for honoring the tradition of those before you."

"No, you don't understand," Ember explained. "It's because of things like that that every group before us was discovered and uprooted. We leave no trail. Everything we do is secret and random. Our routes, targets, times, and movements are completely spontaneous. We can't give Rychus any sort of leeway or heads-up regarding our actions. We don't engage the enemy, spread propaganda, use scouts from our ranks, or show ourselves to the public. We don't even have a name."

"Well, technically we do," Anvil said.

"Yeah, but we didn't come up with it, so it doesn't count."

Mousetrap shrugged. "The Legion started calling us the Echo out of the blue one day, and it stuck. Nothing we can do about it."

"Anyway," Falcon continued. "We operate on a strict protocol with no give. A 'my way or the highway' approach. We scout out families that we believe we can safely smuggle out, and we move on them. A team will show up at their house in the middle of the night with zero warning. They're told to pack everything they can carry, and we move. If they make it to this room, that's their first and only pause for breath. Once they're ready, or we need to clear them out, we give them as many provisions as they can carry, and take them out through the portal. That's what we call the door you came in through. After that, there is no returning under any circumstance.

We never let them go back for anything. We've actually had to kill a few that tried to force their way back or make a run for it after chickening out."

"You four are the only ones outside our group that have actually come *in* through the portal," Mousetrap said, almost grudgingly.

Elaethia looked around the room. "Then why are you telling us all of this?"

Mousetrap sighed. "Because we have no choice but to trust each other now. The fact you all risked your lives to rescue your friend there, and haven't killed us all yet, proves you aren't with the Legion. If we haven't made it obvious yet, you guys terrify us. Just by looking at you, we can tell we have a snowball's chance in hell against you."

Shiro leaned against a pillar. "What of that phrase Falcon said back in the tunnel. 'Your Blood Will Make the Grass Grow,' was it?"

"That's an altered version of the Legion's motto. If someone under Rychus's command hears that, they give themselves away through facial reactions. They're *stupidly* bound to the correct way of saying it. Whether because of fear or honor, they can't seem to bear hearing it differently."

Falcon nodded. "Your companions' reaction was enough to prove you weren't Legion. But I didn't know what you were, so I couldn't trust you. I *still* don't know what you are. Except for your warrior there. She's proven herself Arminian."

"Guess it's our turn for introductions," Geran sighed. "I'm Geran, the mage is Lilian. She and I are both Linderrian adventurers. Shiro there is—"

"Woah, woah, hold up," Anvil said, and he put his hands up. "You guys are Linderrian? What are you doing *here?*"

Lilian folded her arms behind her head. "Elaethia's gonna pick a fight with Rychus. We're tagging along."

"So you just, willingly, left safety for hell on earth, to fight Rychus? *Why?*"

"Dunno. Friendship, boredom, adventure. Any mix of the three, really."

"I don't … *what!* What even *are* Linderrians?"

Shiro raised his hand. "I'm not Linderrian."

Falcon snapped his fingers. "I thought he looked odd. I've heard of another country that's even farther north than Linderry. You're *really* far from home."

"Um, no, I'm not from Svarengel. I'm Osakyotan."

All members of the Echo stared at him.

"What's an Osakyotan?" Mousetrap asked.

"Someone from Osakyota. That's the nation I was born and raised in. I came to Linderry because my sister was mur—"

"Wait, wait, wait," Ember held out a hand. "So there *isn't* another country above Linderry?"

"There is." The samurai nodded. "That's Svarengel. Osakyota is an island nation to the east of Linderry, across the ocean."

The room went completely silent.

"What?" Shiro looked around. "What'd I say?"

"Show me," Falcon suddenly spoke up.

"Huh?"

"I said show me!" he demanded. The human grabbed a parchment and charcoal and slammed them on the bar. "Draw it! All of it! As accurate as you can, show me what you're talking about!"

Geran held his hands up and unslung his rucksack. "Easy, man, easy. I've got a map right here. Got one drawn by the best cartographers in Linderry."

"And this is accurate? You swear on your *life* this is accurate?"

"Yeah, absolutely, but why the—"

"Snake!" the elf shouted over his shoulder. "The map! Get the map over here right now!"

"Yes sir!" a young demibear girl called, and she disappeared up a flight of stairs.

Lilian cocked an ear. "Odd name for a cute girl like her."

"We all use code names, mage," Ember said. "Almost everyone here except Mousetrap and a few others have a life and family outside this. You didn't think my name was actually Ember, did you?"

The demicat shrugged. "I mean, who knows? You guys are foreign; I don't know your culture."

"But that would be such an odd name to give your child!"

"Tell that to Shiro."

"Hey!" the samurai interjected.

Falcon looked up. "Can we copy this map, Galen? Please?"

"It's Geran," he corrected. "And yeah, sure. Just don't mark it up or damage it."

"Not in a thousand years …" Mousetrap murmured as he looked over the large roll of paper with a lens. "This map, if as accurate as you say, is *priceless!*"

"If you're gonna copy it, then make two—one for you, one for us."

The dark-haired elf nodded firmly. "Deal!"

"I got the map, Mousetrap, sir!" Snake called as she rushed in with a scroll in her hands. The little demibear stood on her toes to place it next to the elf.

He patted her on the head. "Good girl. Now all of you scram! I need absolute focus here. Ember, Anvil, can you show our guests around? Limit them to here, the latrine, the meeting room, and the dorms. Ash can decide to reveal more when she gets back. Make them feel at home. We've got a serious asset here, and I don't want to lose them."

Lilian flicked an ear. "Y'know, it kinda defeats the purpose if you say that right in front of us."

Andrew Rydberg

Sixth Era. 140. Miyan 31.

"I don't know what else to call it besides the stars aligning and the heavens hitting me over the head with a sign," Ash said as she rubbed her eyes with the palms of her hands.

She, Falcon, Anvil, Ember, Snake, and a few other members of the Echo sat around a large table in the meeting room. Cataclysm also had seats around the circular stone slab. All had patiently waited for Ash's return from the previous night and were ready to hear the news as she fondled a small vial with an opaque liquid in it around her neck.

"How did the meeting go, boss?" Falcon asked.

She held out a thumb and index finger. "He's this close to coming down to my shop and giving a personal inspection. If I work fast enough on the projects he assigns me, I can't keep acting on our behalf. Not to mention it might even *undermine* us. If I don't have anything substantial for him in two days, he's going to lose it. Stars above, I was so nervous. I was about ready to down my lethal potion here."

Anvil regarded his dwarven leader. "So we have to finish the image-recording device in two days?"

"And begin mass production and distribution. He wants them on every street corner."

Ember balked. "*Every* street corner?"

"Every street corner," Ash confirmed. "Then he wants me to develop smaller ones to put inside every shop, and eventually every house."

Lilian ran her fingers through her hair. "What the hell …"

"Talk about a violation of privacy," Geran muttered.

"Privacy is a luxury, free will an illusion, obedience a necessity," Anvil grumbled. "Words straight from the mouth of his great imperial majesty."

Ash continued. "He's degraded so far from when I was first placed under his charge. The more powerful he becomes, the deeper he slips into insanity."

Shiro leaned forward. "He's getting stronger?"

"Bit by bit, day by day, victim by victim," Ember said.

"What does that mean? Elaethia asked.

"It used to be that he would kill everyone who defied him. But after Marcus, he's been doing … something else …" Ash shuddered. "The victims enter his throne room alive and healthy, and leave as dry, mummified corpses. The only other living person who's knows what happens is his chief advisor, Nurelon."

"What do you think is happening in there?" Geran asked.

Falcon shook his head. "We don't know for sure. All we can tell is that he takes the life force, strength, and soul from his victim."

Lilian perked up. "You've seen his magic firsthand?"

"Only myself and Mousetrap," Ash answered. "The aura and spells he channels and casts originate from and around his body and then return to him. It's nothing anyone has ever seen. It's like a haze … or a fog. His attacks are like tendrils or vines. And that color! A bloodred energy with a warping black aura in and around it. It makes my blood chill just thinking about it."

Falcon shook his head. "It boggles the mind, too. No magic we know of is bloodred like that and seeps into the magician's body. Nobody has ever seen it before."

The members of Cataclysm looked at one another.

"That red magic sounds a lot like the ring we found in the Enchanter's Imperium," Shiro recalled. "Like that glow it gave off before it activated."

Lilian scratched her ear. "Yeah, but it wasn't on the scale they're describing."

"But the description matches almost perfectly," Geran pointed out.

Elaethia rubbed her chin. "And it enabled flight, not the devouring of the essence of another individual."

"What are you talking about?" Ash cut in.

Geran described the ring they had discovered on their quest for Arthur Veldwig. He started with their entrance to the ancient ruin, giving every detail up to returning the ring to the Arcane Sage. He was interrupted several times by the Arminians, who would shoot up from their chairs as they heard the astounding feats of each guild member. By the time the ranger finished the story, even Ash was on her feet, although the dwarf had to stand on her chair to be above the large stone table.

"*Hold up!*" Ember shouted. "A *leviathan?* You four killed a *leviathan?*"

The other members of the Echo began to shout their own questions.

"Elaethia is a *dragon hero?*"

"I thought dragons were a myth!"

"How did you fight atronachs?"

"There's a whole ancient ruin up there with all kinds of magic information?"

"You guys have some *crazy* strong potions!"

Ash slammed a fist into the table to quiet them. "Okay, but how does that connect with Rychus? You said it's the same type of magic, right?"

"We think so," Geran stated.

Falcon groaned. "I still think you're stupid for giving that ring away just for honor."

"We got a pretty neato reward for it too," Lilian said with a grin. "Besides a *ton* of cash, we all got a piece of enchanted gear."

Anvil pointed at them with a shaking finger. "You guys have an enchanted item?"

"We have one each," Shiro corrected him.

Silence filled the room. One of the other member's legs buckled as she fell to the floor. Ash shakily lowered herself back into her seat.

"What … what are they?" the dwarf asked in a small voice.

"My necklace can send forth a burst of energy and a magic-nulling wave," Elaethia started.

"I've got a necklace, too," Geran said. "Although mine makes it hard for people to notice me once I put it on."

"I got a ring that absorbs incoming magic and turns the magical energy back into my own reserves!" Lilian said, beaming.

Shiro drew his sword. "This is Seraph. Its blade has been enchanted so that it will go through inorganic material and only cut organic. That's made it harder to use it in the way that I'm comfortable with, though. Grandfather Ryuuki forged it from the same mountains where my ancestors—"

"Stars above, you talk too much, man!" Anvil laughed. "Forget where it was made; that's unbelievable! I can hardly believe what I just heard!"

"This is a groundbreaking asset!" Ember agreed. "Legionnaire armor is too thick for our gladii to penetrate, but Seraph would just ignore it!"

"Shiro can't fight an entire army by himself," Falcon pointed out.

"Just watch him," Geran said with a grin. "Besides, he's not alone. Lilian can blow them all away, and Elaethia would just wade right through them."

Anvil raised an eyebrow. "What about you?"

Geran shrugged. "I'm a ranger. I just call shots and organize the plans."

"Either way, that's something in and of itself. Hey, boss, what's your take?"

"My take?" Ash sat with her chin resting on her interlocking fingers. The dwarf stared back and forth between the adventurers, deep in thought.

Falcon smiled. "I haven't seen that look in your eye in a while. What plan are you formulating?"

She held up a finger. "Hold that thought. Are all Linderrians as strong as you four?"

Lilian flashed her famous grin. "Not by a long shot."

"Well then," the dwarf sighed. "I guess we can make do with you four if we have to. But maybe we can get some help from your friends up north."

"What are you thinking?" Geran asked, and he caught her gaze.

Ash met it. "I'm thinking I can start putting together an endgame."

Chapter 24
Nemesis

Sixth Era. 140. Jinum 2.

"No way," Falcon murmured as he shakily held the plans Ash handed out. "No way, no how. Did she hit her head or something? Did Rychus hypnotize her? What in the absolute hell is this plan?"

Lilian shrugged and handed her copy to Shiro. "Looks good to me. It's right up our alley, really. Geran's gonna be the only one with an issue."

"I don't think so," the samurai said. "He *did* help come up with it, after all."

Ember sighed and slumped into a chair. "You guys really *are* crazy. Thank the heavens the rest of your country isn't like you."

Elaethia tilted her head. "This is a fairly standard battle plan for Linderrians."

Falcon threw his hands up. "A surprise *frontal assault* on Rychus *himself*?"

Shiro nodded. "It makes sense."

"Yup!" Lilian chirped. "Why bother wasting time and energy slogging through his army and city when we can just cut right to the chase?"

Ember rubbed her fingers through her hair. "Gaaaah, you make it sound almost like a game when you say it like that! Can't you take this more seriously?"

"Don't mistake her positive attitude for joking around, Ember-san!" Shiro assured the woman. "Lilian always looks on the bright side."

"I've never met anyone with that kind of optimism; I'll give her that," Falcon sighed. "I know you guys are amazing and all, but I feel left out. All of this is just a lead-up to getting Rychus against you four."

Anvil made a face. "Honestly, I think I'm fine with that. I don't want to fight him at all. If these guys can and will, I say let 'em."

"I am sure you all would be of aid to us," Elaethia assured him.

Ember shook her head. "Nuh-uh. Anvil and I are the best fighters here, and not even we can stand up to legionnaires. We'll keep them off your back as best we can, but even then we'd like to leave the rest to you adventurers. It would be suicide for us to try to fight him with you."

"Not to mention you might get in Elaethia-sama's way," Shiro thought aloud, rubbing his chin. The three members of the Echo looked rather hurt by that.

"Nice one, Shiro," Lilian said, glaring.

The samurai waved his hands apologetically. "Ah … ah, no! That's not what I meant! Elaethia-sama emits a powerful aura of dragon frost when she's serious, and it would hurt you all as well! Even *we* can't stand near her."

Falcon breathed a sigh of relief. "Why don't we just have her fight him alone then?"

"That would be unwise," Elaethia said. "While I am confident in my power and abilities, we have very little information on Rychus. It would be safer to overwhelm him with numbers as opposed to strength."

Lilian beamed. "That's right! I intercept and redirect his magic, Shiro dices him up in his armor, and Elaethia keeps him occupied by whaling on him like a madman."

"I do not intend to lose myself in the moment. I will maintain discipline and control in my strikes."

"You *know* what I *meant!*"

"What about Geran?" Falcon asked.

"He's with Mousetrap-san and Ash-sama," Shiro reminded him. "They're still making and preparing plans."

"No, I mean during the battle."

"Dunno." Lilian shrugged. "Probably nerd stuff. He likes to observe the fighting and make calls and change tactics."

"Most likely," Shiro agreed. "He's very smart, and he knows us well. He moves the three of us around like shogi pieces, putting us in strategic positions."

Anvil blinked. "Shogi?"

"It's kinda like chess, but Osakyotan," Lilian explained.

"Then why didn't he … ah, never mind."

Ember rested her chin on her palm. "I still don't understand why Geran won't bring that letter to your guild."

"As we said, that would take too long," Elaethia said. "It would most likely be a full year before he could return, convince the guild to aid us, and come back with all those who are willing. Even then there may be none who will help."

"But isn't that what you guys do? Kill things and solve problems to make the world a better place?"

Elaethia shook her head. "Many do not share the same views of the adventurer lifestyle as we do. Most of them use it as an occupation. They will not fight unless there is a reward, and no reward is worth their lives."

"Rychus's treasury has *got* to be chock full of gold," Ember protested. "If they help us win, it's theirs for all I care!"

Lilian perked up. "How much gold we talkin'?"

Anvil ignored her. "If we focus entirely on buttering Rychus up, that would get him off our backs. We can use that time to get your friends down here."

Falcon shook his head. "Those projects are specifically designed to uproot us. If we go full focus into those, we'll be discovered long before then."

Ember groaned and slumped into her hands. "It's just so frustrating. There are hundreds of seasoned fighters and magicians up there, and we can't ask them for help."

"So how do you plan to get to Rychus?" Falcon asked.

Lilian cocked an ear. "Can't we just kick in his front door?"

"Wouldn't that ruin the element of surprise?"

"How?"

"Well you'd have to get past all his soldiers and staff in the castle without being noticed, which is impossible. Except for maybe Geran."

"And he wouldn't be able to take on Rychus by himself," Ember said.

"Do we have any information regarding the interior of the castle?" Elaethia asked.

"Ask Ash," Falcon said, "although she's mostly been restricted to the throne room and workshops. The only other one of us who's been in the castle any time recently was Snake."

"The little girl?" Lilian recalled.

Anvil nodded. "Her family was part of the kitchen staff, and they used her for delivering meals to the other servants. She knows the servant quarters fairly well, but not so much for the upper levels. Besides, she's only eight, so we can't expect her to give us high detail."

"You said she had no family," Shiro said.

Ember played with her thumbs. "Not anymore. Her parents served something to Nurelon, and he got sick from it. We're pretty sure it was bad meat or the like, as everybody else got sick, but Nurelon was convinced they tried to poison him. He had them quartered, but they were able to get Snake out alive."

"Stars above …" Lilian exhaled. "At least they let her go."

"They didn't. She was scheduled for the chopping block. As the legionnaires burst into the kitchen to arrest her parents, they managed to get her out by throwing her down the garbage chute."

Shiro clenched Seraph's hilt. "There is no death I can imagine that would be fit for these monsters."

"Mr. Falcon!" a small voice called from the doorway.

He turned around. "Right here, sweetie."

"Miss Ash said our friends would want these. Mr. Geran made them." Snake trotted into the room with a stack of cards. The little demibear handed them to him, who looked over them in turn.

"Fake citizenship forms." He rubbed his chin and gave them back to her. "And very well done. Why don't you give these to them personally?"

The little girl mumbled quietly under her breath and shifted her feet. She wrung her hands together and slowly looked up to the adventurers with big eyes. After a brief moment of eye contact with Elaethia, she whimpered and hid behind Falcon. A second later, she peeked out from behind his shirt.

Anvil laughed and stood up. "It's okay; they're nice. Come on; I'll do it with you.

The big human gently took her hand and walked her up to Lilian. The mage smiled gently and knelt to Snake. The demibear had soft blue eyes and curly blond hair that rested lazily down to her chin. She clutched a hand to her chest with the cards. After a second, she shoved them forward, looking away with closed eyes.

"H-here …" she whispered.

"Oh, honey," Lilian gently took the cards and put them in her pouch. "You're so cute; you don't need to be shy. I'm Lilian; what's your name?"

The girl slowly took her hand back. "S-Snake."

Lilian smiled warmly. "That's a cool nickname. Did you choose it yourself?"

Snake shook her head. "Mr. Falcon chose it."

"Do you like it?"

She pondered for a moment. "It's okay. It's not cute, but Mr. Falcon says it's important. I want to be helpful, so I work real hard for him."

"He's lucky to have you. How did he find you?"

Snake looked up to Falcon, who nudged her in approval.

"Mr. Falcon was helping some people run away when he found me in the trash. He told me to stay quiet and said he'd come back. He, Miss Ember, and Mr. Anvil took me back here. They gave me a bath and new clothes, and let me eat as much as I want. I know Mama and Papa are gone, but Echo saved me, so I stay here to help them."

Shiro knelt next to her. "That's so noble, Snake-chan! You never gave up, did you? You're doing your best and working hard. Your family would be proud of you."

Snake smiled a little and nodded.

Lilian beamed. "Aw, look at you, Shiro! I never knew you were good with kids."

"Um …" Snake whispered and shuffled her feet. "You can use magic, right, Miss Lilian?"

Lilian grinned. "You bet! Shiro and Elaethia, too."

"Can … Can I see?"

"Sorry, sweetie, my magic is a bit strong to use inside. Oh! I know a cool trick."

The mage held out her hand and channeled a spell into it. The air began to tingle and smell of ozone as her fingers started to crackle. Purple arcs of electricity danced between her extended fingers, and sparks jumped up and around from the palm of her hand. Snake watched with wide eyes and an open mouth as the tiny violet tendrils of energy zigzagged around the mage's open hand. The demibear gasped in awe as she leaned forward, entranced by the magic. A single spark leaped from Lilian's middle finger and suddenly zapped Snake on the nose.

"Woah!" The little girl doubled back and clutched her face. Lilian instantly canceled her spell and was about to rush forward when Snake suddenly giggled into her hands. Her eyes began to water, but a smile was still planted on her lips.

"Are you okay?" Shiro asked and leaned forward. "Didn't that hurt?"

"Mhm." Snake nodded. "But it was so pretty. And it's my fault for getting close. But now I know magic is real, because it touched me."

Lilian smiled. "What a bright kid."

"How do you do that, Miss Lilian?" Snake asked. "Is it your hat? I always saw pictures of magicians wearing pointy hats like that."

"No, silly, we're born with it. Just like you were born with pretty blond hair and blue eyes."

"Oh. Why do you all wear pointy hats?"

Lilian paused and then shrugged. "Because they look cool."

"I think so too!"

"Do you want to wear it?"

Snake's eyes shot open. "Can I? Can I really?"

Lilian flashed her signature grin as she took the wide-brimmed hat off her head and planted it onto Snake's. The cone fell loosely over the little girl's head and caught right on the bridge of her nose. All that showed was the demibear's mouth, which was wide open in an enormous smile. She fumbled around for the brim, found it, and pushed up so she could see. She was met by the grins and chuckles of the adventurers and members of Echo around her. Snake's expression somehow got even brighter.

"Well, look at you," Anvil laughed. "You could be a proper mage."

"Mmh!" Snake nodded fervently. "Can you teach me, Miss Lilian?"

"Tell you what," the mage replied warmly. "If you find out that you can use magic and want to use the same as mine, I'll teach you anything you want to know."

"Yes ma'am!"

"Then I have one other condition. You've got to tell me your real name."

Snake paused and quickly looked up to Falcon.

He nodded. "You live down here with us, so you don't really need to protect your name. And they've proven themselves trustworthy. Go ahead."

Snake looked back to Lilian with a grin and held out the hat. "I'm Celeste!"

Lilian grinned right back and put her hat on her head. "A pretty little name for a pretty little girl. All right, Celeste. Once this is all over, we'll see if you can use magic."

"Okay! Do your best, Miss Lilian!"

She patted the demibear fondly on the head. "I will. Just for you."

Ember leaned in. "So? Are you all friends now?"

"Yep!" Snake giggled.

"Even with Miss Elaethia?"

"She's still scary, but if Miss Lilian says so, I'll be her friend!"

The dragon hero tilted her head. "I am scary?"

Lilian gave her a sideways look. "You still can't tell?"

"I am unable to see my own face."

"Yeah, but you can see how others react to you."

"They do not look the same as those who fear me."

"Elaethia-sama, that's because those who fear you face your axe and magic," Shiro said.

Elaethia nodded. "I see. Geran had mentioned it takes others time to become accustomed to me. I shall work on my image."

"Good luck with that," Falcon laughed. "Snake, honey, could you take this note to Mr. Geran or Miss Ash? It's letting them know we got the cards and are ready when they are, as well as some other plans and stuff."

"Okay, Mr. Falcon!"

Snake nodded and took the paper. She trotted to the archway leading upstairs, turned back, smiled, and bounded up the steps.

Snake ran into Ash's office, which was actually just an old, repurposed wine cellar. The little demibear looked around and clutched the note in her hand. The boss was nowhere to be seen, and neither was Mr. Geran. She tugged on a lock of her curly hair and wondered where they might be. Mr. Geran wasn't with the other three new people, and she didn't know where else he could be.

Miss Ash was usually in one of three places when in the hideout: her office, the planning room, or the workshop. She knew Miss Ash might be working on the machines Emperor Rychus had wanted. She decided to check there. She dashed out the door and to the stairs. Snake was rounding up the spiral staircase when she suddenly bumped into someone coming down. She began to fall backward, but a quick hand shot out and caught her wrist. Snake looked up and recognized who bumped into her.

"Oh, Mr. Chase!"

"Hi there, Snake. Sorry I didn't see you there; are you okay?" he asked.

Chase was a friendly human with short, curly black hair and a matching beard. He wore tan working pants and a deep blue coat with a hood. A pair of black-rimmed spectacles sat in front of his intelligent brown eyes. He was of an average build, but with firm hands and nimble fingers. Chase usually kept to himself but always had great stories.

"I'm okay!" She nodded as she planted herself on the steps. "What are you doing, Mr. Chase? You don't usually come out of the workshop."

"Ah, I'm actually looking for my calipers that I let the boss borrow for one of her new potions. I'm going to her office to get them back."

"Oh, she's not there. I thought she was in the workshop."

"Not right now, she isn't. You don't know where she is?"

"Mm-mm." She shook her head. "But I'm looking for her too! Or Mr. Geran."

"One of the Linderrians? Huh. I'd love to help, but I think I'm at a breakthrough right now, and I don't want to stay away for long. Could you ask her about my calipers when you find her?"

"Yes sir, Mr. Chase!"

The human laughed and tousled her hair. "Good girl. I'd like to get this project done soon."

"Okay!" Snake nodded. "Good luck, Mr. Chase!"

"You too, Snake!" The engineer waved as he went back upstairs to the workshop.

The demibear paused and scratched her ear. She would have to wait for Miss Ash to come back. She frowned. That could take a long time, but maybe that was okay. Snake had something that she wanted to try really badly, but she needed to do it somewhere secret. The only place in the hideout that was empty was Miss Ash's office, but that was no good. If the boss found her, she would be in *super* big trouble.

There was only one place. Outside. It was risky. *Really* risky. But she wanted to try it so badly. *It should be okay, right?* Snake had been outside for errands and food before. This was pretty much the same thing, and she wasn't even going anywhere. Just a quick in and out. Nothing long at all, just a few seconds. After all, that's how long it took Miss Lilian to do it.

Snake tiptoed to the one exit she knew she could come in and out of, and she glanced carefully around to make sure nobody noticed her. Sneaking as quietly as she could, she got to her destination on the other side of the base. She dashed into a dried-up well and carefully grabbed onto the ladder that led up to the boarded-off hole at the top. The old wooden ladder creaked only slightly under her tiny body. The blond girl clambered up, hand over hand, all the way up.

Sunlight poured through the holes and cracks in the cover, dotting her vision as she got to the top. With a push, the trapdoor moved aside, and she emerged into the daylight.

Snake poked her eyes over the brim of the old well. She took a quick look around and then sighed in relief as she saw she was alone. This would be easy. She left the hatch open and hopped to the far side of the stone structure so she wasn't visible from the street. The secret entrance was surrounded on three sides by a sheer cobblestone wall, and a side street on the other. People rarely came by here since the well was dry and this part of Paragon was abandoned. Now she could try in peace.

Snake held out her right hand, palm up and fingers spread. She closed her eyes and thought really hard about what she wanted to do. She imagined everything in her head, down to the tiniest detail she could recall, remembering exactly what Miss Lilian did. Snake didn't know whether she had magic. She had never tried using it, but something inside her bubbled whenever she heard of it. Breathing in slowly, she exhaled and pushed her will into her hand.

Her fingers began to tingle. She opened her eyes to see tiny purple sparks crackle in between her fingers. A wide smile broke on her lips as she felt a new sensation in her body begin to change. She was beginning to use a type of energy she had never felt before. She honed in on it and pushed everything she could into her hands with all her might. A sudden surge and a metallic tinkling sound whined in the air. A purple glow illuminated the walls around her.

Snake's eyes shot open. Her palm erupted into purple arcs of writhing tendrils. Electric bolts of violet lightning swarmed around her, crackling in the air and lighting up the alley. She screamed. She flailed her tingling hand around and kicked away, trying to escape from her own spell. Snake squealed in terror and ran to the sandy road, burying her raging hand in the dust. The ground glowed brightly through the particles in the air, the loud crackling only slightly dampened. It wasn't working. Her tears dripped to the dry ground as she felt the source of energy burn away until it was dried up and gone. Finally her hand stopped sparking and returned to normal. Snake sat back, pulled her knees to her chest, and bawled.

"There!" a sudden male voice bellowed. "That girl right there—she used magic!"

Snake shot her eyes up and met the gaze of an imperial soldier. It was a sight that meant only fear and death: a red tunic, bronze chest plate, and drawn gladius. She shrieked again and tried to scramble away, but it was too late. The legionnaire bore down on her, wrapped a crushing arm around her waist that squeezed the breath out of her, and hoisted her into the air. Snake pounded on the man as hard as she could, but he didn't seem to notice.

"Altir, do you have her?" a second voice called down.

"Yeah. Little runt blew herself out, so she can't even defend herself."

"Easy pickings. Where'd she come from?"

"No clue. I found her just in the road. No sign of where she came from."

Snake gasped. *The well! I left it open!* If they saw that, they would go down, and the Echo would be found. She tried to turn and look, but the legionnaire held her so she couldn't see.

"What's the plan with that one?" the second voice asked.

"Going right to His Majesty. Captain said he only needed one more magician to be ready to launch his campaign. This little brat's gonna be the last drop."

"That scrawny thing? He'd hardly find her more than a snack."

"The magic compensates. Once she's sucked dry, he'll be ready."

Tears poured from the little demibear. She'd ruined it. She'd ruined everything. All the plans Miss Ash had been making. All the time Miss Lilian and her friends had spent. All the work Mr. Falcon had done. The legionnaires were going to find their hideout and destroy it, and then Emperor Rychus was going to eat her and begin his evil plan. As the legionnaire marched her up the trail toward the castle, she took one final look at the well to say good-bye to the people that saved her life, taking the opportunity to apologize to her friends that had trusted her. Through her blurred vision, she saw that the hatch was now closed.

"*Fuck!*" Geran screamed as he landed at the bottom of the dried-up well and punted a moldy bucket against the wall. "*Ash!*"

The ranger sprinted down a hallway and down the spiral staircase. He rounded the corner sharply and nearly collided with the dwarven woman.

"What?" she demanded. "What happened?"

"They got Snake!"

"*What!*"

"I thought she was looking shifty, so I trailed her. She sneaked off to go practice magic, freaked out, and alerted a patrol!"

Ash's face blanched. "By the Sun and Moon. Where is she? Why didn't you stop her!"

"I didn't know what she was up to until it was too late! I followed her because she was looking suspicious. As soon as I heard her scream, I climbed after her. Then I heard the soldiers, and I had to … Damn it all to *hell!* How could I have known what the girl was thinking! I thought you said you were the only magician!"

"I thought so too! Snake never told us she could use magic."

Geran put a hand on his forehead. "Looks like she didn't know either until two minutes ago."

"What is happening?" Elaethia appeared next to them. Shiro, Lilian, Falcon, Ember, and Anvil were with her.

"Snake got grabbed by soldiers after using magic; I just saw the whole thing," Geran said quickly.

Lilian's eyes went ablaze. "And you just *let them* take her away?"

"There was a whole squad of them! If I tried to fight that, I'd get captured too, and they would find the hideout. Then we'd all be in deep shit! Rychus is going to use her to get stronger by absorbing her power, and then it sounds like he's going to launch an assault!"

"Stars above." Anvil put his hands to his forehead. "They'll torture her for information, and then she'll be used as food for that monster. The interrogators are inbrehdar; they'll get everything from her one way or another."

Ash's brow was sweating. "They'll undoubtedly use the truth serum I developed."

Shiro's mouth fell open. "You made a truth-telling potion for the enemy?"

"I had no choice!" she snapped. "In order to maintain my image and keep his suspicion off me, I had to make sacrifices! We can't come out on top every time."

Elaethia gritted her teeth. "Lose the battle, win the war."

"Gaaaah, enough already!" Lilian shouted as she slammed the butt of her staff into the ground, sending a firm *air burst* around the room. "Celeste's been snatched, and you guys are just standing here arguing! We have to *do* something!"

"Of course!" Ember interjected. "Any time like this and we had to let them go, but this is different. The enemy has a plan that's about to be set in motion. If Snake is the last piece they need, we can't let them have her!"

Geran took over. "We're out of time and options; we need to do a frontal assault *now!*"

"Wait, now?" Falcon turned. "As in *now*, now?"

"Yes, you blockhead. *Now!*" Ash commanded. "Get everyone who can fight on standby immediately; we need them to chase after that squad. Geran, lead them. You three follow him. Lilian, Shiro, Elaethia, you need to take advantage of the commotion and get to Rychus. If the Echo causes a ruckus, he'll mobilize everything he's got to take us down. He doesn't know about you yet, so take him out while he's mostly alone."

Geran shook his head. "I've come this far by Elaethia's side. I'm not leaving her when she needs me the most. I'll get Falcon in the right direction. He knows the city better than me, and he can do it."

Ash regarded him for a moment and then sighed in exasperation. "Fine, just do whatever you need to get our little Snake back."

"What about you, Ash?" Lilian demanded.

"Everyone in this organization is ready to die to give that bastard what he deserves, including me. If we die but you kill him, it's an undeniable win."

Shiro nodded grimly. "A martyr to the cause." He suddenly stood at attention and pounded his right fist across his chest. "Ash-sama. You are most fit to lead this battle, and I am honored to work under you. We will not fail."

She smiled weakly. "Thanks, samurai. Now go. All of you! We can't waste any more time. Snake needs us, the city needs us, Armini needs us. It's time for the Echo to go to war."

Over a century before, Paragon was the crown jewel of the country—maybe even the continent. Now it lay mostly empty and barren, crumbling from neglect and time. The once beautiful city was a maze of dilapidated buildings and homes—a mere shell of what it used to be. It was the first time Elaethia had seen her hometown since she was a child, and reminiscence of a more innocent time flooded her mind as they ran through the city.

A bakery where a beautiful woman would always give her a treat when she stopped by with her mother. A fountain she would often play in. The house of a young demiwolf she befriended as a girl. A small playground in a park. All of these were withering away, rotting and rusted from abandonment. Occasional movement from windows and alleys caught her eye. Figures and silhouettes appeared from the shadows, only to duck back into hiding once they saw the four adventurers approach. It was the remaining people of the city.

Shiro gazed on with shock. "Look at them. It's like they aren't even brehdar anymore. Rychus has been so cruel to them; they seem more like animals. What has he done to them?"

Geran gritted his teeth. "Crushed their will to think and resist. They've lived their whole lives in oppression. They can hardly reason for themselves anymore."

Lilian growled. "Don't they hate him then? If they see us fighting, why don't they join us? Why do they just sit and hide? They aren't even cheering us on!"

"Fear of retribution," Elaethia said. "To them Rychus is omnipotent and infallible. The idea of him being defeated is impossible; the notion of uprising, unthinkable. Any action perceived as retaliation to him or anything he stands for means severe punishment. It may be too late to save many of these people."

Your heart is troubled, little one. So much so that its beating like a rabbit's has awoken me. You are significantly further along in your journey than I last remember. The way your soul shakes suggests to me that we near the end of our quest.

"We are, Frossgar. This will be the battle to determine it all."

"He's awake!" Shiro perked up.

"About damn time," Geran muttered.

I will overlook Geran's remark for the time being, as he has a right to feel this way. Much has happened; why have you not woken me sooner?

Elaethia clenched her teeth. "My conversations with the resistance reminded me of where I come from. My father has set everything in motion for me to finish his fight on this day. I needed time to reflect on my family. Please do not be angry with me; I would have called on you at the moment of the battle."

I can see there is no time for scolding, so I will hold my tongue for now. But I am rather wounded that you did not think of me until you were ready to begin combat. Your father may not have known about my existence, but he is my kin now just as he is yours. We may not be one, as we should be, but we are together. Please rely on me more in these scenarios. You are my little one, and it pains me to see you so wrought with conflict.

"Then I apologize for neglecting you, Frossgar. You have guided me thus far just as much as my father. With our friends by our side, let us face our nemesis together."

"*Hell* yeah!" Lilian whooped. "Cataclysm on the move, at full power! Let's blast that sonuvabitch!"

Her enthusiastic demeanor never fails to flourish no matter the situation, does it?

Elaethia felt a hint of a smile. "It does not."

"We're getting close!" Geran called from the front.

Elaethia looked up at Rychus's grand castle. While Geran wasn't wrong, he certainly wasn't right either. It was easily another two kilometers before they reached the front door of the palace. The road to the gates led up a large hill and curved over a cliff to where the enormous palace was held aloft by two natural rock pillars. The formation stood several hundred meters high. Down below was flat, rocky earth, where the ocean would rest during high tide. But that was not the worst issue. It would be an uphill trek, and soldiers were beginning to mobilize from the only entryway.

"Oh, that's just not fair," Geran noted. "I hate to admit it, but Rychus is a genius. That's the most tactically defensive position I've seen in my entire life. He used the natural terrain to its fullest potential. One way in, one way out, and a swarm of enemies the entire way."

Shiro gripped Seraph. "The fight is nearly lost, and it hasn't even begun."

"Elaethia, what's your plan?"

"You are asking me, Geran? Is it not you who usually devises a strategy?"

"Elaethia, you're the only one who can possibly push through that. We've seen what you can do, and we know it isn't even your fullest potential. If you give this everything you've got, we can give Rychus enough attention while you recover some strength. Shiro can rejuvenate you as best he can.

"I will overcast myself to death if that is so needed," the samurai resolved.

"Shiro …" Elaethia said, her voice faltering.

A powerful voice boomed over their heads that resonated over the entire city. *"Legionnaires! My trusted soldiers! Today is the day!"*

Lilian's ears flattened. "No way. Is that …"

Elaethia's eyes flashed. "It is him. It is Rychus."

"Today we begin our conquest!" the emperor continued. "The resistance has reared its pathetic head! Shown its face to us! By the end of the day, I will have devoured every last one of them! My power will grow strong enough that we can fulfill our dream! For too long, Armini has rested in the shadows of the world! For too long my dream has been stifled and postponed. And now, *now*, we have the final piece to the machine that drives our glorious dream to its destination. And soon that piece will fall into my hands."

"He doesn't have Snake yet!" Shiro stated.

"The world has forgotten Armini and the glory that she stands for! But no longer! From this day forth, we will bring Armini to the world! Armini will *become* the world! For as far as the east is to the west, Armini's rule will reign supreme! Go forth, my legion! Show this planet your face! Show them your steel! Show them to their rightful places!"

Geran began to sweat. "This just got way worse."

Shiro responded in tandem. "He wasn't planning to retake Armini; he plans to take the entire world!"

Lilian growled. "Where is he?"

Elaethia shook her head. "We cannot tell."

"Can't Frossgar do some ghost stuff and find him?"

It is possible. For the sake of the moment, I will attempt.

"He will try," Elaethia said.

The dragon hero closed her eyes as she felt Frossgar's presence leave her mind. The dragon's consciousness ascended into the air, invisible and silent. Frossgar went as far as he could and gazed across the chasm to the palace, from which Rychus's voice was emanating. After a moment, he returned.

Elaethia's eyes shot open. "Balcony, at the center of his palace. He intends to lie in wait while his army does his deeds."

Lilian gleamed dangerously. "Doesn't wanna bring himself into the fight, hmm? All righty then. Let's bring the fight to him."

"What's your plan, cat?" Geran asked warily.

"I hope you all weren't counting on a big, grand battle, 'cause I'm about to rock that bastard's world!"

"Lilian," Shiro choked, "You're not …"

"Oh, you bet I am!"

The mage twirled her staff and took the stage. Heat began to swell around her. The air rippled around her legs as her cape flapped from the heat. Lilian took a deliberate step forward and leveled her black staff at the palace as a mirage formed around the weapon's diamond tip.

"I haven't been able to unleash my full power with this staff yet, and I'm feeling *really* pent up! So stand back, ladies and gentlemen, because Cataclysm is about to strike Paragon!"

"Heavens help us …" Geran stepped well behind the mage as she flashed a pose. The demicat wound up, inhaled, and rocketed her dragon-bone staff forward.

History would unfold that the Sun himself descended from the heavens to strike the giant castle on the earthen arch. For the second time in her life, Lilian shook the ground itself with the *explosion* she cast. A flash of blinding light and a sound that caused everyone to go temporarily deaf made it seem that she had cast *flashbang*. In reality, Lilian's detonation would be enough to make the Red Devil himself cackle with glee from the heavens above. The air boiled and churned as the grand palace erupted into the sky and fell to the earth through the inferno. The ancient, rocky formation that held the palace aloft cracked and broke before it tumbled to the shore below. The ruins rumbled and crashed all the way down, until the dust began to settle among the sweltering heat waves. Then the shockwave began to roll. A charging storm of heat, pressure, and dust barreled toward them like a tsunami of raw elemental destruction.

Shiro's face turned pale. "Uh, Lilian. That looks rather close, and fast, and big!"

"Oops," she murmured, and she slumped to the ground. "That might actually kill us. Well, not Elaethia. Probably."

Geran's eyes bugged at the sight of the terrifying shockwave. "Elaethia, Quick! Cast *unyielding ice!*"

"Immediately!" Elaethia agreed, and she thrust her fist up to create a dome of unbreakable crystal around them.

"I thought you were only gonna use enough to just knock it over!" Geran roared at the mage.

"Aheh …" Lilian smiled weakly. "I musta gone overboard."

"You *stupid* motherfu—" his voice was cut off as the blistering wall of force rolled over them.

"Dammit, cat!" Geran lunged forward once the wave had passed and the heat subsided. The ranger grabbed Lilian by the cheeks and began to pinch and pull them apart, shouting and cursing at her the whole time. The demicat weakly tried to retaliate but managed only a slurred "Ow-ow-ow-ow-ow!" After a minute, he released her and slumped to the ground with a heavy sigh.

"Heh-heh-heh," Lilian giggled as she lay on the ground to rub her reddened cheeks. "That was easier than I thought. I planned to overcast myself a little like I did with that fort with the blood sorceress. Man, I love this staff."

Shiro marveled at the sight of the detonation. "What in oblivion …"

"Well," Geran stated, pushing his hair back to look out as well. "That's one way of botching his plan."

Elaethia didn't know whether to laugh or to cry. "Is this how it ends? After all these years, is my journey going to conclude within a few moments of its peak?"

Lilian laughed quietly. "Sorry, Elaethia. Got carried away. I just figured … this was the best … way to minimize … casualties."

"Something I always say in each quest …"

Unease filled her heart. This was not how she had imagined it would end. Granted, she didn't know how it would end. She never put together a set of events in her mind that would lead to the end of her goal. But this was not it. This couldn't be. It was merely a false image to her. Whether it was a dream or a nightmare, she could not say.

Brace yourself.

"Frossgar?"

Something is wrong. Can you feel it? The land in front of us, though broken and scorched, continues to grow with energy.

"Is it not Lilian's spell?"

No. Focus on it, Elaethia. This is not of elemental origin. It is not even of brehdar roots.

It was true. As Elaethia sensed the air around her, she could detect more and more of a malicious aura—a source of energy that made her spine tingle, her blood run cold, and her stomach churn. She peered deeper into the settling rubble and cooling landscape until a single dot of movement caught her eye.

"It is him!" she gasped.

Lilian's mouth fell open. "What!"

Geran stumbled back. "No way …"

Shiro gasped. "Over a hundred years old, can survive that fall, can shrug off that kind of magic, inbrehdar presence. Is … is he …"

Lilian's knees buckled from under her. "A dragon hero …"

Geran shuddered. "Look how he effortlessly walks through those flames. Fire dragons were allegedly only in Armini. Rychus must have met and bargained with one!"

No dragon I know reeks of such malice.

"That is no dragon," Elaethia murmured.

A deep, malevolent roar echoed from the hellish landscape. The distant form of Rychus approached, and with him, the aura of unnatural energy. Cataclysm stood in partial shock as the emperor neared them. His century-old face was still young but was twisted in rage. His white hair was disheveled and singed. His golden skin glowed with power. His bloodred eyes burned with seething hatred. It was the first time Rychus and Elaethia had seen one another, and even though it was the mage that destroyed his world around him, his boiling eyes were fixed into Elaethia's.

"Get away," Elaethia suddenly commanded.

Geran shot her a look. "What?"

"I said get away! Quickly!"

Geran saw the determination in her eyes and helped Lilian to her feet and away.

Elaethia turned to her other side. "Shiro, you must escape as well. There is something about him that tells me you cannot face him!"

"I will not, Elaethia-sama," Shiro announced, his eyes fixed on the approaching enemy.

"Shiro, for once, I am giving you an order. You must flee from this space!"

He drew Seraph and leveled it at Rychus. "Then for once I will disobey. You face the man you swore as your nemesis. And I, as your samurai, will never abandon you. I may not understand much of this world compared to others, but I know a monster when I see one. This man—no, this *thing*—must be destroyed. You may not be able to do this alone, Elaethia-sama. If you die by his hand, I will either follow you by battling him myself and being slain, or by vanquishing him and falling on my sword for abandoning you. This is my code, my life, and my honor. I am your sword, Elaethia-sama. Where you go, I *will* follow."

Elaethia growled, but could not find it in her heart to deny him. "Then stay behind me so I may receive the first blow. If I fall, you must be at full strength to avenge me."

"As you wish," the samurai obeyed, and he paced back. Together the dragon hero and her samurai faced the golden tyrant.

"How *touching*!" Rychus crowed as he neared. "A loving bond shared by two warriors with a passionate goal. I would applaud you by name if I knew who you were."

Shiro spat, "Then I will tell you it, so when I send you to hell, you can te—"

"I'm afraid I couldn't care less, young man," Rychus said with a smirk. "I've never listened to the words of dead men."

Elaethia drew her axe and leveled it. "You are gravely mistaken."

"As a matter of fact, I'm not." An aura of bloodred energy began to radiate from him. Black shadows danced and swirled within the ever-growing crimson mist. "You see, for over a century, all who have opposed me have met a fate worse than death. All have fallen before me, just as you will. Hundreds—no, *thousands*—of souls have stood before me in defiance. Not one has lived to tell of it. So now you see why your words are irrelevant. You are nothing to me but walking corpses."

Shiro stepped forward. "Elaethia-sama, you must not let his energy touch you!"

Rychus stopped. "Elaethia? I've heard that name. Tales of an unstoppable warrior in Linderry, with an Arminian name. I have been preparing my spies to infiltrate Linderry and locate you. I must thank you for saving me the trouble. How serendipitous of you to drop yourself into my lap. Though I must say I applaud you for maintaining your composure at my presence. It has been years since another has dared to step up to me."

"I did not come all this way for your convenience, Rychus," she said, glaring. "Though I am not one for boasting, you are correct in your assumption. I am unstoppable. I have defeated sorcerers, armies, beasts, and monsters—even a leviathan. I do not fear one man."

Rychus threw back his head and laughed. "Oh, but I am not one man! I am many! The souls of those who cower before me are devoured and added to my own. Their lives and power become mine. Each soul I consume is another lifetime I am guaranteed. I have lost count by this point, Elaethia … What was your last name?"

She snarled. "Frossgar, as I have taken the name of the dragon that raised me. But perhaps you would be more familiar with this!"

She reached under her armor and suddenly thrust her gauntlet forward. In it was her gold-and-sapphire pendant—the sign of the resistance, the heirloom of her family, and the final gift from her father.

"Soliano …" Rychus's eyes began to burn as his face turned from arrogance to rage to hatred. "Even in death, Marcus, you still remain a *thorn* in my side! So that's what your plan was, huh? To send your brat after me! To finish what you were too weak to handle!"

"My father was not weak!" Elaethia shouted.

"Your father was pathetic!" the emperor roared. "He thought he could gain my trust, take my promotion, lead my armies, and then thank me by stabbing me in the back with the very sword I honored him with! If your father was any kind of a man, he would have fallen in line behind me, where he belonged!"

"My father belonged anywhere else! He is more worthy to lie in his grave than serve you!"

Rychus began to chuckle deeply. "Lie in his grave, you say? You think he deserved such a simple end? What story have you been told about him having died 'honorably'? Your father was struck down by my hand, clinging to life as I stood over him and spat on his face! Again and again I healed his wounds, nursing him back to health only to tear him apart over and over! He squealed like a dog for months until I was satisfied! He didn't even get the honor of joining the legion of souls within my belly! Not Marcus!"

"You unholy cretin …" Elaethia began to shake with rage as she pulled her visored helmet over her head.

"But don't worry, little Elaethia. You will not suffer the same fate as your weakling father. No, you will follow in the footsteps of your mother. Naomi, was it? The whore that Marcus wanted to make his wife. While my armies ravage the lands, I will give you every treatment I gave her. I will keep you chained to my throne, made a plaything of, until I grow bored and devour you.

I can sense the potency within you that nearly matches my own. Were I not immortal, I might actually fear you."

Shiro gripped Seraph, his rage surpassed only by Elaethia's. "You will die before your unholy hands touch Elaethia-sama!"

Rychus scowled at the samurai. "I see. The heavens always have to interfere."

"How could they not after creating a monster like you?"

"Create? Monster?" Rychus threw his head back again in laughter. "Oh you naive, ignorant paladin. I am no child of the heavens like you. Once upon a time I was, but in the midst of my dream I was offered a deal I could not refuse. Did you really think this power was born from the heavens? The ability to devour another soul and add it to my own? The heavens are too compassionate, too *timid*, to create such a wonderful thing."

Elaethia began to emit a chilling aura. "Your magic, your age, your goals, your appearance … They are not of this earth."

Rychus smiled wickedly. "And so you're starting to understand! And the little friend in your head can feel it too. There is another power within me. Another entity that has so graciously lent me his soul and power."

As he said these words, his aura began to grow thicker. Deep red-and-black shadows swirled around them. Unholy voices whispered among the three brehdars that stood alone in the field.

A dragon's true nemesis. I strived to avoid these conflicts my entire life. But it seems the heavens have decided it is time for me to fulfill my duty.

Rychus chuckled again. "Your scaly addition has figured it out, Elaethia. Now say it! Say it for the world to hear!"

"You truly are an unholy abomination," she growled, and she poised her axe to strike. "You are a demon!"

"Close!" Rychus grinned and willed his aura to expand farther. The shadowy red mist enveloped her and Shiro and seeped into their bones. Elaethia faltered—not because she was in shock, but because she could not stop herself. She turned sharply to her see Shiro crumple to the ground and turn pale.

"Shiro!" Elaethia dared not take her eyes off Rychus for long, but she glanced quickly to Geran and Lilian. Both were far away and yelling indistinguishably to her.

"I must applaud you again, Elaethia." Rychus said. "You have already lasted longer against my demonic ability than any other. But you can't hold out forever. I have a century's worth to give, and your samurai companion fuels it more as we speak. He will be reduced to a shriveled husk within the minute!"

"Your lack of worth for brehdar life makes you nothing but an *animal!*"

"A baseless rebuttal from one who gained her power from a glorified lizard. Frossgar was his name? Such a boring title. But now the real fight begins!"

Rychus reached into the air above his head with both arms and began to pull them apart. In the blank space that was between his hands appeared the shaft of a weapon. As the golden tyrant expanded his arms, the weapon grew larger and larger until it rested fully in his hands—a long war hammer with a thick head on one end and a scythe blade on the other.

"Prepare yourself, Elaethia! For this will be the beginning of hell on earth for you! Let's commence your final battle! Elaethia to Rychus, your dragon to my demon! Frossgar versus Gethevel! Come, dragon hero! Face the wrath of a demonspawn!"

"And so we finally meet, dragon." The echoey voice flowed from Rychus, but it was not his own. While it sounded of the evil man, it reverberated over itself, deepening with ominous energy.

Do not say those words as if you intended this, demon. This is a fated encounter orchestrated by a higher power. Your voice is putrid and vile but drips with fear.

"What do I have to fear? I have bided my time, growing with strength and power. My time on this earth was spent in preparation, not lazing in a cave. You cannot hope to defeat me."

Are you so full of yourself that you forget what I am? I know not your true age, but you are still only a whelp to me. Your barons seem to have neglected to tell you of the one thing they fear.

"Oh yes, I am fully aware of the heavens' reason for creating dragons. But I have grown my host stronger than any of my predecessors, and you are an aging reptile who has not seen combat in millennia. I have thousands of souls at my disposal, while you have only a limited amount of power. You are a half-baked dragon hero challenging a fully-fledged demonspawn. You will not persevere. I only wish to savor this moment before I turn your world on its head!"

Celebrate while you can, Gethevel. It will not last!

"Then come, dragon. Let us see if your claws and frost may stand my horns and souls!"

Elaethia did not need further motivation. She burst forward with astounding speed to slash her battleaxe at the demonic emperor. Rychus hefted his war hammer down and intercepted her strike. With a roar of effort, Elaethia powered through it and staggered the emperor back.

"Good, Elaethia, good!" Rychus laughed. "Your form is solid, and your stance firm. You have been trained well! But I have been at this game over a century longer than you! You have proven capable of dealing blows. Let's see how you can take them!"

Rychus lunged forward with speed equal to her own and swung his hammer to her side. Elaethia maneuvered her axe to stop the blow and collided her shaft with his. The emperor's strike was strong enough to shake the ground beneath them as it shifted Elaethia several meters along the uneven earth. Deep skid marks from where her feet were planted trailed to where she now stood. As the dust cleared, it revealed the dragon hero still standing in her blocking position as her blue eyes burned through her visor.

Before he could prepare again, Elaethia was on him. Her axe hummed through the air as it bore down. Rychus ducked to the side to dodge the strike and wound up to counterattack. In the same moment, he raised the hammer and brought it down on her open side. In a brief moment of satisfaction from his blow, he was just as quickly shocked as Elaethia only shifted in her stance from the impact. A single frost spell launched from the dragon hero's gauntlet. A thick *icicle* shot toward the ground and embedded itself into his right foot, pinning him down. Rychus staggered for a moment and looked up to see the battleaxe fly to his neck.

With the sound of dragonite slicing through bone, the massive axe found its target. The emperor's head was severed from its shoulders and flew into the air, with blood spiraling in every direction. The head fell to the earth with a thud and bounced around on the rocky ground. Elaethia planted her axe into the dirt, glaring at the decapitated form of Emperor Rychus.

It was only a brief moment until she realized what was wrong.

Though his head was severed, the body did not fall. Nor did the demonic aura that continued to sap her strength dissipate. Her hands shook as she felt her stamina and power continue to be absorbed by the demonspawn. The adrenaline had left her veins.

Then the true horror struck.

The head that had just finished rolling to a stop began to move. Laughter suddenly broke over the battlefield. A demonic roar of arrogance cackled with shadowy echoes. The blood that once watered the ground began to rise again. The head floated briefly, until it shot back to Rychus's shoulders and the wound began to heal. Rychus grinned smugly as all traces of his fatal injury disappeared.

"Now you see how hopeless it is for you?" he sneered. "I hold the souls of thousands within me. You have slain only one. In the time it takes you to destroy all of them, I will have defeated you hundreds of times!"

Elaethia growled aloud in fury, hacking again and again into the laughing demonspawn. With strike after strike, blow after blow, and cut after cut, the dragon hero disemboweled the emperor over and over again. But he only stood and taunted her with amused chuckles and remarks. Every wound she inflicted was immediately healed over as if it had never happened. It didn't matter if she only grazed him or cut him clean in two; the emperor rose again in full strength while hers began to fail.

Elaethia! My magic! Make use of it! Gethevel cannot heal his body if it is frozen over!

"I would not do that if I were you," the demon's voice said. "Look behind you, dragon hero."

Elaethia turned to see Shiro's lifeless form on the ground. Seraph lay still in the dirt next to his open hand. The samurai had fallen.

"Shiro …" she choked out.

"He is not dead," Gethevel announced. "Not yet. His putrid holy magic keeps him from being devoured by my ability. No mortal can withstand my aura, but the heavens' blessing leaves him clinging to life by a thread. Any blow or attack that nears him will snuff out the sputtering flame within. Use your magic, dragon hero, and you will kill him."

"Not that it would matter," Rychus added with a smirk. "Your magic would dry out eventually, as it diminishes while we speak. You will be without strength and magic within the minute."

"No …" Elaethia's knees began to quiver as her armor became overburdening. Her arms shook, her axe grew heavy, and her eyes dimmed as her life essence was drained from her.

"Oh yes," Rychus gleamed, strutting up to her. "You have been quite the delicious meal, dragon hero, and have given me a wonderful show of your strength. Now, allow me to return the favor."

Rychus raised the blunt side of his hammer above his head and held it over Elaethia. In a burst of desperation, Elaethia threw her arms up and intercepted the blow with her battleaxe. But she could not stop it. The war hammer glanced off to the side and deflected to the dirt as she gasped sharply. Her ears began to ring as her head throbbed. Rychus wound up a second time and brought the hammer down onto the warrior again.

This time she was not able to protect herself. Elaethia was slammed into the ground by the blunt impact. With quivering arms, she tried to rise, but the crimson energy around her continued to devour her strength. A third blow to her back pounded her into the dirt and crushed the wind from her lungs. Elaethia gasped for breath, choking on blood and dust.

An arrow suddenly lodged itself into the back of the emperor's head. Then another. And another. But the demonspawn didn't seem to notice the ranger's shots that peppered the back of his skull. Again and again, Rychus struck Elaethia on the ground, savoring the pleasure of his victory as he battered the fallen dragon hero with wild, mocking laughter. His hammer breached her dragonite, piercing her flesh. Air no longer came to Elaethia's burning lungs as agony overwhelmed her, and everything went black.

Shiro could not remember the moments before he lost his strength. One second the ominous red energy surrounded him, and the next he lay paralyzed on the ground, unable to move a muscle. The samurai's vision turned dark, and he could hear only the battle around him and the unholy whispers that penetrated his mind. There was the sound of dragonite on flesh, then dragonite on steel, then steel on dragonite, and then laughter from the demon tyrant.

He heard nothing from his master—no sign of her magic, no sound of her armor. A tear flowed from his eye and dripped to the dust below. He had failed. His master was defeated, and all he could do was lie on the ground and die. Regret and anguish rolled over him as the demonic ability completed its course and the samurai prepared to join his master.

"Brother!" a girl's voice echoed in his mind. "Big brother! Wake up!"

Shiro groaned weakly as he tried to open his eyes. "Who …?"

"You have to get up, Shiro! You can do it!"

A light appeared in his distant vision. It slowly grew brighter until he saw the blurry outline of a small hand reaching to him. Shiro gasped painfully with new tears in his eyes as he recognized the figure.

"Mitsuki …"

"You're strong, big brother. Stronger than anyone realizes! I know you can do it; I know you can win. Don't give up! Give it your all!"

"Mitsuki!"

Shiro held out a hand to meet his sister's. As he did, a bright light flooded his vision. The hand that now held his was no longer that of his little sister, but that of an elderly man with a kimono and sword. His calloused and gnarled hand gripped Shiro's with determination and focus. Though bathed in blinding light, Shiro could see the man's features clearly.

"Listen to your sister, Shiro," the elderly man commanded.

"Grandfather Ryuuki … H-how?"

"You will know in time, grandson. But I taught you better than this. Take up your sword and fight! You came with promise to give honor to the Inahari name; now keep it! I taught you your code and the way that our kind lives. I call upon you to honor it now."

"My promise …" Shiro clenched his teeth. "My promise to you, to Geran, to Lilian, and to Elaethia-sama! I *will* honor them!"

Shiro's vision was flooded with a powerful holy aura as his grandfather's fading words resonated in the light.

"On your feet, samurai. Your master needs you."

Through the raging demonic aura that consumed the battlefield, a brilliant flash and a pillar of pure light burst down from the heavens. The beam of blinding holy energy struck the still body of Shiro Inahari and bathed him in its cleansing light. His hand twitched and clenched on the ground. Air was forced into his lungs. His eyes burst open and shone pure white with the heavens' energy. The samurai grabbed Seraph from the dirt, and he pulled himself up to lean on it. With a groan and a gulping breath of air, he rose to his feet. With his entire body glowing with rippling energy and his holy sword at the ready, the Osakyotan paladin's brilliant eyes bored into the demonspawn's.

Rychus faltered and stepped back. "Not possible!"

"How …?" Gethevel trembled. "The heavens never grant divine intervention without consequence and unwavering lifelong loyalty!"

Shiro's words echoed in a chorus of holy voices. "Stay thy words, demon. Thy transgressions on our world hath not been overlooked. Thine evil deeds and unholy desires hath reached us at last. Judgment shall befall thee, Rychus, for thy heart hath blackened beyond redemption."

Gethevel sputtered as Rychus backed up again. "That host is weak! He can't possibly withstand your presence."

"Our child will last as long as he needeth. Repent, demon, and fall to thy knees in submission."

"*Never!*" Gethevel and Rychus roared to the holy entity within the samurai's body.

They weren't given a chance to retaliate.

With a sound louder than a clap of thunder and a flash more blinding than lighting, Rychus gasped and doubled over. He looked down to see that Seraph had pierced his torso and burst from his back. Shiro had seemingly teleported to where he now stood. Shiro dug the holy blade in further, twisting it where it impaled the demonspawn. The holy samurai brought Rychus to his knees and put his shining face directly to the emperor's.

Shiro slowly closed his eyes and offered a prayer. "Be free, my children. I shall guide thee home."

"N-no!" Rychus choked.

But he was ignored. Shiro tore the blade from the impaled demonspawn, leaving a glowing chasm of holy energy in the wound. Instead of sealing itself and healing, it remained open as thousands of tiny glowing lights burst from his gaping chest.

"My souls!" Gethevel wailed "My delicious souls, *no!*"

Gethevel roared in anguish as the lights flew into the holy beam that illuminated Shiro, each soul returning home to the heavens. As the thousands of lights ascended, Shiro rested a hand on Elaethia's haggard form. She still lived. The holy samurai poured his remaining magic into her to refill all that had been stolen from her in the battle and then some.

"And now we leave it to thee, dragon hero. Finish what thy father started all those years ago."

The holy voices faded away to join the lost souls in the heavenly beam of light. Elaethia's eyes shot open as she gasped sharply. The pain left her body. Her magic replenished itself, and her strength slowly returned to her. She heard the gentle voices of the heavens urge her to stand as her broken body repaired itself.

"You …" Rychus glowed again with his unholy energy as the light faded. "You stole them from me! All our souls!"

"I only …" Shiro stopped glowing and crumpled to his hands and knees as the holy energy departed. Seraph fell to the ground as the samurai struggled to stay upright. "I only returned what you stole. You can't use them anymore. You're down to your last life."

"You paladin *dog!*"

Rychus wound his war hammer over his shoulder and attacked in a single, savage swipe. The scythe end of the unholy weapon caught the exhausted samurai in his belly, hooked him, and tore. Shiro was lifted off the ground and thrown through the air, his armor destroyed from the demonic blade that ripped him open from groin to chest. Shiro rag-dolled over the ground, blood splattering the dirt and rock until he lay motionless in a growing crimson pool.

Rychus's wild eyes shot to Elaethia, full of his intent to finish her as he did Shiro. But she was not looking at him. Instead her gaze lay in the direction of where her beloved friend had been thrown. She held her helmet shakily in her hands. Her mouth hung weakly open and trembled. Tears flowed from her anguished eyes as she beheld the now still form of Shiro Inahari. The battlefield was silent only for a moment before a deafening voice dominated the landscape.

"*This shall not stand!*"

A powerful burst of frigid energy exploded from the kneeling dragon hero. A raging blizzard swirled around her as a translucent form began to tower over them. Frossgar's ethereal neck and head loomed over the demonspawn. His enraged eyes chilled Rychus's soul more than the blizzard ever could. Elaethia rose to her feet, and through the unrelenting storm, Rychus witnessed her full transformation. Ghostly dragon wings of jagged frost erupted from her shoulder blades. A tail of equal proportion grew from the back of her waist. The markings around her eyes glowed with draconic power as her irises flared with a blazing blue so bright they created dots in his vision. Rychus tried to scream, but the frozen air seemed to crush his lungs.

"*Nemesis of my child, you have breathed your last!*" Frossgar thundered. "*Your fate is sealed, and my claws will tear you to bloody ribbons!*"

Elaethia strode slowly forward with undeniable intent. Battleaxe in hand, she glared with pure hatred into the demon emperor's paralyzed eyes. Rychus's old human instinct of flight kicked in as he attempted to turn and run. But he found he could not move. Her reptilian gaze was the final catalyst that ensured his doom. Elaethia Frossgar had transformed. Rychus's life was snuffed out in the blink of an eye as his body cracked and fractured from the exposure to *Absolute Zero*.

Elaethia raised her axe above her head and brought it down on the frozen form of the demonic emperor. Again and again, blow after blow, Elaethia hacked and shattered the petrified tyrant, reducing his once human form into powdered ice. Over and over, Elaethia pounded and demolished the once living statue, until all that remained was a pair of boots that stood alone on the ground.

Finally Elaethia released her spell. The dragon hero slammed the spearhead of her axe into the ground. She and the ghostly form of Frossgar turned their faces to the sky and let out an earth-shaking roar. The bellow lasted for several seconds until Frossgar's form dissipated, and the woman's inbrehdar battle cry then slowly turned into a wail of anguish. Elaethia gazed tearfully into the clear sky for a brief moment before she bowed her head in exhaustion and slumped to a knee.

"Father," she whispered, "it is done."

And in that moment of triumph and sorrow, the pendant around her neck seemed to hum and pulse. The chill around her suddenly turned into a gentle spring breeze. Within the warm wind that rolled over her body, she could have sworn she felt a pair of hands rest on her shoulders, until they slowly let go and ascended into the air.

"Elaethia!" Lilian screamed. "Get over here, now!"

"The sword!" Geran called. "Seraph—grab Seraph! Hurry!"

Elaethia staggered to her feet, sheathed her battleaxe, and reached down to her feet, where Seraph lay. The dragon hero pushed through her fatigue and moved as quickly as she could to where Geran and Lilian were kneeling next to Shiro. Elaethia took a knee next to him and saw the haunting spectacle. Shiro lay face up, eyes closed, in the red dirt. Lilian's cape was draped over his open body and stained from blood. Geran held a waterskin to the samurai's lips as Lilian cradled the samurai's head on her thighs.

"Does he live?" Elaethia gasped.

"Barely. I don't think he's got long," Geran choked as water dripped from the skin in his shaking hands.

"The sword!" Lilian pointed to Seraph. "Put it on him, hurry!"

Elaethia complied and rested it gently on his chest. "This will aid him?"

Lilian shook her head as tears fell from her face. "I don't know. He said he needed it. C'mon, Shiro, use your magic; heal yourself!"

"I ... can't ..." he moaned weakly. "No ... magic. Wound is ... unholy. Can't ... heal."

"Adventurers!" Ash's voice broke over them. She, Anvil, Snake, and a few other members of the Echo ran up to them. "We saw what happened! You did it! You killed him! By the Sun and Moon, I never would have thought—"

"Boss ..." Anvil caught her arm and pointed. "Look."

She followed his finger and gasped. "Oh no ..."

Lilian's eyes shot to hers. "You're an alchemist, right? Do you have a healing potion?"

Ash covered her mouth. "There isn't a potion out there that can fix that."

"Please, there has to be something!"

"Let me look." The dwarf dug in her satchel and pulled out a small gray vial. "This won't heal him, but it will stop the pain. We use it for people who are dying and need to give us information. It should give him time to … say his good-byes."

"What are you talking about? This isn't time for that; we have to heal him! If you can't mix up something that will make him better, then just—"

Geran suddenly shot up and took the potion from Ash. "Thank you, Hailey." The ranger took the gray vial in his hands and slowly poured its contents into Shiro's dry mouth. After a moment of silence, the samurai inhaled sharply and opened his eyes.

"The pain … it's gone," he rasped.

Geran put a hand on his friend's forehead. "Easy, samurai, easy. You said it yourself—this can't be healed. Don't try anything drastic."

"I know." He nodded. "Thank you. Nothing except the highest of holy magic could heal this, and I'm already overcast. I wouldn't have enough anyway. The demonic energy is seeping further into me. Gethevel still lives. I fear he is trying to rebuild inside me. It's like he's trying to take over. If I stay living for much longer, he will consume my mind, body, and soul. I don't intend to let him. Where's Seraph?"

"Right here, Shiro," Elaethia said soothingly. She felt for his hand and guided it to his chest, where the katana rested in its sheath. The samurai clasped his fingers around it and smiled.

"Then I'm ready."

"Do what you need to, Shiro," Geran urged.

"Geran," Shiro turned his head and extended his free hand. "I never got to tell you how truly thankful I am for you. All my life, I was the eldest child and had to be the biggest man in the room. Everyone always looked up to me, and those I looked up to didn't always understand me. But you showed me everything. You were always kind and patient, understanding me and guiding me whenever I was troubled. You were the best big brother I always wanted. And a better friend."

Tears soaked into Geran's beard as he firmly grasped Shiro's hand. "I hear you, man. I've never had a junior before, because I always thought they were a pain. But I never looked at you like that. Like you said, you were a brother to me. And I couldn't ask for a more hardworking ally than you. You were more than an asset, and better than any equipment. I'll never have anything as dependable as you in my life. And I'll never have a friend that could be better than Shiro Inahari."

"Thank you." Shiro smiled and turned. "Elaethia-sama. Since the first day, I always swore I was ready to lay my life down for you. While you may not have believed it, I meant it every time. You are a wonderful master. Kind, strong, wise, slow to anger, benevolent. A perfect image to someone like me. If I'm born to serve again and start over, I will find you first. I'm not sad, Elaethia-sama, because I get to die as I lived—honoring you, and at your side."

"I never doubted your words, Shiro," Elaethia said, her voice trembling. "I always knew how strongly you felt. I never wanted you to see me as one who controls you, and I understood after a while what you meant by staying by my side. You were your own man, even whenever you proclaimed to be unwavering to my services. I know how much it meant for you to fight by my side. And I felt equal pride being by yours. I know the heavens call to you now, and you will find a new master with your family where you belong. So now I dismiss you. Return home, good and faithful servant."

"I will honor your final command, Elaethia." A single tear fell from his eye as he looked up to the demicat who gently held his head. "Of all the people in all the places in all the countries, there has never been one that captured me as much as you, Lilian. Your beauty, your power, your grace, your cheerful smile—all of it washed away the sadness and regret I held from home. I was ready to leave it all behind if it meant I could travel the world with you. My family taught me what honor and purpose are, but you showed me something much stronger. You taught me what it means to love and be loved—to enjoy and take control of the life I've been given. I would die a thousand times again just to get a chance to be with you forever. I wanted to bring you home, show you my world, give you your world, and see the world—until I realized I didn't need any of that. Because *you* are my world, Lilian Whitepaw."

"You idiot …" the mage whispered as she bent over him. Her tears fell from her cheeks and softly landed upon his face. "You're not supposed to tell me these kinds of things now. You're supposed to tell me when we go home. You need to say these things when you keep your promise and show me Osakyota. I wanted to hear all those things every day for the rest of my life as I grew old with you. Not while you're dying in my arms. You can't tell me that I'm your world. Because then I have to live in it without you."

Shiro weakly raised his hand to her face. Lilian instantly cupped both hers to his cheeks. "No, no tears, Lilian. What I loved the most in my life was your wonderful smile. If I had to ask you one thing, it would be to never let that smile disappear. You promised me you would never let me be sad as long as I lived, and you kept that promise. Now promise me you will always smile for me and will become the strongest mage ever, as I know you will."

"I will," she whimpered. "I promise you I will."

"Then I have one more request."

He tried to lift Seraph but couldn't find the strength. Both Geran and Elaethia guided his hand and sword to where he motioned.

"Take Seraph," he insisted. "I'm giving it to you, Lilian. Keep it in remembrance of me so that I'm always with you. Never let the two most precious pieces of my life be separate. Remember the part of my code I taught you. I am my sword, and my sword is me. Keep my sword with you, and we can still travel the world together."

Lilian shakily grasped the sheathed katana and gently placed it in her lap. "Of course. I'll remember everything you taught me. When I can't use my magic, or I come across an enemy you would hate, I'll fight them as you would."

Shiro chuckled and coughed. "Just don't do anything crazy, Lilian. I'll eagerly await your arrival in the heavens for when your time comes. But I love you too much for you to be hasty."

Lilian leaned forward and kissed him gently. "Don't you worry. I love you too much to rush. Wait for me, samurai."

Shiro mustered the rest of his strength to press his mouth to hers as the sun began to disappear below the horizon. Its soft and warm rays glinted off the samurai's crimson armor with gentle holy light. As their lips parted, he sighed one last time, and his hand fell limp.

Chapter 25
Sunrise

Sixth Era. 140. Jinum 3.

As much as the surviving members of the Echo and Cataclysm wanted to bury or tend to their dead, they had to regain control of the city. Word of the emperor's defeat spread like wildfire, mostly as a result of the Echo calling it from the streets. Even so, many of the citizens refused to leave their homes. They believed it all to be a lie, a trick—a treacherous test to expose the unfaithful.

While many watched from the shadows, there were a brave few who stepped outside to observe the commotion. Those that did faced the impossible truth. Rychus was dead by Elaethia's hand. The legion was demolished by Lilian's magic. The demonic presence was banished by Shiro's divine intervention. And the crowds were brought under control by Geran's tact.

But Shiro was not the only one lost that day. While Snake had been safely retrieved, Falcon, Ember, and many of the Echo that engaged the single legion squad were killed in action. While the fallen Echo could be buried in their homeland, the adventurers began to prepare Shiro's body for travel back to Linderry. They wrapped the fallen samurai in the most intact cloth they could find from a dilapidated chapel and placed him in a sturdy coffin given to them from the civilians. It was nearly dawn now, and the sun was beginning to cast light over the ocean to the east. Unsure of where to take him, and unwilling to leave him, the three guided their friend in a wagon.

Food lines were set up, the injured were treated, and the sick were guided to Ash as she worked throughout the night to make potions. She quickly ran out of both ingredients and magic. Elaethia silently watched Ash wrap up her work and trudge wearily out of the tent. As she emerged, she saw the three adventurers on a bench in the town square, and she walked over to join them.

"How goes the hospital?" Geran asked as she approached.

"I'm dried up in every way imaginable," she sighed.

"You can say that again," Lilian said, staring at the dirt.

"I can't wrap my head around it," Ash began. "After all these years of planning and gaining trust, working under his nose, and fighting underground. It's just … over. I don't suppose you can relate, but … No, you definitely can. Just not in the same way. You guys have been building up for this, too, right? Especially you, Elaethia."

She nodded. "My life goal is complete, my father is avenged, my homeland is free and yet … Why?"

"Why what?"

Elaethia turned with blurry eyes. "Why can I not feel joy?"

Ash gently rested a hand on Shiro's coffin. "I know what you mean. When I saw what happened to Ember and Falcon, I asked the same question. But then I look around. I see a free city. I see a defeated legion. I see the melted, bloody mess that used to be Rychus. And I see Snake's smiling face again. Celeste, I mean. There's no need for code names anymore, since there's no need for the Echo."

Geran shook his head. "There's always going to be a need for the Echo. All we did was remove the people in charge. If you don't make sure the next ones are trustworthy and know what they're doing, Armini will find itself right back where it was. This city needs a leader. The Echo is its best hope."

"What about you?"

Geran chuckled and then sniffed. "Hell no. I've never wanted to be in charge of a party, let alone a country. Besides, we're adventurers. It's our job to fix problems, not cause them."

Lilian silently nodded with drooping ears. Elaethia just stared at the ground.

Hailey leaned forward. "Elaethia? What about you? What are you going to do now?"

"I do not know. I focused my whole life to achieve this one moment. I never gave any thought as to what I would do beyond it. But there are a few places that have promised me a home to return to. I will reflect on this and stay with my friends for the time being. But I hold no desire to rule as you suggest."

Hailey sighed and leaned back. "It was worth a shot. So are you guys going to leave us so soon?"

Geran rested a hand on the wooden coffin. "We've got to get him home. If you still need our help, you can send me a letter. I'll come if I can."

"I see. When are you heading out?"

"Before the end of the day," Elaethia said.

"It's hardly just started. The sun hasn't even shown his face yet."

"No, but he nears."

Elaethia peered over to the ocean to see the sun poking over the horizon. Suddenly it was blocked by low clouds. She squinted to see that they were not clouds at all. They were sails. Down at the harbor a kilometer away, a single ship had anchored at the dock.

Hailey jumped up. "What in the … That's a ship! No one's sailed into those docks in years; who could that be?"

Elaethia stood as well. "More enemies?"

"I don't know," Geran muttered, "but we ought to go check it out. Let's go."

"Wait," Lilian called as the others began to walk away. The demicat gripped the handles of the cart that held Shiro's coffin.

"It is not right to leave him here," Elaethia agreed.

"But it may not be the best idea to take him, either," Hailey argued.

Geran walked back and took the other handle. "I can't believe I almost forgot him. I'm sorry, Lilian. We're all so used to him being with us. Until we get him home, we won't leave his side again."

The four of them walked from the city square to the harbor, pulling the cart the entire way. Elaethia couldn't help but feel a surge of hope as she looked around the city. The sun still hung below the rooftops, but she could see signs of the population moving again. Civilians looked out and around, curious at the commotion that had been growing ever louder as the hours had gone by since the previous day. This city, Paragon, might be able to come back to life once again.

"Stop!" Geran suddenly shot his hand up and looked around.

Everyone froze, and the group turned their attention to their surroundings.

"What is it?" Hailey asked, reaching for a dagger on her hip.

Geran pointed to a rooftop to his left. "Right there! Who's up there? Show yourself!"

A figure appeared at the edge of the roof and peered down. A pair of brown cat ears and an accompanying tail leaned over the gutter. "What kind of messed-up dream is this? *Geran?*"

Elaethia's eyes widened as she recognized the man. "Roderick Griffith!"

The demicat ranger from Breeze scampered down the drainpipe and leaped from a balcony to land on the cobblestone road. "I thought I was losing my mind when I saw you guys walking down the street! Where the hell have you been?"

"Finishing my journey," Elaethia said. "Why are you here?"

"Why am *I* here? We thought that … you said you'd … why didn't you … Gaaaah!" Roderick ruffled his fingers through his hair. "This really throws a wrench in everything!"

Geran stepped forward. "Why? What's going on, Rod? What happened?"

Roderick sighed in exasperation. "A shit-ton! Listen, I have to go report this right now before Master Dameon has everyone do something stupid. Get down to the docks as fast as you can. I'll go ahead so they don't start burning the city to the ground!"

"Wait, *what?*" Geran lunged forward to grab his guildmate, but the demicat had already turned around. As he ran, Roderick pulled a potion from his pouch, drank it midstride, and shot off like an arrow.

"Who the hell was that?" Hailey demanded.

"Someone from our guild. We have to get to the docks *now!*"

"There's a whole *ship load* of your people down there? You said they wouldn't come! Why are they here?"

"Guess we're about to find out. Let's go."

"This is almost like a dream," Elaethia murmured, and she rubbed her head.

"Hey!" Lilian interjected. "Slow down; you're making the wagon rattle!"

Soon after, they all rounded the last bend at the bottom of the hill to the pier. They halted almost dead in their tracks. Standing gathered on the docks was nearly half of Breeze's guild. Master Dameon, Earth Shatter, Razorback, Heaven's Light, and several other A-level and higher parties stopped what they were doing to look at the three adventurers and Hailey.

"*Guys!*" The collective cheer of over thirty adventurers thundered from the docks.

Every single one of them barreled toward the small group at the base of the hill. Elaethia, Geran, and Lilian walked forward, while Hailey found herself backpedaling in panic. In the blink of an eye, the guild surrounded their three compatriots to rattle off questions so loudly and rapidly that none of them could be understood. After nearly a minute of utter chaos, a voice exploded over all of them.

"Will you all *shut up!*" Master Dameon dominated the crowd and shoved his way to the front. The massive demibear stormed his way to the three long-lost adventurers and glared down at them.

"Nightshade. Explain."

"Uh, explain what, sir?" Geran asked.

"Do you know how long it's been since you left?"

"About four months, maybe a little more."

"And what's the time frame you gave me for the your estimated return?"

"Initially two months, but we ended up taking a detour. Two detours, actually. But I should have explained all this in the lett—" He cut himself off, and his eyes bugged. "I didn't send a letter back to Breeze about the detours …"

Dameon's voice was steady but dangerous. "You do realize that in your neglect to inform us about your whereabouts, many members of the guild, including myself, thought you had died."

"Master, that's something else we need to—"

"And in our ever-growing impatience and anxiety, a lot of us began to form some rather drastic thoughts."

Elaethia stepped up. "Guild Master, we understand your concern, but this is not the time to—"

"Oh, it's not the time to what, Frossgar? You think you're in a position to start making demands now? Look around! You think the rascals in front of you are an illusion? Are you so dense that you can't seem to come up with a reason why we're all here? We thought that emperor got the best of you, so every single one of us decided to come down here to avenge you!"

"By ship?" Geran asked. "But how ... Where did you even get a ship and crew to—"

"Let me tell you the *second* part of why I am this close to grabbing you by the hair and slamming you back and forth! That samurai of yours has a family back home that misses him *oh* so dearly. And when his father appears on *my* doorstep, asks for Shiro, does some *abysmally* embarrassing Osakyotan customs, and then is told we think he might be *dead* ... *that* turns everything into a wildfire! Now, while you four were having a grand time with your happy little adventure, the rest of us have gone through hell these last two months! So go ahead, Nightshade, go on board that Osakyotan ship, and *you* can apologize for causing such a mess. You too, Shiro! Where the hell are you? That's your family on that ship, so go ahead ... and ..."

He trailed off as a very quiet Lilian walked meekly in front of him and buried her trembling head into his torso.

"L-Lilian," he stuttered. "What ...?"

The demicat only sobbed silently with drooped ears.

"So I see you three now. But where is ..."

He looked down again as Lillian tugged his sleeve and pointed shakily behind her. The guild master followed her finger and rested his eyes on the cart with the single coffin. The world went silent as it dawned on the guild where Shiro was.

"Heavens, no ..." The demibear murmured. One hand reached to cover his mouth, and the other to gently cradle Lilian's head. He looked back and forth between Geran and Elaethia.

"Hey!" Liam Barron pushed to the front. "Hey, hey, hey, hey. No way. Nuh-uh. You guys, he's not ..."

Geran and Elaethia shook their heads.

"That's him, Barron," Geran managed to say. "He's in there."

"Son of a bitch ..." the demiwolf muttered. He ran his fingers through his hair and down his ponytail.

"Guys, tell me," Peter pleaded as he appeared. "Tell me he went down fighting. Tell me right now that the bastard who got him is burning in whatever pit of hell he belongs in!"

"He died fighting Rychus," Elaethia choked. "Shiro crippled him but was slain in turn."

The guild's thought process ground to a halt at Elaethia's state. All eyes softened and turned to her as time seemed to stop. Only Angela Bright stepped up to place a hand on the dragon hero's shoulder.

"Can you tell us?" the paladin asked quietly. "Don't force yourself, but can you give us some peace of mind as to what happened? We were all his friends too. You don't have to hold on to this alone."

"Thank you." Elaethia dragged in a shaky breath and began the story.

By the end of her rendition, everyone had knelt. Murmurs and buzzing floated around the guild. Bewildered breaths came from the holy magicians, while there were solemn nods from seasoned warriors. Master Dameon stepped forward to join Angela and Geran to comfort Elaethia. Lilian stood with Cassie Luca next to the wagon that held Shiro. The small priestess whimpered quietly with her tail between her legs as she ran a sleeve over the coffin.

Liam was the first to speak. "Sounds to me like he saved you all."

"Saved the world," Peter agreed. "None of us would have stood a chance if that guy got Elaethia. We would have been screwed."

Angela sighed. "I don't have a choice but to believe it now. Divine intervention. The thing I told him was a myth is the very thing that saved us. That crazy samurai."

"Where is he!" A man with a strange accent pushed through the crowd. "Where is my son? Where are his remains?"

Elaethia looked up to see a middle-aged Osakyotan man with black hair and a pointed beard approach from the docks. He was dressed in an elegant kimono—an outfit she recognized only because it was similar to the one Shiro had worn himself. With simple traveling shoes and two swords at his hip, the Osakyotan walked quickly to Master Dameon.

"Please, Guild Master, I beg you. I understand you asked me to wait so you can handle the situation, but I can't bear it any longer! You said he was here. I will give you anything; just let me have my Shiro!"

The big demibear rested a hand on the general's shoulder. "Hanzo. His friends have brought him down. They are just as distraught as you are, so please be patient with them."

"I will. Please, bring me to him."

Dameon sighed. "Elaethia, Geran, Lilian."

The three silently moved to the cart and gently escorted Shiro to his trembling father. Hanzo Inahari fell forward and collapsed over the casket with a shudder. After several minutes of deep, choking breaths, the northern shogun stood straight with red eyes and clenched fingers.

"My son," he said. "Did he die honorably?"

Geran nodded. "Shiro lived with honor and died with glory, sword in hand. He was able to adjust to any threat thrown at him and made victory assured every time. We'd all be dead right now if it wasn't for him."

Tears formed in Hanzo's eyes and began to trickle down his cheek. "That's him. That's my boy. You must be Geran-san. Or Geran, as you insisted. He spoke fondly of you in his letters home."

"He wrote letters?"

"Yes. Twice a month, sometimes more. I don't know how he did it, but each of them managed to get aboard an embassy ship every month. His loyalty to you three was an inspiration to all of us."

"Shiro's loyalty to his friends and family was unwavering," Elaethia said. "He was always at my side when I needed him. Shiro was bound to his honor, his friends, and his family. He spoke of you often. It was clear he missed you very much. He was the most loyal companion anyone could ask for. I will never have another friend like him."

"You must be Elaethia-sama. He drew a picture of you. Your reputation from Shiro as a kind and noble master, and an invincible warrior, has become famous back home. I am honored, *beyond* honored, to hear these words from you."

He paused and turned to Lilian. "My dear. You must be Lilian, his wonderful girlfriend."

The mage nodded, sniffed, and rubbed her nose with a sleeve. She could only blink with puffy, red eyes in response.

"You don't need to speak," Hanzo assured her. "I understand your pain. By the heavens, I do. My son loved to tell me of the wonderful girl that stole his heart and showed him a side of himself that he never knew. You two must have been inseparable."

"Damn right." Lilian cleared her throat and inhaled with a shudder. "Shiro and I were the power couple of the guild. It didn't matter where he and I went. As long as we were together, it was an adventure. He was also an absolute blast to tease. Even better than the other boys in the guild. But he managed to pull me in before I knew it. Elaethia said it right. I won't ever have another friend like him."

Hanzo couldn't help but smile. "You are everything he said and more. You *are* a little like Mitsuki. It pains me so much to have lost two children now. How terrible a father I must be."

Lilian bumped a fist on his chest. "Nope. Not one bit. Shiro was perfect. An unbeatable swordsman, a brave guy, and a total dork. I wouldn't have had him any other way. So, Mr. Hanzo"—Lilian looked up, rocked back on her heels, put her hands behind her back, and flashed him a fanged grin—"thank you. Thank you for bringing Shiro to us."

"Lilian-chan …" Hanzo's eyes welled up and overflowed as he stepped forward to embrace the demicat. Lilian unhesitatingly obliged and gripped the man's kimono tightly. Geran and

Elaethia joined them almost instantly. The four held tightly together in the center of the pier, silently honoring the man they all knew and loved. After a moment, they all pulled away.

Hanzo sniffed and bowed deeply. "Thank you. Thank you all for giving my son the best year of his life. It pains me more to know how wonderful you truly were to him. I feel almost nothing but guilt to take him from you."

Geran clapped him on the shoulder. "Don't. He's an Inahari. He belongs with his family in his homeland. We'd want the same if we died in Osakyota."

Hanzo smiled. "You truly are a clever and thoughtful man. You all deserve to know that the emperor has fully pardoned Shiro and wished to express this to him personally. He will be most disappointed to hear what happened. But I don't worry. Shiro will be a beacon of hope and honor for the generations to come, as well as a turning point in international relations. Shiro proved that Osakyota is ready to coexist with Linderry. Are his armor and blade with him? The emperor would wish to have them honored and displayed."

Elaethia exhaled gently. "He wears his armor, but …"

She looked slowly to Lilian, who held Seraph tightly in her hands. The demicat slowly walked up to Hanzo and shakily held out the katana with new tears building in her eyes. The general extended a hand, gripped the sheathed blade, and gently pushed it back.

"He gave it to you, Lilian, didn't he?" he asked.

Lilian gave a small nod.

"Then I cannot take it. It is yours now. It is enough that I have my son. I could never revoke a gift so dear as this. My father would never forgive me if he still lived."

Lilian smiled and brought the katana to her chest. "You know he named this sword after it got magic put into it?"

Hanzo smiled. "I did. It is right he named it Seraph. Especially since it was his grandfather who forged it. Our family believes that Ryuuki lives on in the heavens as a warrior."

"General." A second Osakyotan with a masked helmet appeared. "The tide will shift soon. We must get ready to depart."

"Very well. Thank you, scribe." Hanzo nodded and turned with a bow. "Thank you very much, Cataclysm. Thank you very much, guild of Breeze. I will leave you with my letter of greeting and method to contact me. Shiro's tales of adventure are treasured among our family, especially the children. We would love to hear more from you all."

Elaethia smiled as the scribe handed her a rolled parchment. "We would be delighted to write to you. May you have a safe journey, and honor Shiro in death, as we have in life."

"You do not even need to ask," Hanzo assured her. "Then I will thank you again and look forward to your letters. Farewell, Linderrians. May we meet again." With that, he turned to escort his son's remains down the docks, up the gangplank, and onto the waiting ship.

The adventurers of Breeze watched patiently as the crew prepared the ship to depart. The sun was just above the horizon, dancing gently on the ocean's surface. The crew hoisted the sails, untied the ropes, and pushed off the dock. Once the ship turned east, the guild moved itself into formation, and Master Dameon sounded the call.

"*Bang 'em!*"

The response was the sound of dozens of weapons of steel, wood, and stone rapping sharply on the cobblestone pier. The steady beat started quiet and unsynchronized but grew loud and steady as they continued. This was Elaethia's third time hearing the war cry, and her first time giving it. The dragon hero beat the shaft of her axe into the ground alongside her guildmates. Its dense yet metallic sound rang uniquely into the air.

This is the chant you have told me about before?

"Yes, Frossgar," Elaethia said over the noise. "Though this is not for the guild or even myself. We do this to honor Shiro."

Such a display is in the name of honor and companionship?

"It is."

Then I, too, shall send him off.

The dragon gently materialized his form into the air, being careful not to alarm those around him too much. The air grew chilly as the adventurers stumbled from the sight but quickly recovered. A few seconds later, Frossgar was fully formed.

Hanzo Inahari heard the noise from the shore and peered over the stern of his ship. His breath was stolen from him as he saw not only the army of more than thirty adventurers beating their weapons to the rhythm but also the ghostly form of an enormous frost dragon. Then Master Dameon bellowed over the water, as if to reach his voice to the heavens themselves.

"Shiro! You brought honor to those you served, death to those you faced, and smiles to those you loved. Go forth, samurai! Live on in the stars! *Give 'em hell!*"

"Ah-*ooh!*"

"Give 'em hell!"

"Ah-*ooh!*"

"Give 'em hell!"

"Ah-*ooh!*"

The last beat and war cry echoed over the rippling surface of the ocean. The final farewell to the samurai would reach even the ears of those on the other side, recreated by those who heard it aboard the ship. The guild of Breeze stood guard, right hands held in fists across their chests in salute, as Shiro Inahari sailed home into the rising crimson sun.

Andrew Rydberg

Sixth Era. 140. Jinum 8.

The week following the battle was spent in reconstruction. Though Rychus was dead, his influence on the country and his people was not. Although drawn out of their homes from the colossal battle, it was several days before the populace was willing to trust the strange foreigners. Both remaining members of the Echo and Breeze's guild worked day and night to aid Paragon's citizens. Makeshift hospitals and soup kitchens grew slowly but surely as the week went by.

As much as Lilian wanted to spend the time with her friends, there were more important things to do. Even though most of the legionnaires had been decimated in her explosion, several still survived, though not many were present in the city. Geran formed a search-and-destroy unit with the other rangers that exterminated or captured the scattered remaining soldiers. Many surrendered willingly.

She was surprised at how social Elaethia was being, even though much of the work required a delicate touch she hadn't mastered yet. The dragon hero resorted to odd jobs in manual labor, aided in making food, and otherwise helped where she could. But anywhere she went, every single one of the citizens stared at her. They knew who she was and what she had done. For once, Elaethia looked quite uncomfortable with how much she was being stared at.

Lilian found herself doing a ton of work too. Easily approachable as she was, the demicat spent most of her time coaxing in and taking care of the children—particularly Celeste. The small demibear followed Lilian like a little blond shadow, trying as hard as she could to be helpful to the mage. As promised, Lilian guided Celeste in the art of controlling elemental magic and taught her with the wand that Shiro had hardly ever used. For a brief moment, the city and all those in it seemed happy and full of hope. They even latched firmly onto the strangers from the north. But the guild needed to return home.

"You're going away soon, aren't you, Miss Lilian?" Celeste asked her teacher on the morning of their departure.

Lilian gently patted the demibear's head. "Yes, dear. We have our own home that needs us. We all came down to help, but we can't stay forever."

"What will you do there?"

"Same thing I did before I came here. Go on quests with my friends, help the people, and work on becoming the strongest mage ever."

Celeste frowned. "I thought you already were."

"Now where did you hear that from?"

"Miss Ash ... I mean, Miss Hailey. She said you blew up Rychus's palace in one spell and got all his soldiers with it too."

"Well that might be true, but I don't think that makes me the strongest mage ever. There're plenty of magicians back home that are stronger than me."

Celeste shook her head. "Nuh-uh. There's no way any of them could beat that."

Lilian chuckled. "All right, maybe you have a point. But there's a lot more to magic besides being able to make a big explosion."

"So you think you could beat them if you tried?"

The demicat scratched her ear for a moment. "I dunno. Probably? There are a lot of crazy strong magicians in Linderry. They're powerful in ways you or I couldn't understand. But off the top of my head, there's only one person who I know for a fact I couldn't beat."

"Miss Elaethia?"

"Yep. After seeing her at full power, there's no *way* I could stop that. Come to think of it, Geran could also probably find a way to beat me if he wanted to. That's pretty unlikely though."

"He's finding all the bad soldiers now, right?"

"Yup. Doing his best to make sure the city stays safe after we leave."

"And Miss Elaethia?"

Lilian shrugged. "Dunno. I think she walked off somewhere to be alone."

Elaethia stood on the edge of the cliff where the bridge to the palace used to be. The dragon hero looked over the ocean as she shielded her eyes from the rising sun. The ocean in front of her was calm and rippling. Sunlight glinted off of the hundreds of tiny waves that rolled towards the shore. The shrill call of seabirds echoed and resonated all around her and through the wind that blew her hair in a gentle breeze behind her head. It was peaceful. For the first time in what felt like years, she found her mind calm and her thoughts gathered.

What is it you wished to speak to me about, little one?"

"I have many questions, Frossgar," she said after a moment.

As I expected you would. I am surprised you have not come forward with this sooner. However, as a result, I have prepared myself for them.

"I am not sure where to begin. So much has happened, and my world changed so much. There is still unease within me."

Do you fear this country will fall upon hard times again?

"Yes, but not to the same extent. They will remember this history and hopefully will never allow such tyranny to return."

There is one less monster in the world. Two, actually.

"That is one of the things that has troubled me. What was that conversation you had with Gethevel? The more I try to piece your words together, the less I understand."

That is a deep topic to discuss. But you deserve to know. Are you aware of the reason why dragons exist? More so, why they were created?

"I never thought about it until Gethevel mentioned something of it."

Frossgar's aethereal form appeared next to her. "It is a matter of religion. At the beginning of time, there were only two planes of existence: heaven and hell. The two have hated each other for eternity. Both factions created their own worlds. But hell could not match the marvel and splendor of heaven. Unable to even approach the holy creations, the barons of hell were forced to stay in the darkness and watch with unbridled jealousy. And whether it was out of pride, love, or spite, the heavens created the earth.

"The world was born with balance. Everything had its place and purpose. The strongest of creatures were the dullest. The mightiest, the most reclusive. The weakest, the most numerous. The cleverest, the most inhibited. It was a world built for brehdars, but not so that their lives would be easy. As time went on, the heavens realized brehdars were too weak to live on their own, or too prideful to work together. They were driven near to extinction. And so magic was granted to them. And thus, brehdars began to thrive, and balance was returned. But it would not last.

"Enraged and filled with seething envy, the barons of hell came to a unanimous conclusion. If they could not destroy the heavens, then they would destroy their beloved creation. But they lacked the traits capable of surviving on the earth. So they created demons—creatures of hell, each with its own unique ability—that could connect their souls with those of willing brehdars and wreak havoc on the world as a demonspawn.

"Once again, Earth was in peril—not only the brehdars, but the entire world itself. The demonspawn worked to destroy everything and reduce the planet to ash. The heavens needed to make a hasty action. But like the barons of hell, they could not live on the earth. Unwilling to bargain with brehdars themselves, They needed to create a species that could overtake a demonspawn. but had a will of its own. This is why dragons were born."

"And so the first war ensued," Elaethia said.

Frossgar nodded. "Yes, the Crusade—when dragons and demonspawn first came to the earth. The elemental dragons were the first, as an experiment. The heavens were not fully pleased with the four species, however. Fire dragons lacked the control needed to walk alongside brehdar-kind. Air dragons lacked the discipline needed for commitment. Frost dragons lacked the social mindset needed. And the lightning dragons were too prideful to conjoin with brehdars.

"The heavens realized they needed to implement brehdar-like qualities into dragons and tried once more. The druidic dragons were born to closely resemble brehdars. They were given personalities that would let them be regarded as people. Earth dragons were given a nurturing behavior, wanting to work together, but only for survival as opposed to combat. Forest dragons had the cautious traits the heavens decided was necessary, but as a result, they became timid. Water dragons inherited the curiosity for which the brehdars were so unique, which resulted in them lacking focus.

"Finally, the heavens were able to create dragons in their own image—holy beings of earthly status that would become nearly infallible in both dragon and brehdar culture alike. Sun dragons held the determination and sense of righteousness needed to fight demonspawn. But as the holiest of creations, they refused to conjoin with brehdars who had souls they deemed impure. Moon dragons were sent to stand side by side with their sun cousins, being benevolent and merciful. However, their gentle and compassionate behavior overpowered their will to fight and kill.

"While the heavens were unable to create the perfect species to fight hell's creations, it was enough. This was a world designed to maintain balance. So it was only fair that each dragon had its flaws. Nevertheless, the nine species of dragons and the three species of brehdar were able to come together and push back the armies of hell. The heavens watched with pride as their creations worked together to overcome the enemy. But with the demonic threat gone, and through the constant flow of time, there was little need for dragon heroes to exist. Dragons' views on brehdars, and brehdars' views on dragons, began to shift.

"While defeated, the barons of hell were not deterred. They are devious and merciless in their schemes. They saw the rising tensions on the earth and slowly began to reintroduce their demonspawn again but this time with a new purpose—to find a way to drive a wedge between brehdars and dragons, effectively destroying the one thing that hell feared."

Elaethia was beginning to understand. "And so began the second dragon war."

"The Civil War," Frossgar growled. "I saw the rising tensions, and the reasoning dawned on me. I was reclusive, as my kind was known for, but I never blindly attacked any who approached me like some of my brethren. I began to see what was happening. But by the time I learned of the plans of the barons of hell, it was too late. That is why I retreated so far and sealed myself away from the world of both dragon and brehdar."

"And in the time between that and our meeting, the third war occurred."

Frossgar nodded. "The Genocide—Brehdar-kind's nearly unanimous decision to eradicate dragons. No doubt facilitated by the whispers of demons."

"And the rest is history."

"Indeed. I would never have expected my life to turn out this way. I held no intention of fighting demonspawn, and even less of conjoining with a brehdar. But fate has an amusing way of coming around."

Elaethia chuckled. "For over thirty-four hundred years, you tried to hide from your purpose. But the heavens' will is always done, is it not?"

"Putting it like that makes me seem cowardly, but yes. None of us are above their will. I would go so far as to say they let me live as I did for so long just in preparation for an occasion such as this."

"You are no coward, Frossgar. You are cold, firm, kind, wise, reclusive, and sometimes unpleasant. But as I am your little one, you are my dragon. And I love you through all of that."

"And I you, Elaethia."

Hailey's voice suddenly appeared. "I was wondering where you wandered off to."

Frossgar's form dissipated as Elaethia turned to see Hailey Foot ascend the broken bridge behind her. The dwarven woman crested the top of the incline and strode up next to the warrior. She stood side by side with Elaethia, inhaled deeply, and looked over the scenery. The gentle waves of the ocean, the ruins of the once grand palace, the glint of sunlight bouncing off the shining rocks below—it was beautiful in its own way.

"I did not know you were looking for me," Elaethia said.

"Well, everyone's looking for someone. It's finally starting to calm down a little. I think we can finally start focusing on the country."

"What is it you will do next?"

"I was going to ask you the same thing," the dwarf said. "Are you really going back up north?"

"I am," Elaethia stated.

"After all this? Your life goal? Your victory? Everything you've ever worked for is down here, and you won't stay?"

The warrior nodded. "I understand how shocking that may seem, given current events as well as the direction my life took. But I have been away for so long. I have seen more of the world than I could ever have imagined. My travels have taken me all over the continent, and I cannot see myself staying here. There is a home for me in Svarengel, and a family to call my own in Linderry. I had always strived to destroy Rychus, free my homeland, and avenge my father. The only direction I can see myself walking is the one with my friends."

Hailey crossed her legs and sat down. "I was afraid you were going to say that."

"What do you mean?"

"The people see you as a hero, y'know. The woman that defeated Rychus. In their minds, you're the only one who could possibly be the next emperor."

"I will not even entertain the thought of holding the same title as that monster."

"That's a real shame." Hailey sighed and then smiled. "I don't think that's what your father would have wanted, anyway."

"Perhaps not. Then again, I do not know what his intentions were to be if I succeeded."

"Me neither. The legend lives on saying he was a brilliant man—a little crazy, but brilliant. You're definitely his daughter."

"Yes." Elaethia clutched her gold-and-sapphire pendant. "I am."

"Say … no one ever told you how he died, did they? It's not glorious or legendary, but you deserve to know."

Elaethia whipped her head down. "What do you mean?"

"Well, I wasn't there myself, but the story got passed down from people who were. Namely the priests that were with him. After Marcus knew he couldn't win, he told all the priests to retreat and try to get as many people away as possible. Marcus would go on alone. Rychus drove him back all the way to his balcony. But before Marcus could be captured or defeated, he made the final decision to jump from the edge as opposed to be taken into custody and used as an example. It's a mindset we all adopted so we would be prepared if we ever got captured. I know it's not exactly the glorious or honorable death you probably imagined, but at least it's … Hey, woah, I-I'm sorry. I didn't mean to cause grief; I just—"

"No, no, that is not it." Elaethia ran a hand over each wet eye and sniffed. "This is true, is it not?"

"Well we never could recover his body. But there were witnesses that saw the fall, and the splash from when he hit the water."

"I see." Elaethia smiled and wiped her nose while clearing her throat. "I see. Thank you, Hailey."

"Yeah, of course. Do you need a minute?"

"No. I am quite fine, actually. But I do apologize for refusing to take the position of leadership in your stead."

"Wait, wait, wait. That makes it seem like you think *I'm* going to be empress."

"Perhaps not that title. But you are the most fit to lead the country."

Hailey gawked for a second. "Are you sure your head's all right? Me? I barely held together an underground ragtag group of terrified rebels. What makes you think I can manage a broken country?"

"You have proven yourself a capable leader, as the entire reconstruction operation sits on your shoulders. The people look up to you as much as they do me. You do not have to do it alone, however. In my travels, I have learned that responsibility and hardship are best handled when shared among trusted companions."

Hailey stood and ran her hands through her curly hair. "Well. I guess I don't have a choice but to give it some thought. Nobody else seems to want to do it. Either way, I need to get back down there. And you all need to get home."

"Both of these are true. How goes Geran's hunt?"

"They're done as far as they can tell. Most of the legionnaires that surrendered joined our cause."

"These men were capable of such redemption?"

"Keep in mind that most of them only worked for Rychus so they could support their families. With the threat gone, and no reason to keep fighting us, most of them turned a new leaf. They're now using their combat abilities to help maintain peace and security *for* the people, not against them. At the same time, we'll be keeping an eye on them for a while."

"Indeed. Only time will tell if they are trustworthy."

"Yeah." Hailey nodded. "Hey, Elaethia?"

"Yes?"

"We're friends, aren't we?"

She tilted her head. "Why would we not be?"

The dwarf smiled. "Just checking. If I do end up as the head of this mess, one of the first things after reconstruction is getting better at foreign affairs. I don't have to ask to know that you carry weight in your country. Once Armini is back on her feet, I want to make sure we have good relations with Linderry."

"There is no need to worry. You will not have only my support, but Geran's, Lilian's, and that of the entire guild of Breeze. Our countries will be sure friends."

"That's more than I need then." Hailey grinned and held out a hand. "Here's to Armini and her allies."

Elaethia smiled in return and firmly grasped her hand. "To allies."

"How are you guys getting home, by the way? Everyone came on that ship, but it sailed back to Osakyota. What's your plan?"

"I assumed we would all walk."

"All the way to Linderry?"

"There is no other option."

"Actually, there is."

Elaethia tilted her head. "What do you mean?"

Hailey grinned. "You see, my top engineer and I have been working on a little something for these kinds of problems. We started mass-producing them a few months ago but had to halt them for other projects. I think I'll give a few to you guys as a token of thanks. And for our future cooperation."

The Elaethium

Sixth Era.140. Jalesk 19.

Maya slumped back into the guild master's chair in Dameon's office. It had been two months since he and a third of the guild left on the impromptu quest to avenge Cataclysm. The elf somehow knew they weren't dead, but she was still mostly glad that the guild took this action. Mostly. After all, Master Dameon had plopped all the responsibility on her (practically at a moment's notice) and then disappeared on the same day. Now she was juggling temporary guild master duties on *top* of her head receptionist responsibilities. Talk about stressful! Oh well. It was a little easier with only two-thirds of the guild to worry about. At least Master Dameon sent plenty of letters around to the church, state, and NDG. They would even postpone the tournament until they returned.

Maya reread the letter that Roderick brought back. The ranger made the early trip home on horseback to spread the news. The rest of the guild would be about a month or two behind him, depending on how they traveled. Roderick had delivered the letter about a week ago, so that was enough to gauge a time. She would see everyone in a couple weeks or so.

Well, almost everyone. The news that Shiro wouldn't be returning hit her like a blow to the gut. The receptionist went through all seven stages of grief in a matter of hours, finally accepting it with a sigh. At least he went out like a hero. The head receptionist made copies of the letter and sent them all throughout the church and state. Waves were beginning to be made on not just Shiro's behalf but Osakyota's as a whole. The initially rocky relationship with the island nation was starting to smooth over, with probabilities of becoming even friendly. On top of that, the senate and NDG were starting to discuss assigning a national title to honor Shiro.

A sudden ruckus broke out downstairs. What started off as a loud group of voices and noises quickly turned into riot-level shouts and obnoxiousness that Maya hadn't heard in months. As a receptionist, she could stand it. But with all the extra responsibility thrust on her, she was a lot snippier than before. Grumbling swear words under her breath, the elf pushed her seat back and walked out the door to lean over the railing and yell at everyone to shut up. Her words caught in her mouth before they could come out. The deafening noises were from several carts that had pulled up outside. Each one was the size of a wagon, but they were all filled with contraptions and springs and pipes and adventurers. What was all that metal? And was something burning? *Wait, hold on, adventurers?*

"Wait, wait, how did … Somebody … Gaaaah!" She ruffled her white hair in frustration until she saw someone dependable. "Michael!"

The demiwolf cocked his ear and turned around. "Huh? What? Oh! Maya, you're not gonna believe it! They're back! And they're all riding wagons that can drive themselves! They don't even need horses, just machines, magic, and a special kind of potion."

"What are you talking about? What's going on out there?"

The young ranger laughed. "Just come down here! You'll see!"

Maya sighed in resignation. The elf took her spectacles off, wiped them on her blouse, put them back on, and walked downstairs to meet everyone. As she stepped outside, she was greeted by a parade of adventurers, all jumping down from the strange wagons.

"What in the …"

"Yo! Maya!" Liam Barron walked up with a hearty wave. "Long time no see. How you been, girl?"

"Liam, what on earth is this?"

"Pretty sweet, right? Ya like the rides? Those wacky Arminian engineers made carts that make themselves move forward. All it takes is some funky juice! We got back here in no time!"

"I … I see …"

One of the cart drivers walked up. "Actually, it's not funky juice. The potion is called combustion fluid. And these carts are called automobiles. I would know, since I made them. My boss, Hailey, made the combustion fluid."

Maya blinked. "Oh, well, they're very impressive Mr. …"

"Chase," the black-haired human told her. "I mean, Jak. Ignore that first part."

"Oh, I'm Maya, the acting guild master. It's a pleasure to meet you, Jak. How do these automobile things work?"

Jak cracked his knuckles. "Well it's a cross of a combustion engine with hydraulics and manual controls that—"

"Oh this part's *nuts!*" the demiwolf spearman said, jumping in. "So that combustion fluid stuff? It's a liquid that can catch fire! And the machine, like, drinks it or something, and ignites it, and uses that energy from it to make itself push forward by making a bunch of pistons go up and down! It's kick-ass!"

Jak pushed up his glasses and rubbed his eyes. "That … was probably the worst explanation I have ever heard. Whatever. I've got to refuel these things, including the couple we're leaving with you. Thanks for giving a roadside tour of the country, Liam."

Liam flashed him a smile and snapped his fingers into a point. "Not a problem, J-dog! Thanks for letting me drive! Sorry I crashed a few times. Keep up that nerd stuff, bro, it's awesome! *Oh!* Don't forget to give that combustion fluid recipe to Michelle! She's near the back of the guildhall on the right; you can't miss her!"

"Understood. I'll go talk to her right away. Thank you."

Maya shook her head as Jak walked inside. "He's supposed to report to *Michelle?* That poor man has no idea what's about to happen to him …"

Liam grinned and nudged her. "Wanna watch?"

Maya glared at him, frowned, and then sighed and closed her eyes. "Yeah."

The Elaethium

Sixth Era. 140. Jalesk 21.

"I feel like there's nothing else to cover," Geran said as he took a seat in Master Dameon's office. "What's this about?"

The giant demibear folded his hands. "Just some closure things I need to get off my chest. I've been caught up to date on what happened since I was gone, and two things in particular have stuck with me. Both revolve around you."

Geran raised an eyebrow. "I don't know if I like the sound of that."

"Don't get your cloak in a bunch; I just want to know some things about you."

"You do realize I've been in this guild longer than ninety percent of everyone else, right? If there's something you don't know about me by now, you never will."

"Well, some new things occurred after Elaethia arrived, as you know. You joined a party, became famous, got an enchanted item, and, most importantly to me, trained an apprentice."

"What's your point?"

Dameon's eyes glinted. "Geran. Have you talked to Michael since coming back?"

"Yeah, he told me all about his time while we were away. I bought him and his whole party dinner in congratulations."

"You mean you bought *Undertaker* dinner."

"I did. Who even came up with that name for them?"

Dameon sighed into his hands. "Why are you dancing around the subject, Nightshade?"

Geran shrugged. "I have no idea what you're talking about."

"Stars above, you want me to spell it out? You're gonna make me say it out loud like I'm wagging my stumpy little tail for you?"

"Now that'd be something to see," Geran murmured, rubbing his chin.

"If it weren't for the fact I'm so damn pleased with your work, I'd be throttling you right now. What in the *hell* did you do to Michael to get him where he is?"

"Trained his tail off without the unnecessary hazing bullshit that a lot of veteran mentors love to do."

"He is sixteen and already an A-level adventurer! That pup hasn't even been in my guild for a year, and he's already one of my top rangers! If you hadn't gotten back in time, I would have had him partake in the tournament!"

Geran scratched at his stubble beard. "After a decade of being in the business, I know what works and what doesn't. Plus he's a natural. Michael had a lot of the basics already down; I just had to hone in on them and mix in the key points he didn't know. All he needed was experience in the field."

"What part of ranger training makes him so damn fit? That rascal could pick *me* up and run a klick without a sweat!"

"I did kinda slay him a little in our workouts. Proper nutrition plays a role too."

"By the Sun and Moon," Master Dameon sighed in resignation, leaning back. "It's enough that you created a prodigy. But the kid is so damn good he managed to fix *Hartford's* little party. I didn't think those kids would ever get out of the intermediate level, but they're now a *named* advanced party. Undertaker is on its way to being the next ace once Earth Shatter, Razorback, and Cataclysm retire."

Geran gave his guild master a solemn look. "Cataclysm *is* retired."

"I know." Dameon nodded. "You three are still going strong, but it isn't the same without Inahari. We can assign you guys a new name if you want."

Geran shook his head. "Nah. We're fine just being 'Elaethia's party.' It's not like we really need a name, anyway."

"Is that arrogance? Coming out of *your* mouth?"

"What? No. I'm just glad I'm not being brought up as much. Feels nice to be going out of the spotlight."

"After all that, you still managed to not change very much."

Geran smiled. "Not if I can help it."

Dameon grinned back. "Tell that to Elaethia."

"Hah. Maybe I will."

A knock on the door caused both of them to turn around. Elaethia opened the door and looked in.

"Excuse me, is now a bad time?" she asked.

"Depends," Dameon answered. "What do you need?"

"I was only looking for Geran."

The ranger chuckled apologetically. "Whoops. Sorry, I forgot about our lunch date. Can you give us a few minutes?"

"It is all right. I can see you are in a serious conversation. Do you mind if I join you?"

Elaethia stepped in. She was in her casual outfit: tan pants, white shirt, black outer corset, and black leather boots. Her pendant hung around her neck, and her hair was brushed and braided over her ears. As she sat next to Geran, he could tell she had just come from the baths. She looked and smelled incredible.

"I don't see why not," Dameon acknowledged, smirking at Geran, who was still staring at his girlfriend. "Earth to Nightshade. That means we still have a conversation to finish."

"Huh? Oh! Yeah, what was the second point you wanted to bring up?"

"Ah, yes." Dameon grimaced slightly. "How long do you plan to stay with us?"

"What's *that* supposed to mean?"

"You're an expert on hiding your emotions on the job, Geran. But as your old man, I can see right through you. You've got that air around you that I've recognized over the years from all my late veteran adventurers. You're burning out of the guild life, aren't you?"

Geran stayed silent.

"Nightshade …"

"Not for a while yet," the ranger responded. "But yeah, you got me. Elaethia wants to stick around for a good long while, and I have no intention of going anywhere without her."

Elaethia tilted her head. "If I am making you feel grounded, we can discuss what you are planning to do more thoroughly."

Geran waved a hand. "Don't even worry about it. Guild life's not bad by any means. And as long as we're where you're happy, I'll stay by you."

She smiled. "If you insist. However, I will take your goals into consideration."

"It seems you two have already made plans outside the guild," Dameon mumbled with a hint of pain in his voice.

Geran laughed. "Yes and no. Truth is, I *had* noticed Michael's crazy development. I felt so fulfilled and proud of him while he described his missions to me. I never knew I could feel this way. I want to sit back and watch him grow, and keep mentoring him. But at the same time, I want to see him become his own man. I almost want to start all over with a new apprentice and fix all the bumps I had with Michael."

Dameon leaned forward. "Where is this going?"

"I plan to start a new generation of rangers. If Breeze … no, if *Linderry* could have upcoming rangers just like Michael, we'd be on the road to some of the best intelligence gathering and crime prevention the world has ever seen."

"That's what Nocturnal's for," Dameon said.

"But what if there was a Nocturnal all over Linderry?" Elaethia continued. "A Nocturnal that all citizens knew and trusted. What if there was an organization of rangers that could investigate and deter crime all over the country? Men and women with the skill and intelligence to stop atrocities from ever happening."

Geran took back over. "The business with Rychus got me thinking. It would never have gotten that bad if there was a constant flow of information from down there. If I can start a training regimen of rangers who can act as the eyes, ears, and blade of the country, people could sleep soundly knowing there's no corruption or crime brewing."

Master Dameon thought for a moment. "The church and state won't like that."

"We will work around it," Elaethia assured him.

Dameon opened his mouth to respond, until a sudden burst of shouts and ruckus erupted from the main hall downstairs. Jeers and taunts were accompanied by the sound of metal on metal. Crashing, tinkling, and clanging shook the room as adventurers from downstairs whooped and hollered with approval. Dameon growled into his hands and made his way to the door. The guild master threw it open and stormed to the railing.

"What the *hell* is going on down there!"

Silence was the only answer he was given.

He spoke again. "What in the … *Finway!* How did you … Did you really knock all four of them out? *Again?* For the love of the Sun and Moon, put Theodore back the way he's supposed to be; that's unnatural!"

"Can't, sir!" the black-and-white-haired demiwolf called up. "I know joints aren't supposed to go this direction, but it's what he gets for trying to resist. Could you come help, Master? You're the only one strong enough to pop it back into position."

The guild master rubbed his eyes. "Miss Wilhelm, you need to control your man a bit more than this."

Cathrine's voice responded from the ground floor. "Oooooh, I couldn't have stopped him *this* time, Guild Master,"

"You kids … Hold on, I'm coming down. Quit your blubbering, Theo! You should know better than to tangle with Michael by now, let alone try to touch his girl." Master Dameon closed the door to his office and walked downstairs.

Elaethia turned to Geran. "How was your conversation?"

He shrugged. "Well, you caught most of it. You showed up at a good time. Got to the good part."

"Which part was that?"

He smiled and wrapped an arm around her. "I got to talk about you."

Elaethia blushed and shifted closer to him, resting her head on his shoulder. "That is unfair, Geran. You know I do not know how to respond to such things."

"I'd say this suffices."

He leaned in and kissed the top of her head. She sighed deeply and put a hand to his chest. Her fingers suddenly clenched, and she sighed again, this time in exasperation.

"Frossgar, if you are going to be present at these times, please say so beforehand."

Geran raised an eyebrow. "What's he doing?"

"Observing."

"What's *that* supposed to mean?"

Elaethia was silent for a few seconds, obviously listening to Frossgar.

"Yes," she said to the dragon, and then she looked Geran in the eyes. "I enjoy it very much."

He didn't need to hear what Frossgar said to understand what he had asked. "As do I."

Geran grinned, leaning forward to kiss her. They parted after a moment and nestled into the comfortable couch.

"I wonder what Master Dameon would say if he saw that," Elaethia thought aloud.

Geran shrugged. "He'd probably be pissed,"

"Very true," Elaethia agreed. "Although Master Dameon seems to like us enough that his anger toward us slows."

"One of the perks I do enjoy of being a star member."

A loud crash from the door slamming open behind them made both Geran and Elaethia jump from the couch to their feet. Expecting to see a giant, angry demibear, they were instead met with a sleek, cheerful demicat. The mage who burst the door open was in her questing gear: her black cape and hat with orange embroidery, her one orange and one purple thigh socks, and her brown hip pouch. She held the dragon-bone staff in one hand, and Seraph rested longways above her fluffy tail behind her back. In her other hand was a quest flyer.

"Guys!" Lilian said before pausing and looking back and forth between the two.

"What?" Geran demanded.

A devious grin enveloped her face. "Oho? I'm sorry, did I interrupt something?"

"No."

"Yes," Elaethia sighed. "What is it, Lilian? I have not seen you so excited in a while."

"Maya just posted an R-level quest!"

"What about it?" Geran asked, and he slowly leaned forward.

"A behemoth just got spotted to the southwest. It trampled through a farming village and is still going! I snatched it just now; let's go!"

Geran gave her a look. "You want to solo a behemoth?"

"No, dummy! Elaethia and I are gonna tag-team it!"

"Uh-huh. Sounds great. What am *I* supposed to do?"

"You get to carry me back if I overcast myself."

"Lucky me," the ranger grumbled.

Elaethia stepped forward. "You say the behemoth has destroyed one community and is still on the move?"

The mage winked and pointed a finger at her. "Bingo!"

Geran headed for the door. "Looks like we're gonna need a rain check on that date, Elaethia. Lilian, gimme that flyer. I need to make a plan to cut it off. Elaethia, will you be ready in ten minutes?"

"I do not know what rain has to do with our date, as the skies are clear. But I will be ready in half that time if you need."

"Perfect. Lilian, go get this approved. We'll take this one."

"Hm-hmm." The demicat flapped her cape and grabbed the brim of her hat. "Consider it done! My rent is overdue, and I'm out of money. This is gonna give me *bank!*"

"Are you kidding me?" Geran shouted over his shoulder as he opened his room.

"Whaaaaat? You act like this has never happened before! Hurry up and get your nerd stuff ready. Let's go!"

I fail to understand how Lilian's funds are depleted. From what I understand, she obtained a moderate fortune before we reconnected.

"I do not know, either," Elaethia said as she entered her room. "Her reasons are beyond my understanding, but her goal is to become famous. It seems this goal requires a considerable amount of money."

Such an odd source of motivation.

"I concur," Elaethia agreed as she shut her door and began to disrobe. "But it is harmless and pushes her to better herself indefinitely. I have no qualms with it."

She also seems intent on increasing your fame as well.

"In the way that by being friends with me she can become even more popular."

This seems shallow.

Elaethia laughed. "That was a joke, Frossgar."

I will never comprehend any of your senses of humor.

"Give it time. One day you will understand my friendship with Lilian."

I am more curious as to how long it will be until you copulate with Geran.

Elaethia nearly fell over. "F-Frossgar!"

What is the issue?

"That is improper!"

It is a natural action for living beings. Reproduction is a necessary key to survival, and leads to properly raising and defending the next generation. How could it be improper?

"Well, you see …"

Elaethia began to explain the process of brehdar reproduction to Frossgar, as Ingrid had with her three years ago. The dragon seemed to understand the process fairly well until the topic of intimacy and attraction came up. Frossgar asked several uncomfortable questions every time Elaethia tried to modestly explain a subject. She was forced to use her relationship with Geran as an example. Unfortunately, she soon found herself forced to describe certain actions and reactions in embarrassing detail. By the time she had her armor on, her face was quite flushed.

What an interesting notion. Brehdars find emotional comfort and physical pleasure in mating. I wonder why the heavens designed you all this way.

"I could not tell you."

Elaethia sighed and felt her cheeks. She cleared her throat, opened the door, and froze. Standing in front of her room was a shaking, sputtering Lilian. Both her hands were clamped tightly over her mouth, her cheeks bright red. Her eyes were teared up, blinking quickly as she met Elaethia's. Before the dragon hero could say a word; the demicat doubled over, howling in laughter as she clutched her sides. The mage collapsed to her knees while holding the railing as she burst out into uncontrollable fits of snorting laughter.

And then Elaethia turned to her left.

Two doors down, Geran stood alone with his head buried into the wall. She couldn't see his face, as he had pulled his hood over and hidden behind his hand. Her cheeks went bright red, going so far as to turn the blue scales around her eyes a shade of purple. The dragon hero stood paralyzed with embarrassment as she realized they had heard every word.

"Sh-shall we go?" she managed after a moment.

She was given no answer. Lilian was now on the floor with her hand pressed into the wooden floorboards to keep herself up. Geran had shrunk to a squat, and he muttered something to himself while he banged his head against the wall. It would be another five minutes before the three of them would walk out the front doors of the Breeze guildhall and become the first lone party in history to defeat a behemoth.

Epilogue

Sixth Era. 140. Agrion 30.

Elaethia, Geran, and Lilian walked along the paved cobblestone street toward the dragon museum. As Maya had told them, the annual tournament was delayed to accommodate for Breeze's absence. It had ended just the day prior. While only Geran and Lilian competed out of the three of them, Elaethia still received fervent cheers and attention. This was partially exasperating to her, since she had chosen not to take part specifically for that reason—that and the NDG pleadingly requesting she not partake anymore, mentioning something about an unfair advantage. This, of course, sparked multiple disputes and controversy, all of which were shut down by the dragon hero herself. Elaethia had never felt any desire to compete in the first place. This was a convenient excuse for her.

"Hm-hmm," Lilian hummed smugly as she strutted in front. "What … a … *day! Oh,* I'm so stoked right now, guys; you don't even *know!*"

"We know very well, Lilian," Elaethia acknowledged. "You are right to feel such pride and enthusiasm for your performance. You worked very hard, and it has paid off."

"You did promise you'd take first this year," Geran added. "I just don't think anyone else believed you."

Lilian turned and flashed her signature grin. "Doesn't matter now! How's it feel, Gerry? You're looking at Linderry's number-one mage! *And* I consider you one of my closest friends. You should be honored, you know."

The ranger shrugged. "I've had a habit of making friends in high places. What's one more?"

Lilian cocked an ear. "Wait, you're agreeing with me?"

"Yeah?"

"No snarky rebuttal? No dismissing gestures? No … no sarcastic comments? You're actually giving me genuine praise?"

"Why not? Elaethia said it herself. You had a dream and worked hard to make it a reality. I'm not *that* heartless that I don't feel pride in my friends' accomplishments."

"Well you're still dancing around it in your normal nonchalant way! You haven't said it officially yet!"

Geran sighed and walked up to the girl. "You really want me to say it?"

"Course I do!" she stated, folding her arms.

"Lilian," Geran said, placing a hand gently on the demicat's head. "You worked very hard and gave your absolute best. I'm proud of you."

The mage's face flushed as she fumbled for a response. After a second, she shooed his hand away and doubled back

"That wasn't fair!" she sputtered. "I wasn't ready for it."

Geran laughed. "You still liked it."

"D-did not …" the demicat said with a pout as her tail began to curl.

"And she says *I'm* the one who can't convey my feelings straight, right, Elaethia?"

The ranger turned to see that Elaethia, too, had flushed and turned away. The woman had a hand curled in front of her mouth. Her dragon eyes shifted between Geran's face and hand. She realized that he noticed, and she quickly turned away.

"What? You want one too?"

"P-Perhaps …" Elaethia mumbled into her hand. The expression she gave the man nearly melted him.

"I'm surprised you three got here so quickly," Frederick Borough announced as he guided the adventurers into the dragon museum. "I didn't expect you to escape from the celebration for another hour or so."

Lilian sighed. "Yeah, well, these two party-poopers burned out, so here we are."

"That's one way of putting it," Geran chuckled.

"Is Arthur here as well?" Elaethia asked.

"He is indeed," the curator said. "Sage Veldwig is already at the desk, awaiting our arrival."

"I'd hope so," Geran muttered. "He's the one who asked to see us."

Lilian turned her nose up. "He asked to see *me*, thank you very much."

"Indeed," Elaethia agreed. "But he still mentioned Geran and myself."

"Details." The mage fluttered a hand as they approached the waiting Arcane Sage.

Arthur's milky white eyes glanced up at their approach. "Ah, Titan Slayer, welcome. It is good to see you all again," the old dwarf said as he extended a hand.

Geran shook it. "Looks like even *you've* heard about that. We made our preferences clear, but they just had to go and give us another name."

"You shouldn't be surprised, my dear ranger. You are the first party in history to defeat a leviathan, a behemoth, *and* a demonspawn. All three of you are world-famous now, so the state and guild really had no choice."

Elaethia's face fell. "Not all of us are present who defeated the leviathan and Gethevel, however."

"This is true. But you three still live. Shiro will be remembered for ages to come. Both your actions and the ceremony in his honor at the tournament prove this."

"By the way," Frederick interjected. "How did you manage to kill a behemoth with just the three of you? Not that I doubt your validity; I just wish to hear the story."

Lilian's eyes brightened. "Oh, you're not gonna believe this! So Elaethia and I—"

Geran interrupted. "I came up with the idea of having Lilian tip it on its side by putting a gargantuan *air rune* in front of it. Then Elaethia finished it off by blasting an *ice burst* the size of a cathedral into its gut. Worked like a charm."

Frederick stumbled in place. "Elaethia one-shotted a behemoth?"

Lilian whined and stamped her feet. "Gera-a-a-a-n! Stop stealing my thunder!"

Frederick laughed. "I didn't believe there could truly be a G-level adventurer until I met you, Elaethia. Even the Sun Hammer hasn't gotten that rank yet. Congratulations."

The dragon hero fondled her new guild tag. "I thank you, even though the title means little to me,"

Arthur chuckled. "It's no wonder the tournament ended the way it did, Geran. I suppose another congratulation is in order for you and Lilian regarding that. You finally swept the board. Both of you. The coming years will be exceptionally more difficult for upcoming mages and rangers."

Geran shook his head. "Just mages."

"You're retiring?"

"Only from the tournament. If I'm being entirely honest, I can't get excited for next year like I always have. It doesn't hit the same when there isn't much competition."

"Speak for yourself!" the demicat huffed. "I haven't felt that much adrenaline in *years*! Every year there will be new mages trying to step up to me, and every year we'll see if they have what it takes!"

Elaethia shook her head. "I simply just do not understand the desire for such meaningless accolades."

Frederick chuckled. "But you had another reason, didn't you, Geran?"

"Yeah." The ranger nodded. "I want to give my apprentice the shot he deserves next year. Michael's an up-and-coming prodigy, and it'd be unfair to keep taking his position. He'd pass Byron and Roderick eventually, no doubt, but he's eager to see the stage. But I'll still be running with the guild for as long as Elaethia wants to be a part of it. It keeps us both happy while I build up funds and manpower for my organization."

Frederick adjusted his spectacles. "The state and NDG approved the notion of your organization almost unanimously on the first pass. They obviously have high trust and expectations for you."

"Yeah, but I'd like a different name for it if possible."

Arthur chortled. "I'm afraid it is a little too late for that, my boy. The name caught, and people are already whispering about it."

Geran put a palm to his eyes. "That's the exact opposite of what I wanted …"

Elaethia rested a hand on his shoulder. "You still wished for it to strike fear in the hearts of those beyond redemption. The Nightshade Corps will accomplish just that."

"Hmph." Lilian's tail flicked. "I still can't believe your name's getting national recognition before mine."

Arthur's milky eyes twinkled. "About that, my girl. Do you know the reason I called you here today?"

"Probably something magic related?"

"An astute yet very broad answer. Yes, but do you know what specifically?"

She folded her arms behind her head. "If you're digging around for the reason why my spells are different from everyone else's, I'm not spilling. That's something I worked hard on and call my own, so don't think I'll talk about my—"

"Ability to alter your spells by delving into their very properties and advancing beyond the basic functions?"

Lilian's tail puffed out as her eyes widened. She tried to respond, choked on her own breath, gurgled, and doubled over into a coughing fit.

"Hit the nail right on the head," Geran translated.

Arthur smiled apologetically. "You are not the first to discover such capabilities, Lilian. We have all sorts of information held in the Moon's Pillar, you know. Elemental magic is fairly cut-and-dried compared to the other schools, but we still have a plethora of information about it. The Arcane Sages have been around a very long time. Most of the elemental magicians we invite into our ranks have a similar reaction upon hearing this, although not quite as animated as yours. Sage Revrin was also fairly taken aback."

Elaethia tilted her head. "Mordecai is an Arcane Sage now?"

Arthur nodded. "As of last week. The Sages have almost unanimously agreed that we lack elemental magicians in our ranks, as well as members willing to go out into the field. So our eyes are turning toward the guilds for potential."

"That's the best place to look, after all," Geran agreed.

"Wait!" Lilian shouted. "You said 'other magicians you've invited.' What's *that* supposed to mean?"

"Exactly as I said." The dwarf grinned. "You've been scouted."

The room went dead quiet.

"*What!*" Lilian's shriek reverberated around the museum.

"Stars above, cat!" Geran clutched his ear. "Don't *do* that next to us."

"I concur," Elaethia added, still wincing.

"Well," Frederick said as he rubbed a finger in his ear. "Assuming I can still hear properly, I presume that means the Arcane Sages have decided for Lilian to join their ranks."

"Nearly," Arthur confirmed. "Although not all of us. It must be a unanimous decision from all the current Sages to allow someone to join our ranks. If even a single one of us disagrees, the magician in question cannot join. There are a few of my colleagues who aren't too keen in acknowledging Lilian as a sister. Her somewhat childish demeanor is enough for them to look past her current power."

Geran raised an eyebrow. "What a surprise."

"I don't wanna be a *book-sniffer!*" the demicat exclaimed.

"Are you sure about that?" Arthur pressed. "The benefits are beyond what you know. Most of the information we keep hidden will be open to you. You can record and mark your own discoveries as well. A room and study will be granted to you, along with the food services. And if I recall correctly, you wish to go down in history as a legendary mage. There is no better path to that title than that of becoming an Arcane Sage."

"I …" The demicat faltered. "I don't know. I hate to admit it, but you're right. But I'm not ready to leave the guild yet! I can't be an adventurer anymore if I'm a Sage, and that means I can't be in the tournament anymore. I don't want to be cooped up in that tower for the rest of my life. I want to keep going on quests and adventures with my friends! I'm not ready to give that all up."

"This is not a decision you have to make now, Lilian," Elaethia pointed out.

"Indeed," Arthur assured her. "As I said, you've been scouted, not selected. We are merely contemplating the ups and downs of adding you to our numbers. It would probably take a year or so for us to reach a decision. In that time, you can choose how you wish to be portrayed. You can either grow as an individual to appease the current uncertain members, or you can bolster your power even more to bypass their judgment. At the end of it all, you can still deny the offer."

"I … I'll think about it."

"That's all I ask." The old Sage smiled. "I will always be a voice that speaks in your favor. After all, you used my ring splendidly in the tournament. I got much praise and even more job requests after people saw your performance with it. Ah, that being said, I have some projects and meetings to attend to."

"That is not a problem," Elaethia assured him. "We thank you for taking the time to speak with us. It was good to see you again."

"Likewise, my girl. We will all be watching your growth with interest—all of you. You three are becoming beacons in this country in your own regards. My door is always open to you. Oh, and Lilian?"

The demicat cocked an ear. "Hmm?"

"You do know that being a Sage doesn't mean you are confined to the tower. That is merely where the majority of us prefer to stay because it is quiet, secluded, and houses all we need for our research. There is no rule saying you cannot wander the country as you please. You are free to exercise the title of Arcane Sage as you wish. You wouldn't have to sniff a single book, should you so choose."

"Wait, really?"

"Of course. Now I should be going."

He pulled out a shiny metal ring and slipped it onto his finger. An ominous dim red glow radiated from it before it dissipated and began to shine blue. After a few seconds, Arthur began to hover in the air.

"Hold on one damn minute!" Geran sputtered. "Sage Veldwig, that's not—"

"The very ring you recovered for me from the Enchanter's Imperium. I thought the red glow sounded unearthly, and as I hypothesized, it is."

"What do you mean?" Elaethia asked as the old dwarf began to rise into the air.

"Because this power is demonic in origin. While enchanters cannot copy dragon magic, it seems we are able to do so with demonic abilities—after many purifying processes, of course. A dragon's magic is determined by the species, but a demon's is entirely unique to the individual. This one's ability, as you can tell, was flight. How the ancient enchanters harnessed this power is unknown, but it would be a shame to leave this unused. I'm sure you understand. Take care, adventurers!"

With that, he flew up to the dome ceiling and out through a window.

"Impeccable logic," Frederick murmured as he scribbled into a notepad while the guild members stared at the ceiling. "I'll have to record that into our own databases. As well as this sketch of that ring in action. A demon section should be opened in tandem with my dragon section. I have a new topic to research, and that ring will be the first thing I study!"

Elaethia gave him a sideways look and was about to respond when she froze. She looked over to see that the curator was writing on his notepad in one hand while sketching the ring on some paper with the other.

Geran scratched his stubble beard. "I completely forgot you could do that."

Lilian scampered to the desk to gawk at the human's actions. "Woah, woah, woah, wait a minute! How are you doing that?"

Frederick looked up. "This? Ah, I taught myself to do this many years ago to record everything to the greatest detail in the shortest amount of time. Sometimes I find myself in a situation or location where I shouldn't be, and I need to act quickly. This sort of multitasking helps immensely. I can speak, write, walk, and draw at the same time."

"That's so cool! But so unfair!"

Elaethia walked up as well. "You possess a very remarkable talent. I have never heard of someone able to do several things at once."

Frederick looked back down. "Funny thing, that. I'm not actually doing three things at once."

Geran made a face. "Huh?"

"Through research, experiments, and hearsay, I've found that our minds actually can't do more than one thing at a time. But they can, however, switch between activities quickly. Realistically, I'm not doing three things at one time. My mind is just switching its focus between them at a very rapid rate."

"I see," Elaethia marveled. "Such an intricate ability. One might think it is magic."

"Perhaps. So in summary, I'm doing all three one at a time. It's just switched so quickly it *seems* that I'm actually performing multiple abilities at once."

Lilian rubbed her chin. "Multiple abilities at once …"

"That's what he said," Geran stated.

"Not actually performing it all at once, just switching focus …"

Elaethia nodded. "Yes, Lilian, we understand."

"Abilities, multitasking, focus. Magic, casting, switching …"

Geran's eyes widened. "Uh-oh. I know that look."

Elaethia tilted her head. "I recognize this expression. It is the same as when you learned of the possibility to alter your spells."

Frederick stopped what he was doing and looked up. "What? What is she thinking?"

Lilian's deep focus returned to reality as a wicked grin enveloped her face. Geran exhaled heavily, put a hand to his brow, and leaned on the desk. Frederick turned to give a puzzled glance at the ranger. Elaethia pondered what Lilian could mean until it dawned on the dragon hero what the mage would be attempting to do.

"Lilian, surely you are not—"

Lilian turned to them with gleaming eyes. "Yeah. *Oh* yeah."

"Oh no …"

"Guys," she said with a grin, "I'm gonna need a looooot of magic potions."

Special Thanks

Mom
Dad
Jacob U.
Alvin C. Wible Jr.

In Memory Of
John P.

The Elaethium was a long and eventful journey for me. I was truly blessed to have such enthusiastic support from all my friends and family during the process. I would not have been able to do it without your input, patience, and encouragement. Thank you.